LOST

LOST
ENCYCLOPEDIA

Written by

Paul Terry and Tara Bennett

A Dorling Kindersley Book

FOUR SEASONS: WINTER, SPRING, SUMMER, FALL.

FOUR PRIMARY ELEMENTS: EARTH, WIND, FIRE, WATER.

THE BOOK OF KELLS IS AN ILLUMINATED MANUSCRIPT OF THE FOUR GOSPELS, NOW BOUND IN FOUR VOLUMES.

THE FOURTH BOOK IN THE JEWISH TORAH AND THE CHRISTIAN OLD TESTAMENT IS CALLED "NUMBERS."

LOCKE WAS IN A WHEELCHAIR FOR 4 YEARS.

DURING THE JEWISH SEDER, THE YOUNGEST MEMBER MUST ASK THE 4 QUESTIONS AND ALL ATTENDING THE MEAL MUST DRINK 4 CUPS OF WINE.

THE FOUR HORSEMEN OF THE APOCALYPSE EACH RODE A DIFFERENT-COLORED HORSE: PESTILENCE ON WHITE. WAR ON RED. FAMINE ON BLACK. DEATH ON A PALE HORSE.

THE CHRISTIAN BIBLE INCLUDES FOUR GOSPELS, OR "GOOD NEWS": MATTHEW, MARK, LUKE, JOHN.

THE OBJECT OF CONNECT FOUR IS TO ALIGN FOUR DISKS OF THE SAME COLOR IN ANY DIRECTION.

A BACKGAMMON DOUBLING CUBE INCLUDES A 4.

FOUR CHAMBERS IN THE HUMAN HEART: RIGHT ATRIUM, LEFT ATRIUM, RIGHT VENTRICLE, LEFT VENTRICLE.

THE BEATLES WERE ALSO CALLED "THE FAB FOUR."

MOST HUMANS HAVE 4 EACH OF CANINES, INCISORS, WISDOM TEETH.

4:8:15 IS CARVED INTO EKO'S WALKING STICK.

RICHARD ALPERT READ CHAPTER 4 OF LUKE WHILE IMPRISONED IN THE JAIL IN TENERIFE.

FOUR NOBLE TRUTHS OF BUDDHISM: 1. LIFE IS SUFFERING. 2. ATTACHMENT IS THE CAUSE OF SUFFERING. 3. THE CESSATION OF SUFFERING IS POSSIBLE. 4. THE EIGHTFOLD PATH LEADS TO THE END OF SUFFERING.

IV

LOCKE WAS CANDIDATE #4.

YOUNG MILES FOUND A DEAD BODY IN APARTMENT #4.

THE FANTASTIC FOUR INCLUDES: MISTER FANTASTIC, INVISIBLE WOMAN, HUMAN TORCH, THE THING.

DESMOND LOST 4 YEARS OF HIS LIFE ON THE ISLAND.

FOUR CORNERS IS A POINT IN THE U.S. WHERE THE BOUNDARIES OF 4 STATES MEET AT THE SAME POINT: UTAH, COLORADO, NEW MEXICO, AND ARIZONA.

4 IS AN UNLUCKY NUMBER IN KOREAN, BECAUSE IT SOUNDS LIKE THE CHARACTER FOR "DEATH".

TETRAPHOBIA IS FEAR OF THE NUMBER 4.

THE FOUR LOVES BY C.S. LEWIS DESCRIBES FOUR KINDS OF LOVE: AFFECTION, FRIENDSHIP, EROTIC, LOVE OF GOD.

C4, COMPOSITION 4, IS A VERY COMMON PLASTIC EXPLOSIVE IN THE COMPOSITION C FAMILY.

MR. EKO FOUND A PICTURE OF HIMSELF AND HIS BROTHER YEMI IN CHAPTER 4 OF ISAIAH.

A DIGITAL REPRESENTATION OF THE NUMBER 4 IS COMPOSED OF 4 SEPARATE SEGMENTS.

4/4 TIME IS CONSIDERED COMMON TIME IN MUSIC AND INDICATES THERE ARE 4 BEATS PER MEASURE OF MUSIC.

A MUSICAL SYMPHONY USUALLY INCLUDES 4 SEPARATE MOVEMENTS.

FOUR SUITS IN A STANDARD DECK OF WESTERN PLAYING CARDS: DIAMONDS, HEARTS, CLUBS, SPADES.

THE SYSTEM CRASH IN THE SWAN STATION OCCURRED AT 4:16.

LEONARD SIMMS PLAYED CONNECT FOUR.

WORE JERSEYS WITH #4: LOU GEHRIG, BRETT FAVRE, BOBBY ORR.

A 4-SIDED POLYGON IS A QUADRILATERAL.

FOUR QUARTETS BY T.S. ELIOT IS A SET OF 4 POEMS WRITTEN DURING WORLD WAR II.

423 CHEYNE WALK WAS THE HOME ADDRESS OF PENELOPE WIDMORE.

Title Manager
Tim Cox

Lead Designer
Doug Wilkins

Designer
Carol Stamile

Production Designer
Tracy Wehmeyer

Licensing Director
Mike Degler

Editor-in-Chief
H. Leigh Davis

International Translations
Brian Saliba

Project Coordinator
Stacey Beheler

First American Edition, 2010
13 12 11 10   4 3 2 1

Published in the United States by DK/BradyGames,
a division of Penguin Group (USA) Inc.
800 E. 96th St., 3rd Floor
Indianapolis, IN 46240

ISBN: 978-0-7566-6595-1

Printed by Lake Book, Melrose Park, IL

ABOUT THE AUTHORS

Paul Terry's connection to the world of *LOST* has been a strong, varied, and multimedia one since the show first emerged in 2004. He was the editor of *LOST: The Official Magazine* for the title's entire run and was responsible for the planning and execution of every issue and yearbook.

With Iain Lee and Tom Page, Paul also co-presented The LOST Initiative, UK channel Sky1's official show for *LOST* fans. In 2009, The LOST Initiative was nominated for a Digital Broadcast Award. Paul also conducted numerous on-camera interviews with the cast and crew of *LOST* and was a featured panelist for *LOST: The Complete Third Season's* "Access Granted."

Prior to the world of *LOST*, Paul edited *Alias: The Official Magazine* for the hit Bad Robot/ABC spy show starring Jennifer Garner. He also helmed several other major licensed magazines over the past ten years, including *The Simpsons* and *Futurama* comics, as well as having written for key film publications *ODEON Magazine* and *Sky Movies Magazine*.

Paul is also a songwriter/composer. Under his solo moniker of Cellarscape, his records include the acclaimed 2009 album "Animation, Suspension." He has also written several film soundtracks over the past decade for British writer/director Paul Williams, including the 2006 comedy-drama "The Wake" and 2010's horror-comedy "The Furred Man."

Paul lives in London, England.

Tara Bennett is the author or co-author of several movie and TV companion books including *The Art of 300*, *The Art of Terminator Salvation* and *24: The Official Companion Guide*, Seasons 1 through 6. She has also written nearly a thousand interviews and features for print and online publications such as: *LOST: The Official Magazine*, *Alias Magazine*, *24 Magazine*, *SCI FI Magazine*, *SciFi Wire*, *Fandango*, *Fancast*, *Newsarama* and *VFXWorld.com*. She is also the East Coast Editor for the world's premier sci-fi/fantasy publication, *SFX Magazine*.

Tara frequently appears as an expert guest on a variety of television-related media programs such as "Fictional Frontiers with Sohaib," Shaun Daily's "TVTalk," and she moderated the last two "24" panels at San Diego Comic Con.

Tara is also an adjunct professor at Rowan University in New Jersey, teaching Film and Television studies. As part of her curriculum, Bennett utilizes programs such as *LOST* and *24* to teach her students how to write for television.

Before starting her journalism career, Tara worked as a television producer on the East Coast for outlets such as CN8 and Comcast for almost a decade. She then used her expertise to transition into writing full-time about the industry with a focus on scripted dramas and genre-related films.

Special Thanks To: Julia Hardy and Gordon Holmes for their endless support and understanding; Gregg Nations, Noreen O'Toole, and Melissa Harling Walendy for their incredible knowledge, guidance, skills, and support; the entire *LOST* creative family for crafting such an amazing show and trusting us to write about it; Tim Cox for your hard work and dedication; Sohaib Awan at Fictional Frontiers for his continuous encouragement; our wonderful family and friends for their patience when we suddenly disappeared for six months behind our laptops, and to the fantastic *LOST* fandom who have cheered us on as we've progressed through this momentous project. All the blood, sweat and tears in these pages are for you—we're honored to be part of the Lostie fold. Namasté.

CONTENTS

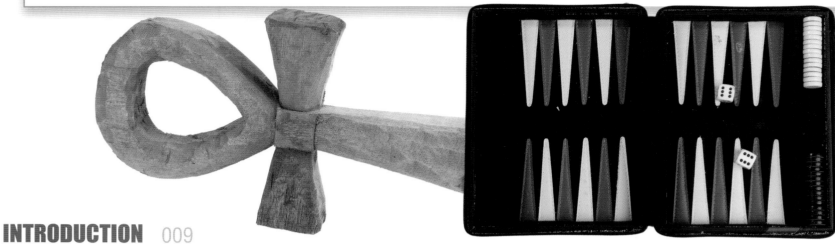

ur numbers are:

MEGA NUMBER

, 8, 15, 16, 23   42

Oceanic AIRLINES

MacCUTCHEON
60
YEAR OLD
SCOTCH WHISKY

THE CRATE HOLDING LOCKE'S BODY IS 823.

"HARD EIGHT" IS ROLLING TWO 4S IN CRAPS.

TOM FRIENDLY PUTS KATE'S DRESS IN LOCKER 841.

SPIDERS HAVE 8 LEGS.

MEDUSA SPIDER POISON PARALYZES FOR 8 HOURS.

A CUBE HAS 8 SEPARATE VERTICES.

JULIET'S BRAND HAS 8 LINES.

FIGURE 8 IS A TYPE OF KNOT.

LOCKE'S FATHER PUSHES HIM OUT OF AN 8-STORY BUILDING.

AN 8-SIDED POLYGON IS AN OCTAGON.

THE DHARMA WHEEL WITH 8 SPOKES REPRESENTS THE EIGHTFOLD PATH IN BUDDHISM.

A CHESSBOARD HAS 8 SQUARES ON EACH SIDE.

SAWYER'S PRISON ID WAS 840.

HURLEY WAS CANDIDATE #8.

OCEANIC FLIGHT 815.

CRAZY 8S IS A CARD GAME.

VIII

BEN'S WHITE RABBIT HAD 8 PAINTED ON ITS SIDE.

THE NUMERAL 8 LOOKS LIKE AN INFINITY SYMBOL.

MICHAEL AND WALT MET FOR THE FIRST TIME IN AN OCTAGONAL ROOM.

THE DHARMA LOGO IS AN OCTAGON.

MAGIC 8-BALL IS A TOY BY MATTEL.

KATE ROBBED SAFE DEPOSIT BOX 815.

8 IS A FIBONACCI NUMBER.

THE BEATITUDES ARE THE 8 "BLESSINGS" JESUS DESCRIBED.

CHARLIE SOLD COPY MACHINE C-815.

ADAM RUTHERFORD DIED AT 8:15.

8 APPEARS ON A BACKGAMMON DOUBLING CUBE.

MICHAEL AND WALT WERE SEPARATED FOR 8 YEARS.

TRICIA TANAKA WORKED FOR ACTION 8 NEWS.

CHARLIE PACE WORE A SIZE 8 SHOE.

SAWYER WAS 8 YEARS OLD WHEN HIS FATHER KILLED HIS MOTHER AND THEN COMMITTED SUICIDE.

TO ALL LOSTIES,

Ladies. Gentlemen. Let's start with a question…and this is one we absolutely promise to answer—

Of all the questions we were asked by fans over the six years we were making LOST, what is the one we heard the most often?

Polar bears, you say? Got it quite a bit, but no.

Further explanation as to Walt and his specialness?

It's right up there…but still not even close.

The number one question was this:

"Are you making it up as you go along?"

From the very early going, over and over again this question would manifest itself. And why shouldn't it? LOST was a show built on mystery and our fans had a right to know that if they invested themselves fully in that mystery then goshdarnit, the people responsible for constructing it better have a plan.

There is a word for this plan in the television business.

It's called a "bible."

A series bible is supposedly a big thick binder that has all the juicy tidbits of information relating to that series. And these bibles not only keep track of what you've already seen, they also (allegedly) keep track of what you haven't seen yet. It is detailed. Specific. A blueprint for what could stretch out into over a hundred episodes of storytelling. But…

Why is it called a bible?

Because it's meant to be a guide. But to us, a bible is something deeply spiritual, something that you take on faith that can be interpreted any number of ways. It is almost never literal. A bible is something that allows the reader to take from it whatever he or she wants to take. It is subjective. And while it is full of exciting stories and oftentimes has a definitive narrative, it is most definitely not a plan.

Sound familiar?

But we digress.

When you consider the above, it seems pretty obvious that LOST was never a show that could have had a literal bible. Certainly, we had a plan but not one that we wrote down and organized. Instead, we began to construct what we affectionately referred to as (cue dramatic music)…

The Iceberg.

When you see an iceberg sticking out of the ocean, what many don't realize is that this is just about one-tenth of its overall mass. The rest of it, most of it, lies below the water's surface. You never see it. But if it wasn't there…well, the iceberg would of course, sink.

What you saw on television, the show itself, was the ten percent of the iceberg above the water. But the majority of our time in the writer's room was spent constructing the part below it. The details. The timelines. The intricate backstories of the passengers of Oceanic 815, not to mention the people who inhabited the island long before them. Then we put them all together and let what happened, happen.

Now that the show is over, there has been great curiosity in our process…a desire to see those details in "official" form. And as an iceberg would just melt and get all over your pants, we decided to call it something else.

And so now you hold the first and only official LOST ENCYCLOPEDIA.

A word of warning before you venture forth…

This text will not confirm nor deny your theories about the show. It will provide clarity, and it's a great reference guide, but what it does NOT provide are answers to the great unknown. It was incredibly important to us to maintain the purposeful interpretive quality of the show. And although it is frustrating at times to puzzle things out for yourself, the show was called LOST for a reason.

As for what this text will do…well, you're more than welcome to dive in and learn more about Alvar Hanso and the ancient game of Senet than you ever thought you needed to know.

So thank you for continuing the journey with us and we hope you have as much fun exploring our iceberg as we did constructing it.

Until we meet again…

Namasté. And Good Luck.

AARON LITTLETON

FACTS & FIGURES

Time On The Island
POST-OCEANIC: 60 days

Connection: Claire Littleton's son

Family: Claire Littleton (mother); Kate Austen (adoptive mother)

Aaron's mother, Claire Littleton, had planned to give up her child to adoptive parents in Los Angeles, but his life was destined for more tempestuous waters. After surviving birth in the middle of the jungle, his mother disappeared and Aaron escaped the island under Kate Austen's care. Back in Los Angeles, known to the world as one of the Oceanic Six, Aaron spent three years with Kate, who told the world he was her son, born on the island. When Kate returned to the island, she left Aaron in the custody of his biological grandmother, Carole Littleton. Aaron was later reunited with Kate and Claire after they escaped from the island via the Ajira aircraft piloted by Frank Lapidus.

PRE-BIRTH

Even before he was born, Aaron was linked to strange events. Richard Malkin, the psychic Claire saw in Sydney, told Claire she needed to raise the child herself or terrible things would happen. Malkin later gave Claire $6,000 to fly to Los Angeles to meet an adoptive couple and insisted that she board Oceanic 815.

Shortly after surviving the crash on the island, Claire had a nightmare. She dreamt she was no longer pregnant and John Locke was berating her for giving up the baby and making everyone pay the price. In the dream, she saw a crib with no child inside—but full of blood.

BIRTH

The night that Boone Carlyle died, Claire gave birth. Kate had formed a strong friendship with Claire and helped deliver the baby with Charlie Pace and Jin-Soo Kwon nearby. During the time flashes on the island, James "Sawyer" Ford also witnessed Kate helping Claire give birth to Aaron.

NEWBORN LIFE

Living in the chaos of the island, Aaron became accustomed to sleeping in a noisy environment. When he couldn't settle, Claire's fellow survivors came to his aid. Charlie, who affectionately called Aaron "Turniphead," fashioned bjorns for him and often looked after him while Claire rested or went for her daily walk and swim. Hurley tried to get Aaron to stop crying by singing James Brown's "I Feel Good," but to no avail. But Sawyer's southern accent proved a hit with Aaron, did reading aloud to him.

Locke fashioned a crib for Aaron out of bamboo, inspiring jealousy in Charlie, who acted as Aaron's father and protector on the island. When Charlie volunteered to turn off the Looking Glass station to give the survivors a chance to leave the island, he secretly left his family ring in Aaron's crib.

ABDUCTIONS

Shortly before Aaron was born, Claire was abducted by Ethan Rom and taken to the DHARMA Staff medical station where she received injections directly into her stomach. She experienced flashbacks of the event when Aaron awoke with a rash and high temperature, which made Danielle Rousseau think he had been infected by the sickness.

Jack examined Aaron and concluded there was no infection. When Claire searched the Staff station, she found a blue bootie she remembered knitting during her kidnapping.

Prior to Claire's memories returning, Rousseau abducted Aaron the night she warned the survivors the Others were coming for them. Danielle misunderstood the whispers she heard in the jungle; she interpreted them as being related to the Others, announcing they were coming for Aaron. Instead, the whispers—the souls of people trapped on the island—were trying to warn Danielle that the Others wanted to abduct Walt Lloyd. Rousseau willingly returned Aaron to Charlie.

Much later, when the Man in Black—in the form of Claire's father, Christian Shephard—lured Claire away from the other survivors, Sawyer found Aaron in a blanket by a tree and Sun looked after him before they left the island.

LIFE AS AARON AUSTEN

When the Oceanic Six escaped, Kate suggested claiming Aaron as her own to help protect those left on the island from Charles Widmore. When Aaron was a toddler, Kate was on trial in Los Angeles. During the trial, Kate's mother, Diane Jansen, offered to drop her testimony against Kate if she could see Aaron, her "grandchild." Kate refused.

During the memorial service for Christian Shephard, Jack met Carole Littleton, who revealed that Claire was Christian's daughter. At the service, Carole inadvertently met her grandchild, commenting that Kate's "son" was beautiful.

When Aaron and Kate met Clementine and Cassidy Phillips, Sawyer's daughter and lover, respectively, Kate revealed the truth about Aaron to Cassidy. A short time later, Kate lost sight of Aaron for a few moments in a grocery store. A woman resembling Claire was on her way to the register with Aaron to have an employee make an announcement, but Kate thought she was taking him away. At this moment, Kate admitted what she had always expected—that Aaron would be taken from her.

Kate decided to return to the island for the sole purpose of rescuing Claire and reuniting her with Aaron. She visited Carole and told her that Claire was alive on the island. Kate confessed that Aaron was just two doors away in Carole's hotel. After a tearful goodbye, Kate left Aaron to embark on her mission to save Claire.

One of Aaron's toys was this Millenium Falcon, which Jack accidentally stepped on and broke.

MATTHEW ABADDON

▶ CONNECTION: Associate of Charles Widmore

A strange soul who had the ability to terrify as well as to comfort, Matthew Abaddon's history was shrouded in mystery. While John Locke was coping from his paralysis, caused by his father Anthony Cooper pushing him through an eight-story window, Abaddon worked as an orderly where Locke was being treated. However, he confessed to Locke that he was "much more than an orderly" and explained he had experienced something miraculous on a walkabout that changed his perspective on life. During this confession, he urged Locke to go on his own walkabout. Although Locke, a broken man, balked at the idea, he embraced Abaddon's challenge later in life, which led to his time on the island as a healed man.

Abaddon had several dealings with Charles Widmore, but it is unknown if he was under his employ, or whether he aligned himself with Widmore's beliefs and ambitions. Abaddon helped assemble the science team for the *Kahana* mission and also took a keen interest in the Oceanic Six. He even visited Hugo "Hurley" Reyes at Santa Rosa—posing as an Oceanic Airlines employee—and probed about the story the survivors told the world about flight 815. This terrified Hurley, who called for help when he became suspicious of Abaddon's true intentions.

Abaddon's last interaction with those on the island was with Locke. Under Widmore's instruction, he became Locke's assistant and took Locke wherever he wanted to go in an attempt to convince the Oceanic Six to return to the island. Shortly after revealing to Locke that his one true love, Helen Norwood, had died, Abaddon was gunned down by Benjamin Linus. Ben insisted to Locke that he murdered Abaddon to protect Locke, but the truth behind Abaddon's overall modus operandi died with him that day.

ABIGAIL SPENCER

▶ **CONNECTION: Sister of Theresa Spencer (Daniel Faraday's girlfriend)**

Abigail Spencer is the sister and roommate of Theresa Spencer. She worked in a local convenience store in Oxford, England and helped care for her invalid sister at home. Bitter about how Daniel Faraday abandoned her sister after his experiments went awry, she was very vocal about her disdain when Desmond Hume visited her. However, she also explained that Charles Widmore was a true benefactor and humanitarian for taking responsibility of Theresa's care, as he funded Faraday's failed experiments. It's through Widmore's generosity that her sister had a live-in nurse who looked after Theresa.

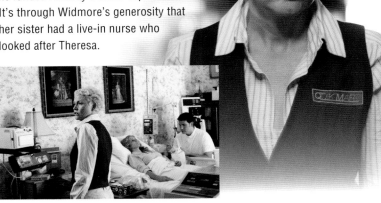

ACHARA

▶ **CONNECTION: Ex-lover of Jack Shephard**

Based in Phuket, Thailand, Achara left her mark on Jack Shephard in more ways than one. During an unknown time period in Phuket prior to the Oceanic 815 flight, Jack and Achara became lovers after a chance encounter on a beach.

She revealed little to Jack during their time together, so one night he followed her and discovered that she was a tattoo artist. She claimed to have an ability to see "who people really are" and declared that her tattoos were an act of definition, not decoration. After categorizing Jack as an "outsider," he forced her to "define" him but she warned him of dire consequences. Jack's persistence led to Achara's brother, Chet, beating Jack up and demanding that he leave Phuket and never return.

Years later on the island, Isabel— the Others' Sheriff—said Jack's tattoo meant: "He walks amongst us, but he is not one of us," but Jack retorted that although the symbols say that, it isn't what they mean.

THE OUTSIDER ✛
The theme of an outsider forcing his way into an otherwise closed group happened more than once with Jack. He attempted to do this with Achara and was punished for doing so. Then while on the island, Jack forced his way into the Others and Juliet paid the price for it. In the end, Juliet received a permanent reminder of her allegiance to Jack over her fellow Others by getting branded.

ADAM RUTHERFORD

▶ **CONNECTION: Father of Shannon Rutherford**

Adam Rutherford was the husband of Sabrina Carlyle, the father of Shannon Rutherford and the stepfather of Boone Carlyle. He married Sabrina when Shannon was just 8 years old. Ten years later, Adam was struck head-on by another vehicle driven by Sarah Wagner (later, Shephard). Adam was pinned inside his vehicle, so the fire department had to pry him out. He suffered major chest trauma and was rushed to St. Sebastian Hospital, where an E.R. intern had a difficult time intubating him. In the meantime, Dr. Jack Shephard worked on Sarah's injuries in the same room. In a matter of moments, Adam succumbed to his injuries and died on the gurney.

BEYOND THE NUMBERS ✛
Adam Rutherford's time of death was called at 8:15.

Although Adam had a very good relationship with Shannon, his vast wealth went into a living trust solely benefiting Sabrina. He left no formal inheritance to his daughter, which caused an irreparable breach in their family.

AGENT FREEDMAN

▶ **CONNECTION: Brokered deal with James "Sawyer" Ford**

Agent Freedman was an employee for the United States Department of the Treasury assigned to recover the $10,000,000 embezzled from the government by Munson. James "Sawyer" Ford was incarcerated in the same Florida prison as Munson and worked a confidence angle on him to gain the location of the hidden money. James agreed to provide that information to the Warden and Freedman in exchange for a full pardon and a cash reward that he had the Feds deposit into the bank account of his daughter, Clementine Phillips.

Freedman and Warden Harris sought Sawyer's help.

AIRPORT GUARD

▶ **CONNECTION: Worked at the main gate at Herarat Aviation**

This employee worked at Herarat Aviation, the airport that Mittelos Bioscience used as a front to transport Juliet Burke to the island. The guard met Juliet at Herarat before contacting Ethan Rom and Richard Alpert—two people synonymous with the Others. Although he could have been part of the Others, it is just as likely that he was an innocent man being deceived.

AIR TRAVEL ✛
Along with Oceanic Airlines and Ajira Airways, Herarat Aviation is yet another travel corporation that unwittingly became associated with events on the island.

HERARAT AVIATION

AJIRA FLIGHT 316

"We're not going to Guam, are we?"

— Spoken by Frank Lapidus

Flight 316 was an Ajira Airways Boeing 737 passenger plane that departed from Los Angeles, California with service to Hawaii and Guam that had to perform an emergency landing on Hydra island. Among its passengers were the Oceanic Six, a contingent of Jacob's people, and the body of John Locke. The flight was only half full and the remaining 78 seats were purchased by Hugo "Hurley" Reyes.

DESTINY CALLS

Ajira flight 316 was handpicked by Eloise Hawking as the flight by which the Oceanic Six would return to the island. Using equations developed at the DHARMA Lamp Post station, Hawking determined 316's route would take it right over the coordinates where the island would be, creating a finite 36-hour window in which the Oceanic Six could "go back."

Jack filled out a form in order to take "Jeremy Bentham" on the flight.

> *"If you...want to return, you need to re-create as best you can the circumstances that brought you there in the first place. That means as many of the same people as you are able to bring with you."*
>
> — Spoken by Eloise Hawking

The flight's captain was Frank J. Lapidus.

Ben's presence on the plane startled Hurley.

PASSAGE 3:16

One of the most popular Bible passages is John 3:16 which says, "For God so loved the world that he gave his one and only Son, that whoever believes in him shall not perish but have eternal life." Some would say it reflects the ultimate destiny of Jack Shephard as he watched Ajira 316 fly overhead with his dying breath.

TURBULENCE

Somewhere over the Pacific Ocean, flight 316 experienced a pocket of extreme turbulence that woke up all the passengers in first class and caused the flight attendant to tell them all to put on their seatbelts. In the cockpit, Frank Lapidus turned off the autopilot and then a white flash encompassed the plane. Seconds later, blue sky reappeared but the engines had stalled. Lapidus and co-pilot Peter Ross found their plane in a dive towards the island, but Ross was able to restart the engines and then under Frank's command divert the power from them to counteract the dive and stabilize them enough to come down for a hot landing on the Hydra island runway. The plane ran out of clear ground and as it hit the jungle trees, a tree limb broke the co-pilot's window and skewered Ross. The plane then came to a full stop, otherwise intact.

A PAWN IN THE WAR

After the emergency landing, the plane remained on the runway untouched until Charles Widmore and his team arrived on the island. His goons murdered the remaining passengers, built a bamboo stairway to access the plane and then rigged the carry-on compartments with four packs of C-4 as a precautionary measure to keep the Man in Black from escaping. However, the Man in Black discovered the explosives and cleared them from the jet.

Miles Straume, Richard Alpert and a water-rescued Lapidus returned to the plane later and hastily performed emergency repairs with the intent to fly off the island. Richard assisted Frank as he welded sheet metal over the broken window and Miles duct-taped a broken hydraulics line in the nose wheel. As the island began to sink into the ocean around them, Lapidus was able to taxi and successfully lift-off with Miles, Alpert, Kate Austen, Claire Littleton, and James "Sawyer" Ford in tow. The plane safely returned them back to civilization.

An Ajira water bottle was found in an outrigger during a time jump by Sawyer and Juliet

BY THE NUMBERS

Ajira Flight 316 departed from Gate 15 at LAX.

Flight 316 coordinates:

Los Angeles — Lat: 118° 14 W, Long: 34° 03 N

Guam — Lat: 144° 48 E, Long: 13° 10 N

As Ross called for Mayday, their radio picked up DHARMA's automated broadcast of Valenzetti's equation: "4, 8, 15, 16."

There were 4 packs of C-4 rigged to explode inside the plane.

KEY PASSENGERS

Sayid Jarrah
Seat 2A

Ilana Verdansky
Seat 2B

Sun Kwon
Seat 3D

Kate Austen
Seat 4A

Hugo Reyes
Seat 5B

Caesar
Seat 5C

Benjamin Linus
Seat 8B

Jack Shephard
Seat 8C

John Locke / Jeremy Bentham
inside coffin in cargo; a proxy for Christian Shephard

15 RED BALLS IN SNOOKER.

JAE LEE'S HOTEL ROOM WAS NUMBER 1516.

CHINESE LUNAR NEW YEAR LASTS FOR 15 DAYS.

15-GUN SALUTE.

JULIUS CAESAR WAS ASSASSINATED ON THE IDES OF MARCH, 15 MARCH 44 BCE.

15 IS A KEY NUMBER FOR SCORING IN CRIBBAGE.

XV IS THE NUMBER ON THE DEVIL CARD IN A DECK OF TAROT.

A 15-SIDED POLYGON IS A PENTADECAGON

15 MINUTES OF FAME.

NUMBER ON THE WHISKY BOTTLE THAT SAWYER AND CHRISTIAN DRANK FROM.

15 MEN ON A RUGBY TEAM.

NUMBER OF YEARS PASSED BETWEEN WHEN KATE AND TOM BRENNAN BURIED THE TIME CAPSULE AND THE CRASH OF FLIGHT 815

DMITRI SHOSTAKOVICH WROTE 15 SYMPHONIES AND 15 STRING QUARTETS.

SAWYER WAS CANDIDATE #15

THE FIRST POINT SCORED BY A SIDE IN A GAME OF TENNIS IS 15.

A WHITE RABBIT WITH 15 PAINTED ON ITS SIDE APPEARED IN THE SWAN ORIENTATION FILM.

ANCIENT NINEVAH HAD 15 GATES.

EACH OPPONENT STARTS WITH 15 COUNTERS IN A BACKGAMMON GAME.

15 BALLS IN A GAME OF EIGHT-BALL.

AJIRA FLIGHT 316 LEFT FROM GATE 15.

JAMES BUCHANAN, THE 15TH PRESIDENT OF THE UNITED STATES, APPEARED ON THE 15¢ STAMP.

ANTHONY COOPER'S SAFETY DEPOSIT BOX WAS 1516.

"FIFTEEN MEN ON THE DEAD MAN'S CHEST" IS THE FICTIONAL TITLE OF A PIRATE SONG FROM TREASURE ISLAND BY ROBERT LOUIS STEVENSON.

THE EARTH ROTATES 15° COUNTERCLOCKWISE EVERY HOUR.

"SIXTEEN TONS," CLASSIC COUNTRY HIT BY TENNESSEE ERNIE FORD.

JAE LEE'S HOTEL ROOM WAS NUMBER 1516.

XVI

16MM FILM.

M16 ASSAULT RIFLE.

WORE JERSEYS WITH #16:
WHITEY FORD,
JOE MONTANA,
BRETT HULL.

MOST CREDIT CARDS HAVE 16 DIGITS.

EACH CHESS PLAYER HAS 16 PIECES.

HURLEY BOUGHT THE AIRPORT SCOOTER FOR $1,600.

DANIELLE'S DISTRESS TRANSMISSION PLAYED FOR 16 YEARS.

JULIET ENTERS 1623 INTO THE KEYPAD FOR THE DHARMA SONAR FENCE.

THE KEYPAD IN THE LOOKING GLASS COMMUNICATIONS ROOM HAS 16 KEYS.

A 1/16TH NOTE IS ALSO CALLED A SEMIQUAVER.

ALEX ROUSSEAU IS 16 YEARS OLD.

AJIRA FLIGHT 316.

JACK'S FIRST PATIENT WAS 16 YEARS OLD.

DESMOND RIDES HIS EXERCISE BIKE IN THE SWAN STATION AT 16 MPH.

ANTHONY COOPER'S SAFETY DEPOSIT BOX WAS 1516.

16 PAWNS IN A CHESS SET.

THE SYSTEM CRASH IN THE SWAN STATION OCCURRED AT 4:16.

16 MEYERS-BRIGGS PERSONALITY TYPES.

SAWYER USED $160,000 TO CON JESSICA.

BEFORE HURLEY WON THE LOTTERY, THERE WAS NO WINNER FOR 16 WEEKS.

SAYID IS CANDIDATE #16.

A 16-SIDED POLYGON IS A HEXADECAGON.

16 APPEARS ON A BACKGAMMON DOUBLING CUBE.

16 DRAMS IN AN OUNCE.

16 OUNCES IN A POUND.

SWEET 16.

ALCOHOL, SEE PAGE 18

ALDO

▶ **CONNECTION:** Temple Other; knocked unconscious by Kate Austen; killed by Claire Littleton.

Although his surname was unknown, it was established that Aldo was an Other working for Benjamin Linus at the Hydra station, located on the small island just off the coast of the main island. He was seen reading Stephen Hawking's *A Brief History of Time.*

His main duty seemed to involve guarding the building that housed Room 23, known as the re-education room, which was the place where Karl was subjected to a barrage of images and statements related to DHARMA and Jacob. Aldo was friendly with Alex Rousseau and even warned her that Ben would kill him if he found out she was trying to help Karl.

Aldo met his demise three years later while accompanying Kate in search of Sawyer. As he attempted to subdue Jin, Claire gunned him down.

LOOKING DEEPER ✛

Hawking's "A Brief History of Time" is an attempt to explain complex subjects such as the Big Bang Theory and black holes, but in an accessible and non-specialist manner. The book's subject matter is therefore strongly linked to time travel.

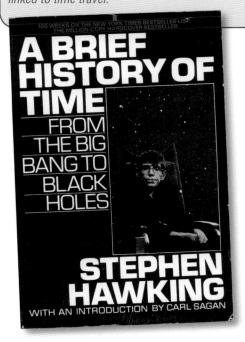

ALEXANDRA ROUSSEAU, SEE PAGE 20

ALVAR HANSO, SEE PAGE 22

ALYSSA COLE

▶ **CONNECTION:** CIA agent who blackmailed Sayid Jarrah

CIA Agent Alyssa Cole, along with Australian Secret Intelligence Service (ASIS) Robbie Hewitt, blackmailed Sayid Jarrah into helping them build a terrorist case against his former college roommate, Essam Tazir. In exchange for his help, they promised to provide Jarrah with the whereabouts of Noor "Nadia" Abed Jaseem.

Sayid confronted Essam about his involvement in the terrorism plot.

AMINA

▶ **CONNECTION:** Lived in the same village as Yemi, Eko's brother

A relief worker at the village clinic near Yemi's church in Nigeria, Amina was the single mother of Daniel, a church altar boy. Amina shared with Eko that she had an arrangement with Emeka, the local drug lord, to keep twenty percent of the Red Cross vaccinations they received at the clinic but the rest were handed over to him to pay for "protection." When Eko murdered Emeka and his men in Yemi's church, Amina accused Eko of being a bad man and that he owed his brother a new church.

AMIRA

After leaving Iraq, Amira and Sami opened a restaurant. Translated, the name means The Garden of the Fertile Crescent.

▶ **CONNECTION:** Tortured by Sayid Jarrah

Amira was an Iraqi citizen who was tortured by Sayid Jarrah when he was a soldier for the Republican Guard. Amira was accused of harboring enemies of the state, a crime that she repeatedly denied. After three months, the pain from the hot oil poured on her arms finally broke her and she proffered a false confession to stop the interrogators. She was eventually released to her husband, Sami, and the couple fled Iraq and set up a new life in Paris, France.

Tracking down a lead on Nadia, Sayid left Iraq, assumed a new name and worked as a chef in Paris. Amira instantly recognized Sayid and told her husband that he was her torturer. Bent on revenge, Sami concocted a scheme to lure Sayid into their restaurant where he chained up the former soldier in their food pantry. Sami then took it upon himself to beat Sayid into confessing his transgressions against his wife. Sami was relentless until Amira called for him to stop. She asked for time alone with Sayid and told him the story of her recovery.

Terrified and a self-imposed recluse, Amira explained that she found the resolve to venture outside only after watching some children torture a cat. After nursing the cat back to health, and despite the cat's tendency to randomly turn on her, she forgave it because, like the cat, she too at times forgot what it meant to be safe. Amira then requested Sayid show her the same respect and acknowledge his sins against her. Seeing her pain, Sayid admitted his misdeeds to give the woman peace. Amira then forgave Sayid and said she would tell Sami she had the wrong man and let him go to stop the cycle of cruelty.

ALCOHOL

DHARMA INITIATIVE
RUM

DI 9FFTR731

DHARMA
INITIATIVE
BEER

960VKKS   R731

DHARMA
GND 94CTP02
DHARMA INITIATIVE
WHISKY

DHARMA
DI 9FFTR731
DHARMA INITIATIVE
CABERNET

Sawyer got drunk on old cans of DHARMA beer before assisting Hurley with the DHARMA van.

Kelvin Joe Inman told Desmond about the Swan station's fail-safe device after getting drunk on DHARMA red wine.

Jacob used a wine bottle to explain to Richard Alpert how the island is like a cork keeping a great evil from escaping and destroying the world.

For the survivors of the Oceanic crash, alcohol had its role as a medicinal item and it served as a comforting crutch for many. Alcoholic beverages served as catalysts for several key events that shaped the survivors' lives. Among the many noteworthy incidents, the following had particularly strong significance for future events.

Desmond Hume lived at the monastery where this brand was produced. He met Penny Widmore for the first time while filling an order for her father, Charles Widmore.

Desmond revealed his premonitions of Charlie Pace's death after drinking a bottle of whisky. This is the same expensive brand of whisky that Charles Widmore used to humiliate Desmond's financial standing.

After the flight 815 crash, the small bottle of vodka that Cindy gave Jack during the flight was used to sterilize his wound before Kate stitched it up.

Kate and Sawyer played "I Never" while drinking spirits, resulting in both of them admitting to murder.

ALEXANDRA ROUSSEAU

FACTS & FIGURES

Connection: Daughter of Danielle Rousseau

Also Known As: Alex

Family: Danielle Rousseau (mother); Robert (father); Benjamin Linus (adoptive father)

In her brief 16 years, Alexandra "Alex" Rousseau's entire existence was bound to the confines of the island. Born to a shipwrecked Danielle Rousseau, Alex was taken from her mother's tent on the beach by 25-year-old Benjamin Linus. Instead of killing the little girl as ordered by Charles Widmore, Ben raised Alex as his own. As she grew older, Alex rebelled against her "father" not only for his strict rules but because she didn't agree with many of the questionable practices he directed the Others to enforce. Whether it was their intention to take Claire Littleton's baby or their overall treatment of the Oceanic survivors, Alex always felt like an outsider with her "people" and made bolder and bolder choices to work against them.

BORN OF THE ISLAND

In 1988, a seven-months pregnant Danielle Rousseau and her fellow French expedition peers ran aground on the island. In the short span of two months Danielle killed her lover Robert and the rest of her crew because of the "sickness," which left her alone to give birth to a baby girl. Danielle named her Alexandra (it was to be Alexandre if a boy) and enjoyed only a week with her before she was abducted by Ben Linus.

BEN'S DAUGHTER

Linus took sympathy on the helpless baby girl with the crazy mother and returned her to the Others' camp. He cleverly kept Alex alive because he challenged Widmore to kill the baby himself, an action that caused the leader to balk and relent. Ben kept the name Alex for his new daughter and raised her with his adopted people in his barracks home.

A sweet little girl who loved her daddy's attention, father and daughter enjoyed a close relationship until Alex became a teenager. Better able to objectively process her father's actions, she pushed back against his rigid rules and aggressive tactics against the Oceanic survivors. She became surly, secretive and combative as she actively tried to subvert his plans. By the time Ben was ready to disown Alex, their relationship was so broken she reverted to calling him Ben.

Despite her anger, Alex was very hurt by Ben's actions and initially ignored him when he attempted to reach out to her after Naomi Dorrit's murder. But not long after when Ben had Locke's gun to his face, Alex stepped forward and tried to save his life which proved she still cared for him. In turn, Ben gave his daughter a map to the Temple so she, Karl and Danielle could be safe.

" Please, Daddy! Please. "

When Alex was seized by Martin Keamy, she came to realize that her father's frantic actions actually had a purpose. Back at the barracks an unsympathetic Keamy forced Alex to her knees as a life or death ultimatum. Although Alex pleaded with her father to save her, he tried a miscalculated plan to manipulate Keamy that resulted in Alex's death.

After Alex's death, Ben cradled his daughter in his arms and kissed her goodbye with utter regret.

STOPPING THE CYCLE
Morally offended by Ben and the Others' intention of making Claire's baby their own, Alex infiltrated the Staff station to warn Claire of their plan and then helped her escape. Even more compelling was the fact that Alex was unaware that the baby-napping she was so passionately attempting to thwart was exactly how she came to live with Ben and the Others, a karmic irony that she would learn a short time later.

REBELLION
Emboldened by the success of Claire's rescue, Alex moved onto springing her boyfriend Karl from Ben's security thugs. She unsuccessfully faced off against Pickett with her slingshot and as she was carried away by his team she warned Kate that the Others were liars and would kill Sawyer. Resilient, Alex then unlocked Jack's cell door in the Hydra so he could stop Juliet's trial.

MOTHERS AND DAUGHTERS
Although Alex was deprived of her birth mother, she always had a feeling there was something more to the story of her mother's death. When she learned the truth from Sayid, it intensified her hatred of Ben. Her father admitted the truth later, when he dismissively introduced mother and daughter for the first time during the *Kahana* crisis. Amazed by the revelation, Alex immediately helped her mother tie up her "father."

Alex handed Locke her weapon against Ben's wishes.

Alex used this rudimentary slingshot against Pickett in an attempt to free Karl.

YOUNG LOVE
While Alex's adventures against the Others were quite dramatic, in reality many of her actions were simply motivated by her feelings for Karl. A fellow Other, they were friends who fell in love. After learning about the relationship, Ben separated the two. Incensed, Alex used her manipulation skills learned from her father to break out Karl. She secured the help of Kate and Sawyer to assist after releasing them from their cages, and together they freed Karl from Room 23. When Karl was injured, she helped him to the beach and sacrificed her own safety so he could escape to the survivors' beach camp. The young couple was reunited later and clung to one another for support until Karl and Alex's mother were murdered by Keamy's mercenaries.

SMOKE MONSTER
The Man in Black knew how much Alex meant to Ben, so he appeared in her form to force the haunted man into obeying all of "Locke's" commands. He used Ben's guilt as a worthy tool to assure his compliance.

ALVAR HANSO

▶ CONNECTION: Founder of the Hanso Foundation

Alvar Hanso was a reclusive industrialist, philanthropist and entrepreneur who created the Hanso Foundation, a non-profit organization used to fund scientific and technological programs such as the DHARMA Initiative. Alvar's only known progeny was his daughter, Rachel Blake.

THE MAN BEHIND THE MYSTERY

Born sometime in the early 1900s in Denmark, Alvar was the great-grandson of 19th century shipping magnate Magnus Hanso. He received an undergraduate degree in chemistry in Denmark and enrolled at the University of Michigan in Ann Arbor twice: for a year as an undergraduate when he lived with the DeGroot family, and then years later to pursue a master's degree in engineering.

During World War II, Alvar carved out his own niche in industry by providing munitions to a variety of Resistance groups throughout Europe. Post-war, Hanso positioned himself as the future of military armament by providing NATO with the latest and greatest high-tech equipment. Over a span of decades, Hanso made it his company's mission to research and develop cutting-edge weapons systems to ensure peace around the globe. While it was a lucrative endeavor, in the late '60s Hanso's focus shifted to the fields of science and technology; more altruistic arenas that he felt were vital in bettering all mankind. Thus, he created the Hanso Foundation.

THE HANSO FOUNDATION

Established in 1967, the Hanso Foundation was created to fund forward-thinkers actively working to better the human experience. Its mission statement explained: "The Hanso Foundation stands at the vanguard of social and scientific research for the advancement of the human race. For forty years, the foundation has offered grants to worthy experiments designed to further the evolution of the human race and provide technological solutions to the most pressing problems of our time."

The Foundation awarded research grants to study life-extension research, electromagnetic research, human genomes, mathematical forecasting, mental health advancements, and global wellness programs.

> *"From the dawn of our species, Man has been blessed with curiosity. Our most precious gift, without exception, is the desire to know more—to look beyond what is accepted as the truth and to imagine what is possible."*
>
> — Alvar Hanso, Address to the U.N. Security Council, 1967

THE VALENZETTI EQUATION AND THE DHARMA INITIATIVE

The Foundation project closest to Hanso's heart was the DHARMA Initiative, or the **D**epartment of **H**euristics **A**nd **R**esearch on **M**aterial **A**pplications. Deeply affected by the Cuban Missile Crisis in 1962 (which almost resulted in a nuclear conflict), Alvar felt compelled to help quell any future escalations through scientific advancements. He soon discovered that right after the crisis the U.N. Security Council had commissioned noted Italian mathematician Enzo Valenzetti to create a top-secret equation that "predicts the exact number of years and months until humanity extinguishes itself." It became known as the Valenzetti Equation, which applied the numerical values of 4, 8, 15, 16, 23 and 42 to core environmental and human factors that were key to world annihilation. The U.N. was deeply disturbed by Valenzetti's work and tried to bury his theorem, but Hanso and University of Michigan doctoral candidates Gerald and Karen DeGroot used it as the basis to build their DHARMA Initiative. The DeGroots asked Hanso to fund their Initiative research projects as a means to scientifically discover ways to change any of those six numeric values with the intent to avert the destruction of humanity. In 1970, Alvar underwrote the project through his Hanso Foundation and personally helped them create their multi-disciplined social science research facility on a special island in the South Pacific.

Hanso was so invested in the project that he emerged from seclusion in 1975 to host one of the DHARMA Orientation films shown to new scientific recruits who had just entered the program. He explained in his own words DHARMA's connection to the Valenzetti Equation and the importance of the invaluable work being done at the top-secret island compound.

Aside from his personal and financial contributions to DHARMA, not much else is known about Alvar's life or work outside of brief anecdotal information. It was rumored that his obsession with the Valenzetti Equation caused him to purchase all copies, and reprint rights, to author Gary Troup's only non-fiction book, *The Valenzetti Equation,* which detailed the mathematician's theories. Hanso's last known public appearance was in 2002, it was said due to a particularly nasty internal power-shift at the Foundation between Alvar and his second-in-command, Thomas Werner Mittelwerk. It's also been said that Hanso's unusually robust longevity is due to his participation in the Foundation's life-extension experiments, however, that has never been confirmed.

ROOM 23 AT THE HYDRA STATION WAS THE RE-EDUCATION ROOM.

23 FLAVORS IN DR. PEPPER.

DUOTRIOPHOBIA IS FEAR OF THE NUMBER 23.

SAYID WAS 23 WHEN AMERICAN FORCES INVADED HIS HOMETOWN.

OCEANIC 815 DEPARTED FROM GATE 23.

KATE HAD A $23,000 BOUNTY FOR HER CAPTURE.

WIDMORE TOLD LOCKE TO CALL 23 TO REACH HIM ON THE INTERNATIONAL SATELLITE PHONE.

FARADAY SET HIS RADIATION DEVICE TO 2.342.

PSALM 23 BEGINS, "THE LORD IS MY SHEPHERD."

DAVE SAID LEONARD WOULD CALL HURLEY "23" IF HE STOLE HIS GRAHAM CRACKER.

JIN CHASES A TAXI WITH THE LICENSE PLATE NUMBER 2369.

HUMAN CELLS HAVE 23 PAIRS OF CHROMOSOMES.

BEN TOLD JACK TO MEET HIM AT SLIP 23.

JACK WAS CANDIDATE #23.

JULIUS CAESAR WAS STABBED 23 TIMES.

THE *BLACK ROCK*'S FIRST-MATE'S JOURNAL WAS LOT #2342 AT THE SOUTHFIELD'S AUCTION.

THE GERONIMO JACKSON EUROPEAN TOUR POSTER LISTED THE KICK-OFF TIME AT 23:00 HOURS.

A 23-SIDED POLYGON IS AN ICOSIKAITRIGON.

JULIET ENTERS 1623 INTO THE KEYPAD FOR THE DHARMA SONAR FENCE.

23 PEOPLE WERE ON THE DECK THAT COLLAPSED WITH HURLEY ON IT.

EKO RECITES THE 23RD PSALM WHEN ATTACKED BY THE SMOKE MONSTER.

PENELOPE'S HOME ADDRESS IS 423 CHEYNE WALK.

THE 23 ENIGMA.

23 IS A PRIME NUMBER.

JACK, ROSE, AND BERNARD SAT IN ROW 23.

THE *BLACK ROCK*'S SLIP WAS #23 IN PORTSMOUTH.

WORE JERSEYS WITH #23: MICHAEL JORDAN, LEBRON JAMES, DON MATTINGLY.

HURLEY'S HOTEL ROOM IN SYDNEY WAS 2342.

THE CONTAINER HOLDING LOCKE'S BODY IS 823.

ANA LUCIA CORTEZ

FACTS & FIGURES

Time On The Island

POST-OCEANIC: 64 Days

Hometown: Los Angeles

Year Of Birth: 1975

Skills: Weapons, Bilingual (English & Spanish)

Drink of Choice: Tequila and tonic

Oceanic Seat: 42F

On the surface, Ana Lucia Cortez was the definition of tough. A former LAPD cop and the de facto leader of the Oceanic 815 tailies, Cortez was fearless when faced with the kind of dire situations that would make most people run. But the hard veneer that she projected to the world was just a front used to protect herself from letting anyone see her vulnerable side. Deeply wounded physically and physiologically from being shot by a perp who took the life of her unborn child, Ana Lucia closed up emotionally and forever again had trouble trusting anyone.

TO SERVE AND PROTECT

Ana Lucia followed in the footsteps of her mother, police Captain Theresa Cortez, and joined the Los Angeles Police Academy. She became a patrol officer in Los Angeles and monitored some of the more troubled neighborhoods with her partner Mike "Big Mike" Walton. She was loyal, strong and respected by her fellow officers, but all it took was one on-the-job mistake and everything changed forever.

While responding to a burglary call with Big Mike, the partners split up to cover the exits when suspect Jason McCormack appeared. She ordered him to put his hands up but he claimed to be a student and went to grab his student ID. In that split second, he shot her four times with hollow-point bullets that pierced her bulletproof vest and killed her unborn child.

She was taken off the streets for four months to recover and met with a psychologist to deal with the devastating trauma. But Ana Lucia closed herself off emotionally from the world, which caused turmoil with her boyfriend, Danny. He eventually left and her trust issues got more entrenched. To cope, she asked to return to her patrol against her mother's wishes.

Back with her partner Big Mike, they headed to the quiet community of Westwood. Unfortunately, a local domestic disturbance call put them in the thick of the action again. While trying to calm down a bickering couple in a heated argument, Ana Lucia noticed a baby on the woman's hip. This propelled her into overdrive, as she drew her gun on the man. Big Mike had to talk her down, which disturbed him greatly.

Things got worse when Ana Lucia was alerted that Jason McCormack confessed to her shooting. However, Ana Lucia claimed he wasn't the shooter because she wanted to exact personal vengeance. Released a week later, she followed Jason to a bar and waited for him to leave. In a deserted alley, she told him she had been pregnant and pumped five bullets into him. Although Ana Lucia created an alibi, her mother knew the truth. At the morgue, Theresa made her daughter look at Jason's body and admit what she did. Ana handed over her badge and her life all in one moment.

"TOM" AND "SARAH"

After she resigned, Ana Lucia felt betrayed by the force, her mother and the world. She still defined herself as a cop so she took a job as an LAX security screener. Attempting to drown her sorrows in booze, she met a gregarious drunk, Christian Shephard, in the airport bar. After learning she had been a cop, he asked her to be his bodyguard in Australia and she accepted. The odd couple then gave each other pseudonyms and went on their way.

THE LOST SHEPHARDS

After a four-day drinking binge and a meeting with a mysterious woman, Ana Lucia revealed her real name and asked Tom to explain himself. He didn't reveal his true name or explain the situation, but admitted he was pathetic because he couldn't apologize to his son and had run away.

LOS ANGELES
POLICE

Ana-Lucia Cortez
NAME

Ana-Lucia Cortez
SIGNATURE

50187
SERIAL NO.

35403

CHIEF OF POLICE
CITY OF LOS ANGELES

"Are you going to try to convince me that everyone here doesn't hate me?"

After parting ways, Ana Lucia sat in the Sydney airport bar before her return flight home on Oceanic 815 where she met Jack Shephard, Christian Shephard's son. He explained that he was in Australia to retrieve his father's body. They were interrupted by her cell, but she promised to share another drink with Jack on the plane. And so it was that without knowing it, Ana Lucia had been the silent connector between the Shephards on their most fateful journeys.

SURVIVOR

Knocked unconscious by a suitcase in the crash, Ana Lucia awoke in the ocean and dragged herself out of the surf in one piece. Her emergency training immediately kicked in, as she performed life-saving CPR on a young girl named Emma. Ana Lucia was integral in establishing the beach camp and created some order out of the chaos. The spark of purpose was back in her life, which was why she quickly became so territorial when the Others started their night raids. Ana Lucia took it as her personal mission to protect her fellow survivors.

VIOLENT PATTERNS

In her quest to protect herself and her fellow tailies, Ana Lucia wasn't afraid to unleash her inner rage and go to some dark places all in the name of survival. Twelve days after the crash, Ana killed an Other and found their master list, which confirmed there was a spy.

Ana Lucia's badge when she worked security at LAX.

VISIONS

Ana Lucia was buried at Boone Hill, but even after death her spirit had great impact on some of those left behind.

Before anyone knew about her death, Ana appeared to Eko in his dream about Yemi and relayed that he needed to "help John find the question mark," which referred to the hidden blast door map.

While a fugitive for murder in LA, a dead Ana Lucia pulled over Hurley and warned him to lay low and go somewhere safe with an injured Sayid.

"Libby says hi."
—Spoken by Ana Lucia to Hurley

Suspicious of Nathan, Ana built a tiger pit, dumped Nathan into it and began her interrogation of him.

After collecting evidence, Ana Lucia found her perp in Goodwin, got her confession and then killed him.

Feeling paranoid after the Goodwin situation, Ana threw Jin, Sawyer and Michael into her tiger pit to get some answers.

On edge because of the whispers in the jungle and Cindy's disappearance, Ana Lucia shot an innocent Shannon as she emerged from the foliage.

OUTCASTS

While Ana Lucia tried to remain isolated from anyone so she only had to rely on herself, she couldn't help connecting with some kindred spirits on the island.

Overwhelmed by the crash and killing an Other, Ana crept away to a stream and broke down. Eko found her, held her and spoke for the first time in 40 days.

Despondent after she killed Shannon and abandoned by the tailies, Ana offered Sayid the chance to avenge his love. He declined and said they were "both dead already."

With an ulterior motive to gain a weapon, Ana had angry sex with fellow black sheep Sawyer.

When Jack learned that Ana killed an Other, he asked her how long it would take to build an Army.

Unable to kill again, she handed her gun to Michael to take out Ben but he used it to shoot her and Libby.

ANA LUCIA CORTEZ

ANCIENT DAGGER

This ancient dagger was used over a span of two millenia by both Jacob and the Man in Black as a tool against one another in their ongoing battle for island dominance. The blade was of Roman origin and came to the island the day before the twin boys' births by way of a group of Latin-speaking castaways. The shipwrecked survivors created their own small village and used their weapons to hunt and build shelters.

When he was 13, the dark-haired twin was visited by the spirit of his slain mother, Claudia. She guided him to the village to show him the truth of his heritage and origins. Appalled by the lies told to him by Mother, he left her and his brother Jacob to live with his people.

In the 30 years he spent with them, the Man in Black came to acquire and use their tools and accoutrements like the dagger he wore on his belt. He first revealed it to Jacob as they talked about a possible way off the island. In a dramatic illustration, the Man in Black threw the dagger at the foundation of a well to which it stuck like a magnet. He explained the discovery of something special in the well that would be his way off the island. He then resheathed the dagger on his hip.

After the Man in Black discovered the massacre of his brethren by Mother, he returned to the caves for the first time in decades and plunged the dagger through her in an act of rage. His act in turn set the stage for the violent face-off between the brothers and their ultimate individual roles as island protector and the seething smoke monster.

THE BLACK ROCK LINK

The next time the dagger came into play was in the late 1860s after the *Black Rock* crashed into the island. In Ricardo, the lone survivor, the Man in Black found a potential pawn to aid in his quest to leave the island. Initially he appeared in the hull of the boat to Alpert as the smoke monster to terrify the man. He later returned in his human visage and released the desperate man from his shackles and fed him. As they sat, the Man in Black unfolded a piece of canvas wrapped around the dagger and then offered it to Alpert as the implement to kill "the devil" (i.e., Jacob). His orders were explicit:

> ### *"Put this right through his chest. Don't hesitate—do not let him say a word. If he speaks, it will already be too late."*

Alpert reluctantly sought out Jacob by the destroyed statue of Taweret and attacked him with the dagger. However, Jacob easily deflected the attack and demanded to know who gave him the knife, which he recognized as his brother's. Alpert was then swayed to Jacob's side and the dagger remained in their possession until it was remanded into the care of the Temple guardian, Dogen.

DOGEN'S DAGGER

At some point during the next 150 years, the dagger was placed inside an intricately carved wooden box and given to Dogen to use when it was time to fight the Man in Black. Dogen buried the box inside a stone herb planter. He dug it out when he challenged Sayid to use it to kill the Man in Black to prove there was still a shred of good inside of him. Using words almost identical to those the Man in Black used with Alpert, Dogen commanded, "As soon as you see him, plunge this deep into his chest—you cannot hesitate. Do not let him say a word. If you allow him to speak, it is already too late."

Sayid embarked upon the mission unaware that it was a setup created by Dogen to get the Man in Black to kill Sayid. When Jarrah plunged the knife into the Man in Black, he quickly realized the entity inside Locke's body was immortal. For his part, the Man in Black immediately recognized the knife, handed it back to Sayid and explained that Dogen had set him up to be killed. Preying upon Sayid's betrayal, he offered Sayid whatever he wanted in exchange for going back to the Temple with a message. Sayid agreed, warned the Others and then went to confront Dogen. Sayid drowned him in the Temple's pool and then slit Lennon's throat with the dagger—an act that essentially sealed his fate as a follower of the Man in Black—and brought the violent legacy of the dagger full circle.

Dogen asked Sayid to plunge the dagger into the Man in Black's chest.

ANCIENT ROMAN DAGGERS ✛

Roman soldiers were often equipped with two weapons, a sword for the initial attack and a smaller dagger called a pugio that was carried in a sheath on the hip. Pugios were shorter than swords with a leaf-shaped blade that ran anywhere from 7 to 11 inches long. They sometimes had very ornate scabbards and hilts, crafted in bronze or other metals including iron and other alloys.

ANGELO BUSONI

▷ **CONNECTION:** Patient of Jack Shephard

An affluent businessman from Italy, Angelo Busoni traveled to St. Sebastian Hospital in Los Angeles for a surgical consultation with spinal surgeons Christian and Jack Shephard. Busoni brought his daughter Gabriela with him for support and to translate his Italian to English for the doctors.

Diagnosed with an inoperable spinal tumor, Busoni hoped Jack would perform his highly complicated surgery and save his life. Christian said the tumor was too difficult to remove and it would take a miracle to remove it. However, Busoni read an article in medical journals about Jack's successful operation on his wife Sarah Shephard's crushed spine and believed the doctor could do the same for him. Jack explained the risks were different, but flush with his previous success, he agreed to admit and operate on Angelo.

Through his daughter, Angelo told Christian they came for Jack, not him.

With his daughter by his side, Busoni spent months in the hospital boosting his immune system and receiving treatment to shrink the tumor before undergoing surgery. After seven hours of painstaking work, Jack successfully removed the tumor but Angelo went into cardiac arrest on the operating table and died.

ANKHS

An ankh is an Egyptian hieroglyph that has been translated to mean "eternal life." It is most often associated with sacred Egyptian burial practices, as Egyptians would leave ankhs in the tombs of the dead. It was their belief that a god or goddess would bestow it upon the mummified remains of the dead to bring them back to life so they could then travel into the afterlife.

There were several instances where ankhs appeared on the island, either blatantly or more subtly, to underscore the symbol's ancient origins.

The Statue of Taweret: Representing the Egyptian goddess Taweret, the island statue featured her holding an ankh in each hand. Taweret represented fertility and childbirth to the Egyptians, an important piece of the revered life cycle of their culture.

Paul, the former DHARMA Initiative Head of Security, wore an ankh necklace that went to his wife Amy after his death.

> **"It's not a guitar, man."** — Spoken by Hurley

ANUBIS

The Egyptian god Inpu (or Anubis, his more commonly known Greek name) was one of the most important gods associated with death, as he protected the tombs of the deceased. He, along with other Egyptian gods, was often depicted carrying an ankh. For Anubis, the ankh was used to wake the dead for their journey to the afterlife. Eventually, he also became the patron god of burial embalmers.

There was a large wooden ankh inside Hurley's guitar case that contained a hidden piece of paper with the list of Jacob's "candidates."

REYES

SHEPHARD

FORD

JARRAH

KWON

LOCKE

ANN ARBOR, THE UNIVERSITY OF MICHIGAN

One of the premier public research universities in the world, The University of Michigan, Ann Arbor campus was where Gerald and Karen DeGroot founded the DHARMA Initiative in 1970. As doctoral candidates at the school, they secured research funding for their project through Alvar Hanso and used the school as their home base for collecting data from their remote outpost.

It was at the Ann Arbor campus that the DeGroots recruited Dr. Pierre Chang, a professor of Theoretical Astrophysics, to join their DHARMA Initiative and relocate to the island. Chang eventually became the primary face and voice of the project through his work on the various orientation films.

After the time flashes on the island stranded Daniel Faraday in 1974, he left the island to work at the Ann Arbor DHARMA Initiative headquarters. For three years, Faraday re-created his life's work at their facilities where he pored over his equations in hopes of finding a way to course correct. His work at the university

also paralleled the path of one of his scientific heroes, early quantum physics and nuclear physics pioneer Enrico Fermi who lectured about Quantum Electrodynamics at U of M in the 1930s. Faraday even cited Fermi's work in his own time travel equations at Queens College in Oxford. Faraday remained in Ann Arbor until he finally returned to the island in 1977.

ANNIE

▶ **CONNECTION: Benjamin Linus' childhood friend**

Annie was a young girl who, with her parents, lived as a member of the DHARMA Initiative in 1973. In the DHARMA processing station on the island, Annie introduced herself to a shy Benjamin Linus. She gave him an Apollo bar and told him they could have as many as they wanted.

They became classmates, where Annie proved to be an inquisitive student. On the day they learned about volcanoes, Annie compared the model to the one that existed inside the island. Moments later, the Hostiles alarm sounded and Annie locked the classroom door and grabbed a frightened Ben to join her in the corner.

Ben and Annie's friendship bloomed. On his birthday, she made wooden dolls. She kept the boy doll and Ben kept the girl doll so they never had to be apart. Annie was Ben's first love and as such she influenced the type of women he gravitated towards for the rest of his life. Sometime around the Incident evacuation of women and children, Annie left the island and never returned.

ANTHONY

FACTS & FIGURES

Connection: Father of John Locke

Occupation: Con man

Aliases: Alan Seward, Louis Jackson, "The Man from Tallahassee," Paul, Ted MacLaren, Tom Sawyer

A cold-hearted, remorseless con man, Anthony Cooper was on the grift his entire life. In his six-decade con career, Cooper never met a person he wanted to keep around, be they lover, spouse, friend or even child. For a hardcore narcissist and swindler only interested in his own needs, attachments to people were unnecessary distractions that could potentially interfere with his cons. As such, he cut a swath of emotional and financial destruction across the 50 states, with ruined lives and broken relationships left in his wake.

COOPER

"If this isn't hell, friend, then where are we?"

CATALOGUE OF CONS

▸ *Jimmy Bane, criminal. Cooper stole $700,000 from him in a retirement con.*

▸ *Mrs. Talbot and Peter Talbot, widow and her son. Cooper tried to marry Mrs. Talbot for her money, but Peter figured he was a scam artist. Cooper had Peter killed and then fled to Mexico.*

LOCKE'S DADDY

Anthony Cooper ranked as one of the all-time worst possible candidates for fatherhood, but that didn't stop him from getting young Emily Locke pregnant. He abandoned them both, but Cooper's bad genetics lived on in a son named John Locke. While an innocent, orphaned John dreamed of reconnecting with his parents, he could hardly know that distance from Emily and Cooper was the best gift they could have given him. Sadly, when John was in his late 30s, his birth mother and father re-entered his life and scammed their own child in a particularly cruel con that changed John's life forever.

ANATOMY OF THE SCAM

▸ *Anthony sent a now-aged Emily to John's work to catch his attention. When John confronted her in a parking lot, she admitted she was his mother and said he was immaculately conceived.*

▸ *John hired Frainey, a private detective, to get information on Emily's and Cooper's backgrounds.*

▸ *John found Anthony's gated residence. Cooper allowed him in and the two men bonded over scotch. He invited Locke back to hunt several times, until one day he "screwed up" John's arrival time and was forced to reveal his dialysis machine and need for a kidney transplant.*

▸ *Locke offered his own kidney, which Cooper gratefully accepted.*

▸ *After the transplant, Cooper had himself discharged into private care and left John without speaking a word.*

After the transplant, John stalked Cooper until he told his son he wasn't wanted. Soon after, Cooper faked his own death to scam an associate out of his part of a con. Anthony saw Locke at his funeral and approached him on the sly and asked him to retrieve the money for a payout of $200,000. Locke did it but declined the money and Cooper disappeared again.

After John confronted his father about Peter Talbot's death, Cooper pushed him through the window of an eight-story building.

John stumbled upon another Cooper scheme years later which he convinced Anthony to stop, but not before the con man killed his mark's son in retribution for ruining his grift. When Locke went to confront him, Anthony threw John out an eight-story window and ran to Mexico. When the fake Oceanic 815 was found underwater, Cooper assumed Locke died with everyone else.

Cooper preyed upon Mrs. Talbot in one con.

MR. SAWYER

In 1976, Cooper, under the alias of Tom Sawyer, seduced Mary Ford out of $38,000 and left town. When Mary's husband found out, he went crazy and killed her and himself in a terrible murder/suicide. It left their son, James Ford, scarred and hell-bent on revenge.

> **BY THE NUMBERS** ✛
> *Anthony Cooper's high-rise apartment number was **3801**.*
> *Cooper's lockbox was **1516**.*

THE ISLAND'S RECKONING

Almost three months after the Oceanic 815 crash, Anthony Cooper was driving in Tallahassee, Florida when he was rear-ended by another car and sent into a highway divider doing 70mph. He was picked up by an ambulance operated by off-island Others who injected him with a sedative and shipped him off to the island.

When Anthony woke up, he was bound and gagged inside the basement of Ben's house at the barracks. Assuming he had died and gone to hell, Cooper bit the hand of John when his son took off his gag. The Others then moved the feisty old con man with them to their alternate camp where they tied him to a column. Ben tasked Locke with killing his old man in order to become an Other. Anthony mocked John, called him spineless and said he would never kill him because "he wanted his daddy."

Courtesy of Richard Alpert, Locke made the connection between his father and Sawyer's lifelong enemy. He lured Sawyer to the brig of the *Black Rock* and put him inside with Cooper to do his dirty work and give the man his own closure. In his typically nasty way, Cooper explained to Sawyer his connection to Locke and his con man past, which made Sawyer realize who this man was to him. Forced to read Sawyer's letter, Cooper mocked it along the way until he finally shredded it without a lick of guilt or remorse. Furious, Sawyer pounced and choked the hateful old man to death.

APOLLO CANDY BARS

Branded chocolate confections, the Apollo Bar was first seen on the island when Boone Carlyle offered one to Shannon Rutherford after the crash. The candy was later discovered in the Swan pantry by Kate Austen as she explored the available food in the stock room.

The bars were manufactured by The Apollo Candy Company and sold around the world. Their history dates back to 1962 when M. David Benson used his grandfather's Benson Bar chocolate recipe to create the first Apollo Bars. He sold his first bars out of J.Pickersweet's Five and Dime in San Francisco and by 1968 the company expanded their candy to a national audience. However, the company's rapid success created huge financial problems. So in 1970, Alvar Hanso of the Hanso Foundation stepped in and saved the company from bankruptcy. It was through Hanso's connection that the DHARMA Initiative had Apollo Bars included in their regular island provision shipments.

While on the island, many of the survivors were partial to Apollo Bars. Hurley offered bars to Rose, Sun, and Ben when they sat outside of Jacob's cabin. Locke even kept Apollo Bars on the desk near the Swan station's computer.

There were plenty of Apollo Bars stacked alongside the other food rations.

INGREDIENTS: DESIGNER WHEY PROTEIN BLEND (WHEY PROTEIN CONCENTRATE, HYDROLYZED WHEY PROTEIN, POUF WHEY PROTEIN ISOLATE), WATER, **YAK BUTTER** (99.7% USP GLYCERIN, L-LEUCINE, L-TAURINE, CLAY), CHOCOLATE COATING [SUGAR, PARTIALLY HYDROGENATED PALM KERNEL OIL, NONFAT DRY MILK SOLIDS, COCOA POWDER PROCESSED WITH ALKALI, WHOLE MILK SOLIDS, SOY LECITHIN, NATURAL FLAVOR, SALT, ARTIFICIAL **FLAVER**], PEANUTS, CARAMEL, **LARK'S VOMIT**, GELATIN, CALCIUM CASEINATE, **INULIN (NOW JUST WHAT THE HELL IS THAT)** RICE FLOUR, **MOUSE TOES**, SALT, SUCRALOSE, POTASSIUM SORBATE. CONTAINS PEANUTS.

ARCTIC STATION

Hurley discovered Apollo Bars in the Swan station's food pantry.

Henrik and Mathias reported any findings directly to Penelope Widmore.

Annie gave a young Benjamin Linus an Apollo Bar when he first arrived on the island.

A remote monitoring station positioned at an undisclosed location near the North Pole. Penelope Widmore hired two men from Brazil, Henrik and Mathias, to man the station, which was stocked with sophisticated equipment that scanned the globe for significant electromagnetic disturbances.

The station was very spartan and small, with barely enough square footage to provide living space for the two men. It featured one main room with several portholes, which let in a small amount of natural light to augment the minimal overhead fluorescents within. Furnishings included bunks and two desks that flanked the walls. A yellow telephone on one desk provided a direct line to Penelope. The men passed their time by frequently playing chess.

ARLENE & JOSEPH STEWART

▶ CONNECTION: Australian couple who attempted to adopt Claire's baby

The Stewart's lawyer, Mr. Slavitt, presided over the meeting.

in·u·lin noun *Chemistry.* a polysaccharide, $(C_6H_{10}O_5)n$, obtained from the roots of certain plants, esp. elecampane, dahlia, and Jerusalem artichoke, that undergoes hydrolysis to the dextrorotatory form of fructose: used chiefly as an ingredient in diabetic bread and as a reagent in diagnosing kidney function.

Melbourne-based couple Arlene and Joseph Stewart met with Claire Littleton in Sydney, Australia in September 2004 to discuss adopting her baby. The Stewarts were prepared to fly Claire to Melbourne and pay for her to stay in a two-bedroom apartment for the rest of the pregnancy. They promised to cover all of Claire's medical and living expenses up until the birth. After her discharge from the hospital, Claire would also have received an additional $20,000.

THE CONTRACT

Arlene and Joseph stipulated in the contract that once the baby was born, Claire would release all rights to see the child again. In return, Claire asked the Stewarts to sing the Perry Como song "Catch A Falling Star" to the baby on occasion, as her father sang it to her.

In a perfect example of coincidence or fate, no matter how hard Claire tried, the pen she used to sign the contract wouldn't work. The lawyer, Mr. Slavitt, gave her a different pen, but it didn't work either. Having a keen interest in astrology, Claire felt that this was a bad sign, so she rescinded the offer and fled the office.

Claire met the Stewarts to sign over the rights to her baby.

THE ARROW

Labeled as station number two by the DHARMA Initiative, the Arrow was a remote bunker in the jungle that served as an observation outpost. According to the recovered portion of the Arrow's orientation film hosted by Dr. Pierre Chang, the station was used to "develop defensive strategies and gather intelligence on the island's hostile indigenous population."

The door to the Arrow was nearly covered by vines.

The tailies used the abandoned station for shelter.

DHARMA HISTORY

It is unknown when exactly the Arrow was constructed, but sometime around the 1973 truce between the DHARMA Initiative and "the hostiles," it was utilized as an observation station to collect recon. Horace Goodspeed was originally stationed at the Arrow (as reflected by his jumpsuit patch) where his knowledge and insight into hostile activities no doubt contributed to his eventual promotion to island DHARMA leader. Subsequent station assignees are unknown, but at some point after the Purge, Stuart Radzinsky placed excised footage of the Swan orientation film inside a Bible left within the abandoned Arrow station.

THE TAILIES

About one month after the crash of Oceanic flight 815, the surviving tailies discovered the Arrow while hiking inland to find safety from the raiding Others. They uncovered the station's door, which was virtually obscured by vine overgrowth. Once they found the inside dry and secure, they used the bunker as temporary shelter for about 20 days. Much later, Michael Dawson and James "Sawyer" Ford were released from the pit and brought to the Arrow to join the rest of the tailies before they packed up and hiked to the main survivors' beach camp.

Radzinsky's ominous warning to the world after the Purge.

INSIDE THE ARROW

On the inside of the station door, the word "Quarantine" was stencilled in paint by Radzinsky in his post-DHARMA paranoia. Despite 15 years of dormancy, the Arrow still had basic, functional electricity thanks to an old battery that powered a few lights. Little else remained in the station except for a metal chest. The contents of the chest included a glass eye, a hollowed-out Bible with a reel of film, a U.S. Army-stamped knife, a radio and blankets.

THE ARROW ORIENTATION FILM

In 1977, Dr. Pierre Chang hosted the Arrow orientation film using the alias name of Dr. Marvin Candle. The film was shot at the barracks, but only a brief snippet of the film's introduction was ever recovered.

" What is this place? "

— Spoken by Elizabeth "Libby" Smith

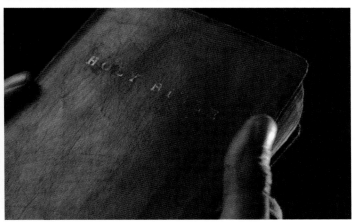

Hidden inside the Bible was a missing portion of the Swan orientation film.

ARROW RADIO

Sayid and Hurley picked up a signal from the '40s using the radio.

This handheld radio was found inside the Arrow station by Oceanic flight 815's tail-section survivors. The radio picked up various broadcast signals, the significance of which remained a mystery to those who heard them.

Bernard Nadler unwittingly made the first connection between the tailies and the other survivors of flight 815 by using this radio. The signal from Bernard's radio was picked up by Boone Carlyle, who was using the radio inside the Beechcraft. Sadly, they never made a connection as Ana Lucia Cortez took the radio from Bernard, fearing that the Others were trying to trick them.

A MYSTERIOUS SIGNAL

After the battery in the Arrow radio failed, Sayid attempted to fix the device and experienced the first sign of time travel on the island. After initially picking up Danielle Rousseau's message, they acquired a signal to the radio station WXR. When questioned about the clarity of the signal, Sayid explained that radio waves bounce off the ionosphere and can travel thousands of miles, meaning the signal could be coming from anywhere. In truth, they had tapped into a radio broadcast from the 1940s thanks to the island's unique properties connecting the two time periods. After several failed attempts to tap into a functional frequency, the Arrow radio only played static.

Bernard made contact with Boone using the Arrow station's radio.

ASH

Of the many mysteries on the island, the use of certain kinds of ash was one of most fascinating. Ceremonial circles of ash were directly tied to some of the island's most significant and terrifying events.

A PROTECTIVE BARRIER

A circle of light gray, powdery ash was laid around Jacob's cabin. The ash served as a protective perimeter designed to keep the Man in Black out. At some point, though, the circle was broken, which made it unsafe for Jacob's advisor to visit him. On the other hand, this breach in the circle allowed the Man in Black to enter the cabin whenever he pleased.

When Dogen, Lennon, and the Others at the Temple learned about Jacob's death, they prepared ash around all of the entry points to the Temple's courtyard as added protection to keep out the Man in Black.

On the island, the ash was utilized as more than just a protective obstacle. Dogen used the ash as part of a series of procedures on Sayid Jarrah that included electrocution and burning. Dogen claimed that it helped determine whether or not Sayid had been "claimed" by a darkness.

Ilana stored Jacob's ashes in this pouch.

ARTHUR GALZETHRON

▶ **CONNECTION:** Judge in Kate Austen's murder trial

Arthur Galzethron was the Los Angeles judge who presided over the murder trial of Kate Austen after she returned from the island as one of the Oceanic Six. District Attorney Melissa Dunbrook argued that Austen was a flight risk, to which the judge agreed and placed Kate in custody for the duration of the trial. The judge made the call to allow Jack Shephard on the stand to vouch for Kate as a character witness. Later when Diane Jansen declined to take the stand against her daughter for "medical reasons," Galzethron recessed the case for lunch, during which Kate agreed to a plea deal.

ARTURO

▶ **CONNECTION:** Lover of Tom Friendly

After Michael and his son Walt left the island, one of the Others, Tom Friendly, visited a then-suicidal Michael. Tom explained to Michael that the island would not let him die because it still had work for him to do.

When Michael visited Tom later in his penthouse hotel room, he encountered Arturo, Tom's lover. Arturo left the hotel room to give Tom and Michael some privacy, but not before Tom kissed him on the cheek. This exchange shed light on a situation that occurred between Kate Austen and Tom, when Kate was asked to remove her clothes on Hydra island. Tom had laughed at Kate's refusal to undress, claiming she "wasn't his type," something that the appearance of Arturo later explained.

JACOB'S REMAINS

After Jacob's death, Ilana ventured inside the Taweret statue and retrieved his burned remains from the fire. She gathered all of his ashes and placed them inside a cloth pouch. After Ilana's death, Hurley took control of the pouch until a young version of Jacob stole them from him. As Hurley attempted to catch up to the young Jacob, he ran into the adult Jacob. After pouring his own ashes into a fire, Jacob explained that once the ashes had completely burned away, he would never be able to appear again. This ceremonial burning of his last remains prompted the remaining candidates to meet with Jacob's spirit to finally understand why they had been brought to the island.

After Jacob's death, Ilana retrieved his ashes.

A young Jacob took the ashes from Hurley.

Jacob finally revealed why the candidates were chosen prior to his ashes burning away.

CONNECTIONS ✛

A "protective circle" is quite common in ritualistic magic and other belief systems. Oftentimes, the circles are carved into the ground around the practitioner, drawn with chalk, or created with salt—considered a powerful substance in many religions.

The notion of it being a sacred circle is a bit imprecise. In fact, the process creates a sphere of energy or protection encompassing the person within it. The drawn circle simply determines its perimeter.

ASTHMA INHALER

When Jack and Sayid tied Sawyer to a tree in order to get the inhaler, it revealed the extremes that both men would go to learn the truth.

Asthma, a chronic inflammation of the lungs where the airways become narrowed, is exacerbated by poor air quality and psychological stress. The loss of a simple item such as Shannon Rutherford's asthma inhaler (which she dropped during the severe turbulence of flight 815) brought several castaways' personality traits to the surface after the crash:

Boone Carlyle's concern for Shannon's health didn't seem to match what one would expect for a half-sister and hinted at the complicated relationship that he and Shannon shared.

Sawyer's agreement to give them the inhaler for a kiss from Kate—and her compliance—exposed their attraction.

Sun's ability to improve Shannon's breathing by using crushed eucalyptus leaves exposed her botanical interest prior to her garden tending.

Sawyer's admission to never having the inhaler brought to light his love of a con.

AUSTRALIA

The smallest continent on Earth (in terms of area), Australia is comprised of the mainland, the island of Tasmania and hundreds of other small islands that surround the continent in both the Indian and Pacific Oceans. Its largest city is Sydney, which is located on the east coast of the country and is home to more than four and a half million people. Oceanic flight 815 originated from Sydney Airport on September 22, 2004 at 2:15 p.m. Australian Eastern Standard Time with an intended destination of Los Angeles, California. The flight broke apart in mid-air over an uncharted island in the South Pacific.

HISTORY

Australia was a nation created out of two diverse and conflicting cultures: its ancient, spiritual indigenous peoples, better known as Aborigines, and the Western pioneers who followed the lead of English explorer Captain James Cook after he claimed the country for Britain in 1770.

As an island with its own mystical history, it's interesting to note how Australia's evolution parallels the island's in many ways. The original indigenous Australians were nomadic people who lived in balance with nature. They created a rich oral history of their origins that was synonymous with the land's animals, flora and fauna called "Dreamtime." They understood this sacred state, or "dreaming," existed in tandem with their everyday lives and would continue after they died. Their spiritualism and connection to the land proved to be in stark contrast to the goals of British colonization, which were entirely focused on bringing European economic and cultural structure to the "wild" nation.

Similarly on the island, Mother's and then Jacob's goal of keeping the light at the heart of the island protected, ran into serious problems as more humanity arrived. The people who made the island their home became curious about what made the island special, which led to exploration and experimentation. The closer they got to discovering—and then exploiting—the light, the more desperate Mother's and Jacob's job became to keep it untouched.

ISLAND CONNECTIONS

Many of the passengers on Oceanic 815 either hailed from Australia or had connections there through business or pleasure. In particular, some of the passengers seemed absolutely fated to spend time in Oz, the outcome of which resulted in their being booked on a flight destined to change the course of all 324 passengers' lives.

IN AUSTRALIA

- ▶ *Ana Lucia Cortez:* Came with Christian Shephard as his bodyguard.
- ▶ *Bernard Nadler:* Brought his wife, Rose, to see Isaac of Uluru on their honeymoon.
- ▶ *Boone Carlyle:* Intended to return Shannon back home.
- ▶ *Charlie Pace:* Visiting his brother, Liam, in hopes of reuniting Drive Shaft.
- ▶ *Eko:* Investigating the "death" of Charlotte Malkin.
- ▶ *Hugo "Hurley" Reyes:* Searching for Sam Toomey and information about the numbers.
- ▶ *Jack Shephard:* Returning his deceased father home.
- ▶ *Jin-Soo Kwon:* Delivering Mr. Paik's Rolex watch to an associate in Sydney.
- ▶ *Kate Austen:* On the run from the authorities; was working for Ray Mullen.
- ▶ *John Locke:* Attempting to participate in a "Walkabout" in the Outback.
- ▶ *Michael Dawson:* Went to pick up Walt after his mother's death.
- ▶ *Rose Nadler:* On her honeymoon with Bernard.
- ▶ *James "Sawyer" Ford:* Looking for the original Sawyer, the man who conned his mother.
- ▶ *Sayid Jarrah:* Recruited by Alyssa Cole and Robbie Hewitt to infiltrate a terrorist cell in Sydney.
- ▶ *Shannon Rutherford:* Living in Sydney with her boyfriend.
- ▶ *Sun-Hwa Kwon:* Traveling with Jin.

Kalgoorlie: Hugo Reyes visited Sam Toomey's widow, Martha Toomey.

CAPITAL: Canberra   POPULATION: 22M

NATIVES

❶ SYDNEY: Claire Littleton, Cindy Chandler, Thomas (Claire's boyfriend), Rachel (Claire's Australian friend), Richard, Joyce and Charlotte Malkin, Laurence, Robbie Hewitt, Lindsey (Claire's aunt), Officer Barnes, Malcolm, Caldwell, Ian McVay

❷ MELBORNE: Arlene and Joseph Stewart, Ray Mullen

❸ CENTRAL AUSTRALIA: Isaac of Uluru

❹ KALGOORLIE: Sam Toomey and Martha Toomey

RESIDENTS

❶ SYDNEY: Liam Pace, Susan Lloyd, Brian Porter, Vincent, Frank Duckett, Essam Tasir, Haddad, Yusef, Imam, Walt

Uluru: Isaac the faith healer met with Bernard and Rose Nadler.

Queensland, Great Barrier Reef: Site of Joanna Miller's scuba diving excursion.

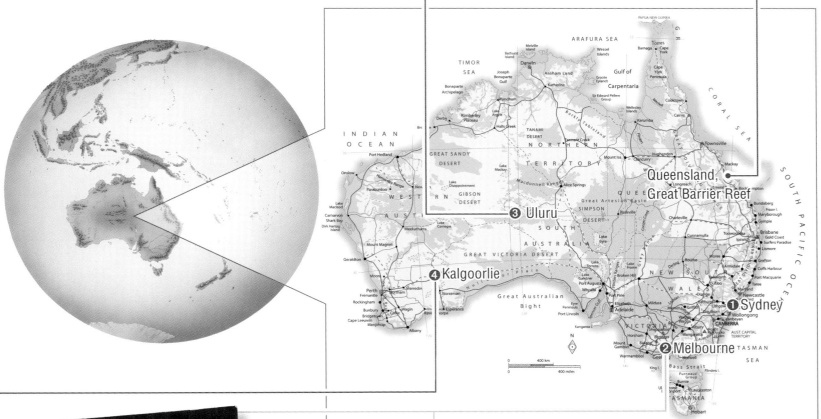

Melbourne: John Locke attempted to participate in a Melbourne Walkabout Tour.

Melbourne (100km outside): Kate Austen worked for farmer Ray Mullen.

BACKGAMMON

A classic board game of strategy, backgammon is played by two people who roll a pair of dice with the goal of getting their counters off the game board before the other player.

Backgammon was of particular interest to John Locke prior to the island and during his time on the island. As a young foster child, he was seen playing the board game right before Richard Alpert visited him for his school aptitude "test." Then shortly after the Oceanic flight 815 crash, Locke found an undamaged backgammon board in the wreckage and proceeded to set up a game. An intrigued Walt Lloyd asked Locke about how to play. He explained its basic, ancient origins and the essence of the game as such: "Two players. Two sides. One is light, one is dark." During his time on the island, Locke played the game with other survivors, including Charlie and Sawyer.

Aside from Locke, others also showed an affinity for the game. While detained at the barracks by the Others, Kate is seen playing a game of backgammon by herself. And most notably, Walt and Hurley engage in several matches together for promissory money. Despite Hurley's confession that he once ranked seventeenth in a backgammon tournament, Walt bested him to the tune of $83,000 in losses.

BY THE NUMBERS

In a traditional backgammon set, a participant chooses to play either white or black counters and is given a total of 15 to set up according to the rules of the board. The alternate doubling cube features the numbers 4, 8 and 16.

◼ Locke explained the rules of backgammon to Walt.

Outer board

The board is grouped into four quadrants, each with six triangles.

Each board consists of 24 triangles called points.

ANCIENT ORIGINS

The modern game of backgammon can trace its origins back to circa 3100 BC with the ancient Egyptian game of senet. Also a two-player strategy game, senet became a standard accoutrement in Egyptian tombs for the dead to take with them into the afterlife. The English translation of the Egyptian word for senet means "game of passing." The game board consists of 30 squares with square 15 marking the traditional start point.

*" **Two players. Two sides. One is light, one is dark.** "*

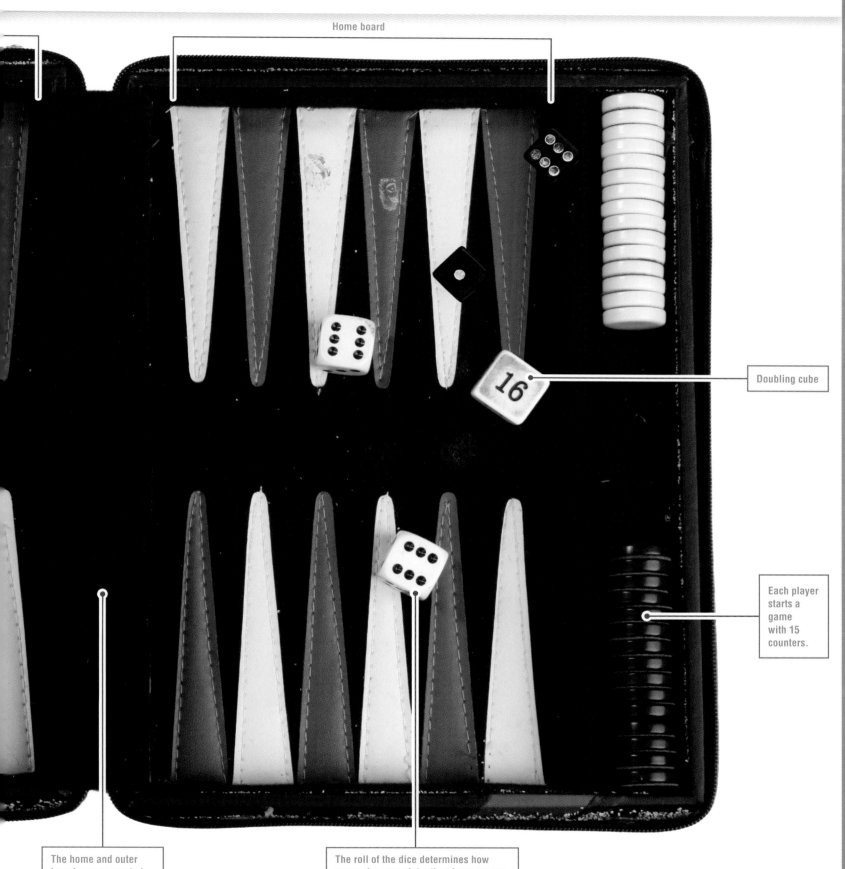

Home board

Doubling cube

Each player starts a game with 15 counters.

The home and outer boards are separated by the bar.

The roll of the dice determines how many pips, or points, the player moves his counters.

THE NUMBER OF PIPS ON A PAIR OF SIX-SIDED DICE.

JACKIE ROBINSON WORE JERSEY #42.

IN JEWISH KABBALAH, GOD CREATED THE WORLD IN 42 DAYS.

THE ADDRESS OF DESMOND'S JAIL WAS 42 BERECHURCH ROAD.

AT THE BUTCHER SHOP, BEN'S NUMBER IS 342.

ANA LUCIA SAT IN ROW 42.

KATE'S POST-ISLAND ADDRESS WAS 42 PANORAMA CREST.

42 PRINCIPLES OF MA'AT WERE AN ANCIENT EGYPTIAN CODE FOR LAW AND MORALS.

THERE ARE 42 PLAYABLE SPOTS ON A CONNECT FOUR BOARD.

42 IS THE ANSWER TO THE ULTIMATE QUESTION OF LIFE, THE UNIVERSE, AND EVERYTHING.

THE MEGA NUMBER ON HURLEY'S LOTTERY TICKET.

A 42-SIDED POLYGON IS A TETRACONTAKAIDIGON.

JIN WORE A HANDCUFF ON HIS WRIST FOR 42 DAYS.

42 IS A PERFECT SCORE ON THE USA MATH OLYMPIAD.

PENELOPE'S HOME ADDRESS IS 423 CHEYNE WALK.

XLII

42 MOVES TO MATE IN THE CHESS GAME IN THE FLAME STATION.

A GUEST AT HURLEY'S BIRTHDAY PARTY WEARS A 42 JERSEY.

KWON WAS CANDIDATE #42.

42 LAWS OF CRICKET.

CLAIRE WAS INJECTED WITH AN UNKNOWN DRUG FROM A CONTAINER LABELED CR 4-81516-23 42.

FARADAY SET HIS RADIATION DEVICE TO 2.342.

RAINBOWS FORMED BY RAINWATER APPEAR AS A 42-DEGREE ARC.

KATE'S TRIAL DOCKET NUMBER WAS 42231615.

DESMOND NEEDS $42,000 TO BUY A BOAT.

THE ORION NEBULA IS OBJECT M42.

LEWIS CARROLL'S FAVORITE NUMBER.

TEXAS 42 IS A DOMINO GAME.

THE BLACK ROCK'S FIRST-MATE'S JOURNAL WAS LOT #2342 AT THE SOUTHFIELD'S AUCTION.

HURLEY'S HOTEL ROOM IN SYDNEY WAS 2342.

MS. KLUGH (BEA)

▶ **CONNECTION:** Member of the Others; interrogated Michael Dawson

Beatrice "Bea" Klugh was a trusted member of the Others assigned by Benjamin Linus to help set up an elaborate ruse in order to gain information from Michael Dawson about his son, Walt Lloyd, and other key survivors of Oceanic flight 815. Together with Tom Friendly, Pickett, Alex and a large contingent from the barracks, Bea helped construct a fake Others camp by the ocean.

The camp was supposed to resemble the Others' permanent settlement in order to maintain the secrecy of New Otherton.

In her late 30s, Klugh was extremely intelligent (fluent in English and Russian), a shrewd interrogator and quite capable of defending herself. Her ability to lie masterfully, along with her absolute dedication to protecting the Others, made her the ideal person to lead the faux camp operation.

Klugh first revealed herself to Michael when he was brought into the camp by Tom's raiding party. Klugh immediately started to interrogate Michael about Walt. She specifically asked if they were biologically related, at what age Walt started to speak, and if he suffered headaches as a child. Most importantly, she wanted to know if there was ever a time that Walt appeared in a place he was not supposed to be.

Ms. Klugh wore aged clothing in an attempt to conceal her identity from Michael.

After a week of continued interrogation, Bea revealed to a despondent Michael that one of her people (Benjamin Linus) had been captured by the Oceanic survivors. She admitted that they could not get him back alone, so in exchange for Michael's help they would facilitate the father and son's release from the island. Distrustful of her offer, Michael demanded to see Walt and she acquiesced to a three-minute meeting.

She supervised their reunion and censored Walt from talking about the tests they performed on him in Room 23. When Walt cryptically revealed that Klugh and her people were pretending, she ended the meeting and had the pair forcibly separated. As Michael sobbed, she handed him a list and explained that she also needed him to bring only the four listed—Jack Shephard, Kate Austen, Hugo Reyes and James Ford—back to camp or he would never see Walt again.

Three days later, Klugh was part of the Others group who collected Michael and his quarry at the capsule dump and brought them to the Pala Ferry. She revealed Mr. Friendly's first name, Tom, when a gagged Kate called him out for his fake beard. Annoyed, he in turn revealed her first name.

HER DEMISE

Several days later, when Kate, Locke, Sayid and Danielle Rousseau hiked into the jungle in search of the Others, they discovered the Flame station. Bea was there with Mikhail Bakunin. As the group approached, Klugh hid in the station basement and waited for the right moment to attack. As Kate and Sayid investigated the underground space, Bea ambushed Kate. The women scuffled for control of Kate's gun until Sayid entered the room. Kate recognized Bea from the Pala Ferry and punched her in the face. She remained eerily silent until they marched her outside the station. To their surprise, Mikhail held Locke by gunpoint and demanded they trade their people and go their separate ways. As Locke and Mikhail argued, Bea addressed Mikhail forcefully in Russian until he took his gun off Locke and shot her in the chest. The single bullet took her life.

> **IN TRANSLATION** ✚
> *Rather than compromise her people, Bea communicated with Mikhail in his native Russian and ordered him to take her life to protect the Others.*
>
> **MS. KLUGH:**
> *Mikhail.*
> *You know what you have to do.*
>
> *Ti znaesh shto delat.*
>
> **MIKHAIL:**
> *We still have options.*
> *U nas estche yest vybor.*
>
> **MS. KLUGH:**
> *We cannot risk the repercussions. You know the protocol --*
>
> *Mi ne mozhem riskovat posledstviyami. Ti znaesh uslovia --*
>
> **MIKHAIL:**
> *No. There's another way --*
>
> *Net est drugoy vykhod --*
>
> **MS. KLUGH:**
> *They have us, Mikhail.*
> *We can't let them use us to breach the compound!*
>
> *Oni vsyaly nas. Mi ne dadim im a proyti un territoriu!*
>
> **MS. KLUGH**
> *You know what you have to do. That's a direct order --*
>
> *Ti znaesh shto delat. Eto prikaz --*
>
> **MIKHAIL:**
> *-- We still have options!*
> *U nas estche yest vykhod!*
>
> **MS. KLUGH:**
> *JUST DO IT, MIKHAIL!*
>
> **MIKHAIL:**
> *Forgive me!*

THE BARRACKS

NEW OTHERTON, DHARMAVILLE AND OTHERSVILLE

The barracks was the official name of the settlement built on the island in the early '70s by the DHARMA Intiative. Planned similarly to a suburban neighborhood, it consisted of a collection of buildings and services that made the enclave a self-reliant community on the island. This compound allowed DHARMA founders Gerald and Karen DeGroot to carry out their dream of creating a communal society where its scientists, researchers, teachers, workers and their families could live together in utopian harmony.

THE GROUNDS

During the DHARMA era, the entire complex was surrounded by a sonar fence that ostensibly served to "keep out the island's abundant wildlife." In reality, the fence functioned as a means to keep out the Hostiles and the smoke monster. However, the Others/Hostiles were well aware of the ancient tunnels that ran underneath the barracks and could access the inside of the DHARMA perimeter at any time.

BY THE NUMBERS ✛
*According to the truce signed by Richard Alpert and Horace Goodspeed, only 216 (**108** x 2) DHARMA members could exist on the island at any one time.*

INHABITANTS OVERVIEW

DHARMA inhabited the barracks from the early '70s until the Purge. The mass genocide left the buildings available for the Others to utilize and they moved into the compound soon after.

The Others turned the community into a thriving island suburbia until 2004 and the crash of flight 815. John Locke discovered they were living there with electricity and running water, communicating with the outside world, coming and going as they pleased. He even accused Ben of cheating, calling him a hypocrite. Disgusted, Locke said Ben didn't deserve to be on the island. His rebuke inspired Ben to move the Others back to living in the jungle as they had done previously, abandoning the barracks.

The initial design plans of the barracks.

1 Welcome Center

2 Security Office

3 Recreation Room

4 Playground

5 Infirmary

6 The Gazebo

Charles Widmore attempted his first return to the island via the *Kahana* freighter. Thinking the barracks was the only place with any type of security, Locke briefly moved into them after he and a select group of his supporters broke off from Jack Shephard's leadership. This faction remained there until Martin Keamy and his fellow mercenaries infiltrated the barracks and killed Ben's daughter, Alex. Ben ordered his people to retreat to the much safer Temple, which left the barracks abandoned once again.

No one inhabited the barracks again until Ajira flight 316 landed on Hydra island, at which point Ben, Sun and Frank Lapidus returned to the long-neglected facility. During the final machinations of the Man in Black, the barracks served as the staging ground for some of his interactions with Sawyer, Ben, Richard Alpert and eventually Charles Widmore. It's unknown how Hugo "Hurley" Reyes used the community during his tenure as the island's protector.

BENJAMIN LINUS

FACTS & FIGURES

Time On The Island

IN DHARMA: Approx. 14 years

AS AN OTHER: Approx. 20 years

DURING HURLEY'S REIGN: Many years

Date Of Birth: December 19, 1962

Likes: Playing the piano, reading, chess

Known Aliases: Henry Gale, Dean Moriarty

Weapon Of Choice: Telescopic steel baton

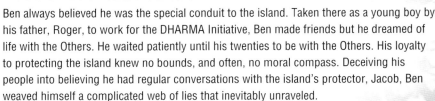

Ben always believed he was the special conduit to the island. Taken there as a young boy by his father, Roger, to work for the DHARMA Initiative, Ben made friends but he dreamed of life with the Others. He waited patiently until his twenties to be with the Others. His loyalty to protecting the island knew no bounds, and often, no moral compass. Deceiving his people into believing he had regular conversations with the island's protector, Jacob, Ben weaved himself a complicated web of lies that inevitably unraveled.

Even after murdering Jacob in an emotional rage of frustration and disappointment, Ben risked his own life to help his family of crash survivors and Others. The day the Man in Black was defeated was the day he finally got the position he'd worked tirelessly to achieve: Ben became the advisor to the new man in charge, Hugo "Hurley" Reyes.

DHARMA DAYS

Ben's mother gave birth alongside a road outside of Portland and died shortly after. Horace Goodspeed and his friend Olivia took the Linus family to the hospital. Both Horace and Olivia went on to work for DHARMA and they recruited Roger and his son Ben in 1973.

Roger vented his anger over his wife's death at his son, mostly on the anniversary of her passing, Ben's birthday. On the island, Ben made a firm friend in Annie.

Due to his relationship with his father, Ben always felt like an outcast, so Ben sympathized with Sayid Jarrah when he was captured by DHARMA in 1977. A teenage Ben brought Sayid sandwiches and books and he was curious about whether the Others had sent him. But the night Ben broke Sayid out of prison, Ben was shocked at a further betrayal—Sayid shot him in the chest.

With DHARMA's chief doctor stationed at the underwater Looking Glass station, Jack refused to help Ben. Juliet fought to stop the bleeding, but even a transfusion from Kate didn't help. Juliet suggested contacting the Others and they delivered young Ben to them. Richard Alpert warned Kate and Sawyer that if the Others took Ben, he would never be the same.

He was healed in the Temple waters, but Ben wasn't ready to live with the Others yet. However, Charles Widmore assured Ben that he could still consider himself an Other. Many years later, and after DHARMA had broken far too many rules of the Truce, Ben murdered his father with a lethal gas canister the day of the Purge, Ben's birthday.

" *Everything I did, I did for the island.* "

BEN'S LONG CON

Several days after a malignant tumor was discovered on Ben's spine, Oceanic 815 crashed onto the island. Ben immediately put several steps into motion and orchestrated a very long con to save his own life.

■ Ben watched Oceanic flight 815 break up.

"Two days after I found out I had a fatal tumor on my spine, a spinal surgeon fell out of the sky."

1973

MASQUERADING AS HENRY GALE

Ben told the following lies as he masqueraded as Henry Gale:

▸ *Ben snagged himself in one of Danielle Rousseau's traps. He claimed to be Henry Gale, a hot air balloonist from Minnesota. He claimed he crashed on the island four months ago with his wife trying to cross the Pacific. He recalled the stats of the balloon: large smiley face on its top; 140ft high, 60ft wide; and 550,000 cubic feet of helium and 100,000 cubic feet of hot air kept it in the sky.*

▸ *He and his wife Jennifer (maiden name Murphy) met at the University of Minnesota. They lived in a cave on the North shore. They had an ADF (Automatic Direction Finder) beacon, which they wanted to use for flyovers. Jennifer died three weeks after they crashed. Her decline began as a fever and, after being delirious for two days, she passed away. He buried her with his bare hands next to where the balloon crashed.*

▸ *He was rich from selling his company that mined non-metallic minerals. He shaved regularly as he felt he needed something normal to distract him from the trauma. He was caught in the net, about a two day walk from this cave.*

▸ *When the real Gale's body was discovered, Ben changed his story rapidly and emotionally. He said he'd found Gale dead, hanging out of the basket with his neck broken.*

MANIPULATING THE SURVIVORS

Being captured and interrogated by the flight 815 survivors led to physical pain, but the end goal of coercing Jack to remove the tumor was worth any amount of suffering. After he manipulated many of the Oceanic survivors like chess pieces, Jack agreed to perform the surgery.

WALT: *Was kidnapped primarily to investigate his "special gifts," as requested by Jacob. He turned out to be useful to emotionally blackmail the survivors of flight 815.*

MICHAEL: *Led Jack and the other survivors to the Others, in exchange for his and Walt's freedom.*

JACK: *Was told he could go home if he performed Ben's surgery.*

SAWYER: *Was tricked into believing he had a pacemaker device inserted in his chest that would kill him if his heart rate got too high, purely to keep him under control.*

KATE: *Was manipulated into telling Jack the Others were going to kill Sawyer. Her attachment to Sawyer fueled Jack's desire to leave the island, and therefore to perform the procedure.*

BEN'S ISLAND CONNECTIONS

THE MAN IN BLACK

The smoke monster took Alex Rousseau's form to pass judgment on Ben. Alex's images preyed upon Ben's guilt and his desire to do whatever she asked, which drove him towards killing Jacob.

Once he realized the person he thought was Locke was actually the smoke monster, Ben knew he had become nothing more than a pawn. Knowing how unstoppable the smoke monster was, Ben played a final, dangerous manipulation. He pretended to follow the Man in Black, while he struggled to find a way of escaping him.

ALEX ROUSSEAU

While in his twenties, Ben defied Widmore's instructions to kill Danielle Rousseau and her baby, Alexandra. Instead, Ben took Alex and raised her as his daughter. When Alex became a teenager, Ben's parental concerns became amplified by his trepidation for the island. He locked up her boyfriend Karl and attempted to brainwash him in Room 23, eventually driving his daughter away.

When the freighter's team arrived on the island, Ben drew a map to guide Alex, Danielle, and Karl to safety at the Temple. The mercenaries killed Danielle and Karl, then used Alex to coax Ben out of hiding. Attempting a bluff, Ben told Martin Keamy that she was just a baby he stole from an insane woman, that Alex meant nothing to him. Keamy shot Alex point-blank in the back of the head. Ben's lie was the last thing Alex ever heard.

JULIET BURKE

Juliet reminded Ben of his childhood friend Annie and he quickly became obsessed with the doctor. He assigned Juliet to one of the nicer homes in the barracks and supplied her favorite operas on CD. Ben was out to impress and on a friendship level, he achieved that goal. The two enjoyed dinners together, but Juliet quickly became aware of his non-platonic intentions.

Jealous that Goodwin and Juliet were having an affair, Ben tasked Goodwin with infiltrating the tail-section survivors of flight 815, a mission that led to Goodwin's death. Ben took Juliet to the site of Goodwin's death and made it clear that he considered her his. From that point onwards, Ben treated Juliet more like something for him to use. When Juliet diagnosed the tumor on his spine, he gave her more false promises of going home. He even used a promise to restore Juliet's sister's health to manipulate her to stay.

With full knowledge of how badly he treated her as an adult, Juliet was the one who saved young Ben's life. In 1977 DHARMA it was Juliet who treated him and she suggested Ben be taken to the Others, who in turn, saved his life.

JACOB

Jacob preferred not to get directly involved, so he gave many lists and instructions to Richard Alpert who, in turn, gave them to Ben when he was the leader of the Others. Alpert always explained that Ben would have to be patient before meeting Jacob himself.

Not meeting Jacob frustrated Ben, but he remained utterly loyal to Jacob's cause. He sacrificed friendships, relationships, and even his daughter for the sake of protecting the island. When Ben finally saw Jacob in his Taweret home, he was furious that the person he thought was Locke (the Man in Black) had been granted counsel with Jacob so swiftly.

Ben felt cheated and worthless and pleaded for an explanation from Jacob, but he received only a dismissive response that made him feel worse. This sparked revenge in Ben's heart and he plunged a knife straight into Jacob's chest.

Ben realized afterwards that losing his position of authority with the Others wasn't important. With Alex dead, he'd lost the only thing that truly mattered to him. But he never expected anyone to forgive him for murdering Jacob, because he never forgave himself.

JOHN LOCKE

Just like John Locke, Benjamin Linus came into the world prematurely and suffered from a fractured family unit. Both lost their mothers, ironically named Emily. Ben's mother died during his birth and Locke's mother gave him away. Both also suffered at the hand of a cruel father. Ben spent years manipulating and tormenting Locke, when he was the person who would've sympathized with his demons more than any other.

From the first time Ben encountered Locke, he toyed with language and twisted the truth just enough to keep Locke intrigued. This stemmed largely from Ben's jealousy. He grew more frustrated as time went by that Locke appeared to be in tune with the island. Then when Locke tried to die on his own terms, by hanging himself, Ben convinced him not to before he strangled Locke to death himself. Here are some of the many ways Ben manipulated Locke:

▶ *Ben made Locke promise to protect him, after he helped during the Swan's lockdown.*

▶ *He taunted Locke's belief in the importance of the Swan, claiming he never pushed the button.*

▶ *Locke was convinced the submarine was vital to Ben's leadership, but blowing it up helped Ben keep Jack on the island.*

▶ *By constantly telling Locke he was special, Ben kept Locke hungry and desperate to learn about the island from him.*

▶ *Ben claimed that Locke brought Cooper to the island, and that he had nothing to do with it.*

▶ *He derided Locke's inability to kill his father, telling the Others that Locke was "not who he thought he was."*

▶ *After humiliating Locke's leadership at the barracks, Ben struck a deal for freedom in exchange for information about the freighter.*

CHARLES WIDMORE

Ben's confrontations with Charles Widmore began before they even met. In 1977, Widmore's girlfriend Eloise Hawking was the current leader of the Others, so Widmore assumed their relationship gave him authority. When he heard Alpert had healed young Ben at the Temple, Widmore was furious, but Alpert stated that Jacob wanted him saved.

After the Purge, with Widmore now in charge, Ben defied his orders to kill Danielle Rousseau. Instead, Ben let her go and abducted her baby, Alex. Many years later, after Widmore had been banished from the Island, Ben took over as leader. Widmore hated Ben but was convinced he'd one day be banished too. Widmore then spent the next 20 years trying to find the island and reclaim what he believed was his. The freighter Widmore sent to find the island was successful, but it didn't manage to deliver Ben to him. After Alex's death, Ben visited Widmore at his London penthouse to accuse Widmore of breaking the gentlemanly rules to which they had agreed: to never harm one another or their families.

As vengeance for Alex, Ben attempted to kill Widmore's daughter, Penny. But when he saw her son, Charlie, he couldn't continue the suffering of another child growing up without a mother. After returning to the island, Ben stopped Widmore from revealing to the Man in Black crucial information that would've threatened the safety of the island. Ben shot Widmore dead.

HUGO "HURLEY" REYES

When Hurley became the next protector of the island, Ben was shocked to be asked to assist him. He accepted the advisory role, similar to Alpert's, and felt genuinely honored to work alongside Hurley. Ben even gave Hurley the confidence to consider that the way Jacob ran the island was simply Jacob's way—and that Hurley should embrace protecting the island the way he thought he should.

In 2010, Ben traveled with Hurley back to California, to the Santa Rosa Mental Health Institute, to collect a 17-year-old who'd become a patient. It was time to bring Walt Lloyd back to the island where he truly belonged.

"That's how Jacob ran things. Maybe there's another way. A better way."

— Spoken by Ben to Hurley

BEN'S OFF-ISLAND CONNECTIONS

❚❚ **Jill** (Butcher, associate)

❚❚ **Dan Norton** (Associate)

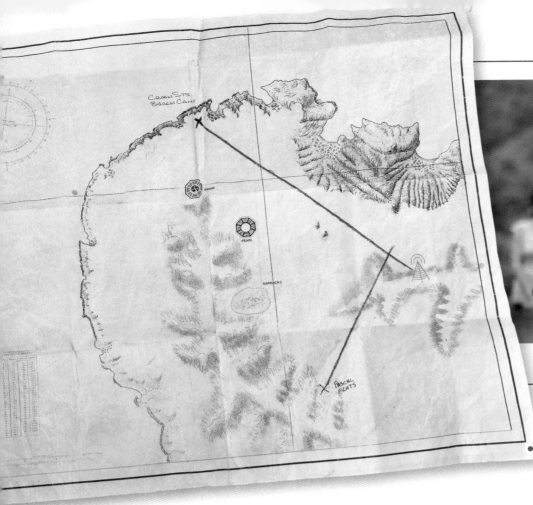

Ben showed compassion for Alex, Danielle, and Karl by giving them the map to the Temple.

Ben's hand-drawn map showing the location of the radio tower.

THE KAHANA

Ben instigated a series of tactical plans when he learned that his nemesis, Charles Widmore, was sending a freighter full of mercenaries to remove him from the island:

► *He tasked Tom Friendly with heading to New York and recruiting Michael Dawson to have a man onboard the freighter.*

► *Mikhail was sent to the Looking Glass to make sure its jamming signal stayed on, but he failed.*

► *Alpert was instructed to lead the Others to the Temple for safety.*

► *Ben tried to acquire the satellite phone by threatening to kill Sayid, Bernard, and Jin, but his Others didn't carry out the execution.*

► *He shot Charlotte Lewis (a member of the science team on the freighter), but she was wearing a protective vest.*

► *Locke was shown footage of Widmore attacking one of Ben's people on the mainland to emphasize Widmore's plan to take the island by force.*

THE MAN BEHIND THE CURTAIN ✚

Henry Gale is the fictional uncle of Dorothy Gale in the "Oz" books by Frank L. Baum. In "The Wonderful Wizard of Oz," the Wizard arrives and leaves Oz in a hot air balloon.

> Isabel,
> I hereby commute Juliets Sentence. Exicution is off of the Table.
> The normal Rules do not apply here. I will however order that Juliet Be Marked and I suggest that Tom carry out this order.
>
> Ben

Ben's letter to Isabel, the sheriff.

PURSUING THE OCEANIC SIX

Ben's myriad passports, currencies, and clothes hidden in the secret room of his barracks home aided his various trips off-island. No one knows how many times Ben left the island, but his extensive contacts—and preferred guest status at a Tunisian hotel—suggested he'd done so many times.

He used the donkey wheel to reach the Tunisian exit point, and he began investigating the whereabouts of those who had left the island. He swiftly convinced Sayid to kill dozens of men Ben claimed were employed by Widmore, supposedly to protect the Oceanic Six. His Los Angeles contacts Jill, Gabriel, and Jeffrey helped Ben store Locke's body and make the final preparations for the return to the island.

Ben read this book on Ajira flight 316.

When Ben, pretending to be Henry Gale, was being held inside the Swan armory, Locke offered him this book to read.

The name Dean Moriarty is in homage to Jack Kerouac's character of the same name in his classic American novel "On the Road."

Ben's various passports and currencies.

BERNARD NADLER

FACTS & FIGURES

Time On The Island

POST-OCEANIC: 101 days

DHARMA YEARS: 3+ years

POST-INCIDENT: Many years

Hometown: Buffalo, New York

Skills: Morse code, surgery

Likes: Phil Collins

Bernard Nadler was a successful private practice dentist and the beloved husband of Rose Henderson Nadler. A bachelor for 56 years, Bernard was content in his life, resigned to the fact that he would never meet "Miss Right." But fate stepped in on a cold winter evening when he discovered a woman who needed help getting her car out of a snow drift. He helped rock her car free and face-planted in the snow. She introduced herself as Rose and offered to buy him a cup of coffee. And just like that, Bernard found his soul mate in Rose. Regardless of cancer, plane crashes, attacking Others or time skips, Bernard and Rose remained focused on the quiet, potent power of their love which was all that mattered to them on the island that would forever become their home.

WHIRLWIND ROMANCE

Instantly smitten, Bernard continued to court Rose for five months. While on a trip to Niagara Falls, he got down on bended knee to propose to Rose. Sadly, she revealed the cancer she had been battling was back and terminal, but Bernard asked Rose for an answer anyway. She agreed and they got married soon after. Frightened of losing her, Bernard concocted his own desperate plan to save Rose. For their honeymoon he took Rose to Uluru, Australia where he arranged for her to meet with Isaac, a reputed faith healer. Bernard was full of hope and Rose fed that when she informed him that Isaac healed her cancer. Desperate to believe, Bernard was ready to start anew when they boarded Oceanic flight 815 bound for home.

> ## "So we die. We just care about being together. It's all that matters in the end."

FOUND IN A TREE

When the tail section of the plane separated, Bernard was thrown into the jungle still strapped into his seat. He landed in a tree and was later rescued by Ana Lucia Cortez and Goodwin Stanhope. Unhurt, Bernard was beside himself since he couldn't find Rose, alive or dead. Eventually, he had to refocus on survival with his fellow tailies as they were hunted by the Others. When they discovered the Arrow station, Bernard got the radio found inside to work and he briefly communicated with Boone Carlyle before Ana Lucia turned off the transmission.

BY THE NUMBERS ✚
Bernard's seat assignment on Oceanic 815 was 23E.

When Jin, Sawyer and Michael washed up onshore, Bernard finally learned that Rose was alive at the main beach camp. Elated, Bernard made the hike to merge with the other camp and 50 days after the crash, the Nadlers were finally reunited.

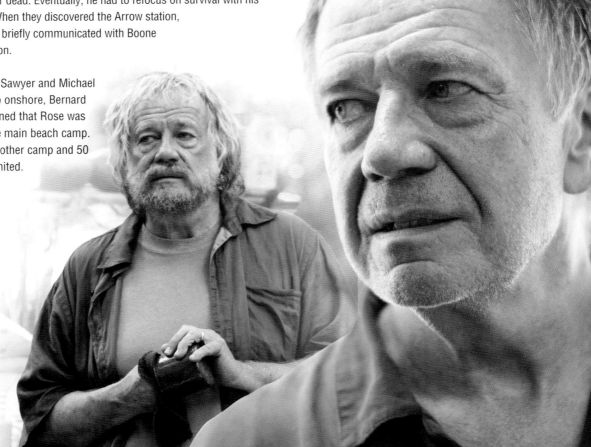

" I am a dentist, not Rambo. "

HE MEANS WELL

As he settled into life with the beach survivors, Bernard ruffled some feathers with his exasperated disappointment in what he considered their complacent attitude about being rescued. At one point, he tried to get volunteers to create a massive S.O.S. on the beach made of rocks. Fifteen people showed up, but that number quickly dwindled after they tired of Bernard's micromanaging. Frustrated, he talked with Rose who revealed the lie she told him in Australia and that she felt the island had healed her. Bernard understood her reluctance to leave and promised they never would.

When Jack Shephard came down with acute appendicitis, Bernard assisted Juliet Burke with her surgery and put Jack under with chloroform due to his prior experience with local anaesthesia as a dentist.

When Benjamin Linus moved the island, Bernard lost Rose for a while but they eventually found one another on the beach and decided to stay put with the other survivors. Bernard had a tough time making fire, which he finally created only to have the wind blow it out. The Others then attacked with flaming arrows and the Nadlers escaped into the jungle.

ISLAND BLISS

When the couple found themselves back in the 1970s, they decided to separate from the rest of the survivors and essentially built a new life off the island grid. Bernard built a small cabin and they scavenged assorted materials from DHARMA to get by. Bernard grew a beard and let go of his angst so he could just love and appreciate every moment with Rose and their adopted pooch Vincent.

"They found us."

Much later, Bernard and Vincent found Desmond in the bottom of a well. He hauled him out and took him home where they offered Hume a brief respite. Bernard took Vincent with him to fish, but returned with the Man in Black, who threatened to kill them both if Desmond didn't leave with him. Des acquiesced only after he secured the couple's safety.

Sawyer, Juliet and Kate thanked Rose and Bernard for their help prior to continuing their search for Jack.

BILLY

▶ **CONNECTION:** Desmond Hume's friend

Desmond Hume received more opposition than support during the periods in which his consciousness became unstuck in time. However, one of his friends in the Royal Scots platoon became an incredibly important believer despite their brief exchange during Desmond's flash to the past.

Billy was part of Desmond's regiment and was the one who he confided in about the bizarre phenomenon he was experiencing. Although Billy was not entirely convinced, he indulged Desmond long enough to learn if there was anyone who Desmond recognized in the strange "dream."

This question from Billy is the key, because it made Desmond recall holding the photo of Penny. Desmond then attempted to call Penny from a phone booth, but the fluxing through time ripped his consciousness back to the freighter in the future. Without Billy pushing Desmond to remember Penny, he would not have ventured further down the path to the discovery of his "constant" (Penny), the importance of it, and ultimately how it saved Desmond's life.

BILLY DEE WILLIAMS

▶ **CONNECTION:** Actor in the TV show *Exposé*, along with Nikki Fernandez

The legendary actor of film and television, Billy Dee Williams was one of the co-stars of the action drama series *Exposé* that featured actress Nikki Fernandez in the episode "The Cobra." Williams played Mr. LaShade, the owner of the strip club that employed the stripper crime-fighters named Autumn and Crystal.

The script for season 4 of *Exposé*.

BLACK ROCK

Portsmouth, England

Tenerife, Canary Islands

Thailand

Il Sainte Marie, Madagascar

The path of the *Black Rock*

The *Black Rock* was one of 15 sailing ships owned by Magnus Hanso of The New World Sea Traders based in Portsmouth, England. The exact year it was commissioned, and when it sailed its maiden voyage, were lost but other records revealed that the *Black Rock* was a fully rigged wooden frigate used for trade expeditions throughout the Indian Ocean.

According to records, the ship's last voyage departed its home berth on March 22, 1845 and was captained by Hanso with a full company of officers and materials for trade. For two years, the ship traveled the Indian Ocean shipping routes to eastern Africa and the Kingdom of Siam amongst other ports of call. While most of Hanso's trade was standard fare, three of his ships—including the *Black Rock*—were secretly used for illegal slave trade. In 1867, Hanso gave the *Black Rock* and its crew an extended break at Tenerife, Canary Islands. However, some of his officers, including Jonas Whitfield, were tasked with acquiring prisoners, debtors and the like for slave work in the mining colonies of Africa. When they left Tenerife a few months later, they carried a full hold of Spanish slaves but neither the ship nor its crew were ever seen again.

BY THE NUMBERS
The Black Rock's slip was #23 in Portsmouth, UK and was one of 15 owned by Hanso.

The first-mate's journal was lot #2342 at the Southfield auction with an opening bid of 150,000 pounds.

Shackles used to keep the slaves from escaping the ship.

THE FATE OF THE BLACK ROCK

In late December 1867, the *Black Rock* found itself moored near the shores of an uncharted island in the South Pacific. In less than a month's time, the boat and all the men aboard (save Ricardo Alpert) were dead. For 15 years, the *Black Rock*'s fate remained a mystery, assumed by family and colleagues as merely lost at sea. It wasn't until 1852, when the journal of the first-mate of the *Black Rock* was found amongst the artifacts collected by pirates on the island of Île Sainte-Marie (off the coast of Madagascar), that a small piece of the truth was finally revealed. The journal was remanded back to the Hanso family where it, and all its contents, remained private until 1996. In that year, Torvo Hanso allowed Southfield's of London to auction the journal to the public. Charles Widmore was the highest bidder. In particular, the last pages of the journal revealed much about what the *Black Rock*'s crew experienced before the ship was thrown and grounded on the island by a massive storm.

A portrait of the *Black Rock* was sold at Southfield's.

CONNECTIONS ✛

Danielle Rousseau referenced the Black Rock, or the Rocher Noir, in one of her looped radio tower distress calls.

In 1977, Jim "LaFleur" Ford told Horace Goodspeed that he and his people were from an expedition that crashed on the island looking for the remains of the Black Rock.

ON THE ISLAND

After the storm, the *Black Rock* was left aground in the dense jungle, an area that Danielle Rousseau would label in the future as the "Dark Territory" due to its proximity to the smoke monster's territory. Alpert survived in the hold for a week before the Man in Black liberated him and the ship was abandoned for more than 120 years.

In early 1988, survivors of the French expedition of the crashed *Bésixdouze* discovered the remains of the *Black Rock* and explored what little it still contained. Danielle Rousseau, the eventual sole survivor of the group, notated the location of the ship on her island map and returned to it several times in her 16 years on the island, both alone and with survivors of Oceanic 815, to obtain sticks of dynamite.

Hurley used the last of the dynamite to blow up the ship.

MORE REVELATIONS ✛

Claire Littleton wrote in her diary about recurring dreams that she had of a "black rock" which might have been a prescient reference to the ship or to the Man in Black.

Stuart Radzinsky ventured out into the "Dark Territory" and discovered the remains of the Black Rock and Captain Magnus Hanso. He noted both finds on the Blast Door Map.

In 2004, John Locke used the brig of the *Black Rock* to bind and restrain his father, Anthony Cooper, as part of an elaborate plan to get James "Sawyer" Ford to kill him. Cooper was murdered there and his corpse was taken by Locke back to the Others.

For over three years, the ship remained in the jungle solitude until Alpert returned for the first time in 140 years. Desperate, he tried to commit suicide via dynamite in the hull that brought him to the island. However, the plan was thwarted because the island wasn't done with him. A few days later, Hugo "Hurley" Reyes blew up the ancient ship with the dynamite that remained inside in an attempt to protect the Ajira plane from being blown up by Alpert.

𝒮
755
Southfield's

Southfields Auction House

Premier auction

Charles Widmore's bidder number at the Southfield Auction, where he purchased the *Black Rock*'s ledger.

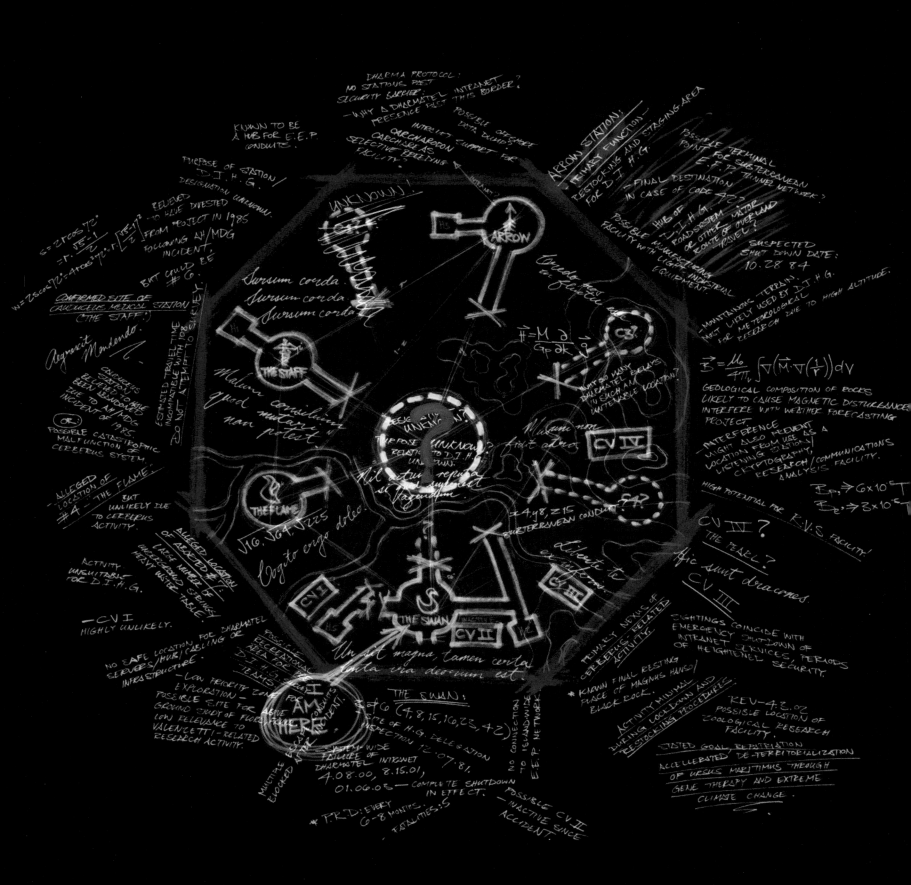

Locke's drawing of the blast door map.

? (The Pearl)

▶ Question mark refers to Radzinsky's inability to determine the station's occupant.

▶ *Nil actum reputa si quid superest agendum* = Don't consider that anything has been done if anything is left to be done.

The Swan

▶ *Ut sit magna, tamen certe lenta ira deorum est* = The wrath of the gods may be great, but it certainly is slow.

The Flame

▶ *Cogito ergo doleo* = I think therefore I am depressed.

The Staff

▶ *Malum consilium quod mutari non potes* = It's a bad plan that can't be changed.

▶ *Sursum corda* (repeated three times) = Lift up your hearts.

▶ *Aegrescit medendo* (outside the Staff boundaries) = The remedy is worse than the disease.

▶ *Alternate name is the Caduceus station named after the winged staff, intertwined serpents symbol of medical practitioners.*

The Arrow

▶ "Intranet support for Carcharodon carcharias selective breeding facility?" = Refers to the great white shark breeding done via the underwater Hydra station.

C3

▶ References an unseen and/or un-built meteorological station located at a high elevation.

▶ *Credo nos in fluctu eodem esse* = I think we're on the same wavelength.

▶ *B* equation refers to magnetic flux density, or the amount of magnetism induced into a body.

▶ *H* equation refers to magnetic field strength, or the magnetizing force.

C4

▶ *Mus uni non fidit antro* = A mouse does not rely on just one hole.

▶ *Liberate te ex inferis* = Free yourself from hell.

▶ *Hic sunt dracones* = Here be dragons.

C1 (The Orchid)

▶ Unknown = Radzinsky was unaware of the function of this station.

This map was the creation of DHARMA Head of Research and Swan architect Stuart Radzinsky. Created on one of the Swan's heavy blast doors, it illustrated a secret, geographical breakdown of the DHARMA stations, their functions and the compound boundaries. Radzinsky drew the map over time using a paint brush dipped in DHARMA laundry detergent and coloring agents so it was only visible after a lockdown under black light. All of the details on the map came from his photographic remembrance of the island and it included some of his cryptic personal musings in both Latin and English. His hatch mate, Kelvin Inman, also worked on the map and continued to do so after Radzinsky's suicide.

John Locke saw the map when his leg got caught under the door after a lockdown.

After the Purge, Radzinsky quarantined himself inside the Swan as he feared exposure to the toxins that killed his peers. His inherently paranoid, Type A personality coupled with his long-term seclusion spurred Radzinsky to create the map to aid his future offensive maneuvers against the Others. However, that plan never came to fruition as he devolved into madness.

WHAT IT ALL MEANS

The abbreviation "CV" indicated a cerberus vent, or the DHARMA name for the Others' smoke monster security system.

"DharmaTel" is the Intranet connection between the stations used for communication.

The abbreviation "E.E.P." was short for Emergency Escape Protocol, or routes of escape for DHARMA members in case of emergency.

The DHARMA Initiative Hanso Group was abbreviated with "D.I.H.G."

The acronym for the island's periodic resupply drops was "P.R.D." This involved air-lifted drops of food and medical supplies to the island from a mainland location by the DHARMA Initiative.

The "X" marks indicated entry points into the various stations.

Lastly, they used the polar bear's scientific name, "Ursus Maritimus" to denote the research being done on Hydra island.

BOONE CARLYLE

FACTS & FIGURES

Time On The Island
POST-OCEANIC: 41 days

Hometown: Malibu, CA

Year Of Birth: 1982

Skills: Lifeguard (CPR), Tennis

Candidate: #226

An earnest young man, Boone Carlyle was the affluent son of a successful businesswoman. He experienced no great tragedies or challenges that helped guide him into manhood, either for good or bad. Boone was content to do what people told him, whether it was his controlling mother or his high-maintenance stepsister, Shannon Rutherford. It wasn't until he came to the island that he discovered his lack of functional skills. It was through his friendship with John Locke that he discovered his own independent spirit blossomed outside of his toxic relationship with his stepsister. However, his potential remained unfulfilled as he became one of the island's first sacrifices.

Boone and Locke bonded right away.

MERGED FAMILIES

Boone was raised by his single mother, Sabrina Carlyle, the head of a successful clothing company. Because of work demands, Sabrina hired nannies to watch Boone. At the age of six he was watched over by a woman named Theresa, whom he liked to torture by calling for her to come up and down the stairs all day long. On one occasion, she tripped on the stairs and broke her neck. Even as a little boy, Boone felt responsible and adjusted his attitude to become more of a people pleaser.

When he was 10 years old Boone's mother married Adam Rutherford, which suddenly gave the little boy a father figure and a stepsister, Shannon, two years his junior. However, Boone could see that his mother didn't like the little girl, so he stepped up as her protector.

Boone traveled to Australia to save Shannon from an abusive relationship.

"We found a hatch."

THE SHANNON TRAP

As Boone grew up, he was groomed to become part of his mother's company. He was 20 and in New York City when Adam Rutherford, Shannon's father, was killed in a car accident, so he returned home for the funeral to comfort Shannon. While there he let Shannon know that he had accepted a job with Sabrina as the Chief Operating Officer of one of her bridal subsidiaries. Shannon became upset and angry because that left her no recourse for a dance internship in New York. He tried to ask his mother for money but was denied, so he offered to loan Shannon some of his trust fund money which she rejected.

> *I know you made a promise, but I'm letting you off the hook. Let me go, Jack.*

Shannon seduced Boone after Bryan, her boyfriend, left her.

By this time, Boone also harbored a secret love for Shannon, so he couldn't just abandon her even when her conduct got worse. He continued to enable her bad behavior to show her that he loved her regardless of her actions.

- ▶ *While on a date at his tennis club, Shannon called and pleaded with him to rescue her from an abusive man in Australia. He left immediately and found a bruised Shannon who wouldn't leave her boyfriend, Bryan. In the end Boone was set up by the pair for the money and he was violently thrashed to add insult to injury.*

- ▶ *In a combative mood at the Sydney airport, Boone blamed Shannon's bad attitude on his inability to get them an upgrade to first class. When he questioned her immoral behavior, she shocked him when she filed a false report about a suspicious Arab (Sayid Jarrah) with security.*

- ▶ *Even at her worst, Boone still looked out for her and packed her asthma inhaler when she forgot it. He also offered her an Apollo candy bar soon after the crash.*

- ▶ *Angry with Shannon's lack of initiative to do anything for herself on the island, he challenged her to get a fish, and much to his chagrin, she achieved it by manipulating Charlie Pace.*

- ▶ *Boone created a huge rift in the camp between Sawyer and Sayid when he accused Sawyer of hoarding all the medicine, including the inhaler Shannon desperately needed.*

GOOD INTENTIONS

While Boone had a good heart, the island quickly showed him, and those around him, that he wasn't particularly equipped to do much of anything on his own. That knowledge frustrated Boone to no end, and coupled with Shannon's continued emasculation of him, it eventually led him to John Locke's tutelage.

- ▶ *In the aftermath of the crash, Boone tried to perform CPR on Rose Nadler but he had her positioned incorrectly. Desperate to help Jack, he offered to find a pen for an emergency tracheotomy so he canvassed all the survivors and brought back a handful, that weren't needed.*

- ▶ *On the hike back from the jungle, Boone swiped Sawyer's gun and offered to be its guardian when found out. His fellow survivors handed it to Kate instead.*

- ▶ *On the sixth day, Boone tried to swim out to save Joanna, who was drowning, but he got caught in the riptide so Jack had to save him. Joanna died as a result.*

- ▶ *Boone tried to take control of the water rationing but almost got himself killed when it looked like he was stealing it.*

Boone tried to save Joanna Miller, a fellow survivor, but failed in his attempt.

LOCKE'S RIGHT-HAND MAN

Impressed by Locke's confidence, survival skills and his knife collection, Boone found himself spending more and more time with the older man. They quickly slipped into a teacher/apprentice relationship as they embarked on their secret scouting trips in the jungle.

- ▶ *When Claire was kidnapped, Locke and Boone split up from the main search party and literally stumbled upon the Swan hatch door.*

- ▶ *Under Locke's direction, the two built a trebuchet to smash the glass on the hatch but it failed.*

- ▶ *Locke and Boone took Walt Lloyd under their wing and showed him how to throw knives. When Vincent disappeared, the duo went out to find the dog and found Claire instead.*

LISTENING TO THE ISLAND

Locke forced Boone to become his own man and not answer to everyone else around him, especially Shannon. Locke counseled the young man that he needed to listen to the island so he drugged him and tied him to a tree to force Boone to connect to the island's will.

In a drugged state, Boone attempted to "save" Shannon from the smoke monster, but she was killed. In reality, it proved to be a hallucination.

THE DRUG PLANE

After his vision of Shannon allowed him to let go of that relationship, Boone followed John to the site of his vision quest—the Beechcraft. It was there that Boone learned of Locke's paralysis and how the island had healed him but the symptoms were returning. Acting as Locke's legs, Boone climbed into the plane and found the heroin statues and a radio that he used to talk to a tailie (Bernard Nadler) until the transmission stopped. Tragically, the plane shifted and fell, crushing Boone. Locke regained the use of his legs again and carried Boone back to camp, where Jack attempted to save his life but failed. Sayid performed Boone's eulogy, after which they buried him in the makeshift burial area they renamed "Boone Hill."

BPO BPO

▶ **CONNECTION:** Puppy that Jin gave to Sun

Bpo Bpo is a Shar Pei owned by Sun and Jin Kwon. The dog was originally purchased by Byung Han, the South Korean Secretary for Environmental Safety, for his young daughter as a family pet. Jin was sent to Han's home by Mr. Paik to deliver a "message" in the form of a beating, however, Jin just verbally warned the man on behalf of Paik. Han was so appreciative that he gifted Jin with their extremely valuable pet as a token of his thanks.

Jin wrapped the puppy in a box as a gift for Sun to keep her company while he was at work. Sun was initially put off by the gesture, since all she wanted was Jin's time, but she grew to love the dog and named him Bpo Bpo, or "a kiss" in Korean. Sun cared for Bpo Bpo throughout her marriage and became part of their family. She intended to take him to America with her, so she made special arrangements for her interior decorator to look after him. When Sun returned to Korea after leaving the island, she took custody of Bpo Bpo once again.

BPO BPO & ✛ JI YEON

When Charles Widmore gave Sun's camera to Jin, it contained pictures that featured his daughter Ji Yeon and Bpo Bpo.

ABOUT THE SHAR PEI
The Shar Pei breed originated in China as a farm dog that was raised to kill pests, herd and track. Translated, its name means "sand skin" which refers to their beige coats. These dogs are known for their distinctive wrinkled faces and blue-black tongues.

The breed was almost completely wiped out when China was under Communist rule and domesticated dogs were eliminated from the populace. The ancient legacy of the Shar Pei was essentially saved by Taiwanese and Hong Kong breeders. In general, these dogs are known to be very stubborn and cautious with strangers, but extremely protective of their families.

BRAM

▶ **CONNECTION:** Passenger on Ajira flight 316; associate of Ilana Verdansky

After Jacob tasked Ilana Verdansky with bringing the last six candidates back to the island Temple, she enlisted the help of a few other trusted associates, including Bram. A big, brawny man with tactical skills and knowledge of the island, Bram was a willing participant in Jacob's mission to protect the island. However, his own relationship to Jacob and the island are unknown.

THE WINNING SIDE
In 2004, one week before the *Kahana* embarked on Charles Widmore's mission back to the island, Bram and three other cohorts kidnapped Miles Straume outside a Los Angeles taco stand. As they drove, a gregarious Bram told Miles that it would be a bad idea to leave with Widmore's crew. Instead he asked Miles to join him, which would in turn lead Miles to answers about his "gift" and his father. Miles feigned indifference to anything but money and demanded $6.4 million to switch teams. Bram declined and had Miles thrown out of the van. In parting, Bram suggested that Miles was on the wrong team instead of the one that was going to win.

BACK ON THE ISLAND
Bram survived the crash of Ajira flight 316 and remained calm as he and Ilana retrieved a large Ajira cargo box from the plane's hold. Ilana, Bram, and their three guards quietly recovered a cache of guns and asserted their control over the Ajira survivors. Back on the main island, Ilana and her team found Jacob's cabin, discovered the Man in Black had been using it, and burned it. They used a leftover fragment of tapestry to lead them to the Taweret statue.

Bram and several others lugged the crate through the jungle to show Jacob.

Under the cover of night, the group arrived at the base of the statue and found Richard whom they asked, "What lies in the shadow of the statue?" He answered correctly and they opened the crate to reveal Locke's corpse to everyone on the beach. Bram argued with Richard about entering the statue, since Richard claimed no one was allowed inside unless invited by Jacob. Bram took Ben and his three armed guards and entered the statue.

With guns drawn, they faced off against the Man in Black. The Man in Black transformed into the smoke monster and violently killed the three bodyguards as Bram poured a ring of ash around himself. The monster was stopped until it knocked some of the ceiling down on Bram. Once outside of the ring, the monster propelled Bram into Jacob's loom where a large piece of wood killed him instantly.

BRENNAN

▶ **CONNECTION:** Part of French expedition team led by Danielle Rousseau

Brennan was a member of the six-person French science expedition traveling from Tahiti in 1987. When their boat, the *Bésixdouze,* ran aground during a violent storm, they paddled ashore in a raft, only to become stranded on the island. Brennan's specific duty within the group was never revealed.

During the time jumps after the island moved, Brennan and his colleagues helped pull a time traveling Jin-Soo Kwon from the ocean. They allowed him to trek with them as they sought the source of the numbers transmission emanating from the island's radio tower. When the smoke monster attacked their party and dragged Montand into the declivity in the wall surrounding the Temple compound, Brennan and the other men ventured into it to rescue Montand despite Jin's warnings.

Sixteen years later, Danielle Rousseau explained to Sayid Jarrah that all the members of her team who entered the declivity came down with a "sickness." Not long after, she shot Brennan and Lacombe on the beach to protect her unborn baby's life. She recorded a new message at the radio tower after the killings.

BRIAN PORTER

▶ **CONNECTION:** Husband of Susan Lloyd; Walt Lloyd's stepfather

A prominent American attorney at a law firm in Amsterdam, he hired Susan Lloyd to join his team in the Netherlands. It wasn't long before their relationship shifted from professional to romantic.

About two months after Susan's ex, Michael Dawson, was in a car accident, Brian was offered and accepted the opportunity to run his firm's office in Rome. He proposed marriage to Susan, but stated that he wasn't interested in being a father. Susan refused to accept his position and demanded that he adopt Walt. Susan traveled to New York and asked Michael to relinquish his parental rights so Brian could become Walt's legal father. She framed the request to sound as if Brian wanted it in order to strengthen her argument with Michael.

A NEW LIFE

By all accounts, Brian and Susan had a happy eight-year marriage. He was a doting husband, supportive of her career and provided for Walt. But Brian never bonded with the boy and failed to warm to the idea of being a father.

It troubled Brian when odd things, like the bird hitting a window, occurred when Walt was around.

The family eventually relocated to Australia, but Susan became ill with a blood disorder not long after that killed her in the span of a week. The day after her death, a very distraught Brian left Walt with his nanny and flew to New York to contact Michael. Initially, he lied to

After Susan's death, Brian asked Michael to take custody of Walt.

Michael and said Susan requested that Michael should regain full custody of Walt. Brian confessed the truth about the adoption and his discomfort with keeping the boy. He provided Michael with roundtrip tickets on Oceanic flight 815 from Sydney to New York and travel money to take back Walt.

When Michael arrived in Australia to meet Walt, Brian made sure he wasn't present. Unwilling to hurt his son with the truth about Brian's callous behavior, Michael lied and told Walt that Brian loved him very much and would still keep in contact.

BROTHER CAMPBELL

▶ **CONNECTION:** Desmond Hume's supervisor at the monastery

Brother Campbell was the head monk at Eddington Monastery in Scotland. As part of their initiation, he placed Desmond Hume under a vow of silence for an undisclosed period of time to test his depth of faith and patience. Despite Campbell's concerns, Hume passed and became a novitiate brother in their abbey.

During a conversation with Desmond about the origination of Moriah as their wine label name, Brother Campbell revealed his appreciation for sacrifice to divine God's will. Desmond's aversion to that concept made Brother Campbell question Desmond's calling. When he later found Desmond drunk on their vintage wine, Brother Campbell fired Des from the abbey. He recognized that Des was running from his past and that despite his calling, God had a much bigger plan for him. Still on good terms, Brother Campbell asked Desmond to help load some crates of wine into a client's car before he left the abbey. Desmond agreed and, as fate would have it, the client turned out to be Penny Widmore.

BY THE NUMBERS

*The monks of Eddington produced very exclusive wine under their Moriah Vineyards label to help fund their monastery. Each vintage, like their 1995 Cabernet Sauvignon, was limited to a production of only **108** cases, so they could set their prices at a premium of 100 pounds per bottle.*

BRYAN

▶ **CONNECTION:** Boyfriend of Shannon Rutherford

The Australian boyfriend of Shannon Rutherford, Bryan conspired with his girlfriend to get back the money her stepmother denied her from her father's estate. Shannon called her stepbrother Boone Carlyle to help her in Australia. She pretended not to want him there but casually revealed a bruise on her head. Boone took the cue and tracked down Bryan at the harbor where he offered him $25,000 on the condition that he would never see Shannon again. Bryan negotiated up to $50,000. Later, back at Shannon's, Bryan showed up

and revealed to Boone that he had been played and proceeded to beat him up much to Shannon's dismay. In a self-fulfilling prophecy, Shannon revealed that Bryan later stole the money and ditched her.

BYUNG HAN

▶ **CONNECTION:** Suffered a beating at the hands of Jin-Soo Kwon

As the Secretary for Environmental Safety in South Korea, Byung Han was responsible for inspecting factories and businesses for safety or environmental infractions. A family man, Han was married with a young daughter.

Han inspected one of Mr. Paik's factories and found violations that warranted its closing. When Paik learned about the results, he summoned Jin to his office and tasked him to visit Han's home with the personal message: "I'm very displeased."

Jin was cautiously welcomed into Han's home where he delivered Mr. Paik's verbal message. A very relieved Han apologized to Jin and handed over his daughter's championship breed Shar Pei puppy in thanks for receiving only a verbal warning.

The next day, Han closed Paik's factory. Incensed at Han's nerve and Jin's failure to sway his actions, Paik sent his son-in-law back to Han's along with one of his thugs. Well aware of the trouble that Han was in, Jin barged into his home and violently beat him. As Han lay motionless on the ground, Jin told him, "The factory opens tomorrow. I just saved your life."

CONNECTIONS ✛

As Han's daughter watched television with her puppy Bpo Bpo at her side, the Korean news broadcast aired a feature on lottery winner Hugo "Hurley" Reyes.

THE CABIN

"Once I open this door, there's no turning back. You sure this is what you want?"

— Spoken by Ben to Locke

The cabin was constructed at an unknown point in time by Horace Goodspeed during his years in the DHARMA Initiative. Originally planned to serve as a private getaway for Horace and his partner Amy, the cabin eventually took on a much more intimidating and paranormal presence in the years that followed.

After the Purge that wiped out the DHARMA Initiative, Benjamin Linus (the leader of the Others) learned that the cabin functioned as the dwelling for the mysterious figure to whom Richard Alpert answered—Jacob. The cabin was encircled by a protective barrier of ash to prevent any hostile intrusions.

■ The cabin was surrounded by a circle of ash.

STRUCTURE & ENVIRONMENT

Although the cabin's outward appearance was ominous, unsettling and utterly foreboding, its interior consisted of only a wooden table and chairs, oil lanterns, glass storage jars, old ropes and several chains. There was absolutely no hint of modern technology present inside the cabin. One object that seemed out of place, though, was an old painting of a dog that hung on the wall, but the significance of the painting remains unknown.

"HELP ME…"

When Benjamin Linus took John Locke to the cabin, they failed to notice a breach in the circle of ash, meaning the protective shield against the smoke monster's presence was useless. Ben, who had never seen or heard from Jacob, created a ruse to trick Locke into believing that Jacob was inside the cabin. Ironically, Ben didn't realize that something sinister was actually inside.

Locke heard a low, ghostly tone say, "Help me." Further convincing Locke that this was an elaborate hoax orchestrated by Ben, Locke took his flashlight and scanned the room. But this made the cabin violently shake, causing a lantern to crash to the floor and starting a fire. As they fled the burning cabin, a figure was visible in a chair. This event left Ben extremely shaken, but Locke was convinced that Ben created the entire thing.

HURLEY'S HAUNTING

Hurley also experienced a shocking, paranormal event involving the cabin. Unlike Locke's experience, Hurley became enveloped in the whispers prior to entering the cabin. Hurley witnessed a light from inside the cabin and saw Christian Shephard sitting in a chair. Even more alarming was the appearance of a human eye in the window.

As Hurley attempted to back away from the cabin, it inexplicably reappeared behind him. Just as quickly, it disappeared from sight completely as Hurley pleaded out loud for it to go away.

LOCKE'S RETURN

Leading a group of survivors away from the freighter team's impending arrival, Locke discovered the circle of ash but the cabin was nowhere to be found. After a dream in which Locke saw Horace building the cabin did Locke realize that he needed to revisit the mass grave of the DHARMA Initiative. Once there, Locke found Horace's skeleton along with a blueprint of the cabin's architectural design and location.

Locke's second visit to the cabin was completely different than his first. This time around, he was greeted by Christian Shephard and Claire Littleton.

Christian, dressed in tattered clothing fitting of the Others, claimed he was speaking on Jacob's behalf. He instructed Locke that if he wanted to save the island, he would have to move it.

UP IN FLAMES

Ilana, Bram and several other people hiked to the cabin with John Locke's body in tow. They planned to tell Jacob that if someone resembling Locke appeared that it clearly wasn't the "real" John Locke. Upon their arrival, the cabin had obviously sustained damage, it was charred on the outside, and the interior was trashed. Most importantly, though, Bram noticed that the circle of ash had been broken.

Ilana found a piece of cloth pinned to the wall with a picture of Taweret, indicating Jacob's whereabouts.

CAESAR

> **CONNECTION:** Passenger on Ajira flight 316

A passenger on Ajira Flight 316, Caesar survived the emergency crash-landing on Hydra island and for a short time became the *de facto* leader of his fellow travellers. Caesar's first encounter with any of the Oceanic Six occured at the check-in line for Ajira Airlines in Los Angeles.

He overheard Jack Shephard speak with the ticket agent about escorting the body of Jeremy Bentham to Guam. Caesar politely offered his condolence, which slightly surprised Jack.

On the plane, Caesar was seated in the first class cabin in the fifth row, near Hugo Reyes, unaware of the silent reunion that was going on around him. After the plane went down, Frank Lapidus assembled the survivors and briefed them on their situation. Caesar immediately asked where they were, to which Frank could not answer. Incredulous, Caesar observed that the island had buildings and there was a larger island nearby that they should immediately search. He asked if anyone would join him and Ilana followed him to the abandoned DHARMA compound.

Caesar entered Ben's old office alone and spotted a loaded shotgun attached to the underside of the desk. He put it and a flashlight in his bag just before Ilana entered the room. When she asked what he had found, Caesar only offered the flashlight. Ilana then told him that one of their group had discovered an odd man alive on the beach.

Curious, Caesar followed Ilana to the beach to question the man who no one recognized. At the beach fire, "Locke" introduced himself to Caesar.

CURIOSITY KILLED THE CAT

The next day, Caesar returned to Ben's office where he met "Locke," who revealed he had spent 100 days on the island and wasn't sure how he had returned. Caesar asked how several people on the plane disappeared. "Locke" asked to see the people injured on the plane, so Caesar took him to their makeshift medical area where "Locke" immediately recognized Benjamin Linus as the man who killed him.

The next morning, Caesar asked Ben what he knew about "Locke." Caesar promised that he had Ben's back and showed him the hidden shotgun. Later "Locke" was prepping an outrigger to go to the mainland with Ben, when Caesar ordered them to stop. He claimed that he was "calling the shots" and he needed to know more about "Locke's" history on the island. As he reached for his bag with the gun, Ben revealed that he had it instead and promptly used it on Caesar.

CARMEN REYES

> **CONNECTION:** Mother of Hugo "Hurley" Reyes

The matriarch of the Reyes clan, Carmen was the estranged wife of David and the mother of Hugo and Diego. A strong Latina woman with a staunch Catholic faith, Carmen guided her family through the good times and bad. She raised her boys as a single mother when David deserted the family. Protective but a bit overbearing at times, she always worried about a rudderless Hugo not finding his path and the love of a good woman.

Perhaps her biggest challenge with Hurley came in his early 20s when he was involved in a tragic accident. He swore that his weight caused the collapse of a deck that killed two people. Things got so bad with Hurley that Carmen eventually had him committed to Santa Rosa Mental Health Institute to help him break through his debilitating depression.

THE CURSE

After leaving the institute, Hurley moved back home and subsequently won the lottery. Carmen was excited about the opportunities it presented until more bad luck consumed the family. Despite the fact that she watched her father die of a heart attack at a press conference, her son Diego was dumped by his wife, she broke her ankle at the new house her son bought her (which subsequently went up in flames), Carmen refused to believe that her son or the money was cursed. She hoped to dispel her son's irrational beliefs when she called her estranged husband,

David, to set their son straight. David moved into the family home, but Hugo resented his father's long absence and asked Carmen to make him leave. She refused to do so, as their marriage had been rekindled.

In the time that Hugo was supposedly dead after the Oceanic 815 crash, Carmen and David continued to build a life together. When Hugo was rescued as one of the Oceanic Six, an elated Carmen and David met him in Hawaii and took him back home. However, the island experience and the subsequent lies caused Hurley to become extremely paranoid. Even Carmen's attempt to throw him a tropical-themed surprise birthday party failed, because of Hurley's fear of what he thought were the "island whispers." After another stint in Santa Rosa, Hurley escaped and returned home to his mother. Worried, Carmen asked him to tell her his troubles and he revealed the true story of the island to which she replied with true empathy, "I don't understand you, but I believe you."

THE CAVES

Mother took Claudia to her living quarters in the caves.

CAROLE LITTLETON

▶ **CONNECTION:** Mother of Claire Littleton

Like her daughter Claire, Carole Littleton had an emotionally challenging experience while bringing up her child. Carole's affair with Christian Shephard, a married man, resulted in the pregnancy that brought Claire into the world. Unfortunately, Carole never fully recovered from the pain of falling in love with someone who already had a family.

When Claire was about two years old, Carole asked Christian to stop visiting them at their Sydney, Australia home, as she found it too upsetting when he returned to his wife Margo and son Jack. To save Claire the same pain, she told her that her father had died.

THE ACCIDENT

Carole and Claire generally had a great relationship, but during a heated argument in Claire's tempestuous teenage years, a car accident left Carole with extensive injuries. She remained in a coma for several years.

Shortly after she slipped into the coma, Christian began paying for Carole's medical expenses. He also revealed to Claire, much to her Aunt Lindsey's displeasure, that he was her father.

CAROLE & AARON

Carole had fully recovered from her coma when the Oceanic Six returned home. She flew to Los Angeles to attend the funeral held for Christian and revealed to Jack that he had a half-sister named Claire. At the funeral, Carole unknowingly met her grandson, Aaron, for the first time.

Jack and Carole met for the first time at Christian's funeral.

Jack later confronted Carole when he grew concerned she had hired Dan Norton to disprove Kate's maternity to Aaron. However, Carole was simply arranging her settlement fee for the Oceanic disaster and had no idea Aaron was her grandchild. Prior to Kate's return to the island, she informed Carole that Aaron was Claire's little boy and left him in his grandmother's care.

Located about a mile inland from the survivors' beach camp, the caves had a long history of serving as shelter for various inhabitants throughout the centuries. Several of its geographic features, which included a flowing fresh-water spring, a canopy of shady leaves, and a cool interior, made them a natural choice for habitation and protection from the harsh sun and elements.

MOTHER'S ABODE

Sometime around the first century AD, a Roman woman named Claudia drifted ashore on the island after her vessel wrecked during a storm. Late in her pregnancy and severely dehydrated, the woman wandered inland until she discovered a stream. An older woman appeared, spoke to her in Latin, and took Claudia into the caves, which served as her spartan home. Claudia then went into labor and the older woman helped her give birth to twin boys. Moments later, the older woman murdered Claudia by crushing her skull with a rock and then raised the boys as her own.

The family of three spent thirteen years in the caves and lived their modest lives as Mother and sons. However, after he discovered the truth about his birth, the Boy in Black left the caves to make a life away from his mother and brother Jacob.

For thirty more years, Mother and Jacob lived together in the caves with their loom and sparse personal belongings. Only after Mother passed her power to Jacob did the Man in Black return to the caves. Livid that Mother killed the villagers he cohabitated with for three decades, the Man in Black killed her. Jacob then beat the Man in Black unconscious, dragged his body to the sacred pool and threw him into it. It destroyed the Man in Black's mortal body, which Jacob then carried back to the caves. He placed the corpses of his Mother and brother together and intertwined their hands for their eternal repose as the island's Adam and Eve. Jacob then placed the black and white pawns of the senet game into his pouch and left it with them.

OCEANIC SURVIVORS

In 2004, Jack Shephard found the caves while chasing the ghost of his father, Christian Shephard. Inside he found his father's empty coffin, luggage and pieces of Oceanic flight 815. Jack lobbied his fellow survivors to move with him to the caves for better shelter and fresh water. Hurley, Claire, Charlie, Locke, Sun, Jin, Michael, Walt, and Artz agreed, while the rest remained on the beach. For the survivors who chose to live in the caves, life was relatively safe and quiet. Jack did the majority of his medical examinations from there, including his unsuccessful attempt to save Boone's life after his fall from the Beechcraft. Danielle Rousseau appeared at the caves once to warn of an impending attack from the Others, which led Jack to collect the beach survivors into the caves for safety. After the Swan hatch was opened, the remaining cave dwellers abandoned the caves either to do shifts with the button or to transfer the Swan's resources to the beach camp.

On their way to the lighthouse after leaving the Temple, Jack and Hurley stumbled upon the caves once again. Jack went back inside to look around, while Hurley pondered the origin of Adam and Eve. He wondered if their time travel could mean the bodies were actually them. Fixated on his father's coffin, Jack then revealed to Hurley how he initially came to find the caves.

Artist: Jack Bender
Title: Black Scale/White Scale #2
Location: Charles Widmore's office (flash sideways).
Significance: Underscores the dark-light themes and recalls the scale in Jacob's cave.

Artist: Thomas Hannsz
Title: Jacob's Dog
Location: Cabin on the island
Significance: Unknown

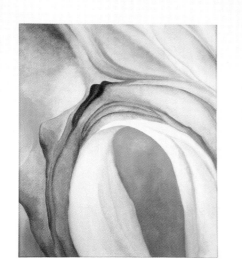

Artist: Georgia O'Keefe
Title: Music—Pink and Blue, II
Location: Hanging in the Staff station surgery room
Significance: O'Keefe's work is often associated with female reproduction.

Photographer: Unknown
Title: Unknown
Location: Dr. Brooks' office in Santa Rosa Mental Health Institute.
Significance: An eerie reminder of Hurley's South Pacific adventures.

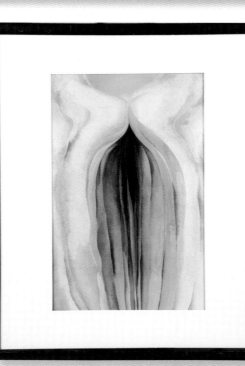

Artist: Unknown
Title: Joshua Tree National Park near Palm Springs
Location: The Swan
Significance: Religious overtones; trees are so named for their resemblance to a praying Joshua's outstretched arms.

Artist: Georgia O'Keefe
Title: Grey Line with Black, Blue and Yellow
Location: Hanging in the Staff station surgery room
Significance: O'Keefe's work is often associated with female reproduction.

CHARLES WIDMORE

FACTS & FIGURES

Connection: Former leader of the Others

Occupation: CEO of Widmore Industries

Family: Eloise Hawking (former lover); Daniel Faraday (son); Penelope Hume (daughter); Desmond Hume (son-in-law)

A former leader of the island Others, Charles Widmore was banished for breaking the rules of his position as established by Jacob, the island's protector. Widmore relocated to England and reinvented himself as a successful business entrepreneur with a consortium of companies known as Widmore Industries. However, the only purpose of Widmore having massive wealth was to bankroll his true passion: returning to the island. For the better part of two decades, Widmore extorted, assaulted, lied and connived to gain any kernel of information that would allow him to overthrow his enemy, the island's new leader, Benjamin Linus. As their personal war escalated over the years, it only served to push the two men further away from what should have been their joint priority, keeping the island safe from the outside world.

A young Widmore learned under Richard Alpert.

EARLY ISLAND YEARS

Charles grew up as an Other under Richard Alpert's island leadership. In 1954 Widmore was only 17 but he was already fearless and ruthless when it came to ridding the island of intruders. As the island skipped through time, it placed Juliet, James and Locke in Widmore's era. By chance they captured Charles and his friend, Cunningham. Unwilling to share any information, Widmore snapped Cunningham's neck to prevent him from talking. Alpert was frequently at odds with Widmore about his hyper-aggressive style, but Jacob appreciated his loyalty and allowed him to rise to a leadership role along with Eloise Hawking, his lover and the eventual mother of his child.

LEADING THE OTHERS

After Eloise left the island to have their child, Widmore took over full leadership of the island with his ruthless style fully entrenched. When the DHARMA Initiative didn't abide by the letter of the Truce, Widmore executed the Purge in retribution. Filled with the success of that endeavor, Widmore became more and more possessive of the island and everything on it. He brazenly left the island for personal matters and even maintained a relationship with a woman who became the mother of his second child, Penelope. More concerned with his own satisfaction than his island responsibilities, Jacob had Alpert strip away his leadership and banish him from the island forever as punishment.

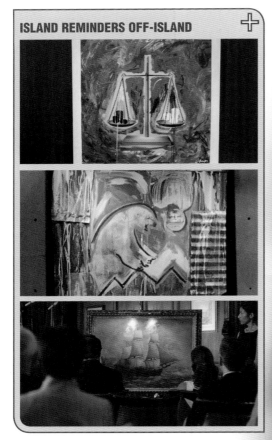

ISLAND REMINDERS OFF-ISLAND

1977

1954

> **"That island's mine, Benjamin. It always was... it will be again."**

WIDMORE INDUSTRIES

Widmore Construction billboard

Widmore Labs Pregnancy tests

Widmore Corporation on Gale's balloon basket

Widmore Industries Building

RELATIONSHIP WITH ELOISE HAWKING

The exact depth and breadth of Charles Widmore and Eloise Hawking's love affair on the island remains a mystery, but as they were two strong personalities with different views about the island, it was no surprise that it ended badly.

Widmore Industries
London, England

Charles Widmore
Managing Director

020.7946.0328

ATTEMPTS TO RETURN

Before Widmore stepped off the Pala Ferry dock the last time, he was already working on ways to return to the island that he felt was rightfully his to lead. Widmore tried every avenue possible and mandated that no price was too high, no life was too sacred and no lead was too small if it meant he could return to where he wanted to be.

Ben showed Locke proof about Widmore's tactics

Widmore tracked down any off-island Other he could uncover and even resorted to physical intimidation to get them to spill information about the island's location. That the Lamp Post station was under his nose in Los Angeles provided Eloise and Ben a great deal of satisfaction.

Six months after the Oceanic 815 crash, Widmore purchased a Boeing 777 fuselage, retrofit it to resemble an Oceanic airlines plane and staged it in the Sunda Trench. He even dug up the graves of 324 people in Thailand and placed them inside. All of it was done so that the official hunt for the wreckage and survivors would be called off and the island would be safe from discovery.

The staged crash was shown on TV.

When Widmore's surveillance of the island's exit in Tunisia revealed John Locke, Charles sent his people to retrieve him. In a field hospital, Widmore offered to finance and support Locke's goal of returning the Oceanic Six to the island. Widmore gave Locke the alias of Jeremy Bentham and the use of Matthew Abaddon's services. While initially put out by Sun Kwon's brazen approach of him in front of his colleagues, he quickly forgave her when he found out she wanted to join their resources to find and kill Benjamin Linus.

Soon after the faux Oceanic wreck footage was leaked to the world, Widmore commissioned the *Kahana* expedition to include a science team contingent and the mercenary contingent to cover all the challenges facing his potential return. He told the people on the freighter that Linus planted the fake wreckage and that's why they had to capture him. The overall mission ended in failure.

After he claimed he was visited by Jacob and told how to get back to the island, Widmore collected his son-in-law, Desmond, as a fail safe tool to prevent the Man in Black's plan to leave the island, and set off in a submarine. Full of himself that he had received a sanctioned return ticket to the island, his hubris did not let him recognize that the situation on the island would most likely not end in his favor.

Emboldened by his return to the island, Widmore again faced a hard choice when the Man in Black threatened to kill Penny unless Desmond's purpose was explained to him. As Widmore went to whisper in his ear, Ben pumped his mortal enemy with a clip full of bullets and simply stated, "He doesn't get to save his daughter."

"You wouldn't dare."

In Widmore's attempt to find Ben, Martin Keamy used Alex as bait to draw out Ben; it didn't work and Keamy killed Alex.

Ben called Widmore and told him he was going to kill Penny.

CHARLIE HUME

▶ **CONNECTION:** Son of Desmond & Penelope Hume

Charlie Hume is the only child of Desmond Hume and Penny Widmore Hume. The boat on which Charlie was born was anchored in the bay of a small, undisclosed Filipino town. Local doctor Efren Salonga delivered the healthy baby with no medical assistance. The Humes named the baby Charlie after Desmond's former friend, Charlie Pace.

For two years, the Humes raised Charlie on their boat as they sailed around the world. In 2007, the family returned to Great Britain, which Desmond introduced to Charlie for the first time. Desmond had returned to fulfil Daniel Faraday's request that he contact Eloise Hawking and give her a message.

The family then sailed to Los Angeles so Desmond could complete his task. While docked there, Benjamin Linus approached the boat in an attempt to kill Penny in retribution for Widmore's assassination of Alex. Penny's frightened voice caused Charlie to come up on deck. Affected by the sight of their young boy, Ben lowered his gun and the distraction allowed Desmond to attack Ben from behind. After Ben shot Desmond at the dock, Penny and Charlie raced to the hospital to find out his condition.

Penny and Charlie watched as Desmond was wheeled away to surgery.

MABUHAY
The word Mabuhay is seen at the docks where Charlie was born. It is a Filipino word in the Tagalog dialect that translates to "long live" in English. It's also used as a term to say "Welcome" to tourists new to the Philippines.

CHARLIE PACE

FACTS & FIGURES

Time On The Island
POST-OCEANIC: 91 days

Skills: Bass, guitar, piano, singing, songwriting

Loves: Banoffee Pie, nature documentaries, The Kinks

Hates: Bees

Desmond encountered Charlie on the streets in England.

The troubled young rock star led a colorful, erratic, and challenging life. Drug addiction, self-doubt, and guilt from his Catholic upbringing plagued Charlie Pace, but he struggled to prevent them from defining him. Charlie was loyal to both his biological family and his island family—especially Claire Littleton and her son, Aaron. Charlie strived to prove himself worthy of love, but he ultimately gave his life to save his friends.

DRIVE SHAFT

Charlie's love of music began when he was very young. His parents encouraged him by giving him a piano on Christmas. Charlie went on to write all of Drive Shaft's songs on this piano and before the band's inception, he tried out the material as a street performer with his acoustic guitar.

Drive Shaft's first gig was a show at the Night & Day café on Oldham Street in Manchester, England. A slew of gigs followed, but Charlie decided to quit the band during a troubled journey to a headline gig in Clitheroe, Lancashire. But when he heard their debut single "You All Everybody" playing on the van's radio, he changed his mind.

Success brought further media exposure and good album sales for their *Draft Shaft* debut, but it also brought groupies and drugs. Charlie, Liam, and their guitarist Roderick all became addicted to heroin. When their second album, *Oil Change*, couldn't match the success of their first, Drive Shaft went on an indefinite hiatus.

Desperate to create some kind of comeback—and to pay the record label what they owed—the band completely sold out and allowed their hit "You All Everybody" to be used for a diaper product. They also agreed to star in the commercial, but Liam's troubling behavior on the set caused them to get fired.

When Liam missed the birth of his daughter, Megan, he made a decision to clean up. Without telling Charlie—who was already writing new Drive Shaft material—Liam sold Charlie's beloved piano. Liam used the money to buy plane tickets to take his family to Australia to start a new life.

Left on his own, Charlie couldn't get clean and he was desperate for a Drive Shaft comeback. In September 2004, he secured an 8-week tour, opening for Meat Coat, with the first gig planned for Los Angeles. Thrilled, Charlie flew to Sydney to convince Liam to do the shows, but his brother refused, leaving Charlie to board Oceanic flight 815 alone.

GREATEST HITS

When Charles Widmore's faked 815 crash convinced the world that Charlie was dead, a public memorial was held for him. A greatest hits album was released and suddenly Drive Shaft was huge. Charlie was once again a big-time star.

DRIVE SHAFT

THE DRIVE

" Guys...Where are we? "

DRUG ADDICTION

When Charlie landed on the island, he was still using and he knew his stash would soon run out. When Locke revealed Charlie's guitar case was wedged high up in a tree, Charlie decided to take Locke's offer for help. He threw his remaining supply of heroin into a fire. But this clean period was short-lived, thanks to the huge supply of heroin left in a plane that had crashed on the island years before. Charlie discovered numerous Virgin Mary statues that concealed heroin, the source of all his troubles, and his demons began growing ever stronger.

As Charlie's behavior became more erratic, it changed several survivors' views of him. Initially sympathetic to Charlie's situation, John Locke took a sterner approach when he feared for Aaron's safety in Charlie's presence. When Claire learned the truth behind Charlie's "religious" statue from Eko, her impression of him soured

a great deal. This hit Charlie hard, as Claire's friendship meant the world to him. As such, Charlie had to dig deep to drag himself away from the constant temptation of the drugs in order to gain back Claire's trust. Eko took a different approach with Charlie when he discovered that the Virgin Mary statues were the ones he loaded onto the plane in Nigeria. He helped Charlie rediscover his spiritual side by getting him to help build the survivors a church on the beach.

Charlie previously attended Catholic mass and confession regularly, but his Drive Shaft career drew him away from his faith. On the island, Charlie had a crisis of faith, but his drug addiction and experiences with Claire and Aaron nudged him back in the right direction.

GOOD VIBRATIONS

After finding his guitar, Charlie spent many hours jamming new material on the beach. This included "Monster Eats the Pilot" which he planned to include on a new album. During his infiltration of the Looking Glass station, Charlie sang Drive Shaft songs aloud to annoy and distract Bonnie and Greta from discovering Desmond Hume's arrival.

Charlie learned that the Looking Glass signal-jamming software was created by a musician. His knowledge of "Good Vibrations" by The Beach Boys enabled him to determine, note-by-note, the correct code to disable the software and communicate with Penny Widmore.

> ### CHARLIE & POLAR BEARS ⊹
> *Charlie faced polar bears several times on the island, but he already knew how intelligent they were. During his Drive Shaft days, he frequently watched BBC nature documentaries while he was high. A stuffed polar bear even made an appearance in the commercial Drive Shaft made for Butties Diapers.*

> Charlie's demon, heroin, was stashed inside Virgin Mary statues.

> ### BY THE NUMBERS ⊹
> *The Drive Across America Tour poster shows the date **8/15/2000**.*
> *The photocopier model Charlie promotes is the **C-815**.*
> *Charlie's life is saved **4** times before his death.*

FAITH

While on the island, Charlie initially had a crisis of faith, but became more spiritual as he shed the hang-ups and guilt that previously weighed him down.

▶ *The cramped space of the cave-in Charlie was trapped in with Jack reminded him of a confessional booth. After he escaped, he began to feel spiritual again.*

▶ *When Ethan abducted Claire, Charlie found solace by praying with Rose. She guided him through his trauma and guilt he felt for stopping Ethan.*

▶ *Just prior to his death in the Looking Glass station, Charlie mustered the strength to cross himself, his faith restored.*

CLAIRE & AARON

Charlie formed an attachment to Claire very quickly. In the early days after the crash, he gave her blankets, moved her luggage, and brought her drinking water. After Claire returned from her abduction by Ethan Rom, Charlie gently helped her battle amnesia.

Charlie showed a romantic side when he brought Claire an empty jar, claiming it was full of peanut butter. The two pretended to eat and shared a moment of contentment on the island. Much later, he surprised her with a real jar of her favorite treat.

Aaron's birth cemented the bond Charlie felt for mother and son. Charlie loved Aaron, but he went through a dark period where Claire feared for Aaron's safety. Claire learned about Charlie's heroin stash and banished him from her tent. Charlie insisted he wasn't using heroin, but his behavior made his friends think otherwise. Charlie became convinced that he needed to save Aaron. He started a fire, causing a distraction, so that he could take Aaron to the ocean's edge to perform a baptism. This bizarre behavior further alienated Claire.

Charlie tried to prove his worth to Claire when he tested the pallet drop's vaccine on himself in case she wanted to give some to Aaron as a precaution. By the time Desmond described his premonitions of Charlie's death to Claire, the two had reconciled and worked together to create the seagull rescue message. After Claire's reaction to the implant the Others placed in her, Charlie became fearsomely protective once more, especially as his family unit was threatened again. When Claire recovered, it was only a matter of time until Charlie resigned himself to his fate—he would have to die to fulfill Desmond's premonition that Claire and Aaron would be saved.

HUGO "HURLEY" REYES

Charlie bonded with his closest friend, Hurley, while they fished together shortly after the crash. The pair quickly developed an honest, wise-cracking relationship. Even when Charlie was ostracized by other survivors, he knew that Hurley hadn't given up on him. Even when he knew about Desmond's premonitions of his death, Hurley was able to slap Charlie out of his depression.

After his death, Charlie still managed to visit Hurley at the Santa Rosa Mental Health Institute after Hurley had left the island. Charlie explained that he was dead, but that he could also be there with Hurley. To prove he was really there, Charlie returned the slap Hurley had given him on the island and told his dear friend something that had future significance: "They need you."

EKO

After the DHARMA pallet drop of supplies, Charlie took wood from the pallet to Eko and helped him with building the church. Eko's decision to move into the Swan station and abandon the church deeply upset Charlie, so he continued the project alone.

DESMOND HUME

Desmond saw Charlie busking in London while singing "Wonderwall" by Oasis. The song's refrain includes the line: "You're gonna be the one that saves me." Once he started seeing images of the future, Desmond prevented Charlie from being killed many times: being hit by lightning; drowning while trying to save Claire; one of Rousseau's traps firing an arrow into his throat; and falling off rocks and into the ocean.

- ▌ **Liam Pace** (Brother)
- ▌ **Megan Pace** (Mother)
- ▌ **Simon Pace** (Father)
- ▌ **Karen Pace** (Sister-in-law)
- ▌ **Megan Pace** (Niece)
- ▌ **Lucy Heatherton** (Ex-girlfriend)
- ▌ **Roderick** (Drive Shaft guitarist)
- ▌ **Tommy** (Friend)

LOOKING GLASS HERO

Desmond had another vision of Charlie drowning—this time in the Looking Glass station. Charlie volunteered to break into the underwater station and disable the signal-jammer. He lied to his Oceanic friends that he could hold his breath for four minutes and was the junior swimming champion of Northern England, just to make sure they let him go.

After Mikhail blew himself up by the porthole to the Looking Glass communications room, Charlie closed the door to prevent Desmond from drowning. Using the same pen with which he'd written his "Greatest Hits," Charlie managed to scrawl on his hand "Not Penny's Boat." He pressed his hand against the window to alert Desmond that the freighter had not been sent by Penelope Widmore, Desmond's girlfriend. Just before his lungs filled with water, Charlie mustered the strength to cross himself.

▌ Charlie exacted revenge against Ethan for kidnapping Claire.

FATED FUTURE

From the beginning, Charlie seemed destined to die on the island:

▶ *Ethan Rom kidnapped both Charlie and Claire, as part of monitoring Claire's pregnancy. Blindfolded and hung by his neck, Charlie died, but he was miraculously resuscitated by Jack.*

▶ *When Charlie discovered a rope bridge, Hurley made it across safely. When Charlie tried, the rope snapped and he nearly fell to his death.*

▶ *Charlie barely survived both the dynamite explosion inside the Swan and its eventual fail-save implosion.*

▶ *Charlie got the words wrong when he sang the Itsy Bitsy Spider song to Aaron. Charlie sang, "Down came the rain, and drowned the spider out," but Hurley reminded him that it should've been "washed" instead of "drowned."*

Jack and Kate struggled to save Charlie after he was hanged by Ethan Rom.

DESMOND & CHARLIE

Once he started seeing images of the future, Desmond saved Charlie's life many times.

Desmond constructed a make-shift lightning rod.

Desmond rescued Claire to prevent Charlie from drowning.

Desmond caught the seagull for Claire so Charlie wouldn't die.

Charlie changed the writing on the tape from "Fate" to "Late."

DS RING ✚

During Drive Shaft's hit tour of Helsinki, Finland, Liam gave his brother the DS ring, which was a family heirloom from their ancestor, Dexter Stratton. Years later on the island, Charlie left it inside Aaron's cot before he embarked on his one-way mission to the Looking Glass station. Sun found the ring years later, but it never made its way into Claire's care.

#5 THE FIRST TIME I HEARD MYSELF
ON THE RADIO
#4 DAD TEACHING ME TO SWIM
AT BUTLINS
#3 THE CHRISTMAS LIAM GAVE
ME THE RING.
#2 WOMAN OUTSIDE COVENT
GARDEN CALLS ME A HERO.
#1 THE NIGHT I MET YOU.

Charlie's "Greatest Hits" list.

The "DS" on Charlie's ring stood for the initials of Dexter Stratton, an ancestor, not Drive Shaft.

DRIVE SHAFT

DRIVE SHAFT

THE DRIVE ACROSS AMERICA TOUR

COBO HALL — MOTOR CITY — AUG 15 2000

CHARLOTTE LEWIS

Charlotte Staples Lewis was an accomplished cultural anthropologist hired to be a part of Widmore's science team aboard the *Kahana*. She was born on July 2, 1971, the daughter of David and Jeanette Lewis and the oldest of their three girls. Her parents were former DHARMA Initiative members and they lived on the island until Charlotte was 6 years old. She was evacuated from the island with her mother before the Incident, and thereafter Jeanette told her daughter that her memories of the island were a figment of her imagination. However, Charlotte believed the island was real and dedicated her professional life as an anthropologist to finding it. Her wish was granted 27 years later when she returned to the island that would be her final frontier.

DHARMA YEARS

When Charlotte was 3 years old, she first saw the man who would become her soulmate, Daniel Faraday. It was another three years until she saw him again. A naughty 6-year-old Charlotte was eating a chocolate bar on her swing set before dinner when Daniel gently approached her with a dire warning: if she left the island and ever returned she would die. The stranger scared Charlotte so much that she suppressed the memory for years. A few days later, Charlotte was evacuated with her mother on the submarine.

Faraday met Charlotte as a young girl during a time skip.

ALWAYS CURIOUS

After the Lewis family left the island, they relocated to Bromsgrove, Worcestershire, England. At some point her father returned to them and her parents had two more daughters. Charlotte earned her undergraduate degree in anthropology from Kent and her Doctorate of Philosophy in cultural anthropology at Oxford University. She specialized in Ancient Carthage studies, which led her to follow rumors to a secret dig in the desert of Tunisia in 2004. Together with another colleague, they traveled to the suspected site and paid a bribe to be allowed into the closed dig. There they found the partially exposed skeleton of a polar bear. Charlotte pulled out an excavation hammer and went to work on the area around the bones and unearthed a collar with a DHARMA Hydra logo. It was her first tangible connection to the actual existence of the DHARMA Initiative.

All the while Widmore was researching potential members to recruit for his *Kahana* science team. Aware of her prior involvement with DHARMA when he was leader of the Others, her award-winning anthropology expertise and her appearance at the Tunisian exit point dig, he had Matthew Abaddon and Naomi Dorrit secure her for his five-person team.

"I'm not allowed to have chocolate before dinner."

1977

80

" *This place is death!* "

CHARLOTTE'S NAME   +

Charlotte's name is a homage to author Clive Staples Lewis (or C.S. Lewis) who wrote the "Chronicles of Narnia" saga about a family of children who can access a magical world through their wardrobe.

FULL CIRCLE

Charlotte was extremely excited and relieved to be back on the island, even if she had to abandon Frank's malfunctioning helicopter via parachute to reach it. She was doubly thrilled to run into Locke's group, whom she peppered with enthusiastic questions about their survival. When she offered escape via the freighter, Locke angrily declined and then took her hostage as future leverage. He attached her transponder to Vincent to throw off their trail. When she attempted to run, Ben shot her twice which she only survived due to her concealed bulletproof vest. In trouble with Locke, Ben explained he had detailed information about Charlotte and her team provided by his mole on the *Kahana* (Michael Dawson) which ensured him more time. At the barracks, Charlotte was traded for Miles Straume by Sayid and returned to her team at the helicopter. She opted to stay on the island with Daniel at the beach camp.

In the dark of night, Charlotte and Daniel packed their HAZMAT suits and gas masks and left for the Tempest. Kate stumbled upon them mid-hike and opened their packs. Panicked, Charlotte pistol-whipped Kate and the pair made haste to the station. There they worked on the computer terminals to make the lethal gas dispersing system used in the Purge inert. Juliet Burke found them and fought with Charlotte as she thought they were up to no good. Charlotte bested her and explained they had stopped the station from being functional anymore.

Back at the beach, Daniel and Charlotte came to understand their freighter brethren had enacted the secondary protocol and they helped evacuate people off the island via the Zodiac raft. Despite Daniel's plea to the contrary, she chose to stay on the island to get more answers about her personal past. He returned to her before the island started to skip through time.

DISPLACEMENT PROBLEMS

Not long after the time skips started Charlotte felt the adverse effects, with nosebleeds and headaches that immediately worried Daniel. As the jumps increased, her symptoms grew worse to where she eventually blacked out for ten

minutes. She was revived by Daniel and Juliet and was able to hike back to the beach with them. They decided to head to the Orchid, but two more flashes laid out Charlotte. She spoke to Jin in Korean and then regressed to moments in her past amongst moments of clarity when she told Daniel about her history on the island. As her mind raced, the memory of Daniel's warning when she was a child came to her just before she died. She told Daniel who wept as he helplessly watched her die…

The time skips eventually caused Charlotte's death.

CHARLOTTE MALKIN

▶ **CONNECTION:** Daughter of Richard & Joyce Malkin; had encounter with Eko

Young and energetic, Charlotte went on a boat trip with her parents, but fell into the river and appeared to have drowned. Her body was taken to coroner Dr. Ian McVay for an autopsy but before he could begin, Charlotte "woke up." Joyce believed a miracle brought her daughter back from the dead and sought verification from the Australian Catholic church via an investigation by Father Tunde.

Richard was quick to debunk the theory and instead asserted that his daughter's body went into hypothermia while in the cold water, which made it look like she had died. Eko left the Malkin residence without interviewing Charlotte and closed the case. While at the Sydney airport just prior to boarding Oceanic flight 815, however, Charlotte approached Eko and said she had a message from Yemi. Charlotte explained that she met Yemi while "between places" and that he said he was proud of his brother and would see him soon. Her vision proved at least one person in the Malkin family had the gift of second sight.

CHET

▶ **CONNECTION:** Achara's brother; beat up Jack Shephard

Chet was the brother of the enigmatic tattoo artist Achara in Phuket, Thailand. Not generally a fan of tourists, Chet however took a liking to Jack Shephard for being brave enough to try an unusual "special Thai dish" at the restaurant where he served. But their friendship went south when Chet discovered that Achara had marked Jack, an outsider, with a tattoo. He collected his friends and they found Jack. They beat him and told him to leave their beach and country.

CHRISTIAN SHEPHARD

FACTS & FIGURES

Connection: Father of Jack Shephard

Occupation: Spinal surgeon

A highly skilled surgeon, Christian Shephard was a tragic soul who fathered both Jack Shephard and Claire Littleton. Although he spent time as Chief of Surgery at Los Angeles' St. Sebastian Hospital, Christian's lack of faith in himself as a father, coupled with an extramarital affair that produced a daughter, resulted in Christian turning to alcohol as a way to hide from the consequences of his choices.

FATHER AND SON

Before his alcoholism, Christian tried to be a good father to Jack. He enjoyed reading Lewis Carroll's *Alice's Adventures in Wonderland* to his son and also taught Jack chess, which the two loved to play. In Jack's adult life, Christian was responsible for guiding him through his first major medical procedure—one that prevented a young girl's paralysis. After a surgical mistake, Christian directed Jack to pause during the operation and count to five to let the fear in for only five seconds, so Jack could compose himself and complete the surgery. The event left Jack angry. He had always felt that his father didn't believe in him. Jack's accusation was incorrect, but it was something Jack never fully understood.

Jack's decision to tell the truth cost Christian his job.

Christian knew Jack had extraordinary skills as a surgeon but lacked the ability to disengage his emotions. He did what he felt was necessary to harden Jack and enable him to help more people even after the loss of a patient. Jack misinterpreted his father's actions, however, and assumed his father was simply telling him he didn't have what it took to become a great surgeon. Despite this firm handling, Christian made Jack understand that even if there is only a one percent chance of a patient recovering, there is still hope.

SUPPORTING SARAH & JACK

Christian's father, Ray, didn't approve of Christian's marriage to Margo, so Christian never wore the watch his father gave him as a gift on his wedding day. To show his approval of Jack's marriage to Sarah Wagner, however, Christian gave Jack the family heirloom, which he wore with pride.

During the Angelo Busoni case, Jack become close to his patient's daughter, Gabriela; but Christian kept telling Jack to go home to his wife. When her father died on Jack's table, Christian intervened and told Gabriela to stop Jack from repeating the same mistake of an affair that he'd made. After Sarah left Jack— as a result of Jack favoring fixing patients over fixing their marriage—Sarah called Christian repeatedly, concerned about how badly Jack was taking their divorce. Tragically, after being sober for 50 days, a huge fight with Jack—where he falsely accused Christian of sleeping with Sarah—pushed Christian back to the bottle.

DAUGHTER CLAIRE

Christian had a brief affair with Carole Littleton. Carole became pregnant and told Christian that she wanted to keep the baby. He visited her home in Sydney, Australia as often as he could when Claire was young and brought her toys and enjoyed singing to her. However, the interval between his visits grew longer, and then the visits stopped altogether.

Claire was in her late teens when a car accident put Carole into a coma. Christian flew to Sydney immediately, but he argued with Carole's sister, Lindsey. Finally, he admitted to covering Carole's medical bills and told Claire he was her father. Christian suggested ending Carole's life-support, as he believed there was no chance for her recovery. But Claire disagreed and disowned her father.

> *"Some people are just supposed to suffer. That's why the Red Sox will never win the damn series."*
>
> — Spoken by Christian to Sawyer

" *Let it go, Jack.* "

ALCOHOLISM

Christian's alcohol abuse reached uncontrollable levels after Jack's rise through the ranks of the St. Sebastian surgical team. While under the influence, Christian performed surgery on a patient named Beth. His unsteady hands and poor judgment led to cutting open a vital artery. In a strange reversal of Christian stepping in to save Jack's career, a nurse informed Jack that Christian had made an error. She added that his father was operating while drunk, but by the time Jack took over, and even though he repaired the hepatic artery, the damage led to Beth's death.

Christian convinced Jack to sign official documentation stating that Beth died as a result of the severity of her injuries sustained from her accident. During the formal hearing, however, Jack told the committee the truth, costing Christian his job at St. Sebastian and his medical license.

Christian's Alcoholics Anonymous support was ruined by a fight with Jack.

A TALE OF "TOM" & "SARAH"

Shortly after Christian lost his license, he met Ana Lucia Cortez in the LAX airport. Ana Lucia, a security guard at LAX, was a former officer in the LAPD, and Christian asked her to be his bodyguard for a trip to Sydney, suggesting fate might have thrown them together. Charmed, and feeling just as lost, Ana Lucia agreed and the two adopted the monikers of Tom and Sarah for their trip. After four days of solid drinking, Christian and Ana Lucia tried to visit Claire, but her Aunt Lindsey refused to allow him in her house.

Christian could be completely honest about his feelings with total strangers—especially after several drinks—but never to his son. He confided in Ana Lucia that he fled to Australia because he couldn't apologize to Jack. He understood that Jack reported his on-duty drinking to help him, but he didn't have the strength to thank his son.

Although Ana Lucia was inspired to head home on flight 815 to reconcile with her mother, Christian had convinced himself that fate led him to another bar. The drinking session Christian started at The Last Call and shared with James "Sawyer" Ford was the beginning of the end for Christian. He died later that day.

COFFIN TO AMERICA

Jack's mother, Margo, insisted that they have Christian's funeral as soon as Jack landed with the body back in Los Angeles. After Jack collected Christian's body in Sydney, he realized his father didn't have any suitable shoes for his casket attire. Jack decided that, as no one would see his feet—and because he felt his father wasn't worth the cost of nice shoes or the time it took to get them—he put a pair of old white tennis shoes he had on Christian's feet, instead.

After flight 815 crashed on the island, the smoke monster then used Christian's physical form for a succession of manipulations over many years that affected Jack, Claire, John Locke and many others. The smoke monster's first act in Christian's form was to alert Vincent, Walt Lloyd's Labrador Retriever, to wake up Jack. From then on, the smoke monster's long con had begun. Although Jack found his father's coffin near the caves, he never located the body.

The Man in Black appeared in Christian's form several times on the island.

The shoes Christian wore in the casket. Jack was so upset with his father he didn't want to buy a new pair for the funeral.

CINDY CHANDLER

▶ **CONNECTION:** Flight attendant on Oceanic flight 815

When the plane broke apart over the South Pacific, Cindy was in the tail-section and miraculously survived the water impact. During the chaotic aftermath, she drew upon her training and kept a level head as she helped others including the two young sibling passengers, Zack and Emma. At separate times she and the children were forcibly taken by the Others, but they bonded with their captors. Cindy and the kids chose to stay with the Others and lived among them peacefully for three years until the Man in Black made his final push to leave the island.

FLYING THE UNFRIENDLY SKIES

Based in Australia, Cindy loved her job and was adept at dealing with all the challenges long-haul flights offered. Even before the crash, Oceanic flight 815 proved to be a particularly eventful journey. About mid-flight as Cindy operated the drink cart, she flirted a bit with passenger Jack Shephard about his weak drink. When the plane hit turbulence, she put away her cart in the back of the plane where she noticed a passenger, Charlie Pace, acting very stressed. She went to him and offered him water, which he refused. Concerned, Cindy consulted with her fellow attendants about him, which sent a panicked Charlie to the first class lavatory. Cindy and her fellow attendants calmly followed and asked him to stop. As the turbulence continued, Cindy announced over the PA system that passengers should put on their seatbelts. Cindy then made it back to her seat before the plane went down.

Cindy remained strong as more of their injured either died or were taken.	Cindy ran to alert the sleeping survivors that Nathan was gone.	Tailies united with Michael, Sawyer and Jin to hike to the fuselage beach together.		

Day 2 • **Day 12** • **Day 19** • **Day 24** • **Day 27** • **Day 45** • **Day 47** • **Day 48**

| Cindy argued the need for the beach fire because before the crash the pilot had lost communication and the plane was two hours off course. | Cindy hiked with the survivors inland and supported Ana Lucia's decision to put Nathan in a hole as she didn't remember his face from the plane either. | Cindy helped explore the Arrow station for resources. | As Cindy and Libby fashioned a fishing net, Cindy spotted Jin's body and helped drag him to shore. | As the hike grew more difficult, Cindy grew more frightened of being exposed to the Others and urged their continued movement. Her fears were proved right when she was plucked from the jungle without a sound. |

TAILIE LIFE

Cindy swam to shore with her fellow survivors and after the initial chaos, sat on the beach to quietly compose herself. Eko came to her with Zack and Emma and asked her to look after them. She agreed as she introduced herself to the children and they watched as Eko pulled dead bodies out of the ocean.

ONE OF THEM

When Cindy was taken by the Others, she quickly learned that the dirty, shadowy figures they were so frightened of were just people—civilized people—who lived in the barracks and protected the island. Ben Linus reunited her with Zack and Emma, as well as the other passengers who were taken per Jacob. They clothed her, fed her and after they explained their purpose, even welcomed her into their fold as had been done with many others before her.

By the time Jack was held in the Hydra cages, Cindy had fully sided with the Others. Therefore, it wasn't odd for her when she, along with about 10 Others, were called by the Sheriff to witness Juliet Burke's trial. They assembled outside of Jack's cage and as some stared he grew frustrated. Cindy calmly came forward to say hello and he recognized her from the plane. She explained they were there to "watch" but his ire seemed to fluster her. And when Cindy voiced Emma's question about Ana Lucia, that only served to confuse and incense him more.

Later, when Ben collected the Others to leave the barracks for the Temple, Cindy and the kids were part of the group. As they made camp, Locke helped a more ruggedly dressed Cindy put up her tent. He couldn't help but notice the stares directed towards him and Cindy explained it was because they were excited to finally meet him—as some had waited a long time.

TIME ON THE ISLAND ✛
POST-OCEANIC: 101 days
As an Other: 3+ years

At some point Cindy and the kids made it to the Temple, where they lived under the guidance of Dogen. She let her hair grow long and dressed to blend into the natural environment. When the Oceanic survivors returned, Cindy vouched for Jack, Sayid and the rest. Later when the Man in Black recruited Sayid to speak to the Others, it was Cindy who questioned what would happen if they stayed.

"It's not that simple…"

CLAUDIA

▶ **CONNECTION:** Mother of Jacob and the Man in Black

Claudia was a passenger on a ship that was destroyed in a violent storm off the coast of the island during early Roman times. When the pregnant Claudia washed up on the island's shore, she found debris but no other survivors.

The mysterious woman known as Mother found Claudia and offered to help. Mother spoke Latin—the language of preference of the Others—as did Claudia, so the two were able to communicate. Claudia questioned Mother on how she came to be on the island, to which Mother answered she arrived there by accident, just like Claudia.

The answer made her collect the children and together they left to follow the Man in Black. The small group relocated to Claire's camp, where the Man in Black promised to protect them as Jacob had. However, he lied and abandoned them as his goal to kill the candidates took precedence. When Widmore launched his mortar attack on the Man in Black's group on the beach, Cindy, Zack and Emma survived and escaped into the jungle. Along with Rose and Bernard, Cindy is one of the few to survive the island's tumult to join Hurley and live under his guard.

THE TWINS

Claudia's plans to search for additional survivors from her ship were cut short by the sudden onset of labor. Her son, whom she had always planned to name Jacob, was born quickly, delivered with care by Mother. Moments later, Claudia's unexpected second baby—she had no idea she was carrying twins—came into the world. As her children lay near Mother—Jacob swathed in a white cloth, and his brother, in a black cloth—Claudia barely got to ask to see her newborn children before Mother violently caved in her head with a rock.

SPIRITUAL CONNECTIONS

Thirteen years after Claudia's murder, Jacob and his brother were young men under the impression that Mother was exactly that to them. But one day, the spirit of Claudia appeared only to Jacob's brother and beckoned him to follow her. Claudia showed him a place on the island that he had never seen, where survivors from her ship had set up a village and made a life for themselves on the island. She explained that it was where he had come from, that she was his mother and had been murdered by the woman who the boys knew as Mother. This ghostly confession set in motion events that changed her sons, and life on the island, forever.

CLEMENTINE PHILLIPS

▶ **CONNECTION:** Daughter of James "Sawyer" Ford & Cassidy Phillips

Clementine Phillips was the illegitimate daughter of Cassidy Phillips and James "Sawyer" Ford. She was conceived in the waning days of a doomed affair in which Sawyer conned Cassidy out of $600,000. Cassidy pressed charges against Sawyer, which resulted in his arrest and subsequent imprisonment with an eight-year sentence.

While visiting him in jail, she explained that she was raising Clementine in Albuquerque, New Mexico and asked him to write his daughter. Sawyer denied paternity at first, but later established an anonymous trust fund in Clementine's name using the money he earned from turning state's evidence for the Treasury Department against a fellow prisoner named Munson.

AN ISLAND CONNECTION

Not long after Kate returned from the island as one of the Oceanic Six, she visited Cassidy and Clementine to fulfil a promise she made to Sawyer. Kate gave Cassidy a portion of her Oceanic settlement to help raise Clementine to show that Sawyer cared about his daughter. Cassidy was unimpressed, but the meeting restored the close friendship between the women. Over the next three years, Clementine came to know Kate as "Aunty Kate" and they often visited Kate and Aaron.

After she returned to the island, Sawyer asked Kate if she looked out for his daughter. After she confirmed her relationship with Clementine, he asked Kate what she was like. Kate said that she was beautiful, had a smile like her father's and a bit of his attitude.

FACTS & FIGURES

Time On The Island

POST-OCEANIC: 101 days

POST-FERAL YEARS: 3+ years

Date Of Birth: October 29, 1981

Likes: Astrology, Peanut Butter

Dislikes: The Temple Others

Former Occupations: Tattoo shop assistant, server at Fish'n'Fry

Sweet in nature, headstrong in her beliefs, and heavily pregnant, Claire Littleton got a unique first-time mother experience after boarding Oceanic flight 815 in her home city of Sydney, Australia. Prepared to give up her child for adoption in Los Angeles, Claire's interest in astrology didn't predict any of the horrors she would face after surviving the plane crash onto the island. With fertility problems plaguing the Others, Claire's pregnancy made her the subject of abductions and medical experiments.

Claire's traumas didn't end with the safe birth of her son, Aaron. After the Man in Black drew her away from her child, Aaron was rescued from the island and remained in the care of Kate Austen for three years. Without her child, Claire's state of mind fragmented. Under the "parental" guidance of the Man in Black, Claire descended into a feral psychosis. It wasn't until Kate returned to the island to rescue her that Claire began her long, hard road out of hell.

Claire's necklace means love in Chinese.

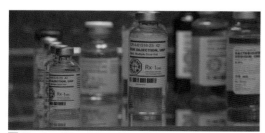

The drug Ethan injected into Claire contained all of "the numbers" on its label.

CHILDHOOD

Claire was raised by her mother, Carole, and her Aunt Lindsey in Sydney. She was conceived as a result of her mother's affair with Christian Shephard. Claire spent most of her life believing her dad died when she was 2 years old, which was actually the point at which Carole decided she couldn't bear continuing her relationship with Christian. Claire had a good relationship with her librarian mother and the two spent many evenings watching nature documentaries.

Claire became rebellious in her late teens and the two were involved in a serious car accident during a heated argument. Claire escaped with a few cuts and bruises, but Carole was thrown through the windshield and entered a coma. Christian came to Sydney immediately, but when he suggested ending Carole's life-support, Claire disowned him and didn't even want to know his name. Claire visited her mother regularly during the years she remained in a coma and always felt she was to blame for her mother's condition.

Claire unexpectedly became pregnant during her relationship with Thomas, a painter, in early 2004. At first, Claire worried about having only a low-wage job at Fish'n'Fry, but Thomas invited her to live with him and have the baby. Three months later, however, Thomas panicked about the responsibility and broke off their relationship. After a series of strange experiences with psychic Richard Malkin, Claire decided to fly to Los Angeles to give up her baby for adoption, believing it would be the best choice for the child. After visiting her mother one last time in the hospital, Claire boarded Oceanic flight 815 on September 22, 2004, ready to experience a new stage in her life.

> **BY THE NUMBERS**
> *The appointment for Claire's adoption meeting was at **8:15** a.m; Claire was **8** months pregnant when she crashed on the island; Claire was injected with an unknown drug from a container labeled CR **4-81516-23 42**.*

PREGNANCY

Claire's pregnancy was an extremely rare success on the island, as pregnant Others routinely died during that time. Ethan Rom, one of the Others, covertly took blood samples from Claire after the crash to assess her health. Although Claire had conceived off-island, blood tests showed Juliet Burke that Claire's symptoms were consistent with previous pregnant women on-island who eventually died. Juliet had developed a serum that could reverse the condition and Ethan began administering injections to Claire while she slept.

FERTILITY TEST SUBJECT

Claire became aware of Ethan's visits, which alerted the survivors to the possibility of an intruder. When Hurley ascertained that Ethan was not part of the flight manifest, Ethan went off-mission. His own wife and child had died during childbirth on the island. Without consulting the Others, he kidnapped Claire and took her to the Staff medical station, where he kept her drugged and continued injecting her with the serum.

Locke fashioned this crib for Claire on her birthday.

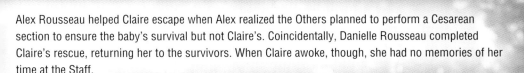

"That's not John. This is my friend."

Alex Rousseau helped Claire escape when Alex realized the Others planned to perform a Cesarean section to ensure the baby's survival but not Claire's. Coincidentally, Danielle Rousseau completed Claire's rescue, returning her to the survivors. When Claire awoke, though, she had no memories of her time at the Staff.

GIVING BIRTH

Several days later, Claire went into labor. Fearful of the Others, Claire headed into the jungle. By the time Kate ran into Claire, her contractions were too close together to head back to the survivors' camp. With Charlie and Jin's help, Kate delivered Aaron on the same night that Boone Carlyle died.

Much later, with the aid of Libby Smith's guided meditation, Claire began recalling her time at the medical station. With Kate and Danielle's help, Claire returned to the Staff to fill in the gaps of her suppressed memories. There, she found a blue baby bootie that she had knitted for Aaron.

Claire's connection with Kate was strengthened when Kate helped deliver her baby.

The Others also gave Claire a subcutaneous implant. Once activated, a time-released drug created symptoms, indicating that Claire was going into withdrawal from the previous injections. This ruse was created so that Juliet could appear to save Claire and win the trust of the survivors.

MESSAGE OF HOPE

When the survivors' bottle of messages washed up on the beach, Claire hatched a plan to use a migrating seabird to seek rescue. Just like Charlie, Claire enjoyed nature documentaries and she recalled how scientists often tag the birds' feet. Desmond caught a seagull and Claire and Charlie attached the following letter to its foot, hoping it would lead to their rescue.

"To whom it may concern:

We are survivors of Oceanic flight 815. We have survived on this island for 80 days. We were six hours into the flight when the pilot said we were off course and turned back towards Fiji.

We hit turbulence and crashed. We've been waiting here, all this time, waiting for rescue that has not come. We do not know where we are, we only know you have not found us.

We've done our best to live on this island. Some of us have come to accept that we may never leave it. Not all of us have survived since the crash, but there is new life too, and with it, there is hope.

We are alive. Please don't give up on us."

CLAIRE LITTLETON

CLAIRE'S ISLAND CONNECTIONS

JACK SHEPHARD

Although it would be years before they knew they were related, the first person to help Claire after the crash was her half-brother, Jack Shephard. Jack discovered their connection once he left the island and met Carole Littleton at his father's memorial service. But Claire was left on the island, processing the revelation alone, when the Man in Black, in the guise of Christian, told her about Jack.

When he returned to the island three years later, Claire got to acknowledge Jack as her brother face-to-face. Soon after, Claire escaped in the Ajira plane while Jack gave his life on the island to secure his friends' departure.

CHARLIE PACE

Claire's relationship with Charlie was rocky, but dramatic events brought them together time and again. After Claire's kidnapping, it was Charlie who killed Ethan. When Danielle kidnapped Aaron, Charlie got him back. Charlie also worked hard to give Claire home comforts too, from handmade baby slings for Aaron, to fake—and later real—jars of peanut butter.

When Claire discovered a Virgin Mary statue in Charlie's knapsack, she assumed it was a religious object. But when Eko proved it held heroin, Claire was no longer sure whether she could trust the Drive Shaft star. Charlie's subsequent visions of Aaron in danger and his growing jealousy over John Locke spending time with the baby caused further concern for the new mother.

By the time Charlie laid his heroin demons to rest, and after he survived the implosion of the Swan station, their relationship was on the mend. Claire was happy to have the Charlie she knew and loved back camping next to her and her son.

While Claire was working with Desmond to catch a seagull, he revealed that he had been trying to prevent Charlie's death that he continued to see in his visions. Attaching the message to the seagull and setting it free was one of the last acts the two would share.

When Charlie went to the underwater Looking Glass station, Rose teased Claire that she'd better treat him nicely when he returned, but this time, he didn't. Hurley broke the news to Claire that Charlie had died to save them all. Even after his death, Claire honored her love for Charlie. Because Charlie had used his last moments to warn them that the freighter was "Not Penny's Boat," she chose not to go with Jack to the *Kahana*. And when explosions at the barracks knocked her unconscious, Claire murmured Charlie's name as Sawyer lifted her into his arms and rescued her.

FATHER FIGURES

Both of John Locke's forms were potent father figures for Claire. On Claire's birthday, a few weeks after the crash, Locke handcrafted a cradle for Claire's unborn baby. During Charlie's darkest hours, plagued by visions and his heroin addiction, Locke moved his camp area next to Claire's and watched over her closely. He even beat up Charlie the night Charlie stole Aaron. Claire also turned to Locke when Aaron's rash and fever developed.

The last time Claire saw Locke, she was inside Jacob's cabin accompanied by the Man in Black in the form of her father, Christian. For the next three years, Claire kept the company of the Man in Black. After he finished using Christian's form, he took on Locke's. Claire understood that the Man in Black wasn't really her father or Locke. But the strange entity she simply called "my friend" was just that—a loyal companion who had kept her safe on the island after her friends had abandoned her.

DARK NIGHTMARE

After arriving on the island, Claire had a terrifying nightmare. Several elements of her dream foreshadowed future events:

Locke is a dark, malevolent version of himself, with a black and a white stone replacing each of his eyes.

The sound of a knife being sheathed echoes the Man in Black's weapon that killed Mother and Dogen.

Locke's table had a piece of tapestry on it, a favorite pastime of Jacob.

The bloody, plastic doll Claire finds in the crib mirrors the substitute "baby" she would later create out of dead animal parts.

The Oceanic flight 815 baby mobile was part of the Staff's nursery, but Claire hadn't been to the Staff yet.

> ## "We'd better get that cleaned up. If there's one thing that'll kill you around here it's infection."
>
> — Spoken by Claire to Jin

A FERAL LIFE

Claire set up a home camp in a clearing with debris from the plane wreckage and surrounding jungle. Her self-made squirrel baby was a disturbing substitute for Aaron, and she fought tirelessly to find her son.

Claire's alliance with the Man in Black was fraught with pain. He told her that the Others had Aaron, which kept her loyal to his cause. The Others tortured and branded her at the Temple to determine whether she had been claimed and they dismissed her as someone who would be better off dead.

When the Ajira flight survivors returned and saw Claire for the first time, they were shocked at how her appearance had changed from a vulnerable, sweet, and open-hearted mother to a paranoid, bitter, and demented woman.

Claire became a feral, angry woman under the Man in Black's care.

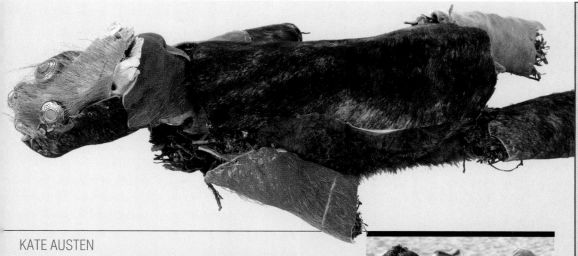

KATE AUSTEN

In the last days of her pregnancy when she was the most vulnerable, Claire bonded with Kate. The two sorted through the practical and impractical salvaged clothes, and Claire guessed correctly Kate was a Gemini, although Claire's passion for astrology wasn't shared. But their strongest bond was created when Kate delivered Claire's baby in the middle of the jungle.

Shortly before Kate took Aaron off the island for his own safety, Claire had suggested Kate try being a mother sometime—highly appropriate considering Kate became Aaron's guardian.

When Kate returned to the island, Claire was excited to see her dear friend. Upon hearing that Kate took Aaron, however, Claire turned vicious. When Kate inquired about the makeshift squirrel baby creation, Claire made it clear it was all she had and put a knife to Kate's throat. In their friendship's bleakest moment, Claire was ready to kill Kate, but the Man in Black pulled Claire away.

Claire eventually relented and thanked Kate for keeping Aaron safe, especially when Kate explained that reuniting her with Aaron was the only reason she returned to the island. In the end, Kate persuaded Claire to board the Ajira plane and head home to be with Aaron. Claire was terrified about being a mother in her current mental state, but Kate promised she would be by her side.

CLAIRE'S OFF-ISLAND CONNECTIONS

- **Carole Littleton** (Mother)
- **Christian Shephard** (Father)
- **Lindsey Littleton** (Aunt)
- **Thomas** (Aaron's father)
- **Rachel** (Best friend)
- **Richard Malkin** (Psychic)
- **Arlene & Joseph Stewart** (Prospective adoptive parents)

COLLEEN PICKETT

▶ **CONNECTION:** Wife of Danny Pickett; member of the Others

Colleen Pickett (or Coll for short) was a trusted member of Ben Linus' security contingent. Stationed on Hydra island, Colleen was the first person to alert Ben that Sayid had found their decoy village and that the survivors were in possession of a sailboat (the *Elizabeth*). Ben tasked Colleen to immediately assemble a team to retrieve the sailboat. Before she left, Colleen found her husband, Danny, to explain the mission and kissed him goodbye.

Colleen enlisted Tom Friendly, Matthew and Ivan to accompany her on the *Galaga* to overtake the sailboat. As Sayid and Jin hid in ambush near the Pala Ferry dock, the Others boarded the sailboat. As Colleen entered the galley, Sun surprised her by pointing a loaded gun in her direction. Both women stood their ground until the sound of the boat's engine startled Sun. She impulsively pulled the trigger and shot Colleen in the stomach.

THE FUNERAL ✚

As Colleen's body was set out to sea, Brenda Lee's "I Wonder" played.

"I wonder my little darling, where can you be this moonlit night? Are you holding someone tight? I wonder. My heart, my heart is aching. And I'm a fool. I'm a fool to let it go on breaking."

Funeral pyres are part of the ancient rite of cremation considered obligatory in the religions of Buddhism and Hinduism. At the moment of death, both religions believe that the soul leaves the body so it is no longer a sacred vessel. Sikhism also follows the cremation custom, but primarily for cultural reasons rather than religious. Eastern religions often drape a body in white cloths and some monks wear white at the cremation service.

The Others rushed Colleen back to the Hydra so Juliet Burke could treat her wound. Juliet removed the bullet but Colleen continued to bleed out. Desperate, Juliet rushed out of surgery and pleaded with Jack to help her save Colleen. He agreed

and at the table quickly identified that there was a retro-hepatic caval bleed behind Colleen's liver. At that moment, Colleen's heart stopped and Jack was unable to restart it because the CPR machine was broken. He tried manual CPR, but it was too late. That evening after dark, several Others dressed in white garments assembled at the beach as Colleen's covered body was placed on a small raft. Ben memorialized her and then the raft was placed in the water, set afire and pushed out to sea.

CONSTANTS, SEE PAGE 92

90

THE CRATE

BY THE NUMBERS ✚
The crate is labelled AA823. The AA stands for Ajira Airways, while 8 and 23 correspond to the numbers.

This large, rectangular metal crate was stored in the cargo hold of Ajira Airlines flight 316 after Jack Shephard checked in "Jeremy Bentham's" coffin. After the plane crash-landed on Hydra island, Ilana and her counterparts immediately

Ilana's men found the crate and set about taking it to Jacob.

claimed the undamaged crate from the belly of the plane. They attached bamboo poles to the crate and carried it to Jacob's cabin and then to his four-toed statue dwelling. Upon their arrival at the statue, Richard Alpert revealed himself to Ilana and she asked him, "What lies in the shadow of the statue?" Alpert answered in Latin, "Ille qui nos omnes servabit." She then opened the crate to reveal the dead body of John Locke, still attired in his funeral suit, proving to Alpert that the man walking around whom he thought was John Locke was something else entirely.

THE PROTECTOR ✚
In response to Ilana's riddle about what lies in the shadow of the statue, the Latin phrase that Richard provides, "Ille qui nos omnes servabit," translates to "He who will protect us all."

Ilana revealed the contents of the crate to be John Locke.

DAGNE

▶ **CONNECTION:** Nanny for Walt Lloyd

After the death of Walt's mother, Susan Porter, Dagne watched over the little boy when Susan's husband, Brian Porter, traveled to New York City to restore Michael Dawson's full custodial rights to Walt. Dagne welcomed Michael when he arrived at the Porter home to pick up Walt. She handed him some of Susan's effects that Brian wanted him to have and a small wooden box that held all the letters Susan had intercepted from Michael and never gave to Walt.

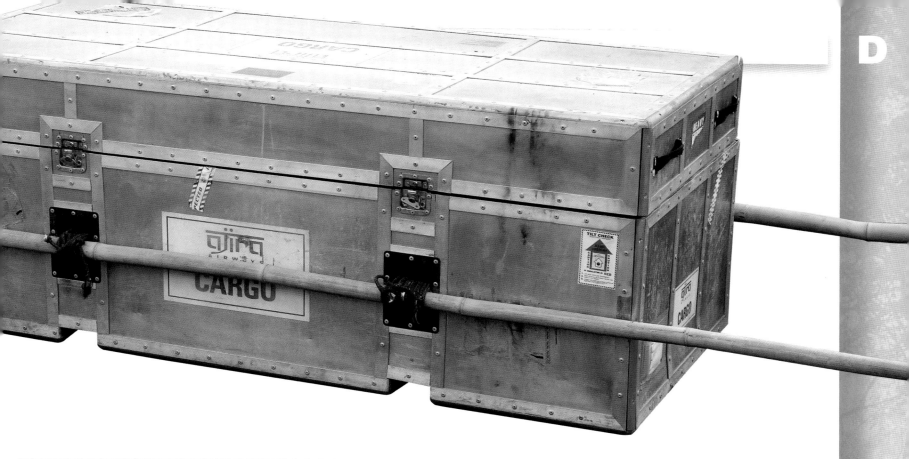

DAN NORTON

▷ **CONNECTION:** Off-island acquaintance of Benjamin Linus; lawyer for Agostini & Norton

A partner in the Los Angeles law firm of Agostini & Norton, Dan Norton was hired by Benjamin Linus to handle several legal matters that pertained to members of the Oceanic Six. The outcome of each case had a direct impact on Linus' ability to successfully persuade each of them to return with him to the island. Linus hired Norton to pursue his interests about three years after the Oceanic Six returned to the their regular lives.

Norton approached Kate Austen at her home to obtain blood samples for a paternity test to prove Aaron Littleton's parentage. When Kate asked whom he represented, Norton would only offer that his client preferred to remain anonymous and stressed that he had obtained a court order for her to comply. Norton's aggressive approach did exactly as Linus hoped, which was to push Kate into a panic so he would have the power with which to leverage. After secretly leaving Aaron with Sun at a hotel to keep him safe, Kate made an appointment at Norton's office and offered to take the test in exchange for a meeting with his client. Instead, Norton played hard ball and said he would pass the offer to his client later that day, but the answer would be no and that Kate should be prepared to lose the boy in a custody exchange.

Norton then traveled to the motel room of another client, Carole Littleton, who had previously hired him to sue Oceanic Airlines in a wrongful death suit on behalf of her daughter, Claire. Norton successfully won a settlement for Carole and hand delivered it to her so she could return to Australia.

After his meeting with Littleton, Norton then rendezvoused with Linus in a parking garage where he briefed Ben on the status of Hurley's incarceration for murder. Hired by Ben to represent Hurley, Norton was confident there would be no case as he determined the victim was killed before Hurley escaped from Santa Rosa. Norton got the charges against Reyes dropped the next morning.

BY THE NUMBERS ✚
Norton's California license plate is 4PCT382

DANIEL

▷ **CONNECTION:** Altar boy at Yemi's church

Daniel resided in the Nigerian village where Yemi was a priest. After Yemi was accidentally killed in the crossfire at the airstrip, Eko maintained the village's belief that Yemi had been called away suddenly because of an emergency at a refugee camp. When Eko returned and replaced his brother as the priest, Daniel continued to attend the church. However, the day Eko killed criminals who attacked him inside the church, he was approached by Daniel who looked down on Eko as he bathed his bloody hands in Holy water. Daniel asked him if he was a "bad man."

Later when Eko became stranded on the island, this conversation with Daniel played on his mind. Just before Eko was brutally killed by the smoke monster, he saw an image of Daniel who said, "Confess."

CONSTANTS

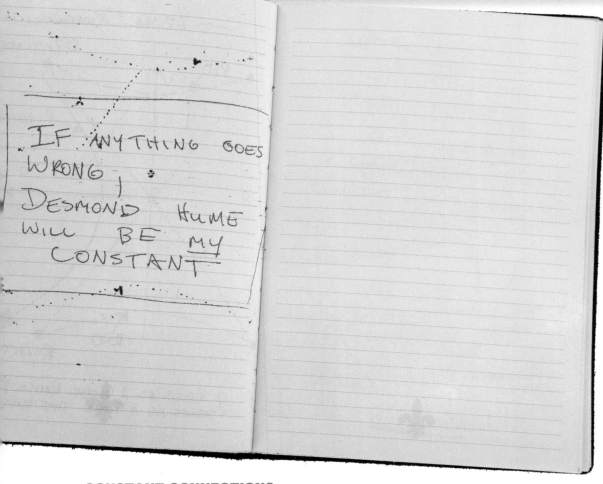

> IF ANYTHING GOES WRONG, DESMOND HUME WILL BE MY CONSTANT

As Daniel Faraday developed his theories about time travel while researching at Queen's College in Oxford, he realized that stability was required in order to anchor the person's consciousness as it moved through time. Daniel called this stability a "constant," or a thing or person who existed in multiple time periods for which the traveler deeply cared. This person or object tied them to the familiar despite all the changeable variables.

Faraday's maze experiments at Oxford University using Eloise the rat helped him determine that if a time traveler's consciousness was allowed to jump between the past and the future without a constant, the subject's brain could be short-circuited. Without the anchor of a constant, the subject would be "unstuck in time" and unable to determine whether they were in the past, present, or the future. As the progression of jumps continued, each subsequent jump would become more difficult on the subject's consciousness, so much so that it could precipitate a fatal brain aneurism. As Faraday exposed the rat to radiation, the rat's consciousness jumped from the present to the future without benefit of an anchor. But when Faraday hit Eloise with the radiation settings provided by his future self, her mind became unstuck and she finally ran the maze perfectly, a task he had to teach her in the future. Not long after, the rat succumbed to the accumulated effects of the temporal displacement and died.

CONSTANT CONNECTIONS

DANIEL FARADAY'S CONSTANT = DESMOND HUME

After the Daniel Faraday from 1996 met Desmond Hume and accepted their connection in both the future and the present, Daniel noted in his journal: "If anything goes wrong, Desmond Hume will be my constant." He recognized the predestination paradox of their situation in which the cause-effect of their meeting in both times (1996 and 2004) made them interdependent in attaining the knowledge to understand and overcome their individual temporal displacement issues.

IMPROPER ISLAND BEARINGS

Kahana crew members George Minkowski and Brandon via the zodiac raft.
Outcome: Both died.

Regina, the *Kahana* communications officer, suffered extreme side effects from improper island bearings.
Outcome: Death by suicide.

RADIATION EXPOSURE

Theresa Spencer was exposed to excessive radiation while working with Daniel Faraday. She never secured a constant.
Outcome: Persistent vegetative state.

TIME TRAVEL

The movement of the island via the frozen donkey wheel caused those on the island to experience time shifts that caused various degrees of temporal displacement.

Daniel Faraday and Jin: headaches.

Outcome: Cured by John Locke returning the wheel to its axis.

Charlotte Lewis: headaches, disorientation, memory problems, and nose bleeds.

Outcome: Died after a time jump.

John Locke: headaches.

Outcome: Cured by when he returned the wheel to its axis.

> ## *Every equation needs stability, something known. It's called a constant.* — Daniel Faraday to Desmond Hume

DESMOND HUME'S CONSTANT = PENNY WIDMORE

When Desmond triggered the Swan's fail-safe, the intense radiation exposure caused his consciousness to start jumping through time. This was later exacerbated when Desmond flew from the island to the *Kahana* freighter. It was only after Faraday explained his theory of constants to Desmond in 1996 that Hume selected Penny as his constant. As his consciousness continued to jump, he followed the lead of the Daniel Faraday from 2004 and crafted a communication plan with Penny through time. It culminated in a phone call from Desmond on the freighter to her on December 24, 2004. Their call not only confirmed his love for her, but it also created his constant connection with her: that anchor finally stopped his consciousness from time travelling and bound him once again to the year 2004.

BY THE NUMBERS ✛

*While on the island, Faraday called Desmond on the satellite phone and said to find him at Oxford in 1996 and relate the message to set his radiation device to **2.342**, oscillating at 11, which effectively made Eloise's consciousness unstuck.*

*Penny Widmore's London-based phone number was 7946-**08**93.*

TEMPORAL DISPLACEMENT

Faraday called the detrimental effects of consciousness time jumps (time travel) without a constant "temporal displacement." He also determined there were two other ways to experience temporal displacement: an improper fixed bearing approach to/from the island, or intense exposure to radiation and/or electromagnetic fields.

Certain tell-tale signs would manifest in a person as the displacement took hold. The effects included disorientation, headaches, double-vision, memory problems, and if not remedied properly with a constant or time realignment, eventual death by sudden brain aneurism.

Desmond Hume was hit with intense electromagnetic exposure by Widmore's scientific team that allowed his consciousness to gain awareness of his flash sideways existence.

Juliet Burke, Sawyer and Miles Straume: headaches and nosebleeds.

Outcome: Cured by John Locke returning the wheel to its axis.

When Benjamin Linus used the frozen donkey wheel, it caused the island and those on it to time skip. Daniel surmised that the intensity of the displacement symptoms was in direct correlation to the amount of time someone spent on the island. The length of time or frequency a person had been on the island, the more acute the progression of the symptoms. In contrast, less time on the island resulted in slower symptom manifestation.

SLAUGHTERHOUSE-FIVE

Daniel's term "unstuck in time" was originated by author Kurt Vonnegut in his classic 1969 science fiction novel about time travel, "Slaughterhouse-Five." The story's protagonist, Billy Pilgrim, becomes "unstuck in time" and travels in non-linear fashion through periods in his life and in the future.

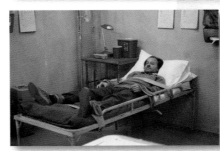

DANIEL FARADAY

FACTS & FIGURES

Time On The Island

POST-KAHANA: 10 days

POST-SUBMARINE RETURN: 1 day

Arrived On The Island: Recruited by Charles Widmore to join the *Kahana* freighter team.

Connection: Charles Widmore (father); Eloise Hawking (mother)

A brilliant physicist who specialized in the study of spacetime, Dr. Daniel Faraday was the son of two Others, Eloise Hawking and Charles Widmore. While he was conceived on the island, Faraday was born off-island and raised in Essex, Massachusetts by his mother. Hawking gave him the surname of a famous scientist whose path she made sure her own son modeled closely. Daniel had a natural affinity for complex scientific and mathematical theories that in the future would allow him to understand his birthplace like few ever would. Faraday discovered that his two decades of specialized study and research were all in preparation for his journey to the island that would provide him the unique opportunity to put the esoteric theories of his work into practical application.

SCHOLARLY PURSUITS

At a young age, Daniel's mother pushed her son to excel academically in math and science because she said he had a gifted mind that needed to be nurtured. So, Daniel spent the bulk of his youth in accelerated academic programs and courses that allowed him to perform at such a high level that he became the youngest doctorate to ever graduate from Oxford University.

After he received a large sum of grant money, Faraday started his research in a private lab at The Queen's College, Oxford University. In 1996, he became a professor and taught relativistic physics and juggled his time between curriculum and his off-the-grid experiments that revolved around a machine he created that facilitated a living creature's consciousness to travel through time. After Desmond Hume visited his lab and provided the correct setting for the machine to work, Daniel moved forward exponentially with his research which also included an exhaustive knowledge of the DHARMA Initiative. Faraday collected any information he could about the secret scientific enclave and documented it all in his journal for future reference.

Daniel's experimentation with his machine quickly graduated from the lone test subject of Eloise the lab rat to include himself and his girlfriend/research assistant, Theresa Spencer. While they protected their bodies with lead covers, their minds were exposed to the effects of temporal displacement, which played havoc with their cognitive abilities. Theresa's mental faculties degenerated to a vegetative state from which she rarely improved. Appalled by the irreversible impact on the woman he loved, Daniel immediately abandoned his work at the University. In the aftermath, the university finally discovered the extent of Faraday's unsanctioned work and they expunged his name and history from their halls and history.

" *Whatever happened, happened.* "

MEMORY MOMENTS

The effects of the time-consciousness experiments to which Daniel exposed his own mind manifested as a form of dementia that severely hampered his ability to research anything, much less spacetime. He needed a caretaker as he couldn't live alone. Soon after the fake Oceanic crash was found, Faraday's former benefactor at Oxford, Charles Widmore, paid him a visit. He explained to his mentally unstable son that he had staged the wreckage and that he wanted Daniel to travel to an island that was the real location of the crash so he could further his research and, more importantly, heal his muddled mind.

Every step that brought Daniel closer to the island also improved his mental abilities as the effects of the temporal displacement were dissipated by the special healing qualities of the island.

▶ *Days after Widmore's initial visit, Daniel attempted to remember the Chopin music he played as a boy. Eloise arrived and reiterated Widmore's offer and told Daniel she would be proud if he accepted—an action that nudged Daniel back on the path he was meant to follow.*

▶ *Charlotte tested Daniel's ability of memory recall with a deck of cards to measure his mental improvements, if any.*

A young Eloise Hawking escorted Daniel to their camp at gunpoint.

BY THE NUMBERS

*When Daniel played the piano, he counted 864 beats on the metronome, which broken down is **8** x108.*

*Upon graduation, Faraday won a £**1.5** million research grant underwritten by Widmore Industries.*

*The proper setting for Daniel's machine provided by Desmond was **2.342**, with an oscillation of 11 Hertz.*

THE CHICKEN OR THE EGG?

Daniel inserted himself into the lives of certain key people, both on and off the island, in an attempt to influence their future actions towards a destined path.

▶ *In 1954, Daniel explained to a young Eloise how to contain Jughead's radiation leak with lead and that she must then bury it to ensure the future of the island. However, his actions made it possible for him to use the bomb in the future to attempt to "correct" time.*

▶ *In 1977, Faraday dressed in a DHARMA jumpsuit and intercepted Dr. Pierre Chang to tell him that he should evacuate the DHARMA community because of an impending electromagnetic disaster under the Swan construction site. He told Miles Straume it was to ensure that he did what he was supposed to do.*

▶ *Daniel warned a six-year-old Charlotte Lewis that she must never return to the island or she would die in an attempt to save her future self.*

DANIEL FARADAY

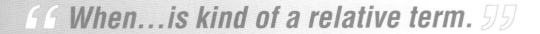

" *When...is kind of a relative term.* "

"The record is spinning again. We're just not on the song we wanna be on."

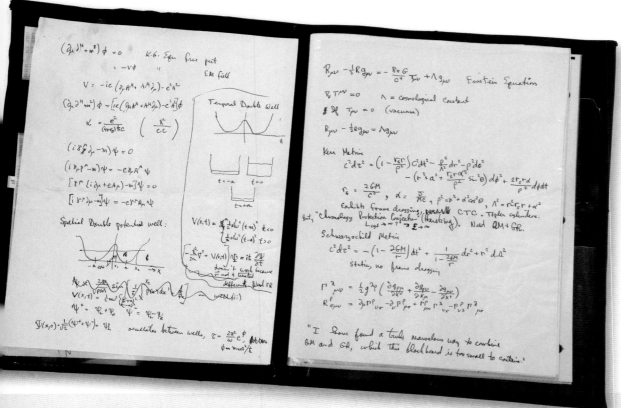

DANIEL'S RULES OF TIME TRAVEL

Daniel's rules about spacetime travel based on research from his youth to the day he left the island in 1974 to research at Ann Arbor:

"Time is like a street.

We can move forward on that street,

We can move in reverse,

We cannot ever create a new street.

If we try to do anything different, we will fail every time.

Whatever happened, happened."

Daniel's revised rules about spacetime travel based on what he learned from 1974 to his 1977 return to the island:

"I studied relativistic physics my entire life. One thing emerged over and over—can't change the past. Can't do it. Whatever happened, happened.

But then I finally realized I had been spending so much time focused on the constants, I forgot about the variables. We're the variables. People. We think. We reason. We make choices. We have free will. We can change our destiny."

Daniel's shift in perspective was a sea change event for the scientist who had been trained to think in the absolutes of fact and rigid theory. Faraday's epiphany that there were variables that could massively impact a prescribed course was his acceptance of chaos, the intangible, that which science can't define. For Faraday, his discovery was as life-changing as if one had just experienced a divine theological epiphany. As implausible as it was to believe Faraday would shift theoretical gears, so too was it for his ideological disciple, Jack Shephard. As an entrenched man of science and student of the tangible, Jack's acceptance and belief that he needed to continue Faraday's nuclear detonation plan after his death represented the moment that shifted Jack to the path of faith. However, Faraday's theory didn't entirely work out. After Juliet detonated the hydrogen bomb, everyone was returned to their proper time period but the past had not changed.

HEARTS AND MINDS

Another distraction that Eloise did not want vying for Daniel's attention was women, as she told Daniel over and over again they were not a priority. Upon his graduation from Oxford, she warned him that any woman in his life would only be terribly hurt by him. Her supposition turned out to be true as Daniel never experienced the kind of long-term romantic relationship he longed for in his brief life because of the all-consuming, and dangerous, aspects of his work.

THERESA SPENCER
Daniel's girlfriend and research assistant at Oxford University.

Problem: Daniel used both himself and Theresa as test subjects for his consciousness time machine, which triggered temporal displacement issues for both of them.

Outcome: Theresa never recovered from her symptoms and was stuck in a vegetative state with only moments of lucidity, which meant she needed constant care. Dismayed and ashamed by what his research did to her, Faraday fled to the United States.

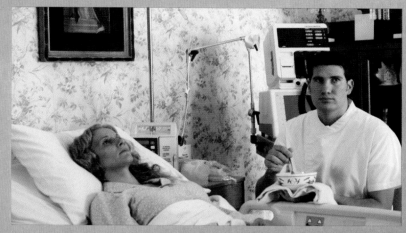

CHARLOTTE LEWIS
Both graduates of Oxford, Daniel met Charlotte on the *Kahana* as they traveled to the island and he quickly fell in love with his beautiful peer.

Problem: The chaos of their mission didn't allow Daniel and Charlotte to truly explore the potential of a relationship, but Daniel bravely admitted he was in love with her.

Outcome: Charlotte never had the chance to reciprocate Daniel's admission of love as she quickly succumbed to the effects of temporal displacement and died as he helplessly watched.

"The light…it's strange out here, isn't it? It's kind of like, it doesn't, it doesn't scatter quite right."

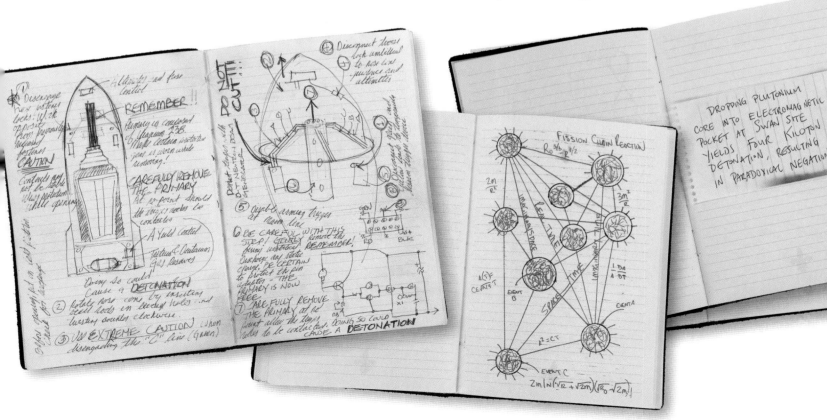

DANIELLE ROUSSEAU

FACTS & FIGURES

Time On The Island: Post-*Bésixdouze* shipwreck: 16 years, 10 months

Arrived On The Island: Shipwreck survivor of the *Bésixdouze*

Family: Alexandra Rousseau (daughter)

Candidate: #20

A French scientist who was shipwrecked on the island for over 16 years, Danielle Rousseau's tale was a particularly sad and tragic footnote in the island's history. Seven months pregnant and in love with a fellow researcher named Robert from the expedition, Danielle's future was filled with promise. However, in early 1988, that potential was snuffed out the moment she and the five other members of the *Bésixdouze* expedition set foot on the island. In the span of two months everyone but Danielle was dead and she was left alone to give birth to her baby girl, Alex.

THE DOOMED EXPEDITION

The *Bésixdouze* sailed out of Tahiti on November 15, 1987 and three days later intercepted the DHARMA-originated, looped audio transmission of the numbers. Curious, the expedition re-charted their course in an attempt to find the source of the message. Out of nowhere a huge squall hit the boat and their navigational instruments malfunctioned. Off-course the ship ran aground and its hull was breached. The six-person science team escaped on the emergency life-raft and drifted towards the beach. On their way in, they discovered an unknown man (who turned out to be Jin) floating in the water and they took him into their boat. Once on shore, Danielle communicated with Jin in basic English and established that he knew the island and could lead them to the radio tower. En route, Nadine's (a fellow member of the expedition) lifeless body was thrown on their path by the smoke monster. The entity then dragged Montand into a declivity of the Temple and everyone but Danielle entered to try to save him. A concurrent time jump then made Jin disappear before her eyes.

The men eventually returned and initially seemed fine, but the sickness had invaded their wounds and over time they became so violent that Danielle feared for her safety and had to kill them. Two months later, Jin reappeared just as a desperately fearful Danielle was forced to shoot an infected Robert. She then hiked alone to the radio tower and changed the transmission to her message. She had her baby three days later. A week after the birth, Benjamin Linus was sent to murder both of them, but he took the baby instead and left Danielle to suffer in isolated misery for years.

1988

98

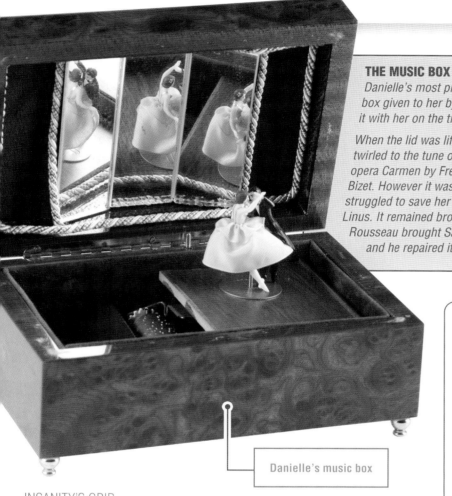

THE MUSIC BOX

Danielle's most prized possession from her pre-island life was a small, wooden music box given to her by Robert before they embarked on the Bésixdouze expedition. She brought it with her on the trip and managed to save it when their ship ran aground.

When the lid was lifted, a dancing couple twirled to the tune of "Intermezzo" from the opera Carmen by French composer Georges Bizet. However it was broken when Danielle struggled to save her baby from Benjamin Linus. It remained broken for 16 years until Rousseau brought Sayid back to her camp and he repaired it for her.

Danielle's music box

INSANITY'S GRIP

After killing her friends and lover, and then having Alex stolen from her, Danielle spiralled into a dark depression. She became incredibly paranoid and found a place away from the beach to create a protected camp for herself. Around it she built snare and net traps to catch any intruders.

Warned by Ben to run when she heard the "whispers," she made it her rule to avoid contact with anyone. She did that by mapping the island and noted the places to shun, which included the Dark Territory and the smoke monster security system. Since she arrived on the island after the Purge, only the natives lived in the barracks and she came to call them the Others. Isolated for so long without anyone to talk to, she became slightly mad which affected the accuracy of her memories such as her not remembering that it was Ben who took her daughter.

THE SEARCH FOR ALEX

Danielle never recovered from the loss of her daughter, so she was particularly affected after she stumbled upon a pregnant Claire Littleton on the island. It renewed her hope of finding Alex and paved the way for their reunion.

▶ *Danielle created a pillar of black smoke to boost fear about the Others, and then took the opportunity to kidnap Aaron in hopes she could trade him for Alex. She returned him to Sayid and Charlie.*

▶ *Claire asked Danielle to take her back to the Staff, where Claire remembered being saved by a young girl named Alex. Danielle's hope was strengthened.*

▶ *Kate confirmed for Danielle that Alex was at the Hydra station. Later she expressed her fear to Kate that Alex would not want to know the woman she had become—a fear Claire would later feel about Aaron.*

▶ *On the way to the radio tower with Jack, Ben introduced Alex to Danielle for the first time. Later, Rousseau punched Ben in the face when he called Alex his daughter.*

▶ *When Danielle led Alex and Karl to the Temple for safety, she and the boy were murdered.*

DANNY PICKETT

▶ **CONNECTION:** Husband of Colleen Pickett; member of the Others

Known primarily as Pickett, Danny was a member of Ben's trusted circle of Others. Married to Colleen Pickett, he served a variety of functions from security muscle to reconnaissance agent. While Danny's behavior often fell on the sadistic side, he revealed his softer side to his wife. His origination to the island is unknown, but he was considered for candidacy at some point by Jacob. Right after the crash of Oceanic 815, Benjamin Linus sent Pickett and Tom Friendly to find the tailies, but they were unsuccessful and returned to New Otherton.

PICKETT UNDERCOVER

Pickett was assigned to Bea Klugh's team, who created a faux Others camp to manipulate Michael Dawson. Danny, Tom, and two Others hiked into the jungle to intercept Michael as he searched for his son, Walt. After Michael found Pickett, he taunted Dawson when he asked, "You're Walt's old man, aren't ya?" The exchange was enough for Tom to sneak up from behind and grab Michael's rifle. Michael ran and Pickett fired on him, much to Friendly's dismay. Pickett missed, however, and Tom felled Michael with a slingshot, then blindfolded him, and took him with them.

Pickett was assigned the task of getting a blood sample from Michael.

As they marched Michael to their camp, Pickett discovered that Kate had followed them at a distance. He was able to subdue her and they held her captive with Michael. Later, when Tom confronted Jack, Sawyer, and Locke in the jungle, he called for Alex to bring Kate out as leverage. She pleaded with Pickett to do it instead and he begrudgingly agreed.

The next day, they arrived at Klugh's camp, Pickett forcibly took a blood sample from Michael and handed him over to Bea. Later on, Danny brought Walt into Michael's hut so the two could speak, but when the conversation got out of hand, he dragged the young boy away. Four days later, Pickett was part of Ben's security team that oversaw the hand-off of Walt to Michael for Jack, Hurley, Sawyer and Kate. When Sawyer struggled, Pickett kicked him the stomach.

AN OTHER'S LIFE

Back on Hydra island, Pickett was assigned the armed security detail over Sawyer and Kate in the cages. As he marched them out to a work site, they were interrupted by Pickett's wife, Colleen, who alerted her husband of her mission to overtake the *Elizabeth*. He gave her a tender kiss and told her to be careful. Danny explained that Sawyer and Kate would be breaking and moving rocks, and if they attempted to run, touch, talk, slack off, or do anything to piss him off they would be shocked with an electrical charge. When Kate refused to do anything until she saw Jack, Pickett shocked Sawyer with a one-quarter charge. That began in earnest an increasingly violent rivalry between the men that included rifle butt hits, mano-a-mano pummellings and more taser shocks for Sawyer.

Colleen returned from her mission mortally wounded, and she died on Jack's surgery table. Wracked with grief, Pickett screamed "They did this!" and ran to Sawyer's cage to beat him until Kate admitted that she loved James. A broken Pickett left them and prepared for his wife's funeral. On the beach, Colleen was laid out on a pyre where Pickett wept before she was set aflame out to sea.

REVENGE

Enraged by how badly the Oceanic survivors had impacted their lives, Pickett focused all his hatred on Sawyer. While Jack operated on Ben, Danny enlisted Jason to follow him to the cages where he planned to kill James as revenge for Colleen.

> ## *"This is for Colleen, you son-of-a-bitch!"*
>
> — Spoken by Pickett to Sawyer

A nasty struggle ensued, but Sawyer backed down to save Kate. As the rain poured, Pickett shoved James to his knees, cocked his gun and said, "This is for Colleen, you son-of-a-bitch," but a radio call from Tom ended the standoff. Jack made a deal that allowed Sawyer and Kate to turn the tables on Pickett and Jason. After almost beating Pickett to death, Sawyer locked the two men in cages, and he and Kate ran. After being released by Ivan, Pickett was hell-bent to stop Sawyer and Kate by any means possible. On the beach, Pickett caught up with his quarry and raised a gun to finally kill Sawyer. Juliet appeared, called out, "Danny!" and then pumped two bullets into him.

DARLENE

▶ **CONNECTION:** Sold a T-shirt to Hugo "Hurley" Reyes

Darlene was the pink-haired gas station clerk who waited on Hugo "Hurley" Reyes when he was on the run with Sayid Jarrah. She teased him about buying an "I heart Shih Tzus" T-shirt and after some banter recognized Hurley as the Mega Lottery winner and one of the Oceanic Six. He denied it but she was adamant as he ran out.

Hurley: "I like Shih-Tzus."
Darlene: "It looks like you heart them."

Hurley found Dave's slipper in the jungle.

DAVE

▶ **CONNECTION:** Imaginary friend of Hugo "Hurley" Reyes at Santa Rosa Mental Health Institute

Dave, Hurley's balding, bath-robed buddy, personified his id impulses in the form of a fellow mental patient at Santa Rosa Mental Health Institute. As Hurley entered therapy with Dr. Brooks, Dave also came into his life as a new friend who often appeared when Hurley confronted his various issues.

When Hurley was asked to create a list of things he liked about himself and he didn't complete the assignment, his excuse was that Dave said it was a stupid idea. Brooks suggested that Dave was a negative influence that blocked Hurley from true change. When Hurley had the opportunity to join a basketball game to get some exercise, Dave talked him into hitting Taco Night instead. At other times, Dave coerced Hurley to drop his celery snack and steal Leonard's graham crackers and to stop taking his Clonazepam so they could break out of the hospital for an adventure.

One night, Dave woke Hurley so they could escape. As they prowled the halls, Dave prompted Hugo to eat some leftover lasagna and then produced the keys from Brooks' office. Troubled by Dave's constant suggestions about food, Hurley stopped and confronted Dave with the statement, "You wouldn't care if I ate myself to death." This was Hurley's moment of clarity, after which he said goodbye to Dave.

ISLAND REUNION
As Hurley bonded with Elizabeth "Libby" Smith, his food issues began to trouble him again. With her encouragement, he made strides to regain restraint until a pallet drop of food challenged his resolve. As the survivors divvied up the food, Hurley caught a glimpse of a man in a bathrobe who left his slipper behind. As he pursued the figure into the jungle, Hurley found a box of DHARMA crackers that he started to binge on until Dave threw a coconut at him and ran again.

At another meeting, Hurley protested that Dave was imaginary, but the figure just asked for his slipper back. Dave was adamant that he existed and he described the crash, the island, and the

Dr. Brooks showed Hurley a Polaroid he took of the "two" friends in an attempt to show Hurley that Dave wasn't real.

survivors as a manifestation in Hugo's mind created when he slipped into a coma at Santa Rosa. Dave explained that he was the part of Hurley's subconscious that wanted him to wake up, which he could do if he went over the cliff with him. Persuasive in his argument, Dave took a backwards step off the precipice and laughed as he disappeared. But finally with Libby's help, Hurley was able to let go of Dave.

DAVID REYES

▶ **CONNECTION:** Father of Hugo "Hurley" Reyes

David Reyes was the estranged husband of Carmen Reyes and the father of Hugo and Diego. A free-spirit, David was a fun-loving parent who fished and worked on a classic Camaro with his young son, Hurley. From an early age, David instilled in his son the idea that all you needed in life was hope and "You can make your own luck."

When Hurley was 10, David told his son that he was heading to Las Vegas for work but he would return to complete the car renovation so they could drive to the Grand Canyon together. David didn't return home for 17 years.

As a belated birthday gift after returning from the island, David presented his son with the restored Camaro, a symbol of his love and belief in his son.

After Hurley won the lottery and began to obsess about being cursed, Carmen secretly summoned David to return home to help their son. An enthusiastic David moved back into the Reyes home and reconciled with his wife. Despite awkwardness between father and son, David was moved to find out that Hurley had kept the Camaro all the years he was away. However, Hurley remained bitter about his father's abandonment and was convinced that his father only wanted to get a share of the lottery winnings.

"You can make your own luck."

Under the guise of concern, David set up a fake meeting with a psychic named Lynn Karnoff in the hope that an "exorcism" would convince Hurley that the curse was banished. However, Hurley bribed the psychic into telling him the truth. David finally confessed to Hurley that initially his return was based on greed, but that he would still support his son if he gave away all the money. His one request was for Hurley to keep enough money to buy a carburetor so they could finish the Camaro together and visit the Grand Canyon. Hurley declined the offer and instead opted for a trip to Australia.

Years later after Hurley escaped from Santa Rosa, David took Hurley and a wounded Sayid into his house. Fearful for his son's sanity, he lied to the police about Hurley's whereabouts and then drove Sayid to Jack Shephard to protect his son.

DESMOND HUME

FACTS & FIGURES

Time On The Island

POST-ELIZABETH SHIPWRECK: 3 years

FORCED RETURN BY WIDMORE: 6 days

Connections: Manned the Swan station computer with Kelvin Inman

Family: Penelope Hume (wife); Charlie Hume (son)

BY THE NUMBERS ✛

In 1996, Desmond's clock in his flat read *1:08*.

The postman had a delivery for **815**.

As his life faltered, Desmond joined the Royal Scots Regiment.

While Desmond Hume seemed like an average bloke from Glasgow, Scotland, he was actually uniquely and miraculously special. Born with the ability to withstand the direct effects of intense electromagnetic exposure, Desmond discovered that his resistance made it possible for his consciousness to travel through time.

For the majority of his life, Hume had no idea that he possessed any abilities as he lived a rather aimless existence that, aside from supporting his three brothers early in life, had no grand purpose. However, destiny was calling Desmond, and as much as he meandered away from it with excuses about his fear of commitment or bouts of self-pity about his lack of worth, eventually a boat, an underground hatch and the love of a woman made it all very clear.

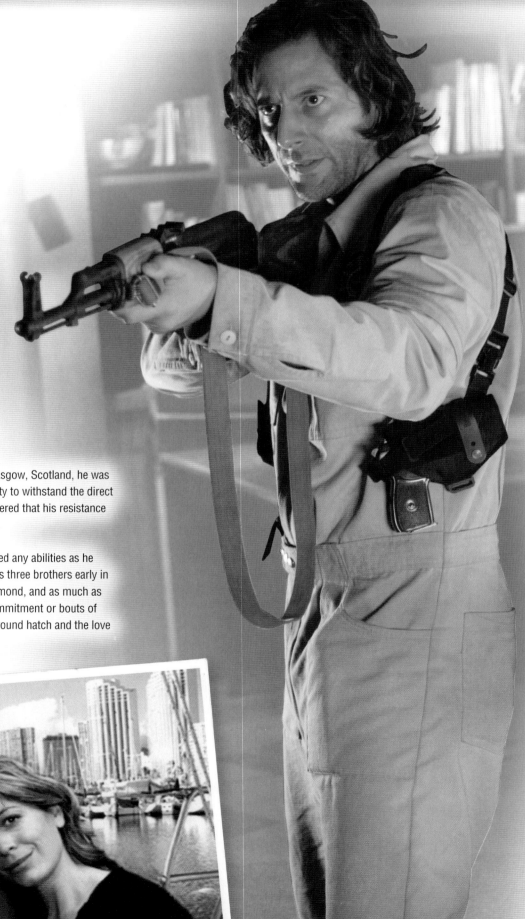

" You've killed us all, brotha! "

A HUME OF ALL TRADES

During his vagabond life, Desmond dabbled in a variety of professional trades and pursuits all without much success:

Set designer, Royal Shakespeare Company (RSC)

Novice monk

Lance-corporal, Royal Scots Regiment

Sailboat race captain

Button pusher, DHARMA Initiative

THE REAL DESMOND HUME

Desmond Hume's name is in homage to the influential Scottish philosopher David Hume (1711—1776) who was a prominent figure of the Scottish Enlightenment. He was a skeptic and argued that humans were guided by beliefs rather than reason. In that vein, he also believed that human freedoms and moral responsibility (or free will) could be balanced with the concept of determinism (fate).

FATED TO THE WIDMORES

When Desmond fell in love with Penny Widmore, he made his first move toward the island—the place that would reveal his life's purpose. Interestingly enough, each member of Penny's family would either push Desmond further down his path or offer explanations about what he was made to do.

Desmond serendipitously connected with Penny shortly after he renounced his orders at Eddington Monastery. She picked up an order of wine from Moriah Vineyards for her father, Charles Widmore, and offered to give Desmond a lift. They remained together for two years.

While she was Desmond's soul mate, it took him a long time to get past his pride, poor judgment and fear to come to terms with it. All the while, she suffered through their long separation and waited for him to come back to her for good. In the end, she was Desmond's one true motivation for everything that mattered in his life.

An arrogant man with high expectations for his daughter, Charles Widmore took one look at Hume and immediately knew he was far beneath what he wanted for Penny. Widmore went straight for Hume's pride and insinuated that he was worthless and undeserving of his daughter's hand in marriage. Widmore's words obliterated Desmond's already low self-esteem and, in the short term, achieved what Charles wanted—the end of their relationship. In the long run, it lit a fire inside Desmond to become worthy of Penny and inspired him to take a journey that would land him on the island—the very place Widmore would have given anything to be.

Eloise Hawking inserted herself into Desmond's path to make sure he stayed on course to carry out his destiny. Because of her knowledge of what he would mean to the island and her son, Daniel Faraday, Hawking was very much in tune with destiny and had to get Desmond in tune with his own. When she told him that "pushing that button is the only truly great thing you will ever do," Desmond may not have understood what that actually meant, but it stayed with him and helped frame the choices he would make from that point forward.

Daniel Faraday, Penny's half-brother, was the man who finally explained the special abilities that Desmond possessed. As Desmond bounced back and forth through time, it was Faraday who provided him information that would eventually save Hume's life. He prompted Desmond to select a constant, Penny, which grounded his subconscious and kept his brain from scrambling due to temporal displacement. With Daniel's guidance, Hume was able to accomplish what he needed to do to get back to Penny.

" I think I crashed your plane. "
—Spoken by Desmond to Locke

THE ELIZABETH

In Desmond's mind, winning Widmore's global sailing race represented an act of defiance and chivalry that would ultimately restore his damaged pride, put Penny's father in his place and make him feel worthy of Penny's love. In reality, none of that mattered because the *Elizabeth* only had one real purpose—getting Desmond to the island.

A suprise gift to him from Elizabeth "Libby" Smith, the sailboat was the key to connecting him to his destiny on the island, where pressing a button would in turn set off a chain of events that would become crucial in determining the outcome of countless lives and the fate of the island.

INSIDE THE SWAN

For three years, Desmond lived in service of the button. Every 108 minutes around the clock for more than 1000 days he took Kelvin Inman's word as law and entered the numbers. For Desmond it provided him an opportunity to do a bit of penance for his previous poor choices and to clarify his perspective on what was truly important in his life (love) which he had allowed to be obscured in his pride-induced challenge to beat Widmore at his own game. But when he was at the point of despair, ready to take his own life, Desmond regained his hope in the instant John Locke thumped on the hatch door, asking for a sign, which Desmond inadvertently provided by turning on a light. Twenty-three days later when Desmond had to use the fail-safe key, he would move himself another step closer to his destiny by activating his own powerful ability to shift his consciousness through time.

"I push this button every 108 minutes. I don't get out much."

BACK TO THE ISLAND

After Desmond was rescued by Penny on her boat the *Searcher*, the pair promised to keep the Oceanic Six's secret and they were finally free to live the life they both had waited years to begin.

Desmond visited Faraday at Oxford University.

However, the island wasn't finished with Desmond and his gifts. After three years of peace and the birth of their child, Charlie Hume, Desmond was struck by a memory from Faraday that spurred him to return to Oxford and ultimately to Los Angeles so he could meet Eloise Hawking who had concocted a plan with Ben to return the Oceanic Six to the island.

He was then shot by Benjamin Linus as part of his personal war against Charles Widmore. It put Desmond in the hospital and within the grasp of Widmore once more, who finally found value in his son-in-law. Having discovered that Hume was a necessary ally thanks to Jacob, Widmore returned him to the island as a fail-safe in the ongoing battle to save the island from the Man in Black. Widmore and his science team set up a rudimentary electromagnetic room that they used to test the resistance abilities Desmond possessed. It again triggered Hume's spacetime consciousness, but this time instead of jumping to the past, Desmond accessed the transitional state after death. While there for only seconds, Hume experienced a rich and complicated consciousness that gave him great peace and certainty.

Altered in an almost Zen-like way, he allowed the circumstances of his island situation, with the Man in Black battling Jack Shephard and the other survivors, to dictate his fate without any input. It was a destiny that he'd been moving towards for a decade and it finally revealed itself to him in the heart of the island—a cork within an electromagnetic pool that kept evil at bay. Only Desmond was able to move it without harm, and he accomplished the task with the expectation that it would send him back to the other consciousness he had experienced. However it did not, as it was Jack's place to restore the cork and move on. Desmond had done his part to save the island and help Jack move on as destined and his reward was to return to Penny and Charlie with Hurley's help.

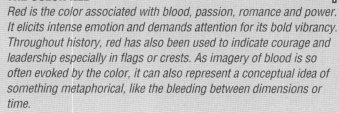

THE COLOR RED

Red is the color associated with blood, passion, romance and power. It elicits intense emotion and demands attention for its bold vibrancy. Throughout history, red has also been used to indicate courage and leadership especially in flags or crests. As imagery of blood is so often evoked by the color, it can also represent a conceptual idea of something metaphorical, like the bleeding between dimensions or time.

The color red appeared over and over in Desmond's life; a silent harbinger of key moments and events that would impact his destiny.

▸ *Penny's door.*

▸ *The freighter phone that Desmond used to call Penny on Christmas Eve.*

▸ *The color of the paint Desmond woke up soaking in at his flat.*

▸ *The man who got randomly crushed wore red shoes.*

▸ *Desmond wore a red shirt in his Thames picture with Penny.*

▸ *The spine color of Our Mutual Friend.*

▸ *MacCutcheon Scotch is an amber red.*

▸ *The lever color on Widmore's magnetization machine.*

▸ *The color of the Swan stationary bicycle.*

▸ *The Swan critical countdown symbols.*

▸ *Desmond was naked and covered in bright red blood stains post-Swan implosion.*

BACK AND FORTH

2004

Desmond turns the fail-safe key

2004

Lapidus bursts into the sick bay with Sayid. Faraday is on the phone and wants to speak with Desmond. He tells Desmond to go to Oxford and find him and gives Desmond info to convince himself. Keamy and Omar break in. Keamy tries to wrestle the phone away from Desmond and then…

1996

He's back outside the pay phone and calls Penny again. She tells him to leave her alone, then…

1996

Desmond talks to Penny and asks for her phone number and tells her not to change it because he'll call her in eight years on Christmas Eve 2004. She gives it to him and he leaves…

2004

Minkowski takes Desmond and Sayid to the radio room. Then Minkowski's consciousness goes away and he dies. Desmond is afraid the same thing will happen to him, then…

2004

Desmond's back on the boat. Keamy and Omar escort him down to the sick bay and lock him inside. He meets Minkowski. Doctor Ray enters and talks to Desmond. While checking his eyes, …

2004

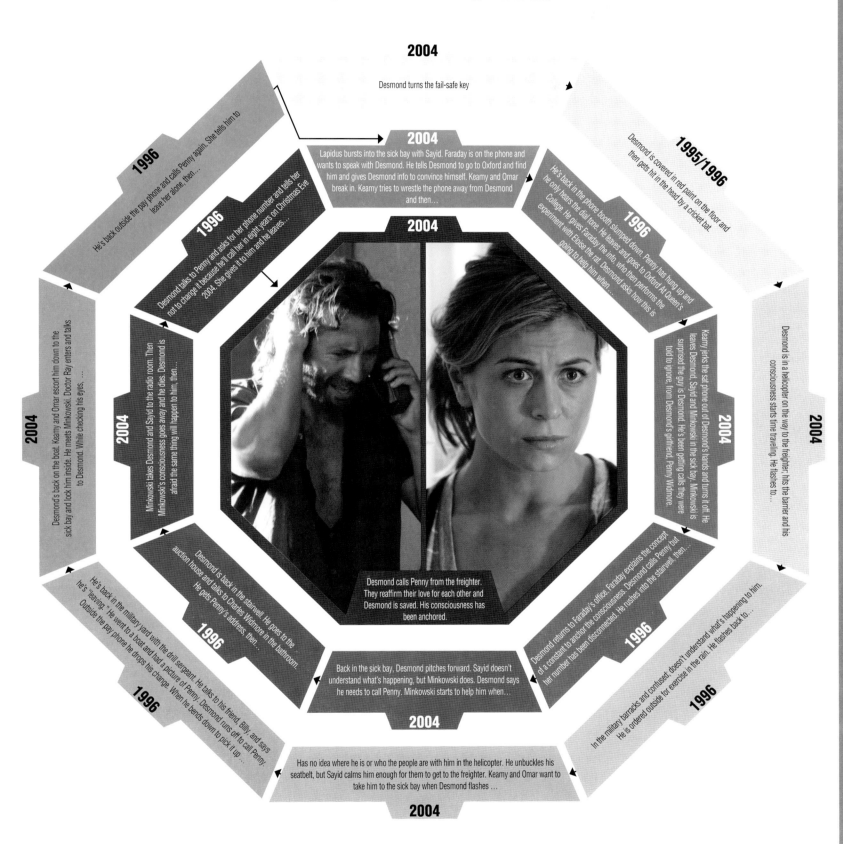

Desmond calls Penny from the freighter. They reaffirm their love for each other and Desmond is saved. His consciousness has been anchored.

1996

Desmond is back in the stairwell. He goes to the auction house and talks to Charles Widmore in the bathroom. He gets Penny's address, then…

1996

He's back in the military yard with the drill sergeant. He talks to his friend, Billy, and says he's "leaving." He went to a boat and had a picture of Penny. Desmond runs off to call Penny. Outside the pay phone he drops his change. When he bends down to pick it up …

2004

Back in the sick bay, Desmond pitches forward. Sayid doesn't understand what's happening, but Minkowski does. Desmond says he needs to call Penny. Minkowski starts to help him when…

2004

Has no idea where he is or who the people are with him in the helicopter. He unbuckles his seatbelt, but Sayid calms him enough for them to get to the freighter. Keamy and Omar want to take him to the sick bay when Desmond flashes …

1995/1996

Desmond is covered in red paint on the floor and then gets hit in the head by a cricket bat

1996

He's back in the phone booth slumped down. Penny has hung up and he only hears the dial tone. He leaves and goes to Oxford At Queen's College. He gives Faraday the info, who then performs the experiment with Eloise the rat. Desmond asks how this is going to help him when…

2004

Keamy jerks the sat phone out of Desmond's hands and turns it off. He leaves Desmond. Sayid and Minkowski in the sick bay. Minkowski is surprised the guy is Desmond. He's been getting calls they were told to ignore, from Desmond's girlfriend, Penny Widmore.

2004

Desmond is in a helicopter on the way to the freighter; hits the barrier and his consciousness starts time traveling. He flashes to…

1996

Desmond returns to Faraday's office. Faraday explains the concept of a constant to anchor the consciousness. Desmond calls Penny but her number has been disconnected. He rushes into the stairwell, then…

1996

In the military barracks and confused, doesn't understand what's happening to him. He is ordered outside for exercise in the rain. He flashes back to…

2004

"I'll see ya in another life, brotha."

— Spoken by Desmond to Jack

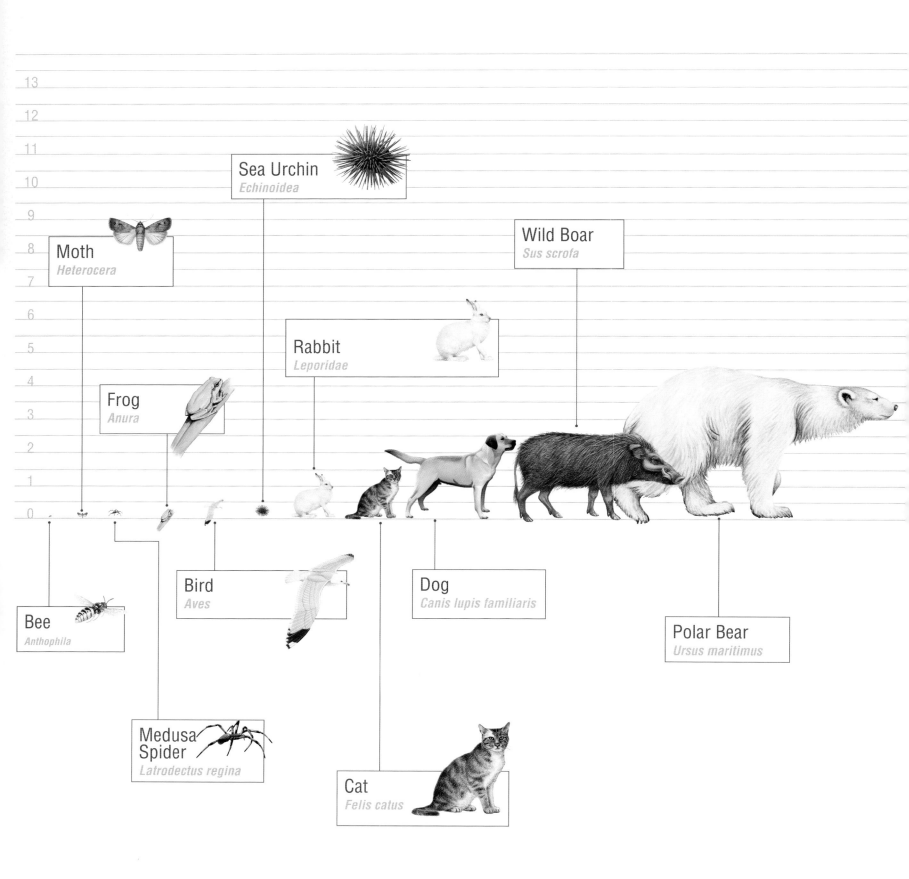

13

12

11

10 Sea Urchin
Echinoidea

9

8 Moth
Heterocera

7

6

5 Rabbit
Leporidae

4 Frog
Anura

3

2

1

0

Wild Boar
Sus scrofa

Bird
Aves

Dog
Canis lupis familiaris

Bee
Anthophila

Polar Bear
Ursus maritimus

Medusa
Spider
Latrodectus regina

Cat
Felis catus

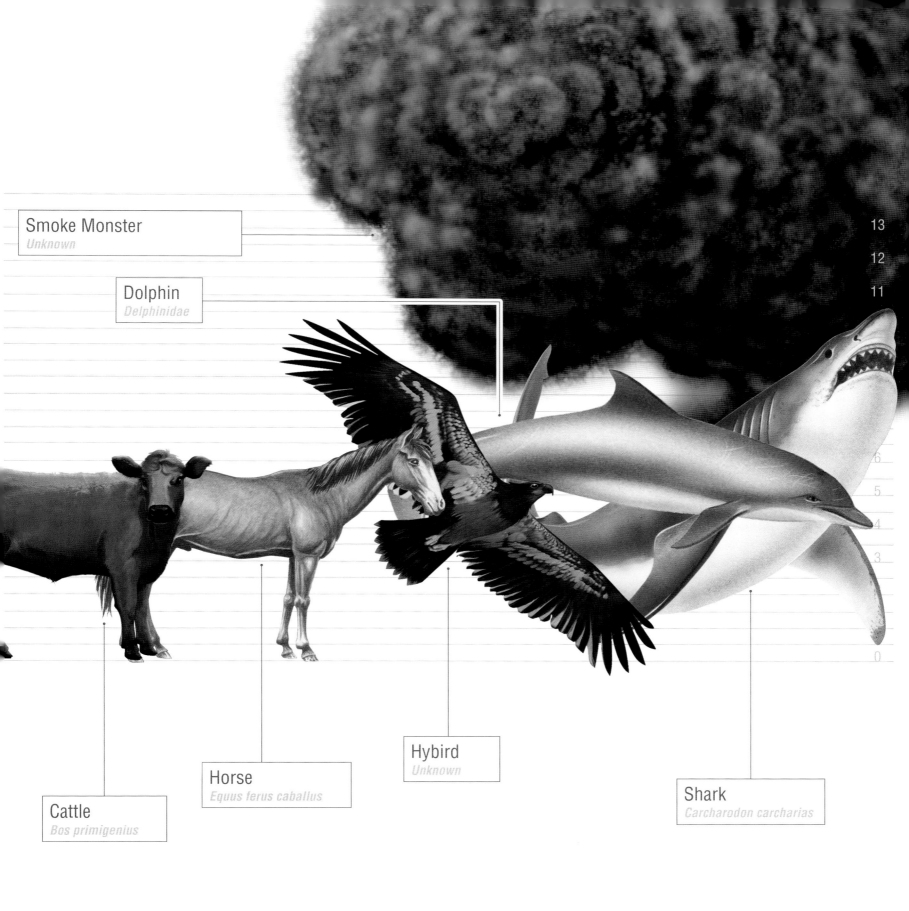

Smoke Monster
Unknown

Dolphin
Delphinidae

Cattle
Bos primigenius

Horse
Equus ferus caballus

Hybird
Unknown

Shark
Carcharodon carcharias

13

12

11

6

5

4

3

0

DHARMA INITIATIVE

Following in the footsteps of visionaries such as American psychologist and author B.F. Skinner, the DeGroots founded the DHARMA Initiative. They imagined a large-scale communal research compound. There, scientists and freethinkers from around the globe could pursue research in meteorology, psychology, parapsychology, zoology, electromagnetism, and utopian social studies for the benefit of mankind. Danish industrialist and munitions magnate Alvar Hanso's financial backing made their dream of a multi-purpose, social-science research facility a reality.

FINDING THE ISLAND

The Lamp Post, located in Los Angeles, CA, was constructed by DHARMA over a unique pocket of electromagnetic energy that connected to similar pockets all over the world, including the island. As the island was always moving through spacetime, the Lamp Post calculated equations that indicated—to a high degree of probability—where the island would be next, or its "event window."

Now defunct, the Lamp Post sent information automatically to the warehouse in Guam that revealed the grid reference that indicated where to deliver the next aerial food pallet drop.

Definition: **D**epartment of **H**euristics **A**nd **R**esearch on **M**aterial **A**pplications.

Intention: Scientific research unit that attempted to manipulate scientific laws. The overall purpose of their experiments was to change the Valenzetti Equation, which allegedly denoted the end of the human race.

Location: Headquarters—Ann Arbor, Michigan
Main site of scientific study—the island
Other facilities—Los Angeles, CA and Guam

History: Created in 1970, it was the brainchild of Gerald and Karen DeGroot, two doctoral candidates at the University of Michigan.

THE TRUCE

The truce was a signed contract between DHARMA and the Others, negotiated by Horace Goodspeed and Richard Alpert. It was created so that the DHARMA Initiative and the Others could co-exist on the island.

RESEARCH FACILITIES

#1, HYDRA
Zoological research and genetic experimentation.

#2, ARROW
Development of defensive strategies against the Others.

#3, SWAN
Containment and regulation of the electromagnetic energy leak caused by the Incident.

#4, FLAME
Communications hub.

#5, PEARL
Psychological research.

#6, ORCHID
Development of manipulating spacetime.

STAFF
Medical bay for DHARMA staff's births and emergency operations.

LOOKING GLASS
Used to guide the submarine back and forth and for secondary communications.

TEMPEST
Experimental facility that studied toxic gases.

LAMP POST
Used to calculate the coordinates of the island.

DI 90M1654-21644
DHARMA INITIATIVE
MEDICAL SUPPLY LOG
PL390
960VKKS

DI 9FFTR73
960VKKS PL390

"NAMASTÉ"

STAFF MEMBERS

GERALD DEGROOT

Job: Founder of DHARMA Initiative Gerald, along with his wife Karen and Danish industrialist Alvar Hanso, were the founders of the scientific research project called the DHARMA Initiative (1970). Gerald was a child when he first met Alvar, who was a foreign exchange student at the University of Michigan while staying with Gerald's family. The two maintained a life-long friendship, with Gerald even following in Alvar's footsteps by attending the University of Michigan as a doctoral candidate. It was at the university that Gerald collaborated with Karen, who was a fellow doctoral candidate, and together they initiated the concept of creating a communal, scientific research compound.

The DeGroots wanted to create a place where scientists could explore all disciplines including "meteorology, psychology, parapsychology, zoology, and electromagnetism." In graduate school, Gerald reached out to Hanso for financial backing of the project and the three became partners in the DHARMA Initiative project.

Aside from the initial DHARMA start-up, not much else is known about the work of the DeGroots. They are seen in passing during the DHARMA Initiative orientation films for the Swan and the Pearl, but the couple's current whereabouts are unknown.

BUDDHISM & DHARMA ⊹

The word Dharma has several meanings and significances in different religious and spiritual beliefs, all of which relate to the DHARMA Initiative beliefs, practices and causes.

In Buddhism, Dharma mostly refers to the wisdom and teachings of the Buddha. It also refers to a basic unit of existence and/or experience called a "phenomenon." A core concept of Buddhism is that all phenomena are interlinked and interdependent.

Buddhists believe that only through the practice of Dharma will they discover the greatest peace, happiness and fulfillment. While there are many different schools of Buddhism that focus on individual aspects of what the Buddha taught, the concept of Dharma unites them all. The DeGroots infused that idea into the heart of their DHARMA Initiative experiment that was created to unite many different scientific disciplines and research schools of thought together on the island with one united goal.

OUTSIDE INFLUENCES ⊹

One of the many influences on the research methodology embraced by the DeGroots was the renowned American psychologist B.F. Skinner. He founded a school of research psychology called the experimental analysis of behavior, which is reflected in the DHARMA experiments including those with the polar bears. Setting up a reward system with food after completing tasks tied into Skinner's theories of reinforcing consequences, as did the observation of the button pressing every 108 minutes.

KAREN DEGROOT

Job: Founder of DHARMA Initiative Karen is the wife and research partner of Gerald DeGroot. Together with Danish industrialist Alvar Hanso, the three founded the alternative scientific research project called the DHARMA Initiative (1970). Karen met Gerald when they were both doctoral candidates at the University of Michigan. They discovered they were of like mind in their determination to create a communal scientific community where varied scientists could pursue broad avenues of research in one place.

With the financial backing of Alvar Hanso, the DeGroots funded and started the DHARMA Initative. Their own personal scientific goals, outside of the initial DHARMA setup, remain unknown along with their current status.

CASEY

Job: Gemologist Casey worked as part of the DHARMA Initiative during its heyday on the island in the 1970s. She specialized in Gemology, the science of identifying gemstones, which is a branch of mineralogy.

She also welcomed newcomers to the island, including Roger Linus and his son Ben. Casey was also present at the critical vote that determined whether Sayid should be executed or not. She was known to spend time with her colleague Rosie and actually left the island with Rosie in the Galaga submarine the day that Pierre Chang ordered the evacuation of all DHARMA women and children from the island.

CRAIG

Job: Unknown A member of the DHARMA Initiative, Craig was present during the 1974-77 time period during which some of the survivors of flight 815 fluxed through time. His job occupation and duties with DHARMA were never formally revealed. When Sayid was under investigation by DHARMA, Craig helped extinguish a catastrophic fire that was deliberately set using one of the DHARMA Initiative's vans as the trigger to start the blaze.

CONTENTS
FOOD DROP PROTOCOL

1 1 General Guidance
P.N a. Tactical Mission Planning
3 ALL b. Checklist Procedures
5 ALL c. Escorting Dharma Safeties
7 ALL d. High Velocity Container Airdrop Using
8 3/4-Inch Plywood Skidboards
12 ALL e. 26 Foot High Velocity Ring Slot Restrictions
16 P.N f. Low-Level Route Restrictions and Pudgy
21 DZ Escape Procedures
28 P.L # g. Passengers on Tactical Flights
37 2 Low-Level Operations
43 P.N a. Operational Requirements
45 P.N,L,M 3 # Jumpmaster Directed
Airdrop Procedures (JMD)
53 ALL 4 High Altitude Airdrop Missions
76 ALL 5 Airdrop/Miscellaneous Information
79 P.N a. Drop Zone Communication Procedures
95 P.N b. Drift Down Information

CONTENTS
MEDICAL SUPPLY LOG

THE INCIDENT

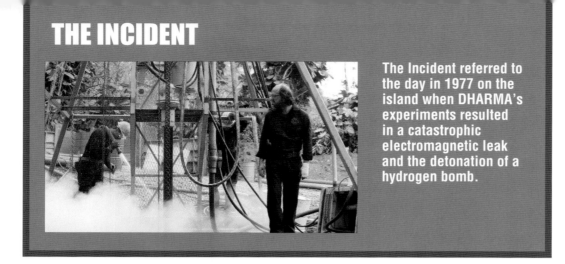

The Incident referred to the day in 1977 on the island when DHARMA's experiments resulted in a catastrophic electromagnetic leak and the detonation of a hydrogen bomb.

DEBRA

Job: Nurse Debra helped Juliet Burke when Benjamin Linus entered the DHARMA hospital area with a gunshot wound to the chest. She followed Juliet's directions and packed the wound with gauze to stop the hemorrhaging. When the bleeding didn't subside, Juliet told Debra and Sawyer that Ben desperately needed the attention of a proper surgeon—namely Jack.

Debra later introduced Kate into the operating room as she volunteered to give blood to help Ben. When he went into hypoxic shock, Debra escorted Roger, Ben's father, out of the operating room so that Juliet could deal with the situation and stabilize Ben.

DORIS

Job: Mycologist Mycology was the area of expertise for Doris, who worked for the DHARMA Initiative on the island during the 1970s.

MYCOLOGY DEFINED ✛
Mycology is the branch of biology that specializes in the study of fungi. Scientists study their genetic and biochemical makeup, their taxonomy (the science behind classification) and their use to humans as fuel. It also includes a fungi's use as a medical agent (penicillin), a consumable (beer, cheese, edible mushrooms) and their poisonous properties, and also entheogens.

ERIC

Job: Construction A construction worker, Eric was part of the team excavating the ground beneath the Orchid station's botanical area. He stopped Dr. Pierre Chang during the shooting of the orientation film to inform him of the problems at the Orchid.

FERN

Job: Video assistant An employee from the 1970s-era DHARMA Initiative, Fern assisted in various events. She was on hand during the filming of Dr. Pierre Chang's orientation film for the Arrow station. Aside from the orientation video duties, Fern assisted the doctor who was treating fellow DHARMA member Amy during her early labor.

FLOYD

Job: Cook Very little is known about this member of the DHARMA Initiative. He was part of the group stationed on the island during 1977, around the time that members of DHARMA were deciding what to do about their discovery of Sayid. Floyd even worked as a cook in the cafeteria with Hurley.

GLENN

Job: Field supervisor While working at the Swan station construction site, Glenn was involved in the development of the Swan location. During the construction at the Swan in 1977, one of Glenn's co-workers asked for the serial numbers for the hatch door—the first piece of DHARMA construction that Locke and Boone discovered. Glenn responded to the request and called out the numbers (4, 8, 15, 16, 23, 42). Hurley was nearby and recognized the numbers and the hatch door.

HEATHER

Job: Unknown A member during the 1970s, Heather lived in a house within the main DHARMA village. One night in 1974, the alarm sounded, signaling that a Hostile had crossed the boundary line and entered DHARMA territory. Her colleague, Phil, came to Heather's house along with Daniel, Jin, Juliet, Miles, and Sawyer and asked Heather to keep an eye on them. Heather was armed with a Ruger Mini 14 rifle.

JAY

Job: Videographer Considered the unofficial videographer of the DHARMA Initiative, Jay worked on visual documentation projects during the '70s era on the island. In particular, he directed the Arrow orientation video that featured Dr. Pierre Chang explaining the station's purpose as an observatory and defensive strategy center against the Hostiles. The shoot was interrupted by Eric, an Orchid worker, who was sent to retrieve Dr. Chang due to a problem at the station. The video was never completed. Jay was also responsible for the DHARMA new recruit photographs seen hanging on the wall inside a barrack's building.

JERRY

Job: Security In 1977, Jerry was a member of the DHARMA Initiative security staff, although he was not as dedicated or focused on the job like his colleague Phil. A fan of the 1970s Tony Orlando and Dawn hit "Candida," Jerry was dating fellow DHARMA co-worker Rosie, a big Geronimo Jackson fan. Jerry was known to neglect his duties especially when Rosie would drop by the security station. It is believed that Jerry remained with DHARMA until its demise.

THE PURGE ✛
The Purge was a response by the Others to DHARMA constantly breaking the terms of the truce. They ultimately wiped out DHARMA using the toxic gas from their own Tempest station.

KYKER

Job: Videographer assistant Kyker is the surname of one of the behind-the-scenes videographers of the Arrow orientation film. The name appears on the official slate that is snapped before Dr. Pierre Chang (speaking in the video as Dr. Marvin Candle) starts to explain the defensive strategy and observational functions of the station in monitoring the "island's hostile indigenous population." However, the film is interrupted shortly after Dr. Chang begins by an agitated DHARMA worker named Eric who explains there is a problem at the Orchid station. The completed piece is never seen in its entirety.

MITCH

Job: Security Mitch was a member of the 1970s DHARMA Initiative security detail. When "LaFleur's" deception about the true origins of Kate, Hurley and Jack to the DHARMA compound started to unravel, Mitch helped corroborate inconsistencies in their stories to Horace Goodspeed and Stuart Radzinsky. He confirmed that the three were late additions to the submarine manifest, which in turn made the leaders more suspicious to their presence on the island.

After the ruse completely fell apart, Mitch was assigned to forcibly escort Sawyer and Juliet onto the next submarine back to the mainland. Mitch then added Kate to the sub after she was captured by security at the barracks. Assigned to provide all passengers with a liquid sedative for the trip, Juliet overwhelmed Mitch and knocked him unconscious. She then stole his keys and freed Sawyer and Kate from their handcuffs.

OLIVIA

Job: Schoolteacher A close friend of Horace Goodspeed, Olivia worked for the DHARMA Initiative as a teacher. She was also connected to the birth of the man who would grow up to slaughter DHARMA's staff during the Purge, Benjamin Linus.

In a wooded area miles outside of Portland, Oregon, Emily Linus gave birth to Benjamin. Emily began to hemorrhage badly, so husband Roger flagged down a passing car driven by Horace Goodspeed and Olivia. Sadly, Emily died shortly after Olivia and Horace's arrival, but the pair helped take Roger and his newborn son to the nearest hospital.

During the early 1970s, Olivia worked as a teacher with the DHARMA Initiative's children who lived on the island. Her students enjoyed her teaching methods, such as her papier-mâché volcano experiment using bicarbonate of soda that illustrated how volcanic eruptions occur. Among her most notable students were Ben and his friend Annie.

During one lesson time in particular, the Hostiles (as the DHARMA Initiative referred to them) triggered an outside alarm indicating that they had crossed a boundary line. When this occurred, Olivia followed a standard procedure by padlocking all the doors and moving the students to safety.

ISLAND HISTORY
When questioned by Annie, Olivia explained that the island's volcano erupted a long time ago. Although this shred of island history came to light, it is unknown when the eruption occurred on the island.

OPAL

Job: Nurse Opal served as a nurse and a job coordinator who doled out positions to the new recruits on the island. Opal's position had a particular impact on Roger Linus, who arrived on the island with his son Ben and expected to have an important job in the DHARMA Initiative. Instead, Opal handed Roger his uniform emblazoned with the title of "Work Man," which translated to a janitorial position. Unmoved by Roger's anger at the assignment, Opal impassively told him he could apply for another position if anything opened up.

Jack, Kate and Hurley were part of DHARMA's new recruits in 1977.

PAUL

Job: Head of Security While on a picnic in 1974, Paul and his wife Amy were approached by two members of the Others. Paul was murdered and they attempted to abduct Amy, but she was rescued when Sawyer and Juliet killed her captors.

When Richard Alpert entered DHARMA territory demanding Paul's body as "justice" for the killing of his two men, Amy acquiesced. Before relinquishing his body, she kept the small wooden ankh that hung around Paul's neck. The theme of fate and destiny is significant with the relationship between the death of Paul and the arrival of Sawyer and his friends into 1974 DHARMA. When the Others killed Paul, Sawyer was instrumental in getting Paul's wife back home. In turn, Sawyer—under the assumed name of Jim LaFleur—eventually donned the mantle of head of security for DHARMA.

THE ANKH
The ankh is an Egyptian hieroglyph that symbolized eternal life and Paul's ankh is the same as the colossal carvings held in each hand by the statue of Taweret.

PHIL

Job: Security Dedicated to the DHARMA Initiative, but also quietly devious, Phil worked in the security detail under the leadership of Jim LaFleur, a.k.a. James "Sawyer" Ford. Phil's loyalty to Sawyer turned to treachery, however, when he learned that his boss had sympathies for the Hostiles and turned against DHARMA.

Phil suspected something was awry when DHARMA's newest recruits—Jack, Kate, and Hurley—were not on the original list. He became more suspicious when Jack seemed to know too much about Sawyer. Phil's discovery of the videotape that showed Sawyer and Kate taking a young Benjamin Linus, was the final straw.

Something in Phil snapped when Sawyer, the man he trusted for so many years, tied him up to prevent the truth from getting out. While Radzinsky beat Sawyer for answers, Phil joined in and struck Juliet to make Sawyer confess. Phil immediately pledged his allegiance to Radzinsky's plan to dispose of Sawyer's friends.

At the Swan construction site, Phil fought to protect the project and kill Sawyer's group. Although Sawyer had sworn he'd kill Phil for hitting Juliet, the electromagnetic leak did that job for him. As Phil attempted to shoot his former superior, he was impaled by a set of magnetized metal rods.

ROSIE

Job: Nurse Rosie worked as a nurse during the 1970s at the Looking Glass station, the underwater structure that was used primarily as a beacon to guide DHARMA submarines toward the island.

On one occasion, Rosie visited her boyfriend Jerry, a DHARMA security officer, during working hours. While the pair danced around to the song "Candida" and ate brownies, she unknowingly almost caused Jerry to miss a serious situation on the security monitors. Rosie indentified the subject on the monitors as Horace Goodspeed. She left the island prior to the Incident, as a result of Dr. Pierre Chang's insistence that all women and children be evacuated.

GERONIMO JACKSON
Rosie was a fan of the band Geronimo Jackson, as indicated by one of her shirts.

CANDIDA
Tony Orlando and Dawn's "Candida," their debut single and a hit in August 1970, was a very appropriate song choice for the opening of the LaFleur episode. The episode focused on the duality of James "Sawyer" Ford's important role as head of security for the DHARMA Initiative in 1977, a role that he was performing under the false identity of Jim LaFleur.

The song's lyrics also mirror other themes, especially Sawyer's struggles: "And, oh, who am I? Just an ordinary guy/Tryin' hard to win me first prize." In addition, the lyrics reflected Sawyer and Juliet's attempts to leave the island."We could make it together/The further from here girl the better/Where the air is fresh and clean/Just take my hand and I'll lead ya/I promise that life will be sweeter/'Cause it said so in my dreams."

Dharma Recruits
1977

DIANE JANSEN

> **CONNECTION:** Mother of Kate Austen: ex-wife of Sam Austen: widow of Wayne Jansen

Diane had a strained relationship with her daughter because of her unhealthy love for Wayne. Besotted with him despite his violent behavior and problems with alcohol, Diane often made excuses or turned a blind eye to his abusive tendencies. She effectively destroyed her bond with her daughter when she chose to remain loyal to Wayne, even after his death, rather than protect Kate.

From a working-class background in Iowa, Diane married young to an Army soldier named Sam Austen. When Sam was stationed overseas in Korea, Diane engaged in an extramarital affair with Wayne Jansen. Diane got pregnant with Kate and Sam returned home a few months before she was born. Aware that he was not the father, Sam decided to stay with Diane and his baby. As Kate grew up, Diane let her daughter believe that Sam was her father.

However, Diane and Sam broke up when Kate was 5 years old. Diane refused custody of Kate to Sam, but she allowed him visitation to reinforce their daughter's belief about her parentage.

> **CONNECTIONS** ✛
> Diane once served Sawyer and his associate Gordy some beers and sandwiches at a roadside diner.

After the divorce, Diane and Wayne reconnected and they eventually married. Wayne proved to be a heavy drinker who would often get violent with Diane, but she grew very adept at blaming the injuries on something else to protect him. Kate noticed this behavior over the years, creating a wedge between mother and daughter.

KEITH'S Diner

> Diane worked for years at a local diner to help pay the bills.

When Kate was 24, the situation hit a boiling point when a drunken Wayne made sexual advances toward Kate. While Diane was at work, Kate rigged a gas leak that caused the house to explode with Wayne in it. When she later met her mother at the diner, Diane lied when asked about her recent wrist injury and said, "I made my bed, Katherine," to explain her enabling ways. Kate then slipped her mother an insurance policy that indirectly explained what occurred. Incredulous, Diane asked Kate several times, "What did you do?" but her daughter just kissed her and went on the run.

When the police arrived, Diane stated that her daughter was involved in the incident. She showed them the insurance policy taken out in her name, at which time the U.S. Marshals became involved.

BRIEF ENCOUNTERS

Kate kept tabs on Diane as she continued to waitress in Iowa. Desperate for answers, Kate even managed to talk to her mother several times despite constant monitoring by the Feds.

> ▶ *With the help of Cassidy Phillips, Kate orchestrated an impromptu meeting with her mother in the diner's bathroom. Kate asked her mother why she told the police about her involvement. Seeking an apology, Diane reiterated about Wayne that "for good or bad, I loved him." Diane made it clear that she had no forgiveness for Kate and that she didn't accept that Kate's actions were for her benefit.*

> ▶ *When Diane was diagnosed with cancer, Kate contacted her childhood friend and doctor, Tom Brennan, to allow them to meet. A sickly Diane was disturbed by Kate's appearance and fearfully cried for "Help!"*

When Kate went to trial for her crimes as one of the Oceanic Six, the prosecution enlisted Diane as their star witness. But after hearing testimony about Kate's "heroics" on the island and the news that she had a grandchild (Aaron), Diane second guessed her choice to testify. Through Kate's lawyer, Diane requested a meeting with her daughter. Although Kate remained bitter, Diane had softened and even admitted her attitude changed when she thought Kate had died and as she faced her own mortality. Diane asked to see Aaron in exchange for not testifying, but Kate ended the conversation. Ultimately, Diane was not present at the trial to testify. Diane's decision provided Kate with the ability to work out a deal for a lesser plea and probation.

DIEGO REYES

> **CONNECTION:** Brother of Hugo "Hurley" Reyes

Diego was present when Hurley was interviewed by reporters about winning the lottery. After stating that the winning numbers had "just come to him," he introduced his family to the cameras: his mom, Carmen; his grandpa, Tito; and his brother Diego with his wife Lisa. When Diego screamed, "Wooo! We're rich!" Hurley told the journalists to ignore his "idiot" brother. Later, Diego moved back home after his wife Lisa left him.

DONOVAN

> **CONNECTION:** Best friend of Desmond Hume

A good friend of Desmond Hume, Donovan was also a physics professor in London who was knowledgeable—but indifferent—to the theory of time travel.

After turning the fail-safe key in the Swan station, Desmond confided in Donovan about his experiences on the island. It was his hope that Donovan could help him determine if he had in fact gone back in time. Quite skeptical of Desmond's story, Donovan challenged his friend while at a pub to predict a future event to prove that Desmond wasn't being delusional. Desmond balked at first, but then predicted the outcome of a football goal during a game on television. Desmond's prediction for this particular game turned out wrong and Donovan resoundingly asserted "There is no such thing as time travel, Des."

Desmond failed to predict the outcome of the goal in this football game.

"There is no such thing as time travel, Des."
— Spoken by Donovan to Desmond

DOGEN

"Do not let him say a word. If you allow him to speak, it is already too late. We have only one chance to defeat him..."

▶ **CONNECTION:** Master of the Island Temple

As the leader of the island Temple, Dogen was responsible for guarding the sacred space and spring within it from the Man in Black. He was given the job by Jacob and served in the position for over 15 years before he was killed by the Man in Black's "claimed" emissary, Sayid Jarrah.

ORIGINS

Before he came to the island, Dogen was a successful businessman at a bank in Osaka. He had a wife and a 12-year-old son. In a sad twist of fate, what should have been a benchmark in his life turned into a nightmare. Dogen was promoted at work, so his colleagues took him out to celebrate. Afterwards, he picked up his son from baseball practice, but Dogen was intoxicated and caused a car accident that put his son in critical condition. At the hospital, Jacob approached Dogen and offered him a deal: he would save the boy if Dogen left his family forever to become the new Temple master.

NEW DESTINY

Dogen chose to live a solitary existence in the Temple and distanced himself from the Others. He continued to speak in his native Japanese almost exclusively and relied upon Lennon as his translator despite the fact that he spoke English quite well. In fact, he informed Hugo "Hurley" Reyes that he didn't like the way English tasted on his tongue.

Jacob eventually shared with Dogen the stakes of his job and explained that the master was the only person who could keep the Man in Black out of the Temple. If he were to fall, the Temple's defenses would fall as well. Dogen was provided the tools by which to test people's corruption by the Man in Black, ash to protect the barrier of the Temple and use of the natural spring for its healing abilities.

INFILTRATION

The arrival of Jack, Kate, Hurley, Jin and Sayid at the Temple sparked a series of events that would change the destinies of Dogen and the Others forever. Initially, Dogen ordered their cumulative execution but Hurley's revelation that Jacob had sent them swayed the protector. When Dogen discovered Jacob's list hidden within the ankh in Hurley's guitar case, he spoke to Hurley and learned that Jacob was dead. Dogen immediately sprang into action aware of the impending war with the Man in Black.

After Sayid's resurrection, Dogen exposed the Iraqi's wound, blew ash over it, and attached acupuncture needles connected to an E-meter to Sayid's body. The results of the tests told Dogen that Sayid had been corrupted and that he needed to be killed to protect him from the Man in Black's influence. Sayid later demanded answers from Dogen about the tests and his "death." Dogan admitted the machine measured the good and evil within a person and Sayid tipped to the wrong side.

When the Man in Black sent Claire Littleton to insist an audience with Dogen, the master refused and sent Sayid in his stead. To test Sayid's true nature, Dogen gave him an ancient dagger and tasked him to kill the Man in Black to prove the good in his soul.

Sayid returned to the Temple and explained it didn't work, which Dogen accepted. He then told Sayid how he almost killed his own son in a car accident after he had too much to drink and how Jacob offered to save his son's life if Dogen came to the island and accepted a new job. The catch was that Dogen could never see his boy again.

Sayid was held underwater in the Temple spring until the hourglass emptied.

Dogen asked if Sayid was offered a similar bargain by the Man in Black. Sayid said yes, but he chose to ignore the Man in Black's ultimatum. Dogen believed they had finally become allies in this war and said he was wrong about Sayid. He was a good man. However, Sayid's story proved to be a lie. In a surprising twist, the Iraqi grabbed Dogen and pushed him into the pool, drowning him.

Dogen used this bowl to grind up the ingredients that were combined to create the poison pill.

This baseball served as a reminder of Dogen's son.

BUDDHISM ✚

Dogen Zenji was the founder of the Soto school of Zen Buddhism. Born of a noble family in Japan, he lived from 1200 to 1253. The loss of his parents at a young age challenged his understanding of life and death, so at the age of 13 he became a Buddhist monk to learn the path to enlightenment. Dogen taught enlightenment through meditation, specifically through shikantaza (which means "just sitting") and hishiryo (which means "not thinking").

DOCTORS

Logo for St. Sebastian Hospital

DR. EVELYN ARIZA

▶ **CONNECTION:** Encountered Jack Shephard and Sayid Jarrah at St. Sebastian Hospital

Three years after the Oceanic Six returned home, Sayid was shot with a potent tranquilizer during a skirmish with a nemesis. After Hurley brought Sayid's unconscious body to his family home, his father, David, took Sayid to see Jack at St. Sebastian Hospital. Jack tended to Sayid, but was ultimately confronted by Dr. Evelyn Ariza, the hospital's Director of Clinical Services. Ariza reminded Jack that he had been suspended from the medical profession because of his substance abuse problem. Although Jack pleaded with Ariza, she stated that, regardless of his good intentions, the hospital was liable for whatever he did to any patient.

DR. BAE

▶ **CONNECTION:** Delivered Sun Kwon's baby

An obstetrician at Choogdong Hospital in Seoul, South Korea, Dr. Bae was the attending at the hospital when Sun Kwon arrived in labor. He asked if there was anyone she wanted him to call and she asked for Jin. As the labor progressed, he determined the baby was under distress and wanted to perform a C-section. However, a delirious Sun wanted to wait until Jin arrived so he could watch his baby come into the world. The doctor ended up delivering the little girl naturally.

DR. DOUGLAS BROOKS

▶ **CONNECTION:** Doctor who treated Hugo "Hurley" Reyes at Santa Rosa Mental Health Institute

A psychiatrist at Santa Rosa Mental Health Institute, Dr. Brooks treated Hugo Reyes when he became nearly catatonic after he blamed his excessive weight for a deck accident that killed two people. Patient yet determined, Brooks tried for two months to address Hurley's weight issues and talk about the accident. He even assigned homework to Hurley, but all Dr. Brooks received in return was passive-aggressive resistance in the form of Hurley's imaginary friend, Dave. After some time, Hurley started to open up about his guilt and obsessive eating. Brooks took the opportunity to show Hurley a Polaroid he had taken of him and Dave that revealed Hurley all alone. It was a breakthrough moment for Hurley as he came to understand that Dave didn't exist and then embraced Dr. Brooks' therapy to get well enough to leave.

Eventually, Dr. Brooks' therapy helped prove that Dave was imaginary.

DR. CURTIS

▶ **CONNECTION:** One of Hurley's former doctors

Dr. Curtis was a practicing psychiatrist who worked at the Santa Rosa Mental Health Institute. Believing the lottery numbers were cursed, Hurley tried to visit Leonard Simms but was denied entry. Dr. Curtis saw Hurley in the lobby and allowed him to enter and speak with Leonard.

DR. JE-GYU KIM

▶ **CONNECTION:** Fertility doctor for Sun and Jin

A practicing doctor based in Seoul, South Korea, Dr. Je-Gyu Kim knew how powerful—and dangerous—businessman Mr. Paik was. Therefore, when he initially received the results of Sun's fertility tests, he concocted a lie to protect himself and his business.

Kim reported to Sun and Jin that she could not conceive due to advanced endometriosis (scar tissue) that was blocking her fallopian tubes. He added that surgery would not make conceiving any less impossible. However, when Sun was later walking her dog, Kim approached her and was happy to tell her the truth now that Jin—an employee of Paik—was not with her. Kim revealed that there was nothing wrong with Sun; it was Jin whose low sperm count meant the couple could not have children. Kim explained he was terrified that if he told someone who worked for Paik that he was in some way less of a man, that he would burn his practice to the ground.

DR. STILLMAN

▶ **CONNECTION:** Doctor at Santa Rosa Mental Health Institute; treated Hugo "Hurley" Reyes

When Hugo "Hurley" Reyes was re-institutionalized on the recommendation of LAPD Detective Mike Walton, Dr. Stillman was one of the professionals assigned to Hurley's case. While under the care of Stillman at Santa Rosa, Hurley claimed that he was visited by the ghosts of people who had perished on the island. Furthermore, he began to doubt the existence of the people who were actually alive and spending time with him, including Stillman.

SANTA ROSA
MENTAL HEALTH INSTITUTE

NAME
Dr. Stillman

75626-67
EMPLOYEE NO.

Fearing that Hurley's mental state was failing, Stillman called upon Jack Shephard for help. Since all other treatments had failed, he hoped that Hurley's Oceanic Six friend could bring about the change needed to help Hurley's psychological issues improve.

SANTA ROSA
MENTAL HEALTH INSTITUTE

◀ VISITOR ENTRANCE

◀ ADMISSIONS

SHIPPING & DELIVERIES ▶

DR. WOODRUFF

▶ **CONNECTION:** Australian doctor who treated Carole Littleton

Dr. J. Woodruff was the Australian neurosurgeon who dealt with Carole Littleton's coma after her car accident. He explained to Claire and Lindsey, Carole's sister, that Carole had suffered a severe head trauma and that widespread damage was almost a certainty. Carole was kept on life-support during her coma and Dr. Woodruff tried to gently make Claire understand that Carole may not awaken.

He assured Claire and Lindsey that Carole's medical expenses were being taken care of, but due to confidentiality agreements, he could not disclose that Claire's father, Christian Shephard, was covering the bills.

DUNCAN FORRESTER

▶ **CONNECTION:** Criminal defense attorney for Kate Austen

After Kate Austen returned to civilization as one of the Oceanic Six, she hired Duncan Forrester as her defense attorney for her criminal trial. Supportive but realistic, Forrester knew that defending Kate would be a huge challenge considering her laundry list of past crimes. However, he believed in Kate's remorse and even coached her on how to deal with the media and protestors who surrounded the courthouse.

At Kate's arraignment and bail hearing, Forrester argued persuasively that Austen was not a flight risk due to her celebrity as one of the Oceanic Six. Based on Kate's prior history of running, however, the judge disagreed and she was incarcerated. Later when lawyer and client met to discuss their defense strategy, Forrester revealed that the District Attorney would be personally handling her case. Clearly worried, he suggested Kate consider accepting a plea deal of 15 years incarceration with seven years served. Kate declined and asked to be put on the stand in own her defense. Forrester balked but asked that she let him try the case based on character and place Aaron on the stand to gain jury sympathy. Kate agreed on the character approach, but refused to expose Aaron to the trial.

When the case opened, the prosecution came out strong and immediately damaged Kate's defense strategy. Unwilling to go down without a fight, Forrester went behind Kate's back and called Jack Shephard to the stand as a character witness from her time on the island. In an even bolder move, the day prior to her scheduled testimony, Forrester allowed Kate's ailing mother Diane to speak to her daughter privately. The conversation caused the older woman to second-guess her decision to take the stand, which crippled the prosecution's case. Forrester sensed the D.A.'s panic and was prepared to go in for the kill, but Kate accepted a plea of 10 years probation as long as she remained in the state.

DYNAMITE

THE SCIENCE BEHIND THE BLAST

Dynamite was invented and patented by Swedish industrialist and chemist Alfred Nobel in 1867. He began experimenting with nitroglycerin in the early 1860s in an attempt to find more effective explosives to blast rock for large-scale industrial construction projects. Nobel found that he could stabilize the volatile liquid nitroglycerin by mixing it with an absorbent kieselguhr (or diatomaceous earth) into a paste that could be molded into cylinder-shaped rods. For increased detonation safety, he also created a blasting cap that could be ignited with a fuse. Before it became known as dynamite, it was sold as "Nobel's Blasting Powder."

Nitroglycerin, the key component of dynamite, in its pure form can detonate on contact. Even stabilized with the inert absorbents in dynamite, it degrades over time and can become volatile. If dynamite is left to sit over an extended period of time, it is common for the nitroglycerin to sweat out of its casing, which can then collect in its storage container with potentially deadly results. Over time, crystals can form on old sticks of dynamite that can ignite once moved, even without a blasting cap, which makes transportation of the aged explosive extremely dangerous.

During a drunken episode, Horace Goodspeed detonated dynamite near the sonic fence.

Hurley planned to detonate the Swan food pantry, but was talked out of doing so by Rose.

1867

1977

Circa **1990**

November **2004**
(44 days post-crash)

November **2004**
(46 days post-crash)

The *Black Rock:* Captain Magnus Hanso stocked several crates of the new explosive called dynamite in the *Black Rock's* cargo hold. It remained dormant in the hold for more than 100 years.

Danielle Rousseau secured dynamite from the *Black Rock* and used it to tripwire traps to protect her shelter from the Others.

Dr. Leslie Arzt helped extract six sticks of dynamite from the *Black Rock* and placed them into two separate bags held by Kate and Locke. A volatile stick exploded, blasting Arzt to pieces.

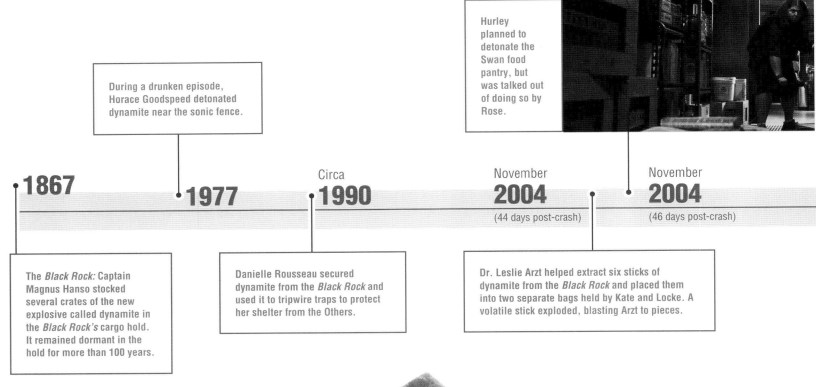

Rousseau took a
crate of dynamite
from the *Black Rock*.

Claire ventured to the
Black Rock to collect
sticks of dynamite.

November
2004
(65 days post-crash)

November
2004
(89 days post-crash)

November
2004
(90 days post-crash)

2005
(post-Oceanic Six leaving)

Day 10 (post-Incident)

Eko used the last of the dynamite
hidden inside the tree in an
unsuccessful attempt to destroy the
Swan blast doors.

Richard Alpert returned to the *Black Rock* to ignite a stick
of dynamite in a failed suicide attempt.

Ilana hiked to the *Black Rock* to retrieve dynamite with the
intent to blow up Ajira flight 316. Ilana dropped the volatile
sticks on the ground, resulting in her gruesome death.

Per Michael's message, Hurley ignited the last of the
dynamite on the *Black Rock*, which destroyed the ship and
prevented the destruction of the Ajira plane.

Jack and Rousseau
test-ignited
dynamite in a plan
to halt the Others.
Sayid and Bernard
ignite two of three
dynamite traps
on the beach,
resulting in the
death of seven
Others.

EDDIE COLBURN

▶ **CONNECTION:** Undercover police officer; infiltrated commune in which John Locke was a member

Edward "Eddie" Colburn was an undercover police officer in the Humboldt County, California Sheriff's Department. He was investigating a local commune that was under suspicion of growing and distributing marijuana. Colburn made contact with commune resident John Locke that allowed him to infiltrate the group and collect first-hand evidence.

THE SET-UP

Colburn connected with Locke while posing as a young man hitchhiking to Eureka for timber-cutting work. Locke picked him up on a rural road and offered to drive him to Bridgeville. After a brief conversation, Sheriff Williams pulled them over for a broken tail light. When the officer threatened to ticket Locke for picking up a hitchhiker, Eddie piped up that John was his uncle and he had called him for help. That lie helped John trust the young man enough to bring him onto the commune's property.

Once inside the gated private property, John showed Eddie the sweat lodge and introduced him to the community founders, Mike and Jan. They welcomed and introduced Eddie to the entire family, for which Eddie seemed to show sincere gratitude to John for facilitating.

Eddie posed as a hitchhiker to ensnare John.

GERONIMO JACKSON ✚

The day John picked him up, Eddie was wearing a vintage Geronimo Jackson band T-shirt that belonged to his father.

HUMBOLDT COUNTY **SHERIFF**

NAME	EDWARD F. COLBURN

SIGNATURE

Officer   84023
RANK   EMPLOYEE #

LOS ANGELES SHERIFF

During his stay, Eddie's friendship with John deepened. He once joked that everyone at the commune was looking for a daddy; a joke that Locke didn't appreciate. Frustrated, Eddie took the opportunity to ask John about secrets—both personal ones and physical—like what was behind the closed doors of the greenhouse. He told John he wanted to assist with whatever they planned to blow up with the fertilizer inside the greenhouse. John laughed and said he would talk to Mike and Jan. However, the couple discovered through a background check that Eddie was a cop.

John took Eddie out for a morning deer hunt to force him to tell the truth about the sting operation. With a gun pointed at him, Eddie admitted he had intentionally targeted John because they determined he had no criminal record, was new to the commune, and would be amenable to coercion. Eddie backed away from Locke unconcerned about being shot because he knew Locke was a good man who didn't have it in him to kill or be a hunter. Correct in his assessment, Eddie slipped safely into the woods and joined his officers who were arresting Mike and Jan.

EDMUND BURKE

▶ **CONNECTION:** Ex-husband of Juliet Burke and her boss at Miami Central University

Edmund Burke was the ex-husband of Juliet Burke. Professionally, he was also her colleague at the Miami Central University Medical Research Laboratory. Although the reasons for their divorce were never revealed, their personal problems carried over into their professional relationship. Arrogant and smug, Edmund kept Juliet under his thumb by threatening to expose the possible moral and legal implications of the "cutting edge" fertility research she used on her sister. He also implied that Juliet should collaborate with him on the research because his exemplary reputation would add credence to her work and bring them both industry acclaim.

Richard Alpert, working under the auspices of Mittelos BioScience, attempted to recruit Juliet in order to bring her fertility expertise to their Portland-based research group, but she declined citing that Edmund would never allow her to leave. Offhandedly, she remarked the only way she could leave was if "he was hit by a bus." Later that day, she revealed to Edmund that her research had resulted in a pregnancy for her sister. Moments later, Edmund was hit by a bus and killed.

EDWARD MARS

"Where is she?"

▶ **CONNECTION:** U.S. Marshal in charge of escorting Kate Austen back home

Edward Mars was the U.S. Marshal assigned with tracking down fugitive Kate Austen for the murder of her father, Wayne Jansen. Mars was relentlessly dogged in his pursuit of Austen and relished the fact that even if she eluded him, he was always hot on her trail. Mars personally escorted Kate back to the United States on Oceanic flight 815. He carried a Halliburton case with four guns onto the plane. When the plane hit turbulence, Mars was knocked unconscious by dislodged luggage. In the crash, his body was impaled by a piece of metal. Jack removed the metal and stitched up the cut, but it wasn't enough to stave off a deadly infection and his residual internal bleeding. Aware he was dying slowly and painfully, Mars asked to speak to Kate one last time. Curiously, he asked what favor she wanted from him. She wanted Mullen to get his reward money. Incredulous, he asked if she would shoot him. She walked away, but Sawyer obliged and missed his heart. Jack then took pity and put Mars out of his misery. Several days later, Kate and Jack dug up his body to retrieve the Halliburton keys.

WHAT'S IN A NAME? ➕

The JRM-2 Mars was the largest flying boat ever put into production. Five were used by the US Navy to ferry cargo between the Pacific Island and Hawaii. In 1950, one of those planes called the Marshall Mars burned up from an engine fire; its crew evacuated safely.

TIME ON ISLAND ➕
POST-OCEANIC: 3 days

THE CHASE

Kate was apprehended at a Missouri bus station by Mars the same night of the murder.

En route to her arraignment, Mars swerved to avoid a black horse in the road and crashed.

Mars put Diane Jansen under 24-hour surveillance. Kate used Cassidy Phillips as a decoy to see what Mars had set up.

Kate called Mars several times on Catholic holy days. She asked him to stop the chase when she married Kevin Callis. He refused and she ran.

Mars tempted Kate with Tom's toy plane as bait in a New Mexico safety deposit box.

Mars caught Kate again in Australia with help from Ray Mullen.

EKO, SEE PAGE 120

THE ELIZABETH

▶ **CONNECTION:** Sailboat given to Desmond Hume by Elizabeth "Libby" Smith

Owned by David Smith and named after his wife Elizabeth "Libby" Smith, the *Elizabeth* was a sailboat that experienced quite a bit of bad luck. As an avid sailor, David bought the Newport Beach, CA-based yacht with the intention of sailing it to the Mediterranean, but he died before he could embark on the trip. Libby and Desmond Hume's chance encounter in a coffee shop revealed Desmond's intention to enter a sailing race around the world in order to prove his worth to his girlfriend's father, Charles Widmore. Moved by his romanticism, Libby handed the boat over to him and Desmond set sail soon after.

During a large storm at sea, the *Elizabeth* was thrown off course and ran aground at the island. Desmond was found by Kelvin Inman and brought to the Swan station, where he remained trapped for years in service to the button protocol. During that same time, Inman kept the *Elizabeth* secretly moored in a cove and made repairs to it in hopes of escaping the island. When Desmond finally left the hatch, he confronted Kelvin and accidentally killed him.

In reality, the *Elizabeth* was anchored in a cove where it remained until Sawyer and Kate were tasked by the Man in Black to retrieve it so they could collect the candidates and sail it to Hydra island together. Led by Sawyer, the group of Kate, Jack, Lapidus, Hurley, Sun and Claire evaded the Man in Black and journeyed to the smaller island together—until Jack second-guessed his decision and jumped off the boat to return to the main island.

Sawyer moored the sailboat about 100 yards off the Hydra beach and later it was anchored near the cliffs for the Man in Black's getaway. After his death, though, Sawyer and Kate sailed it back to Hydra island just in time to get on the repaired Ajira plane.

ELIZABETH MOWEE
NEWPORT BEACH

EKO

FACTS & FIGURES
Time On The Island

POST-OCEANIC: 72 days

Family: Yemi (brother)

The Nigerian man known as Eko lived a life that was a study in contrasts. As an impoverished young boy in Africa, Eko had nothing to call his own, yet he was willing to steal, cheat or lie to provide for his beloved little brother, Yemi. While the church called those things sins, for Eko they were necessary tools required to survive streets run by ruthless guerilla fighters and drug lords. Yet when faced with the choice of entering a life of violence as a militia member so that his brother could be free, Eko took the darker path so Yemi could follow the light.

Eko grew up to be a vicious drug lord, while Yemi became a pious priest. Isolated in a violent existence, Eko forgot his humanity and ignored his bond with Yemi when he forced his younger brother to help him smuggle heroin on missionary planes. Initially Yemi would have none of his older brother's plan, and was disgusted by the monster he had turned into. However, Eko threatened Yemi's church so a deal was made. Having compromised the one person he had loved most in the world not only condemned Eko's soul but also cost him his brother. When the authorities showed up to stop the plane, Yemi was caught in the crossfire. His lifeless body was thrown into the plane, while Eko was left on the tarmac to suffer the consequences of his terrible choices.

MAN OF THE CLOTH

Because he wore a priest's collar, the soldiers at the airfield thought Eko was a legitimate man of God so they returned him to Yemi's church. Remorseful about what he had done to his brother, Eko took over the church and said his brother had been called away to an emergency in the south. He didn't take the job seriously until he desecrated the church by murdering three drug thugs inside. Horrified, he began a lengthy journey of repentance through his work with the church that continued until his death.

▶   *Eko went to London to study and adopted the name of Father Tunde. After that, he ran a small parish in England, where he heard the moving confession of a little boy who killed a dog to protect his sister.*

▶   *As a pastor in Australia, Eko was assigned by the diocese to investigate the reported miraculous resurrection of Charlotte Malkin.*

▶   *Eko's first official act as a priest on the island was to baptize Aaron and Claire.*

▶   *To make right what he did to Yemi's church, Eko drafted Charlie to help him frame out a replacement church by the beach. It was never finished.*

THE SMOKE MONSTER'S JUDGEMENT

After the smoke monster looked inside of Eko, it knew that manifesting as Yemi would allow it to find a way to get rid of a potentially dangerous adversary it did not want on the island, and so it lured him to his fate.

▶   *Injured by the Hatch implosion, Eko was in a coma for two days when he was awakened by Yemi as he snapped open a lighter and told him it was his time to be judged. In the next instant, Eko's tent went up in flames but he was saved by his friends.*

▶   *Bleeding and weakened, Eko hiked out into the jungle as the smoke monster manifested along the way in its natural form, as the drug dealers Eko killed, the altar boy Daniel, and finally, as Yemi.*

▶   *Unhappy that Eko remained defiant in his confession to Yemi, the smoke Monster attacked Eko as it slammed him into trees and dropped him to the ground.*

▶   *Eko's last words to Locke, Sayid, Nikki, Paulo and Desmond were a whispered "You're next." All of them, except for Desmond, died.*

Yemi retrieved Eko's silver necklace from the ground when his brother was conscripted into the militia. He wore it always to remind him of his brother. On the island, Eko found it on Yemi's body and placed it back on his own neck. When he faced the smoke monster in Yemi's guise, he offered the necklace back.

" Don't mistake coincidence for fate. "

EKO'S ISLAND CONNECTIONS

ANA LUCIA CORTEZ

Eko's fellow tailie, she cried in his arms in a rare moment of vulnerability. Eko prevented Sayid from shooting Ana Lucia after she shot Shannon. He comforted her again as she felt ostracized by the survivors for what she did. When Ana and Libby were killed, Eko chose not to attend their funeral and mourned in his own way.

CHARLIE PACE

Eko demanded Charlie be his guide to the drug smugglers' plane, where they found Yemi's body and had an encounter with the smoke monster. Impressed by Eko, Charlie became his acolyte and helped him build a church. They also worked together to try to blow their way into the Swan to hit the button. After the Hatch blew, Charlie helped John find Eko.

EKO AND LOCKE

Eko arrived in Locke's life just as he began to have a crisis of faith about pressing the button in the Swan. While they were both men of faith, Eko showed little interest in the Hatch or the computer until he had a dream that told him to help Locke. Eko forced John to take him to the question mark on his blast map door sketch. More dreams led them to find the Pearl station under the drug plane fuselage. This station's orientation film hinted at the reason for the button protocol and it destroyed Locke's faith in the island. However, Eko was ready to step in during his crisis of faith and moved into the Hatch to take John's shifts. The two men battled over the computer, as Locke wanted to destroy it. Their fight escalated when Desmond and Locke locked Eko out of the Hatch. It triggered a system failure, which restored John's faith and caused Desmond to trigger the fail-safe key to discharge the electromagnetic build-up. Afterwards, Locke helped track a severely injured Eko to the polar bear cave and brought him back to camp. It was John who found a broken Eko after his smoke monster ordeal.

"Things I need to remember."

THE JESUS STICK

As self-imposed penance for killing an Other with a rock, Eko remained silent for 40 days and selected a large branch from a bush on the beach that he turned into a walking stick. At the top of the stick, he carved scriptures with a piece of metal. Noticing the scripture, Charlie Pace dubbed it Eko's "Jesus stick."

INSCRIPTIONS	23 PSALM	"HATETH"	TITUS 3	LUKE
	4:8:15:16:23:42	COLOSIANS [sic]	A cross	PSALM 144
	JOHN 3:05	GEN 13:14	REVELATIONS 5:3	T:4
	LIFT UP YOUR EYES AND LOOK NORTH	ROM 6:12	9:22	
		ACTS 4:12	HAB 1:3	

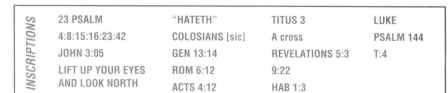

VISIONS OF YEMI

Yemi proved to be an extremely potent motivator for Eko, and his dead brother seemed to reach out from the grave to send him messages through several different conduits:

Charlotte Malkin found Eko at the Sydney Airport where she related that she had seen Yemi in the between places and he had asked her to tell Eko to have faith.

In a dream, both Ana Lucia and Yemi told Eko that he needed to help John, who had lost his way. In particular, Yemi said Eko must make John take him to the question mark.

John Locke dreamed that he was Eko and Yemi took him to the top of the cliff where the drug plane was perched. When he woke up, Eko seemed to know what John saw.

PSALM 23

The 23rd Psalm is a scripture passage that resonated with Eko as he carved it on his stick and recited it as he and Charlie burned the drug plane with Yemi's body inside. It reflects the penitent path that Eko sought in his own life to make right all of his many sins. Eko made several errors as he recited it, as noted below.

The Lord is my shepherd; I shall not want.

He maketh me to lie down in green pastures.

He leadeth me beside the still waters.

He restoreth my soul.

He leadeth me in paths of righteousness for His name's sake.

Yea, though I walk through the shadow [sic] of the valley [sic] of death,

I fear no evil: for thou art with me;

Thy rod, thy staff, they [sic] comfort me.

Thou preparest a table before me in the presence of mine enemies:

Thou anointest my head with oil;

My cup runneth over.

Surely goodness and mercy shall follow me all the days of my life,

And I will dwell in the house of the Lord forever. Amen.

THE ELIZABETH, SEE PAGE 119

ELOISE HAWKING

"Sacrifice? Don't you talk to me about sacrifice, Charles. I had to send my son back to the island, knowing full well that --"

Eloise was one of the select few to lead the Others. Whether she was born on the island or came to it in some other fashion was unknown, but she proved her leadership abilities at the tender age of 17 during the Jughead crisis. When she was 40, an unexpected and fatal encounter guided the actions she took for the rest of her life.

AN UNAVOIDABLE FATE

By the '70s, Eloise was the leader and worked closely with Charles Widmore and Richard Alpert when it came to defending the island against outside threats. However, the defining moment of Eloise's existence happened in 1977 when she unknowingly shot and killed her own time-travelling son, Daniel Faraday. As if that wasn't tragic enough, 40-year-old Eloise still had to give birth and raise Daniel with the knowledge of his

Eloise met Penelope Widmore after Desmond was shot.

unavoidable death at her hands. She understood that the universe would unfold as it was destined, so she took on the mantle of "temporal policewoman" and made sure that all the players were in place for the events to happen as they should.

Eloise relocated to Essex, Massachusetts where she gave birth to Daniel. Knowing that he was destined to be a great scientific mind she gave him the last name of Faraday, in honor of English physicist Michael Faraday. The new last name also gave her son some anonymity should Charles ever look for him.

Fully aware of her son's fate, Eloise chose to raise her son with a cold, authoritarian air. Perhaps to save herself the pain of being too attached to Daniel, she maintained a rigid focus and dissuaded him from wasting any time with pursuits outside of science and math.

"For the first time in a long time, I don't know what's going to happen next."

1977

1954

> ## " Destiny means that if one has a special gift, then it must be nurtured. "

FAMILY CONNECTIONS

Daniel grew up and followed his path by becoming the youngest doctorate to graduate from Oxford. At his graduation Eloise was surprised to hear that he had been given a $1.5 million grant from Charles Widmore; proof that Daniel's father had finally tracked him down. After Daniel was thrown out of Oxford, Eloise learned that Charles had visited their son and offered him a job on the *Kahana* science team. Daniel declined due to his temporal displacement problems, but Eloise told him he needed to take the job as it would make him better, as well as make her proud. Inside, she also knew it was his death sentence.

The day after Ajira flight 316 departed, Eloise met Charles Widmore face-to-face at the hospital where Desmond was treated for his gunshot wound. She suggested he talk to Penny and was livid when he said he had sacrificed relationships with her and Daniel for the island. Eloise smacked him across the face and walked away in disgust.

PAYING HOMAGE ✛
*Eloise Hawking's surname is in homage to the great British theoretical physicist Stephen Hawking, who wrote the seminal popular science book, **A Brief History of Time**. The modern scientific classic distilled some of the most complicated scientific questions, like the nature of time, into layman's language.*

ISLAND TIMELINE

1954 (Age 17):
Met Daniel and his science team. While holding them at gunpoint, she made Daniel disable the Jughead bomb.

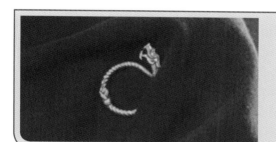

OUROBOROS ✛
Eloise wore a golden broach pin called an ouroboros, an ancient symbol of eternal cyclicality. Its origins date back to hieroglyphs found in a sarcophagus chamber of the Pyramid of Unas in 2300 BC. The traditional symbol consists of either a dragon or a serpent with its tail in its mouth to create an infinity circle.

TEMPORAL POLICEWOMAN

Outside of influencing Daniel, Eloise continued to position herself in places that would help motivate some of the key future island players, like Desmond, in the right directions. She took a job as a salesperson at the antique store where Des was supposed to purchase an engagement ring for Penny. When he attempted to purchase one, Hawking demanded he give it back. She then explained his future in detail and gave him a lesson in the irrevocable nature of fate.

As an off-island Other, Eloise eventually took a position as the keeper of the Lamp Post station so she could help Ben Linus get the Oceanic Six back to the island. She specifically tasked Linus and Jack with reproducing the elements of their Oceanic flight as closely as possible to ensure success.

DANIEL'S JOURNAL ✛
In 1977 after Eloise killed Daniel, she looked through his leather journal and was thrown by the opening dedication made in her own handwriting: "Daniel, No matter what, remember I will always love you. Mother." The journal was a gift to him from her informed future self as a graduation present. She knew it would hold all of his important theories and formulas about time travel.

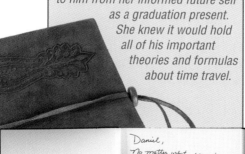

1977 (Age 40):
Shot Daniel when he invaded the Others' camp and demanded to talk to her. His dying breath revealed him to be her son from the future.

1978 (Age 41):
Eloise left the island to give birth to her baby. Leadership of the Others transferred to the father of her child, Charles Widmore.

Eloise predicted the crushing fate of the man in the red shoes.

Charlie Pace's guitar

Danielle's music box

The album cover of Geronimo Jackson's album, "Magna Carta"

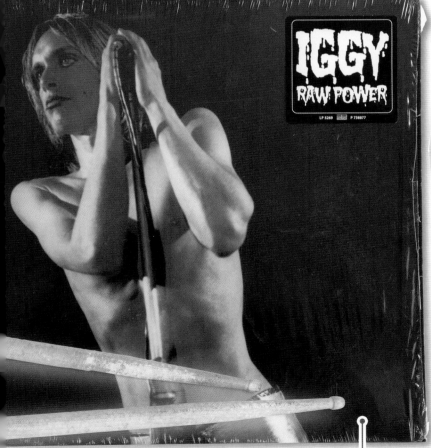

After Juliet's death, Sawyer mourned while listening to the song "Search and Destroy" by the Stooges.

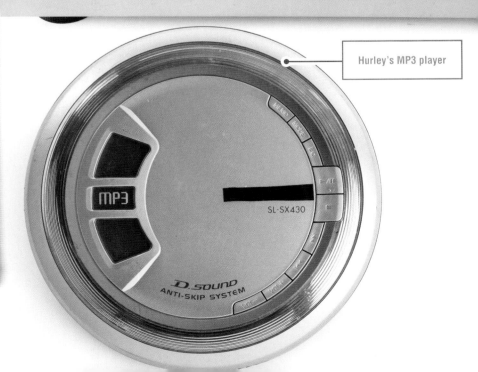

Hurley's MP3 player

ELSA

▶ **CONNECTION:** Hired by the "economist" to kill Sayid Jarrah

A secret assassin who worked for a mysterious individual known only as "the economist," Elsa was born and based in Germany. Beautiful, blonde and extremely savvy at her profession, she was assigned to execute fellow assassin Sayid Jarrah and his boss, Benjamin Linus.

Elsa first met Jarrah in a Berlin café. The pair struck up a conversation and Elsa explained that she worked as a personal shopper for an international economist who specialized in emerging markets. Elsa was unaware, though, that Sayid had initiated contact because her boss was his next target.

> **BY THE NUMBERS**
> *When Sayid suggested they go to dinner, Elsa pointed on a map to the restaurant of choice and suggested a meeting time of **8** p.m.*

The pair dated for several weeks with the ulterior motive to gain confidences for the information needed to kill their employers. Elsa went so far as to engage in a sexual relationship with Sayid. Later, Sayid warned her to leave town as something was about to happen to her employer. Elsa took the opportunity to shoot Sayid in the shoulder and called her boss. Drawn back to Sayid by the sound of a crash, Elsa was shot square in the chest twice by his own hidden gun.

> **CONNECTIONS**
> *A bracelet worn by Naomi Dorrit served to remind Sayid of the bracelet worn by Elsa. Sayid was present for the death of both women and was the person to close their eyes after they expired. Two of Sayid's lovers died of a gunshot wound to the chest: Elsa and Shannon Rutherford.*

EMEKA

▶ **CONNECTION:** Leader of Nigerian militia; killed by Eko

A Nigerian warlord who terrorized the village where Yemi's church was located, Emeka regularly shook down the residents in exchange for "protection." Whether it was taking much-needed Red Cross vaccinations or shooting blind women selling Virgin Mary statues, he routinely proved to be a horrible individual. Eko refused to bow to the thug, so Emeka gathered his men and attempted to cut off Eko's hands. Eko wiped out the henchmen and then drove a machete into Emeka's skull. Later on the island, Emeka haunted Eko's conscience.

EMILY ANNABETH LOCKE

▶ **CONNECTION:** Mother of John Locke

The mother of John Locke, Emily's life was defined by a string of poor choices that led her down a path of discontent and mental illness. A rebellious 15-year-old teen in the '50s, Emily blatantly ignored her mother's rules and started dating an older man named Anthony Cooper. After a quarrel with her mother one evening, Emily fled the house and was hit by a passing car.

At the hospital, Emily revealed that she was six months pregnant. Born prematurely, Emily named her baby John but she fled the hospital and Mrs. Locke, her mother, forfeited her daughter's parental rights.

In adulthood, Emily was diagnosed with a form of schizophrenia that led to a stay at Santa Rosa Mental Health Institute. In the early '90s, Cooper talked Emily into tracking down John so he could con his son out of his biologically matched kidney. Emily needed the money, so she agreed to help out her former lover. Emily told John that he didn't have a father because he was immaculately conceived. Later, John hired a private detective who confirmed their biological link and provided details about his father's whereabouts. After the kidney transplant, Emily explained the ruse that she and Anthony Cooper had perpetrated on their son. A devastated John Locke never saw his mother again.

> **MOTHER ISSUES**
> *John Locke and Ben Linus had mothers named Emily and both men were greatly impacted by the fact that they were not raised by them. John was abandoned by his mother, while Ben's mother died from complications during his birth.*
>
> *According to Emily's medical records, she received her medications from Skadden's Pharmacy, the same pharmacy used by Jack Shephard to get his Clonazepam.*

EMILY LINUS

▶ **CONNECTION:** Mother of Benjamin Linus; wife of Roger Linus

During the seventh month of her pregnancy with Ben, Emily went into premature labor while hiking with her husband in Portland, Oregon. Without access to medical care, Roger delivered his son but Emily continued to hemorrhage. Roger helped his wife and newborn child to the main road and flagged down passing motorists Horace Goodspeed and his friend Olivia, but it was too late. Her last words to Roger were to name the baby Benjamin.

As a youth living with the DHARMA Initiative, Ben remained haunted by his mother. She appeared in a vision outside his window and in the jungle on the Others' side of the sonar fence. She stopped Ben from crossing, saying, "It's not time yet, Benjamin."

ESSAM TAZIR

▶ **CONNECTION:** Former friend of Sayid Jarrah

The former University of Cairo roommate of Sayid Jarrah, Essam was widowed when his wife was killed by a U.S. bomb in a civilian area of Iraq. Bitter about his loss, Tazir joined a terrorist group in Sydney that was working remotely to cause insurgent violence in Iraq. Reunited with Sayid in Australia, Tazir revealed that he was selected to be a suicide bomber but he believed this course of action conflicted with the peaceful tenets of his Islamic faith. However, Essam did not know that Sayid was working as a coerced mole in an effort to infiltrate the group. Sayid wanted to talk his friend out of the plan, but was forced by the CIA to do the opposite. At the last moment, Sayid told him to flee, but a betrayed Tazir committed suicide.

ETHAN ROM " Charlie, I want her back. "

▶ **CONNECTION:** Member of the Others; infiltrated the survivors' beach camp

Born Ethan Goodspeed in 1977, he was the son of Horace and Amy Goodspeed. As a two-day-old infant, Ethan was taken off the island when the women and children of DHARMA were evacuated prior to the Incident. However, because his father ran the island Initiative operations, he and his mother returned soon after. Much like Benjamin Linus, young Ethan was drawn to the native people on the island and yearned to be part of their community. He reached out to their leader Charles Widmore and was told that he would be welcome if, in exchange as a DHARMA insider, he helped carry out elements of the Purge. When Ethan's people were all dead, including his parents, the young boy changed his name from Goodspeed to Rom and officially became one of "them."

AS AN OTHER

While still young, Ethan proved to be an enthusiastic recruit who was well-liked by Widmore. In 1988 Charles even sent Rom and Linus out to kill the shipwrecked French woman, Danielle Rousseau and her days-old baby girl. Yet again displaying a chilling enthusiasm for Widmore's dark bidding, Ethan offered to kill them both when Ben seemed to hesitate. However, Linus took charge, and spared the Rousseaus' lives. Ethan avoided Widmore's wrath when Ben took full responsibility for what happened in one of his first power struggles with Charles.

Per Ben's orders, Ethan assimilated into the survivors' camp remarkably well.

For the next decade, Ethan grew up on the island and was one of Widmore's trusted few allowed to travel on and off the island for schooling and specific recruiting missions. Rom eventually trained as a surgeon and assisted in the ongoing research to solve his people's fertility and childbirth issues. When Widmore was banished and Linus took over leadership of the Others, Ethan didn't have any problems with lingering loyalty because his overall commitment was to the well-being of the Others.

One of Ethan's most important recruiting efforts was Juliet Burke. When Richard Alpert contacted Juliet with a formal job offer under the ruse of the Others' front business, Mittelos Bioscience, Rom joined him at the meeting to persuade her to help them. When she eventually agreed, it was Ethan who administered the sedative for her trip, and later monitored her on the submarine headed to the island. Rom later worked side-by-side with Juliet as a surgeon trying to bring an Other pregnancy to full term.

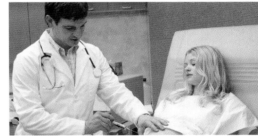
WORD PLAY...
Ethan Rom is an anagram for Other Man, which is exactly what he became after the Purge.

Ethan was often used by Ben to scout out new arrivals or investigate odd occurrences on the island to gauge their impact. When the Nigerian drug plane crashed on the island in 2001, Rom was dispatched and came upon an injured, time-jumping John Locke. Ethan was ready to kill him, but another jump prevented that. Three years later when Oceanic 815 broke up in the sky above the island, Ben quickly assigned Ethan to head out to the fuselage crash site and pose as a survivor. He was to listen, learn and compile a list of survivors in three days; a task he failed to complete.

CONNECTION WITH CLAIRE

Although Ethan observed everyone, Claire became his immediate focus. Having lost his own wife and child in a failed island delivery, Rom became obsessed with bringing new life into the Others' fold. He took a shine to Claire, and started administering their island vaccine to Claire under the cover of dark. About 15 days post-crash, Claire caught him and it triggered Hurley's manifest project. Rom knew his cover would be blown so he kidnapped Claire and Charlie. When Jack followed, Ethan became angry and violent and put him down with a warning to stay away. He then hung Charlie from a vine to reiterate his threat.

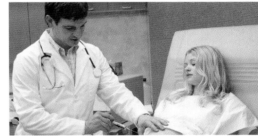
Ethan administered shots to Claire on a regular basis when she was held captive at the Staff.

After the kidnapping, a much gentler Ethan worked with Claire at the Staff station. He kept her drugged and was able to persuade her addled mind that she wanted the Others to have her baby. He told her she couldn't be saved but he would take good care of her child. Without permission he allowed her to go outside for some air, which opened the door for Alex Rousseau to help her escape.

Incensed, Ethan went off the deep end and threatened to kill a survivor every day unless they returned Claire to him. As proof of his word, he murdered Scott. Ethan's fixation with Claire tempered his common sense and he was captured in a trap. He was subdued by Jack while Locke hoped to interrogate him for information but Charlie, fueled by a need for revenge, unloaded six bullets into Rom.

EVELYN

▶ **CONNECTION: Nurse for Lara Chang**

Miles Straume's mother, Lara Chang (wife to Dr. Pierre Chang), became housebound during Miles' teenage years due to a severe illness. Evelyn was the nurse who cared for Lara in her Encino apartment, number 7. This was the same home that Miles and his mother moved into when he was a child, years after they both left the island. Evelyn was shocked to see Miles visit his mother, as he hadn't in a long time.

FALAH

▶ **CONNECTION: Tortured by Sayid Jarrah**

Falah was a Shiite terrorist suspect who was interrogated and tortured by Sayid Jarrah in an Iraqi prison. The suspect was accused of detonating a bomb that killed two men at the Baathist headquarters. Sayid worked him over to get a confession, which included the threat of chopping off the man's hands instead of killing him.

FATHER CHUCK

▶ **CONNECTION: Priest who presided at Anthony Cooper's funeral**

A Christian denomination priest, Father Chuck performed the funeral service at the unknowingly fake gravesite of Anthony Cooper. Only John Locke and his girlfriend Helen Norwood attended. At the end, the priest asked John if there was anything he wanted to say, to which he replied, "I forgive you."

FATHER SUÁREZ

▶ **CONNECTION: Catholic priest in Tenerife prison**

Father Suárez was a strict man of the cloth who made his own decisions about absolution. When Richard Alpert was imprisoned in 1867 for murder, Father Suárez visited him in his prison cell for his confession. A seemingly kind soul who brought Alpert food, Father Suárez's demeanor changed drastically once he learned that the death was merely an accident. Upon hearing Alpert's declaration, Suárez decided he would not absolve him of the sin. Suárez elaborated that Alpert would have to suffer a form of penance to win back the grace of God. He cruelly added that there would be no time for such a thing, as Alpert was to be hung the next day.

Absolution wasn't the only thing on Father Suárez's mind. Having realized that Alpert was reading an English version of the Bible, he determined that Alpert could become a profitable commodity. The next morning, Officer Jonas Whitfield, on behalf of Captain Magnus Hanso, purchased Alpert from Suárez. Richard would soon join the other slave workers onboard the *Black Rock* as it sailed to the New World.

CLARK FINNEY

▶ **CONNECTION: Attorney for Michael Dawson's custody case**

Michael Dawson hired Finney, a budget lawyer, to represent him in a custody case against Susan Porter and her new husband, Brian Porter. Finney informed his client that Susan wanted Michael to relinquish his parental rights so Brian could legally adopt Walt. When Michael asked to file an injunction to keep Susan in town, Finney laid it out bluntly that a fight in court was going to cost a great deal of money and asked if he was prepared to embark upon a "David vs. Goliath" war. Later in a face-to-face meeting with their lawyers, Susan and her lawyer baited Michael into anger, which Finney tried to temper, but it didn't end well.

This orange, fish-shaped food was created by DHARMA's Hydra island scientists and given to the research polar bears as a reward for their correct use of the cage feeding mechanism. When the correct elements were pressed, one biscuit, some grain and water would be dumped via a chute into the cage.

FISH BISCUITS

After Sawyer was imprisoned in one of the cages, he spent quite some time figuring out how the elements worked and was eventually successful. Tom Friendly teased Sawyer that it only took the bears two hours to figure out the puzzle. During the five days that Sawyer and Kate were held captive in the cages by the Others, the biscuits were an important source of sustenance for them.

THE TEACHINGS OF SKINNER
The food reward mechanism that the DHARMA scientists used is an example of a rather extreme experiment to determine animal cognition, or the mental abilities of a non-human animal. The setup of the puzzle, cage and reward system is in line with the scientific methodology of B. F. Skinner, the father of experimental behavior analysis, or radical behaviorism—the science that inspired the DeGroots, driving their creation of the DHARMA Initiative.

■ The button in the Hydra cage that Sawyer pushed to get the fish biscuit

■ Once Sawyer figured out the puzzle, the machine would spit out a fish biscuit as a reward.

THE FLAME

The fourth of six DHARMA Initiative stations on the island, the Flame was their communications hub. Through an intricate cable system it connected all the stations on the island and was outfitted for off-island communication. For a period of time, Stuart Radzinsky manned the Flame. After the Purge, Mikhail Bakunin was assigned there by the Others to monitor all the island stations and to communicate with the Others in the outside world.

HISTORY

The DHARMA Initiative built the Flame in the early 1970s; it was one of the first built so they could establish necessary contact with the outside world as their operations grew on the island. Radzinsky both resided and worked in this station in the '70s. He created the blueprints and a scale model of the Swan during his tenure there. He also noted the location of the Flame on the blast door map.

In 1977 when the Oceanic survivors returned to the island, Jin had Radzinsky monitor all the stations for an airplane that might have flown overhead. Instead they discovered a perimeter breach, which Jin determined to be Sayid. He was placed in the station's pantry until Sawyer, posing as LaFleur, escorted him to the barracks brig.

BY THE NUMBERS ✛
*The Flame's small water tower is labelled **4**.*

" *There's something I need to show you.* "

— Spoken by Ben to Juliet

After the Purge, Mikhail operated the Flame on behalf of the Others. He moved in with his cat, Nadia, and maintained the livestock and his personal garden. As part of his duties, he would use communications equipment to create files on anyone Benjamin Linus requested, such as Juliet Burke's sister Rachel Carlson and the flight 815 survivors. He also patched video feeds to the island, such as outside news reports on the disappearance of Oceanic 815 and live video via Richard Alpert of Rachel and her son Julian in Acadia Park, Florida.

THE STATION LAYOUT

A single-story structure, the Flame was painted blue and featured a large satellite dish on its roof for off-island communication. Outside, there were pens for cows and horses, as well as alarm towers in several spots used for warning alerts in case of Hostile attacks or other emergencies. Inside, there was a large living space and kitchen. Most notable was the anteroom that featured a large bank of five black-and-white monitors connected to a computer display monitor. The communication center of the station received video feeds from surveillance cameras on the island, as well as external feeds from the outside world. On another wall were the electronics that operated the system, including reel-to-reel machines for recording data and large mainframe computers of the '70s era which were state-of-the art at the time. The video wall could be disassembled when necessary so as not to reveal too much about the capabilities of the station to intruders. After he was seen in the Pearl via a video feed, Bakunin took down the video wall. Emergency functions were instead routed to the faux chess computer.

In the hidden basement, there were manuals and schematics for all of the operations that took place in the Flame, like the pallet drop protocols, and for the other stations. Sayid took some of the schematics for future use. It was also rigged with packets of C-4 that were connected to the Flame's main operations computer as a fail-safe in the case of a Hostile insurgence.

FLAME OPERATIONS COMPUTER

Seemingly an old-school computer loaded with basic chess software, in reality it was the main operations computer coded to a manual override system that allowed a user to perform the basic communication functions of the station.

CHECKMATE

If a checkmate was achieved by the user, the computer brought up a video of Dr. Pierre Chang who revealed the codes to perform manual overrides:

Code 2-4 = Pallet drop

Code 3-2 = Station uplink

Code 3-8 = Mainland communication (the satellite was down in 2004)

Code 5-6 = Sonar access (sonar was inoperable in 2004)

Code 7-7 = Hostile incursion protocol (time-delayed C-4 trigger)

FLORENCE

▶ **CONNECTION:** Foster mother of John Locke; introduced Locke to Richard Alpert

Florence took responsibility for the young John Locke after he was given up for adoption by his birth mother. Florence was protective of John, but not overly affectionate with him. When John was 5 years old, Florence welcomed Richard Alpert into their home to conduct a test to see if John had the capability to earn admission into his special school. Florence sternly asked John to be on his best behavior for Alpert and his questions. After he left the house in a disappointed rush, a clearly frustrated and exasperated Florence asked John what he did to earn such a reaction.

FRAINEY

▶ **CONNECTION:** Private investigator hired by John Locke

When a strange woman named Emily approached John Locke and claimed to be his mother, he hired a private investigator to look into her story. Frainey told Locke what he had discovered with an air of caution. Hair samples taken from Emily's car proved with 99 percent accuracy that she was his biological mother. Frainey's work also uncovered that she had been institutionalized a few times with a form of schizophrenia. Remarkably, Frainey's work had also unearthed that Emily spent time at the Santa Rosa Mental Heath Institute, where Locke's future friend on the island, Hugo "Hurley" Reyes, had also been.

Frainey was uncertain about telling Locke the name and address of his biological father, Anthony Cooper. In Frainey's past experience, he knew that in cases where the parent may not even have known he had a child, it often had an unhappy ending. Sadly, Locke ignored the investigator's advice and used the information to introduce himself to his father, which lead to unfortunate consequences for Locke in the future.

FRANCINE

▶ **CONNECTION:** Attended the same anger management class as John Locke

Francine was a young woman who was part of the same therapy group as John Locke in Tustin, California. She had issues with her alcoholic mother stealing money from her for booze. Locke mocked her "pain" when compared to his mother abandoning him at birth and his father "stealing" his kidney.

"You want your $30 back? I want my kidney back!"
— Spoken by Locke to the group

FRANCIS HEATHERTON

▶ **CONNECTION:** Father of Lucy Heatherton, who dated Charlie Pace

Francis Heatherton was the owner of the Heatherton Corporation, a successful U.K. office supplies company, and the father of Lucy Heatherton, who briefly dated Charlie Pace. A widower, Heatherton lived with his daughter in a large house in Knightsbridge, where he housed his collection of personal effects from great leaders of the empire, like Winston Churchill's cigarette case. He and his daughter hosted Charlie for dinner at their home and Heatherton admitted he had his own band as a young man called Protestant Reformation. When Charlie revealed Drive Shaft was in retirement, Lucy's father offered him a job selling paper copiers. He even told Charlie's first client to buy two copiers to boost the young man's selling confidence. Unfortunately, Charlie was discovered with Heatherton's valuable case on him, which got him fired and earned him Lucy's scorn.

FRANK DUCKETT

▶ **CONNECTION:** Killed by Sawyer after being duped by Hibbs

An American expatriate in Australia, Frank Duckett ran a sweet shrimp stand out of a truck near Sydney. His menu was limited: shrimp cooked in either hot or mild sauce.

Back in the U.S., Duckett fell into deep debt with a confidence man named Hibbs. Fearing reprisal, he fled and settled overseas. When Hibbs finally got a lead on Duckett's location, he crafted an elaborate story to trick James "Sawyer" Ford into carrying out his dirty work. Hibbs told Sawyer that Duckett was actually Frank Sawyer, the man who worked a romance angle on his mother and swindled his father out of their savings. The con was the impetus for his parents' murder-suicide.

> **WHISPERS** ⊞
> *As James raced through the jungle to find a boar, he heard jungle whispers that resembled the voice of Frank Duckett uttering his last words.*

Sawyer traveled to Australia to exact his revenge. He found Duckett's truck and ordered a plate of shrimp with hot sauce. As Duckett cooked and engaged in small talk about the South, Sawyer held his gun below the counter and tried to convince himself to pull the trigger. But by the time Duckett turned around to hand him the order, Sawyer had sped away in his rental car.

Hibbs conned Sawyer into believing that Frank Duckett was the real "Sawyer."

Fortified by alcohol shared with Christian Shephard at a local bar, Sawyer returned after dark to the truck during a driving rainstorm. As Duckett threw out the nightly garbage, James walked up to him, called him "Sawyer" and shot him at point-blank range. Duckett slumped to the ground and James attempted to read aloud his childhood letter. As he bled out, Duckett denied that he was Sawyer and pieced together that his assassin was sent via Hibbs for his unpaid debts. Duckett's last words to an incredulous Sawyer were,

"It'll come back around." — Spoken by Frank to Sawyer

FRANK LAPIDUS, SEE PAGE 134

GABRIELA BUSONI

▶ **CONNECTION:** Father was a patient of Jack Shephard

Hailing from Italy, Gabriela Busoni was the daughter of Angelo Busoni. She traveled with her ailing father to St. Sebastian Hospital in Los Angeles to seek the advice of surgeon Jack Shephard. Gabriela served as her father's interpreter as she pleaded on his behalf with Jack to remove a debilitating tumor from Angelo's spine. Aware of Jack's miraculous success with his patient—and wife—Sarah, the Busonis saw Jack as Angelo's last hope. Beautiful and persuasive, Gabriela connected with Jack and he agreed to perform the surgery. During the weeks of tests and pre-surgery consultations, the pair grew closer, a slippery complication that Christian Shephard warned his son against. Unfortunately, Angelo did not survive the hours-long surgery due to his advanced age and weakened heart. The failure devastated both Jack and Gabriela. Outside the hospital, their shared grief turned into a romantic kiss that Jack quickly stopped by saying, "I can't," thus bringing an end to their dalliance.

Gabriela connected with Jack during their consultations.

THE GALAGA

The submarine known as the *Galaga* served as the means of transportation for the DHARMA Initiative—and later for the Others—between the U.S. and the island. The exact bearing of the sub's route from the island to the mainland remains a mystery. The sub was used on a regular basis for more than 30 years, starting in the 1970s. In 2004, John Locke appeared to have blown up the *Galaga* using C-4 explosives, but there was no hard evidence to prove that it was successful. During the DHARMA Initiative's time on the island, the *Galaga* was an integral part of DHARMA's operations. With Captain Bird serving as the vessel's commander, it transported key staff members to areas such as the Looking Glass station and Hydra island.

THE BEACON

A special beacon system helped the *Galaga* find the island during its return journeys. After the Swan hatch imploded, Benjamin Linus claimed that the beacon was damaged beyond repair, along with all of the former DHARMA equipment that was used to communicate with the outside world. Although Ben insisted that if the *Galaga* ever left the island it could no longer return, there was no evidence to support his claim. However, the fact that the underwater Looking Glass station functioned to jam any signals being sent or received to the island contradicted Ben's assertion.

KNOWN JOURNEYS

There are several significant instances in which the Galaga played a huge role in creating circumstances that lead to major changes on the island.

Along with a group of new DHARMA Initiative members, Roger Linus and his then eight-year-old son Benjamin journeyed to the island via the Galaga in 1973.

All of DHARMA's women and children, as well as non-essential personnel, left the island in 1977 just before the unstable pocket of electromagnetism caused "the Incident."

Prior to taking the Galaga to the island, Juliet Burke was given a glass of orange juice laced with a tranquilizer to make the trip smoother.

After the Purge, Benjamin Linus exiled fellow Other Charles Widmore via the Galaga.

In 2004, the Others used the Galaga to capture Desmond's sailboat, the Elizabeth, from the survivors of flight 815.

GOLDEN PASS

As part of the restitution for the survivors of Oceanic flight 815, Oceanic Airlines presented each member of the Oceanic Six (Jack, Kate, Aaron, Hurley, Sayid, and Sun) a special golden pass that allowed them to fly for free on any of their flights for life.

At the height of Jack's post-island alcoholism and depression, he used the golden pass every Friday night and flew roundtrip from Los Angeles to Tokyo, Singapore, or Sydney. He hoped that the flight would crash somewhere over the Pacific and return him to the island so he could correct his mistake to leave behind the other survivors. As for the other members of the Oceanic Six, it's unknown how often—or if ever—any of the other five used their golden passes.

LIFETIME PASSES

At one time, several airlines offered Lifetime Passes that could be purchased for a large sum of money that in turn offered its customers free tickets on its airline for life. American Airlines offered its last AAirpass in 2004 for $3 million. Today, some airlines offer unlimited free flight periods (usually weeks or a month) that can be purchased for a set fee.

GOLDIE

▶ **CONNECTION:** One of Eko's loyal cohorts

Named because of his prominent gold tooth, Goldie was one of Eko's most trusted men. He was present in Yemi's church when Eko tried to force his brother to ordain him and his men as priests so they could use the Catholic missionary plane to fly their drugs out of the country.

As Goldie and Eko loaded the plane posing as priests, Yemi arrived. Soon after, the military arrived and a gun battle erupted. After Yemi was shot, Eko and Goldie dragged Yemi into the plane, but Goldie kicked Eko out as he attempted to get on the plane too. As the plane flew over the island, it went down. Goldie parachuted out but he landed in a tree and died.

After the Oceanic 815 crash, Locke and Boone found a rosary on the ground in the jungle and when John pulled a vine, Goldie's decayed corpse fell to the ground. The skull featured a single gold tooth. Eko and Charlie found the corpse later and the gold tooth clarified for Eko that it was not Yemi. Eko said a small prayer and told Charlie that this man had inadvertently saved his life.

FRANK LAPIDUS

FACTS & FIGURES

Time On The Island

POST-KAHANA: 10 days

POST-AJIRA: 14 days

Occupation: Commercial airline pilot

A pilot adept at flying a variety of vehicles from helicopters to commercial airplanes, Frank Lapidus found himself entangled in the strange destinies of the survivors of two major commercial crashes: Oceanic 815 and Ajira 316. Lapidus—a man with his own demons, especially those found at the bottom of an empty bottle—was a bit of a gypsy who took jobs as they came. In 2004, Frank was a pilot for Oceanic Airways and was assigned to pilot flight 815 from Sydney, Australia to Los Angeles. However, an errant alarm clock caused Lapidus to oversleep, so his good friend and peer Seth Norris stepped in as his replacement. While he dodged that tragic bullet, fate caught up with Frank three years later when he piloted the ill-fated Ajira 316 flight.

CONSPIRACY THEORIST

Shaken by the Oceanic crash, Lapidus packed up and relocated to the Bahamas. In Eleuthera, he was hired by Caribbean Dreams Island Travel to fly tourists around the islands. One day in the office, Frank caught a news story about how Oceanic 815 had been found in the Sunda Trench. Underwater cameras showed the remains of a body they said was positively identified as Captain Seth Norris. Frank observed that there wasn't a wedding ring on his hand, a detail that proved to him it wasn't Seth. Frank called the NTSB Oceanic Hotline and reported the discrepancy, but they dismissed him.

However, Charles Widmore heard that Lapidus knew the truth so he sent Matthew Abaddon to hire him to join the *Kahana* science team as their helicopter pilot. Three months after Oceanic 815 went down, Frank and the *Kahana* were bound for the real location of the crash. While onboard the vessel, Frank met Kevin Johnson (Michael Dawson) and informed him that the news footage of the crash was false.

Frank revealed his knowledge of the fake crash to "Kevin Johnson."

THE ISLAND'S UNFRIENDLY SKIES

Lapidus quickly discovered that any approach to or from the island wouldn't be an easy journey. As he neared the island by helicopter the first time, it was hit by lightning that caused the electronics to fail and forced his team to parachute to safety. He landed the bird on a hill near the Flame, but he sustained a blow to the head.

He was later found by Daniel, Miles and Jack's group. Juliet treated Frank's head injury, while Sayid negotiated a spot on his helicopter if he found Charlotte. As they waited, Frank handed over his satellite phone to Daniel so he could perform an experiment coordinated with the freighter. Sayid returned soon after with Charlotte, and per the agreement Frank brought Sayid, Desmond, and Naomi's body back with him to the *Kahana*.

" Hands and feet inside the vehicle! Let's go for a ride! "

After Frank's emergency landing in the helicopter, Juliet tended to his wounds.

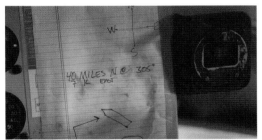

Daniel provided Frank with the proper coordinates for the flight back to the *Kahana*.

Frank flew the helicopter back on a specific trajectory provided by Faraday, which put them in a thunderhead. Despite an addled Desmond and bad turbulence, Frank landed them in one piece. Keamy then killed Ray and Captain Gault to force Frank to pilot them back to the island two more times. On the second trip Keamy was ambushed by the Others and Frank took Jack, Sayid, Sawyer, Hurley and Kate back toward the *Kahana*.

When a fuel tank leak threatened to bring an early end to their flight, Ford volunteered to jump out to save his friends. Frank then landed the helicopter and had it repaired before the freighter exploded. To Frank's astonishment, the island disappeared and he was forced to land in the water. Hours later they were picked up by Penny's boat the *Searcher*, where Frank agreed to keep the Oceanic Six secret.

AJIRA 316

For the next three years, Lapidus kept the secret and returned to his pilot's life. He was hired as a commercial pilot for Ajira Airlines and eight months into his new gig, he was assigned the Ajira flight 316 Los Angeles to Guam route. After a smooth take off, Frank did his courtesy address to his passengers over the PA, which spurred Jack to ask the flight attendant if he could say hello to his old friend.

Much to Frank's dismay, turbulence hit and the plane was enveloped in a white light. When the light faded away, the instruments were dead and the plane was in a dive. Lapidus spotted a nearby island and landed the plane on a rudimentary runway.

Frank then became a bewildered observer to a course of strange events that included the Man in Black's use of Locke's form, the burial of Locke's corpse, the Temple massacre, and meeting Widmore's team on Hydra island. Frank helped Jack and Sawyer overtake Widmore's submarine captain and by gunpoint Lapidus forced the man to dive. However, the Man in Black's planted bomb sunk the sub and Frank went down with it. Miraculously, he made it to the surface and survived on some floating life jackets until Miles Straume and Richard Alpert found him. Frank offered to fly them all out on the Ajira plane and frantically spent three hours repairing, clearing and prepping to take off as the island trembled beneath them. In the nick of time, Frank managed to pilot Miles, Richard, Sawyer, Kate and Claire back to civilization.

Frank's security badges.

Frank was happy to see Jack, but quickly blanched when he saw the rest of the Oceanic Six onboard.

"I'm seeing it but I'm not believing it."

GERONIMO JACKSON

Geronimo Jackson was an obscure '70s psychedelic, bluegrass folk rock band that recorded one studio album, "Magna Carta," which was highly respected in the music world. The band's founder was Kentucky native Keith Strutter, who as a young man of the '60s left his home state and relocated to Detroit, where he founded Geronimo Jackson. Strutter played lead guitar for Jackson, but details on the rest of the band members is scarce. However, it was rumored that another band member named Floyd left to work in the South Pacific for the DHARMA Initiative in the '70s.

At its inception, Geronimo Jackson performed in small Michigan burlesque clubs and before they headed out west to San Francisco where they eventually graduated to more renowned venues like the Avalon and the Filmore. Geronimo never gained enough steam to headline a national tour, but they did translate their modest live success into their lone album, "Magna Carta." Their second album was to feature the single "Dharma Lady." Keith wrote the song about a girl he met in Oregon and the band recorded the track in the home reportedly owned by Gerald and Karen DeGroot. In 1972, the band relocated to Woodstock, New York to record their second album, but they were never heard from again.

ISLAND CONNECTIONS

On the island, Hurley and Charlie browsed the record collection inside the Swan station and discovered Geronimo Jackson's album. While Charlie, a self-professed audiophile, proclaimed to have never heard of the band, several others on the island were fans of the cult group:

▶ *A 16-year-old John Locke had a poster of the band in his high school locker and shared an appreciation of the band with commune leader Mike.*

▶ *Eddie Colburn wore a Geronimo Jackson T-shirt that belonged to his dad.*

▶ *Charlotte said, "Turn it up! I love Geronimo Jackson!" during one of her time displacement flashes.*

▶ *A DJ at Hurley's birthday party spun a Geronimo Jackson album.*

▶ *In 1977, DHARMA Initiative member Rosie wore a band T-shirt and Jin played "Dharma Lady" in the DHARMA van during his security rounds.*

"Dharma Lady" lyrics:

'Dharma Lady, how ya been?
Are we lovers, or we just friends?
I believe, Oh I believe
I'm in love again.

Yeah your kissin', it feels so right
But you had another man holed up last night
Oh I believe. Yeah I believe
I'm in love again.

I can always tell when you've been drinking
But I never know just what you're thinking
Oh I believe. Oh I believe
I'm in love again

You say one thing once, and two things twice
I'm so confused, I can't take my own advice
Oh I believe, Oh I believe
I'm in love again
Oh I believe, Oh I believe
I'm in love again'

A LITERARY LINK

The 1969 Geronimo Jackson European tour poster that hung in the DHARMA Initiative cafeteria featured an "Alice in Wonderland" theme as a basis for the psychedelic artwork. "Through the Looking-Glass and What Alice Found There" is the name of the Lewis Carroll sequel to the original story, which focused on Alice's ability to step into an alternate world by means of a mirror. The poster also featured a white rabbit, an animal used by the DHARMA Initiative to test time travel theory.

The rabbit skull artwork featured on the "Dharma Lady" single is similar to Claire's surrogate island child, Squirrel Baby.

BY THE NUMBERS

*The Geronimo Jackson European tour poster featured the kick-off date of August (**08**) **15**, 1969 at **23**:00 hours.*

*The San Francisco address of DeGroots' home was **108** Cliffwood Place.*

DHARMA LADY DISCOVERY

In 2006, Kent Maltman moved into a house on Laurel Canyon. While wiring his stereo, he uncovered an old recording of "Dharma Lady," recorded between 1970-1972. Geronimo Jackson recorded the song in the San Francisco house they were "reportedly" living in one summer that was owned by Gerald and Karen DeGroot (co-founders of the DHARMA Initiative), who were away in Ann Arbor. How the recording got from the San Francisco house to the Laurel Canyon house is a mystery. Kent gave the newly discovered recording to his music friends where it was traded around but not officially released. Eventually, it landed in the hands of The Donkeys, who re-recorded the song as a tribute to their favorite band.

GOODWIN STANHOPE

▶ **CONNECTION:** Husband of Harper Stanhope; lover of Juliet Burke

Goodwin Stanhope was very intelligent and thus a valued member of the Others. At some point during his time on the island, Goodwin married Harper Stanhope, the island's therapist. Their relationship soured to the point that they coexisted under the same roof, but he slept on the couch for the better part of a year. Things got so bad that he engaged in an extramarital affair with Juliet Burke.

ROMANTIC TRIANGLE

Prior to the Oceanic flight 815 crash, Goodwin worked at the Tempest station where he was privy to its capability to release toxic gas into the environment. After sustaining a chemical burn while working at the station, he was treated by Juliet. Empathetic to one another's struggles (his broken marriage and her failure to save island pregnancies), the pair developed a friendship that eventually evolved into a sexual relationship. Goodwin fell deeply for Juliet and told her that he wanted to tell his wife. Juliet pleaded with him to keep it secret because of Ben's possessive feelings toward her.

LIFE AS A TAILIE

Goodwin arrived at the wreckage of the tail section just as the survivors washed up on the beach. Several minutes later, he emerged from the jungle pretending to be a survivor trying to save Bernard. Goodwin assimilated into the group of survivors all the while observing and compiling a list of "good" candidates for the Others. The first night on the beach, a band of Others used Goodwin's recon to kidnap three survivors.

On the day that flight 815 crashed on the island, Ben consciously sent Goodwin on the dangerous task of infiltrating the tail section survivors.

Scared by what they determined to be an attack by indigenous people, the survivors considered moving inland but Goodwin, Nathan and Cindy convinced them that their best chance of rescue was to remain by the beach fire. As the days progressed, Nathan's behavior seemed more erratic to de facto leader Ana Lucia, and she began to suspect he was part of the Others. Goodwin used her suspicion to deflect attention away from his own subterfuge.

Several days later, the Others penetrated the camp again at night and took nine more survivors. Ana Lucia killed a female Other during the raid who carried a list of the nine people they took. In order to keep up his charade, Goodwin agreed they should all pack up and go inland. At this point, Goodwin's job was complete but he sent word to Ben that he saw great potential in Ana Lucia and that he wanted to attempt to change her so she would be worthy of the list.

After a long hike, the tailies made camp and Ana Lucia started to dig a large pit. She forcibly tossed Nathan into the pit, accusing him of being the mole. Cautiously, Goodwin tried to calm the situation but he backed off to protect his crumbling ruse. Several days later, Goodwin talked to Ana Lucia alone and appealed to her civility to release Nathan. She refused, so in the dark of night Goodwin lowered a rope into the pit for Nathan, but then killed him.

After another long journey, the group discovered the door to the Arrow. Inside, Bernard found a radio transceiver. Goodwin volunteered to trek to higher ground to get a signal and Ana Lucia pushed to go with him. As the two hiked, Ana Lucia grilled Goodwin about why he thought they were being targeted and why he wasn't wet when he exited the jungle after the crash. Rather than continue to lie, Goodwin confessed that he killed Nathan to cover up his own lies. They fought in the grass and Goodwin grabbed a sharpened stake. He dropped it and the pair tumbled down a steep hill. At the bottom, Ana Lucia grabbed the stake and ran it through Goodwin's chest.

After an intense struggle, Ana Lucia drove a stake through Goodwin's chest.

FALLOUT

Two members of the Others, Tom and Pickett, found Goodwin's lifeless body in the jungle. In a cold-hearted move, Ben took Juliet to Goodwin's corpse so she would realize the repercussions of her crossing him for another man.

GOOD-WIN STAN-HOPE ✚
The "good" and "hope" of his name is illustrative of the Others' idea that they're the good guys.

GORDY

▶ **CONNECTION: Ran a con with James "Sawyer" Ford**

A professional con artist and one-time long con partner of James "Sawyer" Ford, Gordy found Cassidy Phillips as a potential mark to fleece out of her large divorce settlement. Sawyer and Gordy set her up for a long con scam in which Sawyer took Cassidy as his lover and then under his wing as he taught her to work small-time scams. After about six months together, Gordy met James at a roadside diner to discuss the status of the con. James said he had Cassidy's trust and would get her $600,000. However, Gordy astutely read James' body language and saw that his partner had fallen for their prey. As Sawyer got up to leave, Gordy threatened to kill him or Cassidy if the con didn't go down as planned. With great regret, James completed the con and paid Gordy his half of the $600,000.

GUAM

An island in the western Pacific Ocean, Guam is the largest of the Mariana Islands. It is classified as an "unincorporated territory" of the U.S., which means it has its own government.

SUPPLY DROPS

All of the DHARMA Initiative supplies were stored in a warehouse in Guam. DHARMA's Lamp Post station, which was based in Los Angeles, had an automated system that periodically alerted the warehouse team when another pallet drop was required. The coordinates were then sent to the warehouse, detailing where the drop-off needed to occur.

HADDAD

▶ **CONNECTION: Acquaintance of Sayid Jarrah**

Haddad, the suspected leader of a terrorist group in Sydney, Australia, was focused on disrupting the U.S. coalition presence in Iraq. He planned to use 300 pounds of C-4 stolen by his group from an army base outside of Melbourne, Australia, for a suicide bomb attack in Sydney. Sayid was recruited by CIA Agent Alyssa Cole and the ASIS' Robbie Hewitt to help recover the explosives from this terrorist cell. The CIA blackmailed Sayid into helping them and promised to reveal the whereabouts of Nadia if he cooperated.

GUS

▶ **CONNECTION: Owner of a pawn shop in NYC; purchased Jin's watch from Michael Dawson**

Owner of a pawn shop in New York City, Michael visited Gus's shop to acquire a gun and ammunition that he planned to use to take his own life. To pay for it, Michael gave Gus the Rolex watch that Jin had given Michael.

At first, Gus didn't want to accept the watch because of the Korean inscription written on the back of it (which Gus initially mistook for Chinese) and feeling it was stolen. Once he was convinced Michael wasn't a cop, Gus agreed to the exchange.

축	"Congratulations/Thanks"
상호협력	"Doing business with one another and prospering"
사업발전	
백회장	"Chairman Paik"

HAJER

▶ **CONNECTION: Tunisian doctor who helped set John Locke's broken leg**

Based in Tunisia, Hajer worked at a hospital near the exit portal connected to the island's subterranean wheel device. Hajer seemed to be under Charles Widmore's service.

When Locke received a compound fracture to his shin upon exiting the portal, it was Hajer who reset the wound. While force-feeding Locke drugs for the pain, Locke passed out as the bone was snapped back into place. During the procedure, another associate of Widmore, Mathew Abaddon, observed the entire event.

HALLIBURTON CASE

▶ **CONNECTION: Carried by Edward Mars on Oceanic flight 815; contained Kate Austen's toy plane**

U.S. Marshal Edward Mars brought a Zero Halliburton briefcase with him as a carry-on for Oceanic flight 815. A state-of-the-art aluminum briefcase, the Zero Halliburton was designed to be sleek, stylish and incredibly durable. Inside the case Mars stored four 9-millimeter guns, some extra boxes of ammunition, cash and an envelope marked "personal effects." Inside that envelope was a smaller envelope that contained Kate Austen's toy airplane. Because of the firearms, the flight stewards stored Mars's case in the crew's cabin luggage area. It survived the crash in excellent shape and was later found by Kate in a pond on the island.

CONTENTS OF THE CASE ✚

The contents of the case remained a mystery to everyone except Kate, who was well aware of what Mars kept inside it. Jack received the case from Sawyer in exchange for a constant supply of antibiotics to treat his injury. Jack and Kate then dug up Mars's body to retrieve the key to the case and Jack made Kate open the case with him. She finally revealed to Jack the contents and the incredible sentimental value of the toy plane, which was owned by her first love, Tom Brennan.

After that point, Jack used the Halliburton case to store guns and he wore the key around his neck for safe keeping. It wasn't until the Swan was discovered that they swapped the guns out of the case and put them inside the armory.

THE HANSO FOUNDATION

Headquartered in Copenhagen, Denmark, The Hanso Foundation is the brainchild of engineer and philanthropist Alvar Hanso. Established in 1967, the Foundation was created to fund scientific and technology-oriented research programs "designed to further the evolution of the human race and provide technological solutions to the most pressing problems of our time."

"The Hanso Foundation. Reaching out to a better tomorrow."

The Foundation has awarded funding to seven major research programs:

THE HANSO LIFE-EXTENSION PROJECT—CURRENT
A longevity research project that used Joop the orangutan as a test subject for experiments into extending human life. Originally harvested by British explorers in the early 1900s, Joop celebrated his 105th birthday on September 21, 2005, which was achieved through the benign, non-invasive transgenic technologies developed by this project.

PER HANSO WEBSITE: The grand summation of all of the Foundation's work—from prevention and wellness, to the development of new gene therapies and the development of young minds—is nothing less than the extension of life itself."

THE HANSO FOUNDATION ELECTROMAGNETIC RESEARCH INITIATIVE—CURRENT
PER THE HANSO WEBSITE: From the simplest touch to the most complex chemical reaction, electromagnetism is at work. From the most rudimentary compass to the most advanced supercomputer, electromagnetism is at work.

"To understand where our world is going, we must first seek to understand how the world was made." — Alvar Hanso

From the magnetosphere's deflection of cosmic rays to the ionosphere's reflection of radio-waves, electromagnetism is at work. While we know a great deal, there is still much to learn about this fundamental force. Such investigations are the domain of The Hanso Foundation Electromagnetic Research Initiative."

THE HANSO MATHEMATICAL FORECASTING INITIATIVE—CURRENT
This program states "by understanding and modeling the mathematic probability of seismic human events, The Hanso Foundation can illuminate the path ahead and provide a true road map to the betterment of humanity."

HANSON WORLDWIDE WELLNESS AND PREVENTION DEVELOPMENT PROGRAM—CURRENT
PER THE HANSO WEBSITE: The Worldwide Wellness and Prevention Development program may just be the heart and soul of The Hanso Foundation's charitable work: a far-reaching educational initiative designed to teach the basics of sanitation, nutrition and disease prevention to the world. Leading by education and example—and working with local health care providers, growers and utilities, The Hanso Foundation is giving hundreds of thousands of people the means by which to live fuller and safer lives.

THE HANSO MENTAL HEALTH APPEAL—CURRENT
PER HANSO WEBSITE: It has always been the steadfast belief of Alvar Hanso that the mentally ill must be given every opportunity to not only heal but to realize the potential robbed of them by their sickness. Every day, thousands of potentially productive minds are crippled by terrible diseases. The Hanso Foundation is committed to restoring these tragic losses. The Hanso Foundation's Mental Health Appeal is a world-spanning system of clinics seeking revolutionary new treatments. It is nothing short of a crusade to rid us all of the spectre of debilitating illnesses that truly hold hostage the human race's drive to a better future. From gene therapies to radical pharmaceutical treatments and the cutting edge in both surgery and psychotherapy, The Hanso Foundation's Mental Health Appeal is moving forward to fulfill Alvar Hanso's ambitious mandate: the complete eradication of all mental illness by the end of the century.

HANSO INSTITUTE FOR GENOMIC ADVANCEMENT—CURRENT
PER HANSO WEBSITE: The Institute for Genomic Advancement is dedicated to the extension of the Human Genome Project to its most logical conclusions. Believing that once our building blocks are laid bare, the future we build upon them will be without limit. In what may be the most forward-reaching of The Hanso Foundation's active projects, the Institute seeks nothing less than eradication of disease and birth defects through a deeper understanding of the function and mechanisms of the human genome.

The DHARMA Initiative—1970 to 1987

HANSO GROUP
The business subsidiary of Hanso's company, the Hanso Group pursued a strictly corporate portfolio of varied businesses they either acquired and managed or bought outright. Examples include:

Apollo Candy Company: Bought in the early '70s from M. David Benson. The Hanso Group brought the company out of bankruptcy, restructured its operations and made it a player in the global confectioner landscape. Apollo Candy was the official provider of sweets to the DHARMA Initiative.

Allied Copenhagen Marine Merchants: The East Ocean Trade Group was a shipping company purchased by the Hanso Group in the 1950s and renamed the ACMM. The shipping conglomerate was originally owned by Alvar's great-grandfather Magnus Hanso.

"A society should not merely be measured by its brightest lights, but on how the brightest light the way for those who cannot shine for themselves." — Alvar Hanso

HAZMAT SUIT

Kelvin dragged Desmond back to the Swan after the *Elizabeth* crashed on the island.

An abbreviation for the term "hazardous materials," the HAZMAT suit played a role on the island; several people wore a HAZMAT suit for different tasks. Desmond's partner at the Swan station, Kelvin Joe Inman, wore a HAZMAT suit whenever he left the station. He was even wearing one the day he rescued Desmond. Inman constantly warned Desmond of the Sickness, a pathogen so dangerous that the HAZMAT suit was necessary in order to survive.

On September 22, 2004, Desmond noticed a small tear in Inman's HAZMAT suit. Suspicious about Inman's claims of the "Sickness," he followed Inman and learned that he had been secretly repairing Desmond's sailboat in order to leave the island.

Kelvin Joe Inman wore a HAZMAT suit to prevent Desmond from leaving the Swan station.

Desmond found a drunken Inman next to the Swan's fail-safe.

HECTOR & GLEN

▶ **CONNECTION:** Worked at Guam warehouse for DHARMA

Two off-island DHARMA workers, Hector and Glen manned and operated the Guam-based pallet warehouse for 20 years. They labeled food staples, then loaded them onto pallets for regular drone deliveries per automated coordinates via the Lamp Post. In 2010, Hugo "Hurley" Reyes sent Benjamin Linus to close the operation. Linus awarded the pair generous cash severance payouts. He also allowed the befuddled duo to ask one question each and then watch a Betamax dub of the Hydra orientation film. At the end, Ben left them to begin their new lives.

HELEN NORWOOD

▶ **CONNECTION:** Former love interest of John Locke

Helen was the silver lining in Locke's dark days of anger and frustration. She was a regular attendee of the same anger management class that John Locke begrudgingly attended. Although Locke was often belligerent and unsympathetic of others in the class, Helen admired his brutal honesty. She saw past Locke's hang-ups and quickly fell in love with him despite all his issues.

A FAILING RELATIONSHIP

After their six-month anniversary, Helen presented Locke with the key to her house in hope that John would move in with her and stop sneaking out at night to check up on his manipulative father, Anthony Cooper. But Locke's need to make sense of why his father abandoned him slowly corroded the bond Helen worked so hard to maintain. Cooper's hold over Locke was much stronger than Helen had imagined.

Helen gave John this key to her house on their six-month anniversary.

Helen and John attended Anthony Cooper's "funeral" together.

After Helen spotted Anthony Cooper's name in the obituaries, Locke mustered up the strength to forgive his father for all of his wrongdoing and they both attended his funeral. But Cooper faked his death and used it as an opportunity to secretly approach Locke and use him to retrieve $700,000 from a safety deposit box.

Soon after, a criminal named Jimmy Bane and his associate intimidated Helen and Locke at their house demanding to know Cooper's whereabouts. Locke lied to them—and Helen—about Cooper being alive. When Locke went to meet Cooper at a local motel, Helen secretly followed and discovered Locke giving the money to his father. Although Helen hated Cooper for his endless and cruel manipulation of his son, she realized that Locke's desire for his father's approval was far stronger than his love for her. Helen walked out of Locke's life and never returned. Ultimately, Anthony Cooper's "return from the dead" brought Locke's obsession back to the surface and destroyed Helen and Locke's relationship.

Helen left Locke after he lied to her again about his father, Cooper.

HELEN'S DEATH

During Locke's attempt to reunite the Oceanic Six from their locations all over the world, Matthew Abaddon took him to a graveyard in Santa Monica, California. He showed Locke a gravestone inscribed with Helen Norwood's name. This revelation broke Locke's heart all over again.

HENRIK

▶ **CONNECTION:** Hired by Penelope Widmore to find Desmond Hume; stationed at Arctic monitoring station

Henrik was one half of a two-man monitoring team commissioned by Penelope Widmore to search worldwide for any major geomagnetic anomalies. Henrik and his partner Mathias spoke Portuguese to each other but communicated with Widmore in English. From their isolated, mountain-based research facility the pair monitored the globe for three years seeking any sudden, electromagnetic signatures that would reveal the coordinates of the hidden South Pacific island. Penny hoped to use the location to find and rescue Desmond Hume. The plan worked when Desmond used the fail-safe key to engage the Swan's discharge system, creating a massive electromagnetic pulse that was picked up by the monitoring station's anomaly equipment. Sometime later, Henrik was reassigned to Penny Widmore's ship the *Searcher*. When they spotted the ship, Henrik said in his native Portuguese, "Here! Look over here! There's a raft full of people, Ms. Widmore!" The ship rescued at sea the Oceanic Six, Desmond Hume and Frank Lapidus.

BY THE NUMBERS ✛

On the computer monitor, the alarm code read:

*>/ 7418880
Electromagnetic
Anomaly
Detected*

That number is the outcome of multiplying the numbers (4 8 15 16 23 42) together.

HENRY GALE

▶ **CONNECTION: Crash-landed on island via hot air balloon**

Henry Gale was a businessman who was attempting to travel across the Pacific Ocean in a fortified hot air balloon. Somewhere over the island, Gale crashed and he was left stranded. Sometime later, Gale then died from a broken neck. It is not certain whether it occurred by accident or if he was murdered by the Others. He was buried near the site of his crashed balloon and later exhumed by Sayid, Ana Lucia and Charlie.

HENRY'S NOTE TO HIS WIFE ✚

This message was found in Henry's pocket, hand-written on a twenty-dollar bill:

Jennifer,
Well you were right.
Crossing the Pacific isn't easy.

I owe you a beer. I'm hiking to one of the beaches to start a signal fire, but if you're reading this, I guess I didn't make it. I'm sorry, I love you Jenny, always have, always will.

Yours,
Henry

According to the personal effects buried with him, Gale hailed from Wayzata, Minnesota and owned the Minnesota Metallurgy & Mining Company. His craft was a personal endeavor that attracted corporate sponsorship from the Hanso Foundation, Widmore Industries, Mr. Cluck's Chicken Shack and Nozz-A-La cola.

Henry Gale's name and persona was eventually assumed by Benjamin Linus when he acted out a complicated ruse to learn more about the survivors of flight 815 who crash-landed on his island.

> **LOOKING DEEPER** ✚
>
> *Nozz-A-La cola is a fictional drink created by author Stephen King in his "Dark Tower" books.*
>
> *A yellow smiley face is stitched onto the orange silk of the balloon that carried Gale's craft. That symbol was also famously used in Alan Moore and Dave Gibbons' graphic novel "Watchmen."*
>
> *Henry Gale is a character in the 1939 film adaptation of The Wizard of Oz. Gale is the uncle of the heroine Dorothy Gale. The iconic character of The Wizard of Oz is famously revealed to be an average man from Kansas who was blown to and then stranded in Oz when his hot air balloon was thrown off course.*

HIBBS

▶ **CONNECTION: Ran a con with James "Sawyer" Ford**

Somewhere in Sawyer's past he hooked up with a fellow experienced confidence man named Hibbs. The pair worked together for an extended period of time pulling off complicated cons in places such as Atlanta, Georgia. Their partnership deteriorated after a botched job in Tampa, Florida that ultimately ended their association.

Years later, Hibbs appeared at Sawyer's hotel room and presented his former partner a peace offering to make good on his past sins. He showed Sawyer a photo of a man named Frank Duckett, an American expatriate living in Australia. Hibbs revealed that Frank was actually Frank Sawyer, the con man who hustled James' parents and ultimately caused their deaths.

It was this piece of information that motivated Sawyer to travel to Australia and track down Frank for revenge. As his victim lay dying, James read his letter to "Mr. Sawyer" but Duckett was confused and didn't understand. Desperate, Sawyer explained why he was there and it suddenly became clear that Hibbs conned James into killing Duckett for an unpaid debt.

HOWARD GRAY

▶ **CONNECTION: Hired Miles Straume to "speak" to his son**

Howard Gray was a grieving father whose son, Russell, had been killed by a drunk driver. Howard paid Miles to contact his dead son to make sure that Russell knew his father loved him. Although Miles initially told Howard he had passed on the message, Miles returned to the Gray household later and returned Howard's money. He explained that he didn't contact Russell and that Howard should have told his son he loved him while he was alive. Although Miles admitted to scamming Howard, some of his encounters did result in interactions with the dead, adding weight to the notion that Miles could commune with the dead.

HOWARD L. ZUCKERMAN

▶ **CONNECTION: Poisoned by Nikki & Paulo**

The producer of cult stripper-crime-fighting show *Exposé*, Howard L. Zuckerman was the creative force behind it and other TV hits, including *Dr. Kincaid, Esquire* and *Strike Team Alpha*. The British producer, who lived in Sydney, Australia, was well known for his infidelity. He even had a fling with one of the survivors of flight 815, Nikki Fernandez, prior to her being a passenger on the doomed flight. Nikki made a guest appearance as heroine Corvette in the finale of *Exposé*'s fourth season.

Four days before flight 815 left Sydney bound for Los Angeles, Zuckerman was poisoned to death by his chef, Paulo, who was secretly Nikki's boyfriend. Nikki and Paulo murdered Zuckerman to obtain the key he kept around his neck. That key opened a safe containing $8 million worth of diamonds that were hidden inside a Russian doll.

> While intoxicated, Horace tossed sticks of dynamite near the sonic fence.

HORACE GOODSPEED

▶ **CONNECTION: Former leader of the DHARMA Initiative**

A mathematician and leader of the DHARMA Initiative enclave, Horace Goodspeed was a kind-hearted, hippie-ish academic who grew increasingly overwhelmed by the challenges of his leadership role. Goodspeed was the husband of Amy and the father of Ethan (Rom). Horace lived on the island for over 15 years.

Horace offered Roger a job with the DHARMA Initiative and personally welcomed he and his son when they arrived.

DHARMA ORIGINS

In 1962, Horace traveled with fellow DHARMA member Olivia outside of Portland, Oregon when they spotted a distraught Roger and Emily Linus on the side of the road. Roger explained that Emily had just given birth in the woods, so Horace offered to take them to the hospital. But before they could do so, Emily expired in Roger's arms. By all accounts a gregarious and well-liked leader, Horace was content in his role on the island until problems with the Hostiles escalated.

THE HOSTILES

When the island started skipping through time, Sawyer, Juliet, Miles, Jin and Faraday arrived on the island in 1974 where they unknowingly created a treaty breach between DHARMA and the Others. The time travelers were captured by DHARMA security and Horace had a one-on-one with Sawyer, who dubbed himself "LaFleur." Horace met with Richard Alpert to work out a satisfactory resolution to the broken truce and LaFleur clarified the circumstances around the dead Others. He then brokered a deal to restore the peace by giving Alpert Paul's body. No small achievement, the deal earned LaFleur Horace's admiration and trust. In fact, Horace let LaFleur and the other survivors stay on the island and eventually promoted him to Head of Security.

HORACE UNRAVELS

Three years later, Horace had married Amy and she was ready to give birth to their son. However, Horace's insecurity about their relationship led to several quarrels. During one such argument, the usually temperate Horace got drunk and went out to the sonic fence and threw lit dynamite sticks at random trees. After LaFleur took Horace back to his home, Horace revealed that he was jealous of the long-dead Paul and then passed out. Amy went into labor shortly thereafter and gave birth to their son, Ethan Goodspeed, who later assumed the surname Rom.

During a botched attempt to learn more about Sayid, he eventually escaped the DHARMA compound. Stuart Radzinsky blamed Horace's poor leadership and took over the manhunt. The events escalated into "the Incident." Horace remained the leader of the DHARMA compound for more than the next 10 years.

THE END

In 1987, Ben and some DHARMA members collaborated with the Others to perform "the Purge" on the majority of the compound. Found with his eyes still open, Ben closed them in one last gesture of respect for the man who was so kind to him.

VISIONS

In 2004, Locke had a vision of Horace in the woods chopping wood to build his cabin. In an eerie loop, Horace spoke to Locke about Jacob. He then provided clues to the whereabouts of the DHARMA mass grave.

"He's been waiting for you a real long time, man."

— Spoken by Horace to John Locke during one of Locke's dreams

145

HUGO "HURLEY" REYES

FACTS & FIGURES

Time On The Island

POST-OCEANIC: 101 days

POST-AJIRA: 4 days

POST-INCIDENT: Many years

Time As Oceanic Six: 3 years

Childhood Pets: Stuart (turtle), Buster (dog)

Skills: Table tennis, Basketball, Horseshoes

Likes: Star Wars, Xanadu, The Flintstones, comics, fried chicken, Exposé, Backgammon champion

Candidate: #8

Hugo Reyes considered himself cursed. Like many of the 815 survivors, Hurley was negatively affected by a family full of dysfunction. Depression and comfort-eating eventually led to a stay at a mental health hospital. After winning the lottery, Hurley became convinced that the winning numbers were evil, so he traveled to Australia to investigate their origin, which led to his place on Oceanic flight 815.

Hurley's experiences on the island helped him grow from a man full of self-loathing to a man full of purpose. After his friends left the island, Hurley remained, taking on the role of island protector. As the new leader of the island, Hurley was tasked with what he did best: looking after others.

EMOTIONAL ISSUES

Hurley was close to both parents, but his father, David, left the family when Hurley was 10. They were working on their broken-down Camaro the day David fled to Las Vegas to make his fortune. He gave Hurley a candy bar to cheer him up, which started Hurley's habit of eating to comfort himself.

SANTA ROSA
MENTAL INSTITUTE

Years later, Hurley was sent to the Santa Rosa Mental Health Institute. He blamed his weight for the collapse of a deck. Built to hold only 8 people, 23 were on the deck, including Hurley. Two people died, and Hurley was overwhelmed with guilt and depression. After leaving Santa Rosa, Hurley returned to his job at Mr. Cluck's Chicken Shack.

While living with his mother, Hurley played the lottery, using numbers 4, 8, 15, 16, 23, and 42, which he heard from fellow mental patient, Leonard Simms. Hugo won the jackpot. After an absence of 17 years, his father returned upon learning of Hurley's multimillion dollar win. Although he was rich, the bad luck that affected those around him made Hurley convinced the numbers were cursed.

David took his son to see a psychic, Lynn Karnoff, to remove the curse. However, the psychic revealed that David had set up the whole thing after Hurley offered her $10,000 to admit the truth. Hurley went to Australia to investigate the origin of the numbers. He boarded Oceanic flight 815 on September 22, 2004, to make it back to Los Angeles in time for his mother's birthday the following day, the 23rd.

MEGA LOTTO JACKPOT

Your numbers are:

4, 8, 15, 16, 23

MEGA NUMBER **42**

Hurley's winning Mega Lotto Jackpot ticket.

"Dude, I just lied to a samurai."

EVERYONE'S BUDDY

Everybody loved Hurley because he always put everyone before himself. After many selfless acts in the first few days after the crash, Hurley created the Island Open golf course. Although it was only two holes with a 3-par, its purpose was to create a distraction from the trauma the survivors faced daily. Charlie, Jack, Michael, and Sullivan were the first to enjoy Hurley's course, and many more followed. Hurley also created the idea of taking a census to prevent more people like Claire and Charlie from being attacked.

Hurley worried he'd offended Jin by refusing his offer of a sea urchin snack, so Hurley agreed to help Jin fish. Hurley stabbed his foot on urchin spines, and got sick from eating Jin's shellfish. Jin and Hurley continued working together with Michael when tasked with building the second raft.

One of Hurley's greatest ideas was creating a huge feast for the whole camp when they discovered the food stores in the Swan pantry. It prevented any arguments over food and united everybody.

Hurley used the DHARMA van to save his friends...twice—once in 2004 during the Others' raid of their camp and next in 1977 to save his friends during the Incident.

When the *Kahana* exploded, Hurley was great comfort to Sun when she thought the bomb had killed Jin. As part of the Oceanic Six, Hurley even flew to Seoul to meet Sun's baby Ji Yeon, and to support her when she visited Jin's grave.

Even when he was terrified, helping Kate buddy-breathe with him as they escaped Widmore's sinking submarine, Hurley maintained his focus to save her.

HURLEY & THE NUMBERS

*Hurley's connection with the numbers even cropped up at his return birthday party. There were **4** fake palm trees, **8** "Happy Birthday" balloons, **15** presents, **16** party hats and the numbers **23** and **42** appeared on two different kids' jerseys.*

HURLEY'S PLAY-LIST

"Wash Away" – Joe Purdy

"Are You Sure?" – Willie Nelson

"Delicate" – Damien Rice

BY THE NUMBERS

*The entire sequence of **4**, **8**, **15**, **16**, **23**, and **42** appeared to Hurley on several occasions:*

His fellow patient at Santa Rosa, Leonard Simms, kept repeating the numbers.

Hurley won the lottery using the numbers.

He saw the numbers on Danielle Rousseau's papers.

They were stamped into the Swan hatch.

Two car dashboards featured the numbers: when Hurley broke down heading to the Sydney airport and on the odometer of the Camaro Hurley's father restored.

Hurley passed a women's soccer team at Sydney airport whose jerseys displayed the numbers.

CHARLIE PACE

From their first days together, bonding over catching fish, Hurley considered Charlie his closest and most important friend from the island. Even during Charlie's period of addiction, Hurley showed him compassion. He hung out with Charlie when he looked after Aaron.

Hurley and Claire were the only ones who knew about Desmond's premonitions of Charlie's death. Although Charlie became terrified that any time spent with Desmond could spell his death, Hurley fought to keep him smiling. Hurley's insistence that Charlie help him get the DHARMA van working gave him one of his most joyful moments on the island.

Charlie brushed off Hurley's offer to help him with his Looking Glass mission. But he told Hurley he loved him and gave him a huge hug, which was Charlie's way of protecting his friend and saying goodbye.

Hurley was able to communicate with Charlie after his death. His spirit visited Hurley at the Santa Rosa hospital, when Hurley readmitted himself. Charlie's message was simple: "They need you."

SAYID JARRAH

After Sayid and Sawyer's first confrontation, Hurley tried to unite everyone, which led to his friendship with Sayid. It was Sayid who found Danielle Rousseau's writings, which included the numbers that had plagued Hurley for so long. This inspired Hurley to attempt to make some kind of sense of them. Hurley also had great respect for Sayid's technological skills and turned to him when they discovered Naomi Dorrit and her satellite phone.

As Hurley used the DHARMA van to save Sayid and several other survivors, it was appropriate that Sayid went to Santa Rosa in the Oceanic Six period to save Hurley's life. The two grew closest when Hurley became a murder suspect in the death of the man Sayid killed outside the institution. Sayid fought more attackers, but when he was struck with a tranquilizer dart, it became Hurley's turn to protect Sayid.

Sayid needed more help from Hurley when he suffered a serious gunshot wound during the Incident. Although Hurley was squeamish around blood, he vowed to save Sayid. With advice from Jacob, Hurley got his dying friend to the Temple's healing waters. With Jacob dead and the waters murky, it couldn't heal Sayid. Hurley was distraught by his death, but overjoyed when he sat up, alive, hours later. Sayid was under the Man in Black's spell for a long time, but gave his life so that Hurley and his friends could have a chance of surviving the submarine bomb.

JAMES "SAWYER" FORD

"Wasn't a con, dude. If you're gonna be our temporary leader, you need to do some damage control."

The most unlikely of Hurley's close friendships was Sawyer. For the longest time, Hurley was the butt of Sawyer's endless string of cruel nicknames. When Sawyer refused to give Hurley medication to help with what he thought was the start of a breakdown, Hurley erupted. He punched Sawyer for all the nicknames he'd received, which was a turning point in their relationship. As they grew closer, Hurley enjoyed beating Sawyer at every game they played. Contrary to Hurley's belief that he was cursed with bad luck, Hurley would always triumph, whether it was ping pong or horseshoes.

Hurley saw the good in people, and he believed Sawyer was not the sum of his selfish actions. Hurley even pulled off a successful con and convinced Sawyer the beach camp was voting to banish him if he didn't change his horrible ways. When Jack was being held by the Others, Hurley recognized that Sawyer had leadership qualities the survivors needed. Sawyer grew extremely protective of Hurley. When Hurley was distraught from Charlie's death, the two became housemates in the barracks. When Martin Keamy and his freighter mercenaries attacked the barracks, Hurley defied Ben and smashed a window to let Sawyer and Claire get inside. In turn, Sawyer threatened Locke that if he harmed one hair on Hurley's head he would kill him. Hurley and Sawyer were thrilled to see each other in 1977 DHARMA. After a three-year absence from Sawyer's nicknames, Hurley admitted he missed them.

JACK SHEPHARD

Although Hurley often disagreed with Jack's decisions, he always respected this friend who helped Hurley discover his true calling. Ever helpful, at the scene of the crash, Hurley assisted Jack in getting Claire Littleton to safety, and later sought out antibiotics for Edward Mars. Hurley also compared Jack's ability to talk Shannon through her asthma attack to that of a Jedi. When Hurley first told Jack about the numbers, Jack dismissed them as just numbers. Years later, Hurley led Jack to the lighthouse, where Jack witnessed how the numbers were tied to Jacob and to Jack's life.

Hurley also passed along a message to Jack from a dead loved one at a crucial time when Jack's confidence in himself was low: "You have what it takes." Although this came from Jacob, Hurley had no idea this was associated with a conversation with Christian that had created Jack's oft-crippling self-doubt.

Dedicated to the end, Hurley fought side-by-side with Jack to save the heart of the island. He even tried to reject Jack's attempts to make him the new protector, and stressed it was only temporary. Hurley was terrified of his friend dying and the huge responsibility left to him, but he found the strength to deal with both.

"That was awesome. I mean, that was like a Jedi moment."

ELIZABETH "LIBBY" SMITH

From stolen glances over laundry, to beach picnic plans, Hurley and Libby's romance was brief but meaningful. Libby enabled Hurley to open up emotionally and she also saved his life.

A hopeless romantic to the core, Hurley asked Sayid for the Arrow radio. Even if he couldn't get it to work, he wanted to re-create the moment from the seminal 1989 Cameron Crowe film, *Say Anything*, in which John Cusack holds a boom-box above his head to profess his undying love.

During a picnic with Libby, he went to get wine while Libby went to get blankets from the Swan station. When Sawyer went to get a Virgin Mary statue from his stash so that Jack could administer heroin to her as a pain reliever, Hurley found out that Libby had been shot. As he apologized for forgetting the blankets, Libby died. Hurley helped dig the graves for Libby and Ana Lucia and he gave the eulogy. In the years that followed, Hurley sat beside Libby's grave and talked to her. He was frustrated that, of all the dead friends whose spirits visited him, Libby was never one of them.

MILES STRAUME

As they both could commune with the dead, Hurley and Miles got along quite well. To take their mind off the island situation, Miles and Hurley often played games together. These moments sometimes led to debates concerning time travel and their chances of survival.

HURLEY'S OFF-ISLAND CONNECTIONS

- **Tito Reyes** (Grandfather)
- **David Reyes** (Father)
- **Carmen Reyes** (Mother)
- **Diego Reyes** (Brother)
- **Dave** (Imaginary friend)
- **Johnny** (Friend)
- **Starla** (Asked out on a date)
- **Randy Nations** (Former boss)
- **Staff and patients at Santa Rosa Mental Health Institute**

HURLEY'S VISIONS

Hurley had an imaginary friend at Santa Rosa and he saw much stranger things on the island. When he fell asleep at the Swan's computer terminal during a numbers shift, he had a telling dream:

- ▶ *Jin spoke to Hurley in English. Jin went on to learn fluent English after his three years with DHARMA.*

- ▶ *Jin said that Hurley was actually speaking Korean. Hurley visited Sun in Seoul to meet her daughter, Ji Yeon, when they were part of the Oceanic Six.*

- ▶ *Jin said: "Everything's going to change, Hugo." When the survivors entered the Swan, it began a shift in their understanding of the island, the DHARMA Initiative, and the Others.*

HURLEY'S OTHER COMIC BOOK ✚

Hurley read a Spanish copy of Y: The Last Man in the LAX departure lounge before boarding Ajira flight 316.

This comic ran for 60 issues, and was written by Brian K. Vaughan. Y deals with a post-apocalyptic narrative where mankind faces extinction.

ANA LUCIA CORTEZ. Helped Hurley escape from being a murder suspect.

MICHAEL DAWSON. Warned Hurley not to blow up the Ajira plane with dynamite.

MR. EKO. Played chess with Hurley at Santa Rosa.

JACOB. Guided Hurley in several ways to help save the island.

CONVERSATIONS WITH THE DEAD

Hurley discovered he had the ability to talk to the dead. In one instance, Charlie appeared while Hurley was at Santa Rosa Mental Health Institute. Charlie encouraged Hurley to return to the island, but Hurley didn't respond well to the image of Charlie.

When Richard Alpert was teetering between alliances with Jacob and the Man in Black, Isabella spoke to Hurley. Her conversation persuaded Richard to stay with Jacob and help the survivors.

OCEANIC SIX DAYS

When Hurley returned to Los Angeles as one of the Oceanic Six, he pleaded with Sayid to back him up and tell the truth because he didn't want to spend the rest of his life lying. When Sayid sided with Jack, Hurley warned that there would be a day in the future when they would need his help and he would refuse to give it.

Not long afterwards, Hurley deliberately found a way to return to Santa Rosa. He noticed that his newly restored Camaro had the six numbers in the odometer. Then, he saw dead Charlie in a store. Hurley responded by speeding away and getting arrested. He returned to Santa Rosa so that he wouldn't face charges and would feel safe. After visits from the living and the dead, a bust-out by Sayid set Hurley back on the path to the island.

DHARMA 1977

Hurley's prime objective was to bring the guitar case that Jacob gave him to the island. Transported to 1977, he went undercover as a DHARMA chef. Later, he decided to write an improved screenplay of *The Empire Strikes Back* and send it to George Lucas. He also became keen on uniting Miles Straume with his father, Pierre Chang.

Hurley's passport.

"I think you do what you do best, Hugo. Take care of people."

— Spoken by Ben to Hurley

THE NEW MAN IN CHARGE

Hurley became the new protector of the island after Jack passed the mantle to him. Hurley appointed Ben as his number two, in a similar advisory role that Richard had to Jacob. Hurley's first task was to return Desmond safely home to his family, which Ben helped him achieve.

In 2010, Hurley initiated a plan for another important phase in the island's history. He and Ben journeyed to Santa Rosa, which had become the new home for a very troubled Walt. Hurley was overjoyed to take his young friend back to the place they could both call home.

THE HYDRA

Located two miles from the main island, Hydra island served as the base of operations for a series of different experiments. The DHARMA Initiative constructed the Hydra station on this small isle and used it to conduct a variety of experiments over the years, ranging from zoological research to psychological human studies. Surveillance cameras smothered the island, allowing the workers to monitor the wildlife and its occupants' activities.

ROOM 23

One of the most significant, yet disturbing, aspects of the operations on Hydra island was Room 23. Located inside the largest building on the islet, this room was used to test the effects of subliminal messaging on its subjects. Originally, the DHARMA Initiative used it for subversive tests on the Others. The members of DHARMA utilized the room to determine why these people came to the island and, more significantly, why they had pledged an allegiance to a person they called "Jacob."

Once inside Room 23, an individual would be strapped to the chair in the center of the room and a cocktail of unknown chemicals was injected via an intravenous drip. Forced to wear a set of peculiar glasses, the subject was then flooded with a cacophony of deafening sounds and a giddy array of images and statements.

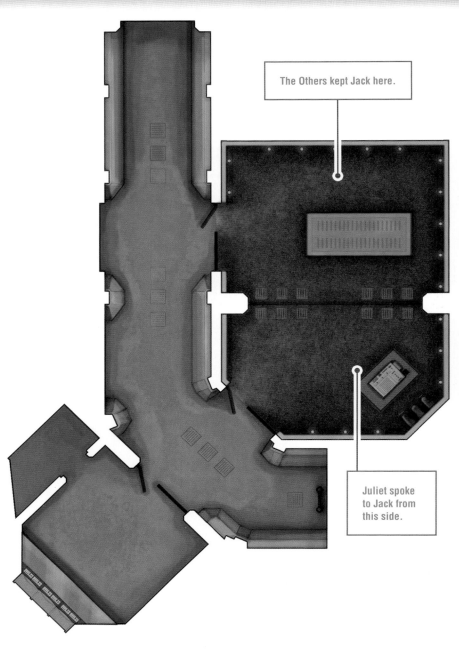

The Others kept Jack here.

Juliet spoke to Jack from this side.

"We do animal research here at Hydra."

— Spoken by Dr. Pierre Chang

ZOOLOGICAL EXPERIMENTS

The DHARMA Initiative constructed a series of different holding pens and areas on Hydra island in order to conduct experiments on wildlife. One of the strangest involved the testing done on polar bears, animals accustomed to living in a far different climate than that on the island. In addition to the climate change, these animals were subjected to gene therapy to determine what kinds of psychological and physical effects would occur.

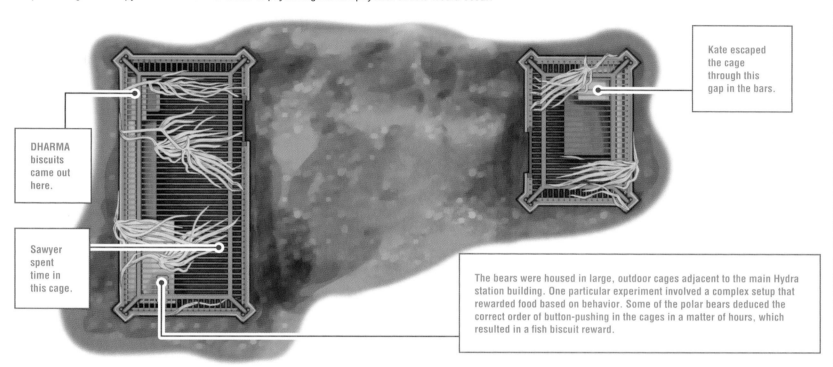

Kate escaped the cage through this gap in the bars.

DHARMA biscuits came out here.

Sawyer spent time in this cage.

The bears were housed in large, outdoor cages adjacent to the main Hydra station building. One particular experiment involved a complex setup that rewarded food based on behavior. Some of the polar bears deduced the correct order of button-pushing in the cages in a matter of hours, which resulted in a fish biscuit reward.

OPERATING ROOM

The Hydra station also had its own medical facility, complete with an operating room. Although crude compared to modern-day setups, the room contained the most necessary medical instruments to perform surgery and treat injuries. There were provisions just outside the main operating room for medical personnel to prep for surgery and examine x-rays.

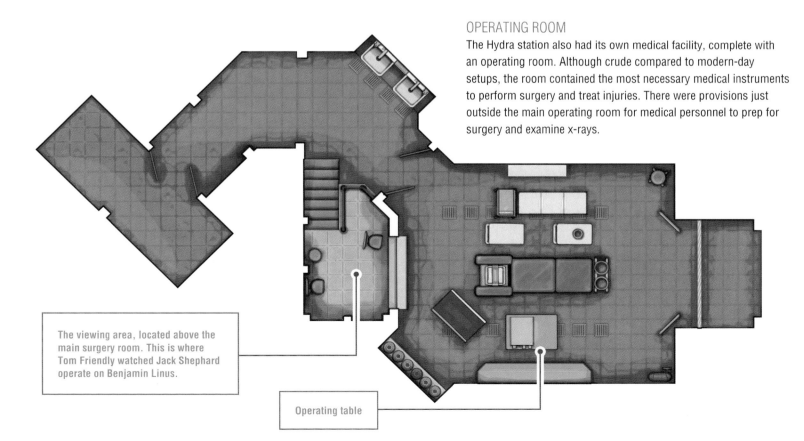

The viewing area, located above the main surgery room. This is where Tom Friendly watched Jack Shephard operate on Benjamin Linus.

Operating table

155

DHARMA also carried out genetic engineering with the intent to create new, hybrid species of animals. They experienced some success, including an impressive chimera tropical bird. An underground chamber below the Hydra station served as an aquarium for the capture and study of sharks and various marine mammals.

HYDRA ORIENTATION FILM

The first DHARMA orientation film to be completed was for the Hydra station. Presented by Dr. Pierre Chang, the instructional film stressed the importance of his name remaining a mystery. This failed to occur, which later led to Chang's aliases in future orientation films.

The zoological research of the Hydra was emphasized in the film, especially DHARMA's genetic manipulations including the hybird. Later in the film, the importance of Room 23 and its psychological tampering of the Hostiles was explained in detail. In addition, those people with the proper clearance were allowed access to the importance of Room 23 and its psychological tampering of the Hostiles.

THE GREAT WHITE SHARK ✛
DHARMA were particularly interested in the great white shark (Carcharodon carcharias), but would have to take great care with their tests as the species notoriously can't survive long in captivity. Sharks have an additional sense that can detect electromagnetic fields. This concept not only fascinated DHARMA, it was an extension of their studies of electromagnetism on the island. They went so far as to tag the sharks with the DHARMA logo before releasing them back into the wild in order to track and monitor the effects of their experiments.

THE RUNWAY

In late 2004, Sawyer and Kate were forced to break up rocks to help the Hydra island's runway. Its construction was a mystery for some time. With Richard Alpert's connection to Jacob, and in turn, Alpert's connection to Benjamin Linus, it's a paradoxical point of interest as to whether someone "knew" Ajira flight 316 would need the runway in the future.

IMPRISONMENT

Several people were imprisoned on Hydra island by the Others once they gained control of the island's resources.

WALT LLOYD

After being abducted by Tom Friendly and his cohorts, Walt was taken to Room 23 for evaluation. Although Ben insisted that Jacob wanted Walt because he was special, Juliet reported that all the Others were scared of him. In fact, no one would enter Room 23 to give Walt food. Among the things that disturbed them was the fact that birds flew into the boarded-up window adjacent to the room, breaking their necks.

KARL MARTIN

Concerned that Karl's relationship with Ben's daughter, Alex, may have led to pregnancy (a fatal condition on the island), Karl was kept in an abandoned polar bear cage. He was also subjected to the subliminal experiments inside Room 23.

WIDMORE'S RETURN

When Charles Widmore and his team returned to the island via a submarine, they set up a base of operations on Hydra island. This gave Widmore a tactical advantage over the Man in Black, who claimed he could not travel across the expanse of ocean as the smoke monster. Widmore also created a sonic fence perimeter as a safeguard against the Man in Black and the magnetizing room to test Desmond Hume's resistance to electromagnetism.

IMMORTAL ORIGINS ✚

The logo used for the Hydra station represents the microscopic fresh-water animal of the same name. Scientists are fascinated by hydras because of their regenerative abilities, resulting in an incredibly slow aging process. This echoes the likes of Jacob and Richard Alpert, both of whom didn't age.

In Greek mythology, the Hydra was a monster with many heads. Like the fresh-water hydra, it had the ability to regenerate after its heads were severed. It was the offspring of Typhon and Echidna.

A fearsome pairing, Typhon and Echidna produced most of the myths' diabolical creatures. Along with Hydra, they created: Cerberus (which is how Radzinsky referred to the smoke monster); a multiple-headed dog that guarded Hades, head of the underworld; Aetos Kaukasios, a colossal eagle (echoing the gigantic, genetically engineered bird DHARMA created); and Chimera, a lion-goat-snake abomination. Chimera is the term used in zoology for an animal that has two or more dissimilar sets of genetically distinct cells. Chimeras occur in nature and also through scientists mixing cells from different organisms, something DHARMA was actively doing.

JACK SHEPHARD

Imprisoned within the Hydra station's aquarium, Jack was coerced to operate on Ben and remove the tumor that was pressing against his spine.

JAMES "SAWYER" FORD & KATE AUSTEN

Held captive in the vacant polar bear cages, their attraction to each other was used as emotional leverage and manipulation against Jack to guarantee he agreed to Ben's spinal surgery. They were also used as manual labor to assist in the creation of Hydra island's runway.

JIN-SOO KWON

After Zoe abducted Jin from the main island, she locked him inside Room 23. Jin was brought to Hydra island to discuss the map that he created in the '70s DHARMA that indicated the location of the island's unique pockets of electromagnetism.

IAN MCVAY

▶ **CONNECTION:** Coroner who examined Charlotte Malkin

Ian McVay worked both as an undertaker and a coroner in Sydney, Australia. An eventful night for Ian began when he received a phone call from his assistant, Ambrose, at 1 a.m. Ambrose had brought in the body of Charlotte Malkin, who had been discovered in a river two hours after she drowned. Charlotte was the daughter of Richard Malkin, a psychic, and his devout Catholic wife, Joyce Malkin.

On the night of the autopsy, Ian's autopsy assistant, Valerie McDervish, washed and prepared the body, but when Ian began the thoracic (chest) incision, Charlotte sat up and began screaming. Eko, under his assumed identity of Father Tunde, was sent to Sydney to investigate the event as a possible miracle at the insistence of Joyce Malkin. Eko's conclusion was that the event was not a genuine resurrection.

IGNACIO

▶ **CONNECTION:** Slave onboard the *Black Rock* with Ricardo

A fellow slave with Richard "Ricardo" Alpert onboard the *Black Rock*, Ignacio helped solidify the idea in Alpert's mind that the island was hell. During their journey, the ship's captain steered the vessel off course and into the path of a terrific storm. As the storm grew more intense, a giant wave thrust the ship and its crew toward the island. Using a small hole in the hull of the ship, Ignacio spotted the island in the distance and the Taweret statue on the shore through flashes of lightning. He declared that the statue was the devil guarding the island moments before the *Black Rock* careened into the statue, smashing it to pieces.

Although Ignacio and three other shackled slaves survived the crash, they didn't live long the following morning. Officer Jonas Whitfield descended below deck and stabbed Ignacio and the other slaves to death with his sword explaining that with no water, limited supplies, and the ship being wrecked in the middle of a jungle, it would only be a matter of time before they tried to kill him.

IMAM

▶ **CONNECTION:** Leader of an Australian mosque

Imam is the leader of a mosque in Sydney, Australia. As he performed a prayer service, Sayid and his former college roommate, Essam Tazir, recognized one another. They both got up and left the service to reunite outside the mosque.

" *What lies in the shadow of the statue?* "

▶ **CONNECTION:** Associate of Jacob, protected the candidates

Ilana was the dedicated and fearless leader of the off-island Others, whose job it was to protect the candidates and return them to the island per Jacob's orders. Ilana lived her life to serve Jacob, who was the closest thing she had to a father. Forever faithful to Jacob, Ilana accepted her mission without question.

TOUCHED BY JACOB ✛

In late 2007, Ilana was recovering in a Russian hospital from severe burns. Jacob paid her a visit and during their conversation touched her face and healed her burns. He then outlined the nature of her mission: to protect the remaining six candidates and get them safely to the island's Temple. He emphasized that this was the task she had been preparing for.

MEETING CANDIDATE JARRAH

Ilana located Sayid in a bar in Los Angeles and flirted with him to gain his attention and trust. After sharing glasses of MacCutcheon whisky over dinner, Ilana seduced him. When he started to undress her, she pulled her gun and held him at gunpoint. She claimed that the family of Peter Avellino, a man Sayid murdered, hired her to take him to Guam to pay for his crime. But the story was all a lie, as Jacob needed her to get Sayid onboard Ajira flight 316.

BEN & ILANA ✛

Ilana was suspicious of Benjamin Linus from the moment flight 316 landed on Hydra island. After learning that Ben killed Jacob, she forced him to dig his own grave. Later, Ilana realized the demons that had driven Ben to this heinous act. She forgave Ben after learning he had chosen to protect the island over preventing the murder of his daughter.

The fake badge Ilana showed at airport security to get onboard Ajira flight 316.

ILANA VERDANSKY

ARRIVAL ON HYDRA ISLAND

As Ajira flight 316 flew over the island, it was consumed in a blinding white light. Ilana realized that Sayid was missing and became concerned that she had failed Jacob. Unbeknownst to her, Sayid had been transported through time to 1977, while she remained on Hydra island in present time. Her fears increased as she became concerned about the discovery of a man who wasn't on the plane when it landed. As they met for the first time, the Man in Black introduced himself to Ilana and the other passengers as John Locke.

When Ilana and her team discovered the corpse of the real John Locke inside the crate, she realized the dire situation: they were up against the unstoppable force of the smoke monster. Ilana knew that taking the crate to Jacob was the only way to prove that a deception was in play.

FINDING JACOB

After Ilana realized the Man in Black had been using Jacob's cabin, she had it destroyed before they headed to the Taweret statue. When Richard Alpert correctly responded to Ilana's riddle with *"Ille qui nos omnes servabit"* ("He who will save us all"), she revealed Locke's corpse. This made it clear to Richard that Jacob invited her to the island. Uncertain if Frank Lapidus was a candidate, she knocked him out and brought him along with her group.

When Ilana discovered Jacob had been killed, she wept by his ashes before gathering some in a small cloth pouch to use for defensive purposes. Things changed dramatically when Miles Straume utilized his ability to speak to the dead to determine who killed Jacob. He revealed to Ilana that Ben had killed Jacob—not the smoke monster—like Ben had stated. This revelation turned Ben and Ilana's world upside down.

RESOLUTION

With the knowledge that one of Jacob's candidates was a "Kwon," Ilana was uncertain whom to specifically protect, so she was keen to help. This made her more determined to help Sun find her husband, thus protecting two candidates in the process and helping her stay true to the task of protecting all of the candidates.

Unfortunately, Ilana met a tragic demise as she and the rest of her party were discussing Richard's plan to blow up the Ajira airplane. With a backpack full of unstable dynamite, Ilana clumsily dropped her bag to the ground causing the dynamite to detonate and blow her to pieces. Sadly, a statement Ben made to Ilana rang true: once she had assembled the candidates, the island would be done with her.

TEMPLE MISSION ✚
At the Temple, Ilana led her new companions inside a secret "panic room," safely away from the smoke monster's devastating rampage.

TIME ON ISLAND ✚
POST-AJIRA: 10 days

IAN MCVAY — IMAM

THE INCIDENT

"THAT DAY" Following is a countdown of events from the day of the Incident:

Daniel Faraday directed Dr. Pierre Chang to order an evacuation from the island and confessed he was from the future. Faraday told Chang that six hours after their conversation, energy 30,000 times stronger than at the Orchid would be released at the Swan site.

Faraday convinced Jack that the Jughead hydrogen bomb could destroy the energy underneath the Swan site, thereby stopping the station's construction and preventing the crash of Oceanic 815.

Chang deduced that Miles Straume was his son and ordered an immediate evacuation.

At the Swan site, Chang pleaded for Stuart Radzinsky and his team to abandon their work; Radzinsky refused.

Temperature exceeded 250 F at the drill tower; RPM hit over 200; Gauss exceeded 20kG.

Phil, a member of DHARMA's security staff, spotted Jack approaching; Radzinsky ordered his men to kill Jack.

Jack's support team arrived in a DHARMA van.

A shoot-out ensued between DHARMA members led by Radzinsky and the rebellion led by Jack.

Sawyer knocked out Radzinsky using the butt of his gun; grabbed Phil by the neck and put a gun to his head.

Chang kept Radzinsky at gunpoint and forced Phil to make everyone drop their weapons.

Chang switched off the drill, but the system didn't shut down. The drill had already hit the pocket of electromagnetic energy and the drill got pulled inside.

Jack dropped the thermonuclear core from the Jughead hydrogen bomb down the drilling shaft toward the source of the energy pocket.

" However, there was an Incident. " — Spoken by Dr. Marvin Candle

As ominous as it sounds, the Incident is how the DHARMA Initiative referred to that day back in 1977 when two of the island's most catastrophic events occurred. First, DHARMA drilled directly into one of the largest pockets of electromagnetic energy on the island. The uncontrollable magnetism that safely existed underground was breached during excavation for construction of the Swan station.

Second, several survivors of Oceanic 815, the *Kahana* freighter, and Ajira 316 had been transported back to 1970s DHARMA as a result of the island's time-flashes and started an insurgence. Dropping the veil that they were part of DHARMA, Jack led the assault on the construction site to detonate Jughead's thermonuclear core in an attempt to change time so that 815 never crashed on the island.

Jack led Kate, Sawyer, Juliet, Jin, Miles, and Hurley to the site, while Sayid lay wounded from a gunshot to the stomach in the back of a DHARMA van. When the electromagnetic leak swelled to gargantuan proportions, Juliet was pulled into the bottom of the drilling shaft, where she bravely struck the bomb's core until it exploded. Time course-corrected, shifting those who should never have been in 1977 back to their present-day time period. But events did not change and the Incident still happened. In 1977, the members of DHARMA who didn't evacuate the island and who survived the Incident realized they needed to fix the situation they caused.

The bomb didn't detonate; the drilling tower and anything metal within the perimeter of the site was dragged into the shaft.

Chang's arm got trapped underneath the collapsed tower. Miles freed him, but Chang's arm is later amputated.

A flying toolbox knocked Jack unconscious.

Phil became impaled and killed by flying metallic rods.

Juliet became entangled in a heavy-duty chain and dragged into the shaft opening.

Sawyer grabbed Juliet, but she was ripped from his grip as the chains around her leg dragged her down.

Jack regained consciousness and helped Kate pull Sawyer away from the collapsing shaft.

Juliet regained consciousness at the bottom the shaft next to the bomb. She hit the bomb with a rock 8 times before it exploded and released a blinding white light.

Jack, Kate, Sawyer, Miles, Jin, Hurley, Sayid, and Juliet returned to present-day. Juliet, however, remained trapped in the Swan site. Sawyer dug through the debris to rescue Juliet, but she died in his arms.

Back in 1977, the DHARMA Initiative began making amends for the accident. Concrete was poured over the entire site, and construction began to make the Swan station a building to regulate the permanently breached electromagnetic pocket.

ISAAC OF ULURU

ISAAC OF ULURU Healer

ISAAC'S ASSISTANT

Isaac of Uluru's female Australian assistant believed in his abilities to heal others by tuning and utilizing life force energy. When Bernard Nadler took his terminally ill wife Rose Henderson to see Isaac, this assistant led her to a room to wait for her appointment.

▶ **CONNECTION:** Spiritual healer who treated Rose Nadler

Isaac was an Australian spiritual healer based in a remote part of the country near sacred Aboriginal land called Uluru. According to his ad in the tabloid "The National Flash," Isaac became world-renowned as a faith healer for his 25 years of successful work helping people with incurable diseases, injuries and emotional distress. He explained that his "gift" was the ability to connect to magnetic hot spots in the Earth, one located directly under his home, which in turn allowed him to harness those energies in order to neutralize severe maladies in others and heal them.

While on their honeymoon in Australia, Bernard Nadler hatched a scheme to take an unwitting Rose to Isaac in hopes of finding a possible miracle to eradicate her malignant cancer. Upon discovering his plan, Rose grew angry and disgusted with her new husband's actions. She explained to him that she had made peace with her diagnosis, but with equal passion and irritation Bernard let her know clearly that he had not.

Mollified, Rose agreed to the meeting, which cost Bernard a donation of $10,000. In a private meeting, Isaac explained his energy channelling powers to Rose and, after a brief aura reading, quickly determined that his location of healing resources were not the right ones to cure her. Isaac then offered to refund their donation, but Rose

An ad appears in the paper for Isaac of Uluru.

declined and admitted she would tell Bernard that she was completely cured so they could both focus on appreciating one another in the time they had left.

> **CONNECTIONS** ✛
> *There are several important recurring symbols inside Isaac's home, including empty wheelchairs from healed clients (a la Locke) and cards featuring the Wheel of Dharma, a Buddhist symbol represented by an eight-spoked wheel that is turned when a milestone occurs (similar to Ben's spin of the frozen donkey wheel).*

Amazing Results...

Over 25 years of Healing Around the World

ABOUT ISAAC

Australian based spiritual healer Isaac of Uluru has been helping to ease pain and to restore people's health as a spiritual healer and masseur for more than 25 years. Born in 1949, Isaac has been in demand for many years for the remarkable results he has achieved in helping people recover from injuries, health issues, emotional issues and so called incurable physical and mental diseases.

TESTIMONIALS

"I received four physical healings: heart, lower back, sacroiliac, and right arm. During the crystal healings, a good deal of emotional healing took place."
-Dean W, Australia

"As a human being you demonstrated some of the best qualities any of us could hope to manifest namely, temperance, patience, compassion and love. Our healing continues and we have returned to a life that holds new promise. Thank you for your love and being such a good friend."
-John M, Japan

"I have had the most amazing experience in the past week. Even though I definitely feel "post-surgical", I feel as if I am vibrating at a much higher frequency. I've been feeling the effects of my surgery and resting a lot, but it hasn't affected the strength of that vibrational frequency."
-Shannon, USA

For consideration, please send your contact information to the email address listed inside this brochure to be contacted about Isaac's healing powers.

ISAAC OF ULURU

ISABELLA

▷ **CONNECTION:** Wife of Richard "Ricardo" Alpert

The love of Richard "Ricardo" Alpert's life, Isabella was a kind and gentle soul. In 1867, she developed symptoms typical of the disease Tuberculosis, better known as "consumption" during the 1800s. Believing medicine for her illness to be expensive, Isabella gave Richard her beloved gold cross necklace as payment.

An apparition of Isabella appeared on the ship as Alpert tried to free himself.

Richard traveled a great distance through a violent storm to visit the doctor, but the physician refused to make the return trip to diagnose Isabella. Alpert's love for Isabella drove him to beg for help, a desperation that cost him his freedom. During a brief struggle, the doctor accidentally hit his head against the sharp side of a table and died instantly. This resulted in Alpert's eventual arrest for murder. Tragically, Isabella died in their home of El Socorro, Tenerife due to complications from her illness, but her spiritual place of rest became another isle entirely—the island.

ISABELLA'S PRESENCE ON THE ISLAND

Alpert inexplicably saw Isabella again after the vessel crashed onto the island during a ferocious storm. She stated that the island was hell, that Alpert was dead, and that she feared the devil. Shortly thereafter, Alpert heard Isabella being attacked on the deck above him.

> **SYMPTOMS OF "CONSUMPTION"**
> *The disease was referred to as "consumption" because it appears to consume the sufferer from within. Symptoms of the illness include high fever, pale coloring, and a cough that produces spots of blood.*

Nearly a century and a half passed before Alpert experienced another spiritual communion with Isabella. When Alpert had lost his way and was deciding to abandon the path of Jacob and follow the Man in Black, Hugo "Hurley" Reyes approached Richard along with the spirit of Isabella. But after communing with Isabella via Hurley, she asked Richard why he buried her necklace on the island, the same necklace that the Man in Black returned to him. Although Alpert could not see Isabella, he could definitely sense her presence. After the couple's powerful emotional and spiritual connection was restored, Richard turned his focus to carrying out his love's plea from beyond the grave: stop the Man in Black from leaving the island to save everyone's life.

> **THE NECKLACE**
> *With the cross on the necklace serving as a religious symbol, this piece of jewelry also represented the powerful love and bond that two people can share. Long after the ship crashed onto the island, the Man in Black returned the necklace to Alpert as a reminder that he would always be waiting for Alpert's allegiance if he ever chose to give it.*
>
> *Richard dug up the necklace some 140 years later to beckon the Man in Black and pledge his loyalty to him. But after communicating with Isabella via Hurley, Richard kept the necklace and restored his faith in himself. With the cross around his neck, it showed him that even in the chaos and trauma of his long life, true love conquers all.*

> **THE CROSS**
> *Another significant religious item that traveled halfway around the world and ended up on the island was the crucifix owned by Yemi, Eko's brother.*

ISHMAEL BAKIR

▷ **CONNECTION:** Hired by Charles Widmore to murder Nadia (Sayid Jarrah's wife)

A shadowy figure, Ishmael Bakir spied on the funeral of Sayid's wife, Noor "Nadia" Abed Jaseem. Ben explained to Sayid that he had photographic evidence of Bakir fleeing the scene where Nadia was killed and that he was certain Bakir was working for Widmore.

After Ben and Sayid's conversation, Ben began spying on Bakir but was caught and held at gunpoint in a nearby alleyway. Before Ben could relay a message that he wanted delivered to Widmore, Sayid appeared and shot Bakir. It was this killing of Bakir that motivated Sayid to work for Ben and take out everyone associated with Widmore who posed a threat to his fellow Oceanic Six survivors and those who remained on the island.

THE ISLAND

Beyond its intoxicating vistas and wild jungles, the island had a purpose far greater than its unparalleled beauty: keeping the sum of the world's evils safely imprisoned. The island acted like a cork, preventing darkness from spilling and covering the world, yet the island was also the central source of benevolence. This intangible goodness exists as ethereal light hidden deep inside the heart of the island.

The role of the island protector was to prevent mankind from exploiting the power of the island. When the smoke monster emerged from the heart of the island, the protector's role became more complicated. The smoke monster indicated a shred of evil had leaked through and its singular purpose was to extinguish the light, destroy the island, and unleash its darkness across the world.

Danielle Rousseau's hand-drawn illustrations of the island.

FACE AU VENT

« LA MER QU'ON VOIT
DANSER LE LONG DES
GOLFES CLAIRS...
A DES REFLETS D'ARGENT... »

A DES REFLETS D'ARGENT LA MER DES
REFLETS CHANGEANT
AU BORD DE LA TANG
UNE INTERBELIK
REGRET BLEUE

The crater

LE CRATÈRE

CÔTE DES MOUSTIQUES

VERSANT
EXPOSÉ

ROC SOU
LES ALIZÉS

LAGON BLEU AZURÉ

ÉPAVE

LA BAIE
DES CRABES

RÉCIFS
CORALLIENS

Blue lagoon

Wreck

LE LONG DES GOLFES CLAIRES
LE LONG DES GOLFES CLAIRES

SABLES MOUVANTS

0   10   20   30   40   50   60 Km

Coral reefs

Bay of crabs

Moving sands

SUBTERRANEAN STRUCTURES

Aside from the heart of the island itself, a complex system of natural tunnels, caves, and catacombs existed deep within it. Over the centuries, some had been expanded and affected by those who came to the island. Some tunnels revealed powerful pockets of energy, such as the one housing the wheel beneath the Orchid station.

MAN-MADE STRUCTURES

From the colossal statue of Taweret, to the Others' Temple, each group of people who arrived left behind their man-made constructions. Most recently, the DHARMA Initiative left its mark with various scientific buildings on the main island and the smaller neighboring Hydra island.

ELECTROMAGNETIC ENERGY

Pockets of unique electromagnetic energy exist all around the world, but none were more powerful than the island itself. All of the Earth's pockets of energy connected back to the source, the island. The two strongest pockets appeared beneath the Swan and Orchid stations. High levels of electromagnetism can cause strange anomalies, which many visitors to the island hoped to harness.

TIME

As the island moved through time and space, there was never a conventional anchor by which its inhabitants could measure time. Consequently, those who experienced time travel found it hard to make sense of what could be determined their "present" and those historical events that could be classified as things that had always happened.

"Think of the island like a record spinning on a turntable. Only now, that record is skipping. Whatever Ben Linus did down at the Orchid station, I think it may have...dislodged us. "
— Daniel Faraday

TRAVEL

Several Oceanic survivors observed that a compass did not read "true north" on the island. Owing to the unique properties of the island, it was very difficult for visitors to leave and return unless they had a specific heading to follow. In order to travel safely from the island to the *Kahana*, the only correct bearing was 305 degrees.

HEALING

For a fortunate few, the island provided miraculous healing. Wounds healed faster than normal, and in rare cases, terminal cancer and paralysis were cured. The Others' Temple was built to protect one of the island's natural springs that had the ability to cure sickness and injury. Symbolically, the island also represented a place that washed away the sins of its guests and often provided them with second chances.

THE STONE CORK

The stone cork was a physical plug for the energy contained in the heart of the island. When Desmond removed the stone cork, the light in the heart changed color, and the water drained from the surrounding pool. Removing the cork caused extreme volcanic and seismic activity. When Jack replaced the cork, the chaotic energy was again suppressed. Numerous symbols encircle the stone cork in a spiral pattern. The meaning of this ancient script follows:

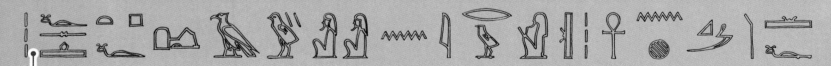

Embrace that which the Balance hath weighed, let a path be made for the Osiris in the Great Valley, and let the Osiris have light to guide him on his way.

He hath reconciled the Two Fighters (Horus and Set), the guardians of life.

Break the immovable yoke that we may sleep.

       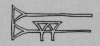

That silence may reign and we may sleep.

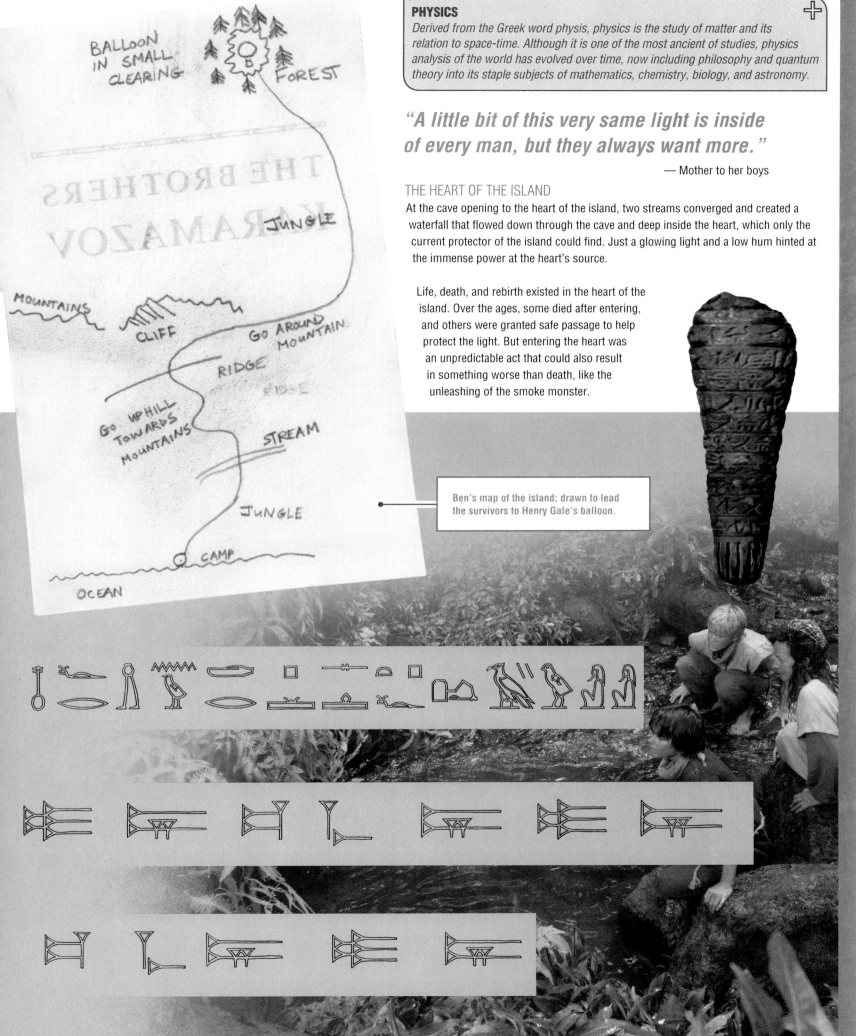

BALLOON IN SMALL CLEARING

FOREST

THE BROTHERS KARAMAZOV

JUNGLE

MOUNTAINS

CLIFF

GO AROUND MOUNTAIN

RIDGE

RIDGE

GO UPHILL TOWARDS MOUNTAINS

STREAM

JUNGLE

CAMP

OCEAN

Ben's map of the island; drawn to lead
the survivors to Henry Gale's balloon.

PHYSICS

*Derived from the Greek word physis, physics is the study of matter and its
relation to space-time. Although it is one of the most ancient of studies, physics
analysis of the world has evolved over time, now including philosophy and quantum
theory into its staple subjects of mathematics, chemistry, biology, and astronomy.*

"A little bit of this very same light is inside of every man, but they always want more."

— Mother to her boys

THE HEART OF THE ISLAND

At the cave opening to the heart of the island, two streams converged and created a
waterfall that flowed down through the cave and deep inside the heart, which only the
current protector of the island could find. Just a glowing light and a low hum hinted at
the immense power at the heart's source.

Life, death, and rebirth existed in the heart of the
island. Over the ages, some died after entering,
and others were granted safe passage to help
protect the light. But entering the heart was
an unpredictable act that could also result
in something worse than death, like the
unleashing of the smoke monster.

THE ISLAND

167

ISLAND OPEN GOLF TOURNAMENT

The "island open golf tournament" was created by Hurley for the Oceanic 815 survivors. There were two tournaments, the inaugural game and a second one that was played for deodorant sticks.

The tournament was created after Hurley found a set of golf clubs in the collected wreckage. He then took it upon himself to create a two-hole, par three golf course in a jungle clearing. It was his intention to provide some fun for the stress-affected survivors.

Jack and Michael were the first ones to play the course, then Charlie joined for the initial three-way tournament. News of the course attracted some beach dwellers to make the hike inland, including Kate and Sullivan. The lively competition created some friendly wagers among the survivors including Sawyer, who offered up some of his stash.

IVAN ANDROPOV

▶ **CONNECTION: Target of hit by Sayid Jarrah, via Benjamin Linus**

Russian Ivan Andropov represented the last of Sayid's assassination targets for Ben Linus. Identified by Ben as one of Widmore's collaborators responsible for Nadia's death and a continued threat to the Oceanic Six, Sayid traveled to Moscow to hunt down Andropov. The men engaged in a street chase not far from St. Basil's Cathedral that ultimately ended at Ivan's apartment. Despite the Russian's best efforts, Sayid burst into the residence with his gun raised. Andropov begged for his life and pointed to a huge stack of money inside an open safe. He offered it to Sayid in exchange for his life, but Sayid showed no mercy and shot him in cold blood. After the kill, Ben released Sayid from his services.

DHARMA CONNECTION ✛

A sign outside Ivan's apartment reads in Cyrillic and translated English as 32 Oldham Pharmaceuticals. In '70s DHARMA, Oldham was the mysterious drug expert who lives outside the compound in the jungle. Per the orders of Horace Goodspeed, Oldham injected Sayid with a serum meant to make him confess his true origins as an Other or someone else.

ISLAND OPEN GOLF TOURNAMENT — IVAN ANDROPOV

The survivors' hand-crafted ping pong paddles.

Games of strategy were a popular diversion among the survivors of Oceanic 815, both on the island and in their previous lives before the crash. Oftentimes the games they enjoyed the most, such as Locke's affinity for Mouse Trap or Shannon's covert enjoyment of crossword puzzles, belied their intelligence and adaptability to survive in their new surroundings.

Leonard Simms played Connect Four at Santa Rosa Mental Institute.

Locke played chess in the Flame station.

Off-island Locke played Risk with a co-worker, and on the island he played with Hurley and Sawyer at the barracks.

Walt's Game Boy.

Shannon worked crossword puzzles prior to boarding flight 815.

puzzle 39

SHOOT SOME HOOPS

FUN WITH CROSSWORD PUZZLES & MORE!

Over 70 Crosswords & Dozens More Mind Bending Puzzles

While working a retail job, Locke explained the rules of Mouse Trap to a young boy.

MOUSE TRAP

Ages 6 & Up

WORD SEARCH SUDOKU

WHITE BELT SUDOKU

MICHAEL RIOS

MARTIAL ARTS SUDOKU

EASY

300 PUZZLES

JACK SHEPHARD

FACTS & FIGURES

Time On The Island
- POST-OCEANIC: 101 days
- POST-AJIRA: 4 days
- POST-INCIDENT: 9 days
- IN DHARMA: 4 days

Time As Oceanic Six: 3 years

Education: UCLA Medical School

Occupation: Spinal Surgeon

Pastimes: Poker, Chess, Red Sox fan

Island Weapon Of Choice: Beretta 9mm

Candidate: #23

A gifted surgeon and natural leader, Jack Shephard's greatest strengths were always tempered by his fear of failure. He adopted his father's technique of overcoming fear in five seconds, but Jack rarely believed in himself. Instead, he wore a heroic mask in many situations, from performing complex surgeries, to calming survivors of the crash.

Rarely letting anyone see his insecurities, Jack faced the physical and emotional traumas on the island with an act of defiance, driven by an obsession to make things better. Although he lost his way after returning to Los Angeles, the man of science gradually increased his belief in the power of the island. When he embraced his destiny, Jack saved the world from being engulfed in darkness, just before his own light flickered out.

THE FIXER, THE SURGEON

As a child, Jack always had the desire to fix things and help others. When his friend Marc Silverman was bullied at school, Jack stepped in and received a beating himself. His father tried to explain that the dilemma in being a hero was that Jack would need to learn to deal with failure. Jack misunderstood his father's message, and concluded his father didn't believe in him. Even after he became a highly regarded surgeon, Jack punished himself and pushed himself to do more.

FAILED MARRIAGE

Running a *tour de stade* to clear his head after operating on Sarah Wagner, his future wife, Jack met Desmond Hume for the first time. After Desmond spoke of miracles, Jack was proud of Sarah's astonishing recovery from a broken back, but he couldn't process this event as being anything more than a scientific anomaly.

In a rare moment of public fragility, during their wedding vows, Jack admitted she had in fact fixed him. However, their marriage was short-lived. Due to Jack's desire to fix people—and his need to prove himself—their relationship deteriorated. After the divorce, Sarah found love with a new man and Jack became obsessed with her new boyfriend. Christian pleaded for Jack to let the relationship go, causing Jack to accuse his father of an affair with Sarah and physically attack him at an AA meeting.

As Christian's alcoholism worsened, so did Jack's relationship with him. The last time Jack spoke to his father was during the hospital inquiry after Christian's drinking caused the death of a patient. Jack's testimony resulted in his father losing his license and his position at the hospital, as well as his subsequent journey to Australia, where he drank himself to death. Jack went to Sydney to bring his father's body home to Los Angeles on Oceanic flight 815.

BY THE NUMBERS

Jack's seat number on Oceanic flight 815 was 23A.

His first major surgery patient was 16 years old.

Jack's mobile phone number as an Oceanic Six member was 323-555-0156.

He was candidate #23; the 23rd Psalm is one of the most beloved Scriptures for both Jews and Christians and it describes God as a shepherd.

" *We have to go back!* "

Jack Shephard
SPINAL SURGEON

OFFICE: (213)555-0189 · CELL: (213)555-0145 · PAGER (213)555-0128

LEADERSHIP

From the beginning, Jack was the accepted de facto leader of the 815 survivors. In addition to his own inclination to take charge, the other survivors also responded favorably to Jack's leadership. He kept the key to the Halliburton case that held the guns and he rallied the troops to help Michael build the raft. However, internally Jack strived to bury his insecurities and bravely battled to keep a degree of order within the chaos on the island. His missteps were always honest, driven by his desperation to honor his promise to get everyone rescued.

Jack struggled so often with his role, because he couldn't accept failure of any kind from himself. Shortly after the crash, one of the survivors drowned while swimming. Boone attempted to save Joanna, but he needed help too. Jack chose to help Boone first, but that didn't stop him from blaming himself that he didn't save them both, however impossible that was.

When conflict with the Others escalated, Jack collaborated with Ana Lucia and later with which Rousseau and Juliet to plan counter-attacks. This strategy was a turning point in Jack's leadership. It dispatched several Others, as Jack led the survivors to the radio tower to await rescue. But when the group realized the freighter wasn't there to rescue them, faith in Jack as a leader faded. He refused to accept that he'd made errors in judgment, and refused to listen to anyone else's counsel.

When Jack returned to Los Angeles as part of the Oceanic Six, his view of himself and his leadership began to change. After he struggled with severe depression and alcoholism, he began believing in fate.

"You've no idea how hard it is for me to sit back and listen to other people tell me what I should do. But maybe that's the point. Maybe I'm supposed to let go."

Jack's time in 1977 DHARMA left him no position of power, as he was assigned the role of janitor. Although he supported Daniel Faraday's plan to detonate the hydrogen bomb, Jack wasn't trying to fix anything. Instead, he was taking a step towards following a feeling, something that he didn't fully understand, but believed was his purpose. Jack's final step on his leadership path was taken by learning to listen instead of shouting orders. Hurley helped Jack realize that when he didn't have all the answers, embracing the unknown would show him the way. Jack finally understood what his father had described during his childhood: If something terrible happens, and you've done everything you can, you need to release the burden of responsibility. You need to let it go.

ISLAND PHYSICIAN

Jack's medical skills frequently helped those on the island. One of the first people he helped at the crash site was the pregnant Claire Littleton, who Jack would later learn was his half-sister.

Boone Carlyle's extensive internal injuries from the fall from the Beechcraft plane tested Jack's desire to be the savior. Jack knew, deep down, that nothing could be done for Boone.

When the survivors shunned Charlie during his days of visions, struggles with heroin and abducting Aaron, Jack remained the faithful doctor and tended to the wounds inflicted by Locke.

Libby's gunshot wound to the stomach was another experience during which Jack had to accept that sometimes he couldn't save his patients.

Jack successfully performed spinal surgery on Ben during his imprisonment at the Hydra station. In return for a guarantee to leave the island, Jack successfully removed Ben's tumor. However, Jack deliberately nicked Ben's kidney to gain leverage to demand Kate's and Sawyer's release from the Hydra cages.

KATE AUSTEN

Jack was immediately attracted to Kate Austen after she mustered the courage to stitch up his wound from the crash. When Jack challenged Kate to a game of skills, he was surprised to learn how good she was and thrilled to find a mutual interest. Her independence both intrigued and annoyed him. This was a woman Jack could never control or predict her behavior.

Aware of the chemistry Kate also shared with Sawyer, Jack often used his medical skills to gain the upperhand. He coerced Sawyer into returning Kate's Halliburton case by threatening to stop giving Sawyer the antibiotic for the infection in his arm wound.

After Sawyer, in a fever-induced delirium, told Jack that he loved Kate, she kissed Jack when she was feeling upset. Jack began falling more in love with her while in front of his eyes she grew closer to Sawyer. The love triangle intensified when all three were imprisoned on Hydra island. Jack was heartbroken when he saw Kate and Sawyer make love at the cages, but he still struck a bargain so that Kate could be safe. Jack didn't want to see Kate with Sawyer, so he made Kate swear not to come back to save him.

Their subsequent rescue changed everything. As part of the Oceanic Six, Jack, Kate, and Aaron became a family. But their engagement and happiness were short-lived. When Jack learned that Claire was his half-sister, his guilt over leaving Claire on the island and watching Kate raise Aaron overwhelmed him. Jack became jealous of Kate and her secretive phone calls. He became convinced she was having an affair and a similar pattern of behavior he exhibited with Sarah began to repeat itself with Kate.

Returning to the island, Jack left their relationship in the hands of fate. Ultimately, they declared their mutual love before they parted for a final time. Jack's last thought was that he did what he promised: He got the woman he loved safely off the island.

JAMES "SAWYER" FORD

Jack and Sawyer had radically different personalities, which led to regular conflict. Jack was frustrated by Sawyer's selfishness, and Sawyer was often jealous of Jack's heroism. When Sayid inadvertently severed an artery in Sawyer's arm, Jack saved his life. Jack also diagnosed his headaches and gave Sawyer a pair of glasses.

In return, Sawyer gave Jack information about his father's last hours. Christian and Sawyer met in an Australian bar the day Christian died. Sawyer told Jack about Christian's confession of regret about his son and how much pride and love he had for him.

The two alpha males shared numerous confrontations from poker and table tennis to gunplay and their rivalry for Kate's affections. Their biggest physical confrontation came during DHARMA 1977. This time, the two disagreed about Jack's plan to change the timeline by detonating the Jughead bomb. Sawyer threw the first blow, but both men unleashed years of pent-up rage in a brutal fist-fight. Juliet's death resulted in a new division between the two men, but ultimately, they were united by a mutual understanding of their fallability. They moved forward with a new respect and a desire to help their surviving friends leave the island.

JULIET BURKE

Although Juliet was one of Jack's original captors in the Hydra aquarium, he swiftly learned that she was not completely loyal to the Others. The two formed a deep connection, fueled by their shared medical background and a desire to go home.

After saving Ben's life by removing his tumor, Jack and Juliet's union became stronger. She began to express feelings for him and the two shared a kiss. Jack realized, however, that he truly loved Kate.

When the two returned to the beach camp, Jack showed his trust in Juliet by warning Sayid that Juliet was under his protection. Later, Juliet diagnosed Jack's stomach pains as appendicitis and performed his appendectomy.

Once Jack left the island with the other Oceanic Six, it was three years until he saw Juliet again. Jack was surprised by her happiness with Sawyer but quickly realized it was genuine. His determination to execute the Swan station plan resulted in Juliet's death, for which Jack accepted the responsibility and guilt.

JOHN LOCKE

As a man of science, Jack found a counterpoint in John Locke, a man of faith. Both men suffered similar internal struggles: each dealt with father/son issues and a desperation to prove their self-worth. When Jack struggled to save Boone's life, he even screamed Locke's mantra, "Don't tell me what I can't do!" Yet it was a long road before they could see eye to eye on much of anything.

In the first few months of knowing Locke, Jack was suspicious of his intentions. Locke's tracking skills and ease within the jungle environment forced Jack to rely on this man who represented a completely different approach to life. At the height of their conflict, Jack tried to murder Locke in front of the whole group. The only thing that saved Locke's life was that the gun Jack fired at Locke's face was empty. Ironically, it was Locke's heartfelt plea for Jack to remain on the island that later contributed to his return.

"You know that you're here for a reason. You know it. And if you leave this place, that knowledge is gonna eat you alive from the inside out...until you decide to come back."

— Spoken by Locke to Jack

Jack's aggressive reaction to Locke's attempts to reunite the Oceanic Six pushed Locke to attempt suicide. The last communication Jack had from Locke was a suicide note that simply read, "I wish you had believed me." Part of Jack did, but refusing to accept it entirely drove him to attempt suicide, before he realized that he had to go back.

MAN IN BLACK

A few days after the crash, the Man in Black appeared to Jack, in the form of his dead father. Jack was manipulated several times by the Man in Black in Christian's form and nearly fell off a cliff while following him. Jack also experienced the smoke monster's devastating power in its natural state several times.

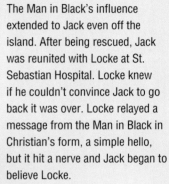

The Man in Black's influence extended to Jack even off the island. After being rescued, Jack was reunited with Locke at St. Sebastian Hospital. Locke knew if he couldn't convince Jack to go back it was over. Locke relayed a message from the Man in Black in Christian's form, a simple hello, but it hit a nerve and Jack began to believe Locke.

Back on the island, the Man in Black in Locke's form was the most intimidating identity to confront Jack. Jack felt responsible for what he thought was Locke's suicide. He began to realize that his man of faith counterpart had been right all along.

After surviving the submarine explosion, Jack made his final moves towards destroying the entity. With the heart of the island's light extinguished, and the Man in Black turned into flesh and bone, Jack's final fight was fueled by his newfound belief for his purpose on the island.

JACK'S OFF-ISLAND CONNECTIONS

- **Margo Shephard** (Mother)
- **Christian Shephard** (Father)
- **Ray Shephard** (Grandfather)
- **Sarah Shephard** (Ex-wife)
- **Marc Silverman** (Best Friend)
- **Gabriela Busoni** (Patient's daughter)
- **Achara** (Thai lover)

DHARMA 1977

The guilt Jack felt for leaving his friends behind—and the realization that Locke was right—drove Jack back to the island. After assuming the role as a DHARMA workman, Jack led the march to the Swan construction site in an attempt to detonate the nuke to reset time so that flight 815 never crashed on the island. In particular, one person who stood in the way was Stuart Radzinsky. His suspicious mind combined with his ambition to tap the pocket of electromagnetism at the Swan site created quite a challenge for Jack. On the other hand, Jack had several sympathetic cohorts like Daniel Faraday, Richard Alpert, Sayid and Kate.

With the core in tow, Jack attempted to detonate it to reset time.

Locke's letter written to Jack.

Jack,
I wish you had believed me.
JL

Ben showed Jack the final game of the Red Sox World Series win.

RED SOX

JACOB'S TOUCH ✛

After his first solo surgery, where his father advised him to let fear control him for only five seconds, Jack met Jacob at a candy machine.

TATTOOS

The Chinese tattoo was created by Achara, who Jack had a relationship with in Phuket, Thailand. The translation "He walks amongst us, but he is not one of us" is a strange echo of Jack's future fate as a protector of the island.

You're not Supposed to raise him Jack

Hurley's note to Jack about he and Kate raising Aaron.

HOFFS/DRAWLAR ✛

When Jack learned of Jeremy Bentham's death (i.e. John Locke), he went to the Hoffs/Drawlar funeral parlor to pay his respects. The name Hoffs/Drawlar is actually an anagram for flash-forward.

THE BEGINNING OF THE END

Jack's island journey began and ended in exactly the same place—within the sacred bamboo forest near the heart of the island. It was where Vincent awoke Jack after the Oceanic 815 crash. It was also where he found himself after disappearing from Ajira flight 316 and it's where he laid himself down to die. After a lifetime of rebuffing faith and surrounding himself with science, Jack let go and embraced something he couldn't calculate—his true destiny.

JACOB

▶ **CONNECTION:** Protector of the island, son of Claudia, assumed child of Mother, brother to the Man in Black

The birth of Jacob and his twin brother on the island led to a struggle for the control of all that is good, all that is evil, and every shade of gray in between. One brother became the protector of the sacred isle, while the other was transformed into an entity of pure, timeless malevolence.

Their opposing views on whether humanity was inherently corrupt spiraled into a contest, each one desperate to prove the other wrong. Although Jacob was killed by an act of misdirection, he had faith that someone would volunteer to replace him and do what he never could: prevent the island—and the entire world—from being cloaked by the darkest cloud, by all that we call hell.

"It only ends once. Anything that happens before that is just progress."

> ## *I chose you because you needed this place as much as it needed you.*
— Spoken by Jacob to the candidates

In their earlier years, Jacob and his brother got along well.

Mother led Jacob to the heart of the island and annointed him as the next protector.

Jacob buried Mother and the Man in Black together in a cave.

LISTS +
The first time the survivors of 815 heard about Jacob and his "lists" was from the Other, Danny Pickett. After bringing Jack to Hydra island, he complained that "Shephard wasn't even on Jacob's list,"—just one of many things Pickett was wrong about.

THE BEGINNING

Jacob was born in a jungle cave on the island, with his twin brother following after. Their mother, Claudia, had survived a violent storm at sea, but her ship was broken apart. Splintered chunks of the bow floated to the shore with Claudia, who, in her heavily pregnant state, was helped to the primitive home of the woman simply known as Mother. But moments after delivering the boys, Mother brutally murdered Claudia with her with own bare hands. She then raised both boys under the ruse that they were hers.

Jacob lived in the shadow of his brother, who Mother loved more. If she left a game by the shore for his twin to find, Jacob would simply be given threads to organize for her loom. Although Mother thought she masked her preference well, Jacob noticed the different ways she loved them, but he buried his jealousy.

Jacob and the Boy in Black enjoyed playing games and hunting boar together. It was during their teens that everything changed. While chasing a boar, the siblings came across a group of men. They rushed to tell Mother that, contrary to what she had told them for 13 years, there were other people on the island.

Jacob hung on to Mother's every word and trusted her warning to stay away from them, but his brother was more intrigued. To explain why the three of them were nothing like the men they saw, Mother blindfolded the boys and took them to the heart of the island. She explained its significance and told them she had made it so that the two boys could never hurt each other.

The ghost of their real mother, Claudia, visited Jacob's brother and revealed, only to him, the truth. She explained the men he'd seen were from her ship. He was furious at Mother's deception, whereas Jacob was simply panicked about change. Jacob beat his brother severely to make him stay, but he was resolute and abandoned them to be with his people. Jacob stayed with Mother, who confessed to everything his brother had accused her of.

DARKNESS FROM LIGHT

Over the next 30 years, Jacob and his brother—the Man in Black—met, talked, and played their game. Jacob was surprised when his sibling openly admitted that—as Mother had warned—the people with whom he lived were very bad. He saw their intelligence and discoveries as purely a means to the end he'd always wanted: to leave the island.

Jacob used the white tapestry to represent happier times, while he created another red tapestry that represented war and destruction.

This Greek phrase quotes Homer's "The Odyssey" and translates to "And may the Gods grant thee happiness."

When the Man in Black showed Jacob the magnetic power near the well, Jacob admitted he was frightened about leaving the island and of Mother dying.

When Jacob reported to Mother what the Man in Black was planning, Jacob created more change than he could handle. Mother filled in the magnetized well, killed all the villagers, and awoke Jacob. Oblivious to what she had done, Jacob was taken back to the heart of the island.

That night, Mother explained that the heart of the island was the source of life, death, and rebirth, but that entering it was forbidden and could cause a fate worse than death. Mother insisted that Jacob was always supposed to be the next protector of the island, but he knew she wanted to give the job to his brother, the Man in Black, all along.

Jacob said that he didn't care about the responsibility and didn't want to protect the island, but Mother retorted that he did not have a choice. Forever desperate to please her, Jacob drank the blessed wine and became the island's next protector.

> ## *Am I good, Mother?*

"That man who sent you to kill me believes that everyone is corruptible because it's in their very nature to sin. I bring people here to prove him wrong. And when they get here, their past doesn't matter." — Spoken by Jacob to Richard

This confrontation between Jacob and the Man in Black led to dire consequences.

The following day, Jacob discovered Mother was dead, his brother next to her with bloodied hands. Once again, Jacob's family unit had been wrecked by his brother's choices. Just like Jacob's reaction 30 years earlier, he flew into a rage. His twin had killed Mother before Jacob had the chance to be loved by her as much as his twin was. Jacob refused to listen to the Man in Black's heartfelt pleas of what Mother had done to his people and unleashed a barrage of blows full of a lifetime of jealousy, rage, frustration, and doubt.

Jacob knew that he couldn't kill his brother due to Mother's prohibition, but he had another idea. Recalling her cryptic warning of dire consequences, Jacob dragged his twin to the stream at the heart of the island and let him float into its core. Jacob was shocked when the light emanating from the cave opening faded. But the terrifying sight of the smoke monster screaming free from the entrance left him dumbstruck. When the spirit of the Man in Black warped into unnamable evil, Jacob was left to weep by his twin's dead body that washed out downstream.

As a young boy, Jacob did whatever it took to please Mother.

"Jacob had a thing for numbers." — The Man in Black in Locke's form

A CHANGE IN THE WEATHER

In the late 19th century, things changed dramatically for Jacob in his struggle against the smoke monster. Ever since his brother's spirit had become a violent, shape-shifting entity, it had frequently met with Jacob in the form of the Man in Black. Jacob argued against his notion that all mankind does is come to the island, fight, destroy, and corrupt.

"OUR VERY OWN ADAM AND EVE" ✛
Jacob was responsible for the "Adam and Eve" corpses that Locke, Jack, and Kate discovered some two millennia later. Jacob collected his brother's body and placed it beside Mother's inside a cave. He placed the two stones—one black, one white—that had fallen from Mother's hand and put them inside a cloth bag. She had picked them up from the senet game Jacob played with the Man in Black before she was stabbed. Jacob wept, kissed the cloth bag, placed it in their hands, and said his final goodbye.

Jacob brought the ship the *Black Rock* to the island in 1867, hoping once again to prove the Man in Black wrong. A ferocious storm crashed the *Black Rock* through the Taweret statue, shattering it, and the ship rested inland.

Jacob waited, and after the Man in Black killed all but one of the survivors, the inevitable happened. Richard Alpert, the remaining survivor, was convinced by the Man in Black to kill Jacob. He told Richard that he was in hell and that he needed to kill "the devil." Jacob explained the nature of the island and the importance of protecting its all-powerful heart from the Man in Black and from mankind.

Jacob's idea of bringing people to the island to see if they knew the difference between right and wrong was itself paradoxical. Jacob had influenced their lives *by* bringing them to the island, but he then stepped away. He left them to make their own decisions, but the test to discover man's core qualities was negated every time the Man in Black flew into a rage and slaughtered them as the smoke monster. Jacob, in part, had forgotten that he himself was once a normal, imperfect, mortal human and that perhaps his plan was inherently flawed.

Jacob submerged Richard to prove he wasn't in hell and was very much alive.

Jacob confessed to Alpert that he'd brought many to the island before the *Black Rock*, and that they'd all died. In the face of Alpert's criticisms, he remained adamant that he shouldn't step in. After Alpert reminded him that the Man in Black would, Jacob offered Alpert the job of being his advisor. The intermediary role would be between Jacob and those he brought to the island.

In return, Jacob granted Alpert the wish that he had the power to fulfill: that Alpert would never die. This was a turning point in the history of Jacob's and the Man in Black's confrontations: from this point, Alpert would be there to assist any others who came to the island.

NOT AT HOME

When Ben took Locke to see Jacob at the cabin, he got more than he bargained for. Jacob was no longer using the cabin. It had been taken over by the Man in Black, who staged a terrifying display, reminiscent of a haunting. The Man in Black only let Locke hear him say, "Help me," another carefully considered move in the long con of both men.

TOUCHED BY JACOB

Jacob knew that one day he would need someone to replace him as the island protector and assume his duties. Using the lighthouse mirror, Jacob created a list of "candidates" to bring to the island to determine who would ascend to the position. The survivors of Oceanic flight 815 had specific encounters with Jacob at varying points of his life.

Jacob touched Locke after his confrontation with Anthony Cooper and his fall from an eight-story building. Jacob came to Kate's rescue after she attemped to steal a lunchbox. Sawyer's encounter with Jacob occured at the funeral of James' mother and father when he was a young boy. Sayid and Jacob met one another at a street corner prior to Nadia's death.

Jacob touched Locke after his fall from an eight-story building.

UNSUBSTANTIATED CLAIMS ✚

Ben told Juliet that Jacob would cure her sister Rachel's cancer if Juliet stayed on the island longer. Rachel was cured, but Juliet never knew for certain whether Rachel's cancer had returned in the first place.

Charles Widmore claimed Jacob came to him and showed him the error of his ways before telling him how to find the island to save it.

Jack and Jacob's meeting took place at St. Sebastian Hospital.

Sun and Jin met Jacob at their wedding.

"I want you to have the one thing that I was never given: a choice."

— Jacob to the candidates

THE END

Until the knife entered his chest, Jacob hoped that Ben would change his mind. True to his belief of self-determination, Jacob didn't try to talk Ben out of killing him. Jacob realized that the Man in Black had found a loophole: if he could not kill Jacob, he would simply carry out a long con and abuse someone's confused feelings about Jacob and the island.

In his final moments alive, Jacob, in many ways, still had the same flaws before he became the protector of the island. He failed to truly listen to the emotional, soul-baring speech Ben gave. It spoke of endless servitude, never once receiving a shred of affirmation, echoing exactly the frustrations Jacob felt from the relationship with his Mother. Ben reminded Jacob that he had done everything blindly for the sake of protecting the island, and Jacob's dismissive response of "What about you?" triggered Ben's fatal action.

After Jacob's death, his spirit sought out Hurley's aid first. Jacob helped Hurley guide everyone toward the Temple to safeguard them from the Man in Black. He then told Hurley how to get Jack to the lighthouse so the doctor would finally realize that Jacob had important plans for Jack his entire life.

Taking the form of Locke, the Man in Black successfully exploited Ben, who felt emotionally distraught and cheated by Jacob enough to want to murder him.

Jacob instructed Jack to drink the blessed water.

Jacob's last moments as a spirit on the island were his most honest. Admitting to his weaknesses and failings, he confessed that he was indeed the cause of not only his own suffering but also the suffering of many others. Jacob's jealousy and human condition had created the monster that made the task of protecting the island so much more difficult. He knew that his mistake could lead to the death of everyone in the world.

Mother's rule prevented Jacob from killing the Man in Black, so Jacob chose candidates who might succeed where he never could. Specifically, he chose them because like him, they were alone, flawed, and the island needed them as much as they needed the island. But Jacob had learned from the mistakes of Mother: she hadn't given him a choice, which is exactly what he gave them; only a volunteer would take his place.

Jacob blessed some river water and initiated Jack, who had chosen to become the next protector. Jacob then left and was never seen on the island again.

JACOB'S CAVE

The cave was a natural grotto that was created by erosion over the eons. Jacob found the hard-to-access space sometime during his existence on the island and claimed the remote hideaway as his private space to work through his list of candidates.

The route to the cave was a precarious 200-foot drop accessible via bamboo ladders attached to the cliff.

INSIDE THE CAVE

Right inside the cave opening was a small space with a rudimentary wooden work table covered with old items that included a compass, an ankh, a mortar and pestle, some rusted chisels, a lute and a box of wooden matches. The centerpiece was an ancient, rusted metal scale with a black stone on one balance plate and a white stone on the other.

When the Man in Black entered with Sawyer, he took the white stone and threw it into the ocean.

"It's an inside joke."

— Spoken by the Man in Black

The small front space opened into a larger, open cavern where Jacob spent the bulk of his time and effort. In chalk, he had written the names of all of his potential candidates—hundreds over the centuries—and then crossed out those who were no longer in the running.

JAE LEE

▶ **CONNECTION: Taught English to Sun-Hwa Paik; had a brief affair with her**

Jae Lee was the general manager of the prestigious Seoul Gateway Hotel in South Korea and the former lover of Sun Paik. Jae was born in South Korea to a wealthy hotelier family and, as such, was afforded all the benefits of a privileged upbringing. As a young man, Jae traveled to the United States to attend Harvard University where he studied Medieval Russian Literature. Toward the end of his studies, he fell in love with an American woman but he had to return home to join the family business. In secret, he made a plan to return to America in six months' time and marry her.

Back in Seoul, Jae was made manager of the Seoul Gateway Hotel and found himself immediately pressured by his father—via his mother and the other women in his family—to find a wife. To humor them, he agreed to meet Sun Paik. The pair was surprised at how easily they connected. As they continued to see one another, Sun grew more smitten with Jae. At one of their lunches, Jae told Sun about his secret love in America, which greatly disappointed Sun and effectively ended their friendship.

A RENEWED RELATIONSHIP

After Sun married Jin, she renewed her friendship with Jae in Seoul after his love affair had ended. Sun asked Jae to teach her how to speak English. Over time, Sun revealed that she wanted to learn English so that she could leave Jin and flee to America. Jae told her that she shouldn't run away from her problems and intimated that she should also stay for him.

Friendship then bloomed into a secret affair, for which Sun had great misgivings. During one of their liaisons, Jae presented Sun with pearls and asked her to leave Jin. Before she could respond, there was a knock at their door and in walked Mr. Paik. Shamed by his daughter's infidelity, Paik told Jin that Jae had stolen from him and tasked his son-in-law to "deliver him a message"—kill him—to restore the family's honor. At the Gateway Hotel, Jin pummeled Jae but showed mercy by not pulling the trigger as he aimed a gun at Jae's head. Jin ordered a sobbing Jae to leave the country or he would finish the task. A few minutes later, Jin was shocked to see Jae's body landed on his car, clutching Sun's pearls.

JAN & MIKE

▶ **CONNECTION:** Owners of a commune that grew marijuana; allowed John Locke to join their "family"

Jan and Mike grew peaches on a farm, which had a very hippy sensibility. There was even a sweat lodge for its "family members" to use for meditation purposes. But most importantly, Jan and Mike constructed a large marijuana greenhouse on the farm.

After Helen Norwood rejected Locke's proposal and ended their relationship, Locke joined the commune of farmers run by Jan and Mike. Later on, Locke picked up a hitchhiker named Eddie Colburn. After bringing him to the commune, Jan

and Mike told Eddie how special Locke was and that any friend of his was welcome. Eddie immediately bonded with Mike as he was wearing a Geronimo Jackson T-shirt, one of Mike's favorite bands.

When Locke approached Jan and Mike to ask about bringing Eddie into the circle of trust—to inform him about the marijuana—the couple

■ Mike and Jan were arrested in part due to Locke's kindness to a stranger.

panicked. They scorned Locke for ruining their family by unwittingly bringing an undercover cop, Eddie, into their lives. Mike mocked Locke's desperate plea that he would fix the situation by shooting Eddie, but Locke couldn't go through with his plans. Eddie let Locke go free as his fellow officers arrived at the commune. It remains unknown what became of Jan and Mike.

JASON

▶ **CONNECTION:** Former lover of Kate Austen

The one-time lover of Kate Austen, Jason was duped by Kate into robbing a bank in New Mexico. They didn't commit the crime for the money, but instead for access to a safety deposit box that contained a memento toy airplane once owned by Tom Brennan. U.S. Marshal Edward Mars stored the toy plane in the box.

Jason was part of a gang, the "Six Foot Five," that knocked over banks. Under the alias of "Maggie," Kate approached Jason for his help. During the robbery, Jason whisked "Maggie" inside an office for a kiss and to praise her play acting. A moment later, Jason planned to shoot the manager, but Kate thwarted him with a gunshot to the leg. She escaped with her plane and left him to rot.

JASON MCCORMACK

▶ **CONNECTION:** Shot Ana Lucia Cortez

A known felon, Jason McCormack tended toward violent crimes, including assaulting an elderly woman in Echo Park. While exiting a home through its front door after a burglary, he was met by a lone police officer, Ana Lucia Cortez. Ana's partner had gone to check the back door and wasn't there to help Ana Lucia when she confronted Jason, who claimed to be a student. He started to reach for a student identification card, but instead pulled out a gun and fired four bullets into Ana Lucia.

Ana Lucia survived the wounds, but her unborn child was killed when the hollow-point bullets Jason fired pierced both the police-issue armor and Ana Lucia's body. During her convalescence, Jason was apprehended. Captain Cortez, Ana Lucia's superior and mother, told her that Jason had confessed to the crime. However, Ana Lucia insisted he wasn't the right man. One week after Jason was released from police custody, Ana Lucia confronted him in a parking lot. She told him of her unborn child before shooting him six times from point-blank range.

JD

▶ **CONNECTION:** Flight attendant on Oceanic flight 815

On September 22, 2004, when Oceanic Airlines flight 815 left Sydney, Australia bound for Los Angeles, JD was working on board the plane as a flight attendant along with colleagues Michelle and Cindy.

During the check-in and boarding process, wheelchair-bound John Locke was informed that the staff could not locate the specially designed wheelchair that was used for transporting disabled passengers onto the plane. Without it, Locke would have to take a flight the following day. However, JD and his colleague, Michelle, carried Locke to his seat so he could make the flight.

Later during the flight, Cindy approached JD for his assistance in dealing with a clearly agitated Charlie Pace. When Charlie locked himself inside the bathroom to inject heroin, the flight experienced turbulence and Charlie exited the bathroom and staggered past JD. When the flight broke apart in mid-air, JD was in the tail section that crashed into the ocean.

JEANETTE LEWIS

▶ **CONNECTION: Mother of Charlotte Lewis**

Jeanette, Charlotte Lewis's mother, and her family background are intertwined with the mysteries of the DHARMA Initiative and the island. Jeanette and her husband, David, had three daughters, the eldest being Charlotte. Jeanette and David had Charlotte while they were living in Essex, South East England. At a certain point in Jeanette's life, she became involved with the DHARMA Initiative and was on the island with Charlotte between the years of 1974 and 1977.

In 1977, Jeanette fled the island with her then three-year-old daughter Charlotte on the DHARMA submarine. The evacuation was triggered during the construction of the Swan when a drill struck a dangerous electromagnetic anomaly underground. When this incident occurred, Dr. Pierre Chang ordered all women and children to evacuate the island.

During Charlotte's adolescent years off the island, she would often recall fragments of memories of her time on the island. For some unknown reason, though, Jeanette always insisted that the island was simply part of her daughter's imagination. Jeanette's involvement with the DHARMA Initiative beyond 1977 remains unknown.

The incident at the Swan construction site led Dr. Pierre Chang to insist that all women and children leave the island immediately, including Jeanette Lewis and her daughter Charlotte.

JED

▶ **CONNECTION: Passenger onboard Ajira flight 316**

Jed survived Ajira flight 316's emergency landing on Hydra island. When Captain Frank Lapidus returned to the plane hoping to fix the radio and call for help, Jed warned him that Ilana and three of the other passengers had found guns and taken charge.

JESSICA

▶ **CONNECTION: Victim of a con by James "Sawyer" Ford**

The focus of one of James 'Sawyer' Ford's many cons before he arrived on the island, Jessica inadvertently reminded him of his dark past. Married to an affluent lumberyard owner named David, Jessica worked at the same auto dealership as Sawyer, and the two had an affair.

During one hotel liaison, Sawyer performed a con game called "the pigeon drop"—pretending Jessica wasn't supposed to see his suitcase full of cash. Sawyer told her the $140,000 was to invest in an oil mining operation in the Gulf of Mexico. $300,000 bought one share, and his investor in Toronto was to make up the rest. Intrigued by the story—especially as Sawyer claimed a government-sponsored fund tripled the share in two weeks—Jessica suggested she provide the remainder instead, via her husband's funds.

After some persuasion, David agreed to the deal. However, at their home, Sawyer saw they had a young son. Haunted by the realization that he'd just performed the same con that the real Mr. Sawyer had, which caused his parents' murder-suicide, he called off the deal and left immediately.

JILL

▶ **CONNECTION: Off-island associate of Benjamin Linus**

Part of a contingent of off-island Others who facilitated the needs of Ben Linus, Jill was a no-nonsense butcher working at Simon's Butcher Shop in Los Angeles, California.

After the Oceanic Six returned to the mainland, Ben enacted his plan to find the six survivors and persuade them to return to the island. Along with Gabriel and Jeffrey, Jill was enlisted by Ben to help facilitate that plan. She was first introduced to Jack Shephard by Ben at the butcher shop, where she curtly referenced the doctor's drug addiction and was rebuffed by Ben for her callous words.

Sometime after Ben murdered Locke, Jill came into possession of the corpse that she then kept in a cold storage room in the back of the shop. After Jack realized the necessity of returning to the island, Ben tasked him with retrieving Locke's body from the butcher shop. Upon Jack's arrival, Jill led him to the back room and set about acquiring a van for the body's transportation to the airport.

JIMMY BANE

▶ **CONNECTION: Victim of a con by Anthony Cooper**

A perfect example of Anthony Cooper's nefarious connections and unscrupulous dealings, Jimmy Bane was conned out of $700,000 by Cooper. Along with one of his associates, Bane visited Helen Norwood and John Locke after the couple had returned from Cooper's "funeral." Helen refused to tolerate Bane's questioning and verbally attacked him for insinuating that Locke was protecting his father. Although Locke convinced Bane that he knew nothing, it was the act of lying to Bane—and in turn Helen—about Cooper that destroyed Locke and Helen's relationship.

JONAS WHITFIELD

▶ **CONNECTION:** Officer on the *Black Rock*; purchased Richard "Ricardo" Alpert

Jonas Whitfield was a British officer who served under Captain Magnus Hanso on the *Black Rock*, an illegal slave trade ship moored out of Portsmouth, England. As one of several ranking officers onboard, Whitfield was responsible for acquiring indentured servants at ports of call, including the Canary Islands, to work in the mines.

While ported in Tenerife, Canary Islands, Whitfield canvassed the local prison for potential recruits with the aid of Father Suárez. Whitfield specifically needed able-bodied men in good health who could perform manual labor and speak English. On the day Richard Alpert was sentenced to hang for murder, Suárez instead diverted Alpert to Whitfield for inspection. Whitfield pressed him to speak English and inquired about his labor skills. Alpert met all of Whitfield's requirements, so he paid Suárez a pouch of silver reales which made Alpert the property of Hanso. Alpert and others like him were shackled and placed into the lower hold of the *Black Rock*, bound for a life of slave labor in a mining colony.

En route, the ship was lured to the island where it crossed paths with a massive storm that smashed the vessel into the Taweret statue on the shoreline. The ship was left landlocked in the jungle. Captain Hanso and most of his crew perished. Only five officers survived, including Whitfield and a handful of slaves. As soon as Whitfield realized the gravity of their situation, he descended into the hold and ran his sword through the surviving slaves to protect their limited resources. His murderous rampage was interrupted by the smoke monster, who wiped out the remaining officers still alive on deck. It then ripped Whitfield from the hold and killed him, too.

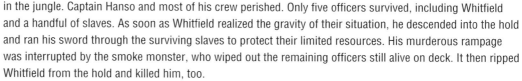

JIMMY LENNON

▶ **CONNECTION:** Friend of Desmond Hume

Desmond Hume knew Jimmy Lennon from when he lived in London with Penny Widmore in the late 1990s. After the Swan station imploded, Desmond's consciousness flashed back to 1996 in London. To prove he'd traveled back in time, Desmond recalled the night Jimmy entered and struck a bartender with his cricket bat before it even happened.

Initially, Desmond got the memory wrong by one night. Twenty-four hours later, he witnessed the event play out just as predicted. Jimmy stormed into the pub, angry that the barman owed him money and raised his cricket bat. As Desmond warned him to duck, Desmond received the blow from the bat to his head. After the impact, Desmond found himself back on the island at the site of the Swan implosion.

JOHNNY

▶ **CONNECTION:** Friend of Hugo "Hurley" Reyes

The happy-go-lucky Johnny was Hurley's best friend during the time they worked together at Mr. Cluck's Chicken Shack. Johnny and Hurley celebrated leaving Mr. Cluck's—and their egotistical boss, Randy Nations—by spelling out "Cluck You" on his front lawn one night. Later that same evening, Johnny discovered Hurley had won the lottery—something Hurley was nervous about telling Johnny as he didn't want his new-found wealth to change their friendship. Shortly thereafter, Johnny ran off with Starla, the girl of Hurley's dreams.

JIN-SOO KWON

FACTS & FIGURES

Time On The Island

POST-OCEANIC: 101 days

IN DHARMA: 3+ years

POST-INCIDENT: 7 days

Year Of Birth: 1974

Jobs: Soldier, fisherman, busboy, waiter, doorman, floor manager, Paik's enforcer

People Killed By His Hand: 2

Candidate: #42

The son of a peasant fisherman from Namhae, South Korea, Jin-Soo Kwon was raised in a meager home by his single father. Jin was told that his mother had died, but in reality she was a promiscuous woman who abandoned him at birth. Unsure if he was even Jin's biological father, Mr. Kwon accepted the baby as his own and kept his son's true heritage a secret so as not to ruin his future.

Jin was an ambitious boy, who saw a life for himself so much bigger than the village where he was raised. Unfortunately, his culture's social caste system made Jin's goal of bettering himself a life-long struggle as his impoverished origins often outweighed anything he accomplished outright. When he was of age, Jin did a stint in the South Korean Army and then moved to Seoul to find work in the hotel industry. His dream was to open a restaurant and own a hotel. To work his way up, he took employment in menial service jobs but none allowed for much upward mobility. Despite his exemplary professional work ethic, his employers commonly discriminated against Jin due to his background.

It wasn't until he met Sun-Hwa Paik that someone finally saw him as an honorable man of great value. Even though she came from the wealthy and powerful Paik family, they fell in love. Naturally Sun's father, Mr. Paik, did not approve of their love and eventual marriage. However, Jin made it his mission in life to be worthy of the woman he adored.

As time went by Jin's tireless pursuit of honor and respect began to poison the thing he cherished most—his relationship with Sun. His position as personal assistant to Mr. Paik was defined by violence and malice, so instead of feeling worthy of Sun, he began to resent what he had to do to have her. Jin began to adhere to the traditional roles that their society demanded and it created a distance between them that was almost irreparable. It took a plane crash for Jin to reconnect with Sun and remember that he had made a vow to protect and love her until death do they part.

THE PAIN OF BEING PAIKS

Desperate to be worthy of Mr. Paik and his daughter, Jin took a job as a floor manager at Paik Automotive. After six months of intense training, he proved to be a go-getter undertaking above-and-beyond tasks like presenting a huge stuffed panda as a goodwill gift to the Ambassador of China when his daughter had a baby.

Unfortunately, things went sour when Jin's mother blackmailed Sun, who then asked for $100,000 from her father to pay off the woman. Unbeknownst to his son-in-law, Paik considered Jin accountable for the debt and used him as his personal assistant responsible for enforcing his more nefarious business practices.

The deeds took a toll on his conscience and his marriage, so Jin made a plan to escape with Sun after one final job in which he hand-delivered Rolex watches to Paik's associates in Sydney and Los Angeles. However, Paik figured out Jin's plan. The controlling patriarch sent a thug in a Hawaiian shirt to the airport to warn Jin not to run.

> *"I do whatever your father tells me. I do it for us."*

Mr. Paik asked Jin to deliver this watch to a business associate.

"She is my dream."

BY THE NUMBERS +

*Jin chased a taxi with the license plate number **23**69*

*It took **42** days for Jin to get the handcuff cut off his wrist*

THE DESTINY BOOK +

According to Tai Soo's grandmother's "destiny book" predicted for Jin:

▸ *He would find love that year,*

▸ *His love would look orange*

JIN-SOO KWON

JIN'S ISLAND CONNECTIONS

Life on the island was a humbling experience for Jin as the proud man lost all of his power. Without language, he was often left frustrated and reliant on his wife to help him communicate with everyone outside of her. The violence and control that was a requirement of his job with Paik translated into dominant behavior with Sun. Without context or language to explain himself, Jin was seen a villain in the eyes of his fellow survivors. He had to overcome cultural perceptions and stereotypes in a brand new environment that was not an equal playing field for him in any way. Jin learned to bridge the communication gap with his natural skills, which allowed him to slowly form friendships and bonds with his fellow survivors.

MICHAEL DAWSON

When Jin saw Michael wearing the Rolex he was tasked to take to Los Angeles for Paik, he became livid and tried to take it back with force. It created a huge rift between the men. It was only when Sun explained to Michael how its loss would dishonor Jin that there was a small glimmer of understanding. When Michael's raft was burned, Jin was ultimately blamed for the fire due to their rivalry. Then when Sun defended her husband in English that he was redeemed but it created another deep gash in their marriage. Jin then shunned Sun and offered to help Michael rebuild the raft. While they weren't similar, they found a way to complement one another's strengths and make an even better raft.

The men bonded more after their harrowing attack at sea and then subsequent incarceration in the tailies' tiger pit. It was Jin who ultimately convinced a frantic Michael to return with them to the main beach camp so they could work together to find Walt. Their friendship gave Jin more empathy and patience that he was able to use to better his relationship with Sun.

JAMES "SAWYER" FORD

The life and death experience that Michael, Sawyer and Jin shared together while on the raft bonded the men in a primal way. While it didn't hurt that Jin couldn't understand James' questionable nicknames for him, the men were all each other had to survive after the Others' attack and they learned to trust one another. When Sawyer's bullet wound became infected on the journey back to the beach camp, Jin became his advocate. After that incident, Jin and James established a friendship that allowed them to appreciate each other's humor. Whether it was ping-pong games for nickname silence or adventures with a DHARMA bus and beer, Jin and Sawyer bridged their language gap with laughter.

Later when they were stuck in 1977 together, Jin became Sawyer's trusted security team member tasked with trying to find their missing friends. Having been taught English by James and a few others, he was finally able to be his own man again on equal footing with his fellow survivors. Later when James grieved Juliet, Jin was one of the first to try to find him. When they reunited on the island, the two men had a new common ground as both missed the loves of their lives. Sawyer made a vow to Jin that they would not leave without Sun.

JIN'S OFF-ISLAND CONNECTIONS

- ▮ **Mr. Kwon** (Jin's fisherman father)
- ▮ **Tai Soo** (Jin's former destiny-believing roommate)
- ▮ **Mr. Kim** (Jin's first boss at the Seoul Gateway Hotel)
- ▮ **Mr. Paik** (Jin's father-in-law and boss)
- ▮ **Jae Lee** (Sun's secret lover and someone "stealing" from Paik)

MAN OF MANY SKILLS

Jin may have wanted nothing more than to leave his humble fishing village roots behind him, but the hands-on skills he learned from his father and in the Army came in very handy on the island.

Initially, Jin used his fishing skills for he and Sun. He later used them to help feed the other survivors.

His fishing boat experience coupled with Michael's engineering talents allowed them to craft a usable raft

Jin's boating experience allowed him to sail the *Elizabeth* around the island's coast.

The Army taught Jin how to handle firearms and tae kwon do, which helped him take down Mikhail Bakunin with a spin kick and then a sleeper hold.

DHARMA 1977

Jin's mission was to reunite with Sun by way of the other Oceanic survivors if they returned to the island.

However, the time skips stranded Jin and his friends on the island in 1977.

Thanks to James "Sawyer" Ford and Hugo Reyes, Jin was able to reunite with his wife.

Jin
Security

JACOB'S TOUCH ✛

In their wedding day receiving line, a stranger placed his hands on both of their arms and offered them a blessing in perfect Korean. Jacob walked away and neither of the newlyweds could place who he was, but they appreciated his kind words that reminded them never to take their love for granted.

LOST IN TRANSLATION ✛

While Sun had secretly learned to speak English in Korea, Jin only knew his native language, which was a huge handicap on the island. Sun tried to help remedy that when she made him a rudimentary Korean to English dictionary to help him learn important words and phrases for his raft journey with Michael, Walt and Sawyer.

Words: Starboard, Aft, Port, Stern, Eat, Sail, Wind, Current, Hurry

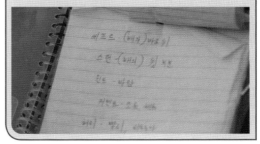

SCENES FROM A MARRIAGE

The Kwon marriage, like any, was complicated with its share of good times and bad. While their union came precipitously close to breaking, ultimately they were able to get past the pain and back to the love that connected them in the first place.

With the prospect of a real future working for Paik, Jin proposed.

Translated, the inscription reads: We will never be apart.

Called into training for his new job at Paik Automotive, Jin had to delay their honeymoon.

Despite his father's absence, Jin and Sun were married in a ceremony with family and friends.

At the beck and call of Paik, Jin found things to fill Sun's time when he was absent.

JI YEON KWON

The only daughter of Jin-Soo and Sun-Hwa Kwon, Ji Yeon (which means flower of wisdom) was born in South Korea seven months after Sun escaped the island. The little girl was loved dearly by Sun and frequently stayed with her grandmother, Mrs. Paik. Sun left her daughter in Mrs. Paik's care when she returned to the island to find Jin. Although Jin never got to meet his beloved daughter, he saw pictures of her via Charles Widmore.

After a violent night, Jin returned with blood on his hands and Sun became aware of the cost of her father's hold on Jin.

Jin hurtfully accused Sun of hiding from him her inability to conceive.

After a long rift, Jin forgave Sun's lie and the two embraced before he left on the raft.

Jin forgave Sun for her affair and took blame for his part in the problems that led her to stray.

Desperate to save his marriage, Jin visited his father who told him to run away to America.

After his ordeal on the raft and with the tailies, Jin returned to Sun.

Sun believed Jin perished on the freighter and mourned him deeply.

After destroying Sun's garden, Jin apologized and admitted he needed her.

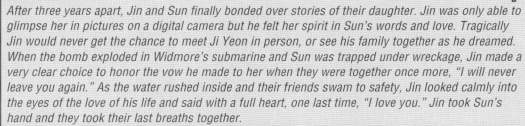

A TRAGIC END

After three years apart, Jin and Sun finally bonded over stories of their daughter. Jin was only able to glimpse her in pictures on a digital camera but he felt her spirit in Sun's words and love. Tragically Jin would never get the chance to meet Ji Yeon in person, or see his family together as he dreamed. When the bomb exploded in Widmore's submarine and Sun was trapped under wreckage, Jin made a very clear choice to honor the vow he made to her when they were together once more, "I will never leave you again." As the water rushed inside and their friends swam to safety, Jin looked calmly into the eyes of the love of his life and said with a full heart, one last time, "I love you." Jin took Sun's hand and they took their last breaths together.

After three years of separation, the couple reunited with a kiss.

Eloise made a personal inscription to her son on the first page of the journal that read: "Daniel, No matter what, remember, I will always love you. Mother."

Hawking already knew that she would kill her own son in the past and there was nothing she could do to change that outcome. She spent all of Daniel's young life pushing him to stay focused and develop his mathematical skills at the expense of everything else. This note was uncharacteristically emotional for Eloise, but it was the one opportunity she took to tell Daniel that despite her cold demeanor, she really did love him.

Daniel,
No matter what, remember
I will always love you.
Mother

This journal belongs to

An embossed leather journal gifted to Daniel Faraday by his mother Eloise Hawking on the day of his graduation from the doctoral program at Oxford University.

Daniel went on to fill the blank journal with his musings, theories, equations and discoveries about time travel, constants, the DHARMA Initiative and hydrogen bomb core removal.

Daniel graphed out the repercussions on the spacetime continuum if a fusion reaction were to split real time into divergent tracks and then how they would come back together again at one point in time. Ben Linus also had a copy of this exact page and kept it in a file in his Hydra island office.

FISSION CHAIN REACTION

DROPPING PLUTONIUM CORE INTO ELECTROMAGNETIC POCKET AT SWAN SITE YIELDS FOUR KILOTON DETONATION, RESULTING IN PARADOXICAL NEGATION.

Other pages of Daniel's journal reference specific equations or theories such as: *Lorentz Invariant*—referred to an unchanged Lorentz transformation quantity that is important to Einstein's theory of special relativity; *Kerr metric*—referred to the non-linear resolution to Einstein's equations of general relativity. It describes the theory of black holes; *Eddington-Finkelstein coordinates*—referred to a pair of coordinate systems adapted to radial null geodesics (or photons moving to or from a central mass). These are used in conjunction with the Schwarzschild radius that is used to explain gravitational singularity (or black holes).

When the island stopped skipping through time and got unstuck in 1977, Daniel left the island on the DHARMA submarine and relocated to Ann Arbor to continue his research. While there, he theorized that detonating a nuclear bomb inside an electromagnetic pocket would create paradoxical negation and, in turn, "correct" time so Oceanic 815 never crashed.

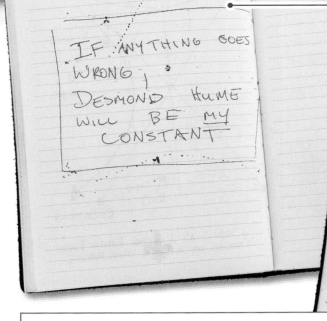

Based on his research at Oxford University and experiments into time travel, Daniel deduced that in order for a consciousness to jump stably through time the person needed a constant that they cared about and remained consistent throughout the period they shifted between. Daniel selected Desmond Hume as his constant and noted it in his journal in red ink to remind himself in case of his own temporal shifts.

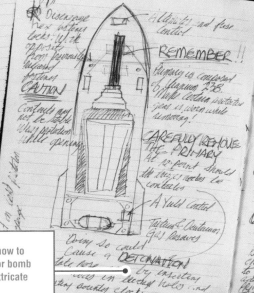

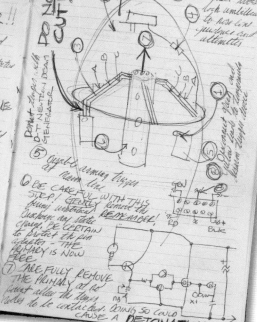

Daniel studied and took copious notes with detailed sketches about how to void and/or detonate a nuclear device. He drew images of key interior bomb components that could trigger detonation so that Sayid could later extricate Jughead's core and then retrofit it into an impact-triggered device.

JOYCE MALKIN

▶ **CONNECTION:** Married to Richard Malkin, mother of Charlotte Malkin

Joyce is the wife of Richard Malkin, the psychic who performed a reading on Claire Littleton, and the mother of Charlotte Malkin. Joyce believed a miracle brought her daughter back from the dead and sought verification from the Australian Catholic Church via an investigation by Eko, who was posing as a priest named Father Tunde. Richard was quick to debunk the theory and instead asserted that his daughter's body went into hypothermia while in the cold water, which made it look like she had died. Eko left the Malkin residence without interviewing Charlotte and closed the case.

JULIAN CARLSON

▶ **CONNECTION:** Son of Rachel Carlson

Julian Carlson was Dr. Juliet Burke's nephew, the miracle child of her only sister, Rachel Carlson. As a fertility specialist, Juliet used her cancer-afflicted sister as a test subject for her experiments and helped her sister conceive. Independently, her sister's illness also went into remission.

Six months into the pregnancy, however, the cancer returned. While working with Benjamin Linus and the Others, Juliet demanded to be released from her work commitment to return to her sister. Ben refused but promised Jacob would cure Rachel as blackmail to keep Juliet on the island. She acquiesced to save her sister.

Rachel lived and gave birth to Julian Carlson. Whether she survived due to her normal cancer treatment, Jacob, or if she even had an actual recurrence, was never revealed. But Juliet was provided proof when Ben later showed Juliet a videotape recorded by Richard Alpert of Julian playing with his mom in a Miami park the day of the Oceanic 815 crash.

WHAT'S IN A NAME? ✛
It is implied that Rachel named her son Julian in honor of her sister by creating a masculine alternative close to the French feminine form of the name, Julienne.

JUGHEAD BOMB

In 1954, a U.S. Army battalion arrived and set up a small camp of nine tents in the Mesa area. Their mission was to construct a firing tower for a hydrogen bomb. Nicknamed Jughead on its casing, the 20-ton bomb was installed by 18 soldiers as part of a bomb testing program by the United States in the South Pacific.

Not long after the soldiers completed the wooden tower and installed Jughead, Eloise Hawking, Charles Widmore, Richard Alpert and the Others revealed themselves to the army. The Others gave the soldiers the opportunity to leave the island peacefully. The soldiers refused and fired upon the natives. To protect the island, the Others waged a calculated war upon the soldiers and picked them off one by one. The soldiers attempted to fight back by placing land mines to defend their small camp, but they were ultimately outwitted. Those who managed to survive ended up dead due to poisoning from the radiation that had leaked from a crack in Jughead's metal housing.

THE RADIATION LEAK

When the island skipped through time, Faraday, Locke, Miles, Charlotte, Sawyer and Juliet found themselves in 1954 about a month after the U.S. soldiers landed. Despite being split up, they were all captured by Others who wore the soldiers' military garb and took up camp in the soldiers' tents.

Faraday observed the burns on some of the natives' hands caused by the radiation, so he talked Alpert into allowing him to view the bomb. A young Eloise Hawking escorted Faraday to Jughead where he found

Daniel Faraday examined the Jughead and found it had a crack.

the crack. After backing away quickly, he told her they had to fill the crack in its housing with lead or concrete and bury the bomb to save the future of the island.

JUGHEAD & SHRIMP ✛
In 1954, the United States created a nuclear testing program with the code name "Operation Castle." Over a period of three months, the U.S. military detonated half a dozen different designs of thermonuclear weapons in the Marshall Islands of the South Pacific. One in particular, the TX-16, was a liquid deuterium-fueled bomb nicknamed Jughead. However, it was never deployed due to the success of the detonation of a solid fuel nuclear prototype called "Shrimp."

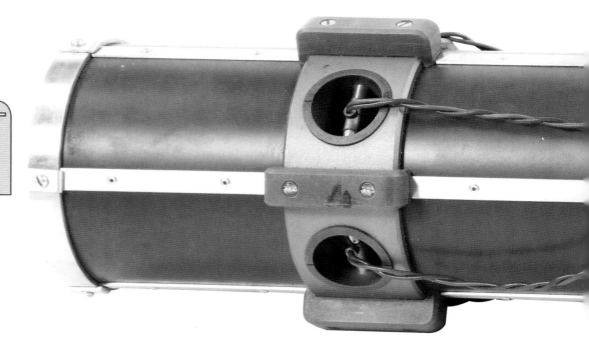

FIXING THE TIMELINE

In 1977, Faraday returned to the island from Ann Arbor determined to detonate Jughead in order to change the future. Based on his study of relativistic physics, Faraday theorized that the detonation of Jughead would wipe out the electromagnetic energy underneath the Swan, thereby negating the need for the hatch. In turn, this would prevent the crash of Oceanic flight 815 and allow the plane to land in Los Angeles. With Jack and Kate in tow, Faraday went to the Others' camp and demanded to speak to Eloise. As he questioned Richard about the bomb, Eloise shot Faraday. With his dying breath, he revealed that he was her son.

> **BY THE NUMBERS** ✛
> *Juliet Burke slammed a rock onto the nuclear bomb core **8** times until it detonated.*

Distraught by her mistake, Eloise confirmed that they buried Jughead in the tunnels that now resided directly beneath the DHARMA barracks. Using Faraday's journal as a reference, she sent Jack, Richard and Sayid to recover the bomb. Sayid consulted the journal to extricate the bomb's core and remove it from the tunnels. The impact-triggered core was eventually transported to the Swan, where Jack threw it into the drill pit. The breached electromagnetic pocket attracted all surrounding metal into it, including a chain that wrapped around Juliet causing her to get pulled into the depths. Broken and bleeding at the bottom, Juliet found the bomb next to her and managed to grab a rock and hit the bomb, causing it to detonate.

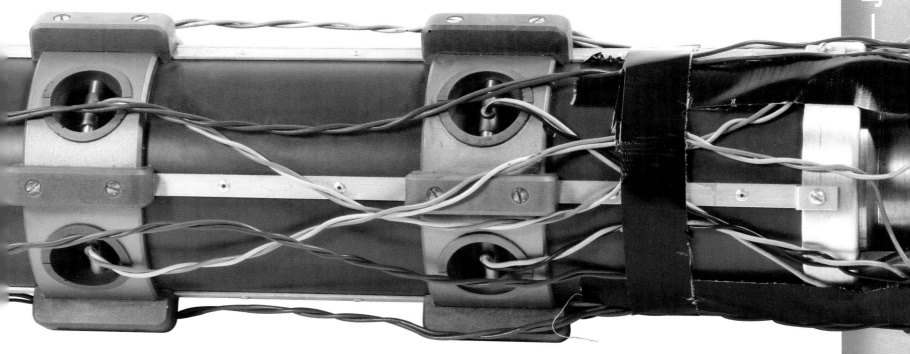

JULIET BURKE

A gifted and empathetic fertility doctor, Dr. Juliet Burke specialized in cutting-edge conception and obstetrics research. Unassuming and dedicated to her work, Juliet wasn't attracted to the fame or money her research could potentially engender. For her, the reward she sought was far more personal. Her beloved older sister Rachel was diagnosed with cancer and her chemo and radiation therapy rendered her infertile. Rachel's one desire in life was to have a baby, so Juliet specifically tailored her research around finding a way to help her sister conceive. After she discovered a way to impregnate a male field mouse, Juliet became more aggressive with her testing, ignoring ethical medical protocols and, with Rachel's support, tested a drug treatment on her sister that resulted in conception.

At this same time, two men learned of Juliet's groundbreaking work and attempted to entice her in dissimilar ways. Edmund Burke, Juliet's ex-husband, used his research assistants to keep tabs on Juliet to track her progress so he could piece together what she was doing outside the lab with Rachel. Wanting to ensure that he could benefit from Juliet's success, Burke threatened to expose her controversial experiments unless she made him an official collaborator.

The same day, Richard Alpert of Mittelos Bioscience arrived in Miami to pitch Juliet a research position at his privately funded facility. They needed her expertise on a special fertility problem that was affecting young women. While intrigued, she declined because of Edmund's threat and her unwillingness to leave Rachel. However, when Edmund was struck by a bus and killed and Richard promised Juliet that she would be home in time for Rachel's delivery, she took the opportunity to free herself and start anew.

OTHER TRUTHS

After working unsuccessfully on the island with nine pregnant women, Juliet determined that a woman could conceive on the island but she would not carry full term. During the second trimester, the woman's immune system would turn on the fetus and her body would naturally terminate the pregnancy at around 100 days. However, if the woman left the island before the 100-day mark, a successful full-term pregnancy could be achieved.

"Don't you understand that every time I try to help a woman on this island give birth, it hasn't worked?"

When she presented her findings to Ben, he would not consider mandatory off-island birth as an option. After three months, Juliet asked Ben if she could to return home. Desperate to keep her on the island, he promised to heal Rachel's newly returned cancer if Juliet promised to stay three more months. Juliet found herself in the same controlled situation that she escaped from with Edmund, but she couldn't risk saying no. Three years later, Juliet was still a prisoner on the island. Ben showed her a video image of a healthy Rachel with her baby boy, Julian, but he again denied her leave to join them. Desperate, she decided to ally with the Oceanic 815 survivors to escape the island and Ben's obsessive clutches.

Juliet used a stealthy videotaped message to convince Jack that she was on his side.

> ## " It doesn't matter who we were;
> ## it only matters who we are. "

BRANDED

When Juliet killed Pickett so Kate and Sawyer could escape Hydra island, she was placed in jail and sentenced to death by Isabel, the Others' sheriff. However, Jack interceded and offered to save Ben's life in exchange for Juliet's life. Isabel agreed but marked Juliet with the brand of a fleur-de-lis so all would be reminded of her crime.

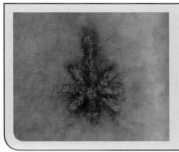

THE FLEUR-DE-LIS

Meaning "lily flower," the fleur-de-lis is an emblem that often denotes royalty. The French adopted the symbol as early at 493 AD with the conversion of King Clovis I. During the height of the French monarchy during the 17th century, certain crimes, such as felony and treason against the state, earned the additional punishment of a fleur-de-lis brand that forever reminded society and criminals of their shameful deeds.

In Alexandre Dumas' "The Three Musketeers" (1844), the character of Milady de Winter is revealed to have the fleur-de-lis brand of a criminal.

LAFLEUR'S LADY

When Jack first brought Juliet to the beach camp, James was distrustful of her intentions. Having read the Others' files about all the survivors, she revealed Sawyer's own transgressions back at him which earned his respect.

"All right, two weeks."

Their trust in one another grew when the island started to skip through time, as an emotional and flustered Sawyer leaned on Juliet as they encountered one dangerous predicament after another. Things started looking up for Juliet when they became stuck in 1974. The DHARMA Initiative's Horace Goodspeed offered them the chance to return to the mainland via the *Galaga,* Juliet's ultimate goal. But Sawyer asked Juliet to wait two weeks so they could find their missing friends. Those two weeks became three years and in that time their friendship turned into a healthy relationship, a first for them both. Juliet saw in James a good man who had finally grown into his potential and she appreciated that he believed and supported her through events like the successful birth of Amy and Horace's baby.

For the better part of three years, Sawyer and Juliet lived together as friends and then lovers.

When the Oceanic Six returned, Juliet could still see a palpable connection between James and Kate. Damaged by her parents' divorce and her own failed relationships, Juliet was convinced she would lose Sawyer to Kate so she supported Jack's plan to detonate the Jughead bomb. When the Incident began, Juliet was dragged into the breached pocket by a heavy chain. James grabbed her arm and desperately tried to save her, but she plummeted into its depths. Broken, bleeding and desperate to have Jack's plan work so she wouldn't have to experience the pain of losing James, Juliet detonated the bomb. She woke only to discover nothing had changed. As James held her tight and she took her last breaths, she finally believed that James' heart belonged to her as she saw her vision of an afterlife with him as she passed away.

THE DOC WILL SEE YOU NOW

Although Ethan Rom was trained in medicine, Juliet was one of the Others' only resident physicians. As such, she was often called upon to use her medical expertise outside of her expertise in fertility research.

- ▶ Juliet treated Goodwin's chemical burn sustained at the Tempest.

- ▶ She consulted on Ben's X-rays to determine the treatment for his tumor.

- ▶ Juliet ran tests on Walt's blood, which led her to label the young boy as "special."

- ▶ Juliet helped Jack during Ben's spinal surgery and provided assistance as he attempted to save Colleen Pickett.

- ▶ She administered Sun's sonogram at the Staff station.

- ▶ Juliet performed an emergency appendectomy on Jack with assistance from Kate and Bernard.

- ▶ When Amy went into labor, Juliet delivered her breech baby.

- ▶ Juliet tried to save young Ben's life in surgery after he was shot by Sayid.

THE MEN WHO LOVED JULIET

Juliet had several significant relationships that impacted her life. Some damaged her self-esteem, while others made her feel whole and loved. They all helped shape the woman who would eventually open her heart to her true soulmate, James "Sawyer" Ford.

▶ **EDMUND BURKE**

Juliet's ex-husband and colleague. He cheated on her with multiple co-workers and marginalized her work to keep her under his thumb.
Outcome: *Edmund was hit by a bus and killed.*

▶ **GOODWIN STANHOPE**

A fellow island Other, Juliet confided in Goodwin after her fertility work failed. In a bad marriage himself, the two bonded and had an affair. Goodwin wanted to leave his wife, Harper, for Juliet but she forbade it because she knew Ben would not allow it.
Outcome: *Ben ordered Goodwin to infiltrate the tailies; Goodwin later died at the hands of Ana Lucia.*

▶ **BENJAMIN LINUS**

Juliet reminded Ben of his mother and his first love, Annie. However, Juliet ignored his advances which made Ben more obsessed. He essentially kept her a prisoner on the island and used Juliet's bond with her sister as emotional blackmail to force Juliet to continue her work and obey his rules.
Outcome: *Lost all control over Juliet when he left the island.*

▶ **JACK SHEPHARD**

Juliet tried to use Jack as a pawn to leave the island, but she quickly came to admire the fellow physician's integrity. An attraction grew and they shared a single passionate kiss, but Juliet knew his heart belonged to Kate.
Outcome: *Jack left the island as one of the Oceanic Six and became engaged to Kate.*

KAHANA

The *Kahana* was a large class cargo freighter owned by Widmore Industries. Its crew of scientists and mercenaries were specifically commissioned by Charles Widmore to locate the island. Once found, the science team was to disable the Tempest station to prevent an assault by the Others, while the mercenaries' clandestine goal was to find and capture Benjamin Linus and kill anyone else found on the island. Unbeknownst to Widmore, Ben infiltrated the crew with his own spy, Kevin Johnson (a.k.a. Michael Dawson), who was used to alert Ben and the Others of the ship once they arrived. The resulting mix of cross-purposes rendered the *Kahana* a very unsettled base of operations for everyone involved. It then ceased to be a resource for escape for the 815 survivors after Martin Keamy rigged C-4 to the ship with a remote trigger that detonated moments after Ben stabbed him.

KAHANA SEARCH MISSION TIMELINE

STARTING PORT: *Suva, Fiji (approximately 76 days after the flight 815 crash)*

SOUTH PACIFIC: *Island location approximated (around the 84th day after the flight 815 crash)*

DROPPED ANCHOR: *Approximately 80 nautical miles to the west of the island*

OCEAN DRIFT: *On day 94, 40 nautical miles west of the island*

LAST DAY OF EXISTENCE: *On day 101, 5 nautical miles from the coast of the island*

KAHANA CREW

CAPTAIN GAULT

▶ **STATUS: Dead, shot by Keamy**

The captain of the Kahana, Gault operated under the impression that he and his crew were on a scientific mission to find the island. It was only when Keamy revealed there was a secondary protocol that included torching the island and its inhabitants that he became fully aware of the truth. A man of action, Gault showed no hesitation in pummeling two of his crew to prevent them from escaping by dingy, or when he pulled a gun on the increasingly violent Keamy. In that heated showdown, Keamy was the victor.

GAULT
Captain Gault's name was inspired by William Hope Hodgson's Captain Gault stories collected into the book "Captain Gault, Being the Exceedingly Private Log of a Sea Captain" (1917). Hodgson's Captain Gault is a morally ambiguous character primarily interested in money and has occult knowledge or arcane religious artifacts.

GEORGE MINKOWSKI

▶ **STATUS: Dead, due to temporal displacement**

Working as the Kahana communications officer, Minkowski served as the voice of the ship when communicating with the island. He spoke with Naomi, Daniel, Jack and Kate by radio at various times. It was his attempt to reach the island via raft that triggered his time displacement symptoms; his lack of a constant led to his apparent brain aneurism on the ship.

MINKOWSKI
George Minkowski shares his name with German mathematician Hermann Minkowski, who theorized that time and space are not separate but one intermingled, four-dimensional entity known as spacetime.

BRANDON

▶ **STATUS: Dead, due to temporal displacement**

Brandon was a crewmember who attempted to reach the island in the Zodiac raft with George Minkowski. They didn't make it due to Brandon's extreme time displacement symptoms. They returned to the freighter where his sickness progressed and he ultimately died.

REGINA

▶ **STATUS: Dead, committed suicide**

She became the replacement communications officer after Minkowski's illness. Regina subsequently had radio contact on the island with Miles and Charlotte. She also helped Daniel perform an experiment from the Kahana by firing a rocket with a timer attached toward the island. After increased erratic behavior, Regina tied herself up in chains and threw herself overboard. Her exact motives were unclear, but it's assumed she fell victim to the time displacement sickness.

COINCIDENCE OR FATE?
Regina is seen reading (upside down) Jules Verne's "The Survivors of the Chancellor," a story about the doomed final voyage of a British ship.

JEFF

▶ **STATUS: Assumed dead after the *Kahana* detonation**

As the ship's mechanic, he maintained the engine and spent much of his time below deck. After Michael secretly sabotaged the freighter's engine, Michael sent Jeff to find a replacement pressure valve in the supply room, then took advantage of the privacy to inform Sayid and Desmond about how he came to be on the freighter and his association with Ben Linus.

" We better get everybody the hell off this boat. "

RAY

▶ **STATUS:** Dead, throat slit by Keamy

A physician on the Kahana, Ray wore a white lab coat and exhibited a rather dispassionate bedside manner. He handled George and Brandon's sickness by strapping them into sick bay beds and injecting them with sedatives. In the end, Keamy slit Ray's throat to prove to Frank Lapidus that he would kill crew members until the pilot took them back to the island by helicopter. Ray's body washed ashore and, in the process, helped Faraday piece together the time anomalies between the freighter and the island.

HENDRICKS

▶ **STATUS:** Assumed dead after the *Kahana* detonation

He served as the Kahana pilot and refused to navigate the freighter closer to the island as it played havoc with his fathometer, which prevented him from seeing the location of the island reef.

KEVIN JOHNSON

▶ **STATUS:** Dead after the *Kahana* detonation

Kevin Johnson was Michael Dawson's pseudonym onboard the Kahana. Per Ben's orders, Michael collected the names and positions of everyone onboard and relayed that information to Ben in preparation for their arrival on the island. He then destroyed the radio room and sabotaged the engine in an attempt to foil Widmore's mission. Michael ultimately failed, as Keamy and his men took the helicopter to the island to face off against Ben. After they departed, Desmond discovered Keamy's C-4 backup plan rigged in the hold and set to detonate remotely. Seeking atonement for his sins, Michael volunteered to spray the explosives with liquid nitrogen in order to delay the eventual detonation. It worked long enough for Desmond and Jin to get topside and the Oceanic Six to escape by helicopter. Right before the explosion, Christian Shephard appeared before Michael and said he could "go now."

MERCENARY TEAM

MARTIN CHRISTOPHER KEAMY

▶ **STATUS:** Dead, stabbed by Ben Linus

A former United States Marine turned elite mercenary for hire. Working for Charles Widmore and with a team of five soldiers, Keamy planned for a tactical invasion of the island with the express intent of capturing Ben Linus and neutralizing all other human threats. Onboard the freighter, he showed little patience for anyone or anything outside of his mission. On the island, Keamy exhibited an even more chilling focus as he killed or facilitated the killing of Karl, Rousseau, and several innocent 815 survivors at the barracks. Yet his most morally depraved act was using Alex as bait to lure Ben from his barracks residence and then shooting her in the head in cold-blood.

Later, Keamy enacted Widmore's "secondary protocol" to track down Ben. He returned to the island and tracked Ben to the Orchid station, where he forced his surrender. After a vicious beating by Sayid and a bullet from Richard Alpert, the soldier reappeared and demanded Ben be remanded to him. In the confusion, Ben appeared and, with Keamy's own knife, finally brought down the assassin once and for all. Upon his death, Keamy's dead-man remote bomb trigger detonated the Kahana out at sea.

OMAR

▶ **STATUS:** Dead, killed by a grenade

He was the implied right-hand man to Keamy, as the two functioned as a highly efficient tactical team that communicated through minimal looks and gestures. Omar went above and beyond to aid Keamy throughout the mission, even providing his own gun to kill Captain Gault and strapping the detonation trigger to Keamy's body for the trip to extract Ben. Omar died when Keamy kicked a grenade thrown at him by the Others in his direction and it then detonated.

MAYHEW

▶ **STATUS:** Dead, victim of the smoke monster

Mayhew was a member of the barracks raid party that intercepted and killed Karl and Rousseau. He helped kidnap Alex and forced her to deactivate the sonar fence. After the smoke monster attack, he was taken back to the freighter by helicopter but perished later from his injuries.

LACOUR

▶ **STATUS:** Unknown, assumed dead

Also a member of the barracks raid party, Lacour attended to Mayhew's extensive injuries after the smoke monster attack and when they returned to the freighter. Lacour returned to the island to capture Ben, but was tripped up by a snare and presumed killed in the melee.

KOKOL

▶ **STATUS:** Dead, neck snapped by an Other

Kokol was the soldier who deployed a missile into Claire's temporary residence. He survived the smoke monster attack and helped bring Mayhew back to the freighter. Upon his return to the island, he helped apprehend Ben, only to be ambushed by the Others and mercilessly killed.

REDFERN

▶ **STATUS:** Dead, killed by a stun dart to the neck

A soldier in the barracks raid party, he was directly responsible for the death of Doug, an 815 survivor. Redfern survived the smoke monster attack and returned to the freighter. On his return to the island to extract Ben, he was ambushed by the Others and killed by an electrified stun dart.

SCIENCE TEAM

Naomi Dorrit, *Science Team Leader*
Daniel Faraday, *Physicist*
Charlotte Lewis, *Cultural Anthropologist*
Miles Straume, *Confirmation Specialist*
Frank Lapidus, *Science Team Pilot*

KAREN DECKER

▶ **CONNECTION:** Facilitator at press conference for Oceanic Six

When Oceanic Airlines discovered there were survivors from its ill-fated flight 815, public relations representative Karen Decker was dispatched to meet them. After retrieving them from the Indonesian island of Sumba, Decker took the six survivors (Jack Shephard, Sayid Jarrah, Sun-Hwa Kwon, Kate Austen, Aaron Littleton and Hugo "Hurley" Reyes) to a military facility west of Honolulu to meet their families and take part in a private press conference. Decker explained that the press was referring to them as the Oceanic Six, but insisted that they didn't have to speak to the reporters.

When they arrived at the facility, Decker led the proceedings and informed the world how the Oceanic Six survived.

KAREN PACE

▶ **CONNECTION:** Wife of Liam Pace (Charlie Pace's brother)

The wife of Drive Shaft lead singer Liam Pace, Karen got involved with Liam when he was at the height of his fame. She became pregnant with their child, a little girl she named Megan in honor of the brothers' deceased mother. When it came time to deliver, Karen was on her own since the Pace brothers were on tour in Germany and too focused on scoring more heroin. However, Charlie made it on a plane to see Karen and the baby first and to cover for Liam's absence. Soon after, Liam's heroin problem was exposed when he dropped the baby. Karen threw him out of the house and threatened to leave him unless he cleaned up his act. She got her uncle in Sydney to offer Liam a job upon his recovery and together they all left for Australia to start a peaceful life.

KARL MARTIN

▶ **CONNECTION:** Member of the Others; boyfriend of Alex Rousseau

Karl Martin found happiness and anguish as a member of the Others. He was often uneasy with the group's leadership and its Hydra station projects, but still managed to find a sense of purpose and even some contentment during his time on the island. He also felt the children taken from the Oceanic flight 815 crash had been given a chance at a better life.

Karl may not have agreed with Benjamin Linus, the leader of the Others, but was very close with his daughter, Alex Rousseau. During the time Karl and Alex spent together, the couple would sit in the backyard of Karl's home in the barracks and create their own names for constellations. Tension between the two men intensified as Karl and Alex grew closer and Ben went to extreme lengths to end their relationship.

LOCKED UP

Karl's life changed drastically when he attempted to free himself and Alex from Ben's controlling nature. To keep Karl away from Alex, Ben had him locked up in one of the abandoned polar bear cages on Hydra island. Ben's rationale for doing so was that he feared Alex would get pregnant and subsequently die, as happened to other pregnant women on the island.

Danielle attempted to comfort Karl after his rescue from Room 23.

Karl was locked up on Hydra island at the same time as James "Sawyer" Ford. After freeing himself, Karl helped Sawyer escape but both were later captured. This failed attempt resulted in a more extreme form of punishment for Karl, as he was confined to Room 23.

> **ROOM 23** ✚
>
> *This disturbing room, located inside a guarded building on Hydra island, was utilized by the Others for re-education purposes. Strapped to a chair, a person was injected with drugs, and forced to endure an audio-visual onslaught to their senses.*

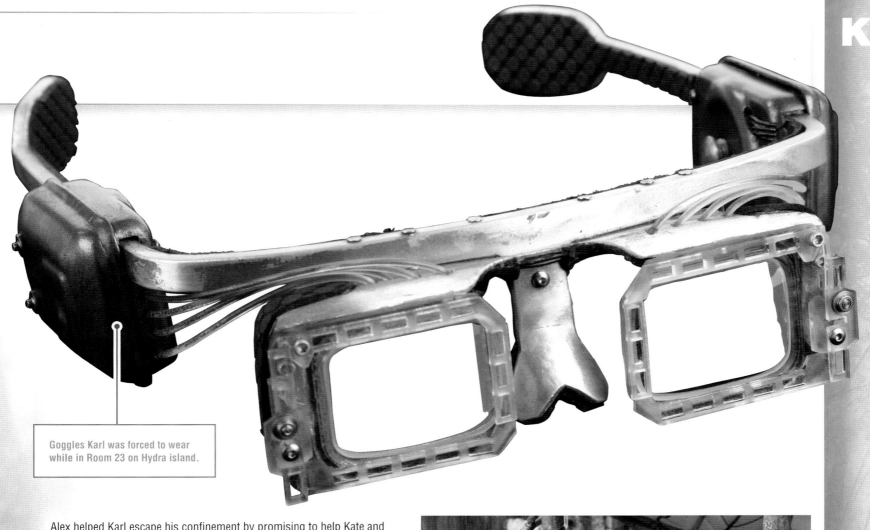

Goggles Karl was forced to wear while in Room 23 on Hydra island.

Alex helped Karl escape his confinement by promising to help Kate and Sawyer leave Hydra island. While Alex stayed behind to pacify Ben's reaction to the escape, Karl left the island on an outrigger with Kate and Sawyer.

TRAGIC DEATH

After reuniting with Alex on the main island, Karl warned the survivors that Ben's plan to invade their beach camp had been advanced. Without Karl racing around the coastline of the main island to alert them, they would not have been prepared to foil Ben's plot to kidnap the women and kill anyone who obstructed them. Karl's tenacity continued right to his final days. Unfortunately, he met his demise as he, Alex and Danielle trekked to the Temple for refuge. Karl was shot dead after taking a bullet to the chest by sniper fire from Martin Keamy's team of mercenaries.

Karl warned the survivors that the Others were planning to attack their beach camp.

KATE AUSTEN

FACTS & FIGURES

Time On The Island
- POST-OCEANIC: 101 days
- POST-AJIRA: 4 days
- IN DHARMA 4 days
- POST-INCIDENT: 9 days

Year Of Birth: 1977

Time As Oceanic Six: 3 years

Days On Hydra Island: 8 days (day 67 – 74)

Years Of Probation Sentenced: 10 years

Candidate: #51

Independent and resourceful even as a child in rural Iowa, Kate always possessed a streak of bravery or defiance that made her a live wire. At a young age, she understood that she was very different from her mother, Diane, who stayed with an abusive husband because she loved him too much. Kate's moral compass got clouded by the violence she witnessed and she learned to be devious to survive. When her rage reached a breaking point, she justified her father's murder as an acceptable exchange for a better future for her mother. It was a misguided call, but one borne out of years of desperation, good intentions, and fierce loyalty to her mother.

As a woman on the run, Kate learned to shield herself from any connections that could tie her down. She became defined by how fast her feet could take her somewhere else. When she survived the crash of Oceanic 815, she had nowhere left to run. Through her relationships with Jack Shephard and James "Sawyer" Ford, she experienced selfless love with two very different men and finally gave of herself as both lover and friend. As a brave and tireless leader to her fellow survivors, Kate discovered that she was capable of behaving honorably for people she cared about. Most importantly, she found the true purpose of her life through mothering Aaron Littleton.

KATE BY THE NUMBERS ✛

Kate's trial docket number was 42231615

The safety deposit box number Kate robbed was #815.

Kate had a $23,000 bounty on her head.

Kate's post-island address was 42 Panorama Crest.

A BROKEN HOME

Katherine Anne Austen was raised by her parents, Diane Jansen and Sam Austen, until the age of five when they divorced. Throughout her childhood, Kate believed that Sam was her biological father; but Kate's biological father was Wayne Jansen, a cruel alcoholic Diane reunited with and married after the divorce. Over the years, she watched her mother accept being physically abused by Wayne. By Kate's late teens, Wayne had even turned his inappropriate drunken sexual advances towards his daughter. When she was 24, Kate rigged a gas explosion in the family home that would kill Wayne. Her objective was to free her mother from the marriage and provide her with a payout from their homeowner's insurance. Livid that her daughter would resort to murder, Diana reported what Kate did to the police, which instigated her daughter's manhunt.

JACOB'S TOUCH ✛

In 1989, Kate and her best friend, Tom Brennan, attempted to steal a lunch box from Mr. Springer's convenience store but were caught in the act. Although he was a stranger to young Kate, Jacob offered to pay for the stolen item in exchange for her promise to never steal again and to "Be good, Katie." He touched her nose and disappeard.

NEW KIDS ON THE BLOCK

This classic '80s-era plastic lunch box celebrates the American boy band, New Kids On The Block. The band was at its most popular from 1984–1994.

" I have always been with you, Jack. "

KATE AND TOM'S TIME CAPSULE

In 1989, Tom and Kate filled the New Kids On The Block lunchbox (paid for by Jacob) with these items and buried it as a time capsule under a shady tree in a cow pasture:

A metal toy airplane—a valued memento of Tom's childhood and a reminder of Kate's first love. The plane is a model of a Douglas DC-3 propeller aircraft and Tom's souvenir to remind him of a solo plane trip he took to Dallas as a boy.

TOM: Is it on? I don't think it's on.
KATE: It's on.
TOM: Okay, this is Kate Austen and Tom Brennan and this is our dedication for our time capsule, here on August 15th, 1989. Hey, give me that back.
KATE: Why are you putting this stupid plane in there?
TOM: Because it's cool, Katie. I got it when I flew to Dallas by myself.
KATE: (sarcastically) That is cool, just like this time capsule.
TOM: It'll be totally cool when we dig it up in like twenty years.
KATE: How do you know we'll be together?
TOM: Because we'll be married and you'll be a mom and we'll have nine kids.
KATE: I don't think so. As soon as I get my license we should just get in a car and drive. You know, run away.
TOM: You always want to run away, Katie.
KATE: Yeah, and you know why.

A cassette tape (see transcript).

An autographed baseball, signature unknown.

ON THE RUN

Her mother's betrayal wounded Kate irrevocably, as she couldn't fathom Diane's loyalty to her abuser. For three years, she was tenaciously pursued by U.S. Marshal Edward Mars, and she never stayed anywhere long. Although she hooked up with several lovers, and even married for love, her past always caught up with her. When faced with the choice to stay or run, Kate always ran. After traveling the U.S., Kate's last strategy was escaping to Australia. While working on a sheep farm, she was turned in to Mars and extradited back to the U.S. via Oceanic Flight 815.

KATE'S KNOWN ALIASES

❶ Lucy: Iowa
Two months post-murder, Kate returns to Iowa due to her car's broken fan belt. Using the name Lucy, she unknowingly connects with Sawyer's former lover Cassidy Phillips.

❷ Kate Dodd: Harrison Valley, Pennsylvania
Where Kate was taken into custody and her federal mug shot was taken.

❸ Joan Hart: Ohio
A blonde-haired Kate receives an anonymous letter that informs her Diane is in the hospital with cancer.

❹ Monica Callis: Florida
In love and married, Kate calls Mars and begs him to leave her alone. He refuses and plays upon Kate's greatest fears. Kate then drugs her husband, Kevin, and disappears.

❺ Mrs. Ryan & Maggie: Ruidoso, New Mexico
Kate teams up with Jason and his gang of thieves. She convinces them to rob a bank for the ulterior motive of regaining Tom's toy plane planted by Mars.

❻ Annie: Melbourne, Australia
Kate works for sheep farmer Ray Mullen for three months until he turns her into Mars for the reward money.

205

KATE'S RAP SHEET

Fraud: For robbing a bank in New Mexico under a false identity and for multiple counts of identity forgery.

Arson: For intentionally creating a gas explosion in the Jansen family home.

Assault on a federal officer: For her assault of Agent Mars on several occasions.

Assault with a deadly weapon: For her use of a firearm during the Ruidoso, New Mexico, bank robbery.

Grand larceny: For the bank robbery in Ruidoso, New Mexico.

Grand theft auto: For stealing Marshal Mars' car after their car accident.

Murder in the first degree: For the premeditated death of her father, Wayne Jansen.

THE BLACK HORSE

Just hours after Kate caused Wayne's death, Marshal Mars intercepted her based on a tip from her mother. Cuffed and placed in his car, the duo set out for a rainy drive to her arraignment. As he grilled her on her motives, an immense black steed jumped in front of the car, causing Mars to swerve and hit a pole. In the chaos, Kate escaped by grabbing the keys and kicking Mars out of the car. As she prepared to drive away, Kate locked eyes with the horse quietly standing to the side of the road, as if he was watching her every move.

Kate's connection with the island horse was a seminal moment for her.

The Secretary of State
of the United States of America
hereby requests all whom it may concern to permit the citizen/
national of the United States named herein to pass
without delay or hindrance and in the case of need to
give all lawful aid and protection.

Le Secrétaire d'Etat
des Etats-Unis d'Amérique
prie par les présentes toutes autorités compétentes de laisser passer
le citoyen ou ressortissant des Etats-Unis titulaire du présent passeport,
sans délai ni difficulté et, en cas de besoin, de lui accorder
toute aide et protection légitimes.

Katherine Austen
SIGNATURE OF BEARER/SIGNATURE DU TITULAIRE
NOT VALID UNTIL SIGNED

The cuffs worn by Kate Austen while onboard Oceanic flight 815.

PASSPORT / PASSEPORT	UNITED STATES OF AMERICA		
USA	Type/Caté gorie **P**	Code of issuing/code du pays State/État USA	PASSPORT NO. / NO. DU PASSEPORT **DEL067294**
	Surname / Nom **AUSTEN**		
	Given names / Prénoms **KATHERINE**		
	Nationality / Nationalité **UNITED STATES OF AMERICA**		
	Date of birth / Date de naissance **03 AUG/AUG 79**		
	Sex / Sexe **F**	Place of birth / Lieu de naissance **INDIANAPOLIS INDIANA**	
	Date of issue / Date de délivrance **24 AUG/AUG 03**		Date of expiration Date d'expiration **24 AUG/AUG 13**
	Authority / Authorité **PASSPORT AGENCY NEW ORLEANS**		Amendments/ Modifications SEE PAGE **24**

P<USAAUSTEN<<KATHERINE<<<<<<<<<<<<<<<<<<<
DEL067294USA42551875HON5PNG4<<<<<<<<<<<<<8

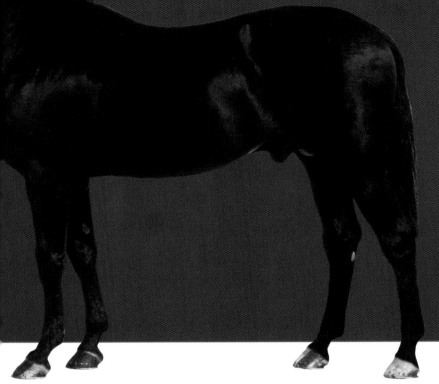

DAY 50 ON THE ISLAND

The island reached out to Kate in the form of a beautiful black horse that mysteriously impacted her life both on and off the island. While picking fruit in the jungle, Kate was shaken when she saw the familiar black horse appear out of nowhere. Plagued by the vision, she confessed to Sayid that she feared she had gone crazy. Later, while Sawyer was delirious, she asked whether he was possessed by Wayne's angry spirit, and revealed her real motivation for killing him. Sawyer woke up and said he heard everything. When the two walked outside together, Sawyer was shocked to see a black horse standing in the jungle. This time, Kate walked over to pet it, an act that further cemented Kate and Sawyer's burgeoning connection.

EQUINE/HUMAN RELATIONSHIP

The horse was an important image for humans even before they were domesticated several thousand years BCE. Since then, horses symbolized many consistent attributes across cultures, including: strength, freedom, grace, beauty, and power. The importance of equines to humans dates as far back as the third millennium BC with ancient Elam slates reflecting their form. Since then, horses have come to symbolize many consistant attributes across cultures including: strength, freedom, grace, beauty and power. The color of a horse also indicates specific meaning, with black signifying death, mystery, and secrets. Native American cultures view the horse as a messenger that brings great wisdom with its wild nature. All of these meanings parallel Kate's own wild story and her restless soul.

OCEANIC SIX LIFE

After the public spectacle of a murder trial and her mother's refusal to testify for her, Kate was sentenced to 10 years probation with enforced residence in California. An ugly chapter of her life was behind her, which allowed Kate to put down roots with Aaron. She found peace in being in one place and joy in mothering a little boy who needed her more than anyone ever had before. It took a dream of Claire warning her never to bring Aaron back to the island to finally understand that she had to go back and rescue Claire for their child's sake.

PATSY CLINE

Kate has an affinity for American country singer Patsy Cline. A huge artist in the early '60s, Cline was known for her big voice that added great depth and heartbreaking emotion to the power ballads of her time. Considered one of the best female singers of all time, Patsy died at the age of 30 in a plane crash.

KATE'S PLAYLIST

"Leavin' On Your Mind" – Patsy Cline

"Walkin' After Midnight" – Patsy Cline

"The End of the World" – Skeeter Davis

"Catch a Falling Star" – Perry Como

"Daydream Believer" – The Monkees

"She's Got You" – Patsy Cline

"Three Cigarettes (In an Ashtray)" – Patsy Cline

DHARMA 1977

Kate's reason for returning to the island was to find Claire and reunite her with Aaron. However, when Sayid shot a young Ben Linus, things got complicated. Kate felt compelled to save his life and gave a donation of O negative blood for a transfusion. Along the way, she enlisted the help of Juliet Burke and Roger Linus in order to complete her mission.

JACK SHEPHARD

From the moment they met, Jack Shephard asked more of Kate than she thought she could give. As she bravely stitched up his gaping wound on the beach, he told her how he found courage by counting to five during a botched operation. In that moment, their mutual admiration began, and they bonded for life.

Kate was ambivalent about Jack's need to fix and find order in the wake of the Oceanic crash. She aspired to be Jack's equal, but inside she suffered with feelings of inadequacy due to the myriad of sins she didn't want to share with him. With Jack, she felt his suffocating need for her to reach her potential, and that caused Kate to do what came naturally—run. Yet their attraction and chemistry was undeniable, and when Kate let her guard down—as she did when she told Jack the origin of the toy plane—she gave him a glimpse of her vulnerable self.

Often, Kate and Jack simply tested one another as they jousted for dominance within the camp. When Kate, Sawyer and Jack were taken by the Others to Hydra island, Kate moved closer to Sawyer romantically, but she was conflicted when Jack found out. When Kate and Sawyer were free, Jack told her to leave with Sawyer; but she fought him because she didn't want her bond with Jack to die. Back on the main island, when Jack admitted to Kate that he loved her, she still couldn't accept it.

Once they escaped the island as members of the Oceanic Six, Kate completed her court trial, and finally entered a real relationship with Jack. Despite their engagement and home-life, Kate's happiness with Jack was short-lived. Jack's dark side ultimately consumed their relationship through alcohol and jealousy and they were finally even in their frailties . Though they slept together one last time before returning to the island, their relationship fate was sealed. Jack realized that his true purpose was with the island; and as he bled for it, and just before Kate headed for home, they declared their mutual love one last time.

JAMES "SAWYER" FORD

Both killers, criminals, and con artists, Kate and Sawyer were kindred spirits, which is why Kate felt more comfortable in her own skin around Sawyer. She wasn't ashamed of her past with James, because she saw herself in his eyes. While she was often offended by his piggish demands, like a kiss in exchange for Shannon's medicine; or selfish actions, like hoarding supplies from the plane, she could still see his true heart despite his often pathetic actions.

They also shared a smoldering chemistry that went to the next level during their captivity on Hydra island. Sawyer tried to protect her from the hopelessness of their situation, which touched her. While in captivity, they made love and Sawyer told her he loved her afterwards. Again, Kate was unable to accept or return his love, as she was torn between her feelings for James and Jack. Back on the main island, their relationship to one another became awkward. Kate used Sawyer to get at Jack; and Sawyer struck back in equally unkind ways. Their feelings remained, however; and Sawyer even jumped off the *Kahana* helicopter so that Kate would have a better chance of escaping the island.

When Kate returned to the island in the DHARMA era, their connection remained, although James loved Juliet. After Juliet died, Kate supported James in his grief. They still cared for one another, but their relationship had evolved into abiding friendship.

JULIET BURKE

Initially, Juliet and Kate were simply rivals for Jack's affections. They were adversaries handcuffed to one another in the jungle, and they had to work together to escape the smoke monster. Juliet didn't mince words when she told Kate the harsh truth about what her actions with Sawyer had done to Jack. Kate continued her hostility until Juliet performed an appendectomy on Jack. Juliet laid down her own laurel leaf when she admitted to Kate that Jack was not in love with her.

When Kate and Jack returned to the island in the DHARMA era, Kate again had to deal with Juliet being with a man Kate had loved. However, Kate quickly saw that Juliet had helped James on his journey of redemption. Juliet had done what Kate could not—be the kind of woman who made James the best man he could be. She admired their love and truly mourned with James after he lost Juliet during the Incident.

"No girl's exactly like me."

— Spoken by Kate

CLAIRE LITTLETON

On the surface, Kate and Claire had little in common; but they formed a lasting bond through Aaron. In the dark of night together in the jungle, the two equally overwhelmed women brought Claire's baby into the world and felt the enormity of the shared experience. Kate then took on the mantle of Claire's protector.

After Claire's disappearance on the island, Kate took Aaron under her wing. And after the Oceanic Six rescue by Penny Widmore, Kate accepted the role of the baby's de facto mother. Over three years, Kate became the only mother Aaron knew; and much to her surprise, she loved him as if he were her own. But the guilt of knowing Claire might still be alive compelled her to give the son she loved so much to his real grandmother, in order to reunite Claire with her son.

While she had hoped for a normal reunion after her return to the island, Kate learned that the years of isolation and the loss of Aaron had damaged Claire emotionally. Claire tried to kill Kate in retribution for taking her son, but Kate understood what the loss had done to her friend. The incident only served to steel Kate's resolve to rehabilitate the broken woman so they could return home together and see her with Aaron once more.

KATE'S OFF-ISLAND CONNECTIONS

|| **Diane Jansen** (Mother)

|| **Wayne Jansen** (Father)

|| **Sam Austen** (Stepfather)

|| **Tom Brennan** (Friend/First Love)

|| **Kevin Callis** (Ex-husband)

|| **Cassidy Phillips** (Friend/Sawyer's Former Lover)

|| **Aaron Littleton** (Foster Son)

|| **Carole Littleton** (Aaron's Biological Grandmother)

|| **Edward Mars** (United States Marshal Service)

|| **Dan Norton** (Ben Linus' Attorney)

KELVIN INMAN

▶ **CONNECTION:** Made Sayid Jarrah a torturer; worked with DHARMA's Stuart Radzinsky; recruited Desmond Hume to the Swan station

Inman's life crossed paths with some of Jacob's candidates long before he arrived on the island. A 10-year veteran of the United States military, Kelvin Joe Inman served in the first Gulf War alongside Sam Austen, the man Kate Austen thought was her real father. Inman was also responsible for convincing Sayid Jarrah to become an interrogator and, more importantly, a torturer.

DHARMA ORIGINS

In the early 1990s, Inman left the army due to his guilty conscience and joined the DHARMA Initiative as a way of atoning for his sins. He eventually ended up manning the Swan station along with Stuart Radzinsky, his paranoid partner who ended up shooting himself while Inman rested. This left Inman alone to enter the numbers.

RECRUITING DESMOND

In 2001, Desmond Hume washed up on the island's shore after his boat encountered a rough storm, presenting Kelvin with an opportunity to finally leave the island. Once back inside the Swan, Inman informed Desmond about the timer and why they needed to push the button. In truth, he was just training Desmond to become his replacement.

The fail-safe is revealed to Desmond by Inman.

Inman claimed that Desmond could never leave the Swan because of a deadly "infection" outside and the fact that there was only one HAZMAT suit. During their three years together, Kelvin would leave the Swan and secretly attempt to fix Desmond's sailboat, the *Elizabeth*, in hopes of escaping the island. But Inman gradually showed his more skeptical side to Desmond. His drunken mockery of the importance of the Swan's function—and especially his reveal of the fail-safe device—fueled Desmond's sense that things were not as they seemed.

Inman told Desmond about his plans to leave the island.

Then on September 22, 2004, Desmond noticed a rip in the HAZMAT suit and followed Inman to the *Elizabeth*. After realizing Inman's plan and the years of deception, Desmond flew into a rage. During a brief scuffle, Inman's skull smacked the rocks, which killed him instantly. It was this event that delayed Desmond from entering the numbers, subsequently causing the crash of Oceanic flight 815.

KEN HALPERIN

▶ **CONNECTION:** Financial advisor of Hugo "Hurley" Reyes

Ken Halperin, Hugo "Hurley" Reyes' accountant, was responsible for investing the majority of his lottery winnings. During one of their standard investment meetings, Halperin gave Hurley a rundown of his financial portfolio that included majority shares of a box company in Tustin, California, all of his stocks on the rise, and an exceptional hike in his Florida orange futures. The lone piece of bad news involved a fire at Hurley's Canadian sneaker factory that killed eight people. However, the company was over-insured and provided Hurley with another monetary windfall. That incident along with a compensatory settlement from the LAPD for Hurley's false arrest ended up doubling Hurley's net worth.

Queried by Halperin about the origin of his winning numbers, it became Hurley's epiphany moment as he finally connected his bad luck to the numbers rather than the money. Hurley labeled the numbers as "cursed" to which Halperin disagreed. To Hurley that protestation was instantly refuted as he witnessed a screaming man falling to his death outside the window behind Halperin.

KEVIN

▶ **CONNECTION:** Ex-fiancé of Sarah Wagner (Shephard)

Before marrying Dr. Jack Shephard, Sarah Wagner (Shephard) was engaged to a man named Kevin. Just eight months before their wedding date, Sarah was involved in a devastating car accident that caused serious spinal damage. The injury was so severe that there was a possibility that she would never walk again.

Prior to the surgery, Jack told Kevin that Sarah would need ongoing physical therapy. Unable to cope with the thought that he may have to care for Sarah for the rest of her life, Kevin cowardly left her at the hospital and never returned. In a cruel twist of fate, Jack fixed Sarah's injury and this chance encounter led to their marriage.

KEVIN CALLIS

▶ **CONNECTION:** Former husband of Kate Austen

Kevin Callis was the husband of Kate Austen when she lived in Florida under the alias of Monica. A handsome and personable police officer for Miami-Dade County, Kevin came from a family of three brothers and a mother named Suzanne. Kevin met Kate when she was a fugitive on the run from Marshal Mars. He was never aware of her rap sheet and took her fabricated history and name at face value as true. The unlikely pair had a whirlwind courtship that resulted in Kevin's quick proposal, which a smitten Kate accepted.

They wed in a church in front of Kevin's family, friends and co-workers. For six months, they lived in marital bliss until Kevin surprised Kate with airline tickets to Costa Rica for their delayed honeymoon. The need for a passport shook Kate's resolve. Not long after, Kate had a pregnancy scare which caused her to go to Kevin and confess the realities of her life. Shocked by her confessions, Kevin got up to follow her for more details when he grew woozy and fell. Kate told him she had drugged him so he would have a cover story and not get fired for her actions. He then passed out. She kissed him, put the Callis family locket in his hand and left, never to see him again.

KILO

▶ **CONNECTION:** Ran a con with James "Sawyer" Ford

A powerful and dangerous American criminal, Kilo lent James "Sawyer" Ford $160,000 for a confidence scam that Sawyer attempted. His play was Jessica, who Sawyer had seduced in order to get the same amount of money out of her husband David, to invest in a non-existent oil deal. However, Kilo was unimpressed that Sawyer had left Kilo's $160k in Jessica's possession—to convince her the deal was legitimate—especially as Sawyer already owed him money from a previous con.

Kilo demanded Sawyer give him his money, plus 50 percent interest the following day or he would make him suffer. However, on realizing Jessica and David had a son, Sawyer was reminded of his own predicament as a child, called off the con, and returned Kilo's money to him.

LARA CHANG

▶ **CONNECTION:** Member of the DHARMA Initiative; wife of Pierre Chang, mother of Miles Straume

Lara Chang lived on the island with her husband and son until 1977. At the time of the Incident, Pierre ordered all women and children to evacuate the island in order to avoid a tragic event. After a terrible fight with Pierre in which he ordered his wife and young son to leave, Lara and Miles boarded the DHARMA submarine and left the island for good.

STATESIDE LIFE

While off the island, Lara was forced to raise Miles on her own. Beyond the usual financial struggles of being a single parent, Lara learned that her son had a strange ability—he could hear the voices of the dead. Miles's inability to come to grips with his ability created a void in his relationship with his mother.

Several years later, Lara became extremely ill. When Miles visited his ailing mother, he asked her about his unusual ability and the whereabouts of his father. Lara insisted to Miles that his father kicked them out when he was a baby and that he was dead. It's not known why Lara lied to Miles about his father, other than to save him the pain.

OTHER FAMILY STRUGGLES

Lara and Miles are part of a long list of families connected to the island's events who have experienced unusual or difficult times with their children. For example, Susan Lloyd knew that her son Walt had an unexplainable "strange" way about him. Also, Claire Littleton was warned that terrible things would occur if she didn't raise her child by herself.

LAURENCE

▶ **CONNECTION:** Sold a gun to James "Sawyer" Ford

The shady and nefarious Laurence ran a workshop near a harbor in Sydney, Australia. His connections to the criminal underworld included Hibbs, the man who had worked confidence tricks with James "Sawyer" Ford in the past.

In September 2004, Sawyer bought a compact .357 handgun (complete with hollow-point bullets) from Laurence to kill Frank Duckett, the man Hibbs had told him was the real Mr. Sawyer. After Sawyer shot Duckett dead with the gun he bought from Laurence, he realized Hibbs had simply conned him to kill a man that owed Hibbs money.

THE LAMP POST, SEE PAGE 212

THE LAMP POST

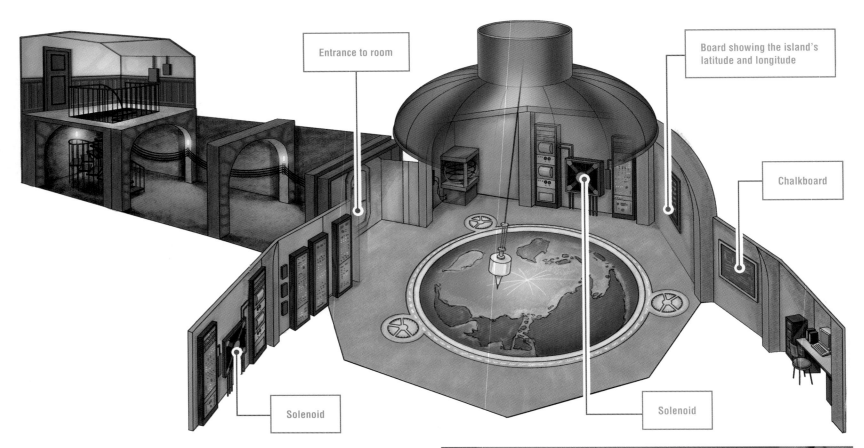

Entrance to room

Board showing the island's latitude and longitude

Chalkboard

Solenoid

Solenoid

The only off-island DHARMA Initiative station, the Lamp Post was also the first station built by the research organization. Located in a secret basement chamber of an unspecified denomination church in Los Angeles, the station's sole purpose was to calculate and locate the current position of the ever-moving island.

HISTORY

Up until 1996, the Hanso family were the only people privy to the recovered journal of the *Black Rock's* first-mate. Inside its pages documented the last voyage of Captain Magnus Hanso and his crew, in particular their last days anchored near the shore of an uncharted South Pacific island that manifested strange physical and navigational anomalies upon the doomed vessel. While Alvar Hanso first became aware of the existence of said island through the journal it wasn't until 1970 that he shared that information with the DeGroots as a potential location for their DHARMA Initiative research project. But first they had to actually find the island, so their scientists researched electromagnetic energy pockets around the globe and determined they were all connected. In particular they found a unique pocket of electromagnetic energy in Los Angeles and built a research room around it—the Lamp Post.

The team gathered evidence the island existed in theory but they were unable to determine any concrete coordinates until "a very clever fellow" in the group built a pendulum in the room based on a hypothesis that "they should stop looking for where the island was supposed to be and start looking for where it was going to be."

Ben relieved Hector and Glen of their pallet drop duties in 2010.

SUPPLY DROP PROTOCOL

The periodic resupply drops (or P.R.D.) originated out of Guam for more than 35 years. The food and supplies were warehoused there in a DHARMA Initiative canning and labelling facility and then packed onto a pallet and airlifted via a drone to the island. However the coordinates for the drops were always generated through calculations made at the Lamp Post which were then automatically teletyped to the Guam Initiative workers who plugged them into the drones according to the approximate station location coordinates provided. After the Purge, the Lamp Post was abandoned but the automated coordinates it generated and the subsequent drops continued until 2010.

> *While the movements of the island seem random... a series of equations tell us, with a high degree of probability, where it is going to be at a certain point, in time.* "" — Spoken by Eloise Hawking

The research team found the island through their calculations and the DHARMA Initiative moved to its remote home. In LA, a contingent remained in the Lamp Post to help navigate their submarines from the mainland to the island. The Lamp Post also calculated the coordinates for the regular supply drops that provided food, medicine and materials to the DHARMA team.

HAWKING'S POST

After Eloise left the island post-Incident to give birth to her son Daniel, she became one of the Others who helped support and protect the island from a distance. Due to her soured relationship with Charles Widmore and his subsequent exile from the island after she left, Hawking made it one of her goals to keep the Lamp Post a secret from him, especially as he obsessively sought a way back. She took on the caretaker's role for the station. In that capacity, she determined the available window for the Oceanic Six to return to the island via Ajira Airlines flight 316. She gave Jack the coordinates in a binder and advised him and the others to re-create the circumstances of the original flight as best as they could for maximum efficacy.

BY THE NUMBERS ✚
The U.S. Army photo of the island on the Lamp Post chalkboard read: "9/23/54 - U.S. ARMY - OP 264 - TOP SECRET - EYES ONLY"

The launch window for the last P.R.D. was: Wed – 24-08-10 – 15:23:09:00 – 12:47:33

FOUCAULT PENDULUM ✚
The pendulum that swings inside the Lamp Post is a Foucault pendulum, which was first used in 1851 by French physicist Jean Foucault to demonstrate the rotation of the Earth. It consists of a weight attached to very long wire that is fixed at the top to a universal joint that allows the pendulum to swing freely and match the Earth's rotation. The pendulum illustrates how the room is actually moving while it's the pendulum that swings in the same motion and direction, much like DHARMA's discovery that the island moves which the Lamp Post pendulum helps calculate.

LITERARY CONNECTION ✚
C.S. Lewis' "The Chronicles of Narnia" tells the evolving story of the Pevensie family of London that were able to travel between two realities—contemporary 1940s England and the magical realm of Narnia. Inside Narnia, a London lamp post grows from a song and is able to burn continuously without oil.

This monitor indicated when and where an event window was found.

AJIRA FLIGHT 316

Jack Shephard finally convinced many of his fellow Oceanic Six survivors to return to the island via Ajira flight 316, which departed from LAX bound for Guam. Each person had a very different arrival to LAX before they boarded the plane.

Jack Shephard brought Jeremy Bentham (John Locke)'s body onto the plane under the guise that he was escorting his deceased friend to be buried in Guam.

While in a cab the day before the flight, Jacob advised Hurley to purchase a ticket.

Sayid Jarrah was brought onto the flight as the handcuffed captive of Ilana Verdansky.

Sun arrived of her own volition in a last attempt to reunite with her husband after three years.

Kate Austen gave Carole Littleton custody of Aaron and then got on the plane in hopes of retrieving Claire.

Oceanic flight 815, which departed from Sydney Airport on September 22, 2004, was scheduled to land at LAX Airport at 10:42 a.m., but the plane went down in the South Pacific. The sixth busiest airport in the world, LAX welcomes more than 59 million people through its gates annually from all over the globe.

CONNECTIONS

Prior to Oceanic flight 815, several passengers flew from LAX to Sydney, Australia for business or pleasure. In particular, Ana Lucia Cortez worked as a security guard at a security check-point where she scanned Christian Shephard. After her shift, they crossed paths again in an airport bar, where Christian asked about how she got her job. Citing fate, Christian offered her a job as his personal bodyguard in Sydney, which she accepted. The pair flew to their destination the same day. The encounter was remarkably similar to how Ana Lucia met Jack Shephard at an airport bar in Sydney on their return flight to LAX.

After the Oceanic Six returned to their lives, Jack Shephard gradually devolved into a depressed alcoholic and used his golden pass to fly from LAX every Friday night to any destination over the South Pacific with the hope that one of the planes would crash and return him to the island. As his desperation escalated, Jack called Kate Austen to meet him outside the gates of LAX near a runway where he told her that they made a mistake and they needed to return to the island.

▶ **CONNECTION:** Dogen's translator; one of the Others who lived in the Temple

The right-hand man of Dogen, Lennon was a member of the Others who kept permanent residence in the Temple. His dress was earthy and ragged, like those of the Others who lived out in the elements, except for his pair of oval, wire-framed glasses similar to the signature ones worn by musician John Lennon. Lennon's origins on the island were never revealed nor how he came to be Dogen's translator, but the duo had an obvious trust for one another's strengths and shared their mutual dedication to Jacob's protection of the island.

INSIDE THE TEMPLE

The beginning of the end for both men began when Jack, Kate, Jin and Hurley arrived. After only a few minutes within the Temple walls Lennon was surprised that Dogen dismissively ordered them to be shot. However, Hurley's desperate admission that Jacob had sent them floored both Lennon and Dogen. It also ignited a heated, translated exchange between the two parties until the list inside the ankh in Hugo's guitar case confirmed their association with Jacob.

Lennon served as Dogen's translator.

Dogen and Lennon then escorted the injured Sayid to the Temple pool where they offered to try to save him. Lennon observed Dogen's submersion test of Sayid with the rest of the group and seemed quite dazed when he explained, "Your friend is dead." Lennon then brought Hurley into Dogen's private garden to speak about what Jacob had shared with him. As Lennon translated, Hurley quickly deduced that Dogen could understand English and he called the man on it. Dogen admitted as much but continued to speak Japanese through Lennon until Hurley revealed Jacob was dead. That news put the men in a panic as they screamed orders to put the Temple into lockdown, as Lennon explained things to Hurley.

Lennon and Dogen questioned Hurley about Jacob's death.

The situation intensified when a bewildered Lennon witnessed Sayid wake up. The bespectacled translator ran to alert Dogen and the pair went to retrieve Sayid for an interrogation in Dogen's chamber where he was summarily tortured.

Later, a friendlier Lennon welcomed Jack into Dogen's room and translated a conversation where they tried to explain Sayid's "infection." Dogen then tasked Jack to give Sayid a pill to cure him; another lie that Jack forced them to admit was really poison. Lennon then revealed Sayid was actually "claimed" and must be stopped.

TEMPLE ATTACK

Things came to a head when Claire was sent into the Temple by the Man in Black with a message for Dogen. After demanding that Dogen speak English, Lennon marched Claire into a prison hole. Chaos continued to build as Sayid returned to tell the Temple Others Jacob was dead. Lennon tried to quell the panic to no avail. Sayid then approached Dogen at the pool, where they talked and Sayid murdered him. Lennon ran in, incredulous, but Sayid coldly slit his throat. Both Temple protectors were gone forever.

"He was the only thing keeping it out! You idiot! You just let it in!"

LEONARD SIMMS

▶ **CONNECTION:** Patient with Hugo "Hurley" Reyes at Santa Rosa Mental Health Institute

Leonard Simms was a former U.S. Navy seaman who went insane and was eventually committed to Santa Rosa Mental Health Institute. He was a patient at the facility when Hugo Reyes was committed and the two spent some time together. One of Simms's ticks involved constantly muttering the numbers 4, 8, 15, 16, 23, and 42. When Hugo was released, he used those same numbers to play—and win—the Mega Lotto Jackpot.

Hugo quickly determined that the numbers were cursed, so he returned to Santa Rosa to speak to Leonard about the origin of the numbers. Simms was still mumbling the numbers and was initially unresponsive to Hurley's queries. But Hurley's admission that he used the numbers to win the lottery snapped Simms out of his stupor, causing him to become agitated as he told Hurley that "he had opened the box." Simms went on to tell Hurley that he had to get away from the numbers. As he continued to press Simms about where the numbers came from, an orderly escorted Leonard from the room. As he was dragged away, Leonard told Hurley he got the numbers from Sam Toomey when he worked with him in Kalgoorlie, Australia.

LESLIE ARZT

▶ **CONNECTION:** Survivor of Oceanic flight 815

Dr. Leslie Arzt was a long-time ninth grade chemistry teacher at a high school in Jersey City, New Jersey. Socially awkward in life, Arzt had a hard time connecting, and staying connected, with people as evidenced by his three failed marriages. However, he never gave up on love, and wooed a woman from Sydney, Australia via the internet. Unfortunately, he used a photo of his handsome friend Nick as his own, which created a problem when he flew out to meet his lady friend.

> **TIME ON THE ISLAND** ✛
> *POST-OCEANIC:*
> *44 days*

Once in Australia, the pair decided to meet in a Sydney restaurant, where Arzt had to fess up to his fib. She initially appeared to forgive him, until he realized she wasn't coming back from the ladies' room after already ordering an expensive lobster dinner. Utterly disappointed, Arzt booked an early flight home on Oceanic 815 which changed the course of his life.

ON THE ISLAND

Arzt was knocked out by the crash and awoken by Nikki, looking for her boyfriend Paulo. Although he helped create the beach camp, his acerbic personality interfered with his social interactions with fellow survivors Boone, Jack, Kate and Jin.

MAN OF SCIENCE

Always happy to show off his intellect, Arzt helped several of his fellow castaways with their scientific endeavors. He helped Nikki map out possible trajectories for her lost luggage and introduced her to the Medusa spider. He also counseled Michael and Sawyer on the best time to launch the raft due to shifting trade winds that predicted the impending monsoon season (which later proved to be a lie as he just wanted them to shove off sooner than later).

Arzt used his spare time to construct a make-shift science lab, and collected 20 new species of insects.

His most profound advice came when he volunteered to hike to the *Black Rock* to help Locke, Jack, Kate, Rousseau, and Hurley properly retrieve some old dynamite to help protect the camp against the Others. Arzt quickly chickened out because of Rousseau's tales of the dark territory and the sickness. He attempted to return to camp only to run back to the group after a confrontation with the smoke monster. Once at the ship, he correctly surmised the boat was ashore due to a tsunami wave, but he refused to go inside. After they brought the dynamite out, a flustered Arzt demanded they all back away as he provided them with a lesson in Nitroglycerin 101. In mid-lecture as he attempted to wrap a stick in Kate's wet shirt, he unceremoniously blew up.

> **WHAT'S IN A NAME?** ✛
> *The surname of Arzt is of German origin and literally translates to mean "physician."*

Arzt's violent death continued to haunt the survivors, both physically with the residual pieces of Arzt and then later when Ilana's dynamite-induced death mirrored his own.

LIAM PACE

▶ **CONNECTION:** Brother of Charlie Pace; lead singer of Drive Shaft

Handsome, gregarious and ambitious, Liam wanted to be a famous rock star so he formed the band Drive Shaft with Charlie. They were signed, recorded an album and toured local clubs and dives in their hometown of Manchester, England with little success. Life in a broken-down van earning no money quickly frustrated the more musically inclined Charlie who was ready to quit. As they stood out in the rain, Liam desperately tried to talk Charlie out of leaving. As fate would have it, the radio blared their first single, "You All Everybody." Drive Shaft stayed alive but Liam often had to coerce his little brother not to leave the band due to the sinful temptations that surrounded them. Liam even promised that they would walk away if things ever got too crazy.

As the band's fame increased on tour, Liam continued to chase the stereotypical hedonistic pursuits of a rock star including women and drugs. Aware that his extreme behavior would probably kill him before he turned 30, Liam even gave Charlie their treasured great-grandfather's DS ring so it would never be lost.

Liam's ego inflated proportionally with the growth of Drive Shaft. In concert he stepped on Charlie's lines, he became too drunk to perform and frequently used heroin. When Liam stopped showing up to sound checks, Charlie finally had enough and threatened to cancel the rest of their tour. Liam screamed that he was Drive Shaft and no one cared about little bass player Charlie. With acrimony Liam added that if Charlie wasn't in the band, then he was a nobody and left the room. Those words finally cracked Charlie's resolve and kick-started his own heroin addiction.

Liam continued to spiral out of control, which caused Drive Shaft to fall from grace. Even their sell-out gigs, like a diaper ad set to their music, fell apart because of Liam's erratic, drug-addled antics. Sometime during this period, Liam married a woman named Karen and they had a little girl named Megan (named after his deceased mother). However, Liam missed the birth as he was strung-out looking for a fix with Charlie. Not long after, Karen threw him out of their house when he dropped the baby while high. She then threatened to leave him and that became Liam's wake-up call.

> **BY THE NUMBERS** ✛
> *Charlie set up a comeback tour for Drive Shaft that would have lasted 8 weeks.*

Desperate to get clean, Liam sold Charlie's beloved piano to pay for plane tickets to Sydney, where Karen's uncle offered to get him a job after he completed rehab. Without regard to Charlie's own addiction or anything else, Liam left to get his house in order. A year or two later, a drug-addicted Charlie flew to Sydney to ask his brother to rejoin Drive Shaft for a reunion tour. Now clean and sober, Liam refused but offered to help his brother get off heroin. Charlie declined and threw Liam's lack of loyalty back in his face.

ELIZABETH "LIBBY" SMITH

▶ **CONNECTION:** Survivor of Oceanic flight 815; fell for Hugo "Hurley" Reyes

Libby helped set a broken bone for one of the tailies.

A passenger in the tail section of Oceanic flight 815, Elizabeth "Libby" Smith survived the crash and endured 64 gruelling days on the island. Libby used her background in psychology to defuse tense situations and she offered support and counsel to anyone who needed it. When she integrated with the main beach camp survivors, Libby bonded with Hugo "Hurley" Reyes.

TROUBLED PAST

Libby was a resident of California. She pursued a medical degree in her 20s, but dropped out after one year. Instead she became a clinical psychologist. During that same period, Libby fell in and out of love quite a bit as she was married three times, two of which were annulled. Unfortunately, her own mental health was tested after her third marriage to a man named David ended with his untimely death due to an illness. Unable to cope with the grief, Libby became unhinged psychologically.

About a month after David died, Libby—already rather manic—had a chance run-in with Desmond Hume at a coffee shop. She fronted him the money for his coffee and the two sat down to chat. Desmond revealed he was on a quest to prove himself worthy of Penny Widmore's hand by winning a sailing race that would take him around the world. Libby started to tear up and demanded that Desmond use her husband's sailboat, the *Elizabeth*. Taken aback he eventually accepted and she handed over the slip soon after.

BY THE NUMBERS ✚
Libby gave Desmond $4 to pay for his coffee.

TIME ON THE ISLAND ✚
POST-OCEANIC: 64 days

On the slippery slope to mental instability, Libby admitted herself to Santa Rosa Mental Health Institute. She was put on anti-depressants but remained relatively catatonic for some time. Coincidentally, Hugo Reyes was a patient at the same time. Three years later, Libby was back to her normal life on a trip to Australia. She booked a return flight to Los Angeles via Oceanic 815. As she prepared to board, she came across the heated conversation between Eko and Charlotte Malkin. She interrupted to offer assistance but Charlotte nodded that all was well, so she kept moving.

MESSAGE FROM BEYOND ✚
When Hurley was back in Los Angeles and he talked to the spirit of Ana Lucia, Libby's spirit told her to tell him "Hi."

SURVIVING THE ISLAND

Hours later, Libby found herself washed up on the island with many other passengers either dead or injured around her. Calling upon her limited medical training, she helped treat the injured, such as setting Donald's broken leg. She was devastated a few days later when he died from the untreated infection in his wound.

Libby settled into a position of support for her camp, especially offering empathy and counsel to Ana Lucia and Eko. As the Others continued to raid and take people from their camp, Libby grew more paranoid. She was one of the first to support Ana Lucia's theory that Nathan might have been behind the kidnappings, and that her tiger pit was a good idea.

Libby lived on edge with the rest of her camp for more than 40 days until Ana Lucia surmised Goodwin was the mole. Their group moved back to the beach where Cindy and Libby discovered Jin washed up on the beach. After they determined Sawyer, Michael and Jin were also from the same plane, the remaining tailies decided to merge with the other survivors.

A NEW BEGINNING?

Libby's alliance with her tail section survivors really dissolved after Ana Lucia shot Shannon. In a panic Ana forced Libby by gunpoint to tie up Sayid, which was the last straw for the psychologist. Libby walked away from the violence and started anew by building a lone shelter on the beach.

Almost immediately Hurley took a shine to Libby and helped her put a home together. She remembered Hurley from Santa Rosa, but she didn't share that with him. Instead she encouraged his attention with mild flirting over laundry and lean-to building. She eventually got him to run with her, and he admitted that he had an eating disorder. Sympathetic, Libby suggested that he destroy his stash of food, which he was ready to do until the pallet drop complicated his resolve. The pair squabbled and Hurley packed up to leave the camp. Suicidal from his self-loathing and visions of Dave, Libby found him close to the cliffs where she tearfully talked him back from the edge. They kissed and returned to camp together.

Hurley made a date to take Libby on a picnic and she offered to get blankets from the Swan. She happened upon Michael as he shot Ana Lucia. Taken by surprise, he fired twice into Libby's chest. Close to death she was discovered by some of the camp leaders. As Jack worked on her, she whispered "Michael" and then died. When Hurley was back in LA and he talked to the spirit of Ana Lucia, Libby's spirit told her to tell him "Hi."

LIGHTHOUSE

"Jack is here because he has to do something. But he can't be told what it is. He has to find it for himself." — Spoken by Jacob to Hurley

The Lighthouse was an ancient, five-tiered stone structure located near a cliff on the island. It was built by the same inhabitants of the island who built the Temple and the Taweret statue. In the two millennia that Jacob was protector of the island, he used the lighthouse exclusively as a special sanctuary where he monitored the off-island lives of his potential candidates.

INSIDE THE LIGHTHOUSE

With an entryway at its base, the lighthouse rose up 80 feet through a succession of steps that led to the open-aired signal room at its apex. In ancient times, the structure was erected as a protective measure, possibly in tandem with the Taweret statue. Egyptians considered fire a protective element that was used by deities to ward off evil and both structures were perched in such a way as to warn outsiders. Over time, the lighthouse may have been used more traditionally for rescue or guidance, considering the inherent navigational issues that always surrounded the island.

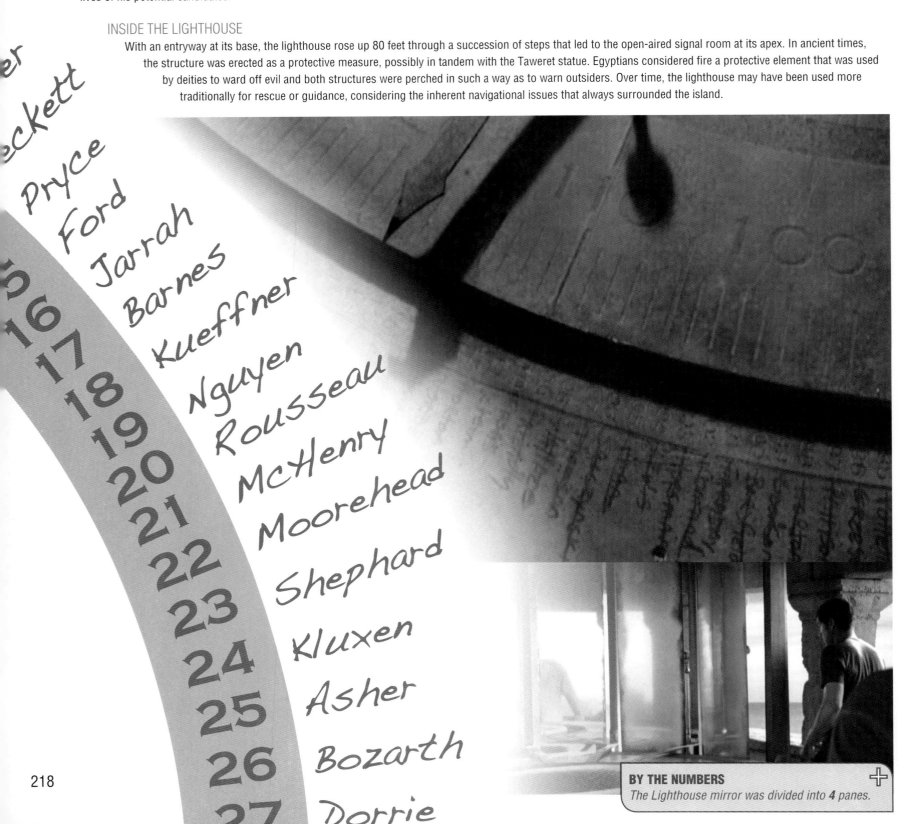

er
ckett
Pryce
Ford
Jarrah
Barnes
Kueffner
Nguyen
Rousseau
McHenry
Moorehead
Shephard
Kluxen
Asher
Bozarth
Dorrie

16
17
18
19
20
21
22
23
24
25
26
27

BY THE NUMBERS
The Lighthouse mirror was divided into 4 panes.

The signal terrace featured a view of the north, south, east and west. There was also an ancient telescope. The room was dominated by a horizontal, wooden wheel with a large, inset brazier bowl that held fire that could then be reflected in the mounted, five-foot-tall mirrors sectioned into four panes. The wheel contained gear teeth along the edges and a rope and pulley system with a gear reduction used to rotate the mirror on the heavy wheel. Jacob labeled all of the gear teeth—from 1 to 360—with the name of a candidate.

JACOB'S PLAN

Jacob gave Hurley instructions on how to find the secret passage out of the Temple by finding the Egyptian hieroglyphic symbol "shen" and directions to the lighthouse once outside. Since Hurley didn't have anything to write on, he used his own arm as a crib sheet. Written quickly and tiny to get it all down, Hurley later couldn't even read the sweaty, smudged sections himself.

Angered by this invasion of their lives, Jack smashed the mirror with the telescope which rendered it useless; however, that didn't matter because Jacob's work at the lighthouse had long been completed. Its final use was to wake up Jack to his destiny.

> **BRAZIER DEFINED** ✛
> *Brazier is a word of Egyptian origination (khet) for a portable grill used to burn items used in funeral rituals. Hieroglyphs often used a brazier image to depict fire or a flame like the famous Egyptian illustration of the Lake of Fire in the Underworld.*

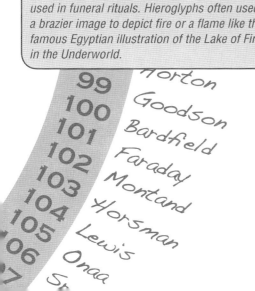

99 Horton
100 Goodson
101 Bardfield
102 Faraday
103 Montand
104 Horsman
105 Lewis
106 Onaa

LILA

> **CONNECTION:** Wife of Munson; Sawyer's mark in prison

When James "Sawyer" Ford spent time in a Tallahassee prison, he cooperated with the prison's Warden Harris and the United States Department of the Treasury to help recover $10 million Sawyer's cell mate, Munson, had stolen.

Lila was Munson's wife, and she was desperate to know the location of the money. Munson refused to tell her, so she hired a private detective to try to find it on her own. When Munson confided in Sawyer about where it was, he passed the information on to the authorities before Lila could find it.

LILY

> **CONNECTION:** Drive Shaft groupie

On the evening of September 21, 2004, Lily met Charlie Pace from Drive Shaft. She pretended to be a huge fan of the band, just so that she could hang out with him, groupie-style, and drink his alcohol and share his drugs. The following morning, when Charlie was running late, he quickly realized that Lily was just sponging off him. She harassed him aggressively to have whatever heroin he had left. When challenged by Charlie, who was convinced she loved Drive Shaft, she called the band Drive Thru. After the row over heroin, Lily stormed out of the hotel room with a champagne bottle.

LINDSEY LITTLETON

> **CONNECTION:** Sister of Carole Littleton; Claire Littleton's aunt

Lindsey Littleton was an important part of the upbringing of her niece, Claire Littleton, in Sydney, Australia. When her sister, Carole, became pregnant by way of an affair with Los Angeles surgeon Christian Shephard—who was married and had a son, Jack—Lindsey helped Carole raise her daughter.

Although Christian flew to Australia and visited often in the early years, Carole couldn't cope with the fact that he already had a family back in Los Angeles, and Lindsey hated how this made her sister feel. Years later, during Claire's late teens, a car accident that involved Claire and her mother put Carole into a coma. Lindsey took this situation very badly, and when Christian arrived to visit Carole—where he immediately covered all the medical expenses—Lindsey was furious. Her anger grew the moment Christian decided to take the opportunity to reveal to Claire he was her father; Carole had told Claire her father was dead.

Carole remained in a coma for many years, and during this time, Lindsey lived with Claire and looked after her. The day before Christian drank himself to death in a bar in Sydney, he drunkenly attempted to barge into Lindsey and Claire's home in the middle of the night, but Lindsey kept him at bay. Her last words to Christian were that he needed help.

LISA REYES

> **CONNECTION:** Former sister-in-law of Hugo "Hurley" Reyes

When Hugo "Hurley" Reyes won the lottery, Lisa was married to his brother, Diego Reyes. She attended the media press conference that announced Hurley's good fortune and, along with everyone else, she witnessed the shocking heart attack of family patriarch, Tito Reyes. This unfortunate event helped spur Hurley's idea that the money was cursed. He later used Lisa as evidence to support his theory when it was revealed that she subsequently left Diego for a female waitress—even more bad luck for the Reyes clan.

ELIZABETH "LIZZY" CALLOWAY

> **CONNECTION:** Attorney for Susan Lloyd

Ms. Calloway was the lawyer employed by Susan Lloyd to help her win the custody battle for Walt over her former partner and Walt's father, Michael Dawson. She was a formidable legal expert, outclassing the representation that Michael could afford. She was relentless with a subtle, but potent, line of questioning that fractured Michael's case for custody.

Ms. Calloway drove home the points that it had been 14 months since the last time Michael had seen Walt, that he didn't know what his favorite food or first words were, and reminded Michael that Susan had paid for all his expensive medical bills during his rehabilitation after being hit by a car.

JOHN LOCKE

FACTS & FIGURES

Time On The Island
POST-OCEANIC: 101 days

Date Of Birth: May 30, 1956

Likes: Silent films, Drive Shaft, Boxing, Mousetrap, Backgammon, Chess, the outdoors

Skills: Tracking, hunting

Former Occupations: Toy store shop assistant; professional home inspector for Welcome Home; assistant at a box company; volunteer farm worker; telephone salesperson

Candidate: #4

Born three months premature in 1956, and strangled to death later in life, John Locke's life began with a struggle for survival. Locke was constantly dogged by both physical and emotional challenges, but he grew to accept that he needed his pain to temper his spirit. In his adult life, his long-lost biological mother spouted a tale of "immaculate conception." His father befriended him, used him, and put him in a wheelchair.

But life on the island was a rebirth. Locke's paralysis disappeared when he awoke among the wreckage. His sense of family, place, and purpose returned. At times, his faith in the island was tested, but Locke always believed everyone had been brought to the island for a reason, long before Jacob's plan was revealed. Locke's mortal end was tragic. The Man in Black used Locke's body to orchestrate Jacob's murder—the one person Locke had never met but was desperate to serve.

Locke's father manipulated him to steal his kidney.

DESPERATE TO CONNECT

Following 15-year-old Emily Locke's affair with a much older Anthony Cooper, John Locke was born prematurely when she was hit by a car. Locke grew up with various foster families, including Florence, his foster mother who had three other children. Locke loved the outdoors, especially his time with the Webelos Cub Scouts. He had a natural aptitude for science, which his teachers encouraged, but science wasn't his passion.

After his father stole his kidney and he lost in love, Locke joined Mike and Jan's commune. Being part of a "family" was one of the happiest and most renewing times in his life. But Locke's misplaced trust in Eddie, who turned out to be an undercover cop, led to the destruction of Locke's commune family.

Helen turned down Locke's proposal becasue of his obsession with Cooper.

Another meeting with his father ended with Locke being paralyzed and confined to a wheelchair. After Locke was turned away from an Australian walkabout because of his physical impairment, he crashed on the island on his return flight home.

John finally found a family at the commune.

BY THE NUMBERS ✚

*Locke was paralyzed and in his wheelchair for **4** years.*

*His father pushed him out of an **8**-story window.*

*The crate that held Locke's body was marked **823**.*

*Locke dialed **23** to contact Charles Widmore.*

" *Don't tell me what I can't do!* "

FATHER ISSUES

Locke's private eye, Frainey, foretold an unhappy ending if Locke visited his long-lost father, Anthony Cooper. Although the two enjoyed hunting trips together, Locke's desperation to be close to his father dulled his senses to the truth: Locke was simply Cooper's prey. After he donated one of his kidneys to his father, Cooper cut off all communication.

But Locke settled for glimpses of his father rather than no contact at all. This obsession cost him Helen Norwood, the woman he asked to marry him. Eventually, this unhealthy relationship deprived Locke the use of his legs. Furious that Locke had ruined his con with the Talbot family, Cooper shoved his son through an eight-story apartment window.

Fully healed on the island, Locke's renewal was almost destroyed when Benjamin Linus brought Cooper to the island. Desperate to crush the man he envied, Ben challenged Locke to kill Cooper. Concerned he didn't have the strength within himself to switch off the need for Cooper in his life, however dysfunctional, Locke sought Sawyer's help. He had learned that Cooper was the original Mr. Sawyer who ruined James Ford's life and conned Sawyer to face his past and relinquish them both of Cooper's sins. Locke was incapable of killing his father, so he turned to Sawyer to finish the deed.

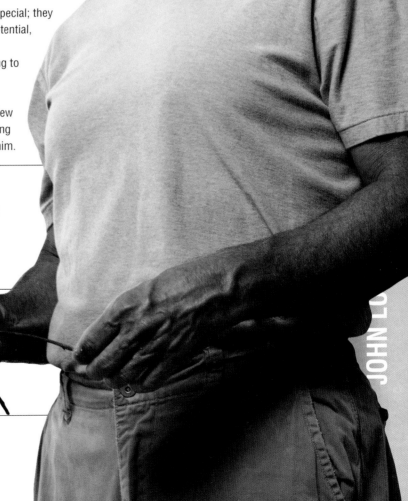

FATHER FIGURE

Long before Locke managed to rid himself of his father, he became a positive role model for the following survivors:

WALT

Locke communicated with Walt as an equal. Like Locke, Walt was special; they were both attuned to the island. Locke wanted Walt to realize his potential, so he taught him to use visualization techniques. The two enjoyed backgammon and Walt often confided in Locke, including confessing to burning the first raft.

When Locke was shot in the DHARMA mass grave, Walt appeared to him—even though he was in New York—and told Locke to get up. Later, when Locke visited him in New York, Walt talked of a disturbing dream that foretold the future. He'd seen Locke on the island in a suit, and everyone wanted to hurt him.

CHARLIE

A big fan of Drive Shaft (although he preferred their debut album *Oil Change*), Locke became a father figure to the band's bass player and chief songwriter, Charlie Pace. Guiding and chastising in equal measures, Locke was key to Charlie kicking his heroin addiction.

CLAIRE

On Claire's birthday, Locke used his craftsman skills to build a cradle out of wood and rendered animal fat. He also showed Claire how to swaddle Aaron to make him feel calm and secure and became incredibly protective of them both during Charlie's dark days.

BOONE

A product of a privileged life, Boone never had to work hard for anything. Locke's back-to-basics, hunter/gatherer approach impressed Boone and resulted in alarming loyalty. With Locke's love of strategy and war games, he gained a soldier who respected and followed his commands.

THE MAN IN BLACK

The Man in Black's plan to use Locke saw him study the man of faith carefully. When Locke first witnessed the smoke monster, he called it the eye of the island. He thought its flashes to pull information from Locke's memories were beautiful. When the smoke monster dragged Locke into one of the island's catacombs, he had complete faith that he wouldn't die. Locke only ever had respect for it and had no awareness of its true guise. Long before Locke ended up on the island, he inadvertently summed up his own fate with the monster during a conversation with his sarcastic boss, Randy Nations, at the box factory. Correcting Randy that a walkabout was not simply hunting and gathering food, Locke described it as "a journey of spiritual renewal, where one derives strength from the earth and becomes inseparable from it." This comment was darkly appropriate for Locke's body eventually being used by the ancient entity that was born from deep within the island's heart.

RICHARD ALPERT

Throughout Locke's life—from the time he entered the world to his resting place on the island— Richard Alpert was a significant presence. Alpert visited Locke on the day he was born because Locke himself had challenged him to do so… two years earlier. The time-flashes had transported Locke to various points in the island's history. Stopping briefly in 1954 gave Locke the opportunity to suggest Alpert visit him to see whether he was worthy of becoming the Others' leader.

Alpert returned when Locke was five with a test. He showed him a baseball glove, a Book of Laws, a glass containing sand, a compass, a *Mystery Tales* comic, and a knife. Locke took the sand first, then the compass, and then the knife. Locke chose the knife, which disappointed Alpert, because the compass was actually Locke's. But Locke had selected sand, recalling the island; considered the compass; and his final choice of the knife signified Locke becoming a hunter.

When Alpert disrespected Ben's attempts to humiliate Locke, he helped him shed the baggage of his father. Alpert believed Ben had been wasting time with the fertility issues; he wanted a leader who would remind everyone of their purpose on the island. Alpert handed Locke Sawyer's file to show him that Anthony Cooper was the real Mr. Sawyer to help Locke plot his revenge.

The Man in Black, as Locke, later manipulated Alpert to remove a bullet from the real Locke during the time-flashes. Repeating the Man in Black's words, Alpert told Locke that he himself said he would have to die to bring back his friends—a paradoxical but perfect manipulation to guarantee the Man in Black's future.

EKO

Feeling useless and depressed after his blast door leg injury, Eko became a metaphorical crutch for Locke. United, the pair discovered the Pearl station, which later divided their faith in the island. Eko thought it heightened the importance of the Swan, but Locke thought it proved the button-pushing was a joke. During one of Locke's dreams in which he was Eko, he saw Yemi in a wheelchair at the top of the hill and then fell. As he hit the ground in the dream, Locke awoke. Crucially, he had never met Yemi and knew nothing about him.

The Pearl revelation was the driving force behind Locke abandoning his faith and destroying the Swan computer. Just before the implosion, Locke realized he was wrong and admitted his mistake to Eko.

In a symbolic renewal of his faith, Locke saved Eko's life from the polar bear cave and returned Yemi's crucifix. During Locke's final trip to the Pearl, Eko was killed by the smoke monster. In death, Eko's passion and belief in the island reignited Locke's faith. John interpreted the "Lift up your eyes and look north, John" inscription on Eko's stick as a compass bearing for rescuing his friends.

SAYID FORESHADDOWING ✚
Locke admired Sayid's skills, especially his homemade compass. Locke warned Boone that they shouldn't make an enemy out of Sayid, as they needed him on their side. Years later, the Man in Black in Locke's form recruited Sayid.

LOCKE'S OFF-ISLAND CONNECTIONS

- **Emily Annabeth Locke** (Mother)
- **Anthony Cooper** (Father)
- **Mrs. Locke** (Grandmother)
- **Florence** (Foster Mother)
- **Randy Nations** (Former Boss)
- **Helen Norwood** (Girlfriend)
- **Noor 'Nadia' Abed Jaseem** (Client)
- **Mike, Jan, & Eddie** (Commune family)
- **Matthew Abaddon** (Assistant)
- **William Kincaid** (Physiotherapist)
- **Gellert** (Childhood Science Teacher)

JACK SHEPHARD

Jack was the first person Locke helped after the crash. Jack called to him for assistance just as Locke realized he was no longer paralyzed. Days later, Locke saved Jack's life. Jack had been following the Man in Black in Christian's form and nearly fell off a cliff. Locke pulled Jack to safety, an inversion of Jack kicking the Man in Black over a cliff many years later.

Often, Locke's faith in destiny and Jack's belief in science resulted in explosive confrontations. At the darkest point of their relationship, Jack desperately wanted to use the freighter to leave the island and Locke attempted to sabotage it. As a result, Jack pulled the trigger of a gun aimed at Locke's face… only the empty chamber saved Locke's life.

Just before Jack headed to the freighter, Locke's belief in the island as a special place left a trace of doubt in Jack's mind. He saw the island move but refused to accept that it happened. Locke's parting words affected Jack deeply, especially Locke's insistence that Jack would have to lie. The story that he convinced his Oceanic Six counterparts to go along with was Jack's penance, his admission that Locke was right.

When Locke failed to convince the Oceanic Six to return, he was a broken man and Jack's volatile reaction pushed him towards suicide. Locke truly believed that Jack was the only person who could convince the Oceanic Six. Locke's suicide note simply lamented, "I wish you had believed me." After Locke's death at Ben's hand, Jack's resistance to faith began to crumble. He fought to reunite the Oceanic Six and return to the island using Locke's words: "We were never supposed to leave."

"You know that you're here for a reason. And if you leave this place, that knowledge is gonna eat you alive from the inside out, until you decide to come back."

— Spoken by Locke to Jack Shephard

Jack.
I wish you had believed me.
JL

Locke's suicide note for Jack.

Locke's compass, which Richard used as part of the test given to a young John.

The knife from Richard's test that young John chose.

THERE ARE TWO PLAYERS...

In one of the most significant speeches Locke gave on the island, his explanation to Walt Lloyd about how backgammon works inadvertently encapsulated the simmering war between Jacob and the Man in Black. It was also very fitting that during the conversation Locke held up the black and white counters, as there ended up being two versions of Locke on the island, once the Man in Black took his form. Locke was plagued by injuries predominantly on the right side of his body. For most people, this is the side of the brain that controls the creative and intuitive abilities. It also handles the sense of the present, the future, philosophy, spirituality, spatial perception, and risk-taking. These are all extremely significant to Locke's island destiny. Examples included:

▶ *The first sign of his cured paralysis was his ability to wiggle the toes on his right foot.*
▶ *He sustained an injury that caused a scar around his right eye.*
▶ *A fragment of the shattered trebuchet pierced his right leg, but he didn't feel any pain.*
▶ *He received a hairline fracture to his right leg after being crushed by the Swan's blast door.*
▶ *Anthony Cooper savagely bit his right hand.*

GAMES MASTER

BACKGAMMON

Locke loved backgammon. Players win by being the fastest to remove all of their pieces from the board. This mirrored the stones from Jacob and the Man in Black's Senet game, plus, their use of people as pieces in their game.

"There are two players. One side is light, and one side is dark."

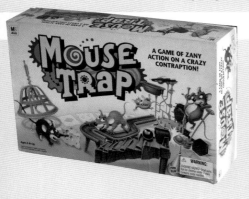

MOUSETRAP

Mousetrap was Locke's favorite game, and he played it with his foster brother when he was young. Years later, he showed the game to a child in a toy store just before he saw his biological mother for the first time.

Locke was manipulated by many people in his life, but none more so than the Man in Black. He slowly put the pieces in place to maneuver Locke to the island's wheel. Once turned, the trap was sprung. Locke wound up dead and his body returned to the island for the Man in Black to use.

"One by one, you build the trap. Piece by piece, it all comes together. And then you wait 'til your opponent lands here on the old cheese wheel. And then if you set it up just right, you spring the trap."

CHESS

Locke beat the computerized chess program at the Flame station, which led to his destroying the station and effectively winning a point over his enemy.

RISK

There was a copy of Risk, a board game about global domination, in the barracks. When Locke, Sawyer, and Hurley played the game, Hurley stated that Australia was the key to winning the whole game.

EMBRACING THE HATCH

The hatch to the Swan station became a spiritual symbol for Locke, something he believed the island wanted him to discover and understand. When

Boone died from exploring the Beechcraft plane, Locke prostrated himself before the hatch and screamed in anger and frustration. He didn't know why the island had killed Boone or why it threatened to take away Locke's ability to walk.

Inside the hatch, Desmond was considering suicide. Locke banging on the hatch door asking for a sign in turn became a spiritual symbol for Desmond. It gave Desmond the courage and determination to live to see Penny again. When Desmond turned on a light in the hatch, it shone brightly out of the small window. To Locke, it was a sign, restoring his faith in the island.

UNITING THE OCEANIC SIX

Once Locke turned the subterranean wheel, he was transported to the island's exit in Tunisia. From there, he embarked on a global trek to reunite the Oceanic Six with the island.

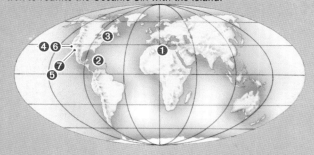

❶ **TUNISIA:** The exit point. Widmore had a specialist flown in to reset Locke's broken leg. Matthew Abaddon then worked as Locke's driver/guide to take him where he wanted to go.

❷ **SANTO DOMINGO:** Visited Sayid, who refused to go back to the island.

❸ **NEW YORK:** Saw Walt but decided he'd been through enough and didn't ask him to return.

❹ **OUTSIDE LOS ANGELES:** Hurley was back at Santa Rosa and initially thought Locke was dead. On seeing Abaddon, Hurley screamed to be taken inside, convinced he was evil.

❺ **LOS ANGELES:** Kate tried to make Locke see how far he'd come and that he shouldn't go back.

❻ **SANTA MONICA:** Abaddon took Locke to Helen Norwood's grave.

❼ **LOS ANGELES.** Following his car crash, Locke was admitted to St. Sebastian, where he inadvertently saw Jack.

THE SWEAT LODGE

When Locke awoke from the Swan implosion, he was unable to speak. With help from Charlie, Locke built a sweat lodge at the site of Eko's church, with the hope that he could "talk" to the island. A sweat lodge is used for spiritual cleansing and insightful visions in many religions. Inside, Locke consumed a hallucinogenic paste, similar to the concoction he gave to Boone. Aptly, Locke then had a vision quest led by Boone. Many of the images he experienced resonated with future island events.

> **WHEELCHAIR:** Boone showed Locke his old wheelchair and said, "You're going to need that," which he did after teleporting off the island with a broken shin.

> **CLAIRE, CHARLIE, & AARON:** Boone said, "They'll be fine, for a while." Later, Charlie died, Claire became feral and disturbed and Aaron lived off the island under Kate's care.

> **JIN & SUN:** The couple argued, but Sayid tapped Jin on the back. Boone said, "I think Sayid's got it." Sayid helped Sun and Jin by sailing the Elizabeth for them.

> **DESMOND:** Boone said, "He's helping himself." This reflected Desmond's very singular mission to understand his time traveling, and later, to resolve being unstuck in time.

> **SAWYER, KATE, & JACK:** Boone stated, "There's nothing you can do for them. Not yet. First, you have to clean up your own mess." Locke needed to rescue Eko from the polar bear cave and then gain intel on the Pearl and the Flame to determine how to help his friends on Hydra island.

> **JACK:** Jack's watch passed through an airport scanner, resonating with the unique way time behaved on the island.

> **SAWYER & KATE:** Locke also experienced Sawyer and Kate's future conversation on Hydra island. Sawyer whispered, "Wipe the stars out of your eyes, sweetheart. Watch and learn, little lady," in Locke's vision. The next day, Sawyer said exactly the same words to Kate.

> **EKO'S BLOOD-COVERED STICK:** Locke heard, "Clean it up, John. They've got him. You don't have much time," as the image of a polar bear roared. This image revealed the peril Eko was in.

C-4

Locke used a block of C-4 to destroy the Others' submarine in late 2004. Three years later, posing as Locke, the Man in Black used C-4 to explode Widmore's submarine.

LOST DOGS

Locke carved a dog whistle that guided Vincent back to the beach to Michael and Walt. In a strange similarity of past and future events, Vincent was the first survivor of the flight 815 crash that the Man in Black manipulated. Years later, the Man in Black took on the form of Locke…the man who helped safely guide Vincent back to the beach.

Locke had other connections to dogs. Many years before he arrived on the island, on the same day he met his mother, he found a "Lost Dog" flyer underneath his windshield wiper.

As a child, Locke's foster sister Jeannie died. Six months after her funeral, a golden retriever appeared at their home. It stayed in Jeannie's room for five years and left the day Locke's foster mother, Florence, died.

AFTER DEATH

After Locke's body returned to the island on Ajira flight 316, the Man in Black used it to take Locke's form. Ilana and her team transported Locke's corpse in a crate to Jacob to show him that the man walking around was not Locke. In Locke's form, the Man in Black exploited Ben's grievances with Jacob to convince Ben to kill him.

Lapidus, Ilana, Sun, and Ben dug a grave for Locke at Boone Hill. Ben gave a eulogy, during which he admitted Locke was a much better man than he would ever be. He then confessed to murdering Locke. Locke was laid to rest where he felt he belonged more than anywhere in the world: the shores of the island.

JOHN LOCKE, PHILOSOPHER (1632-1704)
John Locke was a celebrated English philosopher during the Enlightenment. Locke was the first philosopher to define the self as "consciousness." He said the mind was a tabula rasa (Latin for "blank slate"). This contradicted such philosophers as John Hobbes and Jean-Jacques Rousseau, who believed that the natural state of man was chaotic or bucolic, respectively. A blank slate meant mankind was in charge of his own destiny. In 1666, the philosopher Locke persuaded English politician Anthony Cooper to have an operation for his liver infection that saved his life.

JEREMY BENTHAM, PHILOSOPHER (1748-1832)
Jeremy Bentham was an English philosopher and law scholar, best known for championing "utilitarianism," the idea that the ends justify the means. After his death, Bentham's body was preserved and kept in a wooden cabinet at his request. This "Auto-icon" is still on public display at University College London's.

LEFT BRAIN/RIGHT BRAIN
For most people, the left side of the brain processes information step-by-step in an analytical manner. The right side of the brain processes information in a holistic and intuitive manner. The left brain uses words and numbers. The right brain uses images and patterns. Crudely speaking, the left brain looks at the parts, while the right brain looks at the whole.

THE LOOKING GLASS

The only DHARMA Initiative station built underwater, the Looking Glass was completely submerged about 10 meters deep and located off the shore of the island. The station worked in tandem with the Flame, as both provided conduits of communication to the outside world. Large cables physically connected the Looking Glass to other stations as they snaked through the jungle all the way into the water (as discovered by Sayid Jarrah and then Hugo "Hurley" Reyes). While the Flame used satellite uplink to access incoming and outgoing video and audio feeds, the Looking Glass was primarily concerned with the arrival of the submarines that came to the island. Since the coordinates for the island provided by the Lamp Post were not exact, the Looking Glass served as a beacon for a submarine's sonar navigational system to guide it in as it approached and prepared to dock.

HISTORY

The Looking Glass was built sometime in the '70s once the DHARMA Initiative was established on the island. It was made to either be manned or not, as the communication equipment was built in a water-tight casing that could withstand and operate normally in the event of an accidental flooding. Under DHARMA leadership, the Looking Glass was always staffed by one or two people who were often medical personnel due to the potentially dangerous underwater location.

After the Purge, the Others also recognized the importance of the Looking Glass as a tool in keeping the island (literally) off the radar from the outside world. In particular, after Charles Widmore was banished from the island, Ben Linus made sure that the Looking Glass was always secretly staffed. The last assigned the position were two loyal Others, Bonnie and Greta. Ben told everyone on the island that the pair had left for an assignment in Canada but in truth the women stayed in the station and made sure the jamming frequency was operational at all times. They only communicated with Linus and otherwise remained in radio silence. Their presence was a safeguard since Widmore knew about the station and its ability to guide submarines to dock; as such Ben considered the enabled jamming frequency absolutely necessary in deterring Widmore's return.

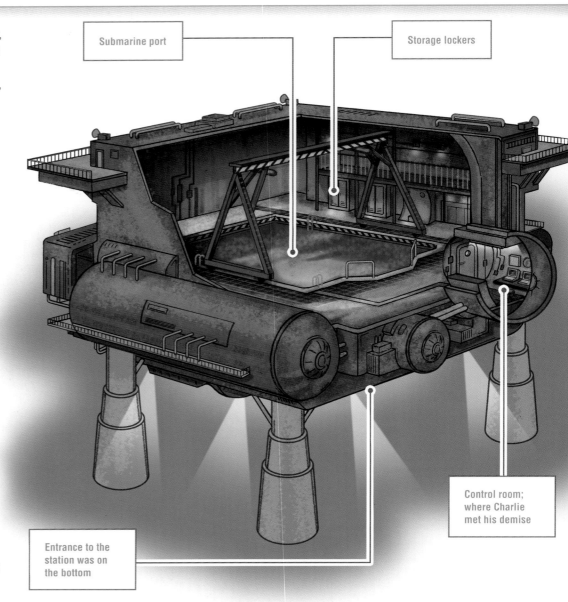

Submarine port

Storage lockers

Control room; where Charlie met his demise

Entrance to the station was on the bottom

INSIDE THE LOOKING GLASS

According to the schematics for the Looking Glass, the station was anchored on the ocean floor by elongated support legs which elevated the operations and living space and allowed for an open moon pool in the center used for submarine or submersible docking. The interior of the station was pressurized to kept the moon pool from flooding the entire rig. Aside from the large pool room, there were several other rooms that included a sleep space, kitchen and the control room which was the communications heart of the station.

The control room featured a dated computer and monitor combination that connected it to the island stations. An operator on duty worked from this station but in case of an emergency, the Flame's secret computer also had remote access to the Looking Glass sonar functions via code input 5-6. The main features of the system were a microphone for audio communication, a small monitor for video feeds and the jamming frequency keypad. The compact room also featured a port hole that looked out into the ocean.

When the station went online in the early '70s, one of the original DHARMA engineers (who also happened to be a musician) programmed the control room security codes. He created a numeric code to turn off the jamming frequency that corresponded to the notes of The Beach Boys song "Good Vibrations": 5-4-5-8-7-7-5-5-4-3-7-7-6-1-1-3.

" *I'm not on a boat. Who…who's Naomi?* "

— Spoken by Penny Widmore to Charlie Pace

BY THE NUMBERS

*The Looking Glass logo features an inset clock face with the hour and minute hands set at **8**:15.*

*The numeric security code used to disable the jamming frequency consisted of a **16**-number sequence.*

THE LAST TRANSMISSION

When Naomi arrived on the island and revealed the *Kahana* was off-shore, Jack and his fellow like-minded Oceanic survivors crafted a plan to radio the vessel for rescue. A key component of that operation was to infiltrate the Looking Glass and turn off the jamming frequency so they could communicate with the freighter. Desmond and Charlie volunteered to paddle out to the station by outrigger and dive down to the Looking Glass. Charlie went down first and was immediately overpowered by an armed Greta and Bonnie in the moon pool room. Ben ordered Mikhail to the Looking Glass to handle the situation. Desmond dodged Mikhail's bullets by diving down to the station where he was able to exit the pool quietly and hide as Charlie was interrogated.

Mikhail used SCUBA gear to dive down to the station and proceeded to kill Greta and fatally wound Bonnie before Desmond shot him with a spear gun. As Bonnie lay dying, Charlie persuaded her to give him the "Good Vibrations" security code which he was able to successfully input because of his musical background.

With the communication frequency opened, Charlie received an incoming transmission from Penny Widmore alerting him that she was not on Naomi's freighter. Outside the port hole, a dying Mikhail performed his last act in what he thought was protecting the island—he waved a grenade at a shocked Charlie, then pulled the pin. It exploded and burst the port hole. Charlie quickly closed the control room's water-tight blast door to protect Desmond. With his last breaths, Charlie wrote one last message to Des. The sealed control room door protected the Looking Glass from flooding and becoming irreparably damaged.

LOGO INSPIRATION

*The Looking Glass logo was inspired by Lewis Carroll's **Alice's Adventures in Wonderland**, which featured a white rabbit that wore a waist-coat and carried a pocket watch. The moon pool opening is similar to the rabbit's own hole.*

LOOMS

A loom is a piece of equipment that is used to weave cloth. It keeps thread under tension and allows the user to interlace threads into desired patterns for use as clothing, rugs, or other items. One of the most popular uses for a vertical loom is tapestry, an ancient art form where different kinds of threads, like cotton, wool, and silk, are combined to create elaborate artistic images. Think of it as painting onto a canvas, but in textiles.

ISLAND TAPESTRY

One of the earliest recorded examples of fabric on the island came from the looms used by Mother. The works she created were painstakingly made over many years and ranged from functional items to tapestries.

During Jacob's adulthood, he craved Mother's approval for his burgeoning loom skills, something for which she rarely gave affirmation. With Jacob's awareness that Mother loved his brother more, his need for her praise with simple things like his loom skills grew more important.

Over the years, Jacob's tapestries became more intricate and impressive. In his room inside the plinth of the Taweret statue, Jacob displayed some stunning examples of his tapestry. He also left a small section of one of his works inside the cabin as an indicator for Ilana Verdansky's team to find him at Taweret.

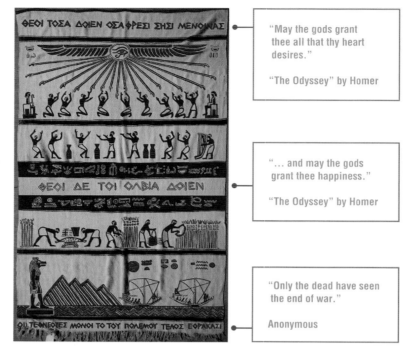

"May the gods grant thee all that thy heart desires."

"The Odyssey" by Homer

"... and may the gods grant thee happiness."

"The Odyssey" by Homer

"Only the dead have seen the end of war."

Anonymous

LOS ANGELES

The largest city in the state of California, Los Angeles was home to, or the final destination of, several passengers on the doomed Oceanic 815 flight that originated from Sydney, Australia on September 22, 2004.

ISLAND CONNECTIONS

Notable residents

Jack Shephard

Hugo "Hurley" Reyes

Eloise Hawking

Randy Nations

Sarah Shephard

Adam Rutherford

Noor "Nadia" Abed Jaseem

PLACES OF BUSINESS

Mr. Cluck's Chicken Shacks—owned by Hugo Reyes

St. Sebastian Hospital—employer of Jack & Christian Shephard

The Lamp Post church— Eloise Hawking

"Now be evil war thy heart's desire."

"The Iliad" by Homer

"And the earth flowed with blood."

"The Iliad" by Homer

"And a black cloud of death enfolded him."

"The Iliad" by Homer

Ana Lucia Cortez

Margo Shephard

Shannon Rutherford & Boone Carlyle

Kate Austen and Aaron Littleton

Teresa Cortez

Miles Straume

Los Angeles Police/LAX—Ana Lucia Cortez

LUCY HEATHERTON

▶ **CONNECTION:** Former girlfriend of Charlie Pace

Oxford graduate Lucy Heatherton was the charming daughter of Francis Price Heatherton, an affluent London-based businessman who owned the Heatherton Corporation, among other lucrative investments. Charlie Pace flirted with her one night in a London pub, purely as a long con to steal her belongings to pay for his heroin addiction, but the two ended up having a relationship.

Lucy cared deeply for Charlie, and he began to fall for her, too. He ended up meeting her father, and even briefly worked for him. Ultimately, withdrawal symptoms from heroin led him to vomit during a presentation. When hospital staff found a cigarette case Charlie had stolen from Francis in his suit pocket, Lucy, feeling distraught and betrayed, ended the relationship.

LYNN KARNOFF

▶ **CONNECTION:** Fake psychic hired by David Reyes; tried to convince Hugo "Hurley" Reyes that he wasn't cursed

Card 1: An unrevealed card said he had recently come into a lot of money.

Card 2: The Six of Swords revealed the money had brought him great misfortune.

Card 3: The Death card revealed death surrounded him and more was coming.

Lynn Karnoff was a store-front psychic hired by David Reyes (Hurley's father) to dupe Hurley into thinking his curse could be exorcised. She created a traditional Tarot card reading for Hurley and selected three cards that set up the need for the exorcism.

Karnoff also recited the numbers (4, 8, 15, 16, 23, 42) and said there was darkness and great tragedy associated with them. While holding his hands, she said he was cursed but it could be removed. Despite her convincing performance, Hurley didn't buy her theatrics and bribed her with $10,000 to reveal that David was behind the scheme.

THE MEANINGS BEHIND THE CARDS

Tarot cards have been used by mystics to divine a person's physical and spiritual pathway since the late 18th century. Over that time, many different tarot decks have evolved but certain cards have remained consistent. On the other hand, interpretations of the cards remain relatively subjective and personalized to the individual reader. A. E. Waite helped develop most modern card interpretations. Taking that approach, Hurley's depicted cards mean:

Death: Deep life changes, intense transition and perhaps the end to something significant.

Six of Swords: The solution of life problems or a long journey.

MACCUTCHEON WHISKY

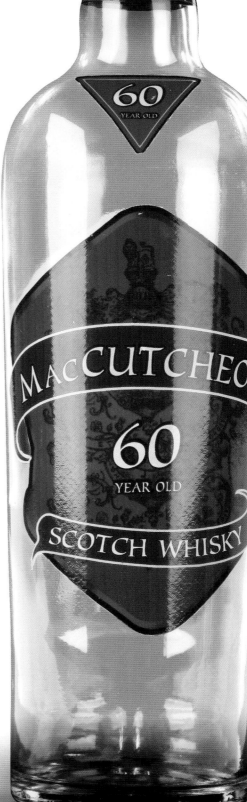

This particular brand of Scotch whisky symbolized wealth in the eyes of many. In fact, it was thought to cost more than $120 a glass in most bars. For Charles Widmore, an extremely wealthy man in his own right, it was his drink of choice.

Widmore used the whisky's exorbitant price tag to mock Desmond Hume the day he asked him for his daughter Penelope's hand in marriage. After Widmore poured himself a drink, he informed Desmond that he didn't earn enough money in a single month to afford one mouthful of MacCutcheon.

OTHER PURVEYORS OF FINE SPIRITS

Although Charles Widmore's great fortune meant he could purchase MacCutcheon whisky with great ease, other figures linked to the island with less means than Widmore were known to have appreciated the fine spirit.

There was at least one bottle of MacCutcheon onboard Oceanic flight 815, as James "Sawyer" Ford salvaged it from the mid-section wreckage and kept it in his camp as part of his secret stash.

Charlie Pace stole the bottle from Sawyer's stash in order to gain information from Desmond. Charlie was completely oblivious to the cost of the whisky, something that Desmond relished considering the way Widmore insulted him with the same whisky years ago.

John Locke's estranged father, Anthony Cooper, owned a bottle of MacCutcheon. He even poured himself a glass moments before he shoved his son through his eighth-floor apartment window.

During the years that Sayid Jarrah lived off his compensation of the Oceanic Airlines crash, he was partial to a glass of MacCutcheon.

HISTORY OF THE WHISKY ✛

MacCutcheon gets its name from Admiral Anderson MacCutcheon, a widely admired and successful Admiral in the Royal Navy. After his retirement from duty, he moved to the Scottish highlands and, at some point, his surname became attached to this 60-year-old distilled whisky. Appreciators of fine whisky often refer to the MacCutcheon scotch as the Admiral's "crowning achievement."

MAGNUS HANSO

▶ **CONNECTION:** Captain of the *Black Rock*

Magnus Hanso was a 19th century British sea captain and shipping magnate. The New World Sea Traders was Hanso's Portsmouth, England based shipping company that at its peak owned and operated a fleet of 15 sea vessels. While the majority of his ships carried traditional merchandise and supplies from port to port, Hanso also kept three trade ships that were used to transport slave laborers from the Indian Ocean trade routes to the East and Mozambique.

BY THE NUMBERS ✚
The Black Rock's home port was Portsmouth in slip **23**.

On March 22, 1845, Hanso commanded his ship the *Black Rock* on a multi-year trade mission from Portsmouth to the Kingdom of Siam. From there Hanso continued his trade to many African mining ports of call. In 1867, the ship docked in Tenerife, Canary Islands where he had his Officers load the hull with Spanish slave laborers who could be sold into mining servitude.

ST. ALBERTUS MAGNUS ✚
St. Albertus Magnus was a late 12th century Roman Catholic bishop from Bavaria who was canonized for his astounding ability to unify the disparate worlds of theology and science in his prodigious writings. Considered a genius, Magnus was a student of Aristotle's scientific theories which he in turn used to explore God's creation. Magnus was one of the first philosophers to prove that science and faith were not mutually exclusive but instead worked hand in hand.

At some point in their voyage, Hanso was compelled to navigate the *Black Rock* off the coast of an uncharted island. Hanso came to realize that his instruments could not determine their location and they were stranded. Moored for more than a week, Hanso began to suffer an onslaught of chronic nosebleeds and mental instability. As his crew also succumbed around him, Hanso grew madder and confided in his first mate that a man named "Jacob" had commissioned their expedition and was to blame for their poor fortune. Hanso never produced any proof of his assertion but it never mattered because a massive storm rolled into the bay and sealed the ship's fate. A fantastic wave threw the boat into a towering ancient Egyptian statue on the shoreline of the island and then into the dense jungle. Magnus Hanso, as well as many of his crew and cargoed slaves, did not survive the impact. However Hanso's family line continued on through his children, specifically through his great grandson Alvar Hanso.

While details of Hanso's death remained a mystery to the outside world, DHARMA Initiative member Stuart Radzinsky documented Hanso's final resting place on the Blast Wall Map. Details of Hanso's death remained a mystery to the outside world until journal pages from the *Black Rock*'s first mate were discovered in 1852 and then auctioned in 1996. However, DHARMA Initiative member Stuart Radzinsky documented Hanso's final resting place by marking it on the blast door map.

MAN IN BLACK

Human. Monster. Pawn of fate. The Man in Black was revealed to be all of these in his two millennium existence. Ultimately, he was defined by his unwavering quest to break free of the island's unyielding boundaries. The result was an epic battle that played out through the stubborn ideology of two very different brothers.

The discovery of the other humans on the island spurred questions in the boys' minds.

A SECOND SON

He was the surprise twin born to Claudia, a Roman woman shipwrecked on the island in the 1st century A.D. Mother, the island's protector, found Claudia and assisted with her birth. The first baby was immediately named Jacob, and he was swiftly followed by a second, unexpected boy. Mother murdered Claudia and adopted her sons as her own. As the boys grew, their distinct personalities were revealed. The dark-haired boy was special and curious about the island and what lay beyond it. Jacob was satisfied with Mother's approval, but his brother was not. The second boy had an insatiable desire to know more. These qualities endeared the boy to his mother, but they worried her too. She vigilantly shielded the boys from knowledge of the outside world and kept them in a bubble of innocence until their thirteenth year when her dark-haired son discovered a Senet game washed upon the shore.

Although he had never seen the game before, he intuitively knew how to play and instructed his brother. He also knew it should remain a secret from their protective mother. The secret didn't last long, however, when the unfailingly honest Jacob revealed their discovery. Mother let her favorite son keep the game, but again had to temper his restless soul that reached out for more.

Soon after, the brothers stumbled upon a group of men on a boar hunt. Stunned to see other humans, they ran back to their mother with the news; it was a moment she had dreaded. Spurred into action, she blindfolded both boys and walked them to their destiny as they peppered her with questions. Mother revealed for the first time that she had made it so the brothers could never hurt one another like regular men were prone to do. At the heart of the island, she removed their blindfolds and explained the special nature of the island and how one of them would become its protector.

Mother eventually took Jacob and the Boy in Black to the heart of the island.

> ## " *Do you have any idea how badly I want to kill you?* "

GAME CHANGER

Not long after their visit to the heart of the island, the spirit of Claudia manifested only to the Boy in Black, who could see her because she was dead. She led the curious young man to the village of humans on the island and explained that they were his ancestors shipwrecked like her 13 years ago, that he was from across the sea, and that she was his true mother. In one moment, the boy's life was turned upside down. Betrayed, he returned to the caves to collect his brother and leave Mother forever. But Jacob stayed loyal to Mother, even when she admitted the truth of their origin. But for the Boy in Black, it was too much to forgive. He walked away from them to join his human family so he could someday leave the island forever.

> ## " *One day you can make up your own game and everyone will have to play by your rules.* "
> — Spoken by the Man in Black to Jacob

THE ISLAND COMES FIRST

For 30 years, the Man in Black lived amongst the humans in their village. Jacob came to visit him privately to play Senet and observe the humans too, but Mother remained estranged which secretly pained the Man in Black. Ironically, he agreed with Mother about the humans and their violent nature. But they were a means to his ultimate end—escaping the island.

The Man in Black told to Jacob that he and his people had found places where metal behaved strangely, so they dug wells. Inside one, they found access to the heart of the island, which he planned to use to get away.

When Jacob shared his brother's plan with Mother, she knew it was time to visit her lost son. Inside the special well, they reunited, and the bitter son admitted his plan to build a wheel that would channel the light and water to enable him to leave. Aghast, she said goodbye and then smashed his head into the stone.

THE MONSTER WITHIN

The Man in Black woke to find the well filled and his entire village murdered. Enraged, he returned to his Mother's cave and stabbed her with his dagger. Seeing her dead body, Jacob was filled with equal rage. Years of frustration and pain ignited within his soul and coursed through him as he brutally ran through her. Jacob arrived to see the carnage and an equal hatred filled his soul as he grabbed his brother, beat him and then dragged him to the heart of the island. A heartbeat later, an unearthly howl erupted from the opening as the smoke monster barreled out with frightening ferocity. Jacob's brother was forever transformed, and all that remained of his former self was his lifeless corpse. Jacob placed the bodies of his brother and mother side-by-side in their former cave home.

The Main in Black killed Mother in retaliation for her destruction of his village.

MEMORIES & MANIFESTATIONS

The Man in Black could read people's memories and temporarily manifest himself as people in those memories.

ISABELLA

When Alpert was shackled inside *The Black Rock*, the smoke monster appeared as Isabella. Being in two places at once made Alpert believe the smoke monster was outside while Isabella was inside.

DANIEL, EMEKA, & YEMI

The day Eko was killed, he was tormented by the smoke monster's manifestations of his past. The smoke monster needed to dispatch Eko, as he was attuned to the island.

ALEX ROUSSEAU

After showing Ben painful memories, the smoke monster took Alex's form to make Ben agree to do whatever "Locke" said.

AS CHRISTIAN SHEPHARD

The Man in Black took on Christian Shephard's form immediately after discovering his dead body flung from the twisted wreckage of flight 815. He became aware of all of Christian's memories, including full disclosure of his son, Jack, and daughter, Claire. This was a crucial move in his master plan of manipulating Jacob's candidates. First, he playfully encouraged Vincent to wake up an unconscious Jack so that the mind games could begin.

Especially when Jack at his lowest, the Man in Black utilized Christian's form to disorientate the candidate further. Although the entity later implored that he looked like his father to help him—Jack did discover the caves and water—there were darker incidents that day. As a result of Jack following "Christian," he slipped off a cliff and nearly died. Finding the caves also meant that Jack had found his father's coffin—empty. This made him more confused and convinced Jack even more that he was losing his mind.

For Claire, using Christian's image was the perfect tool to gain her trust. Because Claire had no idea that her father was dead, she believed that it really was, incredibly, her father on the island.

SMOKE ALARM
Back in Los Angeles, Jack's experience of seeing Christian's form on the island led to him imagining seeing his father. In one such moment, as Jack heard the beep of the smoke alarm, he thought his father was in front of him.

Until Jacob's death, the Man in Black had the ability to take on different forms at will and also be in two places at once. He used this ability when he used Christian's form to manipulate Frank Lapidus and Sun-Hwa Kwon at the Barracks, telling them to follow Locke—the form he had also taken. While in Christian's form, he told Locke to "Say hello to his son" as Locke turned the donkey wheel. This was a smart manipulation, as it ended up exacerbating Jack's feeling that there was something deeply wrong about him leaving the island, especially if his dad was alive.

UNLEASHED RAGE
Being trapped on the island went against the one thing the Man in Black craved even when he was human: to leave. This, combined with the tragedy of his spirit being transformed into an entity shaped by a source of evil, meant he was prone to bouts of extreme rage.

As he wandered the island for centuries and tried to exploit the weaknesses of Jacob's lured candidates on the island, his failures would oftentimes result in him taking on the smoke monster form. Be it uprooting centuries-old trees, or eviscerating people, the smoke monster was a purely an instinctual being that often acted first and didn't think until later. Yet at other times, the entity was purposeful in its pursuit to wipe out those who could help Jacob's mission, or in turn help the Man in Black's goal in any way.

Ben: *During the DHARMA era, the Man in Black recognized Ben's devotion to the island and kept tabs on the manipulative young man who would become the leader of Jacob's people. While Ben used his access to summon the smoke monster as a show of power, in reality it was not something he took lightly or used very often.*

The French Science Team: *After violently killing Nadine, the smoke monster than dragged Montand underneath the Temple's outer wall into a chamber. His friends held onto Montand's arm so tightly that the smoke monster's force tore it off. Robert, Brennan, and Lacombe ventured inside to save him, but were recruited—they returned to the surface with what Rousseau thought was a darkness within them.*

Survivors of Flight 815: *Going from the calm, manifestation of Christian, the Man in Black experienced a delirious rage hours after flight 815 crashed onto the island. The survivors heard the smoke monster tearing through the trees, but it remained unseen. On their second day on the island, the smoke monster yanked flight 815 pilot Seth Norris through the crashed cockpit windshield, eviscerated him and threw him into a tree. It then chased a terrified Jack, Charlie and Kate. Later, it allowed Locke to view it but left him unharmed since he recognized a future pawn in his war with Jacob. At other times, the smoke monster would pursue candidates in an attempt to ruin Jacob's plans, such as when he pursued Juliet, Kate and Eko.*

The Freighter Mercenaries: *Mayhew was thrown 50 feet into the air and had his guts torn out. The rest of the team suffered severe injuries, as the smoke monster raged around them like a dark electrical storm.*

Jacob's Team: *Shortly after the Man in Black used Locke's image to make Ben kill Jacob, he took on the smoke monster form and decimated Bram and his team inside the Taweret statue.*

The Temple Others: *Once Dogen was killed, the Temple Master who was blessed by Jacob with the ability to keep the Man in Black out, the smoke monster raged throughout every crevice, slaughtering those who didn't heed his warning to leave by sundown.*

JACOB'S SPIRIT
The spirit of young Jacob repeatedly appeared to the Man in Black while he was acting out his end game as Locke. The vision taunted him and reminded him of the rules that prevented him from personally killing any of the remaining Candidates after Jacob had died.

"My mother was crazy. Long time ago, before I looked like this, I had a mother, just like everyone. She was a very disturbed woman…"

AS JOHN LOCKE

Bringing Locke's corpse back to the island was the final piece in the Man in Black's master plan to kill Jacob. Benjamin Linus always felt like he was living in the shadow Locke, fearful and jealous of how special he seemed to be. For it to seem like the island had resurrected the man that Ben murdered made him feel terrified, weak, and malleable.

The Man in Black asked for the Ajira flight 316's manifest, establishing the location of the Candidates. Next, Ben's sins were theatrically "forgiven": the smoke monster went inside the Temple wall chamber and promised not to kill Ben, so long as he did everything that "Locke" said.

Although Alpert was suspicious, he followed "Locke" to the location of the real Locke. The entity stressed the importance of telling Locke that he needed to die to save all his friends. Fate confirmed, the Man in Black commanded everyone in the group to come with him to visit Jacob after their years of following him. Inside the statue, Jacob recognized his brother in Locke's form and realized he had finally found a loophole to the prohibition about the brothers killing each other. Playing on Ben's frustration with Jacob, the Man in Black manipulated Ben into stabbing Jacob to death.

With Jacob gone, the Man in Black was stuck in Locke's form, but he didn't care. He knew it was a person who had a huge significance among the candidates. A killing spree saw the smoke monster remove all the Temple Others that didn't choose to leave their safe haven. Those that did were swiftly seduced by the Man in Black's rabble-rousing call to leave the island. Of all the flight 815 survivors, Claire had been his companion for the three years in which she was alone. He brought back Sayid from the dead and recruited him, and Sawyer was loyal to him for a short period of time while he was grief stricken. He resurrected Sayid and recruited him. And Sawyer was loyal to him for a short time.

Charles Widmore's confession that Desmond could withstand a huge amount of electromagnetism made him realize that Desmond could enter the heart of the island and destroy it. This was risky: If the island sunk with no means of escape for the Man in Black, he would go down with it. But when his ploy to kill all of the remaining candidates in Widmore's submarine failed, his rage resurfaced, and he became resolute in sinking what had become his prison.

"...And, as a result of that, I had some growing pains. Problems that I'm still trying to work my way through."

Removing the sacred stone from the heart of the island had an unexpected side effect. It stripped the Man in Black of his immortality, and he became flesh and blood in Locke's form. Jack, who had become the new protector, exchanged brutal blows with the Man in Black while the island experienced devastating seismic activity. Just as he was about to stab Jack in the neck, Kate arrived and shot the Man in Black in the chest. Jack dealt the final blow by kicking him over the edge, of the cliff. He smashed against the cliff face all the way down before landing on his back on a ledge far below. In a darkly poetic way, the entity that had dishonored everything about Locke died on his back after a horrific fall, something that the real John Locke survived.

DESTINED TO USE LOCKE?

Long before the Man in Black assumed the very form of John Locke, there were some strange coincidences—or fate—that seemed to indicate that Locke's life was destined to become intertwined with the smoke monster. When Richard Alpert visited Locke when he was five years old, he noticed Locke had drawn a seemingly prophetic image: a terrified bald man being taken over by a cloud of black smoke.

In less specific incidences, but just a peculiar, when Jack lost track of the Man in Black as Christian, John Locke suddenly appeared from the foliage. A short time later, Kate spotted the smoke monster moving down below her. To express concern for him, she amusingly uttered "Locke" under her breath.

In the early days of their friendship, the Locke also gave Sayid one of his hunting knives and conned him into thinking Sawyer destroyed his triangulation set-up, when in fact it was actually Locke. Years later, the Man in Black in Locke's form gave Sayid his knife and convinced him of things that weren't true.

HAUNTING REMINDERS

The spirit of a young Jacob repeatedly appeared in the Man in Black's presence while he was acting out his end game as Locke. The vision taunted him and reminded him of the rules that he couldn't personally kill any of the remaining candidates after Jacob had died.

MARC SILVERMAN

▶ **CONNECTION:** Jack's childhood friend

Jack's best childhood friend, Marc was by Jack's side from their days on the playground all the way into their adult lives. During their early years, Jack stuck up for his buddy by once taking on two bullies who threatened Marc; unfortunately, they both got beat up for his stance. However, this act cemented their friendship for life.

As Jack prepared to marry Sarah, the still shy Marc was drafted as the best man with duties including a public toast to "the future Mrs. Jack Shephard." Ever the protector, Jack offered his friend an out, which Marc declined admitting he'd be fine after several beers. As it turned out, Marc also offered his friend an out in case Jack had second thoughts about the marriage. Equal in their determination, the pair stood side-by-side on Jack's big day. And Marc even weathered Sarah's post toast teasing him about his boozy breath with a smile.

MARGO SHEPHARD

▶ **CONNECTION:** Mother of Jack Shephard, wife of Christian Shephard

The devoted wife of Christian Shephard, Margo stuck by her husband through his ever increasing alcoholism and suspected infidelity. She was never aware that Christian believed deep down that he made a mistake by marrying her, something Christian's father, Ray, made explicitly clear to him on their wedding day.

TROUBLING TIMES

Things started to unravel after Jack testified against his father at a medical hearing that led to the revocation of Christian's license. This incident caused a huge rift in Jack and Christian's relationship. Margo knew that her husband and son had more in common than they cared to admit and their stubbornness meant neither would communicate unless she intervened.

When Christian left for Australia, Margo became gravely concerned. During an emotional argument with Jack, she pleaded for him to travel to Sydney to bring Christian home. Although Margo blamed Jack for what had happened, she knew in her heart that her husband had brought on the situation himself.

JACK'S RETURN

When Jack returned from his flight 815 ordeal, Margo was overjoyed to see him. Losing her estranged husband was heartbreaking enough, but the thought of losing her only son in a plane crash as he returned Christian's body back home felt too cruel. Margo later attended the belated memorial service held for Christian shortly after Jack's return.

MARK HUTTON

▶ **CONNECTION:** Manager of bank Kate Austen helped rob

Based in New Mexico, Mark Hutton was a bank manager who initially thought he was arranging a bank loan for "Maggie Ryan," an alias used by Kate Austen. Kate's cover story was that she was a photographer who had been commissioned to make a coffee table book of old theaters in small towns. Hutton was charmed by Kate, and even recommended she capture their local theater in Ruidsoso right on Main Street.

When the robbers—who were secretly working with Kate—burst in, Hutton stood up to them. Jason—the robber who was Kate's lover purely for the purposes of the job—decided to try to shoot Hutton, but Kate switched the tables. She stated that no one was to get hurt. She and Hutton activated the safety deposit box that contained a toy plane that belonged to her childhood sweetheart, Tom Brennan. It was the last thing she had to remember him by after she was responsible for his death.

MARTHA TOOMEY

▶ **CONNECTION:** Widow of Sam Toomey, who served in the U.S. Navy with Leonard Simms

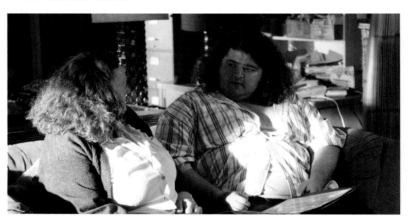

Martha Toomey was the wife of Sam Toomey. After he fatally shot himself, she resided alone in their remote residence in Australia. About four years after Sam's death, Hugo Reyes traveled to Australia to learn more about the origin of the "cursed" numbers (4, 8, 15, 15, 23, 42) from Toomey. Martha welcomed Hurley into her home, offered him a cup of tea and whatever insight she could provide.

When asked about how Sam learned about the numbers, Martha explained that her husband first heard them when he worked for the U.S. Navy monitoring long-range radio transmissions in the South Pacific with Leonard Simms. She said one night, approximately 16 years ago, a voice came through and clearly repeated "4, 8, 15, 16, 23, and 42" in a loop.

A few days later, Sam used those same numbers to crack a local Kalgoorlie carnival scam that involved beans in a jar. They won a huge sum of money, but on the way home they were hit by a pickup truck and Martha lost her leg. Sam was unscathed in the accident and became obsessed with the notion that the numbers had cursed them. Martha was adamantly opposed to her husband's way of thinking and offered Hurley a very definitive pearl of wisdom.

"You make your own luck, Mr. Reyes. You're looking for an excuse that doesn't exist."

— Spoken by Martha to Hurley

MARY JO

▶ **CONNECTION:** Pulled winning lotto jackpot numbers

Mary Jo was the television hostess who pulled the official lottery numbers for the California Mega Lotto Jackpot lottery. The night she pulled 4, 8, 15, 16, and 23, with the mega number 42, they all corresponded with Hugo Reyes' selections and made him the lone winner of the near record jackpot. Outside of work, Mary Jo hooked up with James "Sawyer" Ford who brought her back to his room for a night of passion. The moment was spoiled, though, when Sawyer's former partner Hibbs surprised the pair. James asked Mary Jo to wait for him at the hotel bar, where he promised he'd find her after he talked to his associate.

> **BY THE NUMBERS**
> *Until Hurley won, it had been **16** weeks since the last lottery winner.*

MATHIAS

▶ **CONNECTION:** Worked at Arctic monitoring station for Penelope Widmore along with Henrik

During her desperate search to find her love, Desmond David Hume, Penelope Widmore employed Portuguese duo Mathias and Henrik to monitor for any signs of electromagnetic anomalies. Mathias worked with Henrik in a small monitoring station in a very snowy location. The exact whereabouts of Mathias' place of work remains a mystery.

The two enjoyed playing chess to pass the time and it was during one of their games that Mathias noticed part of their monitoring equipment was flashing "Electromagnetic Anomaly Detected." Mathias wondered how long the message had been showing and vented to Henrik that they had missed it "again." This suggests there may had been another time when the station registered a degree of electromagnetism from the island, but they failed to notice the alert. Mathias called Penelope to deliver the news.

> **PLAYING GAMES**
> *Mathias and Henrik are yet two more characters who played a game that echoes one of the themes of the story. This theme resonates in Locke's explanation of backgammon to Walt: "Two players. Two sides. One is light, one is dark."*

MATTHEW REED

▶ **CONNECTION:** Counselor with LAPD; counseled Ana Lucia Cortez

After LAPD Officer Ana Lucia Cortez was shot four times by convicted felon Jason McCormick, LAPD Captain Teresa Cortez —Ana Lucia's mother— referred her to Matthew Reed, a therapist.

Pregnant at the time of the shooting, Ana Lucia's vest prevented any major injuries, but the massive shock to her system killed her unborn baby. In turn, this incident caused her boyfriend, Danny, to leave her. Reed counseled Ana Lucia for four months before he determined that she was ready to rejoin the force.

MEATHEAD

▶ **CONNECTION:** Bully from Jack's childhood

Meathead is the nickname of the childhood bully who terrorized young Jack Shephard and his best friend Marc Silverman. The friends were once physically accosted by Meathead, who pummeled Jack and then went after Marc. Lying on the ground and angered by their treatment, Jack rose and attempted to defend his friend. That only served to anger Meathead, who then socked Jack in the eye and knocked him out. The event served as an important formative moment in Jack's life.

MEDUSA SPIDER

Several previously undiscovered species of insects and arachnids were discovered on the island. Although it wasn't considered one of the new finds on the island, the Medusa spider (*Latrodectus regina*) was an impressive specimen. The striking spider with its black-and-yellow stripes gets its name from the potent pheromone it secretes, which attracts hoards of male Medusa spiders from great distances.

Beyond its mating chemicals, the Medusa spider also possesses deadly venom. Although the poison isn't fatal to humans, it does cause complete paralysis and slows down the heartbeat to an undetectably slow rate.

During a disagreement about stolen diamonds, flight 815 mid-section survivor Nikki threw a female Medusa spider at her boyfriend, Paulo. As he lay paralyzed, Nikki located the diamonds hidden inside Paulo's underwear.

Both Nikki and Paulo were bitten by the poisonous Medusa spider.

THE SMOKE MONSTER MEDUSA
Although Paulo's paralysis was the result of the bite from a Medusa spider, the swarm of male Medusas that attacked Nikki shortly thereafter were not arachnids. They were actually a manifestation of the smoke monster taking on one of its many forms. The bites from the monster's incarnation still had the same effect, as Nikki collapsed in a paralyzed state. A short time later, their fellow survivors, thinking they were actually dead, buried Nikki and Paulo alive.

> **ABOUT THE MEDUSA SPIDER**
> *The choice of the fictitiously named "Medusa" spider is thematically significant on many levels. Medusa originates from another mythological location that has its fair share of islands— Greece. Medusa was a Gorgon, a terrifying female creature with snakes for hair. Medusa was believed to be the spawn of two sea gods, Phorcys and Ceto. Medusa would lure people to look into her eyes and turn them to stone. In Nikki's life prior to the island, she played the character Corvette on the hit TV series Exposé. On the show, she played the role of a stripper who used her charms to gain information about criminals.*
>
> *Beyond her on-screen persona, Nikki used her femininity to seduce TV producer Howard L. Zuckerman so that Paulo could poison him to death. She also contributed to Paulo "turning to stone" by paralyzing him with a Medusa spider. In a karmic way, a different kind of monster—the smoke monster—then dealt Nikki the same deathblow by turning her into a paralyzed "statue" herself.*

MEGAN STRATTON (PACE)

▶ **CONNECTION:** Mother of Charlie & Liam Pace

Megan Pace was the wife of Simon Pace and the mother of Liam and Charlie. Despite her role as a housewife, Megan always remained a dreamer, which was in stark contrast to her pragmatic husband, Simon. She saw the same spirit in her youngest son, Charlie, and encouraged him to develop and embrace his talent as a musician. When Charlie was a young boy, she even bought him a piano for Christmas and told him he was "special." Megan believed Charlie's talent would be the Pace family's ticket out of their working-class existence. Megan died unexpectedly sometime in her boys' later youth, so she never got to see Charlie and Liam achieve success with their band Drive Shaft. In a sentimental nod, though, Karen (Liam's wife) named his daughter Megan after his mother.

VISIONS

On the island, Charlie once had a vision of his mother and Claire dressed as the two angels in Andrea del Verrocchio's painting "The Baptism of Christ" (a copy of which hung above the stairs in the Pace family home).

BAPTISM OF CHRIST ✛
Andrea del Verrocchio was a fifteenth century Italian Renaissance painter and sculptor who was also the teacher of Leonardo da Vinci. The pair worked on "The Baptism of Christ" together and it's considered del Verrocchio's masterwork. It depicted Christ being baptized by St. John the Baptist, with God being represented by a dove.

MELISSA DUNBROOK

▶ **CONNECTION:** Prosecutor in Kate Austen's court hearing

A tough-minded, rising-star district attorney, Melissa Dunbrook was assigned to prosecute Kate Austen once the Oceanic Six returned to Los Angeles. To build her case for the trial, Dunbrook managed to get some supportive evidence from one witness, Jack Shephard. Unfortunately, she managed to derail the defense by asking Jack if he was in love with Kate. Although Jack responded, "Not anymore," the damage to his testimony was done.

When the prosecution's chief witness, Diane Jansen (Kate's mother) refused to provide evidence citing medical reasons, Melissa's case started to unravel. She claimed that the meeting between Diane and Kate the previous day had wrecked her case, so she offered to stop the trial and make Kate serve four years. But Kate's attorney, Duncan Forrester, argued on her behalf that she was a hero for saving five other people after the accident.

Ultimately, Dunbrook changed the offer to time served plus 10 years probation, with an agreement that Kate stay in the state of California. Kate accepted the plea and stated that she just wanted the trial to end so she could get back to her "son," Aaron Littleton.

CONNECTIONS WITH THE PEARL ✛
At one far edge of the Mesa resided the pneumatic tube dumping ground, which featured piles of canisters from DHARMA's Pearl station.

> ❝ **She's the very definition of a flight risk.** ❞
>
> —Spoken by Melissa Dunbrook about Kate Austen

THE MESA ARMY CAMP

The Mesa is the nickname for an area of the island known for its relatively flat topography and light forestation. The region is nestled in between huge cliffs that rise on both sides, which created the valley-like floor. The area was utilized by various groups, from the U.S. Army to the DHARMA Initiative and the Oceanic 815 survivors. Over the years, it served as a staging ground and a crossroads leading to several important sites.

In 1954, a U.S. Army platoon used the flat, unobstructed space to erect a firing tower for "Jughead," the hydrogen bomb staged for South Pacific weapons testing. However, the bomb was eventually moved and buried below the barracks.

It was during the DHARMA Initiative's time on the island that the area came to be known as the Mesa. On the day of the Purge, Roger Linus offered to take his son, Benjamin, to the area for some father/son bonding over a few beers.

During the time directly after the crash of Oceanic flight 815, the Mesa served as an important locale that connected the survivors to various landmarks on the island. The day after the crash, Jack, Kate and Charlie hiked through the area to locate the separated cockpit of their plane. Another contingent of survivors that included Sayid hiked to the high point of the Mesa in an attempt to dial in Danielle Rousseau's looping radio transmission.

Approximately two weeks after the crash, Hurley created a 2-hole golf course to play the Island Open Golf Tournament on a bluff in the Mesa area, which was located near the entrance to the caves. Two months later, Hurley, Sawyer, Charlie and Jin found the DHARMA van and rolled it down a hill onto the Mesa to get it working again.

THE "REAL" MESA +

The Mesa in reality is the property known as Kualoa Ranch located on the leeward side of Oahu. It's comprised of 663 acres on what was formerly a sugar mill and farm.

MICHAEL DAWSON

FACTS & FIGURES

Time On The Island

POST-OCEANIC: 67 days

Connection: Father of Walt Lloyd

Father to Walt Lloyd, Michael Dawson inherited a difficult situation after he and his son crashed on the island as passengers of Oceanic flight 815. Not around during Walt's upbringing, then reunited with him 10 years later prior to the flight, Michael was forced to learn how to be a parent, all the while learning how to survive. The task proved difficult, as father and son struggled to form a bond on the island. The guilt Michael felt from not seeing Walt grow up resulted in Michael making several morally compromised decisions.

After Walt's birth, Michael and Susan started to drift apart.

RAISING WALT

When Walt's mother, Susan Lloyd, died unexpectedly, his adoptive father, Brian Porter, asked Michael to take him off his hands. Michael travelled to Australia and took Walt and Brian's dog, Vincent, and boarded Oceanic flight 815 on September 22, 2004. But Michael felt the disorientation and confusion of suddenly being with Walt after a decade apart. Michael called his mother from the Sydney airport to ask if she would take care of Walt. Sadly, Walt overheard the conversation.

Soon after the crash, the battle lines between father and son were firmly drawn. Michael didn't know Walt and Walt didn't want to know Michael. Tensions began to quell with Michael's revelation that he had written countless letters to Walt, letters that Susan had never passed on.

Early on, Walt and Michael had a difficult time connecting.

Walt and Michael grew closer during the construction of the raft.

As they grew closer, their project of building a raft together became a cruel and tragic irony: the thing that united Michael and Walt soon tore them apart. On their first night out at sea, the Others abducted Walt and destroyed the raft.

Walt's kidnapping changed Michael dramatically. No longer the methodical, artistic planner, he became fueled by instinct and a singular mission: to get Walt back and leave the island, no matter what.

Once back at the beach camp, Michael was inside the Swan station when he received a message from Walt on the Swan station's computer. Michael ventured out alone, but his subsequent capture by the Others led to a week-long interrogation about Walt and a brief three-minute chat with his son. At this point, the Others set their plan in motion using Michael as the pawn. They threatened he would never see his son again unless he helped free Benjamin Linus.

"Way I see it, there's only two choices: you're either a hero, or you want to die."

"They took my son!"

After Michael's capture, the Others took him to their makeshift camp.

Michael was envious of how his son admired John Locke.

His desperation to save Walt led to Ana Lucia's and Libby's deaths.

Desperate to rescue his son, Michael resorted to murder. He shot Ana Lucia Cortez, then accidentally turned the weapon on Elizabeth "Libby" Smith. Mission accomplished, Ben allowed Michael and Walt to leave the island. However, Michael's confession to Walt about the murders of Libby and Ana Lucia pushed Walt further away. Walt went to live with Michael's mother, as he couldn't bear to be near his father.

VERSUS LOCKE

The person Michael clashed with the most on the island was John Locke. Michael was jealous of the way Walt saw Locke as a warrior and effortlessly looked up to him. Although Michael despised Locke for a long while, he grew to respect him.

Locke was paramount in Walt's rescue from one of the polar bears and, later, became the person who trained Michael how to use a rifle. Driven by blind rage and desperation to get Walt back, though, Michael turned on the man who had trained him. Michael knocked Locke out and imprisoned him with Jack in the Swan's armory before setting off to get Walt from the Others' imprisonment.

DESIGN & CONSTRUCTION ✛

Michael was a deeply creative soul with a huge passion for art, architecture, and construction. Michael's eight years of experience in construction was integral to the survivors dealing with the disastrous cave-in that trapped Jack Shephard and Charlie Pace. After their escape, Michael used his engineering skills to check the integrity of the caves. He later designed a system of basic but highly effective showers for the location.

Eventually, his frustrations and desperation for rescue meant the sense of "making do" on the island was short-lived. Michael refused to construct further water filtration systems and, instead, turned his talents to raft construction.

Although his first attempt was destroyed in a fire caused by Walt, Michael learned from the mistakes of the first design. The second raft consisted of a battery provided by Sayid (supplied by Danielle Rousseau), plus a radar emitter and flare recovered from the Beechcraft.

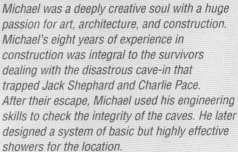

MICHAEL DAWSON

245

CONNECTION WITH SUN

With tension and distance increasing between Jin and Sun after the crash, Sun discovered an effortless chemistry with Michael. Acknowledged with silent looks, the heat between them

Sun and Michael shared several moments together.

was exacerbated when Michael stumbled upon Sun bathing in the jungle. Their friendship developed further when Sun looked after Walt while Michael hunted boar with Locke. The two grew closer when she confided in Michael she could speak English.

Regardless of their attraction, Sun remained faithful to Jin. She slapped Michael when he intervened in their argument concerning Sun's decision to wear a bikini. But Michael's inner rage toward Jin had bigger consequences than just jealousy. When Michael pummeled Jin, convinced he burned his first raft, the violence provoked Sun to scream for Michael to stop in English—something none of the other survivors knew she could speak.

JOURNEY WITH JIN

A combination of their language barrier, cultural differences and Jin's awareness that Michael and Sun shared a connection meant that their relationship began as firm enemies. When Jin assumed Michael had stolen Paik's Rolex watch, Jin

severely beat Michael. But by the time the second raft was launched, the two had formed a strong bond of respect and friendship. In fact, Jin presented Mr. Paik's watch to Michael as a gift.

Michael and Jin failed to bond right away on the island.

After Walt's abduction, Michael drifted away from not only Jin but from all of his flight 815 companions. Then, when Jin and Sun arrived on the *Kahana* freighter later that year, Michael's close friendship with Jin was renewed. Jin stayed by his side as Michael attempted to freeze the freighter's bomb timer until Michael insisted that he leave and become a father.

THE FREIGHTER MISSION

Back in New York after leaving the island, Michael's attempted suicide led to visions of Libby in his hospital room. After his discharge from the hospital, he pawned the Rolex watch that Jin had given him in order to acquire a .38 Special and, once again, tried to kill himself.

NAME THAT TUNE

Things were so bad for Michael when he returned to New York that he attempted suicide by driving his car into a wall. Ironically, the song heard playing in his car is "It's Getting Better" by Mama Cass.

On orders from Ben, Tom Friendly attempted to recruit Michael so that he could redeem himself for his past misdeeds. Michael needed to save the rest of his friends on the island from Charles Widmore. Ben informed Michael that he needed to disable the communications room in the *Kahana* and the vessel's engines.

What followed was the beginning of a downward spiral that led to the death he welcomed. When Sayid first saw

Michael boarded the *Kahana* as deckhand "Kevin Johnson."

Michael, he reported him to the freighter's Captain Gault. Mercenary Martin Keamy then forced Michael to confess giving his name to Ben, but Keamy's weapon didn't fire because the island wasn't done with Michael.

As the survivors proceeded to the freighter, Michael discovered a sizable stash of C-4 rigged to blow. In a display of bravery and regret for his past crimes, Michael stayed with the bomb's timer until its detonation. He repeatedly froze the battery with the only canister of liquid nitrogen on board, giving his friends time to abandon the freighter. Michael died when the C-4 detonated.

Name:	Kevin Johnson
Origin:	Port of Suva, Fiji
Delivery No:	A-2099302
FSR Number:	230 ZD 0200 994 0200
Service Type:	SPECIAL SHIPMENT/OVERSIZE

Paik's watch sparked violence and then a significant friendship between Michael and Jin.

"Time doesn't matter on a damn island!"

INJURY & DEATH

Before his death on the freighter, Michael sustained a variety of injuries:

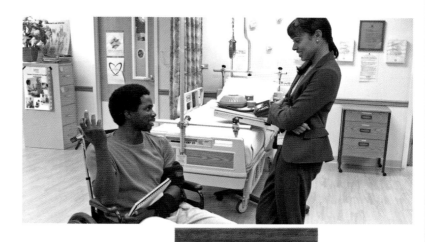

▶ *During the early stages of the custody battle with Susan, Michael was struck by a car and forced to wear a cast on his leg for several months.*

▶ *His right leg was badly sliced open by a rampaging boar's tusks on the island.*

▶ *Michael drowned and died for a short period of time after the Others abducted Walt. Sawyer pulled him onto the raft and resuscitated him.*

▶ *A Great White Shark bearing the DHARMA Initiative logo attacked Michael and Sawyer while they were adrift on the raft wreckage before Michael shot it.*

WHISPERS

When Keamy's device remotely activated the freighter bomb, the whispers surrounded Michael. A vision of Christian Shephard appeared and said, "You can go now," just before the freighter exploded.

Michael remained a restless spirit on the island after his death, becoming one of the infamous "whispers" that warned of impending doom. Michael even showed himself to Hurley to prevent him from blowing up the Ajira plane.

In death, Michael's predicament could still be aided. When Ben and Hurley brought Walt to the island, Walt was told that just because his father was dead, it didn't mean he couldn't help him.

Michael explained the significance of the island whispers to Hurley.

MICHAEL DAWSON
2327 GRIFFITH AVE #610
NY NEW YORK 10007
USA

WALT LLOYD
HEBERGEN 404
1098 SM AMSTERDAM
THE NETHERLANDS

Susan hid all of Michael's letters to Walt

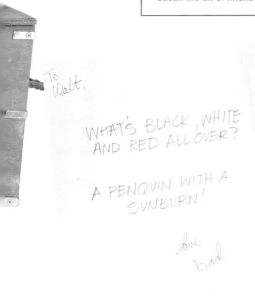

To Walt,

WHAT'S BLACK, WHITE
AND RED ALL OVER?

A PENGUIN WITH A
SUNBURN!

love
Dad

Michael's sketches

MIKE WALTON

▶ **CONNECTION:** Ana Lucia's partner in LAPD

Mike "Big Mike" Walton was a Los Angeles cop who rose up through the ranks to make detective. At one time he was the police partner of Officer Ana Lucia Cortez, who was involved in an officer-related shooting that took her off the job. When she returned to duty, Big Mike was assigned to watch over her by Captain Theresa Cortez.

Under orders for her first day back, Walton took them to the quiet residential neighborhood of Westwood to patrol, but she bypassed his plan and picked up a call for a domestic disturbance instead. As soon as they arrived on-site, Ana Lucia pulled her weapon so aggressively that Walton had to order her to stand down. Angry, Mike was quiet for the drive back to the station but when they arrived the pair argued about her actions until they were interrupted by another officer with news for Ana Lucia. The next day she turned in her badge and Big Mike moved on with a new partner.

By 2005, Walton was promoted to detective and was assigned to the interrogation of Hugo "Hurley" Reyes after he eluded several patrol cars in a high-speed chase in his classic Camaro. Big Mike showed little patience for Hurley and accused him of seeking celebrity treatment because he shouted, "I'm one of the Oceanic Six" to the arresting officers. Walton revealed that Ana Lucia, who was on the plane, had been his partner and asked if Hurley knew her. Hugo lied and Mike went out to get a doughnut. Hurley then screamed and Mike ran back to find nothing, so he threatened to put him back in the nuthouse, which Hurley welcomed.

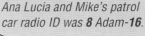

BY THE NUMBERS
Ana Lucia and Mike's patrol car radio ID was **8** Adam-**16**.

MIKHAIL BAKUNIN

▶ **CONNECTION:** Member of the Others; worked at the Flame station

A former soldier in the Soviet Army and dedicated Communications Officer for the Others, Mikhail Bakunin was a formidable man who strived to adhere to Jacob's wishes. Mikhail grew up primarily in Kiev, Ukraine but also spent some time in Afghanistan. After joining the Soviet Army, he gained some medical experience in the field but was mainly stationed at a listening post in Vladivostok, the home to Russia's largest port and its Pacific Fleet navy.

CONNECTING WITH JACOB

Once the Cold War ended, Mikhail's unit was decommissioned. The years spent carrying out terrible deeds against humanity played on Mikhail's mind, so he focused on a single resolve: to do something good. He claimed to have seen a newspaper advertisement that asked a simple but weighty question, one that became interlinked to protecting the island: "Would you like to save the world?" Mikhail would later come to the island at the age of 24.

Mikhail conducted himself as a fervent supporter of Jacob and the island. He was appalled at the lies Benjamin Linus told him about the Looking Glass station and how Ben had been blocking communications. Simply, Mikhail found it difficult to accept the fact that Jacob would tell Ben to lie to his own people.

"Would you like to save the world?"

WORKING AT THE FLAME

Contrary to Jacob's love of life's simple pleasures and dislike of modern advances, Mikhail was a great enthusiast of computers, communications equipment, and all things technological. After the Purge, Mikhail was stationed at the Flame station, the perfect place for him to dwell with its abundance of communication tools. For 11 years, Mikhail used the Flame's satellite to communicate with the outside world for Ben.

NADIA & THE CAT
This former solider was a man who admired strength of character. In fact, he named his beloved cat after Romanian gymnast, Nadia Comâneci.

On the day flight 815 crashed on the island, Mikhail used the resources in the Flame station to garner a full flight manifest of the passengers. Although Mikhail was already aware of the survivors, their first encounter with him was via the camera feed in the Pearl station. He immediately turned off the camera and anticipated the survivors' next move.

When eventually confronted by Kate, Sayid and Locke, Mikhail attempted to deceive the survivors. He pretended that he was, the last remaining member of the DHARMA Initiative after the Purge.

Before its destruction, Mikhail's home provided important resources for the survivors. Sayid stole the DHARMA file that revealed the location of the barracks. Also, Locke stole C-4 from the Flame that he later used to destroy the Others' submarine, the *Galaga*.

KLUGH'S EXECUTION

Beatrice Klugh, a member of the Others who ranked above Mikhail, was discovered hiding in the Flame's basement by Kate and Sayid. Fearing that the survivors would learn too much from her, she ordered Mikhail to shoot her. Mikhail carried out the order, but not without impassioned pleas to find another solution. Fearless and willing to die for the island, Mikhail demanded that Sayid kill him after Klugh's shooting, but the survivors refused and kept him prisoner in hopes of gaining additional intel.

A LIFESAVER

Mikhail's time spent as a Soviet Army Field Medic ended up saving Naomi Dorrit's life. After Naomi parachuted onto the island, he stumbled upon her injured body along with Jin-Soo Kwon, Charlie Pace, Hugo "Hurley" Reyes and Desmond Hume.

Because of his vast knowledge of various languages, Mikhail deciphered Naomi's cries in Italian and discovered that a branch had punctured her lung. He successfully ventilated the injury and dressed the wound.

Mikhail agreed to help Naomi if the survivors would set him free.

BRUSHES WITH DEATH

Due to his army training—or perhaps because the island wasn't finished with him—Mikhail survived a powerful jolt from the sonic fence. Although not set to a lethal level, he still experienced foaming from the mouth and violent hemorrhaging from his ears, which resulted in the permanent loss of hearing in one.

During his assault on the Looking Glass station, Mikhail sustained even more serious injuries that still didn't kill him. Desmond fired a harpoon spear into his chest that

Ben ordered Mikhail to the Looking Glass station and, ultimately, to his death.

knocked him down but not out. Later, he managed to re-enter the moon pool and swim around to the window of the communications room. There, he sacrificed his own life by shattering the porthole to pieces using a grenade, all in the name of Jacob and the island.

MILES STRAUME, SEE PAGE 250

MITTELOS BIOSCIENCE

Mittelos Bioscience was a fake company in the U.S. used by the Others as a front to recruit potential members to the island. Richard Alpert, with the assistance of Ethan Rom and a woman named Diana, headed up the operation. Alpert told those he was interested in "employing" (secretly bringing to the island) Mittelos was a privately funded organization that offered its staff freedom to explore their skills, as well as freedom to enjoy leisure activities with their colleagues. During Alpert's pitches to potential recruits, he would show photographs of Mittelos staff members cycling in the countryside of Portland—which was actually the island.

The branding used for Mittelos Bioscience consisted of two hexagons, curiously similar to the octagonal shape of the DHARMA logos.

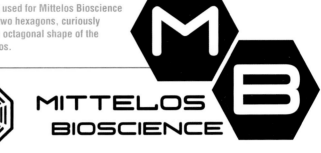

RECRUITING JOHN LOCKE

John Locke's science teacher at Cowin Heights High School, Mr. Gellert, encouraged Locke to attend Mittelos's summer science camp. But even as a teenager, Locke lived for outdoor pursuits like fishing and loved high-energy hobbies like boxing, so he declined to attend the science camp.

John Locke turned down a chance to attend a summer camp at Mittelos Bioscience.

RECRUITING JULIET BURKE

In 2000, Richard Alpert approached Dr. Juliet Burke about an opportunity to work for Mittelos Bioscience. He stated that the company was quite interested in employing her for a period of six months to learn more about her groundbreaking fertility experiments. To pique Juliet's interest further, Alpert showed her a slide of a human womb that resembled a 70-year-old's when the woman in question was actually only 26.

Juliet declined Alpert's initial offer, joking that the only way she could accept it was if her controlling ex-husband—and her boss—was hit by a bus. Soon after her statement, Edmund was struck and killed by a bus. After this, Alpert returned and offered Juliet a second chance at the job. Feeling that there was no one to stop her from accepting the offer, Juliet agreed to work for Mittelos Bioscience.

Juliet later learned that Mittelos wasn't in Portland and was instead in a rather remote location. She arrived at Miami's Herarat Aviation airport and was willingly tranquilized before being taken to the island via the *Galaga*, the Others' submarine.

AN OTHER CONNECTION
Richard Alpert claimed that Mittelos Bioscience was based just outside of Portland, Oregon. This is also the same city near where Benjamin Linus was born. Roger Linus, in his attempt to get help for his pregnant wife, met Horace Goodspeed and Olivia of the DHARMA Initiative on the outskirts of Portland.

MILES STRAUME

FACTS & FIGURES
Time On The Island

POST-KAHANA: 10 days

IN DHARMA: 3+ years

POST-INCIDENT: 9 days

Connection: Son of Dr. Pierre Chang and Lara Chang

Growing up without a father left Miles Straume an angry individual, but it was his ability to ascertain the thoughts and feelings of the dead that set him apart from the rest of humanity. What started as a terrifying curse when he was young turned into a profitable blessing in his adult life—people were willing to pay Miles to speak to their deceased loved ones. However, some instances of supernatural contact highlighted Miles's own issues, especially the messages of love between fathers and sons.

It was a random but extremely well paid booking by Charles Widmore that brought Miles to the island. It was there that he discovered his father's past, and through the power of the island's time-flashes, became a part of it.

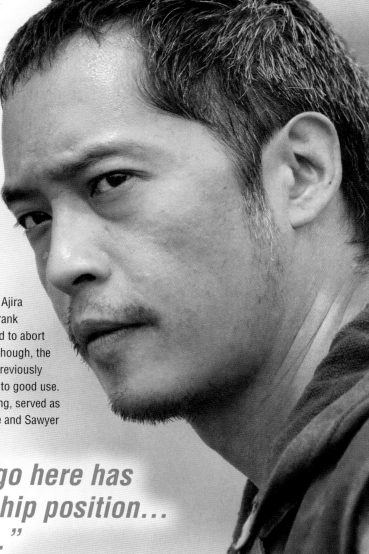
Miles was also approached by Jacob's off-island Others team. Bram attempted to convince Miles to join them, to learn about his father and his power.

FREIGHTER MISSION
Widmore knew that with Miles's gift he could commune with those who were killed by Benjamin Linus and find out where he was hiding. However, Miles was not a courageous soul and the prospect of trying to locate a mass-murderer didn't appeal to him, but Widmore's offer to pay $1.6 million changed Miles's mind immediately.

BACK IN TIME
When the island's time-flashes settled in 1974, Miles became much more of a team player. Although Miles initially hated Sawyer's alpha male presence among the survivors, the time he spent with him during the 1970s DHARMA era changed everything. Miles served under Sawyer as part of DHARMA's security detail and grew to have a great respect for him. The two became good friends and always had each other's back in the ensuing chaos of the Incident. His position within Sawyer's DHARMA security team helped push his development.

Miles realized on the third day there that Dr. Pierre Chang was his father when he saw his mother standing behind him in the cafeteria queue. Three years later, Miles saw his father enjoying a picture book with Miles's three-month-old self. When his father urged his mother to leave the island as part of the evacuation before the Incident, Miles realized that he only wanted to protect them.

TIME WITH HURLEY
Once he discovered Hurley had full-blown conversations with the dead, Miles became quite jealous. The two had several debates pertaining to the time travel they had experienced. Miles became particularly irate when Hurley couldn't understand his interpretation of how it worked: he and Hurley could die, but several things that happened were always supposed to happen.

ESCAPE PLAN
After Miles found Richard Alpert in the jungle, they both headed to Hydra island to destroy the Ajira plane as originally planned. But while paddling their outrigger on the ocean, they discovered Frank Lapidus, who had survived the explosion on the submarine. Frank convinced Miles and Richard to abort that plan and instead use his piloting skills to fly off the island. Before the plan could take off, though, the threesome had to fix various problems, including the plane's hydraulic system. As Miles had previously renovated apartments for a contractor, he had a basic mechanical knowledge that Lapidus put to good use. Miles fixed the hydraulics with a ream of duct tape and, once the plane was back up and running, served as Frank's eyes and helped him back up the plane. Along with Richard, he also helped Claire, Kate and Sawyer onboard before the plane took off and plotted a course back to civilization.

THE NAME GAME ✛
Miles' last name is Straume, as in maelstrom.

"As you can see, Hugo here has assumed the leadership position... so that's pretty great."

> ## " I don't believe in a lot of things, but I do believe in duct tape. "

CONVERSATIONS WITH THE DEAD

Miles's ability to communicate with the dead had nothing to do with speaking to ghosts; it was a sense, a feeling of who they were and what they thought just before they died. Before and during his time on the island, Miles interacted with several people (and even a wild boar) who had passed away. Some were purely for financial gain, whereas others were far more personal experiences that deeply affected Miles and those who knew him.

OFF-ISLAND

MR. VONNER (ENCINO, CALIFORNIA)

This was Miles's first paranormal experience. While his mother, Lara, was looking at an apartment, Miles could hear the dead man's thoughts: he was frightened, alone, his chest hurt, and he wanted his wife, Kimberly, who had died the previous year.

MR. GARDNER (INGLEWOOD, CALIFORNIA)

Miles communed with this murdered dead grandson of Mrs. Gardner. She wanted Miles to exorcise his spirit from her home, as it frightened her. The spirit told Miles where his drug stash and money was hidden, which Miles kept. Afterward, Miles refunded Gardner half of the $200 fee.

RUSSELL GRAY (CALIFORNIA)

Although Miles told Russell's father, Howard, he found out Russell always knew his father loved him, this was an occasion where Miles scammed someone. Miles was angry, as Russell reminded him of his own abandonment issues. Miles later returned Howard's money.

FELIX (CALIFORNIA)

Naomi Dorrit, under Charles Widmore's employ, took Miles to Felix's body to test his skills. Miles passed the test by revealing Felix was killed on the way to delivering paperwork, photos of empty graves in Thailand, and a purchase order for an old plane to Charles Widmore.

ON-ISLAND

NAOMI DORRIT

After spending time next to his freighter colleague's body, Miles ascertained that the flight 815 survivors were telling the truth that they did not murder her.

DANIELLE ROUSSEAU & KARL MARTIN

Miles sensed their bodies as he, Sawyer, Claire, and Aaron trekked through the jungle.

WILD BOAR

Miles's powers came in handy to locate a recently deceased boar that he pretended he killed to provide food for the camp.

FOUR U.S. SOLDIERS

While the Others were escorting him in 1954, Miles sensed they walked over a fresh grave. He revealed three died of gunshot wounds and another of radiation poisoning.

ALVAREZ (DHARMA WORKER)

Miles found out Alvarez was thinking about his girlfriend, Andrea, when a filling in his tooth was yanked out due to electromagnetism at the Swan construction site. The tooth was wrenched violently through his brain.

JULIET BURKE

Sawyer asked Miles to find out what Juliet wanted to tell him before she died. Miles complied and discovered she wanted Sawyer to know that "it worked."

SAYID JARRAH

When Sayid died in the Temple, Miles was disturbed as he couldn't connect or get any information about his final thoughts. Two hours later, Sayid sat up, alive, which troubled Miles even more.

JACOB

Using Jacob's ashes, Miles revealed that Ben murdered him, not the smoke monster as Ben had claimed.

NIKKI & PAULO

Over their graves at Boone Hill, Miles detected they had been buried with $8 million in diamonds, which he later dug up and claimed for himself.

ALEX ROUSSEAU

The last dead person Miles sensed on the island was Alex, who Richard Alpert had buried at the barracks.

MOTHER

▶ **CONNECTION:** Former protector of the island; raised Jacob and the Man in Black

Calm, serene and preternaturally wise, Mother was what Jacob and the Man in Black called the woman who raised them on their island home. Exactly when and how she came to the island was never revealed, but she was certainly placed there by fate to become its protector for a time.

Once she took on her guardian duties, time became irrelevant and mortal aging ceased for her as she lived a solitary existence in the spartan caves that she called home. During her years on the island, she observed from a distance any who landed on her shores and assessed their impact on the landscape. Despite her own human origins, she was clearly disenfranchised by humanity's propensity to destroy and corrupt all that was good, which she watched play out time and time again even within the island's peaceful confines. And so it was with a clear purpose that she kept all men away from the heart of the island.

ONE LIGHT, ONE DARK

Sometime in the early 1st century A.D., a Roman woman who survived a shipwreck washed up on the shores of the island. Close to full term in her pregnancy, the woman, Claudia, blindly sought water inland and was found by Mother. The women discovered they both spoke Latin, so Claudia was able to share her name and the fact that she was entering into labor. Mother took her to the caves and helped her deliver one expected son and his unexpected brother. Claudia named the first Jacob and when she asked to see the second, Mother impassively slammed the woman in the head with a rock until she was dead. After unknown years alone, the haunted woman found a new purpose— to raise and mold two pure sons that the island could choose between as its next protector.

Mother showed no compassion for Claudia.

For 13 years, Mother contentedly raised her sons in their cozy cave home, insulated from any outside human influence that lurked on the island. She shared a close bond with both of her boys. With Jacob she had an honest and devoted son who obeyed her every word. However, she favored her dark-haired son who radiated intelligence and a wistful curiosity she admired. Try as she might though, she could not keep them ignorant of the outside world. When the boys stumbled upon a group of men who hunted in the jungle, she finally had to reveal the destiny for which they were so studiously groomed. With a heavy heart, she blindfolded them and, hand-in-hand, led them to the heart of the island where she took off their blinders and introduced them to the light.

> *"My love. You need to know this. No matter what you've been told…You'll never be able to leave this island."*

BETRAYED BY THE TRUTH

After her revelation, Mother grew despondent with the knowledge that her carefully crafted world would never be the same and she might lose one of her boys. Mother's worst fears came true when her second son assaulted Jacob and revealed to them that he had been visited by the spectre of their real mother who exposed the truth of their origins. Feeling betrayed, he rejected the only mother and brother he ever knew to live with the humans on the island. Devastated, Mother lamented her loss and admitted the reason for her lies to Jacob, who ultimately stayed with her.

DUTY CALLS

For 30 years, Jacob and Mother lived side-by-side in the caves but she was never the same after her family broke apart. Tired and deeply saddened, she worked on her loom and waited for the inevitable, which came when Jacob revealed his brother's discovery of a way to leave the island. Compelled by her duty, she ventured out to confront the Man in Black as he worked in the well. Torn by her love for her son and the island, she expressed her worry about what Jacob had told her about his brother's plans to leave and expose the light to the humans with whom he lived. Defiant, the Man in Black confirmed his plan to build the wheel and escape. Appalled, she told him goodbye and through her tears smashed his head against the wall. Mother then took her unconscious son's body out of the well and proceeded to fill it to the brim with soil and stone. She then moved on to the Man in Black's village where under the cover of dark, she murdered all of the people as they slept and burnt their homes to the ground.

A NEW PROTECTOR

Mother then woke up Jacob and took him back to the heart of the island, a place she made him promise never to enter, and took out a bottle of wine. As she spoke a Latin prayer over a chalice, she told Jacob to drink. Mother returned to the cave which she found upended and her son's Senet game in the fire. As she leaned over to look at the black marker, a dagger ripped through her torso—the Man in Black's bloody vengeance dispensed. Slumped over, Mother serenely whispered "Thank you" to her favorite son and expired. After Jacob confronted and killed his brother, he then placed his body and Mother's next to each other inside their former cave home with a Senet stone in their palms.

"It was always supposed to be you, Jacob. I see that now. And one day you'll see it, too. But until then…You don't really have a choice."

MONTAND

▶ **CONNECTION:** Member of French expedition team led by Danielle Rousseau

Montand was one of six French scientists (along with Brennan, Lacombe, Nadine, Robert, and Danielle Rousseau) who sailed from Tahiti on November 15, 1987 on a science expedition. During their journey, they picked up a strange transmission (the continual repetition of 4, 8, 15, 16, 23, 42) and changed course to investigate it. Unfortunately, their instruments malfunctioned and they were caught in a ferocious storm that forced them to abandon ship near the island.

WHAT'S IN A NAME? ✚
The ship carrying the French expedition team was named the Besixdouzé. This is also the name of the asteroid on which the title character of the book "The Little Prince" lived.

CONNECTION TO FLIGHT 815

The group had an encounter with one of the flight 815 survivors after their arrival on the island. Jin was aboard the *Kahana* when it exploded and his body was thrown from the ship. After the island skipped through time, Montand and the others found Jin floating unconscious. Although Montand didn't trust Jin or his story, he was desperate to locate the source of the numbers transmission and allowed Jin to lead his team to the origin of the signal—the radio tower.

MONTAND & THE SMOKE MONSTER

While searching for Nadine, he ignored Jin's warnings against wandering too far. Shortly thereafter, Montand was attacked by the smoke monster and dragged underground. As his friends struggled to save him, Montand's arm was ripped from his body. Right after this incident, Montand spoke from deep within the hole and stated that the monster had gone, prompting Robert, Brennan and Lacombe to descend inside.

ENCOUNTERS WITH THE ARM ✚
After the incident with Montand and the smoke monster, Jin skipped through time as the island moved and reappeared in the future with the decomposed limb next to him.

Jack, Locke, Kate, Hurley and Dr. Leslie Arzt were the first to hear about Montand's disembodied limb, as told by Rousseau during their trek to the Black Rock to collect dynamite. Rousseau explained that the "Dark Territory" was where her team got infected and where Montand lost his arm. Arzt fled the scene after hearing the story.

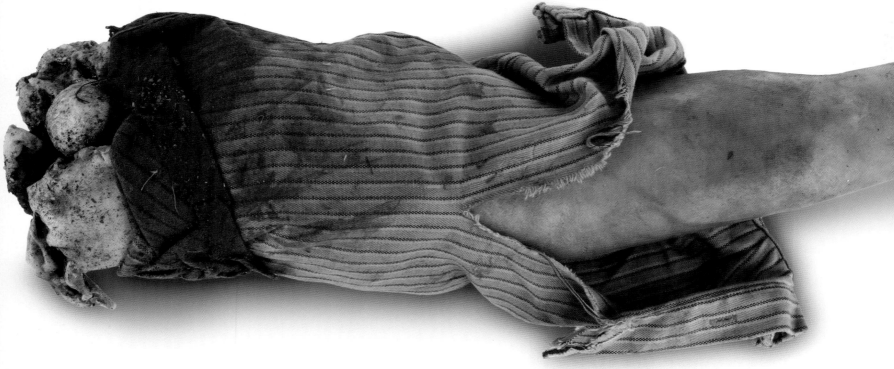

MR. & MRS. CARLSON

▶ **CONNECTION:** Father and mother to Juliet Burke

Juliet's father represented a significant moment in her life, long before she arrived on the island. During her childhood, Juliet's parents announced they were getting a divorce, but it was Juliet's mother who did all the talking, with her father remaining tight-lipped. Rachel, the more vocal of the two sisters, was sarcastic about the way in which her parents tip-toed around the word "divorce." On the other hand, Juliet became terribly upset and confused by the notion of two people being in love and not wanting to stay together. She asked, "But what if you are supposed to be together?" This was an emotional response to a statement her mother made—something that came to mind before the devastating events at the Swan station construction site. Mrs. Carlson explained, "Your father and I...we still love each other. Just because two people love each other, doesn't always mean they're supposed to be together." This resonated with Juliet as she made the decision to follow Jack's plan of detonating the bomb, even though she knew that if the "reset" worked, she and Sawyer would never meet.

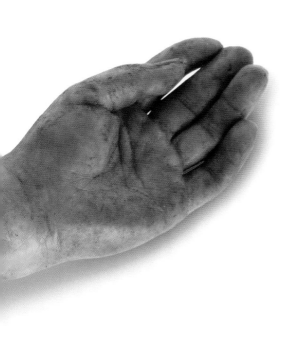

MRS. DAWSON

▶ **CONNECTION:** Mother of Michael Dawson, grandmother of Walt Lloyd

Michael Dawson's mother was fearsomely protective of her grandson, Walt Lloyd. Along with the rest of the world, she witnessed the televised discovery of the submerged flight 815 wreckage and the subsequent appearance of the Oceanic Six survivors.

A DECAYING RELATIONSHIP

Once Michael and Walt returned home, Walt moved in with his grandmother. Michael didn't reveal to her what really happened on the island and she was forced to keep Walt's and Michael's existence a secret. This situation created a deep resentment between her and Michael.

Michael and his mother's relationship started to unravel at the Sydney airport prior to flight 815's departure. Michael pleaded with his mother to take Walt off his hands due to Michael's work commitments and small apartment. He felt it would be better if his mother raised Walt. Unfortunately, Walt overheard the conversation.

When Michael and Walt returned home from the island, Walt immediately moved in with his grandmother. He barely spoke to her, but she would comfort him when he woke up in the middle of the night screaming. She was upset with Michael for not explaining where they were or what happened while they were away, so she refused to let him see his son.

VISITING HURLEY

Years after returning from the island, Walt's grandmother took him to Los Angeles' Santa Rosa Mental Health Institute to visit Hurley. Ever the protector, she made sure Hurley didn't pose a physical threat to Walt before leaving the two to catch up on things.

MR. & MRS. FORD

▶ **CONNECTION:** Mother and father of James "Sawyer" Ford

One of the most significant, if not the most significant, events in James "Sawyer" Ford's life was the death of his parents. Residing in Jasper, Alabama, Sawyer's mother, Mary, was the victim of a long con. The con involved a man named Mr. Sawyer extorting $38,000 from Mary. He wooed her and filled her mind with tales of them going away together. After James's father learned about the affair, however, he changed everything.

On the day of his parents' deaths, Mary made her son hide underneath the bed so that his enraged father would think James was still away at his grandparents. Soon after Mary left James's room, the sound of a gunshot rang in the air. James's father then sat down on the bed that his young son was hiding under and shot himself. Fueled by revenge, James adopted the name of the man he wanted to seek out and kill—"Sawyer."

During Sawyer's time on the island, he came face-to-face with a man named Anthony Cooper—John Locke's father—who chuckled that "Sawyer" had been one of his aliases during his cons. Realizing that James had finally found the man who effectively killed his parents, he demanded Cooper read the revenge letter he wrote as a child. Recalling this particular con, Cooper mocked that Mary had begged him to take her money and rescue her from her sorry life. As a final insult to Sawyer's memory of his father and mother, Cooper tore up the letter. In a blind rage, Sawyer strangled Cooper to death.

MRS. GARDNER

▶ **CONNECTION:** Hired Miles Straume to exorcise the ghost of her grandson

A grandmother from Inglewood, California, Mrs. Gardner hired Miles Straume for $100 to come into her home and exorcise the spirit of her murdered grandson. When he arrived he demanded another $100, which she agreed upon. Once inside the dead boy's room, Miles found a stash of money that he took, so he gave the woman $100 back. As he left, he said her grandson's soul was at peace, which gave the grieving woman some closure.

"No matter what you hear, don't come up." — Spoken by Miles Straume to Mrs. Gardner

2 CLUCKS FOR A BUCK!

GRAND REOPENING
SPECIAL OFFER

SOFT DRINKS
Clucks Got Your Tongue?

Mr. CLUCK'S
CHICKEN SHACK

Mr. CLUCK'S CHICKEN SHACK

MR. CLUCK'S CODE OF ETHICS

- Be on time.
- Follow directions.
- Report to duty with a clean uniform.
- Satisfy the customer.
- Wash hands thoroughly after visits to the bathroom.
- EMPLOYEES SHALL NOT CONSUME COMPANY PRODUCT.
- Smile and say "Thank you".

MR. KIM

▶ CONNECTION: Hired Jin-Soo Kwon as a doorman

The manager at the Seoul Gateway Hotel, Mr. Kim, employed Jin-Soo Kwon as a doorman in the early 2000s, which led to Jin meeting his future wife, Sun-Hwa Paik.

Kim was impressed that Jin had been promoted from doorman to waiter at his former Asiana Hotel position, but quickly ascertained Jin was raised in a fishing village. Kim enjoyed mocking Jin's working-class background, and pulled the tag off Jin's tie—something he'd kept on so he could return it. Jin quickly grew weary of the rude, class-driven attitude his manager displayed. After Kim berated him for letting a poor man's son use the hotel's restroom, Jin quit.

서울 게이트웨이 호텔 • ——— Translated from Korean to English, this means "Seoul Gateway Hotel"

MR. KWON & JIN'S MOTHER

▶ CONNECTION: Parents of Jin-Soo Kwon

Mr. Kwon was a fisherman of modest means from Namhae, Korea and the father of Jin-Soo Kwon. Jin's mother was a prostitute who abandoned Jin after his birth. Even though true paternity was never known, Mr. Kwon accepted Jin and raised him as a single parent. In order to save his son the shame of his true lineage, Mr. Kwon told Jin at a young age that his mother had died.

Mr. Kwon's profession never afforded his household more than the material basics, which embarrassed Jin as he grew into adulthood. When Jin left to make his own way in life, he lied about his impoverished origins and instead told everyone that both his parents were dead.

Not long after Jin and Sun's wedding, Jin's mother resurfaced and followed Sun to a park. She engaged her in light conversation about their recent wedding, which was featured in the local newspaper. Her pointed questions quickly turned into a threat as she revealed Jin's mother's prostitution past.

Soon after, Sun tracked down Mr. Kwon in Namhae, where the humble and understanding man confirmed Jin's unfortunate heritage. Ever the good father, he asked that she keep their meeting from his son.

Sun borrowed money from her father to pay off the woman. She later met the woman and confronted her about actually being Jin's mother. The greedy woman confirmed she bore Jin but was in no way his mother.

Some years into their marriage, and as Jin continued to do Paik's dirty work, Jin returned to his father and apologized for his shameful lies and absence. Disturbed by his broken relationship with Sun and the years of covering for her father's horrible crimes, Jin asked his father for counsel. As they fished, Mr. Kwon sagely advised that Jin perform one last task transporting watches for Paik and then disappear with Sun in America.

MRS. LOCKE

▶ CONNECTION: Maternal grandmother of John Locke

A traditional '50s matriarch, Mrs. Locke was the single mother of Emily Locke and the grandmother of John Locke. Stoic and a bit emotionally cold, Mrs. Locke was frustrated by the challenges of parenting her impetuous teenaged daughter, Emily. Aware that her daughter was seeing Anthony Cooper, a man much older than appropriate, Mrs. Locke confronted Emily and tried to prevent their next meeting. Undeterred, Emily fled the house in a rainstorm and was hit by a car.

At the hospital, Emily confessed she was six months pregnant and gave birth to her son prematurely. Miraculously, the baby named John survived in an incubator and on what was supposed to be his release day, Emily fled, unable to face the enormity of raising a child. A dispassionate Mrs. Locke took out a cigarette and immediately inquired about adoption. Outside the room through a window, she caught the eye of Richard Alpert, a stranger who was fixated on little John Locke.

MR. & MRS. PAIK

▶ CONNECTION: Father & Mother of Sun-Hwa Kwon

The mother and father of Sun-Hwa Kwon, the Paiks couldn't have been more different in temperament...

A fearsome and ruthless man, Sun's father was an extremely powerful and influential businessman based in Seoul, South Korea. The CEO of Paik Heavy Industries, Paik had a working relationship with the Hanso Foundation, the group that financed the DHARMA Initiative.

PRESERVING THE PAIK NAME

Shortly after Jin and Sun's marriage, Jin's estranged mother, a former prostitute, threatened to bring dishonor onto the entire Paik family. She demanded $100,000 from Sun, or else she would tell the media about Jin's background, disgracing Paik Industries in the process. Sun asked her father for the money and he consented, but warned her that the weight of the debt would now rest on Jin's shoulders. Sun's decision to pay off Jin's mother meant that she was largely responsible for her husband becoming her father's personal assistant, and the horrors that followed.

After being hired by Paik, Jin was quickly promoted up the ranks and his nefarious tasks to pay off his debt began immediately. These assignments often involved inflicting physical harm against individuals who crossed Paik. Although Jin always felt guilty for performing these violent deeds, he felt duty-bound to him. This serves as a prime example of Paik's influence over others and it stands in stark contrast to his wife's demeanor.

MAINTAINING HONOR

Utterly focused and dedicated to his sense of family pride and honor, Paik was appalled when he learned about his daughter's affair with Jae Lee. Ironically, this could all be traced back to Paik's insistence on Jin carrying out his orders at all hours of the day. Additionally, the affair caused Paik more embarrassment, as he had originally arranged for Sun to meet with Lee as a prospective husband.

Sun's mother set up a date for Sun and Jae Lee through Mrs. Shin.

Lee's degree from Harvard and the fact that he was from a powerful family fit right into Paik's ideals for his daughter. Ultimately, he ordered Jin to murder Lee for "stealing" from the Paik family. Although Jin went only so far as to beat up Lee, Paik received his wish as Lee died a short time later. Sun's father may have never respected Jin, but this belief system made him keep his daughter's affair a secret from Jin.

Once Sun returned home as one of the Oceanic Six, she used a large portion of the settlement from Oceanic Air to buy a controlling stake in Paik Heavy Industries. She did it to anger her father and get back at him, because she felt he was partly responsible for them being on Oceanic flight 815 and for Jin's supposed death.

Compared to the difficult relationship Sun endured with her father, her connection with her mother was more loving and playful, although it wasn't without tension. During the time when her father wanted Sun to find a husband, his wife was just as focused on the same task. However, Sun's mother acted more like an over-excited and enthusiastic parent compared to her father's reasons. If Mrs. Paik was guilty of only one thing, it was playing matchmaker. Sun was always aware that her mother had high hopes for her, way beyond the life of being married to a fisherman's son.

PAIK'S GRANDCHILD

Mrs. Paik cared for Ji Yeon, Sun and Jin's daughter, when Sun boarded Ajira flight 316 from Los Angeles. While Sun was back on the island, desperately trying to find Jin, Ji Yeon remained with Mrs. Paik.

Translated from Korean to English, this means "Paik Heavy Industries"

PAIK & WIDMORE

Paik's global-reaching business deals involved networking with a major link to the island, Charles Widmore. Paik and Widmore were known to socialize together on occasion. They even shared a similar dislike of the men who pursued their daughters. Like Widmore's disapproval of Desmond Hume, Paik shared a similar dislike of Jin-Soo Kwon. Widmore and Paik both believed that Desmond and Jin were not on the same social standing as their daughters.

Ironically, Paik and Jin believed in the same values. When Sun encouraged Jin to elope with her to America, Jin insisted that he should ask her father for Sun's hand in marriage. Paik knew about Jin's humble fishing village background, but gave his blessing to marry his daughter under the condition that he work for him for one year. This is in stark contrast to Widmore and Hume's relationship.

MUNSON

▶ **CONNECTION:** Fellow inmate of James "Sawyer" Ford

The warden had the other prisoners intimidate Munson in order to gain his confidence.

Munson was an inmate at a Florida penitentiary convicted of stealing $10 million from the federal government. He went to prison without divulging the location of the money, which made him a target of the man in charge of the prison, Warden Harris.

A slightly overweight, doughy man, Munson was physically assaulted by inmates without much recourse for defense. Only Warden Harris would step in to save Munson. Fellow inmate James "Sawyer" Ford observed this and told Munson that he believed the warden was orchestrating the beatings and then coming to his rescue to earn his trust. Sawyer suggested that the warden would probably use Munson's wife to find the money.

Sawyer ended up being right. Munson was devastated about his wife's perceived disloyalty during her visit. Worried she would find the money, Munson asked Sawyer to help him move the money and disclosed to him its location. Munson was unaware that he was being conned all along by Sawyer and the warden.

Sawyer conned fellow inmate Munson while incarcerated in Florida.

NOOR "NADIA" ABED JASEEM

▶ **CONNECTION:** Involved in romantic relationship with Sayid Jarrah

The affluent Noor "Nadia" Abed Jaseem suffered a tragic existence. Although Sayid and Nadia were childhood friends, they were "reunited" for the first time in many years during Sayid's life as an Iraqi interrogator. During the 1990s, Nadia was considered a traitor by the Iraqi Republican Guard due to her alleged involvement in a bombing in the city of Najaf. Sayid was ordered to torture the Najaf bombing suspect, but had no clue it was Nadia.

Over the course of her imprisonment and questioning, Nadia and Sayid grew close once again. After her escape, she wrote Sayid a note on the back of a photo that read "You'll find me in the next life if not in this one."

"Are you going to hurt me, Sayid?"

REUNITED

Nadia fled Iraq in 1997 and took up residence in Los Angeles. During that time, Sayid searched tirelessly for her over an eight-year period. They were finally reunited after he escaped the island with the rest of the Oceanic Six. The pair married soon thereafter.

A year after Nadia and Sayid's emotional reunion, Nadia was the victim of a hit-and-run accident. Curiously, this occurred just after Jacob asked Sayid for directions and touched Sayid on his shoulder. With her dying breath, Nadia asked Sayid to take her home to Iraq. Sayid fulfilled her wish and was a pallbearer for Nadia's funeral, held in their old hometown of Tikrit, Iraq.

ISLAND CONNECTIONS

Nadia's experiences around the world were inexplicably connected to the island's inhabitants. Before flight 815 crashed on the island, Nadia was the victim of an attempted mugging while in London, England. She was attacked in an alleyway off London's famous Covent Garden. During the incident, Charlie Pace happened upon the scene and hit the mugger with his guitar case.

Before John Locke suffered his paralyzing fall, he worked as a Professional Home Inspector for Welcome Home and one of his clients was Nadia. Locke completed a survey of her house with a report of: first-rate seismic bolting, no visible mold, and no dry rot.

REST IN PEACE ✚
The Arabic writing on Nadia's coffin translated to: "The Marhouma (dearly departed) Noor Shammar."

LOCKE, SAYID & NADIA ✚
Although Locke helped Nadia feel safe in her Los Angeles abode when he was a house inspector, he was quick to stop her sweetheart, Sayid, from getting home. During their first week on the island, Locke beat Sayid unconscious and smashed the radio transmitter that he fashioned from wrecked electronics, keen to stop anyone from leaving the island.

NADINE

> **CONNECTION:** Member of French expedition team led by Danielle Rousseau

Part of the French science team who shipwrecked near the island coastline in February 1988, Nadine was a quiet, reserved person who was in charge of the group's water supply. Of all her colleagues, Montand, Robert and Brennan were generally the ones who took charge of situations on the island. As those three argued about what to do next, Lacombe, Nadine and Danielle were left to observe their actions.

Unfortunately, Nadine's stay on the mysterious island did not last long. While searching for the signal that brought them to the island, Nadine went missing. During the group's search, they found her backpack but didn't locate her body until the smoke monster uprooted a colossal tree. It was at this point that they found her bloody and beaten body. The smoke monster likely used a stealth approach and silently took her down, but it is unknown as to why Nadine was a target.

NAOMI DORRIT

> **CONNECTION:** Mercenary onboard the Kahana freighter; assigned to protect the science team

Naomi Dorrit was in charge of the *Kahana* science expedition contingent commissioned by Charles Widmore to find the island. She was approached by Matthew Abaddon on behalf of Widmore to protect the four civilian members of the team: Daniel Faraday, Charlotte Lewis, Miles Straume and Frank Lapidus. While her exact history was not revealed, it is strongly inferred that her prior military tactical experience and multilingual fluency (revealed to be English, Mandarin, Spanish, Portuguese and Italian) played a strong part in assuring Widmore she was the right person for the job.

Naomi distanced herself from the others on the *Kahana* journey and even quarreled with Lapidus about her flying the first helicopter mission to the island solo. She won the argument but not the battle when she was forced to parachute to safety from her helicopter. During her fall, she punctured her lung and was left hanging from a tree. She was found and cut loose by Desmond, Jin, Charlie and Hurley.

Extreme physical injuries defined the thread of Naomi's entire experience on the island. Her lung injury was successfully healed by Mikhail Bakunin, yet only a few days later during a hike to the radio tower to turn off Rousseau's repeating message, John Locke threw a hunting knife into Naomi's back to stop her from bringing the freighter crew to the island. Although it was a mortal wound, Naomi managed to convince Kate to explain why Locke had hurt her. Seemingly satisfied with the answer, she then contacted Minkowski by sat phone and gave him the message, "Tell my sister I love her"—code that meant she did not die of natural causes.

TIME ON THE ISLAND ✛
POST-KAHANA: 5 days.

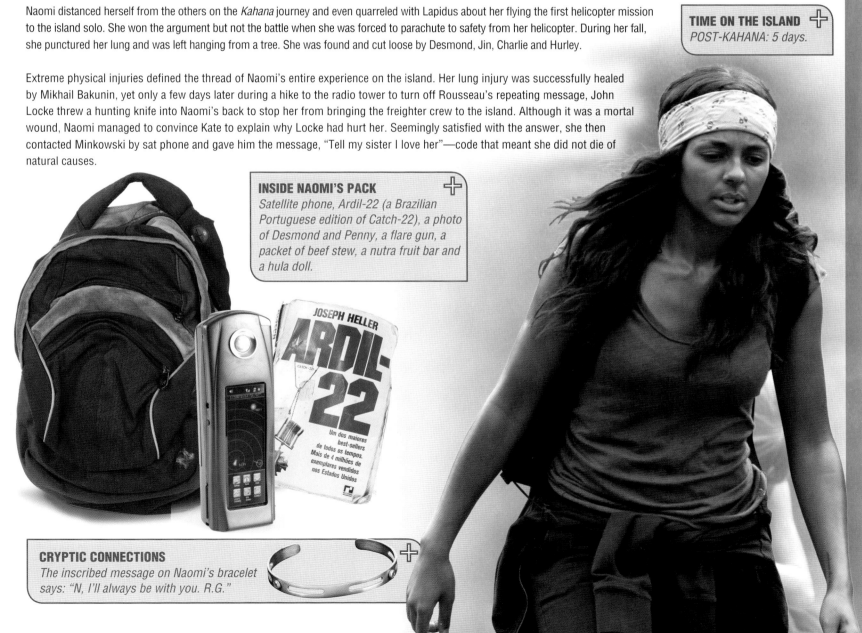

INSIDE NAOMI'S PACK ✛
Satellite phone, Ardil-22 (a Brazilian Portuguese edition of Catch-22), a photo of Desmond and Penny, a flare gun, a packet of beef stew, a nutra fruit bar and a hula doll.

CRYPTIC CONNECTIONS
The inscribed message on Naomi's bracelet says: "N, I'll always be with you. R.G."

NARJISS

▶ **CONNECTION:** Receptionist at hotel in Tunisia, helped Benjamin Linus

Based in Tozeur, Tunisia, Narjiss worked at a hotel as a receptionist. She attended to Benjamin Linus when he visited the hotel on October 24, 2005, after he left the island via the donkey wheel. Linus was already a preferred guest at the hotel where Narjiss worked, but she did not recognize him when he arrived using his actual name.

NEIL "FROGURT"

TIME ON THE ISLAND ✚
POST-OCEANIC: 101 days

Never a fan of making alliances, Neil was a terse and solitary survivor of flight 815's mid-section crash. His nickname, Frogurt, was given to him by Hugo "Hurley" Reyes, although no one really ever knew whether he worked with frozen yogurt or not.

He survived on the island up until just after the time flashes began, when the island's frozen wheel device was displaced. During an attack by the Others in 1954, Frogurt was instantly killed by a flaming arrow—just after he had engaged in another argument with his fellow survivors. He died in another of the island's ironic deaths: the lit arrow burst through his chest just as Frogurt complained that they couldn't even make fire.

FROGURT VERSUS HURLEY

Frogurt managed to upset several survivors prior to his demise, but he definitely saved his best for Hurley. While Frogurt was confrontational with most of the survivors on the island, Hurley bore the brunt of his antagonism. This stemmed from Frogurt's romantic interest in Elizabeth "Libby" Smith. Even when Frogurt discovered that Hurley and Libby were meeting for a date, he still warned that he would be ready to engage what he called "Neil time." After the threat and uncertainty of what the freighter team would bring to the island, Frogurt chose to join Jack's group over Locke's. He agreed with Jack's plan only because Hurley chose to stay with Locke.

NORA

▶ **CONNECTION:** Friend of Shannon Rutherford

During the time that Shannon Rutherford worked at a ballet school, her best friend and roommate, Nora, worked there with her. An affluent Frenchman, Philippe, approached Nora to become his live-in *au pair* for his children who attended the ballet school. However, Nora suspected his motivations were less than professional, and didn't take the job. Shannon ended up accepting Philippe's offer instead of Nora after her stepmother withheld all of her inheritance for herself, leaving Shannon broke.

NIKKI AND PAULO

▶ **CONNECTION:** Passengers in middle section of Oceanic flight 815

One was a successful television actress, the other a gifted chef. However, Nikki and Paulo's joint taste for duplicity was their downfall. A few months before the dysfunctional couple boarded the ill-fated Oceanic flight, they were unified by a long con worth $8 million in diamonds.

TIME ON THE ISLAND ✚
POST-OCEANIC: 81 days

THE CON

In 2004, Nikki Fernandez had an affair with a powerful TV producer named Howard L. Zuckerman. Although Zuckerman believed that the relationship was genuine, it was nothing more than a confidence trick on Nikki's behalf.

The relationship was started when Nikki earned a guest appearance on the TV show *Exposé*, which was being shot in Sydney, Australia. Nikki played Corvette, the stripper/undercover agent who exposed the Mr. LaShade character (played by Billy Dee Williams) as the show's main villain, The Cobra. After being killed off in the series' finale, she politely declined Zuckerman's offer to return for the next season. She later revealed that she wanted to stay with him in Sydney instead of returning to her home in Los Angeles.

Hurley found this script from Nikki's appearance on *Exposé*

ISLAND CONNECTIONS ✚
Exposé was one of Hugo "Hurley" Reyes' favorite TV shows. Hurley later helped bury Nikki after her unfortunate encounter with the Medusa spider.

For his role in the con, Paulo convinced Zuckerman to hire him as his home chef. Compared by Zuckerman to Austrian chef celebrity Wolfgang Puck, skilled Brazilian cook Paulo turned up every day at the producer's office until he scored the job. Zuckerman had no clue that Paulo and Nikki were setting him up. After being hired, Paulo prepared a meal for Zuckerman and Nikki. As Zuckerman professed his love for Nikki, he collapsed from a massive heart attack brought on by poisoned food. The duo took the key hanging from Zuckerman's neck and subsequently retrieved the diamonds worth $8 million.

" *Things don't stay buried on this island...* " — Spoken by John Locke to Paulo

THE SEARCH FOR THE DIAMONDS
Seated in the middle section of Oceanic flight 815, Nikki and Paulo boarded their flight home with the diamonds in tow. After a fruitless search for their belongings on the beach, Nikki used her feminine charms on Dr. Leslie Arzt, a high school science teacher, to find their luggage. After hearing about his project of cataloging the island's species (including the venomous Medusa spider), she convinced him to draw a map of the island.

Nikki and Paulo caught a break when they overheard an argument between Arzt, Shannon and Kate. Learning that the gun case was recovered from a nearby waterfall, they headed there to begin their search. Although Paulo found the diamonds, he didn't tell Nikki because he wanted to keep her interested in him and not the diamonds.

FINDING THE PEARL STATION
During one of their searches for the diamonds, Nikki and Paulo located the Beechcraft. Paulo's refusal to climb up and explore the cockpit turned out to be a good decision, as Nikki spotted the entrance to the Pearl station in the ground.

Desperate to find a hiding place for the diamonds, Paulo returned to the Pearl and hid the diamonds inside the lid of a toilet inside the station. But when Nikki visited the station with Locke, Paulo tagged along and transferred the diamonds from the toilet to his underwear.

A CHANGE OF HEART
Nikki's materialistic side began to wane the moment she realized Thanksgiving had been and gone without any awareness by the survivors. During an emotionally honest moment for them both, Paulo explained how he thought "losing" the bag was a positive thing. Unbeknownst to Nikki that Paulo had hidden the diamonds on himself, she agreed and showed genuine affection for Paulo for the first time in a long while that wasn't driven by their diamond con. But when Nikki discovered a packet of nicotine gum, she realized that Paulo had secretly found the diamonds since the gum was inside their luggage along with the diamonds. Knowing that Paulo had lied to her, she attempted to get a gun from Sawyer but he turned her away. She later confronted Paulo armed with an unusual weapon...

THE MEDUSA SPIDER
Nikki's plan to get the diamonds involved using a venomous spider that was caught by Dr. Arzt. With the spider safely inside a jar, Nikki tossed the spider at Paulo. Once bitten, his paralysis was almost instantaneous, giving Nikki the opportunity to discover the diamonds. As Paulo expressed his feelings for Nikki, and as she was reminded of her feelings for Paulo, her demise was already in play.

Nikki used a Medusa spider from Arzt's collection to get back at Paulo for lying.

Nikki barely had time to hide the diamonds and stagger to the beach before she collapsed. Her last words, heard by Sawyer and Hurley, were "paralyzed," although Hurley thought she said "Paulo lies," implicating her boyfriend as the cause of her death. Their were several disagreements about who or what was responsible for their "deaths." One theory was that the Others were to blame since Paulo had a walkie-talkie similar to the Others'. It was also asserted that poisoned food was the culprit and Sawyer's name was even mentioned as a possibility.

BURIED ALIVE!
Since Nikki and Paulo were still under the influence of the Medusa spider's venom, several of the survivors dug a grave and placed the bodies in it. But as Sawyer poured the diamonds over their bodies, Nikki's eyes opened just as the survivors started filling in the graves. Nikki and Paulo died, buried alive.

As both bodies were being prepared for their burial, Vincent pulled off the blanket covering their bodies sensing they were still alive. Unfortunately, no one understood what he was trying to communicate.

Paulo hid the diamonds inside these dolls.

THE NUMBERS

The numbers—4, 8, 15, 16, 23 and 42—appeared repeatedly both on the island and off and in some way touched the lives of everyone who came to or lived on the island. Some people, like Hugo "Hurley" Reyes and Danielle Rousseau, considered them to be cursed as they seemed to bring harm to those who heard or used them. While others, like the scientific community of the DHARMA Initiative, considered each number to represent a tangible human or environmental factor that could be changed for the better to thwart humanity's demise. For the survivors of Oceanic flight 815, however, the numbers were most significantly used by Jacob, the island's protector, as those specific six were applied to the six people who were eventually given the choice to remain on the island and take over his mantle.

MOST SIGNIFICANT APPEARANCES

Hurley's Winning Lottery Numbers

Connection: Sam Toomey, Martha Toomey, Leonard Simms

Hurley used the six numbers he heard mumbled by fellow patient Leonard Simms at Santa Rosa Mental Health Institute to win the California Mega Lottery. However, Hugo quickly regretted using the numbers as he associated a string of consequential bad luck, including the death of his grandfather and burned down house, to be directly associated with what he called the "cursed" numbers.

NUMEROLOGY

Numerology is an ancient practice that has its roots in the early work of Greek mathematician and mystic Pythagoras. He and his followers used isopsephy (adding the numeric values of letters in words to create a single number) to create connections or make divinations about living things. The practice evolved over the centuries into a branch of pseudomathematics; one that drew upon mathematical principles, but did not adhere to the rigid rules or definitions of standard mathematics. Today the pursuit of Numerology can be applied to those who study numerical patterns and apply them to non-traditional situations, or to what is often considered the occult practice of using numbers to define personality or life probabilities that can determine future outcomes or goals, both good and bad.

The sum of all six numbers equals 108, which is a sacred number in many Eastern religions including Buddhism, Hinduism and within the concept of DHARMA. Mala prayer chains consist of 108 beads that correspond to the recitation of deities, prayers or mantra repetition depending on the individual religion or spiritual practice.

Jacob's Cave

Connection: Jacob, the Man in Black, the lighthouse, Jacob's Cave

A numeric aficionado, Jacob used the lighthouse wheel and its 360 gear teeth to associate a potential candidate to each number. He then transferred the person's name and their associated number to his inner cave wall where he could track those who were still viable candidates over time to replace him on the island.

The Swan Computer

Connection: DHARMA Initiative, John Locke, Desmond Hume

After the Incident, the DHARMA Initiative applied these numbers to their system of releasing built up electromagnetic pressure through the Swan Computer. An operator was mandated to type 4, 8, 15, 16, 23, 42 every 108 minutes to release the pressure, resulting in a never-ending cycle that required operators to be swapped out every 540 days.

The Valenzetti Equation

Connection: Alvar Hanso, the DeGroots, DHARMA Initiative

Mathematician Enzo Valenzetti was commissioned by the UN Security Council after the Cuban Missile Crisis to develop an equation that would avert future global disasters. His equation was said to "predict the exact number of years and months until humanity extinguishes itself." In particular, the numbers 4, 8, 15, 16, 23, and 42 corresponded with core environmental and human factors that if changed could prevent the predicted doomsday scenario. Alvar Hanso funded the DHARMA Initiative so their scientific research could find a means to change any of the six values and ensure the future of humanity. Hanso had the numbers broadcast from the island via radio transmission with the hopes that through their research the values would someday change.

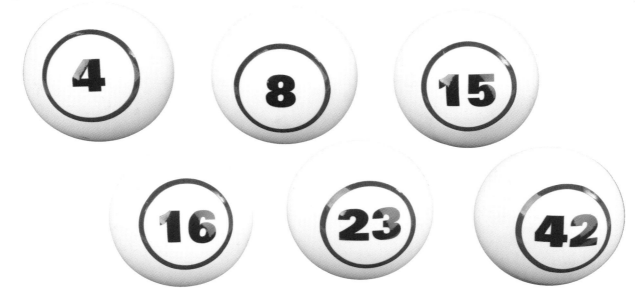

"Jacob had a thing for numbers."

— Spoken by the Man in Black

Some might consider Jacob's connection of number to candidate as a completely random act, while others who are more inclined to believe in destiny might consider each marriage of number to person a more fated occurrence.

OCEANIC FLIGHT

BOEING 777

Oceanic AIRLINES

Oceanic flight 815 was a Boeing 777 class airplane scheduled for transatlantic flight on September 22, 2004. The flight originated in Sydney, Australia at Gate 23 and departed at 2:15 p.m. bound for Los Angeles, California. The flight consisted of 324 people—passengers and a full flight crew—plus one domestic pet in cargo.

Captain Seth Norris flew a standard northeasterly-routed flight plan across the Pacific Ocean and departed Sydney International on time. The flight progressed without note for approximately six hours until the cockpit experienced complete radio failure. Norris notified his flight crew that they were going to reroute to Fiji for repairs. Unable to communicate with air traffic, the captain navigated on the alternate flight path for about two hours, which put the plane 1000 miles off their original flight plan.

Approximately eight hours in the air, Oceanic 815 hit a patch of heavy turbulence that escalated violently in a short span of time. As the passengers were told to strap into their seats, the overhead oxygen masks deployed. At the same moment, a burst of intense electromagnetic energy from the ground disrupted all the cockpit instrumentation which caused the plane to quickly lose altitude, which precipitated a violent mid-air breakup. The plane split into three sections and fell to the ground in pieces on an island below.

815

Oceanic
AIRLINES

THE COCKPIT SECTION

The front portion of the plane landed in the jungle with only one survivor, Captain Seth Norris, who was still strapped into his seat in the cockpit. He died a few hours after impact during an encounter with the smoke monster.

THE FUSELAGE

The center section of the plane separated and then cart-wheeled forward from the interior of the island out to the shoreline where it finally landed upside down. Forty-eight passengers survived, albeit some for just a short time, post-impact.

THE TAIL SECTION

The tail section ripped off the plane and landed in the shallow water off the coast of the island. Twenty-three passengers either swam or washed up alive on the beach, while one man, Bernard Nadler, landed in a tree still strapped into his seat.

Enjoy the clean, crisp refreshing taste of pure Spring water - A taste so good it could only come from protected mountain springs. That's why, since 1894, we've been so proud to share Natural Brand Mountain spring water with you. This bottle is part of a multi-pack unit and should not be sold individually.

SURVIVORS (OCEANIC FLIGHT 815)

BARBARA JOANNA MILLER

Barbara Joanna Miller was a passenger in the middle section of Oceanic 815 who survived the crash, but tragically died later on the island. Miller's demise was especially ironic, as she was an accomplished scuba diver yet she died while taking a morning swim in the ocean.

Prior to the flight, Miller had just finished a diving trip on Australia's Great Barrier Reef. As fate would have it, she picked up an ear infection so severe that Miller's doctor made her wait two extra days before flying home. Because of this delay, she ended up on the doomed Oceanic flight 815.

She went by her middle name Joanna while on the island and struck a friendship with fellow survivor Janelle Granger. Six days after the crash, Joanna ventured out alone for a swim in the ocean and got caught in a powerful riptide. Her screams for help were first heard by Charlie Pace, who said at the time he couldn't swim, so Jack Shephard attempted to rescue her. Jack lost her in the swells but managed to rescue Boone Carlyle in the process, who almost drowned trying to save her. Unfortunately, Joanna was overcome and drowned.

STOLEN IDENTITY

After Joanna's death, Kate found Joanna's passport and burned the picture. Had the survivors' raft voyage been successful, it is likely that Kate would have assumed Joanna's identity once they made it back to civilization.

> ### BONDING ON THE ISLAND
> Janelle Granger was a fellow passenger who kept a journal post-crash that detailed the first 43 days of her life surviving with the other 47 Oceanic 815 passengers. She bonded with Joanna because of their shared love of the water.

BLUE STRIPED SHIRT

An unnamed female passenger on Oceanic flight 815, she was distinguished by the blue striped midriff shirt she wore the majority of her time on the island. Prior to take-off at the Sydney Airport, she had casual interactions with several important passengers like Michael Dawson, Walt Lloyd and Hugo "Hurley" Reyes.

After the crash, she was one of the survivors who helped collect debris and materials to build the original beach camp. She chose to remain at the beach when some of the survivors moved to the caves in the jungle.

Like many of the original survivors, she was an ever-present part of the day-to-day dynamics of the post-crash recovery. It is unknown if she survived the time jumps that occurred once the island moved.

CRAIG

Craig was one of the initial 48 survivors of the crashed mid-section of Oceanic flight 815. After the crash, Craig helped Claire Littleton inspect the passengers' belongings that littered the shoreline and later helped by gathering wood for the difficult task of cremating the dead.

He initially resisted moving to the caves from the beach, but eventually joined his fellow castaways there. He helped construct tents and the raft and, much later, joined the march to the radio tower. He also accompanied Daniel Faraday on the zodiac raft to the freighter.

Craig remained among the castaways on the island for 101 days, but was killed during an attack by the Others in 1954, when the island was skipping through time. Craig, along with his fellow 815 survivor Neil Frogurt and several others, perished when the Others launched a nighttime attack using flaming arrows.

DONALD

Donald was a passenger of Oceanic flight 815 seated in the tail section of the plane. Although he sustained a fractured right leg in the crash, he pulled himself out of the water onto the beach with the help of Ana Lucia Cortez. Later, Libby Smith examined his broken leg and attempted to keep Donald distracted by telling him about an injury she had suffered while skiing. In mid-story, she snapped his bone back into place, which caused so much pain that he immediately passed out. Despite Libby's attempt to fix the wound, an infection set in and, without the proper antibiotics, Donald died five days after the crash.

> ### PROOF THE ISLAND WAS REAL
> After the tailies united with the other survivors, Libby once mentioned Donald's death to Hurley in order to prove the entire crash wasn't a figment of his troubled mind.

EMMA

Emma is one of only three children to survive the crash of Oceanic flight 815. Seated in the tail section of the plane with her brother Zack, the pair were travelling alone to Los Angeles, California to meet their mother.

Emma was pulled from the ocean by Mr. Eko, then given CPR by Ana Lucia. Emma and her brother were then taken care of by Ana Lucia and Cindy while at the tailies' camp. Several days after the crash Emma, Zack, Cindy and six other survivors were kidnapped in the dead of night by the Others. They were singled out on a list created by Goodwin Stanhope so the raiding party could identify and abduct the correct people.

Emma and her brother's whereabouts remained unknown until Juliet mentioned to Ben that she met and spent time with the children while at the Others' camp. When Charles Widmore launched his mortar attack on the Man in Black, Cindy, Zack and Emma managed to escape into the jungle for protection. Along with Rose and Bernard, Emma is one of the few to survive the island's tumult to join Hurley and live under his guard.

GARY TROUP

Gary Troup survived the initial crash of Oceanic flight 815. He was in the midst of the post-crash chaos near the middle section fuselage on the beach. Not long after a fellow survivor was pulled from underneath the wreckage near the still whirling engine, Troup crossed in front of the engine's path. Alarmed by his proximity, Locke warned Troup to move, but he couldn't hear due to all the noise. He hesitated for clarification in the worst possible spot, right in front of the engine. His body was forcefully sucked into the engine, resulting in his violent death.

After the crash, Hurley found a copy of Troup's as yet unpublished manuscript, "Bad Twin," in the wreckage. It was described as a mystery novel that explored "the consequence of vengeance, the power of redemption, and where to turn when all seems lost." Hurley read the manuscript, but later gave it to Sawyer. Unfortunately, he never finished it as Jack burned the manuscript in retaliation for Sawyer's refusal to hand over the stolen guns.

> ### LOOKING DEEPER
> Troup dedicated "Bad Twin" to the woman he loved, Oceanic 815 flight attendant Cindy Chandler, with the following entry: "Cindy, my highest-flying angel."
>
> Hailing from New York City, Troup had previously published "The Valenzetti Equation," a book created by Italian mathematician and Princeton University scholar Enzo Valenzetti. The book explored a radical theorem about mankind's ability to extinguish itself. The book was of particular interest to Alvar Hanso, who purchased every copy of the book to keep the theorem secret from the world.

JACK'S FIRST ISLAND PATIENT

The first person who Jack assisted upon reaching the island beach was a man trapped underneath a portion of the plane's landing gear. Jack got the attention of Locke and another passenger to help him lift the wreckage off the man. After examining his injured leg, Jack applied a tourniquet to stop the bleeding. After the chaos, Jack returned to the man and took off the tourniquet. The next day he told Boone Carlyle the man would recover without any issues. His eventual outcome is not known.

JEROME

Jerome helped build tents, collected the personal possessions from the wreckage with Claire Littleton, and gathered wood for the cremation of those who died in the crash. Jerome declined Jack's suggestion to live in the caves, opting for the beach instead. When Jack became trapped in a cave-in, Jerome was part of the rescue gathered by Michael Dawson.

Jerome contributed to the building of the second raft and even helped launch it. Plus, he contributed a personal letter to his loved ones and placed it inside the bottle that Charlie threw into the ocean. Sadly, the bottle returned to shore and was buried by Sun to keep everyone's spirits up. Much later, Jerome was part of the large group that trekked to the radio tower to seek rescue. When things got perilous, Jerome returned to the DHARMA barracks with Locke. When Martin Keamy and his team of mercs arrived on the island from the freighter, Jerome was killed when they stormed the barracks in search of Benjamin Linus.

JIM

After nightfall on the day of the crash, the Others invaded the Tailie's makeshift camp and kidnapped three people. The event terrified those left behind and set the more aggressive tone for that group of survivors.

Jim survived 11 more days without incident until the Others returned on day 12 and abducted nine more survivors. Unlike other secondary survivors from either the middle section or the tail section of the plane, Jim was never seen. However, he was referenced immediately after the second attack when a survivor screamed during the chaos, "They took Jim and Eli!" Ana Lucia also determined that the kidnappings were not random after reading a list found in the pocket of an Other she managed to kill during the assault. Each person taken was listed and described on the Others' master list.

LANCE

While Lance was never seen on the island, he was mentioned in a key conversation between Hurley and Ethan Rom. As Hurley canvassed survivors for his census, he once mistook Ethan for Lance, whom he described as a "little skinny guy with the glasses and red hair." Obviously a glaring mistake, but it became one of Hurley's first clues in discovering that Ethan was never a passenger on the plane.

MAN ON THE BEACH

When the tail section separated from the fuselage of Oceanic flight 815 and crashed into the ocean, several unnamed passengers safely swam to shore. During that chaotic time, this man was seen helping Ana Lucia pull a fellow passenger clinging to his seat onto the beach. He was also seen screaming for his wife Pam, who was never found. He was never seen again after that first day and it is assumed that he was either killed when the Others raided the camp or died of unknown injuries.

NANCY

When the tail section of Oceanic flight 815 hit the water, several passengers survived the impact and were thrown out of the plane into the ocean. One of those who survived was Nancy, who was pulled from the water by Mr. Eko. Along with a small band of 21 other survivors, they set up camp on the beach and lit a signal fire. On the twelfth night after the crash, Nancy, several of the adults and two children were taken by a raiding party of Others. Her status remains a mystery.

NATHAN

Although Nathan survived when the tail section of flight 815 crashed into the ocean, he suffered a dark fate during his subsequent time on the island. Initially panicked and concerned for his fellow survivors, Nathan's erratic and irritable persona bred suspicion, in particular with Ana Lucia. She began to plant the seed of doubt into the other survivors' minds that Nathan was one the silent abductors who kidnapped several other tail section survivors.

As her suspicions grew stronger, Ana Lucia dug a large pit that would serve as a crude prison. Several days later she shoved Nathan into the pit and closed off the top with a bamboo roof. Although her fellow survivors did not agree with Ana Lucia's suspicions, her false accusations actually helped conceal the identity of the real imposter within the group. Nathan's inability to convince Ana Lucia of his innocence ultimately led to his demise.

SCOTT JACKSON

Scott Jackson was a passenger seated in the middle section of Oceanic flight 815. A salesman for a Santa Cruz, California internet company, Scott was returning home from a two-week Australian vacation. After the crash, he was a proactive member of the survivors who worked to build shelter on the island beach. He was frequently seen collecting materials for camp and even volunteered for search parties, like the ones organized to find Jack during the cave collapse and Claire when she was kidnapped. Unfortunately, Scott became a victim of Ethan Rom's mission to bring Claire back to his people. Ethan beat Scott to death and left his body on the beach as a very clear message that he was willing to kill all of them, one-by-one, to get her back.

Before his death, Scott was most known for his friendship with fellow survivor Steve Jenkins. They shared a very similar physical look, which in turn confused other survivors like Michael and Hurley who often mixed up their names. It happened so frequently that Hurley even apologized for it during Scott's eulogy at Boone Hill.

STEVE JENKINS

Steve Jenkins was one of the 48 passengers seated in the middle section of Oceanic flight 815 who survived the crash. On the night prior to the flight, it was revealed that Steve stayed in the hotel room next to Michael and his son, Walt. He ended up interrupting the pair's loud argument in the hallway in the early hours of the morning.

After the crash, Steve remained with the beach encampment and developed a friendship with fellow survivor Scott Jackson. The two men looked remarkably similar and were often confused for one another by fellow survivors. It was a common occurrence until Scott was murdered by Ethan Rohm.

Steve was a valued member of the beach community. He took responsibility for bringing water to the camp on a daily basis, joined Ana Lucia's forces to combat the Others, and supported Hurley during his DHARMA food conundrum. His ultimate fate after the island skipped through time is unknown.

SULLIVAN

About 12 days after the crash, an anxiety-ridden Sullivan traveled to the caves to have Jack examine his self-diagnosed "tropical disease" rash. After a brief inspection, Jack blamed the rash on a combination of stress and heat. Sun provided Sullivan with some aloe to treat the outbreak, but his overall distrust of the diagnosis and increased stress caused Jack to label him as a possible hypochondriac. It was only at the Island Open Golf Tournament that Sullivan finally loosened up, so much so that he even bet his dinner that Jack would sink a difficult putt.

ZACK

Zack, along with his sister Emma, survived the ordeal of flight 815's tail section crashing into the ocean. The siblings were scheduled to meet their mother in Los Angeles.

According to the information released at the Oceanic Six's press conference, everyone—including Zack and Emma—died when the plane crashed into the ocean. In truth, Eko (a fellow tail section survivor) heroically carried Zack to the shore. Ana Lucia and Cindy, two tail section survivors, cared for Zack and his sister from that point forward. Very little is known about Zack, as he and his sister Emma and seven additional passengers were abducted in the middle of the night by the Others.

ZACK'S "OTHER" LIFE
After his abduction, Zack was cared for by the likes of Cindy and Juliet Burke. The significance of Zack's disappearance stems from both Goodwin and Ben's explanation that he was part of "the list," a mysterious collection of names that Ben insisted came from Jacob.

Zack's toy bear

TRACY

Tracy was another survivor from the middle section of Oceanic flight 815. She resided on the beach camp and lived near fellow survivor Scott Jenkins. According to the note she placed in a bottle that was sent out to sea (which was later read by Sawyer when he was on the raft), she hailed from Fresno, California and was married with two children. Her ultimate fate is not known.

IMMEDIATE CASUALTIES

ELI

When the tail section of flight 815 crashed into the ocean, its survivors had to make their way to the island's shore. Many were injured and the passengers banded together to help everyone stranded at sea make it to dry land.

On the twelfth day of the tail section's survivors' time on the island, the Others stealthily abducted nine of them at night, including Eli. His name was on the list that Ana Lucia found inside the pocket of the female Other who she accidentally killed after hitting her with a rock.

EMMANUEL RAFAEL ORTIZ

Emmanuel Rafael Ortiz was one of the names mentioned during the eulogy that Claire performed shortly after the crash. From his passport, Claire determined that he hadn't traveled much. The only other element found relating to his life before the flight was a video rental receipt. It showed charges had been applied for overdue copies of "Willy Wonka & The Chocolate Factory" and "The Little Princess."

HAROLD WOLLSTEIN

Harold Wollstein was a passenger who perished when flight 815 crashed on the island. Claire Littleton mentioned his name as part of her eulogy at the memorial service for those who did not survive. Claire gleaned his name from Harold's boarding pass.

KRISTEN & STEVE

At the beachside memorial for those who died, Claire remembered Kristen sitting a few rows back from her. Having found Kristen's day planner filled with wedding preparations and photos, she explained that she was engaged to Steve, the man seated next to Kristen and they looked "really in love."

JUDITH MARTHA WEXLER

Judith Martha Wexler was a passenger on Oceanic flight 815 who died on impact. A few days post-crash, Jack determined that the bodies inside the fuselage should be burned to deter foraging predators and further decay. Unable to give the remains a proper burial, Claire and some other survivors decided to give them a fireside memorial. After sorting through discarded possessions from the wreck, Claire then read the gathered materials to honor the deceased's existence in some small way. Judith Martha Wexler was the first to be acknowledged for her connecting flight to Denton, Texas, corrective lenses, and her intention of being an organ donor.

MICHELLE

Along with her colleagues JD and Cindy, Michelle worked as a flight attendant on Oceanic flight 815. Prior to take-off, Michelle helped JD carry John Locke to his seat. Locke was in his wheelchair, but the Oceanic staff could not find the wheelchair they used to transport the disabled onto the plane.

Right before Cindy announced for everyone to fasten their seatbelts due to severe turbulence, Michelle had an exchange with Kate Austen and her arresting officer, U.S. Marshal Edward Mars while she was providing refreshments. Mars requested a black coffee and Michelle headed to the rear of the plane. Michelle was killed as the plane's tail section crashed into the sea.

MILLICENT LOUISE D'AGOSTINO

Millicent was one of the passengers on Oceanic flight 815 who did not survive the crash. During the beach memorial for the victims, Claire mentioned a "Millicent Louise D'Agostino" as being on the plane and originally from Teaneck, New Jersey.

OCEANIC SIX, SEE PAGE 272

OFFICER BARNES

▶ **CONNECTION:** Police officer who questioned Claire Littleton

Barnes was the New South Wales police officer who questioned Claire Littleton in the hospital ER after her car accident. He asked her routine questions about what happened but Claire immediately became defensive as she assumed he blamed her. Her attitude rubbed him the wrong way and he left her alone as soon as he was finished.

OFFICER MALCOLM

▶ **CONNECTION:** Australian police officer, helped Boone Carlyle

Shortly before Shannon Rutherford and her stepbrother, Boone Carlyle, found themselves boarding Oceanic flight 815 in Sydney, Australia, Boone went to see Malcolm, a police officer. He advised Boone that the police could not investigate Shannon's allegedly abusive boyfriend without any physical evidence or a direct complaint from Shannon. On hearing Boone boast of his mother's bridal firm, Malcolm mocked that he was welcome to buy his wife's dress.

At the exact point that James "Sawyer" Ford was dragged noisily through the station, Malcolm used him as an example —if Sawyer was Shannon's boyfriend, he could've acted on Boone's claims.

Boone pleaded with Officer Malcolm for help.

OMER JARRAH

▶ **CONNECTION:** Brother of Sayid Jarrah

In the small town of Tikrit, Iraq, northwest of Baghdad, Omer Jarrah grew up with his younger brother Sayid and their mother and father. During their childhood, their father encouraged Omer to kill a chicken, as he was in his father's eyes approaching an age where he should act like a man even though Omer wasn't even a teenager.

Given a knife, Omer was instructed to stay outside until he did as he was told. However, he could not bring himself to do as his father had requested and it was Sayid who picked up the bird and broke its neck with his bare hands.

Sayid gave the dead chicken to Omer to help his older brother, but when their father returned Omer confessed he didn't do it. Appalled at Omer's cowardice, their father praised Sayid's actions and was pleased that, in his view, one of his sons would grow up to be a man.

OLDHAM

▶ **CONNECTION:** Member of the DHARMA Iniative; chemist

Solitary, quiet, and unsettling, the man simply known as Oldham served as the DHARMA Initiative's chemist. A paranoid soul, Oldham chose to live on his own away from the rest of the DHARMA Initiative village.

> ### PSYCHOTIC OLDHAM
> *Under the assumed identity of Jim LaFleur, Sawyer's role as DHARMA Head of Security in 1977 led to several encounters with Oldham. Sawyer never viewed Oldham as anything other than a "psychopath" and didn't think he should be used as an interrogator.*

Oldham was asked to administer drugs to Sayid so that Stuart Radzinsky could interrogate him to determine why Sayid was on the island. Oldham used a sugar cube laced with some kind of drug to make Sayid confess to everything he knew about the island and his previous time on it.

Also in his confession to Oldham, Sayid revealed the names of the Flame, Pearl, and Swan DHARMA stations. Although these revelations were a cause of concern for Radzinsky, Oldham simply attributed Sayid's ramblings to an excessive amount of his experimental drugs.

OLU

▶ **CONNECTION:** Member of Eko's Nigerian gang

Nefarious criminal Olu worked closely with Eko's Nigerian warlord unit, which also included their associate Goldie. Olu was the first of the group to notice Yemi driving towards the Beechcraft plane that Olu, Eko and Goldie were loading up with heroin concealed inside crates of Virgin Mary Statues.

Although Yemi had alerted the military about the drug run, he didn't reveal the names of those involved to protect his brother. Olu was shot dead by the authorities as they stormed the airstrip. He was not dressed like a priest like Eko and Goldie were, so he may not have planned to leave Nigeria with them.

OMAR

▶ **CONNECTION:** Member of Republican Guard; Sayid Jarrah's superior

Omar was Sayid Jarrah's superior officer during his time with the Republican Guard in Iraq. He was impressed by the way Sayid handled himself, and made a personal recommendation for his reassignment to the Intelligence Division. Omar also ordered Sayid to question and torture his love, Noor "Nadia" Abed Jaseem, whom Omar knew was associated with Kurdish and Shiite insurgents.

After Omar had given Sayid more than a month to interrogate Nadia, he ordered her execution, at which point Sayid orchestrated her escape. Omar witnessed Sayid's defection, and Sayid shot him dead in order to save Nadia.

OCEANIC SIX

"If you have to go, then you have to lie about everything...everything that happened since we got to the island. It's the only way to protect it."

— Spoken by John Locke to Jack Shephard

CRAFTING THE LIE

As the survivors of the helicopter crash waited in their raft for the *Searcher* to collect them, Jack broached the subject of lying about what really happened to Oceanic flight 815 and its survivors. Initially Sayid and Hurley didn't agree to the plan, but over the week Jack, Kate, Sun, Desmond and Penny convinced them it was in the best interest of those left behind to keep Widmore and the outside world away. Lapidus agreed to disappear and support whatever they decided. With everyone resigned to the pact, Penny's crew sailed them 3,000 miles west to Indonesia. The six survivors returned to their life raft so they could paddle to shore to make their story seem more credible.

THE "REAL" WORLD

The outside world learned that the six survivors were found alive on the island of Sumba, Indonesia 108 days after the crash. The survivors were airlifted to Anderson Air Force Base in Guam for medical observation and treatment. A representative from Oceanic Airlines, Karen Decker, was then assigned to escort the survivors via Coast Guard from Guam to Honolulu, Hawaii. She told them about a planned press conference and that the press had already dubbed them the "Oceanic Six."

In keeping with Charles Widmore's phony *Christiane 1* Oceanic 815 Indian Ocean discovery, the survivors stated that eight passengers—Jack, a pregnant Kate, Sayid, Sun, Hurley, Boone Carlyle, Charlie Pace, and Libby Smith—floated on seat cushions and life jackets to Membata, an unpopulated island in the lower Sunda Islands. They indicated that Boone and Libby died of their injuries while Charlie drowned. Kate gave birth to Aaron about five weeks later. Their salvation occurred when a typhoon washed up a battered fishing boat with a survival raft on their 103rd day on the island. They used the raft to paddle to the village of Manukangga.

LIVING THE LIE

For three years, the Oceanic Six went back to their lives. Some rectified old sins, while others moved forward only to fall back. However, each one (sans Aaron) suffered in a self-inflicted silence that tore away at their souls.

RESOLUTION

Each survivor was given an Oceanic Airlines Golden Pass and a large monetary settlement.

SAYID JARRAH

Sayid married Nadia and they shared a blissful nine-month marriage until she was killed by a speeding car driven by one of Widmore's men. Overcome with a need for vengeance, Sayid became Benjamin Linus' paid assassin and together they targeted anyone who threatened the island or the Oceanic Six. After fulfilling his duties to Ben, Sayid headed to the Dominican Republic to build homes until Ben found him with the news that Hurley was in danger. Sayid went back into action to protect his friends.

SUN-HWA KWON

Sun used her Oceanic settlement to purchase a controlling stake in Paik Industries, then installed herself as its managing director. She gave birth to Ji Yeon about seven months later. Eventually, Sun reached out to Charles Widmore about their mutual lie regarding the island and their interest in killing Ben Linus. They worked together to assassinate Linus, whom Sun blamed for Jin's death. However, Ben was able to stay his execution when he presented Sun with Jin's wedding ring as proof that he wasn't dead. With Ji Yeon in her parents' care, Sun was convinced to return to the island.

HUGO "HURLEY" REYES

Plagued by guilt and visits from the dead, Hurley broke down and returned to the Santa Rosa Mental Health Institute. When Jack visited Hurley to make sure he stayed true to their pact, Hugo suggested they made a mistake by leaving. Mrs. Dawson also visited and brought along her grandson, Walt, who knew people were still on the island. Hurley quietly admitted to the young man why they lied. Sayid later freed Hurley from the mental hospital to keep him safe from Widmore's people.

KATE AUSTEN

Kate was tried for her numerous crimes and accepted a plea deal of 10 years probation. She purchased a private home in Los Angeles and raised Aaron as her own, first alone and then with her fiancé, Jack, at her side. Unfortunately, Jack's control issues, guilt and alcoholism ruined their relationship. A frightening dream involving Claire put Kate back on the path to the island.

> *"Don't bring him back, Kate. Don't you dare bring him back."*
> —Spoken by Claire Littleton to Kate Austen in a dream

JACK SHEPHARD

Jack went back to work as a surgeon and eventually moved in with Kate and Aaron. However, his simmering guilt about the lie started to eat at him. He turned to alcohol and abused prescription drugs, which ultimately derailed his relationship with Kate and his ability to work. He had visions of his father and began to fly across the Pacific Ocean every weekend hoping it would crash him back onto the island. John Locke's death finally spurred Jack to make sure the Oceanic Six returned to the island.

THE ORCHID

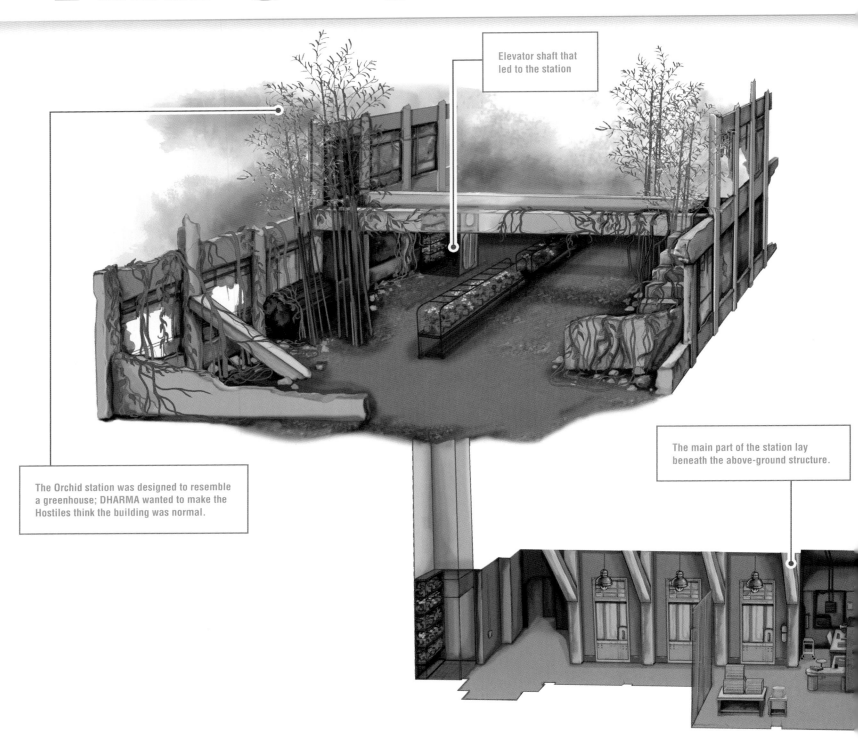

Elevator shaft that led to the station

The main part of the station lay beneath the above-ground structure.

The Orchid station was designed to resemble a greenhouse; DHARMA wanted to make the Hostiles think the building was normal.

"This station is being built here because of its proximity to what we believe to be an almost limitless energy. And that energy, once we can harness it correctly, it's going to allow us to manipulate time..."

— Spoken by Dr. Pierre Chang

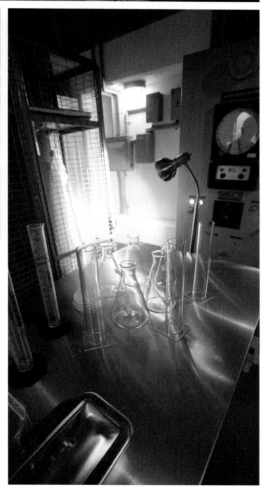

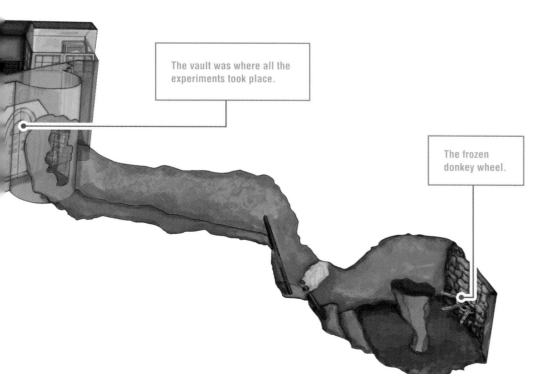

The vault was where all the experiments took place.

The frozen donkey wheel.

The DHARMA Initiative constructed the Orchid station, its sixth such station, above one of the island's pockets of electromagnetic energy. From the outside, the station resembled a botanical research station, complete with a large greenhouse. However, the true station was located far underground, accessible via a hidden elevator.

Designed to harness the island's unique properties and manipulate space-time, DHARMA concealed the true nature of the station to prevent the Others from becoming too suspicious of their actions.

THE DONKEY WHEEL

The hidden, cavernous location of the ancient donkey wheel was located adjacent to the main experimental chamber. When someone turned the wheel, the island moved through time and space. Dangerous and unpredictable, turning the wheel was considered a last resort to protect the island. There were consequences to consider when turning the wheel, like the operator was transported off the island to the exit point in the Tunisian desert. More disastrous, if the wheel wasn't properly turned, the island would erratically skip through time until the wheel was correctly reset on its axis.

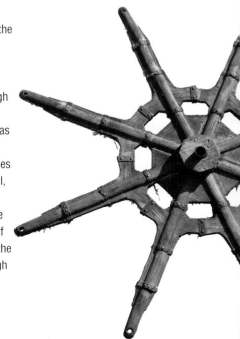

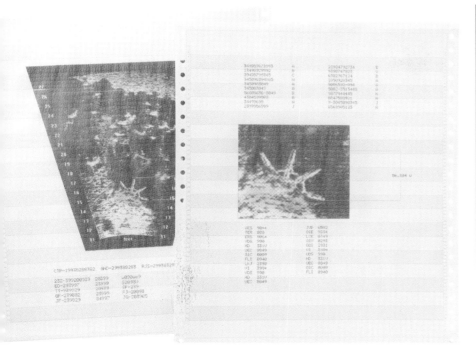

CTP-1998286382 SKC-299588203 RJS-29958529

ZEZ-599200039 20S39 L830we9
ED-290797 21599 S28397
11-029v529 20A54 gP-269
0F-239602 21599 23-10098
3F-239029 04997 30-188W5

UCS 904+   JUD 6862
TER 889   OIE 0034
ERS 9064   LIK 0149
UD6 996   OIU 0291
HD 331U   001 2931
UEC 0649   UI 100v
OIC 0809   UES 590
FLI 0940   HD 331U
LKF 2390   UEO 0049
UI 390v   OIC 0089
VOE 990   FLI 0940
4O 331U
UEC 0049

THE CASIMIR EFFECT

Named after Dutch physicist Hendrik B. G. Casimir, the Casimir effect occurs because space is filled with virtual particle-antiparticle pairs that continuously appear and then vanish.

In one experiment, two metal plates in a vacuum were attracted toward one another. This was because the space between them restricted the range of wavelengths available for the virtual particles, so less of them exist in the gap. Essentially, as there is less than "nothing" in the gap, negative energy and pressure is created that pulls the plates toward each other.

"Exotic matter" is a hypothetical notion in particle physics. The closest known representative of exotic matter is this gap of pseudo-negative pressure density created by the Casimir effect.

Regarding DHARMA's experiments, scientists theorized that the quantum mechanics of the Casimir effect could be used to create a mass-negative area of space-time, which in turn could allow "faster than light" travel, or time travel.

CONSTRUCTION ISSUES

A key breakthrough—both literally and metaphorically—occurred at the Orchid construction site in 1977. While cutting through the subterranean layers of rock according to Dr. Pierre Chang's specifications, the machine's drill bits melted. Even more troubling was the fact that the drill operator experienced severe headaches and a nosebleed.

Sonar imaging revealed the donkey wheel 20 meters beyond the solid rock. Although the foreman at the site was confident it could be reached using explosives, Chang explicitly banned the idea. The scientist explained that the Orchid was being constructed next to what could be almost limitless energy, properties that could allow the manipulation of time. Drilling at the Orchid construction site was halted indefinitely until more research could be conducted to ascertain the safest way to proceed.

THE VAULT

A patch of anthuriums concealed the switch that triggered the elevator door. The switch was located in an alcove by the north wall of the Orchid's botanical façade. The elevator took staff members on a long descent into the real Orchid station beneath the surface. Initially, the exit point was unknown, which led to test subject casualties and polar bear deaths.

The Orchid's orientation video, presented by Chang under the on-camera moniker of Dr. Edgar Halliwax, explained how the unique properties of the island created a kind of "Casimir" effect. The Orchid technology and surrounding computers all led to the vault, a special room constructed next to the pocket of electromagnetism, something Chang termed "negatively charged exotic matter."

Since the Orchid vault involved electromagnetic experiments, no inorganic materials could be placed inside it. Chang then demonstrated with one of DHARMA's albino rabbits, showing how it was shifted 100 milliseconds ahead in four-dimensional space (4-D). The rabbit disappeared on the film, as it had momentarily traveled forward in time and space.

AN EXTRA DIMENSION

Fourth-dimensional space is an abstract idea that mathematicians and philosophers (men of science and men of faith) have studied for hundreds of years. It involves taking the rules that apply to three-dimensional space and simplifying them into a space where an additional dimension exists. This fourth dimension used to be classified as time, but is now referred to as space-time. One of the resulting spaces of study is called the Minkowski space.

THE OTHERS

When Oceanic fight 815 crashed onto the island, its survivors thought the island was deserted. But beyond the abundant wildlife, it couldn't have been further from the truth. When the flight manifest didn't coincide with who was walking among them, they started to realize something wasn't right. Silent abductions of their people under the cover of night confirmed for the survivors they were not alone.

For lack of a better understanding, the survivors began referring to these people as "them" and then adopted Danielle Rousseau's phrase "Others." This term was perfect for capturing her ominous presence that the survivors felt on the island. Considering the dark deeds the Others committed against the survivors, the truth was more sinister than their being supernatural. They were just regular people; people who had pledged their loyalty to protect the island according to the wishes of its protector, Jacob. But this commitment didn't equal a life of spirituality or being "at one with the island." The Others were humans with the same flaws, hang-ups, paranoia, and curiosity as everyone else.

Throughout the years, the composition of the Others changed many times as did their moral compass. Some of them were loyalists to the island and Jacob, while some were rebellious and driven by greed and power. This clash perfectly represented the ongoing debate between Jacob and the Man in Black: is mankind inherently corrupt?

THE FIRST OTHER

1867 was the year that everything changed, that the notion of Others on the island became a reality. Before this, over the past two millennia, Jacob had brought vessels to the island to prove the Man in Black wrong, but the entity would always intervene. Hearts would become blackened, corruption and greed would be encouraged, and the smoke monster would slaughter them. But Richard Alpert changed everything.

Richard inside the *Black Rock* with the smoke monster.

When he arrived on the island via the *Black Rock,* the Man in Black immediately tricked him. But Alpert was a deeply spiritual and intelligent soul. He attacked Jacob, as the Man in Black had suggested, but after talking with Jacob, he showed the protector a flaw in his game. Although Jacob didn't want to influence Man's decisions, Alpert reminded him how his nemesis always would. So to make the rules fairer, Jacob offered Alpert the job of becoming his representative—a halfway, advisory position between Jacob and those he brought to the island. Although Alpert wanted his dead wife back in exchange, Jacob could not resurrect her. Nor could he make it so that Alpert's sins were absolved. But he could make him live forever and be impervious to the smoke monster's attacks.

MORE CAME, MORE STAYED

Over the next 80 years, more people were brought to or came to the island. Alpert approached them when Jacob saw fit, but on the whole, they were left to simply experience the island. Some died, some were corrupt, but eventually, what became the notion of the "Others" that the survivors of flight 815 experienced began to flourish: a group who led a nomadic, simple life, living off the fruits of the ocean and the land, much like Jacob. They also developed a preference for speaking Latin, which they considered the language of the enlightened and would teach it to those who decided to join them.

> *"They've attacked us. Sabotaged us. Abducted us. Murdered us. Maybe it's time we stop blaming 'us' and start worrying about 'them.' We're not the only people on this island and we all know it!"* — Spoken by John Locke

CONFRONTATION & CHANGE

In the 1950s, the U.S. military was conducting hydrogen bomb tests in the Pacific. In 1954, a faction discovered the island and came ashore with their Jughead hydrogen bomb to conduct further tests. Within the Others, Jacob and Alpert had never appointed anyone within the Others as a de facto leader, as she was a fervent believer in protecting the island. They had, in alignment with how Jacob chose to behave, allowed everyone to work things out for themselves. By 1954, a young woman named Eloise Hawking emerged as the Others' leader, as she was a fervent believer in protecting the island. When the Others found 18 members of the U.S. battalion setting up camp, they asked them to leave—peacefully. Determined to carry out their tests, the Army attacked the Others, who in retaliation, killed them all.

SIGNIFICANT OTHERS

ADAM

Not a great deal is known about this Other. Adam attended the Others' book club, held at Juliet Burke's home in the Others' village—the former dwelling of the DHARMA Initiative.

He defended Ben during the book debate about Stephen King's "Carrie" stating that Ben wouldn't even read it in the bathroom. His cross words occurred just before Oceanic flight 815 broke into pieces in the sky above them.

AMELIA

One of the more senior members of the Others, Amelia witnessed Oceanic flight 815 break apart in the sky before its crash.

Amelia was close to Juliet Burke and, just prior to 815's "arrival" on the island, she visited Juliet's home in preparation for their book club gathering. During a conversation before the rest of the club arrived, Juliet confided in Amelia and shared with her the results of Ben's X-ray tests.

Amelia had a good rapport with Ethan and enjoyed the book club's debates, especially when Adam and Juliet disagreed about the quality of the writing in the novel "Carrie." Her whereabouts are unknown, but it's possible that she was killed when Martin Keamy and his team of Mercs stormed the island in search of Benjamin Linus.

BONNIE

Bonnie was an Other who was given a top-secret assignment inside the Looking Glass station. Together with fellow Other Greta, they were tasked by Benjamin Linus to covertly monitor and jam any electronic transmissions leaving the island.

Having a more aggressive personality than Greta, Bonnie was all too happy to pull a gun on Charlie Pace when he swam into the Looking Glass pool. She then tied him to a chair and proceeded to pummel Charlie each time he didn't answer their questions. Eventually, Bonnie left Charlie and entered the communications room where she contacted Ben about their unexpected guest. He instructed them to sit tight until Mikhail Bakunin arrived, which only served to make Bonnie more agitated.

When Mikhail entered the station, he questioned Bonnie and Greta about their blind devotion to Ben's orders. Bonnie said she did so because she absolutely trusted Ben and Jacob and "the minute I start questioning orders, this whole thing, everything that we're doing here falls apart." Her answer made it easy for Mikhail to follow his own orders from Ben: killing both women. In the chaos, Charlie and Desmond were able to subdue Mikhail. Using Mikhail's gun on a dying Bonnie, they asked her for the jamming code. With her last breath, she revealed the code, a set of numbers that corresponded to the tune of The Beach Boys' "Good Vibrations."

"CUNNINGHAM"

Just after the attack by the Others on the castaways (after the island skipped back through time to 1954), Cunningham emerged from the jungle. His associate, whose uniform bore the name Jones (it was actually Charles Widmore), led Cunningham and their group member Mattingly. While Cunningham held Juliet Burke, Mattingly was ordered by Widmore/Jones to cut off Juliet's hand. Instead, Sawyer managed to grab Cunningham and severely beat him.

The castaways gained the upper hand on the trio of Others, as Juliet recognized Cunningham's use of Latin as a language the Others spoke. Juliet's efforts were in vain, however, as Widmore snapped Cunningham's neck just before he revealed the location of the camp.

DIANE

Diane was a member of the elite team that was sent to the castaways' beach camp in order to kidnap any pregnant women and kill the rest. During the raid, Diane carried a device that resembled something used for injecting a drug subcutaneously.

Others who joined her on this mission were Ryan Pryce and Tom Friendly. Diane confirmed with Pryce that Juliet Burke had done her job by marking the tents with coral. Unbeknownst to them, Juliet had already aligned herself with the castaways. On discovering that the first marked tent was unoccupied, Pryce instructed Diane to get away, fearing it was a trap. Sayid fired his rifle and made a direct hit on the explosives, which threw Diane into the air, killing her.

ERIK

Erik was a vicious member of the Others who was initially part of Jack's group who attempted to acquire the Jughead bomb. Eloise Hawking brought Erik into the group, but Sayid killed him when he tried to prevent Kate from leaving. Prior to that, Erik exhibited a violent streak by beating Kate and Jack.

Before Erik's death, he questioned Richard Alpert's decision to take an injured young Benjamin Linus into their group. He insisted that Eloise should be consulted, inferring that Charles Widmore would also be furious.

DHARMA CONSEQUENCES

By the 1970s, Eloise's relationship with her fellow Other, Charles Widmore, had started to add more tension within their group. Being her romantic partner, Widmore began to assume authority in many situations, even though the Others still considered Eloise their sole leader.

Friction escalated further when the DHARMA Initiative arrived on the island in the early '70s. The scientific research group was met by the same caution and concern as the army two decades previous. After several tense confrontations between DHARMA and the Others—who DHARMA termed the "Hostiles"—Richard Alpert liaised with the Initiative's Horace Goodspeed and drew up the Truce on August 16, 1973. This contract stipulated the rules by which both sides should abide.

Eloise Hawking assumed a leadership role in the 70s, but relinquished it after the Incident.

However, in 1977, DHARMA caused what became known as the Incident. While carrying out deep excavations (breaking rules of the Truce) to prepare their Orchid and Swan scientific stations, DHARMA pierced a pocket of uncontrollable and powerful electromagnetism. Eloise later left the island to have her child, concerned that the radiation exposure and escalating violence on the island would put her baby's safety at risk. At this point, Widmore assumed the new role as leader of the Others.

In the late '80s, after DHARMA had continuously disrespected the Truce, Widmore decided to execute the Purge. The majority of DHARMA, except for young collaborators Ben and Ethan, were wiped out by toxic gas released from the Tempest, a facility they themselves created. Shortly thereafter, Widmore and the Others moved into the barracks. This was a turning point for the Others, as they were no longer content to live by the land, as they even used the DHARMA scientific stations, including Room 23. Years later, when John Locke discovered Ben's Others were using the barracks and DHARMA's facilities, he was appalled and truly believed they did not deserve to be on the island.

> "You're cheating! You and your people communicate with the outside world whenever you want to. You come and go as you please. You use electricity and running water and guns. You're a hypocrite! A Pharisee. You don't deserve to be on this island. If you had any idea what this place really was, you wouldn't be putting chicken in your refrigerator!"
>
> — Spoken by Locke to Ben

GRETA

Greta worked alongside fellow Other Bonnie on a top-secret assignment inside the Looking Glass station. They were directed by Ben to monitor and jam any electronic transmissions leaving the island. Their mission was so highly classified that only Ben knew their whereabouts; everyone else was told that the pair were on assignment in Canada.

When Charlie Pace swam into the Looking Glass, he surfaced to find the women pointing their guns at him. Greta was less comfortable with their aggressive stance, but she deferred to Bonnie and they beat Charlie into confessing why he was at the station.

HARPER STANHOPE

Harper Stanhope was the wife of Goodwin Stanhope. On the island, she served as the community therapist for new recruits, including Juliet Burke, and existing members at the barracks. However, Harper exhibited a prickly bedside manner that left much to be desired.

It is unknown whether she was recruited to the island or was part of the original island Hostiles, but she spent enough time off the island to earn a bachelor's degree from Columbia University and a master's in psychology from Yale University. Her other academic achievements included a "Certificate of Recognition" from the Hanso Foundation, membership in the American Association of Social Psychology and the Association of International Psychologists and certification from the "Experimental Social Psychology Society."

The exact duration of Harper and Goodwin's marriage was not revealed, but for some time prior to the Oceanic flight 815 crash, their problems were bad enough that Goodwin strayed outside the marriage with Juliet. She later confronted Juliet and warned that if a jealous Ben also discovered the tryst, he would certainly take out his anger on her husband. Her warning proved correct when Ben assigned Goodwin to the dangerous job of infiltrating the tailies.

After Goodwin's death, Harper tracked down Juliet in the jungle near the survivor's camp and delivered what she stated was a message directly from Ben. Juliet was tasked to stop Daniel Faraday and Charlotte Lewis' mission to reach the Tempest, as the freighter crew was planning to release a deadly toxin onto the island. Harper then disappeared and her whereabouts are unknown.

ISABEL

Shortly after Jack had removed the tumor from Ben's spine on Hydra island, Isabel became significant in helping Ben's post-op condition. She was leading an investigation that questioned Juliet Burke's loyalty to the Others. Juliet had just shot and killed Danny Pickett and it was suggested she also wanted Ben killed during his surgery.

While Isabel was in a meeting arranging Juliet's execution, Jack blackmailed Ben into calling off the punishment, reminding Ben that he was the only person who could treat his infected tissue to make sure he walked again. Ben called off her execution, but Juliet was still punished—she was branded on her lower back.

Isabel was last seen when Jack and Juliet were at the Hydra island's shoreline, preparing to leave with Ben for the barracks. Isabel's parting words to Jack were the English translation of his Chinese tattoo: "He walks amongst us, but he is not one of us." Although Isabel's translation was correct, Jack retorted that even though it's what the characters say, "it's not what they mean." Isabel was later killed in unknown circumstances.

"THE SHERIFF" ✛
The Other known as Tom Friendly referred to Isabel as "the sheriff," but he stated that this wasn't literally her role in their group.

IVAN

Ivan took part in the decoy village ploy and also assisted in taking Hurley, Jack, Kate, and Sawyer to the Pala Ferry. He even took Kate to her breakfast meeting with Ben at the Hydra station.

Ivan had a surgical background and assisted during Ben's spinal surgery, which was led by Jack. Ivan was attacked in the operating room as Jack attempted to help Kate and Sawyer escape. During the Others' raid of the Elizabeth, Ivan attempted to shoot Sun. He was killed when a tent rigged with explosives blew up when several Others attacked the beach camp. Ryan Pryce described Ivan as one of his "10 best men."

JASON

Jason was first introduced as part of the Hydra island contingent. He was a central figure in the ruse to convince Sawyer that they had operated on him and placed a pacemaker in his heart. Jason's rank among the Others was more concretely defined by fellow Other, Ryan Pryce, who called him one of his "10 best men." Further proof arose when Ben took Sawyer on a hike to the Hydra island lookout and Jason and Mathew were the only Others to accompany them.

Jason remained a key player in the Others' campaigns including standing watch over Jack as he operated on Ben's tumor, attempting to avenge Colleen's death with Pickett by trying to kill Sawyer in the cages, and then subsequently pursuing Kate and Sawyer in the jungle after their escape. His most important mission came with Pryce's team as they infiltrated the 815 beach camp to extract its pregnant women. The plan failed and, in the ensuing melee, he helped capture Bernard Nadler, Jin and Sayid. Hurley's van distraction allowed Sayid to trip Jason and, using only his legs, snapped Jason's neck.

LUKE

Luke was a familiar face among Ben's people during Kate and Sawyer's incarceration. Originally assigned to the barracks, Luke was one of Juliet's neighbors. He shared a friendly relationship with her until he was given the assignment of watching Kate and Sawyer on Hydra island and overseeing their work at the quarry. His assignment proved dangerous when, at one point, Sawyer grabbed Kate for a passionate kiss that caused Luke and Pickett to forcibly separate the pair. This intervention earned Luke a face-full of Sawyer's elbow and the con man's grudging respect, as he later referred to him as "the shaggy-haired kid" with the "martial arts training."

Luke was considered by Pryce to be one of his "10 best men" worthy of participating in the beach raid on the survivor's camp. Luke survived the booby-trapped dynamite explosion that took the life of five of his brethren and almost gunned down Jin. He missed his target, though, allowing Jin to return fire and take Luke's life.

JUSTIN

Justin, who resided in the Temple, was trusted enough to carry a rifle and knew about the downed Ajira flight, as well as who was responsible for the recent booby traps set in the jungle. He and Aldo were ordered to retrieve Sawyer from the jungle with the help of Kate and Jin. A kinder soul than Aldo, Justin was less aggressive toward their inquisitive companions. He even prevented Kate from stepping into a cleverly disguised booby trap. But when the opportunity presented itself, Kate triggered the same trap against the duo, allowing Kate and Jin to flee. When Justin and Aldo regained consciousness, they found Jin and retrieved their gun from him. Livid, Aldo threatened to kill Jin despite Justin's protests. As Jin attempted to flee for his life, Claire appeared from the brush, killing Aldo and wounding Justin.

Justin feigned death until Claire returned and discovered him alive. She bound his arms and returned to her hovel to interrogate him about the whereabouts of Aaron. When Justin could not answer Claire's questions about Aaron, her rage intensified. He did admit that the Others took Claire to their Temple, but denied they tortured or branded her. Beside herself with frustration, Claire finished the conversation by driving an axe into Justin's chest.

MATTHEW

Matthew participated in several important campaigns against the 815 beach survivors. He was a member of the raid party that kidnapped Michael Dawson and then marched him across the island to their decoy village. He was also in attendance at the Pala Ferry confrontation that resulted in the Others taking Jack, Sawyer and Kate hostage while Michael and Walt sailed away and Hurley was returned to the beach survivors as a symbolic warning. On Hydra island, Matthew was part of an Others team led by Colleen Pickett that intended to confiscate the Elizabeth from Sayid, Sun and Jin.

One time, Ben ordered Matthew to inject a serum into Sawyer that was supposed to mislead him into thinking his heart would explode if he became over-excited. The following day, Matthew joined Ben and Sawyer for a hike to the lookout that revealed the existence of another island. Matthew's swan song occurred during the fateful raid on the 815 beach camp by the Others as they sought out pregnant women. Despite being one of Pickett's "10 best men," Matthew was felled by a shot from Jin's gun.

"MATTINGLY"

A member of the Others in 1954, the name "Mattingly" was actually an alias taken from the nametag on a U.S. Army jumpsuit acquired by the Others. It can be inferred that it was taken from a member of the Army team that landed on the island to test the nuclear bomb dubbed Jughead.

The Others attacked the time-jumping 815 beach survivors with flaming arrows. As Juliet and Sawyer fled, the pair was discovered by Mattingly, who was ordered to chop off Juliet's hand to force her to talk. Out of nowhere, Mattingly was hit with a rock; shaken, he was about to end Juliet's life when Locke pierced Mattingly's side with a thrown knife, killing him instantly.

VANESSA

Vanessa was a member of the island Others. She was present in the camp when John Locke returned to their secret enclave and was the first person to alert Richard Alpert of Locke's return.

OUTRIGGER

An outrigger is a type of wooden canoe used to traverse bodies of water to transport a small number of people from one land mass to another. Due to its Southeast Asian maritime origins, outriggers are often associated as either Polynesian fishing vessels or for transportation.

USES ON THE ISLAND
The Others utilized outriggers to travel between the main island and Hydra island. There were at least three outriggers strategically placed on the beaches for their impromptu travel needs.

The first time the Oceanic survivors used them occurred when Kate and Sawyer used one to escape from Hydra island. The pair also took an injured Karl Martin along with them back to their camp. Later, Karl used the same boat to return to the main camp again to warn the survivors of an impending attack by the Others.

When Ajira flight 316 landed on Hydra island, outriggers became the principal mode of transportation between it and the main island by the flight's survivors, the Man in Black, and eventually Widmore's contingent. The increased use of these boats during that time was perhaps a key to the mysterious altercation that occurred during a time skip with Locke, Sawyer, Juliet Burke, Miles Straume, Charlotte Lewis, and Daniel Faraday. As that group explored the long-abandoned beach camp, they discovered two large outriggers, one of which contained a bottle of water with an Ajira label. Juliet and Miles recognized the airline as a contemporary one, so its presence inferred a different time frame.

MODERN-DAY OUTRIGGERS ✚
In present day, outrigger canoes are most often used for sport and racing. There are several design variations depending on the number of paddlers in the boat. Whether it features one paddler or 12, all single hull outriggers are distinguished by an ama, or an attached float that provides stability. Most often the ama is attached to the left, or port side, of the boat. Outriggers crafted for longer voyages often have a double hull or multiple amas and are referred to as catamarans.

OXFORD, ENGLAND

MOTTO
Dominus Illuminatio Mea
(The Lord is my Light)

STUDENT POPULATION
20,330

ESTABLISHED
Unknown; teaching existed since 1096

Home to the world-famous Oxford University, the oldest university in the English-speaking world, the city of Oxford is one of the most well-known and historic cities in England. Countless brilliant minds attended the university to hone their skills in the fields of the arts and sciences. One of the university's most renowned students was British theoretical physicist Stephen Hawking.

FARADAY'S EXPERIMENTS
It is appropriate that within its walls, Daniel Faraday perfected his controversial time-travel experiments. Although part of his childhood was spent in Essex, Massachusetts, Daniel Faraday developed into a unique part of Oxford University's history in the mid 1990s. He became the youngest doctorate to graduate and went on to receive a £1.5 grant from Charles Widmore. Sadly, throughout his entire life, Faraday never knew his benefactor was his father.

"Every equation needs stability, something known. It's called a 'constant'."
— Spoken by Daniel Faraday

Faraday's lab was situated in an attic above the Physics Department in the Claredon 142-08 building at Oxford University's Queen's College. This humble environment, with its wooden furniture and blackboards, was rather modest compared to the complexity of the time-travel experiments that were undertaken within its walls.

OXFORD & CHARLOTTE LEWIS
Another member of the Kahana freighter team, Charlotte Lewis, also attended Oxford University. She received a PhD in Cultural Anthropology and used her knowledge to uncover some very important information about the island. It is unknown whether Lewis and Faraday knew each other at Oxford.

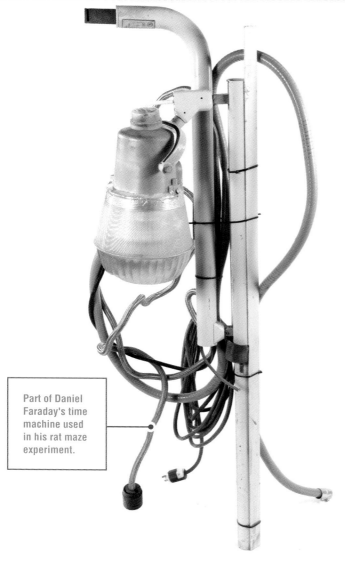

Part of Daniel Faraday's time machine used in his rat maze experiment.

SIGNIFICANT OXFORD ALUMNI

Several of Oxford University's esteemed graduates share names or thematic connections to LOST characters. Along with his groundbreaking studies in chemistry and physics, nineteenth century electromagnetism expert Michael Faraday gained an honorary Doctor of Civil Law degree from the university.

Eloise Hawking, Daniel Faraday's mother, shares the surname of English theoretical physicist Stephen Hawking. Born in Oxford, Professor Hawking studied physics at Oxford University and was fascinated by, among other related fields, quantum mechanics and theories about time travel, subjects close to the hearts of Eloise Hawking and Daniel Faraday.

Charlotte Staples Lewis, a romantic interest of Daniel's, shares more than just a name with the university. Beloved author Charles Lutwidge Dodgson, better known as Lewis Carroll, wrote the labyrinthine novels "Alice In Wonderland" and its sequel "Through the Looking Glass," both of which share common themes with LOST. Alice's journey into the strange Wonderland also echoes Charlotte's island experience, especially the theme of "returning" to the island, much like Alice's experience in the second novel.

Charlotte's middle name comes from Clive Staples Lewis, the Irish novelist responsible for "The Chronicles of Narnia." This beloved series of children's books deals with traveling to a mysterious land and strong themes of destiny and fate. C. S. Lewis studied at Oxford University alongside his close friend J. R. R. Tolkien, author of "The Lord of the Rings."

In yet another connection to the Lewis name, former Poet Laureate Cecil Day-Lewis graduated from Oxford University in 1927. He later wrote more than 20 mystery novels under the pen name Nicholas Blake. One of the novels was even titled "Malice In Wonderland."

Oxford University was also home to two philosophers whose names mirrored two important stages of John Locke's life on and off the island. The real-life John Locke and Jeremy Bentham championed philosophical themes related to the life that John Locke experienced on the island. Philosopher Locke is famed for being the founder of Liberalism, the belief in equality and liberty, while Bentham championed Utilitarianism, the idea of "the greatest good for the greatest number of people."

The centerpiece of Faraday's time-travel studies revolved around a complex wooden maze that he constructed. He successfully transported the consciousness of his pet albino rat (affectionately named Eloise after his mother) forward in time so that the rat could learn the maze's correct path. After the rodent's untimely death upon completing the course, Faraday continued to experiment on other rats to refine the process. To avoid detection by his Oxford University superiors, a colleague of Faraday's disposed of the animals to avoid detection.

At one point, Faraday even conducted experiments on his girlfriend and research assistant, Theresa Spencer, and himself. Unfortunately, the experiment on Theresa went horribly wrong and she was left permanently unstuck in time. As a result, Faraday was dismissed from Oxford University. Heartbroken, he left Theresa in the care of her sister, Abigail Spencer, in Oxford and returned to his childhood home.

DESMOND'S VISITS

Desmond Hume traveled to Oxford twice in his lifetime and both expeditions intertwined with Daniel Faraday's life. The first visit involved helping reset Desmond's consciousness from being unstuck in time. The subsequent trip concerned Faraday's mother, Eloise Hawking, and helping those who were in jeopardy on the island.

RESONATING THEMES

The center of Oxford is called Carfax, a name derived from the French word carrefour meaning "crossroads." This term is very appropriate regarding the lives and times of the survivors converging at the point of chaos and resolution.

For 10 miles within Oxford, the River Thames is called The Isis, an Egyptian goddess. Isis was worshipped as the ideal mother, which is ironic considering Eloise Hawking's manipulation of her son Daniel. Isis was also the patron of magic, appropriate for Faraday's obsession with stretching science into the fantastical realms of time travel. It is said that Isis was a goddess of fertility, much like the Egyptian goddess Tawaret that towered above Jacob's dwelling.

In Saxon times, Oxford was known as Oxenaforda, which meant Ford of the Ox. In Egyptian mythology, Apis was a bull-god. Oftentimes, Apis was depicted with a sun disk between its horns. This image is reminiscent of the ankh symbol of fertility associated with Apis' mother, Hathor—another similarity with Taweret and fertility.

The island was the location of a mysterious "sickness" that affected some of its inhabitants. In 1517 Oxford, a strange epidemic called the "sweating sickness" wiped out half of Oxford's population. The illness resulted in death within hours and its cause to this day remains unknown.

THE PEARL

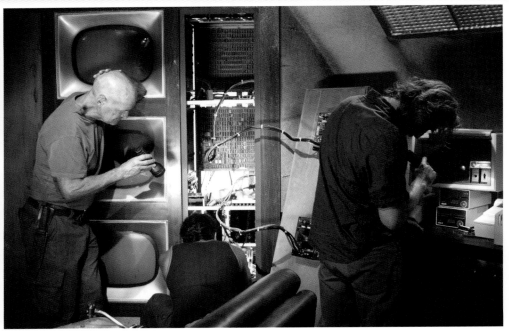

"Careful observation is the only key to true and complete awareness."

— Spoken by Karen DeGroot

Filled with monitoring equipment, the DHARMA Initiative's Pearl station was used to observe activities at its other stations, primarily those of the Staff or the Swan. The Pearl's orientation film, hosted by Dr. Pierre Chang (appearing on-camera as Dr. Mark Wickmund) claimed that the purpose of the monitoring done at the Pearl was to refine the work of DHARMA and serve as a historical log for the group.

A team of two people worked an eight-hour shift for a three-week period. During that time, they noted everything that occurred at the Swan station using a camera feed from the Swan station of which the occupants were unaware. The teams working at the Pearl were told they were watching and logging "a psychological experiment," but no description of the importance of the button pushing that occurred at the Swan station was ever revealed.

Ironically, the Pearl's orientation film stated that they did not need to know what the Swan team believed they were accomplishing, only that Swan workers thought their job was of the upmost importance. This statement mirrored the Pearl staff's mission: logging everything they saw without questioning why.

REVERSE PSYCHOLOGY

Staffers at the station were told that their completed notebooks of observations were carried to DHARMA headquarters and "Dr. Wickmund" via a vacuum tube. However, the tube simply dumped all the notebooks a short distance from the Pearl. The books remained in a clearing undisturbed, suggesting it was the Pearl's occupants who were the subjects of the psychological experiment as surmised by Desmond Hume.

Nikki and Paulo witnessed Mikhail Bakunin's image when it suddenly appeared on a monitor.

A DIFFERENT SET OF RULES ⨁
Unlike at the Swan station, those who worked at the Pearl did not have to remain inside the subterranean station. After each eight-hour shift, the workers returned to the Pala Ferry dock and were taken back to the DHARMA Initiative's barracks.

WHO IS SR? ⨁
Many of the notebooks contained references to observing "S.R.," or "Subject Radzinsky." This referred to Stuart Radzinsky, who was stationed at the Swan. In addition, there were references to "S.I.," or "Subject Inman." This referred to Kelvin Inman, Radzinsky's partner in the Swan.

> ## *"That's not work. That's a joke. Rats in a maze with no cheese."*
> — Spoken by John Locke

THE BIG QUESTION MARK

Paulo was the first survivor to enter the Pearl. Later, he secretly hid diamonds inside a Russian doll inside the lid of the toilet in the Pearl's restroom. After a series of different visions experienced by Eko and Locke, the pair discovered a clearing in the jungle near the crashed Beechcraft. The area within the clearing had been salted to create a circle, like the Pearl logo. However, some jungle overgrowth obscured part of the circle. When the Beechcraft fell, its resting position resembled the dot in a question mark when viewed from above. In one of Eko's visions, Yemi told him to make Locke take him to the question mark. However, Locke struggled to understand what the punctuation mark on the blast door map meant. All the while, neither was aware it actually just represented Radzinsky's curiosity.

Once inside, Locke watched the Pearl orientation film, which had the unfortunate effect of destroying his faith in his island purpose. He became certain that everyone pushing the buttons in the Swan station were just lab rats for a meaningless experiment. However, one of the printouts that Locke took from the station provided the proof needed to confirm that the Swan's task was real. It showed that a "System Failure" had occurred at the Swan on the date that Oceanic flight 815 crashed. This information also strengthened Eko's viewpoint that entering the numbers was important. This change in opinions later led to Locke and Eko's confrontation inside the Swan.

PEARLS

Pearls are natural phenomena formed by mollusks, like oysters. They are created unintentionally when something like a grain of sand gets in between the mantle and the shell. The mantle begins to create tiny layers of shell around the sand grain until a pearl is formed. As the DHARMA Pearl station is underground and its subjects spent years logging the tiniest of details in an attempt to refine DHARMA's work, the Pearl was the perfect name for it.

MIKHAIL BAKUNIN

After Jack, Kate and Sawyer had been captured by the Others, the survivors were intent on finding them. Desmond theorized that all the stations were linked, meaning they could use the monitors in the Pearl station to find some clues as to their whereabouts. After briefly manipulating the dials, an image of Mikhail Bakunin appeared on-screen, broadcast from the Flame station, and likewise, he saw them.

THE BLAST DOOR MAP

The question mark that Radzinsky placed on the blast door map was his way of indicating that he intended to find out who was manning the Pearl station. It had no significance to the question mark on the ground above the underground station.

> ## *"I guess he'll be expecting us."*
> — Spoken by John Locke in reference to Mikhail Bakunin

The station consisted of a bank of monitors, discarded cigarette butts and late-70s era technology in an octagonal-shaped observation room.

PENELOPE WIDMORE HUME

FACTS & FIGURES

Born: Knightsbridge, Britain

Family: Desmond Hume (husband), Charlie Hume (son), Charles Widmore (father), Daniel Faraday (half-brother)

Likes: Color red

Dislikes: The Alps

Phone Number: 79460893

Penelope "Penny" Widmore was a woman torn between two excessively proud men. As the only daughter of Charles Widmore, she was raised with the best schools and amenities, but the price was her father's overprotective and controlling nature. Her love, and eventual husband, Desmond Hume's inferiority complex and commitment issues meant Penny endured his long, frustrating path to self-discovery before their love affair was truly sustainable. Over that time, she displayed a persistence and patience not many women would endure, even for true love.

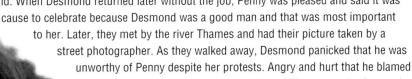

A ROCKY START

Although Penny never worked for her father, she did see her father socially and did favors for him like when she picked up an order of Moriah Wine from the monastery vineyard in Scotland. This is where she first met Desmond, just as he renounced his robes. Intrigued, Penny solicited his help to unload the wine in Carlisle in exchange for a ride. The long ride was the beginning of their two-year relationship.

In 1995, Penny moved into Desmond's small flat. At that same time, Desmond accepted a meeting with Charles about a job, which Penny tried to dissuade him from taking as she said it was her father's loss if he didn't respect her boyfriend. When Desmond returned later without the job, Penny was pleased and said it was cause to celebrate because Desmond was a good man and that was most important to her. Later, they met by the river Thames and had their picture taken by a street photographer. As they walked away, Desmond panicked that he was unworthy of Penny despite her protests. Angry and hurt that he blamed his fears on her, Penny slapped him across the face and told him not to be a coward.

Desmond visited Penny in order to get a constant.

In 1996, she moved out of his flat and into a new place to start over. Still deeply hurt, she was upset when Desmond tracked down her new address and asked to speak with her. He added insult to her injury when he asked for her new phone number so he could call her on Christmas Eve in eight years. Incredulous, she gave him the number and threw him out of her house.

A LONG SEPARATION

Penny learned that Desmond was sentenced to military prison and wrote him a letter she placed in his beloved book "Our Mutual Friend" by Charles Dickens. Over the span of four years, Penny struggled to let go of Desmond. The fact that he never wrote her during his prison stint made it easier. She eventually met someone new and became engaged. However, she was still in love with him so she hired a detective to find out his new residence in Los Angeles. She confronted him at the stadium where he trained for the boat race. Tearfully, she asked if he had read his book and he asked if she was engaged as Charles had told him. He asked for another year to win the boat race and restore his honor. Heartbroken, she let him go.

Penny confronted Desmond as he trained for Widmore's boat race.

Desmond

ISLAND YEARS

Penny broke off her engagement and continued to spend money to keep track of Desmond—an effort she ramped up when he disappeared at sea. At some point, she learned about her father's quest to find a South Pacific island with special electromagnetic properties. She refocused her search on finding the same place and hired two scientists in the Arctic to monitor the globe for any electromagnetic bursts. On September 22, 2004 at 3:05 a.m. BST, they called Penny with a hit.

Penny then spent time tracking down and sending transmissions emanating from the coordinates area. She happened to be monitoring when Charlie turned off the Looking Glass signal jam. From Charlie, she received confirmation that Desmond was alive and she told him that she was not on the *Kahana*. A few days later on Christmas Eve, Desmond called Penny from the freighter as he promised. She told him she knew he was on the island and promised she would find him. Through tears of joy, she reaffirmed her love for him before the connection was broken.

Able to track his location, Penny set out on her boat the *Searcher* to find Desmond. On December 31, Henrik spotted the helicopter lifeboat which Desmond was aboard. Frantic, Penny welcomed her love back into her arms.

Dearest Des,

I am writing this letter to you as you leave for prison. And I've hidden it in the one place you would turn to in a moment of great desperation. I know you go away with the weight of what happened on your shoulders. And I know that the only person who can ever take it off is you.

Sorry to be so dramatic, but these are dramatic times, are they not? Please don't give up, Des. Because all we really need to survive is someone who truly loves us. And you have her.

I will wait for you. Always.

I love you, Pen

FINALLY, A FAMILY

Penny gave birth to Charlie Hume on their boat, *Our Mutual Friend*, in the Philippines.

Penny met Eloise and visited Desmond in the hospital after he was shot by Ben.

HAPPY ENDINGS

After the assault on his daughter, grandchild and son-in-law, Widmore put Penny and Charlie into hiding and took Desmond (against his will) to the island. Des survived his ordeal in the heart of the island, so Hurley and Ben returned him to his wife and son.

PETER AVELLINO

▶ **CONNECTION:** Murdered by Sayid Jarrah

Very little is known about this wealthy Italian businessman, who was from the Republic of Seychelles—one of the archipelago nations that is a part of 115 islands in the Indian Ocean.

Sayid knew next to nothing about his target, except that Avellino had the same thing in common with other people he had killed since he left the island. That common thread being that Benjamin Linus had impressed upon him that these were people associated with Charles Widmore. Until they were all killed, the threat of death loomed over the heads of everyone who was still trapped on the island.

THE ASSASSINATION
Sayid met Avellino on an affluent, private golf course during a sunny afternoon in 2006. After casual banter and a small wager on who could get their ball closest to the hole, Sayid revealed that he had received a substantial compensation from Oceanic Airlines. Upon discovering that Sayid was part of the Oceanic Six, Avellino's demeanor immediately changed. As he attempted to brush off Sayid's insistence that he pay Avellino for losing the bet, Sayid retrieved his gun from his golf bag and shot Avellino dead.

ILANA'S "VENGEANCE"
Years later, in a Los Angeles bar, a woman named Ilana seduced Sayid and took him to a hotel room where she held him at gunpoint. She later claimed that she was hired by Peter Avellino's family to capture him and take him to Guam, where he would answer for his actions.

PETER ROSS

▶ **CONNECTION:** Co-pilot of Ajira flight 316

Peter Ross was the man next to Captain Frank Lapidus in the cockpit on the Los Angeles-based flight bound for Guam. As they flew over the South Pacific, Ross drank a cup of coffee and drew Frank's attention to Hugo "Hurley" Reyes in the first class section. He recognized him as one of the Oceanic Six and commented on how he must have "nerves of steel" to survive a crash and then fly the same flight path again.

Later when the plane hit violent turbulence, Ross disengaged the auto pilot so Frank could manually take the controls. After a flash of white light, the engines stalled, but Ross re-started them and then gave Lapidus enough throttle to pull them out of their dive. Ross made the last "Mayday" call before he threw the throttle in reverse to help the plane land safely. Tragically, a tree branch smashed through Ross's window and impaled him to death.

PHILLIPE

▶ **CONNECTION:** Had an affair with Shannon Rutherford

A wealthy French businessman, Philippe was married to a woman named Dominique. They had two children, Sophie and Laurent, who were both students at the ballet school that employed Shannon and her best friend, Nora. Nora was originally asked to be Philippe's live-in *au pair*, but after Nora turned him down, Shannon accepted the position as an act of desperation—she had no money after her stepmother, Sabrina Carlyle, cut her off following her father's death. Shannon also dated Philippe for a short time during her employment.

FACTS & FIGURES
Arrived On The Island: Recruited by Gerald and Karen DeGroot; member of the DHARMA Iniative

Family: Lara Chang (wife), Miles Straume (son)

Also Known As: Dr. Marvin Candle, Dr. Mark Wickman, Dr. Edgar Halliwax

Ferociously smart and a loving family man, Dr. Pierre Chang worked for the DHARMA Initiative during the 1970s. Chang was a theoretical astrophysicist and his knowledge of cosmology, the study of the universe in its current state, and humanity's place within it, contributed greatly to DHARMA's overall *modus operandi*. Astrophysicists deal with many disciplines of physics and areas such as electromagnetism, quantum mechanics, and relativity were of great importance to studying the island's unique properties.

Although he was dedicated to science, his heart was grounded in the love and safety of his family. Hours before the Incident, Chang ordered an immediate evacuation of all women, children, and non-essential personnel—including his wife Lara and baby son, Miles.

WELCOME TO THE ISLAND
Chang presented an introductory film for new DHARMA recruits who arrived on the island. It covered key issues such as: living at the barracks, job assignment, and uniform rules; recreational activities, such as the annual volleyball tournament; the rules of the sonar fence; and warnings about the environment and indigenous population.

Miles rescued his father during the Incident.

REUNION
Although he didn't realize it at the time, Chang worked with the future, adult version of his son, Miles, for three years on the island. After many hints by Hurley and then a final reveal by Daniel Faraday, Chang realized who Miles Straume really was.

ORIENTATION FILMS
Chang also became the face of DHARMA's Orientation films. These instructional presentations featured Chang describing exactly what the DHARMA members would endure at each of the six main stations. He provided the following information for each Orientation film:

DR. PIERRE CHANG

#1, HYDRA: *Filmed in early 1970s on Hydra island.*

The first orientation film.

The station and its surrounding islet handled biological and behavioral research in animal, bird, and marine life.

Chang insisted no one divulge his real name to any outside parties, or he would have to use an alias in the future.

If the viewer didn't have Tier 2 Clearance, they had to stop the tape. Tier 2 allowed classified access to details concerning the Hydra's Room 23 and its tests on abducted and sedated Others. Test subjects had an amnesia-inducing experience at the end of the Room 23 test.

#2, ARROW: *Filmed in 1977.*

As Chang's name was leaked after the Hydra video, he altered his name from this point forward. The first alias he devised was Dr. Marvin Candle.

DHARMA members with skills in weaponry and developing defensive strategies were stationed at the Arrow to gather intelligence on the island's hostiles.

#3, SWAN: *Filmed in 1980, three years after the Incident.*

Chang maintained his Dr. Marvin Candle moniker and now had a prosthetic left arm.

Pairs of DHARMA staff members were stationed inside the Swan for 540-day stints.

Although the Incident was mentioned by name, the facts surrounding it were not revealed. Viewers were simply told about the protocol of entering a code every 108 minutes, although they were not told why.

#4, FLAME

In the early 1970s, Chang filmed this station's manual override protocol that had the following options for the staffer to enter:

2-4: Let DHARMA headquarters know another pallet drop was required.

3-2: Station uplink

3-8: Mainland communication

5-6: Sonar access

7-7: Signified an incursion on the station by the Others.

#5, PEARL: *Filmed in 1980 after completion of the Swan station.*

Chang changed his name again for this film, this time to Dr. Mark Wickman.

This station involved a psychological experiment on the people manning the station.

#6, ORCHID

Chang used yet another moniker for this film, Dr. Edgar Halliwax.

This station dealt with attempts to manipulate spacetime.

Chang warned not to place any metallic objects inside the vault.

THE INCIDENT

Although Chang fought to prevent the Incident, Stuart Radzinsky was resolute in breaching the electromagnetic pocket. In the chaos that ensued, Chang's left arm was trapped underneath the drilling tower as it collapsed and was dragged toward the energy. Chang's son, Miles, helped pull him free, but his arm was severely crushed in several places. His lower arm could not be saved and he was fitted with a prosthesis. Chang was killed with the rest of DHARMA during the Purge.

POLAR BEARS

English Explorer and Royal Naval Officer Constantine John Phipps named the bear "Ursus maritimus," Latin for "Maritime bear" describing the bear's oceanic existence.

Its large claws, thick fur and body type are suited for cold temperatures, traveling across snow and ice, swimming, and hunting for seals. Day-to-day existence in the tropical conditions of the island would have been extremely difficult and unsettling.

The largest living land carnivores (adult males can weigh up to 1500 lbs. and measure 3m in length, with females approximately half this size), polar bears are curious scavengers known to hunt humans if they're hungry. With their diet of seals absent on the island—along with the disorientating climate and environment—the ferocity the island's polar bears showed toward the castaways was understandable.

Two polar bears are shown in the Swan station Orientation film, as the word "zoology" is mentioned.

Another confusing aspect of island life was that polar bears do not make their dens on dry land, but rather on the sea ice. Therefore, usual cycles such as hibernation and pregnancy would have been greatly affected. Mother and cubs have high nutritional requirements (mainly gained through seal blubber), so even if female polar bears were on the island, pregnancy would have been incredibly problematic—something the human inhabitants of the island also found difficult and, oftentimes, fatal.

SPIRITUALITY

The indigenous people of the Arctic, the Inuit, call the polar bear "Nanook/Nanuq." In their mythology, Nanuq was the master of all bears—he decided if hunters deserved to be successful. It's known that John Locke saw a vision of a polar bear during his meditation inside the sweat lodge. There is an associated theme here: Nanuq gave a blessing to hunters. With John Locke being a believer in the island and a masterful hunter, it could be interpreted that the vision of the bear granted Locke safe passage to overcome the one that mauled Eko—also a very spiritual man.

> ## " *I repeat, the bears are not your friends.* "
> — Spoken by Dr. Pierre Chang

> Hurley's comic book featured a polar bear.

In further connections of language and island events, for the Inuit of Labrador (a region of Atlantic Canada), the polar bear is a form of the Great Spirit called Tuurngasuk. There, it was vital that any apprentice shaman endure a symbolic death if he was to acquire shamanistic powers. The "death" sometimes occurred at birth. Folklore tells of Ava, who was born dead, strangled by an umbilical cord and brought back to life by a shaman who predicted a significant destiny for Ava, giving him protection with the help of the bear. Locke, who himself was strangled by a cord at the hand of Benjamin Linus, was told that he would have to die, after which he returned from death as seemingly something otherworldly.

POLAR DHARMA

It is believed that the polar bears encountered on the island were brought by the DHARMA Initiative. Although they were held in cages at the Hydra station—situated on a smaller island a short distance away from the main island—polar bears, being excellent swimmers, could easily have traveled from shore to shore. In fact, after DHARMA was purged, the polar bears eventually broke out of their cages and swam to the main island.

On the blast door, located inside the Swan station and visible after the emergency "Lockdown" procedure was initiated, writings on the strange map suggested that DHARMA Initiative researchers carried out genetic experiments on polar bears to help them adjust to warmer climates. This theory is strengthened by the fact that Charlotte Lewis found the skeleton of a polar bear in Tunisia at an archeological dig site. Among the bones, a collar was found bearing the DHARMA Initiative Hydra station logo, suggesting that the bears were being prepped for warmer climates. They may have been part of a spacetime travel experiment, sending them from the island to Tunisia, presumably via the Orchid station. The Hydra orientation video confirmed that as fact and it was further supported when Charlotte Lewis found the skeleton of a polar bear in Tunisia at an archeological dig site. Among the bones, a collar was found bearing the DHARMA Initiative Hydra station logo. Dr. Chang also verified the bears were part of electromagnetic studies that were part of a spacetime travel experiment, sending them from the frozen donkey room on the island to Tunisia via the Orchid station.

Walt hid inside a banyan tree while a polar bear attacked him. Michael and Locke came to his rescue.

OTHER SIGHTINGS/OCCURRENCES

▶ *Tom Friendly explained the Hydra cages were used to house bears and that they worked out the food puzzle faster than Sawyer.*

▶ *Pierre Chang threatened to assign Hurley to "shoveling polar bear feces" if he told anybody about the corpse in the body bag delivered to him.*

▶ *Michael gave Walt a stuffed polar bear toy when he was a toddler.*

▶ *Polar bear toys are inside the crib set of Drive Shaft's commercial for Butties nappies.*

▶ *One of the Santa Rosa Mental Health Institute patients has a stuffed polar bear toy.*

ISLAND ATTACKS

Several of the castaways encountered polar bears on the island:

▶ *Boone, Charlie, Kate, Sayid, Sawyer and Shannon were charged by a polar bear in the jungle. Sawyer shot this particular bear dead.*

▶ *While looking for Vincent, Michael was chased by one of the bears.*

▶ *After Sayid was captured and heard a roar, Danielle said, "If we are lucky, it's one of the bears."*

▶ *Locke and Charlie encountered a bear at the cave where Eko was dragged. There they saw bones and torn Dharma jumpsuits.*

Charles Widmore had a painting in his office that featured a polar bear.

THE PURGE

Letter of Truce

RESOLUTION OF 15 AUGUST 1973
The DHARMA Initiative and the indigenous island inhabitants,

Desiring to bring about cessation of hostilities on the island without prejudice to the rights, claims and position of either the indigenous island inhabitants or DHARMA Initiative recruits and employees,

1. Call upon all authorities and leaders concerned to order a cessation of all acts of armed force in perpetuity going forward from this date; *Fix Period - Finite*

GOODSPEED, IS THE "LEGAL" LANGUAGE NECESSARY?

2. Call upon all authorities and leaders concerned to refrain from introducing fighting personnel into the DHARMA Initiative or the indigenous island inhabitants' camps during the cease-fire;

3. Call upon all authorities and leaders concerned to refrain from mobilizing or submitting a military array for training during the cease-fire; *WE'RE NOT THE ONES WITH UNIFORMS*

4. Call upon all authorities and leaders concerned to refrain from importing or exporting war materials into the DHARMA Initiative or the indigenous island inhabitants' camps during the cease-fire; *PLEASE DEFINE "WAR MATERIALS"*

5. Urge all authorities and leaders concerned to take every possible precaution for the protection of the island, including all shrines and sanctuaries used for whatever purposes by those who have an established right to visit them; *I'VE INCLUDED MORE SPECIFIC LANGUAGE ON THIS IN OUR COUNTERS*

6. Call upon all authorities and leaders concerned to respect the established boundaries of the DHARMA Initiative and the indigenous island inhabitants' camps and a zone of five kilometers surrounding each camp, and to not infiltrate or attack these areas during the cease-fire;

7. Urge all authorities and leaders concerned to respect the established right of the citizens of each camp to live freely within their community and to not fear attack during the cease-fire; *REDUNDANT - WE GET IT.*

8. Instruct the DHARMA Initiative and the indigenous island inhabitants to create security teams, in concert with a mediator, to supervise the observance of the above provisions, and provide them with a sufficient number of security observers;

9. Instruct the mediators to make contact with all parties as soon as the cease-fire is in force with a view to carrying out his functions; *I WILL BE OUR MEDIATOR, YOU WILL BE DHARMA'S.*

10. Instruct the mediators to make periodic reports to each party as mutually decided upon during the cease-fire; *Is THIS NECESSARY?*

OUR WILLINGNESS TO ALLOW YOUR PRESENCE SHOULD NOT BE MISTAKEN AS CONTINUED OPPORTUNITIES FOR DIPLOMACY

11. Invite the mediators of the DHARMA Initiative and the indigenous island inhabitants to communicate their acceptance of this resolution not later than sundown on 16 August 1973;

12. Decide that if the present resolution is rejected by either party or by both, or if, having been accepted, it is subsequently repudiated or violated, the situation on the island will be reconsidered with a view to military action and swift reprisal;

13. Call upon all authorities and leaders concerned to take all possible steps to assist in the implementation of this resolution.

SEE MY COUNTERS/ADDENDUMS ON BACK

Adopted this day, 16 August 1973.   Agreed and accepted to.   *RA*

Horace Goodspeed, for the DHARMA Initiative   Richard Alpert, for the indigenous island inhabitants

Pg 1 of 1

The Purge represented a sea of change in the dominant human population who resided on the island, as it specifically determined the "winner" in the long-term adversarial relationship between the DHARMA Initiative's enclave and the island's indigenous dwellers. In 1973, the two groups entered into an official truce that laid out the specific terms of how the two opposing factions would maintain a peaceful existence with one another for a finite span of 15 years. At the end of that time, the DHARMA personnel were to leave the island permanently.

However, the DHARMA members breached the truce in several ways. First, they secretly drilled into the ground deeper than the 10-meter limit outside of their territory in order to build the Swan. They also dug underneath the DHARMA barracks and the Orchid deeper than the 10-meter limit. Lastly, they intended to remain on the island past the 15-year window. These actions provoked the leader of the Others, Charles Widmore, to seek permanent retribution against DHARMA with a plan that came to be known as "the Purge."

THE PLAN TAKES SHAPE

The plan began to formulate in 1977 when 12-year-old DHARMA Initiative member Benjamin Linus was shot by Sayid. Kate and Sawyer then transported the boy to the Others to save his life. Richard Alpert agreed to take him to the Temple to heal with the caveat that Ben would always belong to the Others. After he was healed, Ben was introduced to Widmore who sent him back to DHARMA as his mole inside the organization.

Approximately 15 years after the truce was first signed, Ben helped his Others brethren initiate the Purge on his birthday, December 19 at 4:00 p.m. He drove with his father, Roger, out to the Mesa, put on a gas mask and opened a canister of toxic gas that quickly killed his father. Meanwhile at the Tempest, Alpert and a contingent of Others donned gas masks and released the station's toxic gas into the atmosphere with the intent of killing the majority of the DHARMA community.

More than 40 DHARMA members perished during the gas attack. Aside from Ben and Ethan Rom, a few other unspecified DHARMA associates also defected to the Others. The only other DHARMA member to survive the Purge was Stuart Radzinsky, who was stationed inside the Swan at the time. Somehow he became aware of the attack and stayed underground until the air became safe. Paranoid after the massacre, Radzinsky subsequently labeled the inside doors of the Swan and the Arrow as quarantine due to the gas attack.

While the DHARMA Initiative attempted to recruit new members to rebuild the island community (especially to man the Swan), they were never able to regain their pre-Purge presence and the Others moved into their former compound.

After the purge, Ben, Richard and the Others moved the corpses of the deceased DHARMA into a mass grave they dug in the jungle.

— IF THE DHARMA INITIATIVE ENTERS OR VIOLATES ANY ~~PREEXISTING~~ RUINS ON THE ISLAND, THE TRUCE IS VIOLATED.

— IF THE DHARMA INITIATIVE DIGS OR DRILLS ANY MORE THAN TEN METERS INTO THE GROUND, EVEN IN THEIR DESIGNATED TERRITORY, THE TRUCE IS VIOLATED.

— THE DHARMA INITIATIVE PLEDGES ITS TERM OF RESIDENCY WILL LAST NO LONGER THAN FIFTEEN YEARS. AT THE END OF THIS TERM, ALL FACILITIES AND PERSONNEL ARE TO LEAVE THE ISLAND.

— THE ~~D.I. CAN ONLY~~ MAXIMUM POPULATION OF D.I. MEMBERS CANNOT EXCEED 216 AT ANY ONE TIME ON THE ISLAND.

RACHEL

▶ **CONNECTION:** Best friend of Claire Littleton

Rachel was supportive of Claire's relationship with Thomas, and encouraged Claire when they moved in together. Rachel also arranged the psychic reading with Richard Malkin. She knew Claire was fascinated by astrology and its related subjects so she thought Claire would find a reading interesting. Rachel was also the friend to whom Claire confided about her pregnancy, even before telling anyone from her family.

RACHEL CARLSON

▶ **CONNECTION:** Sister of Juliet Burke

Rachel Carlson was a resilient soul. Stricken with cancer, she managed to fight off the disease and conceive a child with the aid of her sister's experimental fertility treatment. Even during the siblings' childhood, Rachel remained the more stoic of the two sisters when their parents divorced.

Always supportive of Juliet, Rachel encouraged her to take a research job in Portland, Oregon after her cancer went into remission. Unbeknownst to Rachel, that job led Juliet to the island. The last time Rachel saw Juliet was at Mittelos Bioscience headquarters in Portland. The sisters thought they would see each other in a few months, before Rachel's due date, but Ben Linus never allowed Juliet to leave the island.

UNDER BEN'S CONTROL

Six months after Juliet arrived on the island, Ben informed her that Rachel's cancer had returned and that she would not have her baby. He promised that Jacob would cure Rachel's cancer, but only if Juliet stayed and helped solve his people's fertility problems.

Two years later, and just after flight 815 crashed, Juliet saw Rachel playing with her son, Julian, via a live Flame camera feed from Miami, Florida. Since Rachel's health updates came from Ben, it remains unclear whether or not Rachel's cancer returned, or whether Jacob did in fact leave the island and cure Rachel as Ben had promised.

DETECTIVE RAGGS

▶ **CONNECTION:** Co-worker of Ana Lucia Cortez

A caring and dedicated LAPD officer, Detective Raggs was friends with Ana Lucia Cortez. After an extended period of leave, Raggs helped plan a surprise cake for her return to work. Ana Lucia had been recovering from losing her baby as a result of being shot by Jason McCormack.

Raggs worked closely with Ana Lucia's mother and boss, Captain Teresa Cortez. He reported to Cortez on the news of McCormack's arrest and subsequent confession to the attempted murder of Ana Lucia.

RADIO TOWER

"I'm alone now, on the island, alone. Please, someone come. The others, they're dead. It killed them. It killed them all."

— Danielle Rousseau's distress signal broadcast from the island's radio tower, as translated by Shannon Rutherford

The radio tower was built by the DHARMA Initiative along with their myriad other technological facilities and buildings on the island. It was created so that they could send and receive information to and from the outside world. Its secondary purpose was to allow communication to occur between it and the Flame and Looking Glass stations, which each served different communication purposes. The radio tower was also the source of an automated broadcast of the numbers, as well as Danielle Rousseau's distress message.

BROADCASTING THE NUMBERS
The first known broadcast heard outside the island from the radio tower occurred in 1988. U.S. Naval Officers Sam Toomey and Leonard Simms were assigned to a listening post monitoring long-wave transmissions from the Pacific. For quite some time, all they heard was mainly static but that all changed one fateful night. They heard a male voice repeating the numbers 4, 8, 15, 16, 23, and 42 in sequence on a continuous loop.

The same year that Toomey and Simms first heard the numbers, the crew of the French ship the *Bésixdouze* also picked up the same transmission. A group of French scientists (Danielle Rousseau, her partner Robert, Montand, Lacombe, Nadine, and Brennan) changed course to investigate the source of the radio tower's transmission. A vicious storm wrecked the *Bésixdouze*, but all six crewmembers safely made it to the island's shore. Rousseau and the remaining members of the team discovered the radio tower weeks later. After all but Rousseau had been taken over by "the sickness," Danielle changed the transmission to a distress signal in French. Rousseau's distress signal was programmed to repeat on a permanent loop, so it prevented anyone from transmitting messages from the island to the outside world. Thus, once the transceiver was recovered from Oceanic flight 815's cockpit, there was no way for the survivors to broadcast any messages.

Sayid's early attempts to find the location of the radio tower, by triangulating signals from antennas, failed as John Locke knocked him out and smashed the transceiver. Later, Rousseau led the survivors to the radio tower so they could switch off her message and clear the airwaves for Naomi Dorrit's sat phone.

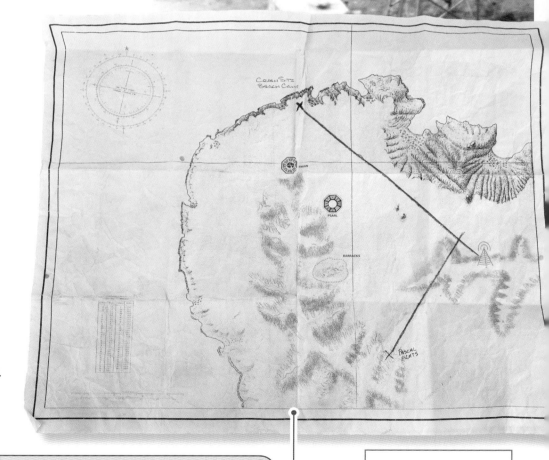

Ben's map triangulating the route to intercept Jack's group walking to the radio tower.

BY THE NUMBERS ✛
*By analyzing the iterations of Rousseau's message, Sayid correctly calculated that the message had been running for **16** years and five months.*

AJIRA EMERGENCY ✛
When Ajira flight 316 suffered major instrument failure while flying over the island, its copilot radioed a Mayday message. Strangely, the only response they heard was the broadcast of the numbers.

RANDY NATIONS

▶ **CONNECTION:** Hurley's former boss at Mr. Cluck's Chicken Shack; Locke's boss in Tustin, CA

During the time that Hugo "Hurley" Reyes worked for Mr. Cluck's Chicken Shack, Randy Nations was his boss. Hurley never felt motivated at his job under Randy's eye. He was chastised for handing out too many napkins and he was also caught eating some of the store's food. During Randy's interrogation of Hurley about this particular incident, Hurley quit; his winning lottery ticket gave him a newfound confidence.

Hurley and his friend/Cluck's co-worker, Johnny, used Randy's gnomes to spell out the phrase "Cluck You" on his front lawn, after Johnny was inspired by Hurley to quit too.

With some of his winnings, Hurley bought Mr. Cluck's and kept Randy as an employee. When reporter Tricia Tanaka arrived for the grand reopening, the camera crew entered the restaurant to shoot some footage. Shortly after, Hurley and Randy watched as a meteor crashed into Mr. Cluck's, killing Tricia Tanaka and destroying the restaurant.

After the accident, Hurley gave Randy a job at a box company in Tustin, California in which Hurley was the majority shareholder. While at the box firm, Randy was the boss of, among others, John Locke. As with Hurley, Randy did not treat Locke very well. He made fun of Locke's age and disability, especially when he found the Australian Walkabout brochure on Locke's desk.

Years later, Randy worked for Circuit House. During a high-speed police chase between the LAPD and Hurley, Randy began videotaping the incident—although he unwittingly left the lens cap on. The chase ended when Hurley crashed his Camaro just outside Circuit House.

RAY MULLEN

▶ **CONNECTION:** Australian farmer, turned in Kate Austen to authorities

Ray Mullen lived on a farm in the rural country outside of Melbourne. A recent widower, Mullen was checking his property early one morning and was surprised to find Kate Austen sleeping inside his sheep pen. He woke her up with a cock of his gun and asked her how she ended up on his remote piece of land. She said she walked and then, exhausted, fell asleep. Lonely for company, he invited her inside for breakfast where she lied and said she was a Canadian named Annie out to see the world. Charmed, Ray offered to keep her on for a fair wage if she helped out an old man with a prosthetic arm with his farm. She agreed and stayed for three months.

One day in town at the post office, Ray saw Kate's U.S. wanted poster with a reward for $23,000. Desperate to keep his farm, Ray called Marshal Edward Mars and worked out an apprehension trap. On her own, Kate got itchy and planned a midnight getaway but Ray caught her in the act of collecting her money and things. He acted hurt and convinced her to stay the night and offered to take her to the train station the next day.

> **BY THE NUMBERS** ✚
> *Ray's wife had been dead for **8** months.*
> *Kate's bounty was worth **$23**,000.*

As they drove, Ray tried to stall and often looked out of his rear view mirror which tipped off Kate that he had ratted her out. Sure enough, the Marshal sped up to their truck and Kate forced Ray to pull off the road. The sudden movement caused the truck to flip, and it went up in flames. Kate managed to drag Ray from the wreckage by his prosthetic arm, but her compassion allowed the Marshal to finally apprehend her.

RAY SHEPHARD

▶ **CONNECTION:** Father of Christian Shephard & grandfather to Jack Shephard

A charismatic soul, even in his senior years, Ray lived at a retirement home but was always looking for a way to escape.

THE WATCH

Never afraid to speak his mind, Ray openly disapproved of the woman Christian married—Margo—and told his son how he felt on their wedding day. Conversely, Christian felt much different about Jack and Sarah's nuptials. Prior to their special day, Christian gave Jack his father's old watch. It was a fitting but ironic display of affection, as Ray had given the watch to Christian just after he expressed his displeasure about Margo. Christian explained how he wanted Jack to wear it as a symbol of his blessing.

Christian passed along the watch given to him by his father to Jack on his wedding day.

BEFORE AJIRA FLIGHT 316

Three years after Jack Shephard left the island and one day before he was to board Ajira flight 316 to return, he received a call from Ray's retirement home. The staff explained that he tried to escape for the fourth time.

Inside Ray's room, Jack discovered a packed suitcase indicating that his grandfather was ready for another escape. While helping him unpack, Jack discovered a pair of his father's shoes. Ray explained that Jack's mother, Margo, had sent him some of Christian's possessions and the shoes must have gotten mixed in while he packed. Recalling Benjamin Linus' advice about faithfully re-creating the original Oceanic flight 815, Jack took the shoes, already deciding that the dead John Locke would wear them.

> **RECURRING THEMES** ✚
> *Jack prevented Ray from escaping, but in turn, discovered a pair of his father's shoes that he believed would facilitate himself getting to the island. Without the accidental discovery of the shoes, the re-creation of the flight may not have been enough for Ajira flight 316 to be a success.*

RECORD PLAYER

Beyond the literal presence of a turntable, the conceptual theme of a record player is significant to the events that occurred to those on the island. The mysterious frozen donkey wheel that was located in one of the island's deep catacombs not only affected the person who turned the wheel, it also influenced the island. Turning the wheel on its axis transported the user to an outlet in a Tunisian desert and moved the island through space and time. Much like a record player, though, the wheel could become stuck—like when the needle of a record player fails to find a footing on a vinyl's stabilizing grooves. When the island started skipping through time and space, someone had to reset the teeth of the donkey wheel so that they were in perfect alignment. The same is true for a traditional record player.

SPIN THE RECORD ✛

Other instances where vinyl made a cameo:

Locke put on "These Arms Of Mine" (Otis Reading) in the hatch while drawing the blast door map; at the pub, a Mama Cass tune was played and freaked out Desmond; Kate listened to "I've Got Your Picture" on a record player; a young Emily Locke played Buddy Holly on her turntable before heading out with Anthony Cooper; and Dr. Pierre Chang listened to "Shotgun Willie" and the needle got stuck.

"MAKE YOUR OWN KIND OF MUSIC" ✛

Nobody can tell ya.
There's only one song worth singin'.
They may try and sell ya.
'cause it hangs them up to see someone like you.
But you've gotta make your own kind of music.
Sing your own special song.
Make your own kind of music
Even if nobody else sings along.

Mama Cass, 1969

SKIPPING RECORDS

While John Locke was detonating dynamite at the Swan hatch, Desmond Hume was down below listening to "Make Your Own Kind of Music." The vibration of the explosion caused the record to skip, repeating the lyrics "You've gotta," over and over again. The skipping records foreshadow the skipping through time that Desmond and others would later experience.

RECURRING THEMES

One day during Rachel Burke's chemotherapy and fertility treatments, her sister, Juliet Burke, found a skipping record with the needle circling the end groove. This is of particular thematic significance to events that followed. Just like the record in Rachel's apartment, Juliet would end up experiencing what it was like being part of a skipping record when the island was fluxing through time. More appropriately, though, is that Juliet brought her sister's record player to a stop. Years later, Juliet smashed the atomic bomb, resetting time for those in 1977 and transporting them to 2007.

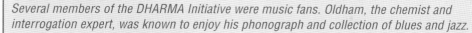

> ## " No more flash. The record is spinning again. We're just not on the song we wanna be on. "
> — Spoken by Daniel Faraday

VINYL COLLECTIONS

Several members of the DHARMA Initiative were music fans. Oldham, the chemist and interrogation expert, was known to enjoy his phonograph and collection of blues and jazz.

Once the Swan hatch was completed, it was stocked with a turntable and an impressive collection of albums. There was music from Geronimo Jackson and the likes of Mama Cass Elliot, Patsy Cline, B.B. King, and Otis Redding.

RICHARD ALPERT

> *"I don't want to die...*
> *I want to live forever."*
>
> — Spoken by Richard Alpert to Jacob

Richard Alpert served as the intermediary between Jacob and the unwitting people he lured to the island. The path that led Richard to the island began with a tragic illness and ended with a shipwreck delivering him to the island's shores.

LOST LOVE

In 1867, Richard Alpert and his wife, Isabella, lived in a humble cottage in rural El Socorro, Tenerife, part of the Canary Islands. Working on the land, the two were blissfully happy. Alpert was teaching himself English, as they planned to head to the New World one day. Unfortunately, Isabella became gravely ill before they could start their voyage. Alpert's desperate attempt to acquire medicine led to a struggle that caused a doctor's accidental death and Richard's subsequent arrest for murder.

BLACK ROCK TRADE

While incarcerated, the priest at the prison discovered Alpert understood English, which made him valuable. Father Suárez sold Ricardo to Jonas Whitfield, an officer of Magnus Hanso's vessel, the *Black Rock*. During the voyage, a storm caused the vessel to crash through the Taweret statue and onto the island.

Alpert suffered a series of horrendous ordeals chained inside the belly of the marooned *Black Rock*. He watched Whitfield run through the other slaves with his sword, paranoid about remaining rations. Alpert first heard the terrible death cry of the smoke monster when it dispatched Whitfield and the other officers, before he watched it creep toward him. Instead of killing him, though, the smoke monster observed him and then left him alone.

THE MASK OF THE DEVIL

Shortly after that first encounter, the Man in Black used Alpert's heartbreak over losing Isabella against him. Taking the form of his dead wife, the Man in Black told Alpert that he was in hell and that if he killed Jacob—whom he called the devil—he could be with his wife again.

After a brief confrontation where Jacob convinced Alpert he was not in hell, Jacob explained why he brought people to the island. Alpert reminded him that, although Jacob didn't want to intervene with their lives, the Man in Black invariably would. Unwittingly, Alpert's suggestion created his eventual role on the island: to serve as an intermediary for Jacob with the people he brought to the island. In exchange for helping Jacob, a distraught Alpert sought immortality, which Jacob granted.

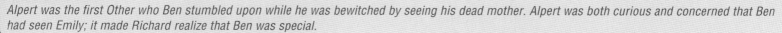

BEN'S PATIENCE ✛
Alpert was the first Other who Ben stumbled upon while he was bewitched by seeing his dead mother. Alpert was both curious and concerned that Ben had seen Emily; it made Richard realize that Ben was special.

OFF-ISLAND VISITS

Alpert visited John Locke in California throughout his life. He was there the day he was born, tested John when he was five, and even influenced Locke's high school science teacher to encourage Locke to join Alpert's Mittelos Laboratories Summer Camp.

Alpert, under the masquerade of Mittelos Bioscience, convinced Juliet Burke to leave her Miami home and come to the island to help with the fertility problems experienced by its inhabitants.

On the day that Oceanic flight 815 crashed on the island, Alpert was in Miami. He reported back on a live feed so Juliet could see her sister Rachel was free from cancer and had a son, Julian.

NUMBER TWO ✛
The Man in Black said, "I'll be seeing you, Richard," which resembled a famous phrase from the cult classic, "The Prisoner." "Be seeing you," was something its central character, Number Six, would often say to Number Two as a provocation and Alpert was very much Jacob's "number two."

DOUBTS & RESILIANCE

Following Jacob's death, Alpert had a serious crisis of faith in his role helping the island. Jacob had not told him anything about the candidates and he felt cheated, considering his 150 years of servitude.

Knowing he couldn't kill himself, Alpert asked Jack to light dynamite and do it for him. However, Jack's faith that they were both there for a reason resulted in the pair watching the ignited fuse sputter out instead of causing an explosion. It was Hurley's communication with the spirit of Isabella that renewed Alpert's faith in believing in the island and not following the Man in Black's path.

▪ Richard asked Jack to end his life.

"I think I just realized I wanna live..."

MORTALITY

After surviving an attack by the smoke monster—and once Jacob's spirit had left the island—Alpert became mortal. Miles was the first to notice Alpert had sprouted a gray hair, which filled Richard with joy. After the message of love from Isabella's ghost, delivered through Hurley, Alpert was ready to embrace mortality; he knew that one day he would be reunited with his true love again.

❝ *Actually...We're not quite in Portland.* ❞

RICHARD MALKIN

▶ **CONNECTION:** Psychic who read Claire Littleton's future

Paranormal phenomena were associated with several island events and one of the strangest remains the Malkin family. Although no one from their family (Richard, wife Joyce, and daughter Charlotte) ever set foot on the island, this Australian family's connections with those who visited the island were very significant.

Richard Malkin, who made his living as a psychic, had a peculiar and alarming interaction with Claire Littleton prior to her doomed Oceanic flight. His readings and conclusions about Claire's future were particularly perplexing when you consider that Richard later claimed that he was a fraud the day before flight 815 left Sydney.

CLAIRE'S READING

Claire's friend Rachel took her to a psychic reading with Richard. He immediately mentioned Claire's pregnancy, although she only learned about it two days prior. Strangely, Richard ended the session and gave Claire a refund and demanded that she leave. When Claire returned later for a second session, more alarming details came to light. During the reading, Richard stated that:

▶ *Claire had to raise the child because it needed her "protection."*

▶ *The father of Claire's baby (Thomas) would play no role in their lives.*

▶ *If anyone else raised the child, terrible things would happen.*

Following the second reading, Richard began calling Claire, begging her to keep the child. But after four months of harassing phone calls, Richard insisted that Claire fly to Los Angeles and give up her child for adoption. Even stranger, Richard gave her $6000 as an incentive and promised an additional $6000 but she had to take flight 815. Claire became convinced that Richard's ploy wasn't to get her to LA at all. She believed it was to get her and her unborn child to the island.

RICK ROMER

▶ **CONNECTION:** Organized walkabout tours in Australian Outback; prevented John Locke from taking part

Working as a travel agent for Melbourne Walkabout Tours, Rick Romer was a straight-talking Australian who called things as he saw them and wasn't afraid to assert his knowledge of what a walkabout entailed.

When John Locke arrived at Romer's office in Melbourne, Romer was visibly frustrated because Locke had neglected to tell the tour operator about his disability. Romer reminded Locke that the experience was grueling, even for a very fit person. Although Locke insisted that he be allowed to take part, Romer explained it was also an insurance issue that would prevent him from allowing Locke to participate.

Romer's company paid for the flight to take Locke back to Sydney. Therefore, Romer's decision was a significant factor in Locke boarding Oceanic flight 815 to return to Los Angeles from Sydney.

Ironically, Romer's insistence that Locke could not handle a difficult walkabout experience in part caused Locke to crash on the island. Locke's experience on the island was much more physically and emotionally challenging than any Australian walkabout.

"Don't tell me what I can't do!"

– Spoken by John Locke to Rick Romer

ROB HAMILL

▶ **CONNECTION:** Employee at St. Sebastian Hospital; had a confrontation with Jack Shephard

Rob Hamill was the Chief of Surgery at St. Sebastian Hospital when Jack Shephard returned with the Oceanic Six. He met Jack Shephard the night Jack had saved Mrs. Arland and her eight-year-old son who were injured in a car accident—an accident that he inadvertently caused while almost committing suicide off a bridge.

Jack insisted that he was to perform spinal surgery on Mrs. Arland, but Rob made it clear that another doctor, Gary Nadler, was booked to do the surgery. The next day, Rob found Jack rifling through a medical cabinet and told him that Mrs. Arland explained she crashed because a man standing on the edge of the bridge distracted her. Jack reacted negatively, but Rob was only interested in helping Jack with his obvious demons; unfortunately, Jack refused Rob's aid.

ROBBIE HEWITT

▶ **CONNECTION:** Australian agent who extorted Sayid Jarrah

Straight talking and intimidating, Robbie Hewitt was an agent who worked for the ASIS (Australian Secret Intelligence Service). Angry that a terrorist faction had stolen C-4 from one of his country's army bases, Hewitt worked with the CIA (Central Intelligence Agency)'s Alyssa Cole to extort Sayid Jarrah into helping them.

They used his previous friendship with suspect Essam Tazir, and hinted at knowing Sayid's lost love, Noor "Nadia" Abed Jaseem's whereabouts as bait. Although Essam didn't know the location of the C-4, Hewitt and Cole extorted Sayid further and forced him to go through with the plan to lure out the person who did know. They threatened to arrest Nadia, at which point, Sayid would never see her again.

When the plan failed and Essam shot himself, Hewitt stated that, even though Essam was a Muslim who should be buried, his body would be cremated. Sayid managed to claim Essam's body to give him a proper burial. Sayid needed to change his flight to do so, which resulted in Sayid being on Oceanic flight 815.

ROBERT

▷ **CONNECTION:** Member of French expedition team led by Danielle Rousseau

Loving partner of Danielle Rousseau, Robert worked with Danielle as part of a scientific research unit. Although it's not known whether the two were married, Robert was the biological father to Danielle's daughter, Alexandra, although he never lived to see her birth.

Robert arrived on the island in 1988 along with Danielle, who was seven months pregnant at the time. They were joined by fellow scientists Nadine, Montand, Brennan and Lacombe. After tracking the broadcast of the numbers from the island, they abandoned their ship during a storm and made it to shore in a life raft.

After rescuing Jin from the ocean and trekking toward the radio tower as a group, Robert did his best to keep the group safe. Even after Montand lost his arm and was dragged underground by the smoke monster, Robert heroically entered the hole next to the Temple wall with Lacombe and Brennan to save his friend's life.

THE SICKNESS

Danielle Rousseau coined the term the sickness to explain what happened to Robert and the rest of her team. The name signified a change that people went through; a transformation that made them something other than themselves; a change that made them dangerous enough to be killed before they killed her.

Due to the island's unstable fluxing through time, Jin witnessed firsthand the devastating effects of the sickness. Robert, who was previously caring and protective of Danielle and their unborn child, turned his gun on her and attempted to fire. Fortunately, the gun jammed and in that split second of time, Danielle shot Robert dead instead.

RODERICK

▷ **CONNECTION:** Member of Drive Shaft

The guitarist for Drive Shaft for the entire length of the band's career, Roderick was a charismatic performer who excelled in a live setting.

ROGER LINUS

▷ **CONNECTION:** Father of Benjamin Linus

A depressed widower, Roger Linus was the single parent father of Benjamin Linus. Roger lost his wife, Emily, shortly after Ben's birth and he never really snapped back into life after that loss. Instead, he drank to excess and kept himself emotionally at arm's length from his son, whom he blamed for his wife's death.

Desperate to start over, Roger packed up and took his then eleven-year-old son to an island to work and live with the DHARMA Initiative. What was supposed to be a grand reboot for his life proved to be another bitter disappointment and the island ended up representing the breaking point between father and son.

DHARMA DREAM

After Emily's death, Roger spent years wandering from job to job. So when he was contacted by Horace Goodspeed, the man who helped him and Emily just after she gave birth to Ben, about a special job, Roger jumped at the opportunity to do what his wife would have wanted for him and their son. He and Ben were welcomed to the seemingly idyllic island by Horace, but the shine quickly dulled when Roger discovered he would have a janitorial position as a "Workman." Instead of fighting for something better, Roger returned to his self-pitying mode and settled for his fate. As Ben looked to his dad for help in transitioning to their new life, Roger just disappeared into his own pain at the bottom of a bottle.

Sawyer, Jin and Hurley found Roger's skeleton inside a DHARMA van.

As years passed, Roger was still cleaning up the DHARMA compound and more estranged than ever from Ben, who was now secretly obsessed with the Hostiles who represented the kind of special family he always wanted. When Ben tried to ingratiate himself to Sayid, a DHARMA prisoner who everyone thought was a Hostile, Roger caught wind of it and threw his son out of the security building. Later when he returned home and drank too much, he punished the boy with a beating. It only served to push his son more towards the island natives.

After the Incident, Roger and Ben continued to live together in an uneasy peace. Ben also took a job at DHARMA as a Workman, but he was just biding his time and waiting for a sign from his "real" family, which came on Ben's birthday. Roger invited his son out to the Mesa to drink some beers and celebrate. Ben asked his father if he really blamed him for his mother's death, and Roger was non-committal. Ben put on his gas mask and dispassionately opened a canister of toxic gas. Confused, Roger immediately choked, bled from the nose and then died at the wheel of his DHARMA van. Years later, Sawyer, Hurley and Jin found Roger's decayed corpse inside the van.

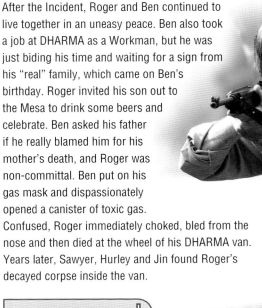

BY THE NUMBERS ✚
Roger was killed on December 23 at 4:00 pm.

ROSE NADLER (HENDERSON)

FACTS & FIGURES

Time On The Island

POST-OCEANIC: 101 days

IN DHARMA: 3+ years

POST-INCIDENT: Many years

Connection: Married to Bernard Nadler

Wise, straightforward and very connected to her beliefs, Rose Henderson Nadler was the voice of reason to so many in her life, from her husband Bernard Nadler to her fellow Oceanic 815 survivors. Having battled and survived cancer later in life, Rose gained clarity and appreciation for the things that she valued most. It's what allowed her to seize the moment with Bernard after they met and opened herself up to an unexpected love with him.

So when she was diagnosed again with terminal cancer, it wasn't something to mourn. Instead, Rose chose to embrace the time that remained, which gave her an enviable aura of peace that she tried to share with others. Even after the crash, Rose was a Zen-like figure for those who were emotionally spiralling like Jack Shephard, Charlie Pace, Hugo "Hurley" Reyes and even Bernard. Through all their years on the island, Rose was and remained the calm amongst the chaos, who kept her focus on the truly important things in life.

"There's a fine line between denial and faith…and it's much better on my side."

A TERMINAL CASE

Rose was saddened but ultimately at peace with the news that her cancer had returned and she only had a year left to live. Initially, she decided to just enjoy her time with Bernard and not reveal her diagnosis, but that all changed when he proposed at a Niagara Falls restaurant. Rose told him everything, but when he still wanted to marry her, she agreed and gave up her beachside honeymoon to follow him into Australia's Outback.

Her attitude changed when Bernard revealed that their ultimate destination involved a faith healer. After he pleaded with her to see Isaac, Rose agreed and skeptically entered his sanctum. Isaac explained about the energy he harnessed and put his hands on her, but quickly determined his pocket of energy couldn't help her. She told him to keep Bernard's $10,000 and she would tell him she was healed.

302

DUAL HEALING

Rose and John briefly met at Sydney airport. Prior to boarding, Rose dropped a medicine bottle that Locke picked up and returned. When they reacquainted on the island and Rose saw Locke walking, they both knew the island was special.

Bernard took Rose to see Isaac of Uluru in hopes of curing her cancer.

Much later, Rose apologized to Bernard and admitted she lied so he wouldn't waste their last days trying to change the inevitable. She also revealed that after the crash she didn't feel the cancer anymore and believed she was in remission. They agreed they were gifted a miracle on the island and they would never leave. In the three-plus years they built a life there, Rose's cancer never returned.

KEEPING THE FAITH

Amongst the wreckage of the crash, Boone Carlyle found Rose close to death. He tried to perform CPR, but Jack stepped in and brought her back. As she recovered and helped others, Rose was very aware that she had escaped death again and was deeply moved by the experience. Later, she clutched Bernard's wedding ring (which she kept when they travelled because his fingers swelled) and stared out at the ocean. Rose bonded with the island and not only felt her illness leave but that her husband was alive too. While her unequivocal faith perplexed some, it also helped refocus those who were lost.

- ▶ *Rose told a faithless Jack that she believed her husband and others were alive, which was later proven right.*

- ▶ *When Charlie wallowed in his fear and guilt after Claire was kidnapped, Rose told him that nobody blamed him and she prayed with him to find his path.*

- ▶ *She worked with Hurley to inventory the Swan pantry, counseled him about his fear of losing friends over the food and talked him out of blowing it up.*

"If you say 'Live together, die alone' to me Jack, I'm gonna punch you in your face."

JACK'S ADVOCATE

Aside from John Locke, Rose also challenged Jack about his lack of faith. But even when he doubted himself, Rose saw a good man who she rallied behind time and time again.

- ▶ *When Bernard wanted to build his S.O.S. signal, Rose said he should talk to Jack.*

- ▶ *She teased Jack that he was practically an optimist after his return from Hydra island.*

- ▶ *Even when she had no intention of leaving the island, she supported Jack contacting the freighter by radio.*

- ▶ *Rose took Jack's need for surgery as a bad sign, since people got better on the island, not worse.*

A SECOND CHANCE

After the island stopped skipping in time in 1974, Rose and Bernard chose to retire from the drama and built a camp by the ocean where they lived in peace. Their simple philosophy to just be together resonated deeply with Juliet Burke and it helped her decide to follow Jack's plan with the bomb.

When Bernard brought Desmond Hume back to their camp, Rose took the opportunity to warn him that he needed to eat and then be on his way as they broke their rule about getting involved. When Bernard was captured by the Man in Black, Rose calmly said they were both way past any fear of dying and that Desmond should not go with him to spare their lives. But Desmond did and secured the couple more time in the life that they truly appreciated.

BY THE NUMBERS

Rose's seat assignment on Oceanic 815 was **23**D.

RUTH

▶ **CONNECTION:** Former fiancée of Desmond Hume

Ruth was a lovely, red-headed Scottish lass from Eddington who Desmond courted for six years before asking her to marry him. She accepted and they set a date. However, a week before the wedding, a nervous Des got drunk one night and woke up in the street with a monk standing over him. He took it as a sign and entered the monastery that very day and left Ruth jilted. As soon as Desmond passed his initiation he went to visit Ruth to apologize. She allowed him in her home and they had tea while he explained his side, but she saw through his story and let him know.

> *"Next time you want to break up with someone, Des, don't join a monastery. Just tell the girl you're too bloody scared."*

RYAN PRYCE

▶ **CONNECTION:** Head of security for the Others

During Ben Linus' era as leader of the Others, Pryce was often trusted with heading reconnaissance missions or creating security teams to enforce Ben's will. At some point, he was brought to the island as a candidate #14 but was eventually crossed off the list after his death.

Pryce kept a tight handle on the security at the barracks. When Kate, Locke and Sayid attempted to infiltrate their camp to rescue Jack, Pryce and his security burst into Jack's home when Kate was inside. Pryce pulled a gun and roughed her up to get some information. He later found Sayid and handcuffed him to the swing set. When the Iraqi attempted to talk to Alex, Pryce knocked him out with his gun.

When tensions came to a head between the Others and the beach survivors, Ben ordered Pryce to collect nine of his best men to infiltrate their camp and kidnap the pregnant women from the tents marked by Juliet. But Pryce and his people weren't prepared for the trap set up for them. Dynamite was rigged inside the tents, which blew up some of their contingent and temporarily caused chaos. However, Pryce was savvy and quickly grabbed Jin as collateral to stop the attacks. He then subdued Sayid and Bernard and tied them all up together. Not long after, Hurley came to his friends' rescue driving the blue DHARMA van. As Pryce stood his ground and shot at Hurley, the van smashed into him, killing him instantly.

SABRINA CARLYLE

▶ **CONNECTION:** Mother of Boone Carlyle, stepmother of Shannon Rutherford

Exhibiting a cold, business-like attitude as the owner of a successful wedding business, Sabrina always made sure her son, Boone, was financially secure. However, she was much less supportive and caring of her stepdaughter, Shannon. Sabrina married Shannon's father, Adam Rutherford, when Shannon was eight years old. However, Sabrina made sure she underlined what was painfully clear to Shannon: that she was not her daughter in any shape or form.

ADAM RUTHERFORD'S DEATH

Sabrina called Shannon and told her about her father's car accident, a head-on collision with an SUV driven by a woman named Sarah—the future Mrs. Jack Shephard. Adam was admitted to St. Sebastian Hospital, where Jack worked. Jack's decision to treat Sarah first ultimately resulted in Adam's death, which occurred at 8:15. After Adam's death, Sabrina's cold nature remained intact. She even corrected the doctor by stating that Shannon was actually her *stepdaughter*.

FINANCIAL DECISIONS

As Shannon experienced financial difficulties and looked to Sabrina for help, Sabrina informed Shannon that she would not receive any of her late father's wealth. Sabrina claimed that Adam never made a will and that the couple's "living trust" was passed along to her as his late wife. She made it clear that Shannon would never receive a dime.

"Oh hell no. Bernard! They found us."

SAM AUSTEN

▶ **CONNECTION:** Stepfather of Kate Austen

A U.S. Army Sergeant Major, Sam Austen was married to Kate Austen's mother, Diane, but they divorced when Kate was five. After the divorce, Diane kept custody of Kate and eventually married Wayne Janssen, Kate's biological father. Although Sam always knew that Kate wasn't his daughter, he never had the heart to tell Kate. In fact, she believed Sam was her real father for over two decades.

HATCH MAN ✛
Sam Austen served in the military alongside Kelvin Joe Inman, the man assigned to the DHARMA Swan station with Desmond Hume. It remains unknown whether Sam had any connection to DHARMA or the island.

CONNECTIONS TO THE ISLAND
Sam's connections to the island extend far beyond his love for his "daughter." As a Sergeant Major in the Army during the first Gulf War, Sam and Sayid Jarrah actually crossed paths. U.S. intelligence learned that a U.S. solider had been captured after his Apache helicopter made an emergency landing deep in enemy territory. This same intel revealed that Tariq, a member of the Republican Guard and Sayid's former

During Sam's conversation with Kate, an image of Sayid appeared briefly on the TV.

Commanding Officer, was holding the U.S. solider hostage. Sam's unit captured Sayid and resorted to blackmail in hopes of getting his former comrade to talk.

They utilized Sayid's command of the English language to translate and interrogate Tariq. It was under Austen's insistence that they forced Sayid to torture Tariq to get at the truth. It could be surmised that Sam Austen's actions contributed to Sayid's dark side.

HONORABLE FATHER
After Kate confronted Sam about her paternity in 2001, he remained loving and respectful of his former wife's decisions. Kate visited Sam during her time as a fugitive, questioning why he never told her the truth. Sam explained that the only reason he never told her was because he knew she would kill Wayne.

SAM TOOMEY

▶ **CONNECTION:** Served in the U.S. Navy with Leonard Simms

Sam Toomey was a former U.S. Navy seaman who relocated to Australia after marrying a local woman, Martha Toomey. In the '80s, he was stationed at a government outpost in the South Pacific where he was assigned to monitor long-range radio transmissions. He shared with his wife that the job was incredibly boring, as he had to listen to static all night long.

During that time, Sam served with fellow seaman Leonard Simms. One night, Sam picked up a voice transmission that repeated a series of numbers—4, 8, 15, 16, 23, and 42—in a continuous loop. The men never ascertained the source of the

Hurley visited Sam's widow to learn more about the numbers.

broadcast, but the numbers remained forefront in both of their minds. So much so that a few days later, Sam used the numbers to crack an "unbeatable" carnival scam that involved guessing the number of beans in a jar. The numbers arranged as 4,815,162,342 provided the exact answer and gave Sam and Martha a financial windfall of $50,000. Unfortunately on the way home, their car was hit head-on by a pick-up truck that resulted in Martha losing her leg due to severe injuries.

Although Sam escaped unharmed, he was haunted by the tragedy and blamed the numbers. He became obsessed and tracked every instance of his family's bad luck back to the numbers. Panicked, he moved Martha to a remote residence in the Australian outback to protect them from further harm. However, normal misfortunes still fell upon them; in order to purge the "curse," Sam took his own life.

SAMI

▶ **CONNECTION:** Husband of Amira, who was tortured by Sayid Jarrah

Sami was married to Amira, an Iraqi national who had been tortured by the Iraqi Republican Guard for harboring an enemy of the state. After she was released, Sami took her to Paris where they attempted to start a new life in the aftermath of her ordeal. Sami opened a restaurant called Le Jardin Croissant Fertile while Amira stayed in their apartment fearful of the world outside. She healed slowly over time, until one night she was out on a walk with Sami when she caught a glimpse of Sayid cooking inside a restaurant. The encounter sent Amira into a panic as she recognized him as her torturer.

Incensed, Sami went to the restaurant later to eat and asked to meet the chef—Sayid. With a smile, Sami spoke to him in Arabic and praised his skills as a cook then offered to pay him twice his salary to cook for him. However, it was all a ploy to lure Sayid to his restaurant where he was then beaten and chained in the back room. Sami demanded Sayid admit what he did to his wife or he would kill him. Over days Sami personally thrashed Sayid as Amira observed, but Sayid maintained his innocence. Finally, Amira dismissed her husband and after a talk with Sayid told her husband she was mistaken and they let him go.

SANJAY

▶ **CONNECTION:** Motel receptionist, spoke to Kate Austen

Located in Ohio, Sanjay worked at the Flightline Motel's front desk as the receptionist. During the downtime of his daily work, Sanjay enjoyed playing handheld video games. He briefly met Kate Austen in 2002, but he would never have realized he did. Kate was using the identity of Joan Hart and Sanjay gave her a letter that had arrived at the motel addressed to that alias.

SARAH WAGNER (SHEPHARD)

▶ **CONNECTION:** Former wife of Jack Shephard

Sarah Wagner, Jack Shephard's ex-wife, was involved in a head-on car collision with Adam Rutherford, Shannon Rutherford's father. Upon arriving at St. Sebastian Hospital, Jack chose to address Sarah's injuries first, a decision that in part led to Adam's death. Sarah's influence on Jack's life was extensive and forced him to face his destructively compulsive need to fix people.

THE ACCIDENT

At the time of the crash, Sarah was engaged to a man named Kevin and their wedding was just eight months away. Jack informed Kevin that Sarah's injuries were so extensive that there was just a slim chance of her regaining full mobility below the waist. After learning of the the hard truth, Kevin stopped visiting her. It was Kevin's unsupportive reaction that spurred Jack to make the bold promise that he would fix her. Miraculously, the surgery that Jack performed reversed Sarah's paralysis.

THE DOWNFALL

Sarah and Jack's relationship could be considered something of a fairytale, the heroic doctor marrying the woman he miraculously "healed." Unfortunately, their marriage failed because of Jack's obsession with fixing things. Jack moved on to new challenges and drifted further away from his wife. Things hit rock bottom when Jack removed a tumor from the spine of Angelo Busoni. Even though the surgery was a success, Busoni's weak heart gave out during the operation and he tragically died. As Jack tried to comfort Gabriela Busoni, Angelo's daughter, she and Jack shared a brief embrace and kiss. Long before this confessed infidelity, Sarah had already met someone else and decided to leave Jack. Ironically, Sarah attributed Jack's need to always "fix" something to the reason she was leaving him.

Sarah tried to tell Jack it was over.

Jack became obsessed with the identity of her new love, someone who he believed for a time was his father, Christian. Still worried about Jack, she went through a period of calling Christian out of concern for Jack's mental health. Jack didn't learn that his ex-wife was completely content with her life without him until he was on the island. While a captive on Hydra island, Juliet Burke told Jack that Sarah was very happy.

Just prior to leaving Jack, Sarah suspected that she was pregnant but a home pregnancy test confirmed otherwise. Tragically, Jack's cavalier response that he was "relieved" she wasn't pregnant was the last straw. In a cruel twist much later after Jack returned home as one of the Oceanic Six, Sarah was called to the hospital after Jack was injured. When she arrived, Sarah was pregnant.

SATELLITE PHONES

The satellite phones used by the freighter team onboard the *Kahana* were at the cutting edge of technology in 2004. Using his far-reaching connections, Charles Widmore secured these next-generation models for the mercenary team's invasion of the island. Unlike radio broadcasts that were affected by the island's unique properties, communication via satellite phones was not disrupted by the island's temporal distortion.

GPS TRACKING

Each sat phone came equipped with GPS (Global Positioning System) technology, a space-based global navigation satellite system. This provided an accurate tracking system of where each sat phone user was located in relation to the rest of the crew.

Naomi Dorrit's satellite phone.

TRANSMISSIONS

Although the sat phones used satellites to send and receive information, they were not completely outside of the Others' innovative ways of controlling broadcasts. As an ex-Communications Officer, Sayid Jarrah determined that Naomi Dorrit's sat phone could not broadcast anything because Danielle Rousseau's looped distress message was overriding the frequency. In addition, Benjamin Linus made the underwater Looking Glass station jam all signals coming from the island, except for their own. Charlie Pace's sacrifice inside the Looking Glass succeeded in turning off the jamming system, while his fellow survivors switched off Rousseau's message from its source, clearing the airwaves.

The sat phones were used often, including a conversation between Charlotte Lewis and Regina that revealed the helicopter hadn't arrived at the *Kahana* yet, even though it took off from the island the previous night. This was the first evidence that indicated time behaved in a strange way on the island. The sat phone was also crucial in helping Desmond Hume anchor his consciousness from being unstuck in time. Daniel Faraday instructed Desmond to head to Oxford and speak with him to save Desmond's life.

305

Bluebeard, by Charles Perrault

Sawyer called Mr. Friendly "Bluebird"

ECG Workout: Excercises in Arrythmia Interpretation, by Jane Huff

On the Swan station bookshelf

The Afro-Asian World: A Cultural Understanding, by Edward Kolevzon

On the shelves in the DHARMA classroom during Ben's flashback

Babar, by Jean de Brunhoff

Sawyer called Hurley "Barbar;" Hurley corrected him by saying it's Babar

Haroun and the Sea of Stories, by Salman Rushdie

Desmond read it on the plane

Deep River, Shusaku Endo

Dogen read it

Heart of Darkness, by Joseph Conrad

Charlie mentioned the character Kurtz to Hurley; Jack referred to the book when talking to Kate

Notes from the Underground, by Fyodor Dostoyevsky

Found in Ilana's backpack

Bad Twin, by Gary Troup

Sawyer read the manuscript

The Godfather, by Mario Puzo

Hurley described the hospital scene to his father

Everything That Rises Must Converge, by Flannery O'Connor

Jacob read it while waiting for Locke to fall

After All These Years, by Susan Isaacs

On the Swan station bookshelf

The Invention of Morel by Adolfo Bioy Casares

Sawyer read it

Rainbow Six, by Tom Clancy

On the Swan station bookshelf

The Oath, by John Lescroart

Inside Ben's tent

The Coalwood Way, by Homer Hickam

On the shelves in the DHARMA classroom during Ben's flashback

The Annotated Alice, by Lewis Carroll

David, Jack's son, read it during the flash sideways

The Chosen, by Chaim Potok

Inside Sawyer's tent

Our Mutual Friend, by Charles Dickens

Desmond's favorite book

A Wrinkle in Time, by Madeleine L'Engle

Sawyer read it

An Occurrence at Owl Creek Bridge, by Ambrose Bierce

On the Swan station bookshelf

The Brothers Karamazov, by Fyodor Dostoyevsky

Locke offered it to "Henry Gale"

The Third Policeman, by Flann O'Brien

Desmond read it

The Turn of the Screw, by Henry James

The Swan orientation film is hidden behind it

Y: the Last Man, by Brian K. Vaughan

Hurley read the Spanish version

Dirty Work, by Stuart Woods

On the Swan station bookshelf

Hindsights: The Wisdom and Breakthroughs of Remarkable People, by Guy Kawasaki

On the Swan station bookshelf

Valis, by Philip K. Dick

Ben read it

The Survivors of the Chancellor, by Jules Verne

Regina read it on the *Kahana*

A Separate Reality, by Carlos Castaneda
Young Ben gave it to Sayid

Fear and Trembling, by Søren Keirkegaard
Hurley found Montand's copy of it in the catacombs below the Temple wall

White Noise, by Don Delillo
It washes ashore in the sub explosion debris

Memoirs of a Geisha, by Arthur Golden
A couple in LAX airport say Sun & Jin's relationship is like this book

Lord of the Flies, by William Golding
Referenced by Sawyer; mentioned by Charlie when talking to Kate

Jurassic Park, by Michael Crichton
Nikkie admonishes Paulo about the smoke monster, saying they're in the South Pacific and not Jurassic Park

The Stone Leopard, by Colin Forbes
On the shelves in the DHARMA classroom in Ben's flashback

High Hand, by Gary Phillips
On the Swan station bookshelf

A Brief History of Time, by Stephen Hawking
Aldo read it

Catch-22, by Joseph Heller
Naomi had the Portuguese edition

The Ugaritic Baal Cycle, by Mark Smith
Caesar found it in Ben's office

Lancelot, by Walter Percy
Sawyer read it

Watership Down, by Richard Adams
Sawyer read it

The Fountainhead, by Ayn Rand
Sawyer read it

Alice in Wonderland, by Lewis Carroll
Jack read the book to Aaron

Island, by Aldous Huxley
The Pala Ferry was named after the fictional island of Pala

Musset: Poesies Completes, Tome 1, by Alfred de Musset
Locke used pages from the book to draw the blast door map from memory

Harry Potter, by J. K. Rowling
When Sawyer tried on some glasses, Hurley said it looked like someone steamrolled Harry Potter

Little Red Riding Hood, by The Brothers Grimm
Sawyer referred to this story when Ana Lucia followed him to a stream and had sex with him

Laughter in the Dark, by Vladimir Nabokov
Inside Sawyer's tent

Are You There God? It's Me, Margaret, by Judy Blume
Sawyer read it

Carrie, by Stephen King
Juliet's book club read it

Of Mice and Men, by John Steinbeck
Sawyer read it while in prison

Evil Under the Sun, by Agatha Christie
Sawyer read it

Shane, by Jack Schaefer
Sawyer read it

A Christmas Carol, by Charles Dickens
Sawyer called himself the "Ghost of Christmas Future"

Ulysses, by James Joyce
Ben read it

JAMES "SAWYER" FORD

FACTS & FIGURES

Time On The Island

POST-OCEANIC: 101 days

IN DHARMA: 3+ years

POST-INCIDENT: 9 days

Year Of Birth: 1968

Education: Dropped out in 9th grade

People Killed By His Hand: 5

Candidate: 15

James "Sawyer" Ford wore his seething anger like a badge of honor as he sat on the beach in the aftermath of the Oceanic flight 815 crash. His rough stubble, annoyed sneer, and aggressive pulls on his cigarette illustrated everything his fellow survivors needed to know about him—stay away. A quintessential bad boy with a chip on his shoulder the size of the fuselage, Sawyer was extremely disturbed that his two-decades-long pursuit of personal vengeance was as obliterated as the chunks of airplane that littered the shoreline. But as he sat on a rock and re-read the letter written by his eight-year-old self to a phantom nemesis who had inspired his life of predatory cons and self-loathing, James could hardly know that the island would be his ticket to achieving emotional closure, redemption and even love.

Forced to eschew his loner status in order to co-exist on the island with the other survivors, Sawyer made sure he was a thorn in the side of anyone who assumed a leadership role. A scrappy self-preservationist and a successful thief, Sawyer looted the plane and luggage for himself content to let everyone else fend for themselves. His selfishness earned him plenty of resentment and eventually a life-threatening stab wound from Sayid Jarrah that put a literal and metaphorical chink in his almost impenetrable emotional armor. He briefly allowed Kate a glimpse at the pain that shaped him and it was enough for her to realize there was more to him than the ugly bravado. This opened the door for Sawyer to connect—even by bribery—with others like Michael Dawson, Jin-Soo Kwon, and John Locke. Those relationships evolved and created even more important connections with Hurley, Claire and Kate. And while he fought his evolution every step of the way, the island eventually chewed up the façade Sawyer had been and resurrected James Ford so he could emerge again.

> Dear Mr. Sawyer,
> You don't know who I am. But I know who you are. And I know what you done. You slept with my mother. And then you stole my dad's money all away. So he got angry and he killed my mother. And then he killed himself, too. All I know is your name. But one of these days I am gonna find you and I am going to give you this letter so you'll remember what you done to me. You killed my parents. Mr. Sawyer

THE GHOST OF MR. SAWYER

Possibly the single most defining moment in James Ford's young life was the sudden and violent death of his parents. The sordid reasons behind the act weren't kept from James and his broken heart immediately wanted vengeance for what "Sawyer" had done to his family. He wrote a letter to the man who instigated the tragedy and vowed to find him someday and personally hand-deliver it. The mission consumed him and ironically turned James into the very callous monster he sought. Without knowing it, his dark pursuit of closure and retribution ultimately opened the door for his redemption.

" *I'm a complex guy, sweetheart.* "

By the time he turned 19, James adopted the name Sawyer and started to run his own cons.

Bitter and angry at life, Sawyer remained haunted by his past even on the island.

Angry at Kate's discovery of his letter, Sawyer admitted the truth about his name and his past.

Locke lured Sawyer to the *Black Rock*, where he confronted the real Sawyer. Mocked by the man who ruined his life, Sawyer exploded in rage and strangled him.

FELLOW SURVIVORS

JACK
Chico, Cowboy, Doc (Quinn, Do-right, Giggles), Amarillo Slim, Sundance, Daniel Boone, Saint Jack, Jacko, Jackass, Hoss

SAYID
Ali, Mohammed, Captain Falafel, Omar, Abdul, Al Jazeera, Captain A-rab, Red Beret, Chief, Iraqi (Genuine, Our Resident), Damn Arab Genius, Buddy, Terrorist, Boss, Brave One

EKO
Shaft

KATE
Freckles, Baby, Girl, Honey (Hon'), Sassafras, Little Lady, Sugarpop, Sweetcheeks, Woman, Belle of the Ball, Shortcake, Kiddo, Pippi Longstocking, Puddin', Boar Expert, Magellan, Sheena, The Mighty Huntress, Thelma, The New Sheriff in Town

CHARLIE
Limey Runt, Oliver Twist, Jiminy Cricket, Amigo, Chucky, Tattoo, Munchkin, Sport, Has-been Pop Star, Reject from Vh-1 Has-beens, Babynapper

JIN
Hidden Dragon, Bruce, Kato, Mr. Miyagi, Sulu, Chewie, Yo-Jin-Bo, Jin-Bo, Jin Senior, Papa-san, Chief, Daddy-O, Old Man, Torchy, Hoss

SUN
Crouching Tiger, Tokyo Rose, Betty, Sunshine

ANA LUCIA
Sister, Hot Lips, Lucy, Ana Lulu, Little Red Riding Hood, Cupcake, Bitch, Rambina, Little Amiga, Muchacha, Ponce de Leon

BERNARD
Norma Rae, Aunt Suzy, Bernie

CINDY
Earhart

DHARMA

AMY
Sister

HORACE
Boss, Chief, Fearless Leader, Bastard, H

OTHERS

BEN
Yoda, Bug-eyed Bastard, The Artist Formerly Known as Henry Gale, Big Kahuna, Captian Bunny Killer, George, Gizmo

JULIET
Blondie, Sweetheart, Wise-ass

ALEX
Sally Slingshot, Sister, Sheena, Lollipop, Underdog

KARL
Bobby, Chachi, Cheech

ETHAN
Ringer, Jungle Boy

TOM FRIENDLY
Zeke, Bluebeard

RADZINSKY
Stu, Quick Draw

COLLECTION OF CONS

Always ready to turn any situation to his advantage, Sawyer looked for any opportunity to take the upper hand. All it took was a savvy setup, a convincing story and the right lies at the right time…

▸ At 19, James first conned an unnamed married woman to pay off a $6000 debt.

▸ Jessica and David: James almost conned the couple out of $160,000 in a fake Gulf of Mexico oil mining investment scam. (pigeon drop)

▸ Cassidy: He attempted the investment scam on her but she saw through it. Instead, he taught her the worthless necklace scam, the Tulsa Bag scam, and the Lookie-loo. He then pulled a long con on her for $600,000. She later turned him in to the cops.

▸ In exchange for a shortened sentence and a cash reward, Sawyer conned a fellow prisoner Munson to tell him the location of his embezzled money.

▸ Sawyer and Hibbs worked a failed scam they called the Tampa job. James came out conned in the end, which created bad blood between them.

▸ Kate Austen: Sawyer made her trade him a passionate kiss for Shannon Rutherford's asthma inhaler, which he never had.

▸ While Jack and Locke squabbled over possession of two guns, Sawyer worked an elaborate con on the camp that gave him possession of the guns and medicine.

▸ Sawyer used the Wookie Prisoner gag to trick Aldo, a member of the Others, and rescue Karl from Room 23.

▸ In 1974, Sawyer conned Horace Goodspeed into believing that his name was James LaFleur and he was a captain of a shipwrecked salvage vessel in search of the Black Rock.

▸ In 1977, James conned his DHARMA brethren for a time that Jack, Kate and Hurley were fresh recruits off the latest submarine.

▸ He tried to con the Man in Black into believing he was on his side, when in reality he was on nobody's side and just wanted off the island.

CONNING A CON

While Sawyer was very good at his swindler schemes, he wasn't impervious to getting conned himself. While Sawyer used greed to topple the majority of his victims, James' most exploitable Achilles heel was his search for the real Mr. Sawyer.

▸ Hibbs, Ford's former partner, tricked him into flying to Australia to kill Frank Duckett (who owed Hibbs money) by saying he was the original "Sawyer."

▸ Ben convinced Sawyer that they had installed a pacemaker in his heart that would explode if his heart rate went too high. He mellowed to protect Kate, but was later informed that it was all a con to gain Sawyer's respect.

▸ Hurley hustled Sawyer in a game of ping pong to make Sawyer stop using nicknames for a week.

▸ In an inspired follow-up con, Hurley got James to believe the camp was going to vote to banish him unless he changed his surly ways. Sawyer found out from Charlie there was no vote and it was all a ploy by Hugo to get James to be nice.

▸ Locke brought Sawyer to the Black Rock to kill Ben, but revealed it was actually Anthony Cooper—the true "Sawyer" of James' past. John set up the perfect scenario to get James to do his dirty work when he killed his father in a rage.

HURLEY

Jabba, Stay-Puff, Jumbotron, Grimace, Montezuma, Kong, Hulk, Mongo, Barbar (instead of Babar), Pork Pie, Hammo, Deepdish, International House of Pancakes, Grape Ape, Pillsbury, Chicken Little, Hoss, Esse, Snuffy, Avalanche, Lardo, Rotund, Rerun, Muttonchops, Number One Draft Pick, Three Men and a Baby (Aaron & Charlie + Hugo 2x)

LIBBY
Moonbeam

LOCKE

Mr. Clean, Bald Bastard, Bald Fellow, Johnny Boy, Johnny Locke, John Boy, Daniel Boone, Hoss, Col. Kurtz, Tarzan, Brutus, Gimpy McCrutch, Wacko

CLAIRE

Missy Claire, Sweetheart, Mamacita, Barbie, Pregnant Girl

AARON

The Kid, Little Baby, Baby Huey, That Thing

BOONE

Metro, Boy, Son

SHANNON

Sweetcheeks, Sticks

MICHAEL

Daddy, Hoss, Boss, Mikey, Pilot, Captain, Chief, Han

WALT

Short Round, Kid, Tattoo, Kazoo, Taller Ghost Walt, Six-year-old

FARADAY

Twitchy, Danny Boy, Geek, Dilbert, H.G. Wells, Dr. Wizard, Mad Scientist, Whiz-kid, Plato

CHARLOTTE

Red, Ginger

MILES

Enos, Mr. I Speak to Dead People, Bruce Lee, Bonsai, Donger

DESMOND

Scotty, Magic Leprechaun

LAPIDUS

Burt Reynolds, Chesty, Kenny Rogers

ROUSSEAU

Frenchie, French Chick

JACOB

Burning Bush

MAN IN BLACK

Smokey, Ghost of Christmas Past

ANTHONY COOPER

Pops

WIDMORE

Chief

AND THE REST...

CON TERMS EXPLAINED ✚

Pigeon drop: A "pigeon" is coerced into giving up a small amount of money in return for a bigger payoff that never happens.

Tulsa Bag scam: A thief enters a public place with a large bag rigged with a catch mechanism and no bottom. The thief puts the bag over someone's bag or purse, snags it, and leaves.

Long con scam: The thief gets their mark to ask the thief to do something believing it's their idea, when it's really the thief's.

Wookie Prisoner gag: By pretending to be a prisoner, you get the trust of another party to infiltrate his territory with his help.

BY THE NUMBERS ✚

James Ford was **8** years old when he was orphaned by his parents' murder-suicide.

Sawyer attempted to con Jessica out of **$160,000**.

James Ford's prison ID# was **840**.

Jack and Sayid created these reading glasses for Sawyer.

JAMES "SAWYER" FORD

SAWYER'S ISLAND CONNECTIONS

KATE AUSTEN

From the beginning, Kate had Sawyer's number. She recognized his wounded soul concealed a prickly exterior, because she had resorted to the same tactics when she was on the run. Even when he did everything to alienate her, Kate still considered him worth understanding. It was persistence that allowed him to open up with anyone. Of course, they also had palpable chemistry, which only pulled them closer even when Kate was torn by her feelings for Jack. When Kate nursed Sawyer back to health from his bullet wound, the pair got even closer. Sawyer became more protective of her, a subtle shift toward selflessness that was monumental for his growth.

They became lovers while incarcerated on Hydra island and, more importantly, Sawyer allowed himself to admit that he loved her. But the pair danced around one another in a triangle that featured Jack as a rival that Sawyer knew in his heart he couldn't best. Ultimately, he made the greatest sacrifice he ever had for another person when he jumped off the *Kahana*'s helicopter to ensure Kate and the others would survive. His love for Kate opened the door for him to grow up in a way he had avoided his entire life. It was so transformative that even three years later when Kate returned to the island, James felt their bond completely intact, which was unsettling because he loved Juliet Burke so deeply. However, Sawyer realized that he and Kate would always be something deeper—friends, catalysts, kindred spirits—as they started anew off the island.

CLAIRE LITTLETON & AARON

The tiny blonde and her newborn son brought out the protective side of James. When Claire allowed him to hold Aaron, it was a connection moment that resonated inside Sawyer. From that moment, he understood how important it was to watch over this innocent woman and her child. When she decided to follow Locke after Charlie's death, Sawyer followed and watched out for them. He helped with the baby when they settled into the barracks and ran to guard them when Martin Keamy invaded the compound. It was James who carried her out from the rubble of her exploded house and later found Aaron after Claire disappeared.

JULIET BURKE

James had no idea that what he learned and loved with Kate would prepare him for Juliet Burke. They started out as adversaries distrustful of one another's motives. He even pegged her as a duplicitous minion of Benjamin Linus. Because of her access to the files on the Oceanic survivors, she knew Sawyer was a killer and told him as much. It created an uneasy stalemate between them until they were left to deal with one another after the destruction of the *Kahana*. In the confusion of the island's jumps through time, James and Juliet came to trust and rely on one another to survive.

By the time the island got unstuck in 1974, James found that he needed Juliet to watch his back and convinced her to stay for two weeks as they tried to find the rest of their missing party. As more time passed, they fell in love. Juliet helped James grow up and become the man who had long been buried inside. James understood what it meant to have an equal partner and someone who accepted him for who he was. And while Kate's return to the island rattled Sawyer's heart, it never made him feel less for Juliet. When Juliet was pulled into the hole at the Swan site, James' sheer terror was laid bare on his face as he desperately clung to her hand. He knew what he had in Juliet and when he lost her, he lost a huge part of what he had regained in himself. The loss almost undid him, but what he had gained from Juliet's love kept him whole through more unbearable losses. When he finally left the island on the Ajira plane, it was as the man who had loved and lost, but would survive to honor her until they were reunited once again.

JACK SHEPHARD

A rival and Sawyer's polar opposite in so many ways, Jack was simply a do-gooder pain in the ass to the con man in the days after the crash. Sawyer's selfish pursuits offended and angered the doctor, much to James' glee. But when Jack still worked just as hard to save Sawyer's life after Sayid cut his artery, a very begrudging respect was born. And while they locked horns frequently, Sawyer learned a bit about leadership and empathy through the good doctor. And those lessons fully bloomed once Jack and the rest of the Oceanic Six escaped the island. James stepped up, despite frustrations, and looked out for the others who were left behind.

When the two men met again in 1977, they were still just as different but James was a lot more self-assured and confident in his own abilities, something that Jack respected. However, Jack's intention to set off Jughead was a breaking point for James. It resulted in a violent fistfight that was equal parts James trying to stop Jack's crazy plan and years of pent-up mutual aggression released in its most primal state. Unfortunately, Jack won and it ultimately cost James the love of his life, Juliet. A remorseful and guilty Jack was stunned as a broken James bitterly spat at him, "You did this." It created a chasm between the men that was only crossed when days later James made the equally poor call of pulling the wires from the Man in Black's bomb that cost the lives of Sayid, Jin and Sun. The deaths equalized the men again and it allowed them to work together to help save the island and those who could still leave the island. As they said their goodbyes, they finally understood they had shared far more in common experience and loss than they ever could have imagined.

HUGO "HURLEY" REYES

James was pretty awful to Hugo Reyes from day one on the island. Be it a nasty comment about Hurley's weight or his generally dismissive attitude to anything the man had to say, Sawyer should have made a lifelong enemy in Reyes. But Hugo proved to be one of James' greatest advocates. It was Hurley who helped James learn (albeit by trickery) the worth of being nice and that there was a leader inside of him. Regardless of the taunts, Hurley believed in James—a revelation to the tough con man. It created a real friendship between the two, one of the first for James. And over games of Risk, viewings of *Xanadu* and Hurley's trip to Jacob's cabin, James came to value Hurley so much that he would kill to protect him.

DHARMA 1974

Sawyer's initial plan was to spend two weeks on the island, wait for the rest of their missing group, and then return to a life on the mainland.

Unfortunately, no one showed up and as he, Juliet, Miles and Jin were accepted into the DHARMA fold, and two weeks turned into three years.

During this time, James LaFleur reinvented James Ford. His counsel and intelligence were valued, so much so that he was made the trusted Head of Security. It resulted in a period of growth for James in which he could respect himself enough to love wholly, which opened the door for the healthiest relationship of his life with Juliet.

SAWYER'S OFF-ISLAND CONNECTIONS

▌ **Mr. & Mrs. Ford** (James' conned parents)

▌ **Uncle Doug** (Relative who helped raise James)

▌ **Cassidy Phillips** (Sawyer's ex-lover and mother of his child)

▌ **Clementine Phillips** (Sawyer's daughter he never met)

▌ **Hibbs** (Former partner in crime and reason for his trip to Oz)

A TRAIL OF BROKEN HEARTS

With his charming smile and movie star good looks, Sawyer figured out early on how to use his assets to get a lady into his bed whether it was for kicks or a con. Over his two decades as a professional grifter, he broke a lot of hearts—including his own—and here are just a few:

KATE AUSTEN

A fellow survivor and kindred spirit, they were lovers with a strong bond that became a strong friendship.

ANA LUCIA CORTEZ

A fellow survivor who he had angry sex with.

JULIET BURKE

The Other who became the unlikely love of James' life during their DHARMA exile.

SAWYER'S LIBRARY

A closet voracious reader, James outed himself with his fellow survivors by always having a book in hand during the quiet times. Far-sighted, he even gave himself headaches by reading too much until Jack rigged him a pair of glasses. Over the years, James went through an eclectic selection of reading material:

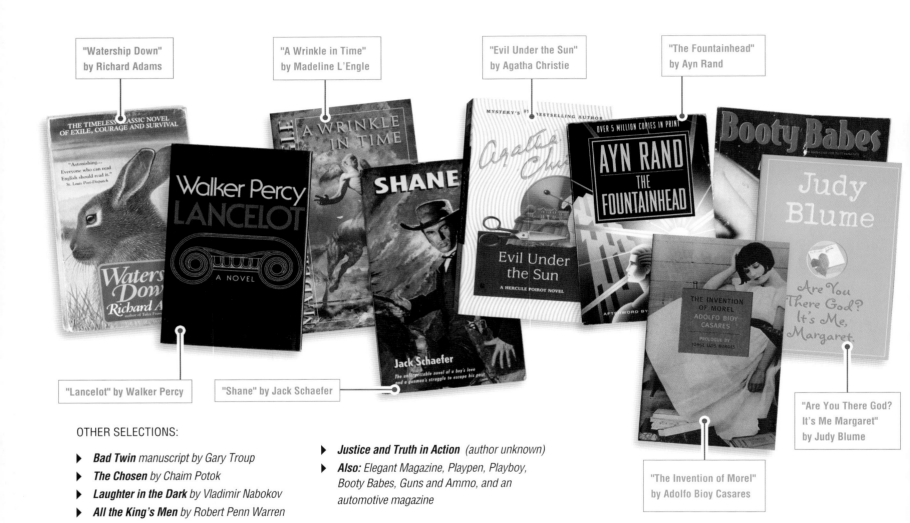

"Watership Down" by Richard Adams

"A Wrinkle in Time" by Madeline L'Engle

"Evil Under the Sun" by Agatha Christie

"The Fountainhead" by Ayn Rand

"Lancelot" by Walker Percy

"Shane" by Jack Schaefer

"The Invention of Morel" by Adolfo Bioy Casares

"Are You There God? It's Me Margaret" by Judy Blume

OTHER SELECTIONS:

- **Bad Twin** manuscript by Gary Troup
- **The Chosen** by Chaim Potok
- **Laughter in the Dark** by Vladimir Nabokov
- **All the King's Men** by Robert Penn Warren
- **Justice and Truth in Action** (author unknown)
- **Also:** Elegant Magazine, Playpen, Playboy, Booty Babes, Guns and Ammo, and an automotive magazine

TOM SAWYER

Considering James' love of literature, it's appropriate that his adopted name of Sawyer is a direct homage to Mark Twain's literary classic "The Adventures of Tom Sawyer." Under the alias of Tom Sawyer, Anthony Cooper turned on the charm and seduced Mary Ford into a con that bilked her and her husband out of all their savings. Mark Twain used the Tom Sawyer character in four novels, where he often portrayed him as an immature, charming and sometimes selfish young man. A product of his Southern antebellum culture, Sawyer was mischievous and came up with a variety of schemes that allowed him to bypass rules to pursue a life of fun. The adolescent con artist even faked his own death and showed up at his funeral. The character's pursuit of pleasure at the expense of others was certainly similar to how James Ford lived life before the island.

JACOB'S TOUCH

On the steps of the church where his dead parents' funeral was held, young James Ford sat with some pieces of loose-leaf paper and a pen that had run out of ink. Out of nowhere, a stranger offered him a pen. The two touched hands as Jacob passed him a gold pen and told him to keep it. As James continued to write his letter to Mr. Sawyer, Jacob expressed his sorrow and walked away.

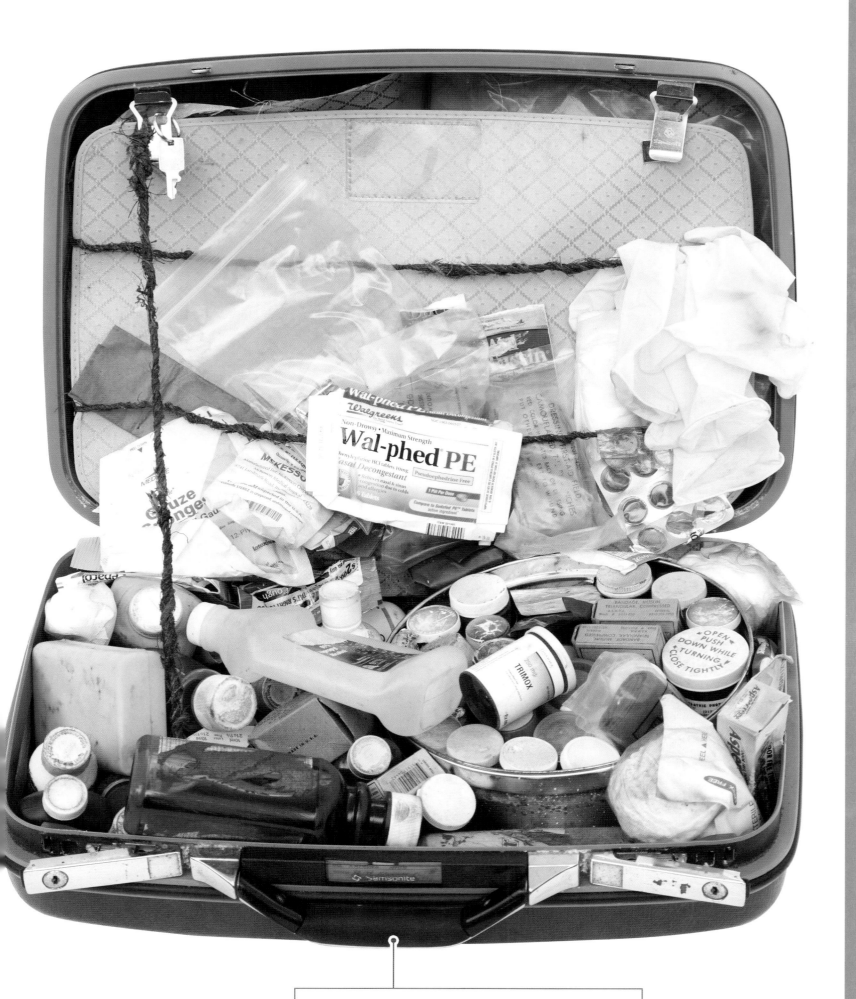

Sawyer kept his collected stash of medical supplies inside this suitcase.

SAYID JARRAH

FACTS & FIGURES

Time On The Island

POST-OCEANIC: 101 days

POST-AJIRA: 4 days

POST-INCIDENT: 7 days

Time As Oceanic Six: 3 years

Year Of Birth: 1967

Country Of Origin: Iraq (Tikrit)

Higher Education: Cairo University

Years In The Iraqi Republican Guard: 5

People Killed By His Hand: 16

Candidate: #16

IRAQI REPUBLICAN GUARD DOSSIER: SAYID HASSAN JARRAH

■ Communications officer, five years

■ Mulazim Awwal, Operation Desert Storm

■ Ra'id (Major), Military Prisoner Interrogation Division

■ Sayid unknowingly tapped into a radio transmission from the 1950s, an early indication that time did not behave normally on the island.

BY THE NUMBERS ✛

Sayid told Ben he waited **8** years to reconnect with Nadia.

Outside of Santa Rosa, Sayid shot one of Widmore's men at **8:15**.

He was **23** when he was captured in the Persian Gulf War.

A trained killer with a tender soul, Sayid Hassan Jarrah spent his life trying to reconcile the two halves of his disparate self. On one hand he was a respected soldier who could torture and kill as duty demanded, but on the other hand it was his first instinct to protect those he loved. His ability to inflict pain on other human beings greatly shamed him; he regretted almost every act of violence he performed. Through the love of two women, Sayid learned to believe in his own worth, yet fate would not let him hold onto happiness for long. Sayid's lifelong challenge was to keep the monster within from swallowing him whole, so that he could see himself as the good man he so desperately wanted to be.

As a member of the Iraqi Republican Guard, Sayid interrogated Falah.

A RENAISSANCE MAN

Mere hours after the plane crash, Sayid proved to be remarkably learned on a variety of subjects, including electronics and cartography. Sawyer dubbed him that "damn Arab genius" because he displayed aptitude in repairing broken items and adapting equipment for different purposes.

▶ He fixed the radio on the transceiver so they could use it on higher ground.

▶ Sayid fixed Rousseau's broken music box.

▶ Using Rousseau's maps, Sayid charted the island.

▶ He repaired the Swan station computer.

▶ With some leftover materials from the plane, Sayid crafted a radar to help the raft navigate at sea.

▶ In the Pearl station, Sayid patched the bank of monitor feeds where they observed Mikhail for the first time.

▶ On the Kahana, he repaired the radio equipment that Michael had sabotaged so Desmond could call Penny.

▶ Under the barracks, Sayid (guided by Daniel Faraday's journal) extracted Jughead's core and reconfigured the warhead to detonate on contact.

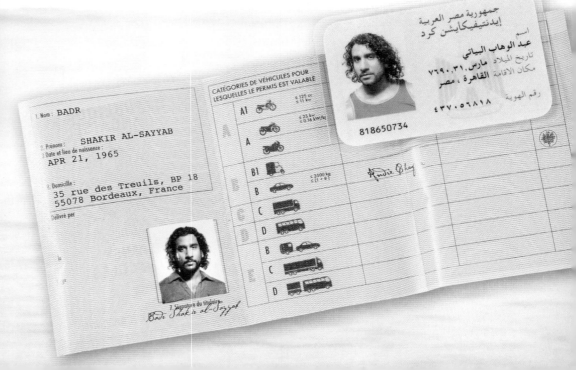

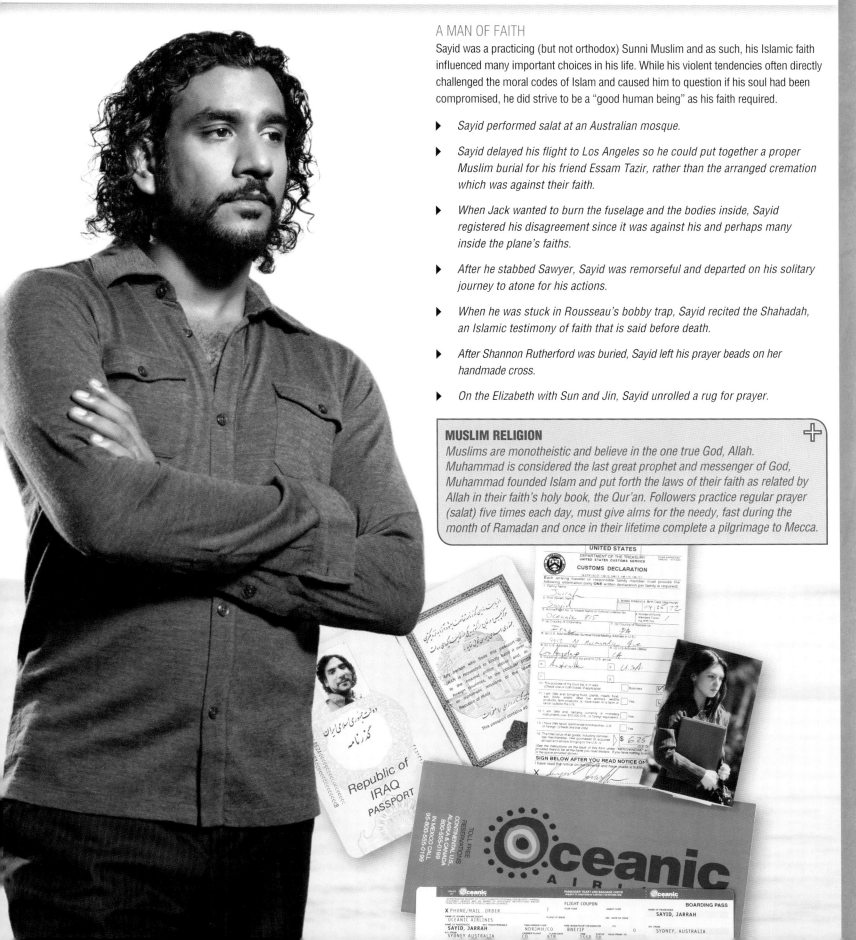

" *My name is Sayid Jarrah and I am a torturer.* "

A MAN OF FAITH

Sayid was a practicing (but not orthodox) Sunni Muslim and as such, his Islamic faith influenced many important choices in his life. While his violent tendencies often directly challenged the moral codes of Islam and caused him to question if his soul had been compromised, he did strive to be a "good human being" as his faith required.

▶ *Sayid performed salat at an Australian mosque.*

▶ *Sayid delayed his flight to Los Angeles so he could put together a proper Muslim burial for his friend Essam Tazir, rather than the arranged cremation which was against their faith.*

▶ *When Jack wanted to burn the fuselage and the bodies inside, Sayid registered his disagreement since it was against his and perhaps many inside the plane's faiths.*

▶ *After he stabbed Sawyer, Sayid was remorseful and departed on his solitary journey to atone for his actions.*

▶ *When he was stuck in Rousseau's bobby trap, Sayid recited the Shahadah, an Islamic testimony of faith that is said before death.*

▶ *After Shannon Rutherford was buried, Sayid left his prayer beads on her handmade cross.*

▶ *On the Elizabeth with Sun and Jin, Sayid unrolled a rug for prayer.*

MUSLIM RELIGION ✛

Muslims are monotheistic and believe in the one true God, Allah. Muhammad is considered the last great prophet and messenger of God, Muhammad founded Islam and put forth the laws of their faith as related by Allah in their faith's holy book, the Qur'an. Followers practice regular prayer (salat) five times each day, must give alms for the needy, fast during the month of Ramadan and once in their lifetime complete a pilgrimage to Mecca.

SAYID JARRAH

SAYID'S ISLAND CONNECTIONS

DANIELLE ROUSSEAU

When Sayid embarked upon his lonely trek around the island to seek some absolution for his dark deeds, he met another sad soul in Danielle Rousseau. On the surface she appeared to be a mad woman, but Sayid saw a kindred spirit behind her sad eyes. As they talked they each revealed the loss in their life that helped shape them. When Danielle worried that he thought she was crazy, he tenderly remarked, "I think you've been alone too long." It was a statement that applied to Sayid as well and he realized that he had voluntarily closed himself off from the world as he pursued the dream of Nadia. In order to move on, he had to embrace the people around him. While Danielle declined to follow his lead, the two remained trusted friends who relied upon one another when needed. It was Sayid who told Alex of her true parentage, which eventually gave Danielle a taste of life as it should have been with her daughter.

SHANNON RUTHERFORD

"I do believe in you."

After Sayid decided to let go of his past with Nadia, he returned to camp and found a connection with Shannon as they translated Danielle's maps. As a man trained to see the truths people concealed inside themselves, Sayid knew that Shannon's selfish exterior masked a vulnerable and loveable woman inside. For him, Shannon represented a completely fresh start. She didn't know about his dark past, so he could woo her as the man he wanted to be—light in heart, romantic and infinitely patient. Together they brought out the best in one another, learned to trust someone outside of themselves, and for Sayid, she made him believe he could be redeemed through love. When Shannon was murdered, though, a good part of his hope died along with her.

BENJAMIN LINUS

Sayid and Ben both proved to be masters of the art of manipulation; it's just Sayid worked in physical violence, while Ben focused on mental annihilation. Their paths first crossed when Ben posed as errant balloonist Henry Gale and Sayid interrogated the little man to see if he really was an Other. Sayid saw through Ben's lies immediately, but Linus was talented at identifying a person's weakest points and exploiting them. Still distraught by Shannon's death, Ben locked into Sayid's palpable loss and pushed the Iraqi to the emotional brink.

When Ben learned much later that Sayid's wife, Nadia, had been murdered by Charles Widmore's men, Linus once again saw an opportunity to exploit the grieving Iraqi. With his Widmore hit list ready to go, Ben convinced an emotionally adrift Sayid that killing and torturing were not a choice, but in his inherent nature. When the job was done and Ben just let him go, Sayid felt the magnitude of how much Ben had used him. When Sayid returned to the island and discovered it was 1977, it was of little consequence that his enemy was only 12 years old; Sayid wanted to exact his revenge from Ben in blood. Sayid then took the role of diabolical manipulator and posed as an Other to lure the young man away from his DHARMA environment. In cold blood, Sayid shot the young boy with a message meant for his older self—"I am a killer."

SAYID'S OFF-ISLAND CONNECTIONS

- **Omer Jarrah** (Brother)
- **Noor "Nadia" Abed Jaseem** (Childhood friend and love)
- **Tariq** (Commanding officer)
- **Kelvin Inman** (U.S. Defense Intelligence agent)
- **Omar** (Superior officer)
- **Amira** (Former torture victim)
- **Essam Tazir** (Former roommate)

A KILLER INSTINCT

Trained by the Iraqi Republican Guard, Sayid could inflict devastating damage on another person with any kind of weapon or even with his own hands. While he constantly struggled internally to keep his dark instincts in check, Sayid often resorted to violence or threats of violence to get results.

"I am a killer."

> *When Sawyer refused to hand over Shannon's asthma inhaler, Sayid put bamboo spikes under his fingernails. Later he put a knife in Sawyer's artery.*

> *After Ana Lucia shot Shannon, Sayid launched himself at her with his gun but Eko and Ana together stopped him.*

> *He interrogated "Henry Gale" and threatened to take off his fingers using a wrench and then beat him bloody. He later returned and almost shot him.*

> *At the Flame, a wounded Sayid engaged in an ugly fight with Mikhail.*

> *During the beach ambush, he shot some of the Others and then snapped one's neck with his legs.*

> *Sayid jumped Martin Keamy in the jungle, beat him and knifed him.*

> *Off the island, Sayid worked as an assassin for Ben. He directly killed five men for him.*

> *To protect Hurley, Sayid threw a thug over a hotel balcony and impaled another killer on a kitchen knife.*

> *Full of vengeance, in 1977 Sayid shot a teenage Ben Linus at point-blank range.*

> *After subjecting him to "the test," Sayid and Dogen engaged in a brutal martial arts fight.*

> *As mandated by Dogen, Sayid stabbed the Man in Black with a dagger but it didn't deter the immortal entity.*

> *Sayid drowned Dogen in the Temple pool and slit Lennon's throat.*

> *On Hydra island, Sayid killed two of Charles Widmore's men and stole Desmond.*

SAYID'S HIT LIST

Peter Avellino: Target acquired at Seychelles golf course

"The Economist": Presumed dead

Elsa: Acquired target's assassin in Berlin, Germany.

Ivan Andropov: Target acquired in Moscow, Russia

Unnamed Widmore goon: Target aquired outside of Santa Rosa Mental Health Institute

"Hope is a very dangerous thing to lose."

AN OCEANIC SIX LIFE

After the Oceanic Six press conference, Karen Decker let Sayid know that an unauthorized guest—Noor "Nadia" Abed Jaseem—was waiting for him outside. Stunned to see her, the two embraced, kissed and finally embarked upon the life they had always dreamed of together. They married and blissfully spent time together as they stayed connected to the Oceanic circle. Nine months into their new life as they discussed the destination of their one-year anniversary at a crosswalk, Nadia was the victim of a brutal hit-and-run and died.

Despondent, Sayid took Nadia's body back to Tikrit, Iraq for her traditional Muslim burial. On a rooftop, Sayid spotted Ben Linus taking pictures of her procession and chased him down. Ben told Sayid he was trying to find Ishmael Bakir, the man hired by Charles Widmore to kill Nadia. A day later, the pair set up Bakir and Sayid emptied his gun into the man. Not satisfied, he asked to join Ben's war against Widmore.

Sayid attended the press conference with the other Oceanic Six.

Nadia and Sayid reunited after his return as one of the Oceanic Six.

ALREADY DEAD

After spending the better part of two years mourning the loss of Nadia through vengeance-fueled assassinations, Sayid was a shell of the man he once was. He sought penance in building charity homes in the Dominican Republic but a threat to Hurley's safety pulled him back into the killing game. However, his heart was sick of it all, and he left his friends once again only to be trapped by Ilana in a sting that forced him to return to the island via Ajira flight 316.

"I have no life. They took it from me."

Just how lost Sayid was became clear when he chose to shoot a young Ben Linus to get back at Ben's future self; the man who would manipulate him 30 years later. It was a step too far and something was never the same inside Sayid again. Even Sayid recognized the karma when Roger Linus shot him for what he did to Ben. When Sayid was later immersed into the Temple pool, he wasn't immediately healed or saved, but he did rise again. His soul infected with the "sickness," Sayid was extremely vulnerable to what the Man in Black later tempted him with. The only thing Sayid ever wanted died in his arms, but the Man in Black promised he would see her again.

Roger Linus recognized a disguised Sayid and shot him to exact revenge for killing young Benjamin.

In an emotionless state, Sayid sleepwalked through the drama between the Man in Black and his friends. It was only when he made the choice to leave Desmond Hume in the well and join his friends on Widmore's submarine that his true soul once again emerged. As the Man in Black's bomb raced to its detonation, Sayid grabbed it, told Jack about Desmond and then raced away from his friends so the bomb wouldn't kill them too. In his last selfless act, the "killer" proved that his own death could free him from his sins and be his honorable path back to redemption.

JACOB'S TOUCH

In Los Angeles nine months after their wedding, Sayid and Nadia were about to cross the street when a stranger asked Sayid for assistance. A moment later, Nadia turned around, triumphantly waved her lost sunglasses at her husband and was violently hit by a car. Jacob put his hand on a shocked Sayid's shoulder and then disappeared as Jarrah rushed to a crumpled Nadia who whispered, "Take me home" in Arabic and died.

A DOOMED LOVE

While two women claimed Sayid's heart, one owned it the longest: Noor "Nadia" Abed Jaseem. The two met as children at their school in Tikrit, where the privileged Nadia resorted to throwing Sayid in mud puddles to gain his affection. Instead, he ignored the pushy little girl. As they grew up, they lost track of one another as Sayid went to finishing school and university, while Nadia went underground as a Kurdish and Shiite insurgent. For that she was tortured repeatedly by the Republican Guard until she found herself in Sayid's interrogation room. Their chemistry was reawakened and that dark reunion would mark the first of several as they randomly wove their way in and out of each other's lives.

"You will see me in the next life, if not in this one."

Sayid staged his own shooting to help Nadia escape her execution. He didn't follow her for fear his family would suffer retribution, so she gave him her photo with a private inscription.

He then left the Guard in 1997 and spent the next seven years on the hunt for Nadia, to no avail. In 2004 he was extorted by the CIA for information about her whereabouts in exchange for his help in a sting operation to bring down Essam Tazir. After that, he was booked on Oceanic 815 to LAX bound for Irvine, CA, where Nadia lived. The plane crash pre-empted their reunion.

In 2005, Nadia met Sayid after his Oceanic Six press conference. After a lifetime of bad timing, they were only given nine months together before her untimely death.

Sayid confronted Nadia during her interrogation.

Ben preyed upon Sayid's grief to get him on his side.

SAYID'S FATHER

▶ **CONNECTION:** Father of Sayid & Omer Jarrah

A soldier in the Iraqi Republican Guard, he was a strict father who encouraged his children to mature fast. He once demanded that his eldest son, Omer, slay a chicken with a knife to prove that he was no longer a child. When Omer's younger sibling, Sayid, killed the chicken with his bare hands, their father commended Sayid's actions, but looked down upon Omer's failure to act.

Sayid's father was viewed by the Iraqis as a great hero to their cause. This view was not lost on an Iraqi soldier named Tariq, who was appalled at Sayid's cooperation with American soldiers who were searching for intel about missing helicopter pilots. He claimed that his father would be ashamed at the way Sayid, a former Republican Guard soldier himself, was colluding with the enemy.

SCOTT WHEELER

▶ **CONNECTION:** Guard at St. Francis Hospital; fought with Kate Austen

In 2002, Scott Wheeler was working as a Security Guard at St. Francis Hospital in Iowa when he had a run-in with Kate Austen. Kate had secretly returned to her hometown to visit her cancer-stricken mother, Diane Jansen. During the visit, Diane began crying out for help. Kate tried to flee, but ran into Wheeler. When he attempted to call for backup, Kate struck him with his own walkie-talkie and escaped with the aid of her childhood sweetheart Tom Brennan, a doctor at the hospital.

SEAMUS

▶ **CONNECTION:** Worked for Charles Widmore during his occupation of Hydra island

Headstrong, focused and loyal, Seamus worked tirelessly to carry out the plans of Charles Widmore. Whenever Widmore's intentions were disrupted or threatened in any way, Seamus was always there to restore order. During his associate Zoe's failed attempt to con Sawyer, Seamus came to her aid and took Sawyer into their custody by gunpoint.

Seamus' post along the Hydra island beach proved important when the Man in Black arrived via the outrigger to deliver his warning to Widmore. Seamus bravely stood firm, protecting his boss, even though Widmore knew how useless Seamus' rifle was against the mysterious Man in Black. Seamus later teamed up with Zoe again during the nighttime abduction of Jin-Soo Kwon from the main island.

Unfortunately, he didn't always get along with Zoe. When Widmore signaled them to bring the "package" (Desmond Hume) from the sealed submarine compartment, Seamus was visibly upset at Desmond's condition. Although Zoe admitted she gave him a large dose for the long trip to the island, Seamus showed disdain for his colleague's decision. Seamus was key in getting the magnetizing room operational for Widmore's test on Desmond. During the smoke monster's nighttime attack on Hydra island, Seamus was killed by the entity as it tossed his body into one of the polar bear cages.

SENET

One day on the island's shoreline, an ancient senet set washed up on the beach where a teenaged Boy in Black found it. Aware that it might be special, he secreted the wooden box secured with leather straps away into the jungle. Under the cover of the foliage, the Boy in Black examined the contents: five white stones, five black stones and four sticks.

The Boy in Black happily shared his new treasure with his brother Jacob. Oddly, the darker-haired boy seemed to inherently know how to play the game. He offered Jacob the white stones, took the black stones as his own, and made his twin promise not to tell Mother what they had found. In truth, Mother lied about the origin of the game to keep her favored son in the dark about the truth of the outside world.

As the boys grew up, senet became one of their favorite pastimes. But the Boy in Black steadfastly enforced his rules of the game with his brother. He explained, "I found it. One day you can make up your own game and everyone will have to play by your rules."

When Mother decided to destroy the human encampment and all who lived in it, the Man in Black's senet game was spared from the full fury of the conflagration. Incensed, he retrieved it and left it in the caves for his Mother to find. When she returned, Mother opened the box for the first time and held the stones as the Man in Black crept up behind her and ran her through with his dagger. Her lifeless body crumpled onto the game board.

After the brothers' fateful violent confrontation at the heart of the island, Jacob brought the Man in Black's body back to the caves. He placed his dead brother and Mother together there in repose with one white senet stone and one black senet stone. Their remains were found by Jack and Hurley two millennia later.

SETH NORRIS

▶ **CONNECTION: Pilot of Oceanic flight 815**

When Frank Lapidus overslept his alarm, his job of flying Oceanic flight 815 was given to Captain Seth Norris. Norris married his childhood sweetheart when he turned 19 and always wore his wedding ring. Years later after flight 815 went missing, his close colleague and friend, Lapidus, saw a news story on television that disturbed him. It reported to show Norris' dead body inside the cockpit—crashed deep underwater at the bottom of the ocean—but Lapidus knew something was wrong: the corpse's ring finger was bare and Norris always wore his band. This was all part of the elaborate hoax by Charles Widmore to prevent anyone from looking for survivors of the missing flight 815.

COCKPIT CRASH-SITE

On the island, Norris was found alive in the crashed cockpit section of flight 815. The cockpit became detached from the main body of the plane and ended up further inland in the jungle. Charlie, Jack, and Kate found Norris unconscious the next day after the survivors of the crash on the beach had rallied together.

When Norris awoke, Jack gave him water and inspected his injuries. He was bleeding profusely from multiple head injuries and his right eye was completely closed and swollen. Norris became more agitated when Jack explained it had been 16 hours since the crash and no rescue had yet appeared. The pilot responded by saying, "Six hours in, our radio went out; no one could see us. We turned back to land in Fiji. By the time we hit turbulence, we were 1,000 miles off course. They're looking for us in the wrong place." Norris showed them the transceiver. It was then that the unearthly roar first heard by the castaways on the previous night—their first on the island—returned.

POST-CRASH DEATH

The first kill by the mysterious smoke monster was swift: Norris was ripped out of the cockpit through the windshield. He was later found dead, bloody, and with several broken bones, tossed into the branches of a tall tree. Since Norris wasn't on Jacob's list of candidates, the smoke monster could kill him without breaking the rules.

A HISTORY OF THE GAME ✛

A two-player strategy game, senet was invented by the ancient Egyptians almost 5,000 years ago. It was played throughout their society, across classes from Pharaoh to peasants. Archeologists have excavated many senet sets from Egyptian burial tombs and found the game first depicted on the tomb walls of Hesy-Ra, the third dynasty physician to Pharaoh Djoser, circa 2650 B.C.

All modern knowledge of the rules is based upon interpretations of hieroglyphics by archeologists over the centuries. Experts have agreed that the basic game board consisted of three parallel rows of ten squares. The two players strategically maneuvered their five game pieces (sometimes up to seven) through the squares with the goal to be the first to clear all of their pieces off the board. Players would throw four sticks to determine the numbers of moves made with their pieces.

The word senet translated in English means "the game of passing," which reflected the spiritual connotations that became synonymous with the game over the centuries. Created as a purely non-ecumenical pastime, Egyptians came to believe that as they played the game they could influence the gods' judgments on their afterlife. The squares were representative of a soul's journey to the afterlife.

Senet's popularity migrated to the Roman Empire and the Greeks, who created their own version called Grammai. With the dawn of Christianity and the end of the Egyptian dynasties, senet eventually disappeared but it influenced many an off-shoot game including what would become the modern-day game of backgammon.

SHANNON RUTHERFORD, SEE PAGE 324

SHAWNA & TRAVIS

▶ **CONNECTION: Caused a domestic disturbance Ana Lucia Cortez investigated**

Shawna and Travis lived together at 2210 South Veteran, Los Angeles, California. One afternoon, a dispute between the couple escalated to the point where neighbors called the police to intervene. Mike Walton and his partner, Ana Lucia Cortez, responded to the domestic disturbance call.

They found Shawna, holding her child, engaged in an explosive argument with Travis as he was attempting to leave her and take a television he claimed to have purchased. Unknown to the couple, Ana Lucia had recently returned to active duty four months after being shot and losing her unborn child. Travis told both police officers that Shawna had hit him, but Ana Lucia's fragile state caused her to overreact. She drew her weapon and ordered Travis onto the ground. Walton immediately stepped in, calmed Ana Lucia, and convinced her to holster her weapon.

SHERIFF WILLIAMS

▶ **CONNECTION: Officer who stopped John Locke and Eddie Colburn**

Sheriff Williams was a member of the Humboldt County, California police department. On his regular patrol, he pulled over John Locke and his passenger Eddie Colburn for a broken tail light. He asked both men to exit the truck and inquired what was under the tarp in the bed of the pickup to which Locke responded "guns and groceries." He explained the guns were legally purchased and documented in a red notebook. The sheriff looked over the paperwork, but threatened to arrest John for picking up a hitchhiker. Eddie immediately covered for John by telling him John was his uncle. With nothing left to pursue, Sheriff Williams let the men go.

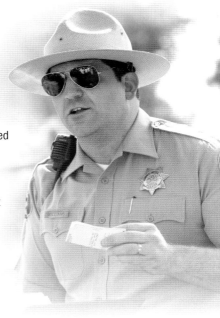

SHERRY

▶ **CONNECTION: Love interest of Edmund Burke, Juliet Burke's ex-husband**

Not afraid to mix business with pleasure, Sherry started a relationship with Edmund Burke in 2001. Sherry and Edmund were not concerned about displaying their affection for one another at Edmund's place of work—the Medical Research Laboratory at Miami Central University—especially as Edmund swiftly employed Sherry as his new research assistant, something that equally infuriated and amused Juliet.

"Jules? Could you please turn off the lights?"

— Spoken by Edmund to Juliet while with Sherry

SHANNON RUTHERFORD

FACTS & FIGURES

Time On The Island

POST-OCEANIC: 48 days

Born: Los Angeles, CA

Ailments: Acute asthma

Oceanic Flight 815 Seat: 9F

Candidate: #31

Shannon Rutherford didn't exactly charm her fellow passengers in the aftermath of their cumulative tragedy. Most of their first impressions were of a young woman shrieking wildly in shock amongst the wreckage. After Shannon pulled herself together, people's esteem hardly improved as she petulantly and selfishly refused to lift a finger as she waited to be rescued. If it weren't for Boone Carlyle, her protective stepbrother, not many on the beach would have had anything to do with her. But like everyone else who brought their demons with them to the island, Shannon's abrasive nature was a carefully crafted wall she erected to protect her from connecting with people whom she feared would abandon her in the end. But as days passed without rescue, Shannon realized she had to start opening up or risk being ostracized by everyone. With the help of Sayid Jarrah, Shannon came to believe in herself again and saw the island as a do-over opportunity. Sadly just as she started anew, her journey came to a heartbreaking end.

Shannon had a rocky relationship with her stepmother, Sabrina Carlyle.

Just as their romance blossomed, Shannon was mistakenly killed by Ana Lucia.

"Everyone gets a new life on this island. I'd like to start now."

A DADDY'S GIRL

Shannon was raised by her single father, Adam Rutherford, until she was eight years old. She was the center of his world until he brought a new woman into his life, businesswoman Sabrina Carlyle. The couple married and, together with her 10-year-old son Boone, they became a blended family. However, Sabrina was jealous of Shannon's relationship with Adam, so they never bonded as mother and daughter.

Shannon grew up without a lot of focus, as her father's money gave her a comfortable life. By the end of high school, she decided to pursue dance professionally and taught ballet on the side. She even applied for a dance internship at the Martha Graham Dance Company in New York City. But Shannon's world fell apart when her father died in a head-on car collision. She found out a few weeks later that she had gotten the internship, but her bank account went into overdraft. Sabrina coldly explained that Shannon would have to take care of herself financially as Adam had not willed his daughter anything and she would not support her. Shannon then asked to stay with Boone, but he revealed he was relocating to work for his mother. Betrayed and angry, Shannon proudly declined his financial support.

USING BOONE

Shannon returned from France with a new disdain for men, especially her stepbrother. She preyed upon his good nature and the feelings she knew he harbored for her to get money from him and Sabrina. Even on the island, she continued to lash out at him until his unexpected death led to her undoing.

▶ Pretended to date three guys who Boone paid off to leave her.

▶ Married and then separated from an unnamed man (buy-off unknown).

▶ Lured Boone to Australia with a con to pay off her "abusive" boyfriend, Bryan.

▶ Got drunk and flirted with Boone in his hotel room, which led to sex.

▶ Screamed at Boone in Sydney for not getting first-class tickets.

▶ Ignorantly refused any of Boone's Apollo bar post-crash.

"I am so not moving to the rape caves!"

SELFISH SHANNON

While Shannon's fellow passengers at least attempted to get along, she clung to her bratty ways, mostly to mask her fears.

▶ Agreed to watch Sayid's bag in Sydney, then walked away. To spite Boone, she lied to security about an Arab leaving his bags.

▶ Loudly whined about Marshal Mars dying too callously.

▶ Flirted with Charlie Pace to get him to catch her a fish.

▶ Desolate after Boone's death, she stole a gun to kill John Locke.

ATTITUDE ADJUSTMENT

Very slowly, sometimes not even for the right reasons, Shannon chose to give of herself on the island, which eventually opened her heart to love.

▶ Hiked to the valley and reluctantly translated the French distress message.

▶ Despite distractions, lit the beach signal bottle rocket on time.

▶ Agreed to translate Rousseau's island map with Sayid.

▶ Agreed to take care of Vincent for Walt.

"LA MER"
Shannon took a job as the au pair of one of her former ballet students, Sophie, and her little brother, Laurent, in St. Tropez, France. She also had an affair with their father, Philippe, the first of many men she learned to manipulate. While in France, she learned the classic Charles Trenet song "La Mer" and the basics of the language she would later use on the island.

UNEXPECTED SAVIOR

Perhaps the most unlikely couple on the island, Sayid and Shannon began a tentative romance about 20 days after the crash. Shannon thawed under Sayid's patient attention and showed him her softer side. However, she was quick to test his loyalty like the time when she defended John Locke in Boone's death. But when he built her a tent and then confessed his love, she finally let herself love him.

"I know as soon as we get out of here, you're going to leave me."

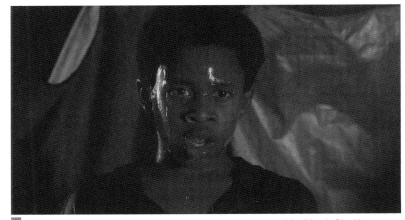

It's unknown if Shannon's visits from Walt were real or part of the Man in Black's con.

WHISPERS AND WALT

Walt's request that Shannon watch over Vincent represented the only time someone had asked her to do something important and, as such, it created a bond between them. At her most vulnerable moments, like Vincent's disappearance or after she was intimate with Sayid, Shannon had frighteningly real visions of Walt. Initially, no one believed her, but Sayid was present and saw Walt's third appearance, which put Shannon in the path of a twitchy Ana Lucia, who shot her dead in a blind panic. Whether it was really Walt with warnings or the manifestation of the Man in Black remains unknown.

THE SICKNESS

The different kinds of "sickness" on the island were very frightening and often meant that an intangible, "spiritual infection" had occurred. From disturbing shifts in personality to a collective belief that, post the Incident, DHARMA had done something to cause a sickness on the island, the variations all had one thing in common—disastrous consequences.

THE SMOKE MONSTER'S DARKNESS

The sickness created by the island's smoke monster was a darkness that would grow inside the host. A wound or entry point meant that the smoke monster could enter the body and darken the host's spirit. This form of sickness caused a change in the carrier's personality, often resulting in malevolent acts carried out with a complete lack of emotion. Those close to the carrier were often killed without any motive.

THE FRENCH SCIENCE TEAM

Danielle Rousseau firmly believed that the sickness took hold of her crew. After Nadine and Montand were killed by the smoke monster, her boyfriend—and father of her unborn daughter—Robert, as well as Lacombe and Brennan, descended into the catacomb underneath the Temple wall. They were convinced that Montand was still alive and could be saved, as they heard his voice—a trick by the smoke monster to lure them inside.

Once the three French scientists returned to the surface, they were never the same again. A sinister calm had descended over them; Rousseau shot all three after they showed homicidal tendencies towards her.

Danielle killed Lacombe and Brennan, fearing they had become "infected."

CLAIMED BY DARKNESS

When Sayid Jarrah was placed in the Temple spring, the Others considered it a test to determine if Sayid was infected. Although he was clinically dead for two hours, he suddenly returned to life. This caused Dogen to be suspicious of what brought him back.

Dogen blew ash across Sayid's body and tortured him with electricity and a hot poker. Although Lennon and Dogen told Sayid he passed their test, they told Jack Shepard the "infection" meant Sayid had been "claimed;" a darkness was growing inside him and once it reached his heart, there would be no hope of bringing Sayid's good side back.

Following his own interpretation of the "sickness," Dogen did not have a complete and total understanding of how it, or the smoke monster's influence, actually worked.

AARON PARANOIA

When Aaron developed a rash and fever shortly after his birth, Rousseau told Claire Littleton she thought her baby had been infected by the sickness. Rousseau even warned that Aaron would need to be killed if he was infected. Fortunately, Aaron's fever broke the next morning.

The word "quarantine" was stenciled on the inside of the Arrow's main door.

QUARANTINE & FERTILITY

Everybody who worked in the Swan station believed that a situation had occurred where something bad was present—a "sickness," hence the fear of infection, the inoculations, and the quarantine warnings. They could not ascertain whether DHARMA caused it or if it was something the Hostiles took from DHARMA and used against them. Before the Incident in 1977 when Eloise Hawking was the leader of the Others, people on the island could safely give birth. When Eloise left the island to give birth to her own child, Daniel Faraday, after the Incident, Charles Widmore assumed control. It was from that point forward that women would tragically die during a pregnancy.

PRECAUTIONS

Kelvin Joe Inman and Desmond Hume took injections while working inside the Swan and Inman also donned a HAZMAT suit as a safeguard when he ventured outside. Inman was aware of the Purge, the time when a gaseous chemical agent was released from the Tempest station to kill off DHARMA. Both the suit and the injections were considered necessary in case some kind of residual toxin remained from the Purge. Over time, Inman grew more cynical about the necessity of the precautions.

Robert threatened to kill Danielle when he became infected.

> **Some of us continued to search for the meaning of those numbers... But then the sickness came.** — Spoken by Danielle Rousseau to Hugo "Hurley" Reyes

FERAL CLAIRE +

Dogen also believed that Claire Littleton had been "claimed" and she was tortured/tested by Dogen in the same way as Sayid. Although she was distraught and maddened by Aaron's absence, Claire's feral side did not quash her morality. She trusted the Man in Black and was manipulated by him for three years, but didn't become his puppet.

SIMMONS AND SIMON PACE, SEE PAGE 330

SMOKE MONSTER

When Jacob threw his brother into the heart of the island, the consequence was the creation of the smoke monster. The Man in Black's spirit became fused with the all-powerful force that lay hidden inside the island's heart, a source of malevolence, evil and darkness. In his purest form of hate and rage, the Man in Black as the smoke monster was a seemingly unstoppable dark force of nature. The smoke monster was a purely instinctual being that simply acted first, with no conscience and no remorse.

SETH NORRIS
Sixteen hours after the crash, the smoke monster pulled flight 815 pilot Seth Norris through the cockpit windshield, eventually resulting in his violent death.

THE FREIGHTER MERCENARIES
Mayhew had his guts torn out, while the other mercenaries suffered severe injuries during the smoke monster's attack.

ILANA'S TEAM
After the Man in Black used John Locke's image to persuade Ben to kill Jacob, he took on the smoke monster form and wreaked havoc on Ilana's team inside the Taweret base.

CREW OF THE *BLACK ROCK*
After Jacob brought more people to the island, the smoke monster tore through the ship's crew. It then found Richard Alpert in the belly of the ship and realized he could be manipulated for his own gains.

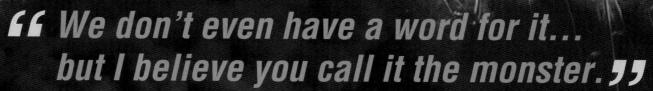

" We don't even have a word for it... but I believe you call it the monster. "

— Spoken by Benjamin Linus

PROTECTION AGAINST THE MONSTER

The Man in Black was immortal and virtually unstoppable. Only a few key elements affected the smoke monster.

SACRED ASH: Encircling yourself with ancient ash protected the person inside from the smoke monster.

SONAR FENCE: When the DHARMA fence was turned on, the frequency prevented the entity from traveling through it.

WATER: Standing in it, being splashed by it and traveling over rivers on the island wasn't a problem. But the smoke monster claimed he could not fly across great expanses of water.

THE FRENCH SCIENCE TEAM

The smoke monster violently killed Nadine, then dragged Montand underneath the Temple's outer wall. The other team members went inside to save him, but emerged seemingly changed. Rousseau was convinced they returned infected with a "sickness" and killed them.

MR. EKO

Refusing to offer his "confession" and repent for his past sins, the smoke monster grabbed Eko and repeatedly threw him against the trees and ground until he was dead.

THE TEMPLE OTHERS

Once Dogen was killed, the smoke monster raged throughout every crevice, killing those who didn't leave.

329

SIMMONS

▶ **CONNECTION:** Worked for Charles Widmore at the Hydra station

Simmons was one of several technicians hired by Charles Widmore to accompany him to Hydra island to test the electromagnetic resistance of Desmond Hume. As Zoe and Seamus attempted to field test their electromagnetic solenoids per Widmore's last-minute orders, a problem with the generator prompted them to send Simmons into the wooden test shed to locate any faulty contacts. As Simmons tested the wiring, another tech inside the monitoring station found the

source of the problem—a bad breaker—and flipped it. That immediately triggered the coils, which essentially fried Simmons to death. Widmore purposely observed Simmons' charred face before the body was taken away for disposal.

SIMON PACE

▶ **CONNECTION:** Father of Charlie & Liam Pace

Simon Pace was the husband of Megan Pace and the father of Liam and Charlie. A Manchester butcher by trade, Simon had no-nonsense, working-class ideals about life and how to rear his boys. When Charlie was young, Simon signed up his son for a summer camp at the Butlins pool to teach him how to swim. He stood in the pool and promised his frightened son that he would catch him if he jumped. After pleading with his son several times, Charlie eventually jumped but Simon let his son sink. When Charlie emerged from the water paddling, they both knew he had learned a valuable lesson about doing things on his own. As the boys got older, it was clear that Simon loved them but he did not love their pursuit of music as a profession and wanted them to learn a proper trade.

VISIONS

On the island, Charlie once saw his father in a bizarre vision in which Simon was butchering meat in the Pace living room. While doing so, he also discouraged Charlie from a life in music. Simon then put a plastic baby doll on the board and cut off its head.

SQUIRREL BABY

▶ **CONNECTION:** Substitute baby created by Claire Littleton

Three years of virtually no human contact on the island took its toll on Claire Littleton's mental health. Although she had the company of the person she referred to as "her friend" (the Man in Black), it was not knowing who had taken her son, Aaron, that drove her mad.

Under the assumption that the Others had abducted Aaron, Claire created a baby substitute to fill the void. The "squirrel baby" consisted of an animal skull with button eyes attached to a crudely sewn-together doll made from the pelts and bones of various small animals Claire had killed and eaten. Although its outward appearance was startling, the creation helped Claire deal with Aaron's absence to a certain degree.

"It's all I had."
— Spoken by Claire to Kate

SPANISH DOCTOR

▶ **CONNECTION:** Doctor who refused to help Richard "Ricardo" Alpert's ailing wife

An affluent doctor on the Canary Island of Tenerife in 1867, his status and occupation afforded him all the luxuries that money could buy at the time. He catered to a clientele of wealthy merchants and plantation landowners, which allowed him to reside in an opulent home staffed with servants.

On one stormy evening, a modest field hand named Ricardo (Richard Alpert) arrived at the doctor's door. Alpert had frantically ridden half a day's journey in the rain to seek the doctor's help in treating his sick wife Isabella. Unfortunately, the doctor refused to travel in the elements to treat Isabella, but he offered medicine for a steep price. Alpert handed over everything he had, including his wife's gold cross, but the scornful doctor refused. Desperate, Alpert begged for the medicine and tussled with the physician, causing the doctor to slip and strike his head on the corner of his oak dinner table. The head injury proved fatal.

SPANISH DOCTOR'S SERVANT

▶ **CONNECTION:** Worked for the Spanish Doctor

The house servant of a wealthy Tenerife doctor, the servant attempted to keep field hand Ricardo out of his master's home. After he was overpowered by the desperate Alpert, the doctor ordered the servant to find blankets to sop up the water tracked in by his unwelcome guest. When the servant returned, he was shocked to see the doctor dead on the floor as a wide-eyed Alpert grasped a bottle of medicine. The servant reported the altercation to the authorities, who then pursued Ricardo.

ST. SEBASTIAN HOSPITAL

Located in Los Angeles, California, St. Sebastian Hospital was the workplace of Jack and Christian Shephard and the location for many significant events before and after the crash of flight 815.

The logo for St. Sebastian Hospital

ST. SEBASTIAN ✛
A Christian martyr, St. Sebastian is the patron saint of athletes and plague sufferers.

ADAM & SARAH

Shannon Rutherford's father, Adam, 57, died at St. Sebastian after a collision with the woman who would later become Jack's wife, Sarah Wagner. Sarah's car blew a tire, flipped over the highway divider, and struck Adam's SUV head-on. Adam suffered massive chest trauma and had stopped breathing when he arrived at St. Sebastian. Jack made the call to attend to Sarah first, because her breathing was deteriorating fast. A piece of the steering column was lodged in her chest, which had pierced her pericardium, the double-walled sac that contains the heart. Adam's heart stopped at 8:15 a.m., just as Jack managed to remove the column from Sarah's chest, saving her life.

Although Sarah suffered a broken back, ruptured spleen, and abdominal bleeding, Jack was able to save her life and restore her ability to walk. Engaged at the time, Sarah married Jack sometime later.

THE BUSONI CASE

Jack attempted to help Angelo Busoni, an elderly Italian man with an advanced spinal tumor. Christian concluded that Angelo wasn't a candidate for surgery, but his daughter, Gabriela Busoni believed otherwise. Through extensive research, Gabriela discovered Jack's successful spinal surgery and she insisted that Jack attempt to help her father. Jack's inability to quit led him to accept the case against his father's judgment.

After a month's worth of tests, Jack advised that Angelo could live a normal life for another year, but Gabriela insisted on the surgery. After seven hours and the successful removal of the tumor, Angelo's heart stopped and he died on the operating table.

Jack's brief kiss with Gabriela and the time he spent away from Sarah damaged their marriage even more.

Emotionally fragile, Gabriela kissed Jack after learning that her father had died. But it was the huge amount of time Jack had spent working on the Busoni case, and away from his wife Sarah, that damaged their marriage beyond repair.

" *Tell him I'm very sorry, but he's not a candidate for surgery.* "
— Spoken by Christian to Gabriela

BETH'S DEATH

In September 2004, Jack struggled to prevent Beth, a woman in a major car accident, from dying on the operating table. Instead of being a simple operation, Beth's case put the final nail in the coffin of Christian Shephard's medical career and pushed him one step further towards his death.

Beth was bleeding out and Jack managed to seal a ruptured artery, but her heart stopped and couldn't be restarted with CPR. Jack refused to call the time of death and desperately tried to resuscitate her. When Christian reentered the O.R., Jack angrily demanded Christian call the time of death, as controversially, Christian had been working on Beth before Jack was called onto the case. A nurse rushed to get Jack as she'd noticed Christian's hands were shaking while working on Beth—a sign he had been drinking. His unsteady hands caused Christian to accidentally cut her hepatic artery open.

After Beth's death, Christian convinced his son to sign the paperwork that stated Beth died as a result of massive internal injuries, despite his best efforts to save her. Conflicted, Jack agreed to sign the statement, but events took a more serious turn when Beth's widower refused to accept the conclusion and threatened to sue St. Sebastian.

Jack questioned Christian's performance in the operating room

Christian went on record during the hearing that followed that Beth went into cardiac arrest as a result of her blood pressure dropping from the massive injuries she sustained from the car crash, and that there was nothing they could have done to save her. However, when it was announced by one of the administrators that Beth was pregnant, this triggered Jack to confess the truth. He revised his statement and made it clear that he entered the O.R. well into the procedure and took over from an incapacitated Christian, who had cut open her hepatic artery that led to her death. Christian was subsequently fired from St. Sebastian, had his medical license removed, and fled to Australia where he died from self-induced alcohol poisoning.

Jack changed his testimony at Christian's hearing, which led to Christian's dismissal.

HOSPITAL STAFF AND VARIOUS PATIENTS

Nurse Andrea	Dr. Erika Stevenson
Dr. Evelyn Ariza	Beth and her husband
Ms. Berenberg	

OCEANIC SIX ERA

Jack returned to work at St. Sebastian after he and the Oceanic Six successfully left the island, but his life in LA wasn't smooth sailing. Jack had doubts about leaving the island, guilt from leaving people behind, and ambivalence about Kate raising Aaron. These doubts and his fear that he would become the same man as his father, led to severe depression, his subsequent alcoholism, and prescription drug addition. Just like his father before him, Jack was terminated from St. Sebastian. Shortly afterwards, Benjamin Linus found him and convinced him to gather the Oceanic Six for their return to the island.

THE STAFF

> ## "You're going to die. They're going to cut him out of you..."
>
> — Spoken by Alex to Claire

One of the most important stations, not necessarily for the DHARMA Initiative, but for the time when Benjamin Linus led the Others, the Staff was a key building for studying the fertility problems on the island. Built by DHARMA in the 1970s, the Staff was an underground headquarters with medical bays that featured nurseries for children, plus rooms with facilities for the delivery of babies.

However, sometime after the Purge, the Others moved into the vacant DHARMA barracks and utilized the stations DHARMA had built. The last birth on the island was Ethan Rom's in 1977. After that, the station was used to study whatever radioactive fallout occurred after the Incident and whether or not it contributed to, or was unrelated to, the fertility issues on the island.

Inexplicably, every woman who conceived on the island never came to term and always died before giving birth. Greatly troubled by this, the Others took every opportunity to kidnap children who arrived on the island to expand and extend their group. They also abducted pregnant women who appeared on the island to try and decipher why the island was no longer allowing them to procreate. During this period, Dr. Juliet Burke was brought to the island because of her extraordinary success and innovative experiments with fertility.

CLAIRE'S KIDNAPPING

Oceanic flight 815 survivor Claire Littleton was kidnapped by Ethan Rom while she was still pregnant, and was taken to the Staff. Two weeks later, she escaped to the beach camp with no memory of what occurred.

With the aid of clinical psychologist Elizabeth "Libby" Smith and her meditative techniques, Claire was able to recall the memories of her abduction. She later returned to the Staff with the aid of Kate Austen and Danielle Rousseau.

Claire was terrified the Others had done something to Aaron and that he needed medicine from the station. On visiting the Staff, Claire gained a greater understanding of her time there and closure on the traumatic experience. She recalled Alex Rousseau helping her escape, their obsession and paranoia with the dire fertility problems on the island driving them to desperation.

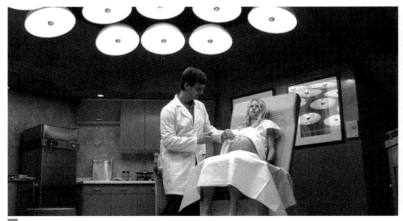

Ethan Rom administered shots to Claire while inside the Staff.

> ## "You're not the only one who didn't find what they were looking for. "
>
> — Spoken by Danielle Rousseau to Claire Littleton

A HIDING PLACE

The Staff's locker room was a holding bay for the fake beards and nomadic disguises used by the Others. They had abandoned this way of life in favor of living in modern clothing in the former DHARMA village, in the barracks. Kate made the discovery of their stash of theatrical costumes and outfits at the Staff while helping Claire.

SUN'S SCAN

The Staff played a positive role in determining the date of conception for Sun's daughter, Ji Yeon. Juliet, concerned for the well-being of Sun and her unborn child, took them secretly to the Staff to use its ultrasound bay. The bay was located in a soundproof room, just off the Staff's locker room. This soundproofing was added because, sadly, it was where pregnant Others were taken to die.

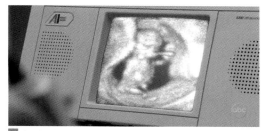

Sun's ultrasound was taken inside the Staff station.

Although Sun's husband, Jin, was infertile back home in South Korea, Juliet explained that sperm count was strangely five times higher on the island. Jin's paternity was confirmed by the ultrasound. Although Sun was pleased, as it proved she was not pregnant before she left Sydney from the affair she had with Jae Lee, conceiving on the island meant she had two months before she would most likely die. Fortunately, Sun escaped the island via Frank Lapidus' helicopter and Penny Widmore's boat.

JULIET'S SECRET MISSION

Aside from Juliet bringing Sun news of her pregnancy, the fertility doctor also used the Staff to record and deposit tapes providing Ben with crucial intelligence on the pregnancies among the 815 survivors. However, she hated herself for giving Ben the information, confessed everything to Jack Shephard and defected from the Others for good.

JACK'S APPENDECTOMY

The final medical use the Staff provided the surviors of Oceanic 815 involved Jack's appendectomy. Although Jack was convinced it was food poisoning, Juliet determined Jack's appendix needed to be removed immediately. She sent Sun and Jin, along with the freighter's Daniel Faraday and Charlotte Lewis, to gather surgical instruments and medical supplies from the Staff so they could perform the operation on the beach. Sun used the opportunity at the Staff with Jin to reveal it was where she had seen their baby on the ultrasound screen.

The medical supplies van that delivered vaccine to Eko's Nigerian village home bore the same logo on its side as the DHARMA Initiative's Staff station. It is the Caduceus, a common emblem often used to represent medicine.

EXPLAINING THE CADUCEUS SYMBOL

In 1902, the U.S. Army adopted the Caduceus symbol from Greek mythology and used it for their medical division and is largely responsible for it being associated with the medical field. However, the origin of the Caduceus symbol does not point to any kind of medical association.

The Caduceus features two serpents wound around a staff, and the staff sometimes features a pair of wings. Originally it belonged to Iris, the goddess who connected the gods to humanity, but the staff became linked to Hermes in later myths.

The correct medical symbol that is similar in appearance—but for which the Caduceus was mistaken and adopted in its stead—is the Rod of Asclepius, or the Asclepian. This is a single rod with a single serpent intertwined around it. It gets its name from the Greek god Asclepius (the son of Apollo) who was the god of medicine and healing. Although many medical professions do use the Asclepian to represent medicine, a large majority of commercial organizations still use the Caduceus.

Echoing themes on the island, Asclepius' medical skills were so heightened it was believed he could resurrect the dead. For this, he was imprisoned in the sky as the constellation Ophiuchus, "the snake bearer."

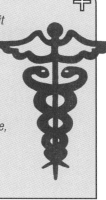

STARLA

▶ **CONNECTION:** Love interest of Hugo "Hurley" Reyes

Music fan and longtime crush of Hugo "Hurley" Reyes, Starla worked at the LA record store Hurley and his best friend Johnny often frequented. When Hurley's confidence was up—after winning the lottery—he mustered the courage to ask Starla out on a date to see one of his favorite bands, The Hold Steady. She accepted and the two dated for a while.

Unfortunately, once Hurley had revealed the news of his windfall, Starla dumped Hurley and started seeing Johnny. Hurley blamed his bad luck on the numbers he used to play the lottery.

SUSAN LLOYD

▶ **CONNECTION:** Ex-girlfriend of Michael Dawson; mother of Walt Lloyd

The former girlfriend of Michael Dawson, Susan Lloyd was pursuing a career in law when she got pregnant. Although Michael supported her dream of becoming a lawyer by taking low-paying construction jobs, her eventual success in her new career led Susan down a more professional path and into more conflicts with Michael.

When Walt was still a small child, she was recruited for a new job in international law by Brian Porter. In effect, this job offer was the beginning of the end of Susan's relationship with Michael. She accepted the opportunity even without consulting with Michael, then moved to Amsterdam with Walt to start a new life.

MANIPULATING MICHAEL
Susan began dating Brian Porter, the man who hired her, while working in Amsterdam. It was during a huge argument on the phone with Michael that Susan stated their relationship was over. It was shortly after their spat that Michael was seriously injured in a hit-and-run accident.

Two months after Michael was hospitalized, Susan traveled back home to visit him. Although she covered all of Michael's medical costs, the main purpose of her visit was to announce her engagement to Brian, his plans to adopt Walt, and their impending move to Italy.

Susan, Brian and Walt eventually moved to Australia. While Michael attempted to stay in touch with his son, Susan kept all of Michael's letters from Walt. It was only after Susan's sudden death due to a deadly blood disorder that Michael learned about the letters.

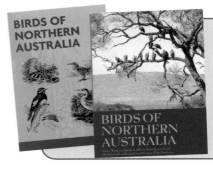

> **WALT'S TROUBLES** ✛
> *Before her death, Susan realized that there was something different about Walt. On one memorable occasion, she witnessed a bird crash into a window and die. This event occurred mere moments after Walt became frustrated because no one was paying attention to him. This all happened while he studied a book about Australian birds.*

SUZANNE CALLIS

▶ **CONNECTION:** Mother of Kevin Callis, Kate Austen's ex-husband

Suzanne Callis, a warm and generous woman, welcomed Kate Austen (a.k.a. Monica) into their family because of her devotion to her son. On the day of their wedding, Suzanne visited Kate as she prepared for the ceremony and presented her with a locket, a family heirloom passed down to the women of the family on their wedding days. Since Suzanne only had sons, she happily gifted it to Kate to continue the tradition. Suzanne witnessed the happy couple's nuptials with the rest of her family and friends.

STUART

▶ **CONNECTION:** Member of the DHARMA Initiative

Paranoid, obsessive, volatile, and extremely intelligent, Stuart Radzinsky contributed both innovative scientific advancements and chaos to the DHARMA Initiative. During the 1970s, Radzinsky was stationed on the island at the Flame, the central communications building connected to all the other DHARMA stations. As he preferred solitude over teamwork, the Flame's isolated location away from the barracks suited Radzinsky. Exceptionally territorial, he insisted that no one else touch any of the Flame's workings except him. He had little respect for his DHARMA co-workers and zero tolerance for any of the Hostiles, especially if they broke any of the terms of the Truce.

PRE-INCIDENT
Radzinsky's hatred of the Hostiles reached its highest level in 1977, when the Flame's alarm signaled that a motion sensor had been tripped in an area of land designated to DHARMA, meaning that the Others had broken the Truce. Jin-Soo Kwon raced to the same site, hoping to find his wife, Sun-Hwa Kwon, but instead found Sayid Jarrah. He had been teleported to 1977 from Ajira flight 316 as it flew over the island in 2007. Radzinsky's armed arrival led to Jin mock-arresting Sayid as a suspected Hostile.

RADZINSKY

Radzinsky wanted to execute Sayid immediately, as the zip-tie handcuffs he wore, courtesy of Jacob-supporter Ilana Verdansky, incriminated him as an enemy. Plus, Radzinsky was panicked that Sayid had seen the model for the Swan station inside the Flame. Under direction from Sawyer—who Radzinksy knew as DHARMA's Head of Security, Jim LaFleur—that the Truce said Sayid would be shot if he didn't identify himself as a Hostile, Sayid quickly confirmed that he was a Hostile, in order to save himself.

Sayid's subsequent refusal to talk, and truth-serum interrogation by DHARMA's Oldham, only fueled Radzinsky's suspicions. Sayid spoke with great familiarity of the functions of the Flame, Pearl, and Swan. Radzinsky was resolute that Sayid must be executed. At a DHARMA council meeting, everyone voted in favor of Sayid's execution; but Sayid had already plotted with a young Benjamin Linus to escape.

The series of events that followed showed Radzinsky at his most volatile. Radzinsky was responsible for the shoot-out between his team and Daniel Faraday, Kate Austen, and Jack Shephard. Radzinsky shot Daniel in the neck, but only grazed him. After discovering Phil gagged in Sawyer's cupboard, he proceeded to beat Sawyer to discover Kate's whereabouts. Sawyer eventually bargained for himself and Juliet Burke to be put on the submarine that was evacuating all non-essential personnel off the island, in exchange for drawing a map to show Radzinsky where the Others lived.

PROJECT SWAN

Aside from his communications job at the Flame, Radzinsky was also a gifted scientist, designer, and artist. He was a key player in the design, development, and creation of the Swan station, and even constructed a highly detailed scale model of it during its six-year development. Regardless of Dr. Pierre Chang's grave concerns over damaging the island's pockets of electromagnetic energy, Radzinsky never wavered from his vision of drilling directly into the one at the Swan construction site.

When the DHARMA excavation team's drill—much like the kind used to tap oil deposits—passed 70 meters in depth, its temperature increased by 60 degrees, and Chang ordered for the machine to be shut down. But Radzinsky cited Thomas Edison and continued drilling.

When the drill tower's Gauss meter exceeded 20kG (20,000 gauss), Chang feared what would happen next, but Radzinsky was thrilled that the drill was directly on top of the pocket of energy. Before the point of entry, the drill's temperature had already passed 250 degrees Fahrenheit, with over 200 RPM (Revs Per Minute)

> **GAUSS METER** ✛
> Gauss strength is a measure of magnetism named after German mathematician Carl Friedrich Gauss (1777-1855), who developed mathematical principles with magnetism.

Phil alerted Radzinsky that Sayid had a bomb and that his team was heading straight for the Swan site. Desperate to preserve the project he had spent so many years pursuing, Radzinsky fought Jack, Kate, Juliet, and Sawyer in a shoot-out. Although Sawyer managed to disarm Radzinsky and hold Phil at gunpoint as Chang trained his gun on Radzinsky, the subsequent leak from the pocket sucked everything metallic into the breach.

> ## "If Edison had been afraid of the consequences, we'd still be sitting in the dark."
> — Spoken by Stuart Radzinsky

Radzinsky ignored Chang's plea to stop drilling.

POST-INCIDENT

After the Incident, Radzinsky went on to complete construction of the Swan, the purpose of which was to regulate and safely release the continuous build-up of electromagnetism. He assigned himself to oversee the station with Kelvin Joe Inman for the two-man job of entering 4, 8, 15, 16, 23, 42 in the station computer every 108 minutes. Radzinsky began to lose his mind inside the Swan station, painting strange, nightmarish murals on the subterranean walls. He would trip the Swan alarm to fake a lockdown, then use fluorescent paint to create a kind of war map on one of the blast doors. For reasons unknown, he also made edits to the Swan's orientation film and kept a removed section of film hidden inside a copy of the Bible at the Arrow station. Ultimately, Radzinsky's decline led to suicide by shotgun while Inman was asleep.

> **RADZINSKY QUOTES EDISON** ✛
> Thomas Edison (1847-1931), also known as the "Wizard of Menlo Park", is considered the American inventor of the electric lightbulb and the phonograph.

SUN-HWA KWON

FACTS & FIGURES

Time On The Island
> POST-OCEANIC: 101 days
> POST-AJIRA: 5 days
> POST-INCIDENT: 7 days

Time As Oceanic Six: 3 years

Year Of Birth: 1980

People Killed By Her Hand: 1

Favorite Soup: Tofu soup

Alias: Dahlia Cho

Candidate: #42

BY THE NUMBERS +

*Sun is advised by her interior decorator/
co-conspirator to flee the Sydney airport at
11:**15** for a waiting limo.*

*Sun received a box with **15** chocolates that
concealed a hidden gun she was to use to kill
Benjamin Linus*

Born in contemporary Seoul, South Korea, Sun-Hwa Paik was a woman stuck between two worlds. On one hand as a strong-minded, educated woman, Sun was clever and determined enough to successfully follow any path available to her. But she also lived in a traditional Asian culture that valued women who were meek and subservient, especially in regards to their fathers and husbands. The wealthy and connected Mr. Paik, Sun's father, raised his daughter to be a good wife and her independent spirit was of little consequence unless she crossed him. Sun grew up and played the roles that were required of her, but when it came to her heart, she resolved to marry for love and not just social connections. And so when she met and fell in love with Jin-Soo Kwon, a modest man of little means who cherished her spirit regardless of her family's social standing, she risked everything to be with him.

THE PAIN OF BEING A PAIK

As the only daughter of the wealthy Paiks, Sun grew up with every privilege money could buy including a large house with servants, piano lessons and private schools. A traditional Korean patriarch, Mr. Paik was always stern with his daughter, but he did not involve Sun or his wife in any of his business pursuits, be they good or bad. However, Sun knew about the darker side of her father's business, she just pretended not to and played by her traditional role. Mr. Paik allowed Sun to get a degree in art history from Seoul National University, but after her graduation he determined it was time for her to marry.

It was by chance that Jin literally ran into Sun on the street in Seoul, but when their eyes locked theirs was an instant connection. Because of their disparate backgrounds they dated in secret. Knowing her father's class prejudice, Sun suggested they elope but Jin was too proud to "steal" the daughter of a prominent and respected man. Jin bravely asked Mr. Paik for her hand, and the savvy elder businessman saw the first of many opportunities to take advantage of the earnest young man in love with his daughter. Paik agreed, as long as Jin worked for his company, Paik Automotive, for six months. With that arrangement, the controlling Paik would retain incredible influence over his daughter and her lower-class husband's life.

After they married, Jin chose not to share with his wife what he was expected to do for his father-in-law, as the men adhered to the established Korean code of honor. But Sun's choice to take money from her father to pay off Jin's mother's bribe created a debt that her father exploited with his daughter's knowledge. Over time the job changed Jin and it put a wedge between them that almost unraveled their union. Only after the couple survived the Oceanic crash and repaired their relationship did Sun come to know how much her father impacted her marriage.

"Being told what to do was my life for four years... I didn't like it much either."

" *You ruined my husband's life.* "

SCENES FROM A MARRIAGE

There are two sides to every story and that's especially true in marriage. For the Kwons, their romance started with equal devotion. When they vowed their lives to one another they were an impressive united front impervious to the discontent of Mr. Paik and even some of their more class-conscious peers. But the complications of their life together, and especially because of the unyielding demands of Mr. Paik, caused the pair to lose one another. Sun felt the betrayal of coming second to her father's demands with Jin, and in turn she created her own a web of lies and betrayal. But Sun and Jin's love was always present and ultimately was what led them back to one another.

Sun and Jin's wedding day was magical, but dire complications were on the horizon.

JACOB'S TOUCH

At the receiving line at their wedding, Jin and Sun were blessed by a mystery man who reminded them to never take their love for granted. Jacob touched both of them and, with a smile, moved along.

The true nature of Jin's violent work upset Sun so much she slapped her husband across the face one evening.

Unable to conceive, Sun and Jin saw a doctor who revealed to her behind closed doors that Jin was sterile.

Sun felt alone and unloved, so she had an affair with Jae Lee.

Ready to flee from her marriage, Jin's gift of a white flower at the airport changed her mind and she got on Oceanic 815 with him.

After the crash, Jin reverted to a very traditional husband role and forced Sun to follow his lead.

When Jin found out Sun could speak English, Sun begged for his forgiveness and to start anew.

With their relationship still in jeopardy, Sun wept in fear for Jin's journey on the raft.

Juliet's confirmation of the length of Sun's pregnancy bonded the couple as they forgave one another.

Devastated when the freighter exploded with Jin still aboard, Sun screamed in abject pain.

THE GLASS BALLERINA

As a little girl, Sun broke a fragile crystal ballerina figurine that belonged to her parents and blamed it on the maid. When pressed by her father that he would fire the maid, she still blamed the innocent woman. It was an early example that the apple didn't fall far from

the tree when it came to the Paik prowess of deception. While Sun wasn't pathological, she was afraid of her strict father and would do anything to avoid his wrath. It was this pattern that continued into Sun's adulthood, when she lied on many occasions to avoid confrontations with the men in her life. Whether it was to hide her affair with Jae Lee, or when she took secret English lessons or the careful plan she worked out to escape Jin at the airport, Sun's lies showed that she was a woman conflicted about being true to herself or following the path she was raised to follow by her conservative culture.

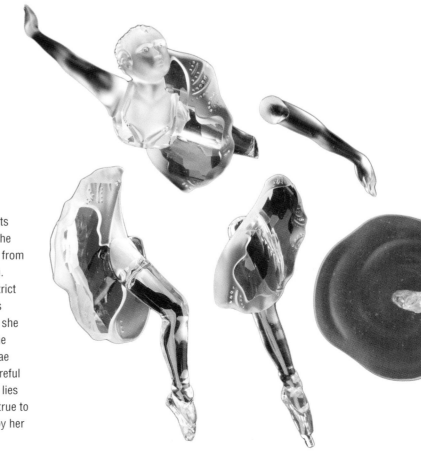

Sun honored her husband with a grave marker that she and her daughter visited often. He was gone but never forgotten.

The Man in Black tempted Sun by promising to reunite her with Jin, but she fled, bumped her head and lost her ability to speak English.

THE OTHER MAN

Originally introduced to Jae Lee by her mother and a matchmaker as a potential husband, Sun was actually smitten by the worldly young man. But Lee quickly confided that he was in love with an American woman, so the two just pursued a friendship.

A few years later they reconnected; Sun was married but Jae was single. He taught her English and during their intimate meetings at the hotel he managed, they embarked upon an affair. Jae tried to gift her an expensive pearl necklace and offered to take her away to America to start anew with him. But Sun's father found out about the affair and told Jin that Jae had stolen from him so he was to "deliver a message" to the man. Unaware that Jae had been with his wife, Jin beat the man and told him to leave the country. Shamed greatly, Jae clutched the necklace and fell to his death. Filled with guilt, Jae's death was another loss for Sun that pushed her to escape her life.

"I don't want to share you anymore."

— Spoken by Jae Lee to Sun

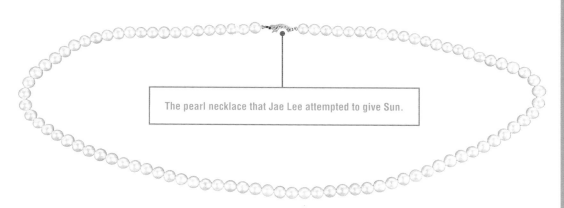

The pearl necklace that Jae Lee attempted to give Sun.

RECONNECTING

After three years of separation, Sun found her husband and her voice again as her heart's greatest desire was miraculously fulfilled. United once more, the couple touchingly discussed their daughter for the first time.

SUN'S ISLAND CONNECTIONS

While the Oceanic crash was disruptive and terrifying, the 101 days on the island also gave Sun the rare opportunity to come into her own as a woman, a wife—and with the confirmation from Juliet Burke, a mother-to-be. The island also provided her the opportunity to connect with a handful of people who would have a transformative impact on Sun Kwon's future.

MICHAEL DAWSON

From the moment they laid eyes on one another, Sun and Michael shared a sympathetic chemistry. He was moved by how she dealt with her apparently dominant husband and was attracted to her as well. Impressed by her strength, he entrusted the care of Walt to her when he went out to hunt; a job she welcomed and appreciated. After Jin attacked Dawson for wearing Mr. Paik's Rolex, Sun had to keep her friendship with Michael secret. But as a confidante she shared with him her ability to speak English and in a moment of particular vulnerability the two almost kissed. As Sun had already gone down that path to no avail with Jae, she pulled back but she remained a source of advice for Michael especially in regards to Walt. Michael also openly defended Sun when Jin was being chauvinistic with his wife. While she appreciated the sentiment, it only caused more problems with Jin. Yet in that way Michael proved to be an important catalyst for the couple as they started being honest with one another about their past so they could move forward on the path of forgiveness.

WALT LLOYD

While Sun had been unable to conceive a child prior to the island, she still had a strong maternal instinct that was evident in her relationship with Walt. She understood the little boy's awkward relationship with his father and patiently took the time to teach him how to use what the island provided. They planted a garden of herbs and aloe for medicine together. She listened to his likes, wants and needs and was able to translate that to an often confused and frustrated Michael. When Walt left with his father on the raft, she was truly sad to see the little boy go.

CLAIRE LITTLETON

After Claire gave birth to Aaron, Sun stepped up to help the young mother care for her baby. The women bonded and Sun was there to help Claire after she was attacked by Danielle Rousseau. As a woman who was very familiar with the vulnerability of not having control of her life, Sun tried to give Claire strength to overcome the difficulties she faced on the island.

HUGO "HURLEY" REYES

Incredibly pained by Sun's loss as she wailed for Jin on the *Kahana* helicopter, Hurley comforted her and remained a source of support for her during the rest of her pregnancy. Sun welcomed Hurley's warm and gracious spirit to the hospital after she had Ji Yeon and together they all visited Jin's grave.

KATE AUSTEN

While on the surface Kate and Sun were nothing alike, they soon discovered they had more in common than expected. They recognized each other's strength and bravery. While Kate was more brash and aggressive and Sun was more low-key in going after goals, they admired one another's approach, as well. After they got off the island, they bonded over their new roles as mothers. Sun kept her heart open and forgave Kate for her part in leaving Jin behind on the freighter.

SUN'S OFF-ISLAND CONNECTIONS

- **Mr. and Mrs. Paik** (Sun's parents)
- **Jae Lee** (A friend who taught Sun English and later became her lover)
- **Bpo Bpo** (Sun's pet Shar Pei)
- **Mr. Kwon** (The gentle fisherman father of Jin)
- **Jin's Mother** (A former prostitute who abandoned Jin; blackmailed Sun for money)

PART OF THE OCEANIC SIX

When Sun returned to Seoul, Korea she was a different woman in mind, body and soul. Having lost Jin, she carried a tremendous sadness in her heart that she was able to reshape into a karmic retribution in regards to her father. When she was given a very large settlement by Oceanic Airways, Sun invested that money and purchased a controlling interest in her father's company. She was able to turn the tables on her father and wrest back the control he had sought to deny her and her husband. She also made him accountable for his actions and retained her honor and dignity all at once.

For three years, she showed how smart she was in business affairs as her father's company thrived and she filled her broken heart with running a company and raising the little girl she and Jin had always dreamed of. But when she was found by Ben Linus, who showed Jin's wedding ring as proof that he survived the fiery explosion, Sun's focus returned to her husband and getting back to the island so she could bring him home to meet their daughter.

Sun and Hurley reconnected after Ji Yeon's birth.

A TRAGIC END

While their time back together was cut very short, Sun and Jin were given the gift to say goodbye. When they chose to stay together while the water rose inside the submarine, they remained calm and spoke of their vows of love to one another one last time. They connected as deeply as they had the first time they set eyes on one another and it carried them through to the other side.

SUSAN LLOYD AND SUZANNE CALLIS, SEE PAGE 336

SUN-HWA KWON

THE SWAN

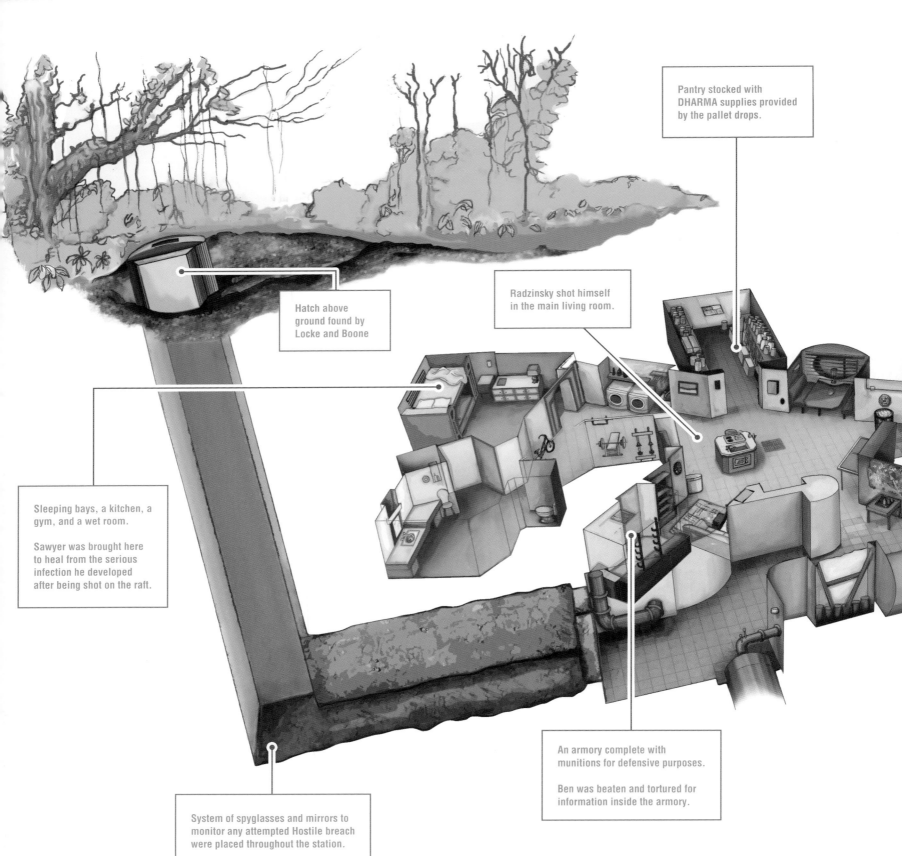

Pantry stocked with DHARMA supplies provided by the pallet drops.

Radzinsky shot himself in the main living room.

Hatch above ground found by Locke and Boone

Sleeping bays, a kitchen, a gym, and a wet room.

Sawyer was brought here to heal from the serious infection he developed after being shot on the raft.

An armory complete with munitions for defensive purposes.

Ben was beaten and tortured for information inside the armory.

System of spyglasses and mirrors to monitor any attempted Hostile breach were placed throughout the station.

> ## *Is this what you were talking about, Locke? Is this your destiny? All roads lead here?*
>
> — Spoken by Jack Shephard to John Locke

A computer to enter the numbers 4, 8, 15, 16, 23, and 42.

Eko set off dynamite to gain access to Locke and make him push the button when Locke threatened to let it go past zero.

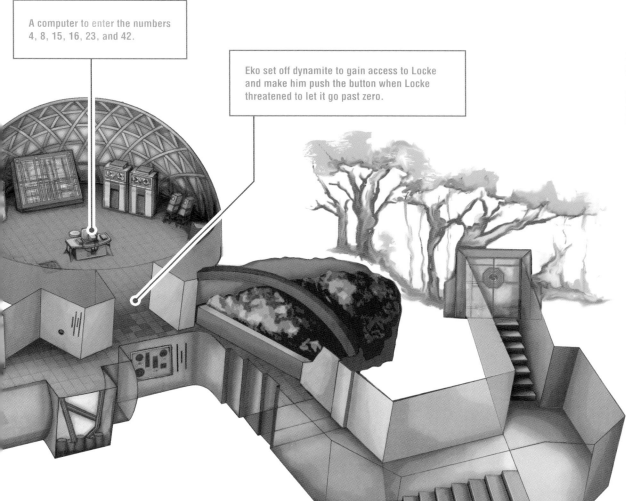

SWAN INTERIOR

All safely protected underneath its geodesic dome, the Swan's interior utilized structural, technological, and architectural advances from the late 1970s.

Of the island's many locations of electromagnetic energy, the pocket underneath the eventual site of the Swan station was the most powerful. Compared to the Orchid station's energy, the Swan's electromagnetism was 30,000 times stronger. Following the Incident, Swan staffers spent 27 years entering a code into the Swan's computer to contain the permanently swelling energy. Desmond's failure to enter the code released a surge of electromagnetic energy skyward at 4:15 p.m. on September 22, 2004, causing Oceanic flight 815 to crash on the island.

DHARMA's Stuart Radzinsky was responsible for the design and development of the Swan.

CHERNOBYL, UKRAINE ✛
The Chernobyl disaster occurred in April 1986, when a meltdown at a nuclear power plant released dangerous radiation over a vast area, with nearly 400,000 people relocated as a result. By December of that year, a large concrete slab sealed off the reactor and its harmful contents.

THE INCIDENT

Radzinsky's campaign to drill directly into the energy pocket underneath the Swan unleashed an uncontrollable surge of electromagnetism in 1977. This energy attracted everything made of metal into the mining shaft, inadvertently pulling Juliet Burke into the cavity. Trapped, she detonated the bomb Jack Shephard had thrown into the shaft in an attempt to reset time, prevent the Swan station from being built, and prevent the crash of Oceanic 815.

CONSTRUCTION & REGULATION

After the Incident, concrete was poured over the entire excavation site, and work began on the construction of the Swan station. Although its original intention was to study the unusual electromagnetic properties of the island, its subsequent purpose was to negate the electromagnetic energy.

Housed inside an underground geodesic dome, the Swan utilized a timer system to keep the energy leak from causing further destruction to the DHARMA Initiative and the island. As the energy swelled, someone had to manually enter the security code 4, 8, 15, 16, 23, 42 and then press the Execute button every 108 minutes, thereby containing the energy.

The light from the hatch restored Locke's faith in the island.

Radzinsky and Kelvin Joe Inman were the last to man the Swan station. Those who stayed inside the Swan station were safe from the poisonous gas the Others unleashed from the Tempest station to wipe out DHARMA. When Radzinsky went insane, he committed suicide inside the Swan. Inman was left on his own, until Desmond Hume washed up on the island's shore and was coerced to help.

THE HATCH

John Locke and Boone Carlyle were the first flight 815 survivors to stumble upon one of the Swan's access points. Locke had taken Boone under his wing while searching for Charlie and Claire, who had been abducted by the Other, Ethan Rom. It was during a seemingly random act—the throwing of a battery-powered torch from Locke to Boone—that appropriately shed some light on their situation. The torch struck the hatch door buried underneath a layer of soil and the metal-against-metal sound alerted them they had discovered something. Locke and Boone had some success in unearthing the hatch, but none in opening it. The glass was too thick to break and Boone surmised correctly that the door had been sealed shut with cement.

After Boone's death, Locke was terrified the other survivors would get involved with something he believed only he was destined to uncover and enter. When Locke eventually showed Sayid and Jack the hatch, Sayid was desperate to rebury it. Due to the lack of a handle, Sayid concluded it shouldn't be opened from the outside.

In a strange twist of Boone and Locke's initial discovery, when Hugo "Hurley" Reyes dropped a torch thrown to him, it landed by the hatch door, illuminating the numbers 4, 8, 15, 16, 23, 42 stamped onto its side. Spooked by the sight of his "cursed" lottery numbers, Hurley tried to prevent Locke from lighting the fuse to the dynamite gathered from the *Black Rock*. Locke ignored his pleas and the hatch door was blown open.

When the survivors returned to the hatch, Locke threw another flashlight to Hurley, who also dropped it by the hatch door, illuminating the numbers 4, 8, 15, 16, 23, 42 stamped into its side.

A BRIEF HISTORY OF GEODESIC DOMES ✛
Broken down into its root words, "geo" means earth and "desic" means divide. When applied to anything spherical in shape, a geodesic is the shortest path between two points on a curved structure, which creates a segment on the surface that is triangular in nature. To create a geodesic dome, one starts with an icosahedron. If its triangular connections are projected out from a central point on a sphere, then the dome pattern emerges.

The first geodesic dome structure ever built was a planetarium created by Dr. Walter Bauersfeld on the roof of the Carl Zeiss optical company in Jana, Germany in 1922. However, geodesic dome structures really didn't come into fashion until American architect Buckminster Fuller first popularized them in the mid '40s. In 1945, the first attempt at constructing one was at Bennington College in Vermont. His first free-standing, unsupported model came in 1949. Fuller was awarded the American patents on geodesic domes in 1954.

Geodesic domes hit their heyday in the '50s and '60s. Since their unique structure didn't rely on any load-bearing supports or structural columns, the process to build them was cheaper. Aesthetically the domes also matched Americans' increased fascination with futuristic minimalism, eco-friendly construction and counterculture idealism. But by the end of the '70s, the dome's broad appeal began to wane and its use was relegated to specific industrial or oddity home-building projects.

Spooked by the sight of his cursed lottery numbers, Hurley tried to prevent Locke from lighting the fuse to the dynamite gathered from the *Black Rock*. Locke ignored Hurley's pleas and the hatch door was blown open.

BLAST DOOR LOCKDOWN

The blast door served two purposes: to contain the Others if they entered the hatch and prevent the Swan staff from witnessing airplane drops of DHARMA supplies. The blast doors were designed to close automatically, but Radzinsky figured out how to fake a lockdown. During his descent into madness, Radzinsky painted his secret UV map on the blast doors, which theorized how he could defeat the Others.

Unaware of the automated lockdown, Locke's leg was crushed underneath a blast door during a pallet drop. While Locke was trapped, the 108-minute timer got dangerously close to zero. Ben Linus—masquerading as Henry Gale—was being held prisoner in the armory, but he was able to access the computer room through the air vents and enter the code. Because Ben was late pressing the button, a moment of blackout and emergency UV lighting revealed the blast door map painting to Locke.

FAILSAFE EXECUTED

One night while drunk, Inman told Desmond about the failsafe option. The theory behind the failsafe switch was that it would destroy the electromagnetic anomaly, thus rendering the Swan and its staff unnecessary. However, the failsafe mechanism was labeled "Caution: System Termination," and the real outcome was completely unknown. After Inman died, Desmond kept the failsafe key with his copy of Charles Dickens' "Our Mutual Friend," which was given to him by Penny Widmore.

When Locke destroyed the Swan computer and the timer had gone past zero, the entire station began to shake and fracture due to the rise of electromagnetic energy. Without knowing the consequences, Desmond turned the failsafe key and terminated the anomaly caused by the Incident. Accompanied by a loud subsonic hum, a bright white light engulfed the island, the sky turned purple, and the hatch imploded.

Desmond's unique resistance to electromagnetism combined with the island's mysterious spacetime properties enabled him to survive the implosion, but the blast knocked loose his consciousness' hold on the present and allowed him to experience the past and have glimpses of the future. On the island, he began to experience future events that indicated Charlie Pace's eventual death.

HIEROGLYPHIC WARNING

Once the 108 minutes from the Swan's timer had counted down, the numerical plates would flip to show Egyptian hieroglyphs. Although they were reputed to indicate a form of "to die," their exact translation and warning remained unknown.

SWAN ORIGINS

The word swan is an Old English word meaning "to sing." Swans form pairs, often resulting in relationships that last for life, appropriate for this DHARMA station where a long-term, two-person task was required. Swans also appear in the mythology of many cultures, including Greek, Irish, and Russian. In Hinduism, swans represent purity of conscience and have an association as Brahma's mount and are compared to virtuous souls whose defining ability is to be in the world without becoming attached to it. This mirrors Desmond's unique ability.

SYDNEY AIRPORT

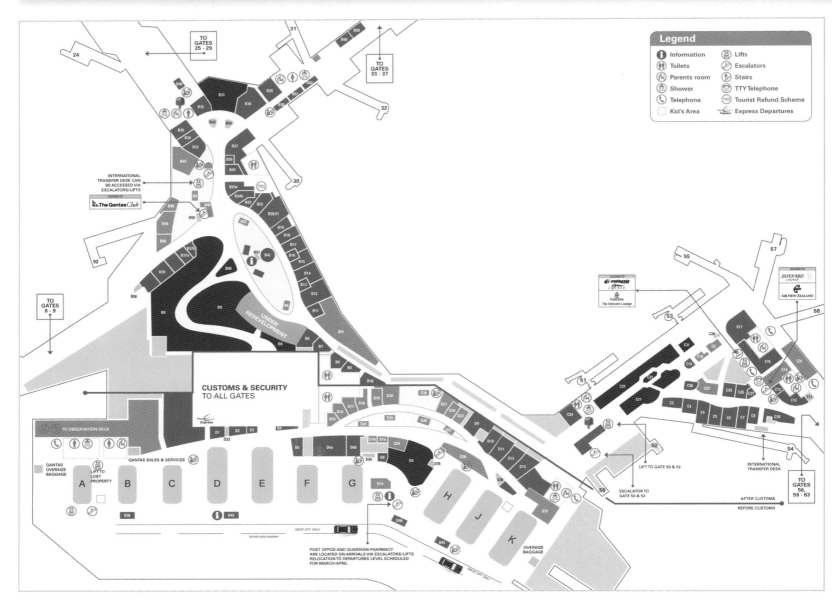

Legend

- **i** Information
- **♿** Toilets
- **👶** Parents room
- **🚿** Shower
- **☎** Telephone
- **□** Kid's Area
- **⬆** Lifts
- **↗** Escalators
- **⬇** Stairs
- **TTY** TTY Telephone
- **TRS** Tourist Refund Scheme
- **Express** Express Departures

TO GATES 25 - 29

TO GATES 33 - 37

INTERNATIONAL TRANSFER DESK CAN BE ACCESSED VIA ESCALATORS/LIFTS

ACCESS TO
The Qantas Club

TO GATES 8 - 9

UNDER REDEVELOPMENT

CUSTOMS & SECURITY
TO ALL GATES

TO OBSERVATION DECK

QANTAS OVERSIZE BAGGAGE

LIFT TO LOST PROPERTY

QANTAS SALES & SERVICES

DEPARTURES ROADWAY

DROP OFF ONLY

POST OFFICE AND GUARDIAN PHARMACY ARE LOCATED ON ARRIVALS VIA ESCALATORS/LIFTS. RELOCATION TO DEPARTURES LEVEL SCHEDULED FOR MARCH/APRIL.

DROP OFF ONLY

OVERSIZE BAGGAGE

ACCESS TO
malaysia
The Emirates Lounge

ACCESS TO
SILVER KRIS LOUNGE
AIR NEW ZEALAND

TO GATES 56, 59 - 63

LIFT TO GATE 50 & 52

ESCALATOR TO GATE 50 & 52

INTERNATIONAL TRANSFER DESK

AFTER CUSTOMS

BEFORE CUSTOMS

International Terminal

Sydney Airport

Oceanic Flight # 815
Destination: Los Angeles
Departure Time: 2:15 pm
Status: Boarding

▶ **CONNECTION:** Best friend of Jin-Soo Kwon

Tai Soo was Jin's roommate in Seoul, South Korea. As Jin dressed for his job interview at the Seoul Gateway hotel, Tai read his grandmother's "destiny book" and said it predicted that Kwon would find love that year with a woman who would look "orange." Jin denied the need for a woman in his life, so Tai teased his uptight friend. He also joked that Jin looked "stunning" and attempted to cut the tag off his necktie, but was stopped because Jin intended to return it. Later Jin met Sun Paik, who wore an orange dress.

Oceanic flight 815 departed Sydney Airport bound for Los Angeles, California on September 22, 2004. As the passengers boarded the airplane at Gate 23, they had no idea that all of the life-changing events that had occurred in their lives prior to this moment were about to lead them to a new destiny on a mysterious island in the middle of nowhere.

Several of the passengers crossed paths in the airport prior to boarding the plane. One noteworthy event occurred between Ana Lucia Cortez and Jack Shephard. Strangers prior to their chance encounter, the pair met in the airport bar, briefly flirted, and even discussed the passing of Jack's father, Christian Shephard.

WHAT IF...?

At one point during their conversation, Ana Lucia suggested to Jack that they trade seats. Jack's seat was in the middle section, while Ana Lucia was seated in the tail section. Before Jack could answer, Ana Lucia received a phone call from her mother. Had she not taken the call, perhaps they would have experienced a completely different dynamic on the island. Their leadership styles greatly influenced the lives of those who followed them, so this change could have altered events on the island dramatically for the survivors of the middle section and the tail section.

Shannon Rutherford and Sayid Jarrah also had a brief encounter prior to boarding the plane. Sayid asked Shannon if she would watch his baggage for a moment while he stepped away. In an attempt to prove to her stepbrother Boone Carlyle how influential she could be, Shannon informed the airport authorities that an Arabic man had left his luggage unattended. After officials questioned Sayid, they decided to let him board the plane. Ironically, Shannon's deceitful act could have resulted in Sayid being arrested and, considering how close Shannon and Sayid became on the island after Boone's death, it would have resulted in her losing her closest friend on the island next to Boone and her future lover.

LOCKE'S VISIONS

On the island, John Locke built a meditative sweat lodge and experienced a chilling hallucination that involved the Sydney Airport. During the vision, Locke was being pushed in his wheelchair by Boone. Locke witnessed several of his fellow survivors around him in symbolic scenes. For example, Benjamin Linus was dressed as a security guard scanning Jack Shephard to see if he could pass through the security gate, mirroring the control Ben exerted over Jack at the Hydra station. He even received clues as to how to save Eko.

ITEMS PROHIBITED BEYOND THIS POINT

Thank you for your cooperation.

Sydney Airport

Ben and Jack appeared together in one of Locke's visions.

349

THE TALBOTS

▶ **CONNECTION:** Conned by Anthony Cooper

Peter Talbot was the son of Mrs. Talbot of Tustin, California. An earnest young man and a good son, Peter grew concerned when his mother became engaged to a suave ladies' man named "Adam Seward" after only two months. Worried that his mother was being played by a grifter for her $200 million fortune, Peter learned that when Seward went by the alias of Anthony Cooper he received a kidney from a man named John Locke, so Peter tracked Locke to his home. Still bitter about being duped, Locke said his donation was anonymous and sent the young man on his way.

However, an angry Locke tracked down Cooper and his fiancée at a flower shop as they planned for their wedding. John took Anthony aside and confronted him about Peter's story and demanded that his father leave the Talbots alone. Two days later, detectives showed up at John's home and told him that Locke's name and address had been found in the now-dead Peter's pocket. A devastated Mrs. Talbot called off the wedding.

TARIQ

▶ **CONNECTION:** Member of Sayid Jarrah's unit in the Republican Guard

During Desert Storm, Tariq was the local intelligence commander for Sayid Jarrah's unit of the Iraqi Republican Guard. As the Americans bombed the Guard's location, Tariq told his men to burn and shred critical documents until the U.S. soldiers burst in and ordered them all on their knees. Sayid lied to protect his superior and repeatedly said Tariq had escaped to Hillah until the soldiers revealed they had Tariq in custody. Sayid was then forced by the Americans to act as interpreter as Sgt. Sam Austen questioned the commander about his missing U.S. pilot.

Later, CIA operative Kelvin Inman revealed to Sayid that prior to Tariq's current command he was head of a chemical warfare battalion in the North that used sarin gas on a village full of women, children and relatives of Jarrah. Sayid was then turned loose on Tariq with torture implements, but the commander never flinched. He defiantly ordered Sayid to kill himself to save his honor. Instead, Sayid took up his pliers until a broken Tariq revealed the location of the dead pilot's body.

TASER

An effective and painful electroshock weapon, the Others used different varieties of Tasers on the island. Charles Widmore's team even used them to incapacitate those they wanted to control or abduct.

While Kate and Sawyer were in the custody of the Others, Danny Pickett used a Taser to enforce discipline as they worked on the Hydra island's secret runway project. Years later, Charles Widmore plotted to abduct Jin from the Man in Black's camp on the main island. Widmore's associates, Seamus and Zoe, used a Taser for the task.

ORIGINS OF THE TASER ✚

The name of the device is an acronym for Thomas A. Swift's Electric Rifle. Swift was a character in a series of books written by Victor Appleton between 1910 and 1941. The inventor of the Taser, John "Jack" H. Cover, was a huge fan of the Tom Swift series and decided to use the fictional character's name for his device.

Fired from a gun-shaped device, the Taser utilizes Electro-Muscular Disruption (EMD) technology. A person hit with a charge experiences involuntary muscle spasms, resulting in their incapacitation, depending on the strength of electrical volts used.

TAWERET

Over the many eons of the island's existence, several distinct cultures made an impact on its landscape. Arguably none was more dramatic than the ancient Egyptian inhabitants who built epic island landmarks like the Taweret statue. The towering, 200-foot, porous stone sculpture of the Egyptian goddess Taweret was built on the island's western shore where it looked out onto the sea until its destruction in 1867.

ISLAND HISTORY

The island's Taweret statue wasn't a strictly traditional depiction of the deity (especially as it wasn't pregnant), however, it retained several of the key aspects such as the animal features, ankhs held in the hands and the four toes of a non-human creature. It's unknown what the ancient island dwellers used the statue for on the island, most likely as part of their death and fertility rituals. Regardless, it's interesting to note that both of those particular issues remained central to subsequent civilizations, none of which ever gained the kinds of population numbers that would have allowed their further generations to gain any permanency on the island.

The statue remained unchanged on the island until 1867, when a massive storm that generated a huge tsunami wave carried the *Black Rock* inland. The violent surge created enough force to propel the ship into the body of the statue, which toppled two-thirds of the structure into the sea. All that remained was the base entrance and the sandaled left foot that rose above it.

EGYPTIAN HISTORY OF TAWERET ✚

In Egyptian culture, Taweret (Great One) was considered a "household deity" because she appealed to the average person rather than being a representative deity of a Pharaoh. She embodied protection, birth and fertility, and was known as a fierce fighter who protected mother and child. Her implied ferocious nature came from her physical depiction, which was an amalgamation of three aggressive maternal creatures: a crocodile, a pregnant hippopotamus, and a lion.

Taweret was also closely associated with the northern sky, which represented rain and darkness to Egyptians. She kept the skies free from evil and also stood as the guardian of the north where she kept the unworthy out of her domain.

When the island experienced time skips after Benjamin Linus turned the frozen donkey wheel, a small band of survivors who included Sawyer, Juliet, Miles, Daniel and Charlotte glimpsed the statue intact sometime before its destruction. The first time the statue was officially seen by any of the Oceanic survivors was by sea in 2004, when Sayid, Jin and Sun witnessed it from the deck of the *Elizabeth*.

INSIDE THE STATUE

After the deaths of Mother and Jacob's brother, Jacob moved out of the caves and at some point made his new residence in the plinth of the Taweret statue. Inside was an open but spartan chamber supported by columns and an overhead vent that provided a view into the statue's remaining foot. In the center of the room was a large fire pit inside a stone bowl.

Jacob installed a large loom on which he created intricate tapestries and a wooden rocking chair. The tapestry featured hieroglyphics of Egyptian origin that depicted the three ancient seasons of Egypt: autumn/inundation, winter/growing and summer/harvest. The bottom row also depicted ships sailing to the island with the cut-out area showing the Taweret statue facing the ocean. Access to Jacob's home by anyone was strictly forbidden. When a newly shipwrecked Richard Alpert was sent to find Jacob by the Man in Black, it was in the shadow of the statue's foot the two men first spoke. Alpert gave his allegiance to Jacob soon after, and remained the sole person who knew how to gain access to his residence with the answer to Jacob's question—"What lies in the shadow of the statue?"—with the response: "He who will save us all" in Latin.

In 2007, the Man in Black, in the guise of John Locke, was able to gain access into Jacob's chamber. Together with Ben, they entered the space for the first time ever and confronted Jacob. Ben stabbed him and threw his body into the fire—a violent end to Jacob's long residency.

THE TEMPEST

Although some inhabitants of the island thought the Tempest served as an electrical outpost that powered the island, the truth behind its purpose was a lot darker. Built by the DHARMA Initiative, the Tempest contained a plethora of chemicals that, when combined in a specific way, could be released as a poisonous gas cloud. However, the reason the DHARMA Initiative built the Tempest is still unclear.

WIPING OUT DHARMA

One significant event in the island's modern-day history was the Purge. During this catastrophic event, the DHARMA Initiative's own Tempest creation was used against them in the most heinous way. After Charles Widmore had colluded with Richard Alpert and the rest of the Others, he gave the order to release the lethal fumes from the Tempest. Only a few DHARMA members besides Benjamin Linus and Ethan Rom survived.

When members of the DHARMA Initiative inhaled this airborne gas, they suffered hemorrhaging from the nose and violent respiratory problems, followed by death shortly thereafter. Bodies littered the grounds after the massacre.

POST PURGE

During Juliet Burke's initial interactions with the Others on the island, her friend (and later, lover) Goodwin Stanhope suffered a chemical burn while working at the Tempest. In his attempt to keep up the pretense that the Tempest was a power plant, Goodwin initially brushed off the injury as a burn caused by leaning against a transformer. However, Juliet knew the burn was one caused by contact with chemicals.

> **JULIET & HARPER** ✚
> *Harper Stanhope served as Juliet's therapist as she struggled to overcome the stress of dealing with all the pregnant women dying under her supervision. Harper was married to Goodwin Stanhope, although the two had virtually separated, prompting Goodwin's relationship with Juliet.*

After Juliet and Goodwin became romantically involved, he revealed that he was working with dangerous compounds that had the capability to kill everyone on the island. This was a chilling nod to the Purge, which Juliet knew nothing about.

HARPER'S WARNING

In one the strangest occurrences that Juliet experienced on the island, after she joined the 815 survivors, she was approached by Harper Stanhope. During a massive rainstorm, Juliet began to hear the eerie and sinister whispers all around her. Then suddenly, Harper appeared out of nowhere. She claimed that Benjamin Linus sent her to warn Juliet about the Tempest. Her message was that Juliet needed to kill Daniel Faraday and Charlotte Lewis, because they planned to release the toxic gas from the Tempest. Just as suddenly as she appeared, Harper vanished once the whispers returned. In reality, it was Ben who wanted to unleash the Purge part two. His intention was to release the gas and kill everyone on the island, including all the crash survivors. So Ben had Harper help set up Juliet for a suicide mission.

MASS MURDER, OR SAVING LIVES?

Charlotte and Daniel knew that Benjamin Linus was involved in the releasing of the Tempest's poisonous gas on the island more than a decade ago. Part of the reason they were dispatched to the island was to render the gas inert and safe. As they reprogrammed the Tempest, the station emitted a warning sound very similar to that heard in the Swan hatch during its lockdown procedure.

> ## *It's safer for you if I don't talk about it.*
>
> — Spoken by Juliet about the Tempest

Daniel and Charlotte attempted to render the gas inert.

Heeding Harper's warning, Juliet tried to prevent Charlotte and Daniel from tampering with the Tempest's inner factory workings. Wearing HAZMAT-style suits and gas masks, Juliet believed Harper's warning that Charlotte and Daniel were planning to kill everyone on the island. However, the two scientists convinced Juliet of their benevolent goal and rendered the gas harmless.

SHAKESPEARE'S TEMPEST   ✛

The thematic associations of the event involving the Tempest are prevalent with William Shakespeare's 17th century play "The Tempest." In the story, an island-bound magician named Prospero creates a storm that brings his brother's ship to his shores. Prospero uses his magic to divide the passengers of the ship so that once on the island, some believe each other to be dead. This is very much like the tail and mid-section survivors of Oceanic flight 815. Much of the play's subtext is about the difficulty of distinguishing between "men" from "monsters." "The Tempest" even features a strange monster native to the island referred to as "Caliban."

The DHARMA station logo for the Tempest featured a single large wave, echoing the concept of a great storm or disturbance, or a tempest.

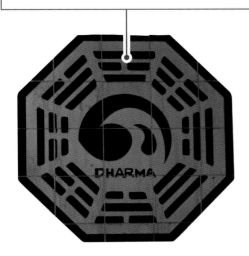

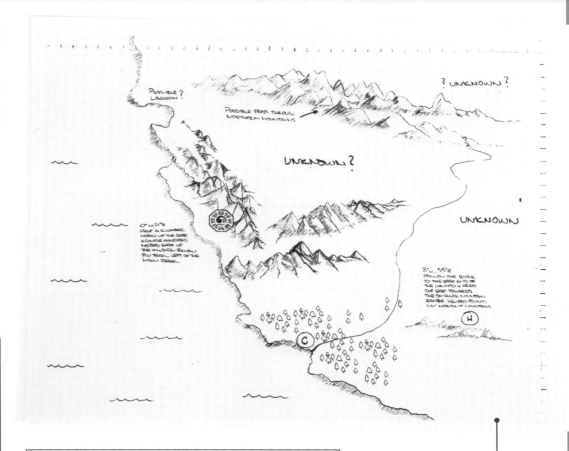

Faraday's map of the island showing the Tempest station.

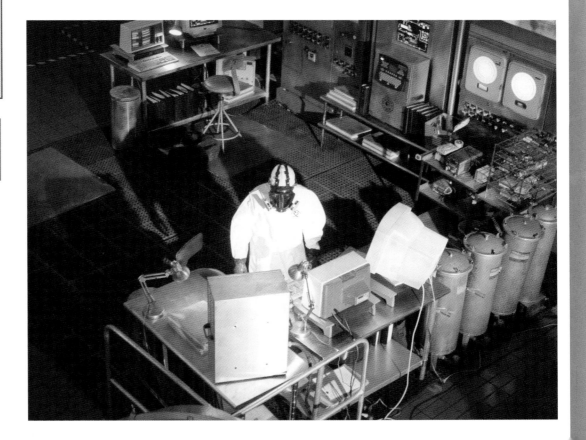

THE TEMPLE

The DHARMA Initiative may have created some impressive man-made structures of their own on the island, but none of them came close to the sense of awe and power that was exhibited by the Others' Temple. Built many lifetimes before the likes of DHARMA ever arrived on the island, the Temple was a colossal fortress, tattooed with symbolic glyphs, and steeped in ancient history.

Although its intimidating outer wall towered above the jungles and helped keep those who found themselves stranded on the island at bay, the sanctuary always required a Temple master. This person not only guarded its significant secrets and protected the Others who dwelled within, he also had the power to keep the Man in Black from entering the Temple.

The north door states "hail, thou beautiful power, thou beautiful rudder of the northern heaven"

The east door states "hail, splendour, dweller in the temple of the ashemu gods, beautiful rudder of the eastern heaven"

The west door states "hail, thou who circlest, guide of the two lands, beautiful rudder of the western heaven."

THE NATURAL SPRING

The Temple was located in an area with one of the island's natural springs. Although not situated near the heart of the island, the Temple was erected in a very sacred place. The entire structure and its surrounding perimeter wall were created to protect this natural spring from being manipulated and abused. The spring was located just beyond the Temple's courtyard, inside its first great hall.

In 1977, when a young Benjamin Linus suffered a near-fatal gunshot wound at the hand of Sayid Jarrah, Kate Austen and James "Sawyer" Ford delivered Ben's body to Richard Alpert. Alpert took Ben inside the Temple and bathed his wounds inside the spring. Ben was healed since he was special and Jacob had deemed him important enough to make him well again.

After Ben killed Jacob some thirty years later, the water turned to a cloudy, murky, rusty hue. Dogen, the Temple master at the time, cut his own palm to test the healing properties of the changed water, but his wound remained open and bleeding.

> ## " It's where the island healed me. "
> — Spoken by Benjamin Linus

Much like Ben, Sayid suffered a serious gunshot wound to the body and Dogen ordered him to be immersed in the newly cloudy spring. Sayid was drowned, instead of being restored to normal. Something that terrified the Temple Others was that after two hours had passed, Sayid sat up—alive. As the spring's water was now tainted and evil was beginning to take over, it didn't heal Sayid the way the Others thought it would. Sayid was cured, but the darkness was still growing inside him.

SANCTUARY

When Ben learned about Charles Widmore's freighter, he ordered a mass exodus of the barracks. He instructed Alpert to take all of the Others to the Temple, a day-and-a-half's trek from the barracks. Ben knew the Temple would become one of the last safe places on the island.

THE OUTER WALL

French scientist Montand was dragged so violently by the smoke monster into the chamber underneath the Temple's outer wall that his arm was torn off and left in the hands of his friends Robert, Brennan, and Lacombe. After they descended into the chamber to retrieve their friend, they returned, changed. Robert pleaded to Danielle Rousseau that it was not a monster, just a security system guarding the Temple. But the smoke monster wasn't guarding it and had spent the longest time trying to enter it.

DESTRUCTION

When Hugo "Hurley" Reyes told the Temple Others that Jacob was dead, they took precautions and prepared sacred ash around the entrances and sent a warning signal that Jacob was dead. The alert indicated that their defenses against the smoke monster could be weakened.

When Sayid (manipulated by the Man in Black) slit Dogen's throat in the spring hall, the Temple's last line of defense was severed. With Dogen gone, the Man in Black in his smoke monster form raged throughout the Temple, desecrating the sacred building and slaughtering those who chose to stay.

TERESA CORTEZ

▶ **CONNECTION:** Mother of Ana Lucia Cortez

Teresa Cortez had a complicated relationship with Ana Lucia Cortez. As a captain in the LAPD, she was Ana Lucia's boss but also her mother. This conflict of interest was the cause of much friction between mother and daughter, especially during the time in which Ana Lucia was shot. After her full recovery, Teresa fought to keep Ana Lucia from patrol work and wanted to give her a desk job. The mother and daughter bond was too strong, though, and Teresa let Ana Lucia back in a patrol car on her first day back on the force.

MOTHER/SUPERIOR

While on duty, Teresa found it quite difficult to see Ana Lucia as "just one of her officers." She was extremely concerned when her daughter didn't positively identify Jason McCormack, the alleged gunman behind Ana Lucia's shooting. Even though Teresa suspected Ana Lucia of lying about McCormack, she still offered to help her daughter. A short time later, Ana Lucia gunned down McCormack in cold blood. This particular incident became a catalyst in Teresa losing her daughter. After the shooting, Ana Lucia fled to Sydney, Australia, but later chose to board Oceanic flight 815 to return home. Sadly, Teresa never discovered the truth that Ana Lucia lost her life on the island.

The last time Teresa spoke to Ana Lucia—prior to Ana Lucia's flight from Sydney—Teresa said, "I'll be there when you land, mija." Mija is a term of affection popular in Latin American culture.

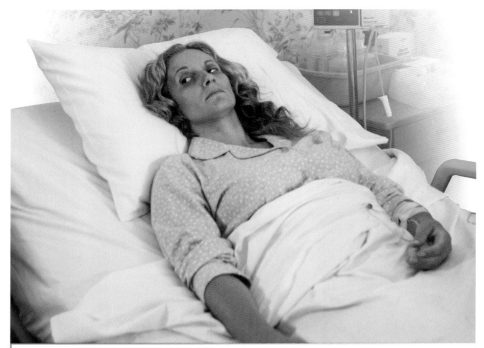

THERESA SPENCER

▶ **CONNECTION:** Ex-girlfriend of Daniel Faraday

A dedicated assistant to Daniel Faraday at Oxford University, Theresa Spencer was also Faraday's girlfriend. Daniel's mother, Eloise Hawking, did not approve of Theresa and was openly rude to her. In fact, Eloise only referred to her as Daniel's "assistant."

UNANCHORED IN TIME

Theresa volunteered to be a test subject in one of Daniel's time-travel experiments. Unfortunately, things went so tragically wrong during one such episode that her consciousness became unstuck in time. Her condition was so bad that her sister, Abigail, had to provide constant care for her while Theresa remained bed-ridden in a vegetative state.

While in this hypnotic condition, Theresa's outward appearance would change from looking completely vacant to alert and energized. She would even recall events from her childhood and various other times in her life. Without the ability to anchor herself during her time fluxes to a "constant," Theresa remained in an extremely detached state of mind.

As Theresa's condition worsened, Daniel fled England and traveled to the United States. Feeling partly responsible for her condition for funding his son Daniel's research, Charles Widmore became Theresa's benefactor by paying for all her medical bills and ongoing care.

> **WHAT IS A CONSTANT?**
> *According to Faraday, a "constant" is an object or person who exists in both periods of time during which a person's consciousness travels through time. If one is not found, the time travel becomes more frequent until the individual eventually dies.*

THOMAS

▶ **CONNECTION:** Claire Littleton's ex-boyfriend; father of Aaron Littleton

Thomas and Claire shared a loft in Sydney, Australia where he hoped to become a professional artist. About six weeks after Claire missed her period, the couple watched as her home pregnancy test revealed two very pink positive lines. While Claire had no intention of going through with the pregnancy, Thomas was excited by the prospect and reiterated his love for her. His reaction changed her mind. However, after three months, Thomas finally woke up to the reality of their situation and panicked and told Claire he wanted out. Upset, Claire told him he couldn't back out so he accused her of getting pregnant on purpose. Then he literally walked out of the loft and her life.

TITO REYES

▶ **CONNECTION:** Grandfather of Hugo "Hurley" Reyes

Tito Reyes was the patriarch of the Los Angeles, California based Reyes clan. He was the loving father of David and the grandfather of Hugo and Diego. Tito was a loyal and self-sacrificing provider for his family. From the age of 18, he worked three jobs for 52 years to take care of his family's needs.

As he got older, Tito developed a heart condition that eventually forced him to get a pacemaker. When Hugo won the California State Lottery, he announced at a press conference that the money would allow his grandfather to finally retire, but that was a short-lived dream as Tito doubled over in pain from what would turn out to be a fatal heart attack. At his funeral, more bad luck occurred when the officiating priest was fatally hit by lighting during a freak storm at the outdoor service. These tragic events were factors in Hurley believing that the numbers he used to win the lottery were possibly cursed.

TOM BRENNAN

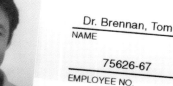

St. Francis Hospital

Dr. Brennan, Tom
NAME

75626-67
EMPLOYEE NO.

▶ **CONNECTION:** *Childhood friend of Kate Austen*

Best friends since childhood, Tom Brennan vowed to always stay together with Kate Austen. At the age of 12, Tom and Kate even buried a "time capsule" that would personify their promise. Unfortunately, time spelled out a much more tragic future for the friends than they planned.

In fact, Tom was involved in several events that led to Kate's troubled future and her connection to the island. As young children, Tom once dared Kate to steal a New Kids On The Block lunchbox from a local general store. The owner of the store confronted Kate about the stolen item and threatened to call her parents. But then Jacob appeared, paid for the lunchbox, and told Kate "to be good."

REUNION

Tom and Kate lost touch with one another as adults. He eventually became a doctor, married Rachel, and had a son named Conner. When Kate was on the run for the murder of her father, she learned that her mother, Diane, was dying of cancer. Kate returned home to Iowa to visit her mother at St. Francis Hospital, the same hospital where Tom worked. Kate asked for Tom's help, so he arranged for Diane's MRI. They also took the opportunity to dig up their time capsule and reminisce. Later, thanks to Tom, Kate spoke to her mother at the hospital, but her mother alerted the authorities.

Thanks to Tom, Kate spoke to her mother at the hospital, but her mother alerted the security. It was during Kate's attempted escape from the police that Tom was tragically killed. He pleaded for Kate to turn herself in, but she drove Tom's car through a police blockade. While sitting in the passenger seat, Tom was struck by a bullet and died.

ISLAND CONNECTION

Tom's presence on the island was felt by Kate. She found the metallic briefcase owned by U.S. Marshal Edward Mars near a waterfall on the island. Kate's sole purpose to retrieve the case was to recover the toy plane inside it, the one that belonged to her long time best friend, Tom Brennan.

Kate and Tom shared a kiss after digging up their time capsule, but Tom reiterated his love for his wife and child.

EXCERPT FROM TAPE:

> **KATE:** *...As soon as I get my license we should just get in a car and drive. You know, run away.*
> **TOM:** *You always want to run away, Katie.*
> **KATE:** *Yeah and you know why.*

CONTENTS OF THE TIME CAPSULE

Tom and Kate filled their lunchbox with personal effects, including among other things, Tom's favorite toy plane. The plane was very special to Tom, as it reminded him of the time he flew to Dallas by himself. The cassette tape they buried contained a recording of Kate and Tom's promise to each other to get married and have nine children. It also, appropriately, contained a conversation about how Kate wanted to just run away and Tom's disapproval of her idea.

As adults, Tom and Kate revisited the hiding spot of their time capsule and dug it up. Tom found the reunion both heartwarming and difficult. The two even shared a kiss at the location.

The toy plane that Kate and Tom placed inside their time capsule.

TOM FRIENDLY

▶ **CONNECTION: Member of the Others**

Although Tom exhibited a gentle, sensitive side, he willingly engaged in such sinister acts as kidnapping and murder. A conflicted soul, Tom believed he lived his life all in the name of Jacob and, for the most part, with complete loyalty to Benjamin Linus. His name even appeared on Jacob's lighthouse wheel at the 109-mark as a prospective candidate.

HIS ROLE WITH THE OTHERS

Tom had a degree of seniority in the ranks of the Others, and he often tasked various members to perform jobs as specified by Ben. Tom was at his most loyal to Ben, even though he was squeamish around blood, when he helped Jack Shephard during the procedure to remove Ben's spinal tumor. However, toward the end of Ben's leadership, Tom's faith in Ben waned. When Tom and Ryan Pryce led the Others' assault team to kidnap the survivors' women, Tom was furious at Ryan for firing three warning shots into the sand, instead of executing Jin-Soo Kwon, Bernard Nadler, and Sayid Jarrah. Tom believed that Ben had lost sight of the greater good.

Tom felt strongly that he and his fellow Others belonged on the island, but that the survivors of Oceanic 815 did not. When Tom faced-off against Jack Shephard, John Locke, and James "Sawyer" Ford, he mocked and criticized their conduct on the island. Tom claimed they had acted rudely, taken things that didn't belong to them, and entered places they did not belong. Tom made it clear that the Others were allowing them to co-exist on the island with them.

> ### THE TRUCE ✚
> The situation between Tom and the survivors of flight 815 mirrors the Truce reached between the DHARMA Initiative and the Others years earlier. During one encounter, Tom warned Jack and his people not to cross a line that he stipulated. Unlike the Truce, though, there was no negotiation or contract with this line—just the threat of killing Kate Austen if the survivors didn't relinquish their weapons and walk away.
>
> During Tom's warning, he quoted Alvar Hanso, the Dutch CEO of The Hanso Foundation, which financed DHARMA. He stated, "Since the dawn of our species, man's been blessed with curiosity." It is unknown whether this was an affectionate recollection that Tom was involved with DHARMA prior to joining the Others, or whether Hanso was being referenced in a mocking way.

KIDNAPPING WALT

Tom embraced the Others' theatrics of dressing in tattered clothing to fool their enemies and keep the location of their homes a mystery. The handmade clothing, weathered by the elements and nothing more than functional, recalled Jacob's choice of clothing and his rustic existence.

Tom added a fake beard to his alter ego when he and three Others attacked the raft on which Michael Dawson, his

Tom and Bea Klugh brought the captured survivors to Pally Ferry.

son Walt Lloyd, Jin, and Sawyer were leaving the island. Tom took Walt from the raft by force, before destroying it and leaving Michael and his friends in the ocean.

OFF-ISLAND PURSUITS

Tom left the island for a special mission ordered by Ben. Fearing that Charles Widmore had discovered the coordinates of the island, Tom tasked Michael to leave his New York home and help the island. Tom successfully manipulated Michael into joining the mission by exploiting Michael's guilt. Michael was distraught because his son, Walt, had disowned him for killing Ana Lucia Cortez and Libby Smith on the island.

" We're gonna have to take the boy. "

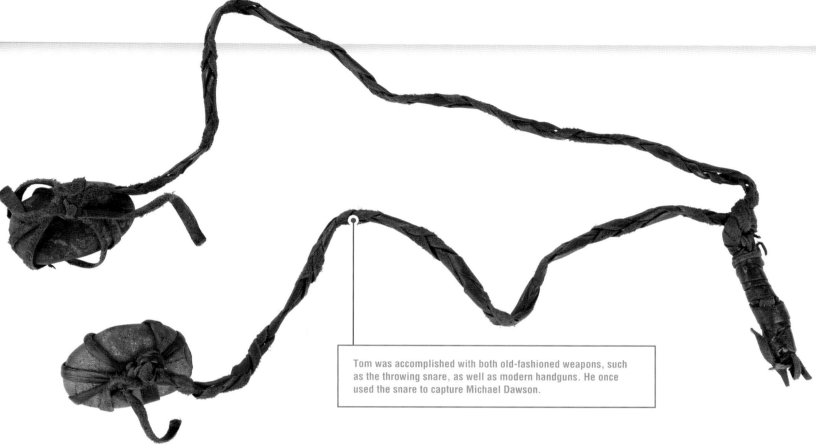

Tom was accomplished with both old-fashioned weapons, such as the throwing snare, as well as modern handguns. He once used the snare to capture Michael Dawson.

When Kate called Tom on his disguise, he decided to take it off.

Tom watched in horror as Jack put Ben's life in danger.

While in the penthouse of the Manhattan Hotel Earle, Tom revealed to Michael he had evidence showing that Widmore had staged a fake Oceanic flight 815 crash. This compelling evidence included a purchase order for an old 777 jet and photographs of a Thai cemetery where more than 300 bodies had been exhumed. Tom had taken these documents from Felix, who he shot and killed. Felix, who worked for Widmore, was on his way to inform his boss of the successful operations in staging the bogus underwater flight 815 wreckage. Tom instructed Michael to board Widmore's *Kahana* freighter in Fiji under the assumed name of Kevin Johnson. He was ordered to kill everybody on board to stop it from reaching the island.

FINAL CONFLICT

As Tom got to know some of the survivors, especially Jack and Kate, he occasionally dropped his guard and showed a kindness toward them. During Jack's time with the Others, Tom played football with Jack and Juliet to pass the time. After Kate had been locked up in the barracks' pool room, Tom warned Jack that the Others were listening to their conversations.

During the raid on the survivors' beach camp, however, all empathy Tom felt for them was soon gone. When seven of Tom's people were killed by explosions, he became resolute on revenge for his friends' deaths, but that opportunity never came to fruition. Sawyer confronted Tom and killed him, stating, "That's for takin' the kid off the raft!"

"That's for takin' the kid off the raft!" — Spoken by Sawyer to Tom

TOMMY

▶ **CONNECTION:** Friend of Charlie Pace

Tommy was a heroin addict from London who researched people he spotted as "plays"—potential victims to con to pay for he and his friends' heroin habits. He met up with Charlie Pace just as Drive Shaft's second album, *Oil Change*, was experiencing poor sales, forcing the band into an indefinite hiatus. Tommy pointed Charlie toward Oxford graduate Lucy Heatherton as a "play." Her family lived in Knightsbridge and were extremely wealthy.

TONY NAGY

▶ **CONNECTION:** Attempted to kidnap Sayid Jarrah

Under the pretense of being a nurse at St. Sebastian Hospital, Tony Nagy attacked Sayid Jarrah there in 2007.

Charles Widmore, Benjamin Linus, or Jacob's off-island protection team led by Ilana Verdansky may have employed Nagy. He was only armed with a tranquilizer dart gun, so his M.O. was to abduct Sayid, not kill him.

Strangely, during a struggle with Sayid, he confessed to an address in his pocket when Sayid gained the upper hand. Written on the paper was Kate Austen's home address. Sayid shot Nagy twice with tranqs from his own gun.

St. Sebastian HOSPITAL

Tony Nagy
NAME

151623-42
EMPLOYEE NO.

TRANSCEIVER

Sayid attempted to locate the distress signal using flight 815's transceiver.

Taking its name from the fact that it is both a transmitter and a receiver, the transceiver recovered from Oceanic flight 815's cockpit may not have led to rescue, but it did provide the survivors with important information about their predicament.

While using the transceiver at a high point on the island, it picked up a distress signal that had been repeating for over 16 years. Translated by Shannon Rutherford, the message revealed that a French woman (unknown to the survivors at the time as Danielle Rousseau) was alone on the island. The mystery behind the message led Sayid to desperately attempt to use the transceiver to locate the source of the transmission.

One of Sayid's most ambitious attempts to discover the radio tower's location involved a plan to triangulate the signal. This involved constructing a series of antennas using equipment stripped from flight 815's wreckage. They erected one antenna on the beach, another further in the jungle, and a third one at higher ground. Sayid planned to turn on the transceiver within the three points of the triangle to create a signal cross-reference. If the source of the message was somewhere within the triangle, it would indicate the location from which Rousseau's message was being broadcast. Although the antenna sequencing was a success—with Sayid, Shannon and Sawyer all setting off rockets to signify each aerial was up—John Locke knocked Sayid unconscious before he could switch on the transceiver, which Locke then destroyed.

TREBUCHET

John Locke and Boone Carlyle built a modified trebuchet to break the glass on the Swan's hatch door. After attempting several other techniques to no avail, Locke told Boone that a trebuchet would deliver "a half ton of force" right onto the glass. Unfortunately, the device did not work. Upon impact, the device splintered into pieces, wounding Locke's leg in the process.

USE IN THE MIDDLE AGES ✚
Trebuchet contraptions date back to the Middle Ages, where armies would use the lever-based machines to propel items at the enemy or objects of obstruction. There are several different versions of trebuchet "siege machines" based on the particular needs of the offensive. Locke's version employed a modification that focused the arm into the glass, rather than the arm sending an object into the air.

His ability to create a trebuchet to "outwit" the hatch harkened back to his love of contraptions utilized in the board game Mouse Trap.

TRICIA TANAKA

▶ **CONNECTION:** News reporter who interviewed Hugo "Hurley" Reyes

If Hugo "Hurley" Reyes was considered by many to be the luckiest person in the world for winning over $110 million in the lotto, then Tricia Tanaka is surely the unluckiest person in the world. A news reporter for Action 8 News, Tricia was assigned to interview Hurley outside of Mr. Cluck's the day before its grand reopening.

THE INTERVIEW
Tanaka began her interview with Hurley by asking him why he purchased Mr. Cluck's. Hurley explained that it was simply because he liked chicken, so Tanaka switched her line of questioning to the provocative subject of Randy Nations, Hurley's former boss but now a current employee. After a mere shrug from Hurley, Tanaka asked what else he had done since his lottery success. At this point, the weight of the numbers "curse" came to the forefront, as Hurley revealed that he had suffered a string of bad luck.

As Tanaka grew more irritated with Hurley's responses, she reminded him that the piece was supposed to be heart-warming. Tricia and her cameraman then entered Mr. Cluck's to get some additional shots for the segment. Visibly uncomfortable with the idea, Hurley let Tanaka and her cameraman go inside. Then out of nowhere a meteor came streaking through the sky, destroying the restaurant and everyone inside, just as Tanaka said, "And then pan through the…"

BAD LUCK ✚
After Hurley won the lotto, his grandfather Tito died from a heart attack and the house he purchased for his mother burned down. To make matters worse, Hurley's best friend Johnny took off with Hurley's crush, Starla.

TUNISIA, SEE PAGE 362

VERONICA

▶ **CONNECTION:** Nanny for Aaron Littleton

During the time Kate Austen was off the island and was caring for Claire Littleton's son, Aaron, Veronica worked as a nanny at their Los Angeles home. She was a kind and dedicated person who helped raise Aaron.

Veronica was unintentionally involved with one of Kate's secret meet-ups with Cassidy Phillips and her daughter Clementine—James "Sawyer" Ford's daughter—when Jack realized Kate was keeping something from him. Jack returned home from work at 6 p.m., and Veronica was still working, when she normally left by 4 p.m.

TUNISIA

CAPITAL: Tunis
POPULATION: 9.2M

Located along the northern coastline of Africa, Tunisia's northern and eastern shorelines border the Mediterranean Sea, giving it a vast coastline over 600 miles long. Conversely, the arid Sahara Desert encompasses a large portion of Tunisia's southern realm. The island Djerba, made famous by Homer's epic poem *The Odyssey*, is nearby in the Gulf of Gabes. Tunisia had a powerful connection to the island. In addition, many of the survivors on Oceanic flight 815 are familiar with the country.

THE ISLAND'S EXIT

The island's donkey wheel—located in a subterranean cavern underneath the Orchid station—was the device used to move the island. When turning the wheel, a blinding light would emerge and the person turning the wheel would be transported to an "exit point" off the island. After traveling through time, the person appeared in the Sahara Desert in Tunisia.

Two people were known to have manipulated the wheel. In 2005, Benjamin Linus did so to leave the island but he understood the consequences of doing so. On the other hand, John Locke set the wheel back in place not knowing what would happen to him or the island.

ISLAND CONNECTIONS

The cities of Tozeur and Medenine in central Tunisia served as hosts to key island-related events. After Ben arrived in the Sahara Desert, he headed to Tozeur, a place famously considered an "oasis" for the region. Using the alias Dean Moriarty, Ben checked in as a preferred guest at a hotel in Tunisia, meaning he had visited the hotel on other occasions.

In her pursuit of information about the island, Cultural Anthropologist Charlotte Lewis bribed archaeologists to give her access to a dig site in Medenine. After a bit of excavation, Charlotte found the skeletal remains of a polar bear wearing a collar from DHARMA's Hydra station. At some point during their experiments on the island, DHARMA made one of the bears leave the island via the donkey wheel and it reappeared in the Sahara Desert.

> ### A NATIONAL ANTHEM
> Poet Aboul-Qacem Echebbi, who was born in the Tunisian city of Tozeur, is responsible for what is considered one of the country's anthems. Titled "To the Tyrants of the World," the emotional and evocative poem mirrors the struggle between good and evil, with lines such as:
> **Wait, don't let the spring, the clearness of the sky and the shine of the morning light fool you, because the darkness, the thunder rumble and the blowing of the wind are coming toward you from the horizon.**

The local Tunisian newspaper's headline focused on the discovery of Oceanic flight 815.

Charlotte Lewis found this collar with the Hydra logo on it in the Tunisian desert.

Hydra station polar bear collar

Translated to English: 815: Found!

When Charlotte returned to the island as an adult, she mentioned having detailed knowledge about ancient Carthage. This series of ancient North African cities outside Tunis became one of the crown jewels of the Roman Empire. The Carthaginian region was historically rooted in Phoenician religion, a form of polytheism. In this belief system, followers worship a series of gods or goddesses, much like the belief system of ancient Egypt. The people of Egypt revered the river goddess of fertility, Taweret, the colossal statue that towered over Jacob's coastal island dwelling.

Like the island after the Purge, ancient Carthage had a burial ground. Carthage also had a walled citadel, the Byrsa, much like the Temple on the island.

Located in the southwestern part of the country, Tozeur is the capital of the Tozeur Governorate. It is one of 24 governorates, or provinces, that comprise Tunisia.

Medenine, the capital city of the Medenine Governorate, is located in the southeastern region of Tunisia. Situated below the island of Djerba (the largest island off the North African coast), it is a land rich in mythological history.

After being paid a visit by Benjamin Linus, former island resident Charles Widmore set up surveillance cameras at the exit to monitor who was being teleported off the island.

Tunisian national flag

VINCENT

▶ **CONNECTION: Walt Lloyd's pet dog**

Walt Lloyd's pet Labrador Retriever, Vincent was the only non-human survivor of Oceanic flight 815. When the plane's mid-section crashed onto the island's shores, Vincent managed to escape the wreckage without sustaining any injuries. Vincent helped the survivors deal with various traumas on the island and he was paramount in kick-starting Jack's journey on the island.

PRIOR TO THE ISLAND

Vincent's first master was Brian Porter, Walt's stepfather. Brian and Vincent lived in Sydney, Australia and were later joined by Susan Lloyd (Walt's mother) and Walt when Brian and Susan were married. After Susan's unexpected death from a rare blood disorder, Brian surrendered custody of Walt to Michael Dawson. Perhaps out of contempt for Brian, Michael took Vincent to console his son.

Thanks to Locke's wooden dog whistle, Michael and Walt found Vincent.

LIFE ON THE ISLAND

Vincent was one of the first survivors to experience an encounter in the realms of the paranormal. While in the jungle adjacent to the crash-site, Vincent reacted to a whistle in the distance. However, the whistle did not come from a survivor of the crash; it came from Christian Shephard, who had died in Sydney, Australia and was stowed on the plane inside a coffin. Vincent could see the apparition and understand him. As if under Christian's direction, Vincent woke Jack from his unconscious state and spurred him into action to help the survivors.

A MAN'S BEST FRIEND

Several of the survivors relied on Vincent for comfort to forget about the chaos of their predicament. For example, Shannon Rutherford became closer to Vincent after Boone Carlyle died. She even tried to use Vincent to locate Walt after the Others abducted him. Sadly, Vincent unwittingly led Shannon into the jungle where an apparition of Walt appeared just before Shannon was accidentally shot by Ana Lucia Cortez.

Vincent was lovingly cared for by different people at different times, including Ana Lucia, Sawyer, and Charlie. Locke had a very immediate, natural affinity with Vincent. Concerned for his well being, Locke hand-made a dog whistle out of wood to help alert Vincent and bring him back to Walt. Like many dogs, Vincent gravitated toward people who were emotionally damaged in order to comfort them.

ROSE & BERNARD

In 1977, Sawyer, Kate, and Juliet appeared back on the island during their quest to find Jack when they were greeted by Vincent. Shortly thereafter, Rose emerged on the beach looking for the Lab. Rose revealed that during the time flashes she and Bernard had taken care of Vincent.

During another situation, Vincent was alerted to Desmond's cries for help. The Labrador got the attention of Rose and Bernard and the couple helped Desmond out of the well that the Man in Black had thrown him into.

A FINAL COMFORT

Vincent came full circle with one of the key survivors of Oceanic flight 815. Bleeding out from his injuries, Jack Shephard dropped onto his back in the bamboo forest in the exact location he awoke in after the crash. As happened years prior, Vincent lay down next to Jack to provide him comfort in his last moments of his life.

> Vincent was placed on Oceanic flight 815 in a pet carrier unit that was stored in the belly of the plane. This is the form Michael signed that allowed Vincent onboard.

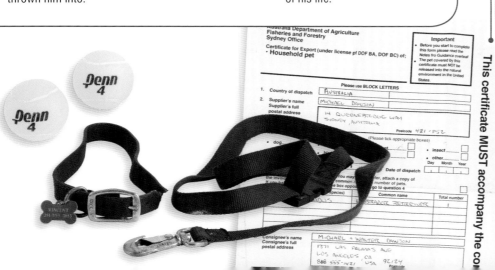

VIRGIN MARY STATUES

Central figures in the Catholic Church, statues of the Virgin Mary are worshipped for being the chosen vessel of Jesus Christ, the son of God. An extremely powerful image, the statues of the Virgin Mary challenged the faith of two survivors on the island. Everything that the statues represented—from their spiritual significance to the heroin contained within—united Charlie Pace and Eko. After bringing them together, the statues took both men on different but equally life-changing paths of self-discovery.

At one point, Eko confronted Charlie about the Virgin Mary statues.

ORIGIN OF THE STATUES

The Virgin Mary statues that were found on the island came from a small Nigerian village in West Africa. In fact, their pilgrimage to the island started in the same Catholic village where Eko and his younger brother Yemi once lived. The villagers sold the statues to raise money to purchase Polio vaccine, but Eko devised a plan to conceal the heroin in the statues and smuggle the drugs out of the country.

Unfortunately, the consequences of using such a holy image for a criminal act were disastrous. After loading a Beechcraft full of statues, Eko's brother Yemi was shot by authorities as the plane departed. The Beechcraft took off with Eko's cohort Goldie and Yemi on board. Eko was left on the airstrip to continue his charade of being a man of the cloth.

ISLAND CRASH-SITE

The Beechcraft and its cargo of statues crash-landed on the island years before the arrival of Oceanic flight 815. There were no survivors of the Beechcraft accident; Yemi either died from the gunshot wound sustained in Nigeria or from the crash. Goldie perished after he parachuted out of the plane and fell into the jungle canopy.

John Locke and Boone Carlyle were the first ones to discover the downed aircraft and the statues. After recognizing the Virgin Mary statues that Charlie had found, Charlie led Eko to the crash-site where Eko was forced to face the errors of his past. Eko found the decayed bodies of his former criminal partner, Goldie, and his brother, Yemi.

The Beechcraft, which crash-landed on the island years prior to the arrival of Oceanic flight 815, was discovered by John Locke and Boone Carlyle.

CHARLIE'S REDEMPTION

Charlie Pace, the Catholic-raised heroin addict, found the duality of the Virgin Mary statues a true test of his faith in his God and himself. Mirroring Charlie's life prior to the island, the statues represented the Drive Shaft bassist's fall from grace. A devout Catholic and former altar boy, the success of Drive Shaft pulled him away from his faith.

When Charlie suffered from waking dreams and strange visions on the island, his faith returned. He became obsessed with the idea that the dreams were spiritual messages warning him that Aaron must be baptized to save him from great danger. After a long struggle battling the temptations of his addiction, Charlie cast the last of the statues and heroin into the ocean. His faith was restored and he helped Eko build a church on the beach.

WALT LLOYD

FACTS & FIGURES

Time On The Island
POST-OCEANIC: 67 days

Likes: Power Rangers, video games, comics

Pet: Vincent, a Labrador Retriever

In many ways, Walt Lloyd was like any other young boy. He loved video games, comic books, and action TV shows, and he didn't get along with his parents. In other ways, though, Walt was a very special boy. He was one of the rare few humans attuned to the island, but he remained unaware of it for a long time.

After surviving a plane crash, encounters with polar bears, and abductions by mysterious Others, Walt was allowed to leave the island with his recently reacquainted father, Michael Dawson. However, their strained relationship was pushed to the breaking point when he discovered the dark deeds his father carried out willingly to secure their departure. It was nearly six full years later that Walt finally returned to the island, a place that he knew, deep down, was where he always belonged.

FAMILY TIES

Like any 10-year-old boy, Walt often craved attention. His early life was unsettled as his family moved often due to the careers of his mother and stepfather, Brian Porter. During the first 10 years of his life, Walt lived in Europe, Australia, and the U.S. As he grew older, living with his mother and stepfather became more difficult. When Susan died of a rare blood disorder, the responsibility of raising Walt on his own became too much for Brian to handle. Brian flew to New York to ask Michael Dawson, Walt's biological father, to take him off his hands.

An image of Walt appeared on this milk carton during one of Hurley's dreams.

MISSING

WALTER LLOYD

Male — DOB 8/24/94
Height: 4'9" — Weight: 75 LBS
Black Hair, — Brown Eyes

Last seen: Middle of nowhere

IF YOU HAVE ANY INFORMATION REGARDING THIS MISSING YOUTH, PLEASE CALL YOUR LOCAL COUNTY SHERIFF'S DEPARTMENT

Walt never learned about the meeting and he found the hand-off between parents incredibly disorientating. To ease the transition, Michael brought Vincent, Brian's dog who was adored by Walt, on the flight to provide a familiar presence from Walt's childhood.

Although Walt was initially full of anger for Michael taking him away from his Australian home, he slowly began to understand the complexities of the situation. Walt was very mature for his age, and when Michael gave him a box of letters that Susan had kept from Walt, he realized his father had always loved him very much. After the crash of Oceanic flight 815, Walt initially felt at home on the island but still resented his biological father. To stop his father's initial escape attempt, he burned a raft Michael

ABDUCTION

After Walt insisted that his father fire the only flare that remained on the raft a team of Others, led by Tom Friendly, approached their small craft. They took a screaming and terrified Walt by force before destroying the survivors' raft with an explosive.

Walt was subjected to a series of tests during his time with the Others, which included time spent inside Room 23 on Hydra island. The Others also wanted to learn specific things from Michael, such as how old Walt was when he started talking; whether he suffered any fainting spells, headaches, or illnesses growing up; or whether he had ever appeared to Michael from the other side of the world.

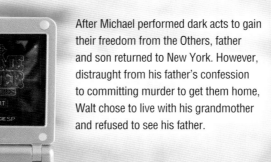

PRESS START

GAME BOY ADVANCE SP

After Michael performed dark acts to gain their freedom from the Others, father and son returned to New York. However, distraught from his father's confession to committing murder to get them home, Walt chose to live with his grandmother and refused to see his father.

Walt's Game Boy

Walt left Vincent in the care of Shannon, a thoughtful gesture as she had just lost her stepbrother, Boone Carlyle.

" *Don't open it, Mr. Locke.*
Don't open that thing. "

TENACITY

Walt was always an inquisitive, steadfast soul. This characteristic led him to discover the handcuffs that belonged to Kate in the jungle, after exploring on his own after the crash.

As an only child, Walt was adept at keeping himself amused. He created a game of sliding shells and stones that he slid down the side of a piece of plane wreckage to pass the time.

He also enjoyed playing Backgammon with Locke and Hurley. Walt was very lucky during his games with Hurley and built an I.O.U. of $83,000 from the lottery winner.

Walt was also unafraid of speaking his mind to intimidating souls. When Sawyer read through everyone's messages in the bottle, Walt was swift to chastise him.

WALT'S OFF-ISLAND CONNECTIONS

- **Michael's Mother** (Grandmother)
- **Susan Lloyd** (Mother)
- **Brian Porter** (Stepfather)

POLAR BEARS

Walt encountered different kinds of polar bears throughout his life. Michael gave him a stuffed bear when he was very small.
A polar bear was featured in Hurley's Spanish comic book (Green Lantern-Flash "Faster Friends, Part One") that Walt read on the island. He was attacked by a polar bear on the island and saved by Michael and Locke.

POTENTIAL UNLOCKED

Being in tune with the island, Walt slowly began to display in different ways his special qualities. Walt idolized Locke and oftentimes showed courage during the island's darker times. Walt wanted to take Vincent with him to sniff out Claire and Charlie after they were abducted. He even guessed correctly that not only was Ethan responsible, but that he and many other people were already on the island, much to Sawyer's initial amusement.

Walt also enjoyed Locke's training him with the hunting knives, and crucially, the art of visualizing (e.g., seeing yourself strike a target before trying). While helping his father build the second raft, a specific concern Walt aired ended up actually happening. He was worried about what they would do if a shark attacked them, which happened to Michael and Sawyer. When Locke held Walt's wrist to assure him he didn't tell anyone that Walt set the first raft ablaze, Walt pulled his arm away and became gravely concerned. He warned Locke not to open "that thing," even though he was unaware Locke had found the Swan hatch.

VISITING HOURS

When he lived in New York with his grandmother between late 2004 and 2010, Walt made friends but never quite fit in. Before his father went on the *Kahana* mission, Michael tried to make contact with Walt. However, his son was still too traumatized by Michael's confession about murdering Ana Lucia and Libby Smith.

Locke visited Walt in New York in 2005, but Walt didn't seem surprised to see him, as he experienced strange dreams about Locke on the island. Walt inquired where his dad was, as he assumed he had returned to the island. Locke confirmed that the last he knew, Michael was on a freighter near the island's shores. Feeling frustrated, Walt asked his grandmother to fly with him to Los Angeles to visit Hurley at Santa Rosa. He questioned Hurley about why the Oceanic Six hadn't come to visit him and why they were lying. Hurley explained they were doing it to protect everyone on the island.

GOING "HOME"

In August 2010, Hurley and Ben visited Walt at Santa Rosa to discuss an important job opportunity with him. This job would take him back to where he always belonged—the island. Although Walt knew that his father was dead, Ben explained that it didn't mean Walt couldn't continue to help Michael.

STRANGE BEHAVIOR

Birds would fly into windows and kill themselves.

Walt, dripping with water, appeared to Shannon and Sayid as a warning.

When Locke was in the DHARMA mass grave, Walt appeared and told him to get up.

WARDEN HARRIS

▷ **CONNECTION:** Warden at prison housing James "Sawyer" Ford

Warden Harris ran the Florida penitentiary that housed James "Sawyer" Ford and an inmate named Munson. Munson was incarcerated for stealing $10 million from the federal government; the location of the money was never revealed.

In an attempt to retrieve the funds, Harris orchestrated a complicated plan to get Munson to reveal its location. He selected convicted con artist Sawyer to earn Munson's confidence, while the warden took the spot of the "heavy" when he protected Munson from intentional beatings. He even enlisted Munson's wife to pry for the money's location.

In return for Sawyer's intel that the money was left inside a red Bronco parked in a Stor-Quik facility in Sawgrass, Harris brokered a deal between the Federal Treasury Agent on Munson's case and Sawyer. The con man got the last six years of his sentence commuted and a cash reward that the warden transferred to an anonymous account for his daughter, Clementine Phillips.

WARREN

▷ **CONNECTION:** Acquaintance of John Locke

Warren worked closely with Locke at the box company in Tustin, California, owned by Hugo "Hurley" Reyes. During their lunch breaks, Warren would play war games such as Risk with Locke. The two even created nicknames for one another: "Colonel" (Locke) and "GL12" (Warren).

Like Locke, Warren despised their boss, Randy Nations. During their war games, "GL12" didn't strategize his moves with the same level of patience as his friend the Colonel. Locke even reminded GL12 that patience was the hallmark of great leadership. Locke also confided in Warren about his walkabout dreams and his friend, Helen.

WAYNE JANSEN

▷ **CONNECTION:** Father of Kate Austen

The biological father of Kate Austen, Wayne Jansen was an abusive husband and alcoholic. He beat his wife, Diane Jansen, on numerous occasions and even made sexual advances toward Kate while intoxicated. Although Wayne never touched Kate inappropriately, his behavior toward her was flirtatious and offensive, often resulting in lewd insinuations. Kate may have never been the victim of physical abuse—like her mom was—but the emotional damage ran deep. Things got so bad that when Kate discovered the truth about Wayne's paternity, she plotted to kill him.

Diane divorced Sam Austen when Kate was five years old. After winning custody of Kate, Diane later married Wayne. Oddly, Kate didn't learn that Wayne was her real father until her mid 20s after seeing some dated photos of Sam. Learning the truth about her real father triggered a downward spiral of events for Kate. While making a scrapbook of photos for Sam's birthday, Kate contacted one of his commanding officers in the U.S. Army to obtain pictures of him in uniform. She received photos of Sam that pictured him in Korea up until four months before Kate was born, proving that he couldn't be her biological father.

THE "ACCIDENT"

Kate purchased an insurance policy for the family home under her mother's name. Knowing that her mother was working the night shift at Keith's Diner, she turned on the gas and sat outside the house with her Zippo lighter. When Wayne arrived home, he was clearly intoxicated so Kate helped him inside and put him into bed. He then made a sexual advance toward Kate, which she rebuffed. Clearly disturbed by his actions, Kate fled the house on her motorcycle as the house exploded behind her with Wayne inside.

> **DIANE'S LOVE** ✚
> *U.S. Marshal Edward Mars, who eventually arrested Kate, suggested that, although Wayne was abusive to Diane, maybe she loved him for all that he was. Diane confirmed this some months later, when Kate—a fugitive after escaping Mars' arrest—managed to secretly meet with Diane. Thinking her daughter had returned to apologize for killing Wayne, Kate stated that she wanted to know why her mother had told the police what she'd done. Her mom simply said that she couldn't help whom she fell in love with. It didn't change the fact that Kate killed Diane's husband.*

MOTIVES FOR MURDER

The fundamental reason that Kate killed Wayne was because she hated that she could never escape the fact that he was a part of her. In her eyes, she would never be a good person. She was destined to never have anything good in her life.

> **PARANORMAL EVENT?** ✚
> *When Sawyer was on the island recovering from injuries sustained while inside the Swan station, Kate experienced a very strange event. As she put "Walkin' After Midnight" by Patsy Cline on the Swan's turntable, Sawyer began to murmur something. When Kate moved closer, his eyes bolted open and he grabbed Kate by the throat and screamed, "Why did you kill me?" This occurred just after Kate had been telling an unconscious Sawyer about the horse she saw on the island. The horse reminded her of the time she escaped from the authorities shortly after killing Wayne.*

THE WELLS

Instead of being used to find water, the man-made wells on the island served as points of scientific exploration. Unlike the common notion of throwing a penny inside a well for good luck, the island's wells became synonymous with Man's desire for harnessing the power of the island.

EXPLORING ELECTROMAGNETISM

In early Roman times, a group of people stranded on the island became curious of its seemingly "magical" qualities. During their studies, they realized that metal was drawn toward the ground in certain areas. Whenever the group found such a location, they excavated to learn more about the cause. Inside one of the wells, the Man in Black showed Mother that he discovered a way to access the light at the heart of the island.

Deep inside a cavern where the donkey wheel became set, the DHARMA Initiative created their nearby Orchid Station right next to the filled-in well. DHARMA's tests concluded this was one of the island's key electromagnetic locations.

WHITE RABBITS

Rabbits are small mammals found in many places all over the world. Wild rabbits existed on the island and became part of the food supply for the Others (who also carried out experiments on the rabbits) and all others who lived on the island over the years.

APPEARANCES

Rabbits appeared several times on and off the island, including:

- *On the Hydra orientation film, six white rabbits were seen with the numbers 2, 9, 17, 54, 33 and 17 painted on them.*

- *Sawyer read the book Watership Down, which belonged to Boone Carlyle, who was very much led "down a rabbit hole" on Locke's fantastical journey in trying to understand the island.*

- *Ben had a white rabbit with the number 8 painted on it that he used to con Sawyer.*

- *Vincent led Hurley to the discovery of the car keys for Roger Linus' DHARMA van; the key chain had a rabbit's foot on it. Roger died in the Purge while sitting in the van.*

- *After leaving the island, Hurley was given a rabbit's foot with the key to his Camaro. It wasn't lucky: the numbers 4, 8, 15, 16, 23, 42 were on the dashboard display.*

- *Ilana suggested buying a rabbit's foot key ring for Sayid, as he was nervous about boarding the Ajira flight when he saw his flight 815 friends at LAX.*

- *When Miles was young, he picked up an apartment key that was located near a rabbit statue. Unfortunately, this is when Miles started hearing dead people "talk."*

- *Widmore brought a white rabbit named Angstrom to Hydra island when he returned. The animal lived in a cage in the Hydra generator room.*

WHITE SUIT

▶ **CONNECTION:** Associate of Mr. Paik, Sun-Hwa Kwon's father

One of Mr. Paik's nameless hired thugs, he was known for his crisp, white suit. After Jin went easy on Byung Han, Paik ordered Jin to drive White Suit back to Han's home so he could "deliver a message" the right way. As Jin stopped in front of Han's home, the thug put on white gloves and gave him specific directions to leave the car running as he would return in two minutes, then to drive the speed limit to the riverbank. As White Suit entered Han's home, Jin rushed past him and took over Han's beating, which actually saved the man's life.

WIDMORE INDUSTRIES

Its headquarters based in London, England, Widmore Industries was the brainchild of British entrepreneur Charles Widmore. Using a keen sense of business, Widmore quickly diversified and expanded his business into a broad range of lucrative and profitable ventures.

With its founder having spent a great deal of his life on the island, it's not surprising that Widmore Industries had several threads that tied it to the island, the people who lived on it, and key events associated with the island. Widmore Construction was renowned for its constant innovations in cutting-edge construction technology and engineering. On the flip side, Widmore Laboratories was well respected for pioneering important pharmaceutical developments.

PUTTING IT ALL TOGETHER

Widmore Industries financed a major global sailing event that was co-sponsored by Oceanic Airlines. Even though Widmore Industries was behind the cover-up of the faked Oceanic flight 815 crash off the coast of Bali, there is no proof that Oceanic Airlines was directly involved in the ruse.

The company even had its name branded with the International Open Ocean Racing Association. The competition, the "Widmore Race Around the World," saw experienced and junior yachtsmen—including Charles Widmore's future son-in-law, Desmond Hume—take part in one of the biggest sailing races ever organized. There were even

connections between Widmore Industries and the Hanso Foundation, which financed the DHARMA Initiative, and Paik Heavy Industries, which owned Phi Yachts.

Widmore Laboratories also sponsored Minnesota-born balloonist Henry Gale's desire to fly around the world in a hot-air balloon. The Widmore company name and logo were emblazoned on the side of the balloon. Ironically, Benjamin Linus, Widmore's life-long nemesis, later assumed the name and identity of Gale when he was captured by Danielle Rousseau and interrogated by the flight 815 survivors inside the Swan station.

The Widmore Industries logo appeared on Henry Gale's balloon.

PREGNANCY TESTS

Widmore Laboratories had a large financial investment in fertility-based research, including the home pregnancy kit. During Charles Widmore's time on the island, he was well aware that women suffered organ failure and ultimately death if they became pregnant on the island. This correlation cannot be overlooked when analyzing the links between Widmore Industries and the island.

WIDMORE LABS HOME PREGNANCY TEST

RESULTS IN 2 MINUTES

easy to use • convenient • confident • accurate

WILD BOARS

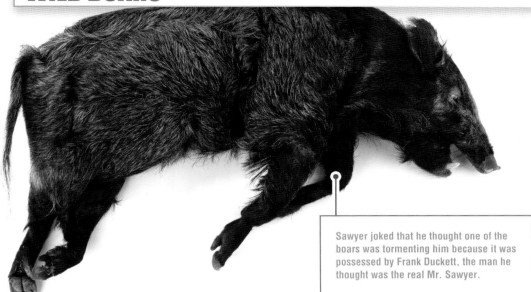

Sawyer joked that he thought one of the boars was tormenting him because it was possessed by Frank Duckett, the man he thought was the real Mr. Sawyer.

An important part of the island's eco-system, the resident wild boars left their mark on those who lived there. Also known as "wild hogs" or "razorbacks," this species of animal *(Sus scrofa)* thrives in conditions similar to those experienced on the island. A dangerous and powerful mammal, the average wild boar measures out at around 180 lbs. and 160 cm in length.

MYTHOLOGY
The wild boar is prominent in several mythologies around the world. In ancient Greek mythology the Greek god of war, Ares, could transform himself into a boar. In Norse mythology, the boar is a sacred symbol that is not only associated with war but, more significantly, fertility.

Boar tusks grow continuously, reaching 12 inches in length. The main expert and leader of the boar hunts was John Locke, although others—including Sawyer and Desmond—were successful in bringing dead boars to their camps, too. Although Charlie Pace and John Locke discovered a boar that looked as if it had been mauled by a polar bear, none of the boars' regular predators were ever seen on the island. In other habitats around the world, the likes of tigers, hyenas, wolves, and crocodiles target piglet and adult boars for sustenance, but in the absence of these larger predators on the island, the animals thrived.

WINE BOTTLE

Jacob used this aged glass decanter of wine as an object to explain the nature of the island to Richard Alpert. As Jacob and Richard sat on the beach by the base of the newly destroyed Taweret statue, Alpert asked if Jacob was the devil. Jacob denied his assumption, but admitted that he brought the *Black Rock* to the island. He then took the half-filled decanter, plugged it with a cork, and turned it upside down. He explained that the wine represented "malevolence, evil, darkness" while the cork represented the island, the only thing that kept the evil at bay.

Later, Jacob and the Man in Black casually convened at an overlook to discuss their recent impasse over Alpert. Jacob gave the Man in Black the decanter of wine to "pass his time" still bound on the island. An irritated Man in Black later smashed the bottle upon a rock in frustration.

EGYPTIANS & WINE MAKING
The Egyptians were the first to document any wine-making process via paintings in their tombs. Archeologists also found many wine bottles and jugs included in burial rooms, meaning it was a drink reserved for the upper echelons of society. As such, wine was often associated with the divine, even the actual blood of the gods poured into the soil that in turn birthed the vines.

WILLIAM KINCAID

▶ **CONNECTION:** Physiotherapist who helped John Locke

After John Locke's father, Anthony Cooper, pushed him through an eight-story window, William Kincaid helped John cope with his paralysis. A kind and patient physiotherapist, Kincaid always encouraged Locke, even when he was at his most depressed. Kincaid was amazed Locke had survived the fall, and was determined to make him see that although he now needed a wheelchair, it didn't mean that his life was over.

WINE BOTTLE

WOODEN SHED

When Charles Widmore returned to the island, his team set up operations on Hydra island and they constructed the wooden shed next to the Hydra station's main building.

Made entirely from wooden panels—except for two huge solenoids and their related cabling—the magnetizing room was constructed to test Desmond Hume's resistance to vast quantities of electromagnetism. Widmore had gained information about the heart of the island's electromagnetic core. He knew that if the stories about Desmond were true, he would be the only person who could enter the island's heart and turn off the light, so that the smoke monster could be destroyed. Desmond survived the colossal amounts of electromagnetism. After Widmore's employee, Simmons, was accidentally killed inside the magnetizing room, Desmond was trapped inside but he survived the colossal amounts of electromagnetism that the device fired through his body. A side effect was that the experience allowed Desmond to experience the flash sideways realm.

YEMI

▶ **CONNECTION:** Brother of Mr. Eko

The younger, devoutly religious brother of Eko, Yemi and Eko were very close as young boys. A turning point in his life occurred when a group of militants stormed their village. One man thrust a gun into Yemi's hand and told him to murder an unarmed villager. Yemi refused to shoot the man, so Eko grabbed the gun and finished the deed. The militants accepted Eko and ripped the crucifix from his neck. Yemi retrieved it, thus creating his future path.

RELIGIOUS ADULTHOOD

Years later, Eko returned to Yemi with a plan to fly a stash of heroin, smuggled inside 300 Virgin Mary statues, out of Nigeria in order to sell it. Yemi was forced into signing the paperwork to identify Eko and his associates as priests. In exchange, Eko gave the church money for medical supplies.

Yemi tipped off the military and raced to the airstrip. Eko and his cohort Goldie were dressed as priests, ably assisted by Olu. As the authorities arrived, Yemi explained to Eko that because he didn't reveal anyone's names that he could just walk away. As bullets started flying, Yemi

"You speak to me as if I were your brother..."
—Spoken by Yemi to Eko

was shot by the military and Eko dragged his brother onto the Beechcraft. Goldie then kicked Eko out and the Beechcraft took off. Somewhere during its flight path to an unknown destination, the Beechcraft nosedived onto the island. It is uncertain whether Yemi died from the gunshot wound or the crash.

REUNION

Eko and Charlie Pace located the Beechcraft on the island and discovered the body of Yemi inside. Stricken with grief, Eko cradled Yemi's body, reclaimed his crucifix, and set the plane aflame while reciting the 23rd Psalm: "The Lord is my Shepherd, I shall not want…"

ISLAND MANIFESTATIONS

Later, Eko's brother appeared in a dream insisting that the Swan station was more important than anything else. Yemi said Locke must be taken to "the question mark" and that he should bring an axe. Yemi also appeared in one of Locke's dreams, just before Eko and Locke discovered the question mark-shaped pattern on the ground that revealed the Pearl station's entrance.

During Eko's recovery from his polar bear attack, Yemi appeared and asked him to confess. Upon further investigation, Yemi's corpse had disappeared from the Beechcraft. Later, Eko refused to repent to the manifestation of Yemi and explained that he did what he needed to do to survive. With a chilling retort, Yemi stated he was not his brother. This vision of Yemi was in fact a manifestation of the smoke monster. It wasn't long before Eko was killed by the monster in one of its most fearsome rages.

The necklace worn by Yemi. Locke found it in the jungle and gave it to Eko.

YUSEF

▶ **CONNECTION:** Member of a terrorist cell; plot foiled by CIA, ASIS, and Sayid Jarrah

Sharing an apartment in Sydney, Australia, with his friends Haddad and Essam Tazir (Sayid Jarrah's former roommate from Cairo University), Yusef was a member of a terrorist cell along with his flat mates. Yusef enjoyed playing video games like *Half Life* with Haddad. He was involved with the suicide bomb plot that was to utilize C-4 that had been stolen from an army base outside of Melbourne; the plot that Sayid helped the CIA and the ASIS foil.

ZODIAC RAFT

The Zodiac was a multi-person, small, inflatable raft that was used by the Kahana crew to travel short distances between the freighter and the island. It was used on several occasions for what turned into ill-fated voyages.

George Minkowski and crewman Brandon set out in the raft to find the island, but Brandon's sudden, acute reaction to the time displacement issues forced the men to abort the adventure.

Two panicked Kahana crew members attempted to steal the raft but were stopped and beaten by Captain Gault to save them from a fate similar to Brandon's.

Gault gave Sayid permission to take the raft back to the island to start ferrying flight 815 survivors to the freighter. The captain warned him to stay fixed on a bearing of 305 out and back.

Daniel Faraday transported Sun, Jin, Aaron and three other survivors to the Kahana.

Faraday returned to the island and attempted to take survivors Craig, Neil "Frogurt" and two others back to the freighter. Still within the boundaries of the island at the moment of the flash, the boat and its passengers were also moved. Although they made it back to the beach, the raft disappeared between one of the time shifts.

ZOE

▶ **CONNECTION:** Worked for Charles Widmore on Hydra island

Zoe was a geophysicist hired by Charles Widmore to lead the scientific contingent of his second attempt to return to the island. Zoe's expertise in the field of geomagnetism was of particular importance to Widmore, as he needed someone to find the island's most magnetic pockets of energy, to determine the breadth of Desmond Hume's special ability to absorb and withstand large amounts of electromagnetism.

WORKING FOR WIDMORE

A rather capable and cagey woman, Zoe proved to be a huge asset to Widmore due to her loyalty, bravery and resourcefulness in a variety of difficult situations. Once they arrived on Hydra island, Zoe posed as the last Ajira flight 316 survivor so she could gain intelligence on the main island situation. Zoe's first such encounter was with James "Sawyer" Ford. She attempted to con the con man into thinking that she was the last remaining survivor of Ajira flight 316, but he saw through her ploy when she slightly faltered before saying the flight was headed to Guam.

Following Widmore's orders, Zoe was also tasked with assembling a covert invasion of the Man in Black's camp to capture Jin-Soo Kwon. She needed him to clarify information on a '70s-era DHARMA map of the island that pinpointed the biggest concentrations of electromagnetic energy. Zoe was also in charge of retrieving a heavily drugged Desmond Hume from the submarine so that they could test him inside their makeshift electromagnetic shack.

HER DEMISE

When Zoe traveled with Widmore by outrigger to the barracks, they encountered Ben, Richard Alpert and Miles Straume. Again following Widmore's order, she returned to their outrigger but caught sight of the Man in Black on his way to the main island. Frightened, she radioed Widmore and returned to the barracks. Ben told Widmore and Zoe to hide inside a secret room, but with Ben's help the Man in Black found the room and asked Zoe who she was. Prompted by Widmore not to speak, the Man in Black then brutally slashed Zoe's throat as she was useless to him.

Zoe confronted several of the survivors on Hydra island.

INDEX

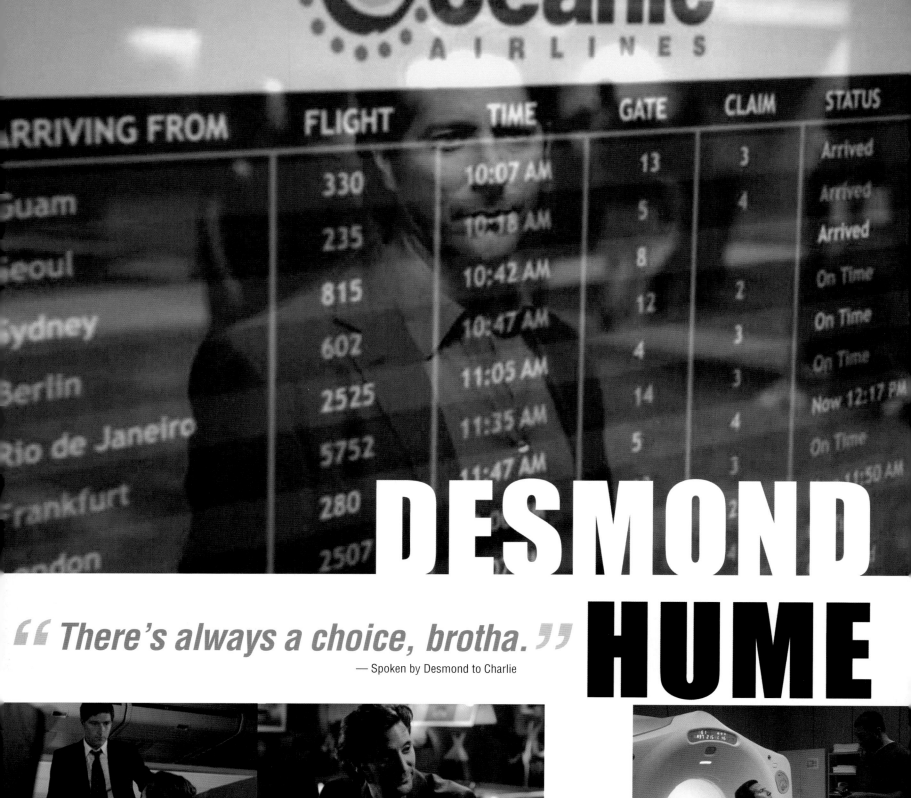

ARRIVING FROM	FLIGHT	TIME	GATE	CLAIM	STATUS
	330	10:07 AM	13	3	Arrived
Guam	235	10:18 AM	5	4	Arrived
Seoul	815	10:42 AM	8	2	Arrived
Sydney	602	10:47 AM	12	3	On Time
Berlin	2525	11:05 AM	4	3	On Time
Rio de Janeiro	5752	11:35 AM	14	4	Now 12:17 PM
Frankfurt	280	11:47 AM	5	3	On Time
London	2507				11:50 AM

DESMOND HUME

"Then enlighten me."

In the flash sideways, Desmond achieved the one thing he thought was most important to him—the respect and friendship of Charles Widmore. But outside of his professional success, he had nothing. No passion, no family, no love…until Charlie Pace, a seemingly drug-crazed musician, awakened him.

When Charlie mentioned the name Penny Widmore, a light turned on inside Desmond's consciousness and propelled him to find her. When Des and Penny touched, his true destiny was revealed. He then made it his mission to pass on his awareness to the other passengers on Oceanic flight 815.

"You can't because you're not ready yet, Desmond."
— Spoken by Eloise to Desmond

"Nothing's too good for you."
— Spoken by Widmore to Desmond

"If I were you, I'd stop worrying about me …and start looking for Penny."
— Spoken by Charlie to Desmond

"Find what you're looking for?"
— Spoken by Minkowski to Desmond

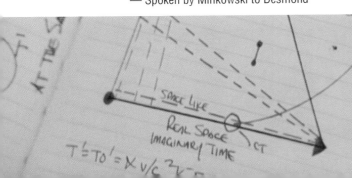

HUGO REYES

> ❝ *Our man of the year...* *Hugo Reyes.* ❞
>
> — Spoken by Pierre Chang to Hurley

Although Hurley was beloved by everyone in his flash sideways, true love was still missing from his life. With the encouragement of his mother, Carmen, and the guidance of Desmond, Hurley started spending time with Libby Smith. Libby had strong memories of a previous existence in which they had spent significant moments together. Hurley believed her, but he didn't have the same memories. A kiss on the beach shared with Libby opened Hurley's eyes and prompted him to help Sayid, Charlie, and his fellow loved ones onto the path of enlightenment.

"The moment that I saw you, it was like I was hit over the head. All these memories came washing back, of my life. Only, it was another life."

—Spoken by Libby to Hurley

"It takes as long as it takes."

—Spoken by Hurley to Boone

"Do you believe that two people can be connected, like soul mates?"

—Spoken by Libby to Hurley

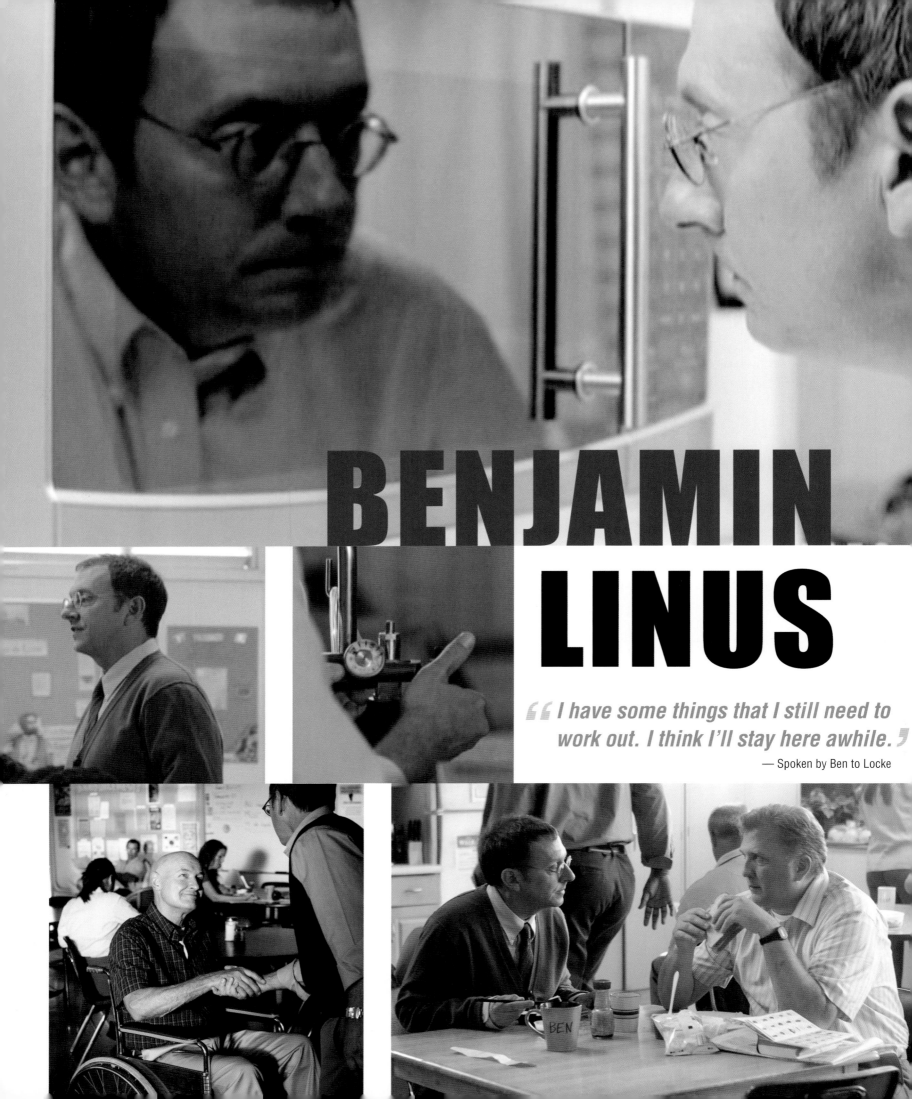

BENJAMIN LINUS

> " *I have some things that I still need to work out. I think I'll stay here awhile.* "
>
> — Spoken by Ben to Locke

> ## "You're the closest thing to a father she's ever had."
> — Spoken by Danielle to Ben

Ben's flash sideways experience was full of events that countered the dark decisions that defined him as a person. Ben initiated the toxic fumes on the island that led to his father's death during the Purge, but Ben cared for his gravely ill father in the flash sideways. Ben went so far as to administer oxygen to his father due to his respiratory illness.

As a high school European History teacher, he showed great compassion for his students' futures. In particular, Ben's kindness for Alexandra Rousseau was apparent, and she viewed him as a father figure.

Through interactions with John Locke, Desmond Hume and Alex's mother, Danielle, Ben discovered the true meaning behind this plane of existence.

SUN-HWA KWON

" Did you see? " — Spoken by Sun to Jin

"Let's run away."

"Maybe you should tell me to button it ...like you did on the plane." — Spoken by Sun to Jin

In their flash sideways, Jin and Sun are hindered yet again by the demands of Sun's father, Mr. Paik. Jin was still the man's lackey and Sun, on the surface, submitted to her father's traditional ways. But Jin and Sun's love prevailed, as they pursued their romance in secret and planned a life apart from Paik's control. As they considered the feasibility of their plot, Sun's pregnancy was revealed. Their child, Ji Yeon, became the physical symbol of their undying love.

JIN-SOO KWON

> ## "I'm pregnant."
> — Spoken by Sun to Jin

> ## "That's a beautiful name. And for the record, you two speak English just fine."
> — Spoken by Juliet to the Kwons

SAYID JARRAH

"I've spent the last twelve years trying to wash my hands of all the horrible things I've done, but they're still not clean. I can't be with you because I don't deserve you."

— Spoken by Sayid to Nadia

In the flash sideways, Sayid has spent more than a decade atoning for the sins of his Republican Guard past. Unable to wipe away the guilt of his past or reconcile the violent part of his nature, Jarrah sacrificed a life with his love, Nadia, so she could be with a better man, his brother Omer. But by defending Shannon when she was assaulted, Sayid recognized the love that allowed him to break from his past and become the man he always wanted to be.

"I can't forget it."
— Spoken by Sayid to Martin Keamy

" I'm sorry. You clearly don't know anything about me. "
— Spoken by Sayid to Hurley

"It's all right. Let me help."
— Spoken by Sayid to Shannon

KATE
AUSTEN

" *I think you should keep him.* " — Spoken by Kate to Claire

"I'm wanted for murder."
— Spoken by Kate to Sawyer

In Kate's flash sideways, she was on the run for murder, but she had embraced her fate and was less empathetic than before. She was looking out only for herself until she found Claire wandering the streets, pregnant and lost after Kate threw her out of their cab. Through this small, defenseless woman, Kate's empathy returned. And their destined connection at Aaron's birth opened Kate's heart to her life with Claire, Aaron, and Jack.

"I missed you so much."
— Spoken by Kate to Jack

CLAIRE LITTLETON

> " *We're not strangers…
> we're family.* "
> — Spoken by Jack to Claire

In Claire's flash sideways, she carried through with her original intention of giving up her unborn child for adoption in Los Angeles. When the adoptive parent changed her mind, Claire found herself facing a reality in which she would be the mother of her child.

Through connections with Kate, Ilana, Jack and Desmond, Claire ended up attending a benefit concert. Once she made eye contact with her one true love, Charlie, it triggered the birth of Aaron. This event not only helped Claire understand where she was, but it also bolstered Kate and Charlie's awakenings.

"A woman…Blonde…Rapturously beautiful and I know her. We're together. It's like we've always been and always will be. This feeling, this love…" —Spoken by Charlie about Claire

"Aaron's a great name."

"I don't know why I said it. It's like, I don't know. I knew it or something." —Exchange between Claire and Kate

"It's just a blanket." "Then go ahead and bring it to her." —Exchange between Kate and Charlie

JOHN LOCKE

" What are the odds of you just running into a spinal surgeon? I mean, who knows …maybe it's destiny?"

— Spoken by Helen to Locke

Although there were differences from Locke's mortal life to his flash sideways existence, he still suffered great traumas for which he blamed himself. In a cruel inversion of how Anthony Cooper caused Locke's paralysis, Locke was responsible for his own paralysis and the brain-damaged condition of his father in the flash sideways.

Locke found happiness with Helen, who helped care for Cooper. Through connections with Jack and Ben, Locke found a new confidence and accepted Jack's offer to try and restore his ability to walk. By letting go, Locke came to understand the true meaning behind this life.

"Push the button...I wish you had believed me." — Spoken by Locke to Jack

"I hope somebody does for you, what you just did for me."
— Spoken by Locke to Jack

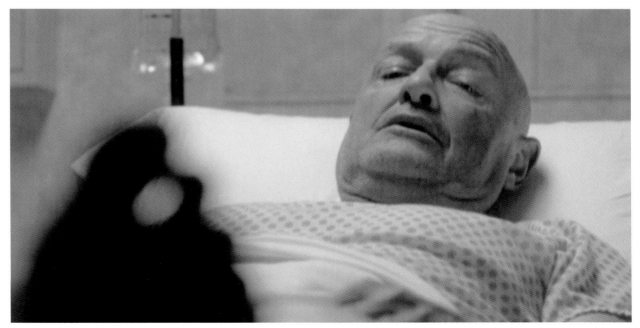

JAMES FORD

> " *I'm sorry Jim…but I gotta ask. Do you wanna die alone?* "
> — Spoken by Miles to James

In James Ford's flash sideways, he's a Los Angeles cop with a best friend and partner in Miles Straume. Still seeking vengeance for his parents' death, James' exhaustive search cost him any kind of real family or love. But due to his bad date with Charlotte Lewis and the disclosure of his history to Miles, James learned that he needed to let go of his past in order to move forward with his life. That revelation opened his heart when he met Dr. Juliet Carlson in the hospital. Their love awakened them both.

"Thanks, Doc."
— Spoken by James to Jack

"We should get coffee sometime… Kiss me, James." — Spoken by Juliet to James

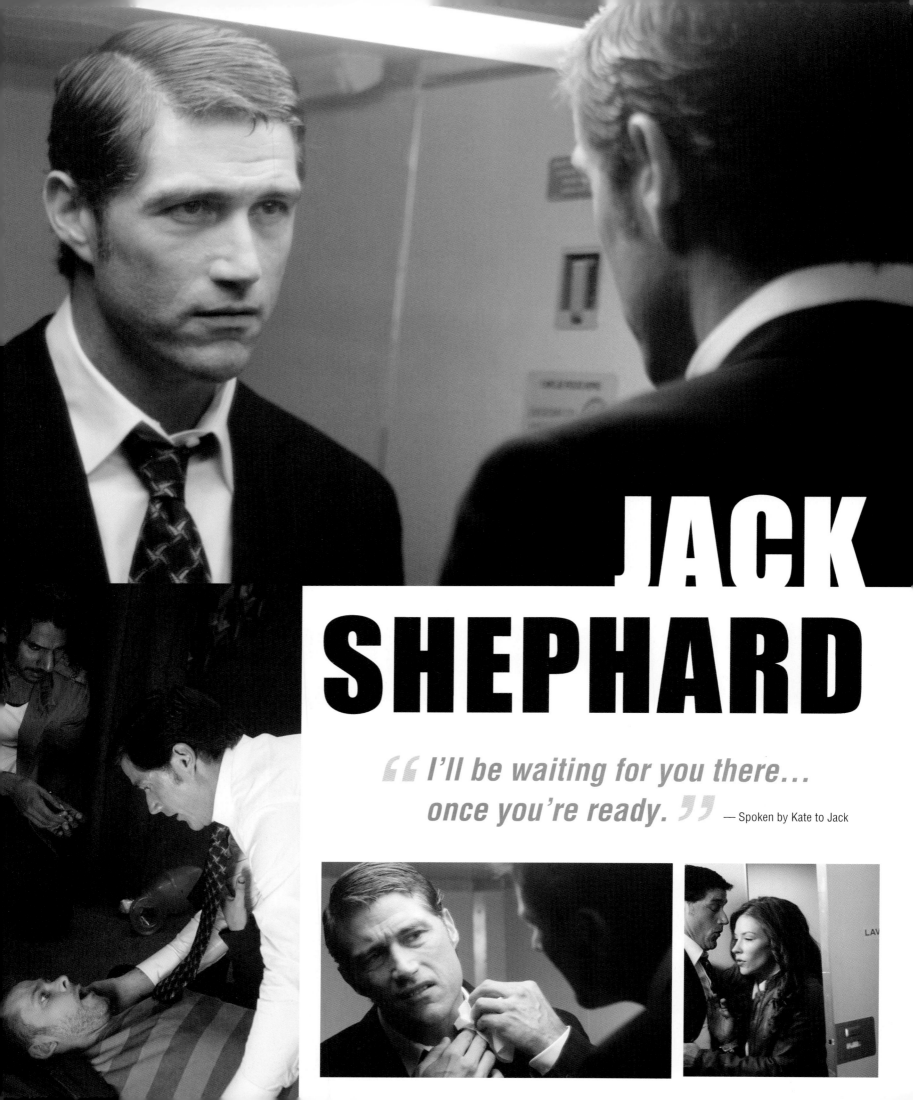

JACK SHEPHARD

" *I'll be waiting for you there... once you're ready.* " — Spoken by Kate to Jack

"They didn't lose your father…They just lost his body."
—Spoken by Locke to Jack

All of the issues Jack experienced with his father, Christian, had a defining influence on his life. But in his flash sideways, Jack's son David helped him process those grievances.

David was an accomplished pianist, something Jack gave up to pursue medicine. Jack read *Alice's Adventures in Wonderland* to David as a child, just as Christian did to Jack. Perhaps most important, Locke pointed out to Jack that David looked just like Jack.

Jack's willingness to help Locke brave an operation to fix his paralysis created a domino-like effect with several others from the island. This process moved Jack toward a place where his true love, Kate, and his father helped him fully let go and move on with his loved ones from the island.

"It's hard to watch and be unable to help."
—Spoken by Dogen to Jack

"Is that your son? He looks just like you."
—Spoken by Locke to Jack

ISLAM

One of the six fundamental Islamic tenets is the belief in life after death, which functions as a primary guide for living a God-conscious life. A Muslim who believes and lives accordingly after death will find their soul in a place between death and resurrection where they will be judged by angels on their actions and faith in life. Their judgment will be individual and not dependent on the intercession of family or loved ones. If they lived true to their faith, they will reside in a garden of paradise. If not, they will be tossed into the fires of hell for eternity.

HINDUISM

Through their ancient books and hymns, Hindus came to define that all humans possess a soul, or the atman, which is the divine breath of life. How Hindus live impacts their afterlife, which consists of three main realms—heaven, Earth and the netherworld. A soul will experience samsara, or the long, cyclical process of death and birth into a new body. The more successful souls accumulate karma in their lifetimes, which helps them end the cycle so they can attain nirvana or an utter oneness with God.

BUDDHISM

Buddhists believe the ever-changing nature of humanity means there can be no eternal soul, as the inherent nature of all life is transient and evolving. As humans go through life, it should be their goal to eschew their material, physical and ego ambitions and seek a transformed state of consciousness that has no anchor in the material. After this lifelong journey, at death a priest will recite from the Book of the Dead so the consciousness can enter the bardo (or in-between) state between death and rebirth. Through six bardo states, the consciousness examines its path as it prepares to begin anew.

JUDAISM

Hebrews believe that the soul returns to a spiritual origin after death where it awaits the return of the Messiah and the Day of Judgment. With the call of the shofar (or ram's horn), all the souls that slumber will be awakened for their judgment by the Lord who will either take them to paradise or be led to Gehenna to atone for a prescribed time for their sins.

CHRISTIANITY

The Apostle Paul explained that all humans have an individual, immortal soul created by God that would be judged after death in heaven. A person who believes and has been redeemed by their faith in Jesus Christ on Earth will spend the rest of their soul's eternity with the Lord. Those who lived sinful and unrepentant lives on Earth would find their soul condemned to hell. Roman Catholics believe that repentant souls can reside in purgatory where they exist in limbo, atoning alone, and with the aid of prayers from their families they can eventually be reunited with God in heaven.

TAOISM

Despite being a collection of teachings with many different branches, Taoists have fundamental beliefs closely connected with the balance of nature. Essentially, humans are but a part of the universe and the more in tune man is to the five elements—fire, earth, water, metal, wood—the more man can understand his place in the whole of existence. Thus, death is seen as a natural transition from being to non-being, or the yin-yang of life, and not an act to be judged or feared. To a Taoist, death just is.

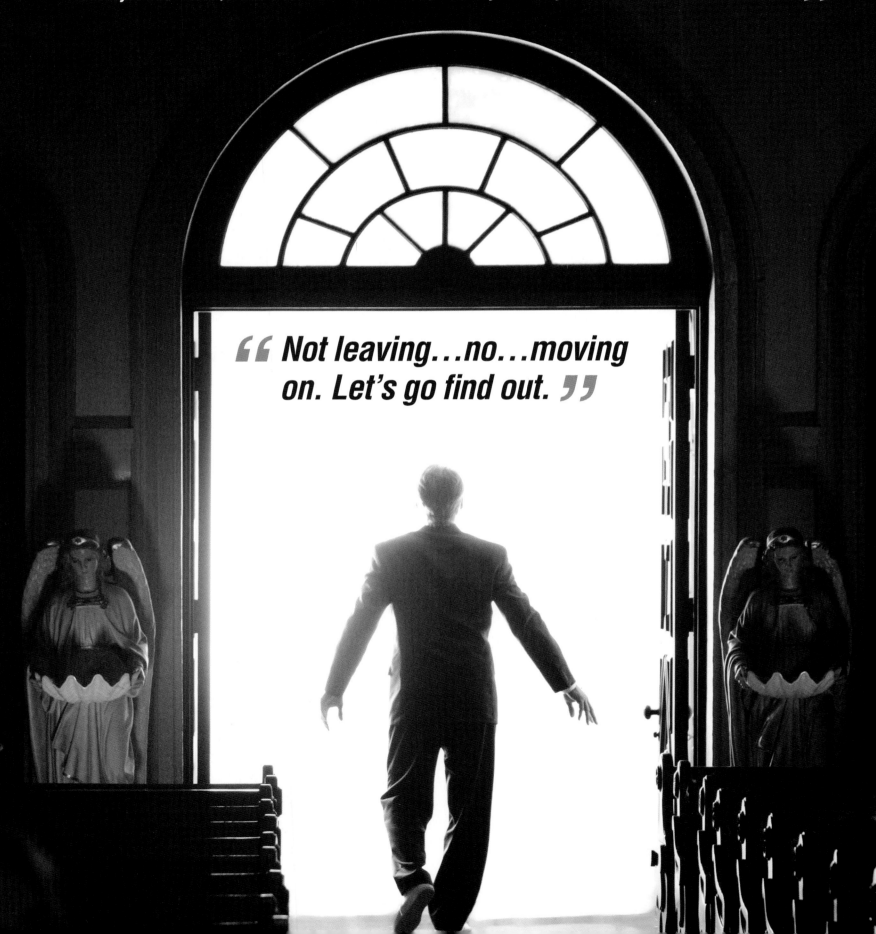

" **Everyone dies sometime, kiddo. Some have been before you, some long after you.** "

" **There is no "now" here…this is the place that you all made together so that you could find one another. The most important part of your life was the time that you spent with these people. That's why all of you are here. Nobody does it alone, Jack. You needed all of them, and they needed you…to remember…and to let go.** "

" **Not leaving…no…moving on. Let's go find out.** "